# SORDANEON
## IS MAKING NEWS!

# SORDANEON

### THE TRIEMPERY REVELATIONS
### BOOK 1

# L. L. STEPHENS

# Copyright Information

## SORDANEON
Published by

## Forest Path Books

Forest Path Books publications may be purchased for educational, business, or sales/promotional use. For information, please email the publishers at:

*info@forestpathbooks.com*
or address:
Forest Path Books, LLC
P. O. Box 847, Stanwood, WA 98292 USA

Stay informed on our releases and news!
Join the reading group/newsletter at:
*https://forestpathbooks.com/into-the-forest*

Front cover art © 2021 Larry Rostant
Map of the Triempery © 2021 Christina Wooden
Cover design @ 2021 Mahli
PR Compass Rose font © Peter Rempel (licensed for use)
Cover content is for illustrative purposes only, and any person depicted on the cover is a model.

Library of Congress Control Number: 2021909138
ISBN: 978-1-951293-41-3 (hardback)
ISBN: 978-1-951293-40-6 (trade paper)
ISBN: 978-1-951293-39-0 (e-book)

*To Steve—*
*For his undying support of my life's work.*

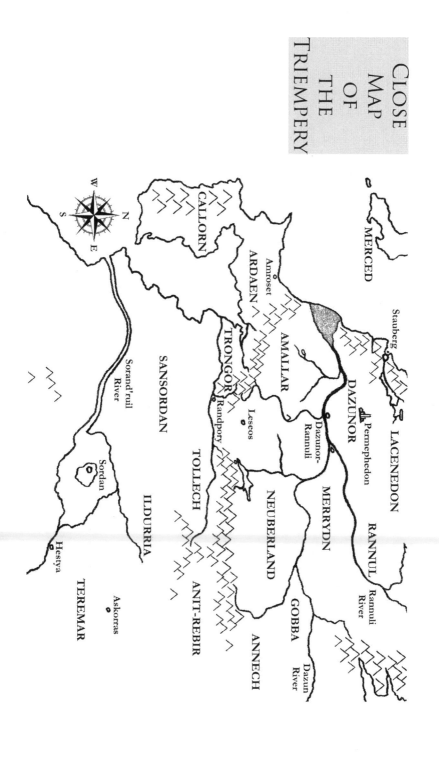

CLOSE
MAP
OF
THE
TRIEMPERY

# SORDANEON

## THE TRIEMPERY REVELATIONS
## BOOK 1

# 1

The Rill grieved, and Dorilian listened.

Other voices drew him along shadowed corridors and into the courtyard. Nights in Sordan were never dark. Rill glow from the City's heights paled the sky and silvered rooftops, walls, and even the flowers in the trees. He'd run barefoot through the immense palace's empty halls and pillared courts and seen no one. Now his shadow raced ahead as he darted up glow-bright steps far below the Rill's luminescent arches and ran toward his mother's room, the gilded chamber of an empress. Though she was Archessa, no guards stood outside her door, and no ladies knelt in attendance. Why had they fled?

Had they not heard the life within her signaling its distress?

He found her not quite gone. Light from the courtyard showed her to be still in bed, unmoving upon waves of silk. Wetness shone in a black pool between her legs and ran in rivulets down the bedclothes. Dorilian stepped forward into the Rill light and toward the bed where sheer curtains billowed, reflected in an argent floor. Nothing in his seven years of life had prepared him to see his mother so silent.

A deep thrum, familiar and only noticed in passing, rolled above the city. More light spilled into the room. The Rill did not cease its operation. But the Rill must feel *something*, surely, if Dorilian could tell it was in pain. His tutors told him that unyielding law forbade him to speak to the Rill—so he did not tell them he could hear it.

Not knowing what else to do, he reached for his mother's mind the way he always had. He found only a sickening swirl.

*Too soon... too soon.*

Her fading thoughts shaped themselves upon his lips—words so naked he flinched. He approached when she caught his eye.

"Dor." She whispered the pet name few others would dare. He smelled licorice on her breath, seductive and sweet. "Tell your grandfather... it was *merethe*." Her fingers, white as fangs, caught his hand and clung to it. "My poor son. My baby? Does he live?"

"He lives, Mother." He felt that life, too.

"Tell me... truly. You are god-born. Give me *truth*—"

"My brother lives, Mother." Her fear frightened him. Darkness ate at her core of light. "See? I will show you—"

The bedcovers between her legs gleamed wet and dark. Dorilian reached into the darkness and lifted the newborn, its tiny body and twiglike limbs barely visible within the dense membrane that shrouded it. A cord thick as his small finger held it to a clump of something black and heavy, so he lifted that, too. He cradled the warm mass in his fingers, slick with blood. His brother. Surely the one she had promised him just a week ago in the sweet-scented gardens of Rhondda.

*Is that my brother?* He had placed his hand on her rounded belly. *Are you making him?*

She had laughed. *Yes, tyrant. But give me time to finish him. He shall come when he is ready. He will be very small and will need his big brother to protect him.*

His brother, then... small, just as she'd said. So small, a lump of blood and ichor, with jelly and not bone for limbs, that didn't cry or breathe or move. Only the baby's heart moved, tapping against his finger. He had never seen a baby so tiny, not even filling his small, boyish hands. Hopeful, he showed his brother to her. But instead of being put at peace, her throat opened with an animal's howling.

He recoiled, driven back by her black wells of pain, her woman's loss he could not understand. Retreating, he tucked himself into a dark corner beside the wide door onto the terrace, cradling his tiny brother against him until the world fell silent.

"Mother?" he whispered. "Mother? Mother...."

His query echoed back to him, as thin and cold as the light that bathed her. Valyane. That was her name, the one his lips had never called her. Valyane, the Archessa Sordaneon—so beautiful, men said, that the moon prostrated itself nightly before her balcony. Even in death and pallor she was beautiful, honey-dark hair strung like webs upon the pillows, gray eyes moon pale and unseeing.

He held his free hand into the Rill light, toward her. Between bloodstains, his hand shone as white as hers had, ghostly, drained of living brightness. Her life had fled. She was cold, and he was cold, and death had not yet left the room. The Rill's pain lingered. He bent his head over the frail, curled mannequin he clutched to his breast and breathed upon it, his lips touching the wet, velvet membrane. Its borders, delicate as new fern, filmed his lips with blood, and he felt it draw upon the moisture in his breath… his warmth, his life.

*Brother. Brother, please don't go. Don't leave me.*

The babe twitched fragile limbs, and Dorilian froze. All at once, he felt large and clumsy. What if he moved and somehow harmed his brother? Light yet pulsed in the tiny body, but he knew so little about babies. His tutors had not prepared him for such things as this. He knew only that the baby's mind was quiet. Not silent—not as his mother's now was, unfindable—merely quiet. He could tell, though, that his brother knew him. Dorilian had felt him many times under their mother's skin. Opening his shirt, he cupped the newborn to the naked skin of his chest, the better to warm him.

*You're with me… stay with me. I will protect you now.* He wrapped his brother in thought, for the babe had no thoughts at all and his nourished it like milk. He sensed its yearning. His brother sought their mother again. Oneness, warmth, and life.

He could offer all three. Dorilian's tutors had told him Highborn kind were one blood, one life. A manifold godhead. Now he felt the truth of their teaching. His bond to his brother called to him as the babe's unfinished body cleaved to his flesh. Red membranes pulsed to his warmth, a flutter of wetness and a prickle of tiny things boring into his skin. Though he could not see them, he felt the tendrils work deeper, like worms burrowing in earth. He gasped as his chest burned and then his heart, but still, he did not pull the baby away. He forced his fingers to relax about the tiny form. His brother would never hurt him. Blood pounded in Dorilian's ears as his heart quickened. So fast! Through a haze of fear, he yielded to its imperative… what his brother sought, Dorilian let him find, afraid of what might happen if he did not.

Unmoving but for rapid breaths, braced against the wall, he watched the baby change. The urgency of it dizzied him. Beneath that translucent skin, new organs blossomed upon stalks of rose; existing buds swelled… the strange eyes, black and round, shrouded in membrane, eyelids fused… a breastbone like glass, the tiny heart beating beneath it like a ruby as crimson filaments became threads. His lungs drew air, and the baby's wet lungs unfolded, tiny ribs sucking in and out like strings with each shuddering breath. There were even bones now, fragile as a baby bird's. That thought frightened him anew—the baby bird his mother had shown him, fallen early from its nest, had died.

*Merethe.* He worked the word into his mind, finding it strange and lovely, but deadly too. She had told him what had killed her. His family had enemies. Somehow, they had torn his brother from her body along with her life.

He detected voices in the courtyard below and turned his head, an edge of curtain caressing his cheek. Men's voices, but his father's not among them.

If they would kill his mother and her baby, might they mean to kill him next?

Under his hand, the babe stirred, much larger and stronger but tiny still. Its delicate, red-laced eyelids appeared closed as before, but the fingernails had grown in. It looked more like a baby now. Dorilian was the one who had shrunken and changed. Bending a leg, he noticed how his bone stood out clearly beneath the skin, like a dog's. Holding the baby to his chest, he tried to stand, but did not have the strength to move. His muscles failed him. He tried again, using the wall for support, and inched onto his feet.

Concealed by curtains and shadows, he watched as the door from the corridor swung open. Two of his mother's handmaidens, the two who should have been with her this night, entered the room. Their dark garments and snoods blended with the shadows, but Rill light painted their faces bright as moonstones. A man followed them, his murky vestments emblazoned with golden crown shapes and the rearing outline of a horse. Dorilian recognized the emblem of Essera's King, who dared think himself Sordan's overlord. A King's Man, then.

The women, more silent than he'd ever seen them, hung back to let the man approach the bed. The King's Man looked down upon the body of the Archessa, then put out his hand, running it down one of her naked thighs, her cold white flesh. Dorilian stiffened. No man touched his mother! Not even his father ever did so. Couldn't this man tell death had already claimed her? With one hand, the man raised her nightdress, studied the blood between her legs… then thrust his hand into it, combing clots and searching the folds of bed linen. He lifted pale fingers black with gore and wiped them on her thigh with a muttered curse.

Choking back a cry, Dorilian bolted from the shadows. Shoving wisps of curtain aside, he fled through the open door into the night. Outside, the terrace shone ghostly white as the Serat raised vast, pale walls around him like sentinels. Above him, immense wings of ethereal Rill structure cradled the sky, bright glow spilling across the heights.

Over the wall was death. To each side of the terrace plunged stairs that would take him to the lower levels. Dorilian knew a hundred places to hide, and there would be people loyal to his family down there. Someone would hear him shout. They would have to come. As he ran, footsteps ran after him. Heavy. Thudding. The babe clutched within his bloodied nightshirt felt his fear and let out its first cry, a thin sound lost in the open place through which he fled. He was halfway down the wide stair leading to the Well of Birds before he saw the soldiers advancing upon the landing, a giant at their head, and the gleaming of drawn swords filled his eyes.

The man running after him stopped when Dorilian reached the bottom. Dorilian hunched over as soldiers charged past him up the stair, then he ran headlong toward the outstretched arm of their tall commander, who froze, wide-eyed, gaze riveting to Dorilian's blood-smeared shirt.

Soldiers had surrounded his pursuer and now dragged their captive down the stair.

The man bellowed in protest. "Unhand me! I was trying to help!"

"Is that why you were chasing one of the god-born, King's Man? Is that why he's covered with blood?"

"It's not his!" Gold bright hair disordered and vestments in disarray, the villain ceased to struggle. "Look at him! See for yourself. He's not harmed in any way."

Unconvinced, Commander Tiflan knelt before Dorilian. "Are you hurt, son?"

Dorilian shook his head. He trusted Tiflan, whose mother was sister to his own. "No."

"What's this?" Tiflan asked softly. He moved an immense hand toward Dorilian, but stopped short of touching. Dorilian pulled aside his fingers to reveal the infant's tiny head pressed to his sticky, red-stained chest.

"My brother." He barely had the breath to gasp out the words. The very world was spinning. Tiflan's concerned face floated before his eyes, losing focus. "My mother... she's dead."

"Your... brother?" Tiflan paled. He turned to the tall man at his side. "Take five men and go to the Archessa's room!" To another, he said, "Get Prince Sebbord! Get him *now*!"

Dorilian swayed as Tiflan wrapped a strong arm around his shoulder and swept him up into both arms. Dorilian held his brother close. Overhead, the sky turned and opened, light streaming like strands of starlight lifted by wind, thousands of unfurling filaments... he blinked, and the sky turned normal again, clotted with stars and slashed by Rill glow from the god structure arranged overhead. The King's Man could not get him now. He was safe with Tiflan, guarded by the Rill.

Voices vied with the darkness. Dorilian heard them, but they washed over his drifting thoughts like waves over rocks. Sometimes he understood the words and tried to listen, but the weight of his safety proved more soothing. Every time he opened his eyes, he saw only chaos and soldiers. The King's Man was gone.

His grandfather arrived, his face so terrible in grief and anger that Dorilian closed his eyes rather than look upon it. Weariness pulled him toward sleep, but he fought to stay above it, wanting to tend the baby's new thoughts. He and his brother shared a silent place, their bodies touching and their minds nestled like clasped hands.

"The bastards broke their word." Sebbord's condemnation was cold as stone. He placed his hand on Dorilian's head. "This is my reward for all my promises. My Valyane is dead, and her sons at the mercy of wolves. This is Essera's gift to me."

"Their father—" Tiflan's voice rumbled through the wall of his chest, vibrating under Dorilian's ear along with the rub of leather armor, the sounds of rapid footsteps and sharp words exchanged in corridors. His cousin's long walking strides rocked Dorilian gently as their grandfather continued to speak.

"I'll give Deben no second chances. He failed to protect her. True, theirs was no love match—but she was his *wife*! And see what they did to my beautiful girl—" Sebbord's words turned ragged. "I care not who is behind this. Marc Frederick or his minions, it matters not. They conspire alike. It was their plan to get Deben to surrender control of his Heir, and now those jackals will tear at him until he yields. 'For the boy's protection,' they will say. 'As surety for Sordan's peace and the withdrawal of our administrators,' they will plead. And Deben will listen, now that Valyane no longer stands like a lioness between them and her son. They know I have no legal standing in this matter."

Dorilian relaxed as the old man's fingers stroked his hair. He understood that they spoke about him, only not in the way adults usually did. If this was any indication, people said more important things—terrible things—when they thought he was asleep. In his mind he repeated the name his grandfather had used, a name he had heard before. *Marc Frederick. The barbarian, Essera's King.*

His enemy.

"So we leave, and we take him with us," Tiflan agreed. "But is Dor strong enough to travel? See how weak he is... the babe sapped his strength. We dare not guess how."

They came into another open place. Exposed, brushed by wind. Briefly, Dorilian's eyes flickered open to a view of the Serat towering above him, all white planes and angles, like an immense ship caught upon the cliffs. They were now on the lower levels, then.

"This newborn thwarts all their plans. Deben has denied Valyane's babe for weeks. He paved that path. Because of him, those vultures saw the way clear to kill her and also rid him of an unwanted heir." Sebbord's words would have iced sword steel.

Dorilian turned just his head, hair snagging on Tiflan's emblems of rank. Tears silvered his grandfather's eyes and stained that aged cheek, trailing down Sebbord's drawn face in glistening threads. Other sounds intruded now, the jangle and creak of harness and the clop of horses' hoofs, sharp on stone. Once he had mounted, Sebbord held out his arms. "Here, give my grandsons to me."

Dorilian did not resist as the old man's arms looped under Tiflan's and lifted him. Other horses were departing. He saw the King's Man bound to one, still dressed in his court finery but for a hood covering his head and shoulders. Another horse bore a long bundle wrapped in black cloth. As Dorilian watched, it too left with more guards.

"They gave her *merethe*." This time Dorilian didn't look away from the pain that touched his grandfather's eyes. "She told me to tell you."

Sebbord shifted him in his arms. "Thank Leur she had someone to tell. It should not have been you."

"Where are we going?" Uncomfortable, he stirred against his grandfather's grip on him but took care not to jostle the infant he still held in the stiffening fabric of his nightshirt. No one had sought to relieve him of his burden, as though they were afraid to take the child from him. Though his eyes wanted to close, he held them open as Sebbord looked down upon him gravely.

"To Teremar, lad." Teremar was Sebbord's domain, separated from Sordan's island by the deep waters of Lake Sarkuan. Dorilian had heard his mother talk of it as a land of grass plains and rich farms. "Young as you are, I think you understand your city has fallen under the sway of men we cannot trust."

"But I am Sordaneon. I must stay in the city with the Rill and my people."

"It's the Rill they want, son, through you. And the Rill I will not give them."

Dorilian saw only determination in the lined face, the way Sebbord's golden gaze shone piercingly beneath stern silver brows. Sebbord would not tell him lies. Their enemies wanted the Rill Entity. Dorilian's mother had told him the same thing, as had his father. He was Rill kind—god-descended, gifted, different from the servants around him though he looked like them in body. Human. Mostly human. But Highborn, too—and he didn't want to do anything that might place his legacy at risk. And now there was his brother to consider.

Sebbord had been a Rill mage, an Epopte sworn to the Entity's service. Sebbord would protect them. Dorilian weighed this against the cold protection of his father, who wanted to send him to live in Essera among men like the King's Man, who he had last seen wearing his mother's blood like a red glove on his hand. And hadn't Sebbord just said his father meant to deny his tiny brother?

"I will go with you," he said. Because he was Highborn and part of the Mind, any act he undertook required his consent.

They left the palace by way of the east garden and the quadrant controlled by Tiflan's men. Dorilian barely remembered departing Sordan, only that they followed a barracks road to the edge of the city. One of his grandfather's men found a wet nurse among the wharf folk's wives and daughters, a plump girl into whose wide brown eyes Dorilian peered for a long moment before he handed over his brother. The girl now cradled the babe to her breast. Dorilian rode with Sebbord. As they set off down a road that would take them to a secure estate and a ship that would carry them to Teremar, they looked back only once.

To a man, the party reined in their horses as a dulcet whine vibrated the graying skies of morning. Silent, they watched a silver bolt born in the heart of the high places they had left behind split the dawn and break above the sleeping city. A massive spear of light tore open the darkness, headed north. Dorilian barely registered the *charys* before the gleaming spindle vanished. The god propelled the vessel far away, to lands that, for Dorilian, were but names. He envisioned the things it carried: passengers bound for distant cities, spices, horses, cascades of golden wheat, all flowing into the coffers of mighty Essera.

"They have not discovered us yet," Sebbord said. "The Rill runs as ordained. They would have held it if they knew us missing."

Dorilian burrowed deeper into his grandfather's arms. He had wanted his own horse, but he was glad of Sebbord's warmth and the strength that held him fast. "I shall ride the Rill one day." He resented that he never had.

"Yes, son, you shall. Ride it and more." Sebbord stared into the distance where the Rill had gone. Loss stained his face with yet another kind of grieving. "And may you wrest it back from the jackals that feast upon its holy carcass."

# 2

The bridge of his nose broke first, then his left cheekbone. Stefan's boot had found its mark. Blood gushed beneath his eyelid along with sharp, blinding pain. Dorilian refused to cry out, but his breathing betrayed him with a gurgle as blood poured from between his lips along with his final expletive. The next kick, aimed at his mouth, broke his jaw.

"Stefan! Stop!" Maybe one voice, maybe more. "He's bleeding! Hells! You know how they are about that!"

Dorilian did not know who had spoken. He didn't care. There were four of them, and he despised them equally. None of his attackers had ever pretended to be his friend. He was more surprised by the attack itself—and the sight of his blood as it splashed on the wood parquet floor in a steady crimson stream. That was new.

"Stefan!" someone shouted again. "Let's go!"

Though Dorilian braced for it, no third kick came. Metal scraped on the floor—plates affixed to the heels and toes of Kheld boots—as the boys wrestled Stefan aside, then away. Dorilian gasped for air, inhaling blood along with it. Coughing, he collapsed, though he managed to turn his face so that his unbroken cheek struck the floor first. Footsteps echoed in the hallway outside, receding. Someone stayed behind and knelt at his side but did not touch him.

"Are you all right?" the Kheld asked.

He recognized the voice now. Cullen Brodheson. A damned barbarian Kheld speaking accented Stauba, trying to sound as if he cared.

"Go 'way," Dorilian snarled as best he could, the words

misshapen. He could barely move his jaw, and it hurt just to open his mouth enough to breathe. In all his fifteen years, he had never felt such pain as now flooded every nerve. "Fuggin' Khelds. Damn fuggin' Khelds."

"You shouldn't have said the things you did—"

"Glad." Dorilian refused to admit his mistake in responding to Stefan's taunts. Especially when the Stauberg-Randolph prince's friends had pinned him by the arms, holding him down on his knees, bent over. He had made matters worse by retorting that Stefan must be especially talented at providing certain oral services to the King or that perhaps he preferred offering up another orifice. At least Dorilian had enjoyed the sight of Stefan's face turning a deep shade of purple before seeing his boot hurtling toward his face. "Go 'way." He opened the one eye not swollen with blood so he could see Cullen's face. Typical of his race, the other boy had dark-lashed blue eyes and wavy hair the color of shit. "Hate him forever... for this. Hate all fuggin' Khelds."

He meant it, meant it with all that was in him. Perhaps Cullen felt that. The boy's concerned expression faded, acknowledging something, maybe merely that Dorilian was not going to die. Nodding, Cullen rose and quickly walked away, leaving Dorilian as he wished to be: alone.

He fought the pain and dragged himself to the tall window. There he wedged himself shoulder first into the corner of the broad, deep frame, tight against whatever invisible force would not let his body pass and fall into oblivion. It was not oblivion he sought but escape. Escape from pain, from knowledge he did not want... from this land and this place. Somewhere out there, the Rill raced toward freedom.

*I hate this place. I hate Essera. I hate them all.*

He cursed the day Esseran nobles had succeeded in pressuring his grandfather and father into sending him and his brother to attend their "exalted" school at Permephedon. For their own good, the bastards had said. Maybe for Lev, who thrived as never before. But not for him. In this Citadel of wonders ruled over and attended by Sordan's oppressors, all he encountered was hate and fear, thick and foul as an apothecary's fog as it seeped through every corridor, glance, and carefully inflected word.

Because of the Rill.

More than just its sheer ability to hurl men, goods, and information across a continent in the time it took to cross a road, the Rill created wealth and hierarchies. Because they sought to keep their hold on the Rill, these Esseran lords and their masters had raped his country and killed his mother. They had allowed the barbaric Kheld folk to slay others of his family in ways monstrous beyond description. The Sordaneon bloodline to which the Rill's life was tethered had been reduced to a handful. Now they wanted to silence him, too. Force him to adopt their habits, their rulers, their words. Only in that way might they render him powerless. And Dorilian refused. He refused to acknowledge their power, refused to fear them, refused to be ruled.

He was Highborn. Sordaneon. What he was *mattered*.

*Holy Leur, it hurts.* He put his hand to his mouth and spit into his cupped palm. Blood and a tooth. It was not the only one. A second rolled against his tongue, and he knew he had lost yet another on the floor. Damn Khelds. Damn fur-faced Khelds. Even their facial and body hair offended him. He would exterminate the lot of them if he could. More footsteps, this time heavier, familiar. *Go away!* he willed, not wanting to be seen this way by any of them, ever.

"Dorilian?"

His kinsman Elhanan Malyrdeon met him daily in this chamber. Even by Essera's laws, only another of Highborn kind could draw a blade in his presence or serve as his instructor in using a sword. They did not let him keep a weapon. But Elhanan had been delayed today, and Stefan had been in the practice room instead with his three friends, waiting in the shadows to catch Dorilian unguarded.

Elhanan's footsteps quickened, paused—perhaps at the sight of the pool of blood on the floor—then ran toward him. "Dorilian! What happened?"

He tried to curl away, but the man would have none of it. Unlike Cullen, Elhanan had the right to touch him, and he did so, pulling Dorilian around by the shoulder.

"Gsch! Who did this?"

By the sound of it, he must look as bad as he felt. Dorilian nearly laughed. "Stefan."

That truth sat between them like lead. Dorilian and Elhanan were both god-born. Highborn. To lay a hand on their kind was forbidden. To spill their blood was a crime. By naming Stefan as his assailant, Dorilian had condemned the Esseran King's grandson and his friends to death.

# 3

"I didn't know you were going to kick him! Hells!"
Stefan flinched as Cullen Brodheson grabbed his
shoulders and spun him against the garden wall. The boys
had split up after fleeing the weapon room, but Cullen had known
Stefan's mind well enough to have followed him. "Stefan." But his
friend ignored the warning look sent his way. "He's bleeding bad!"

"He'll live!" Stefan snarled. Shaking Cullen off, he vaulted over
the garden wall and ran toward the mosaic of shallow pools that
pebbled the lawn. The water reflected the sky, bright blue. "He's
Highborn. They heal. I can break every bone in his body, and it
won't fucking matter!"

"But it still hurts, Stefan."

"I hope the hell it does hurt! I *want* him to feel it. Maybe he'll
think about something except being so high and mighty next time he
wants to start calling me names." Stefan walked into the nearest pool,
his boots splashing. Bright red ribbons of blood curled into the water.

"This is bad, Stefan." Cullen couldn't stop glancing over his
shoulder.

Only now did Stefan duck his head and sigh. "He deserved it."
Even so, he didn't think he would ever forget the look in Dorilian
Sordaneon's bloodied eyes.

He wouldn't admit it to Cullen, but he wished he hadn't kicked
the other boy so hard. And he wished there were more trees in this
garden, more cover. Permephedon was such an overly arranged and
civilized place. Nowhere to run or hide. And even if they did hide,
Marenthro's damned Undying Guard always knew where to find
them.

Stefan marked the Rill rising above the glassy towers. The god-
machine's enormous structures thrust high into the sky, rings and

spokes, arrays of arches and angles in motion. Scythe-like shapes sliced through the air, unfolding and elongating to receive arriving *charyses* or send outgoing ones on their way. No one—not even the Epoptes who ordered the thing—fully understood how it worked.

A series of resonant thrums reached his ears, and Stefan felt the same pang of wonder he always did when the Rill's white limbs unfurled to capture a wide streak of light. Before his eyes, a needle-shaped sliver several times more massive than any sailing ship materialized out of the very air to glide soundlessly into the city. He looked at Cullen and noticed his friend also watched the sight, his expression sick.

Rill blood, it was said, flowed in Dorilian Sordaneon's veins.

Guards wearing the singular headgear and saffron garments of Permephedon's High Citadel approached along an elevated, grass-carpeted walkway leading from the Scholar's Quad. In the distance behind them, another contingent of men emerged from a wooded park between two of the nearer glass towers, dragging two more struggling Kheld youths with them.

"Looks like they got us," Stefan said. Together he and Cullen walked toward the soldiers, their feet pressing tufts of pale green grass between twilight-colored stones.

"You attacked one of the Highborn! A Sordaneon! What in Sharga's ring of hell were you thinking?"

Stefan was not accustomed to seeing his uncle in a rage. Jonthan Stauberg-Randolph had always been the most easygoing of his relations, a pleasant man whose scholarly ways reminded many of his royal father, the King, but without the soldiering part.

"You didn't hear what that bastard said!"

"Nothing he could have said justifies what you did. The Malyrdeons are involved now, trying to find a way to satisfy the Sordaneons and save your life."

Stefan looked up. "My life?"

"Yours. And your friends'."

"He wasn't hurt that badly—"

"You drew blood, didn't you?" Jonthan met his nephew's defiant gaze. "Did you stop to look at him? Did you ask if he was hurt?"

"No, but—" Stefan couldn't deal with this. This wasn't what he'd been trying to do.

"I don't know myself how badly he's hurt. From what I've heard, he's going to live, which means he's going to heal, which means you've made one hell of an enemy. And not just for yourself—for *all* of us."

"He was my enemy already. He was yours! He never spoke a word to me, but it was against our family. He called me a bastard—he called *you* one! He calls Grandfather a barbarian, a usurper—"

"Stefan—"

"—my mother a Kheld outlaw's whore—"

The water hit him full in the face. Stefan gaped at Jonthan, who stood over him holding an empty glass. "Words, Stefan," his uncle said, every word measured. "Just words. And you've ensured that next time it will be more than that. I don't care what Dorilian says about us. He's never *known* us! You are the first of our family he has ever met, and all you did was harden whatever animosity he brought to Essera with him." Jonthan set the glass down on a nearby table, the *thunk* loud enough to punctuate his continued desire for silence. "He might have called you a barbarian bastard, Stefan, but it was you who proved yourself to be one. And it was you who struck a blow against a person who has the King's promise of protection."

Stefan sank back against the wooden slats of the chair. A clerk's chair in a clerk's tiny room. More and more, it felt like a prison cell. As he cooled down, he remembered Marc Frederick's words about Dorilian and the importance of easing the strained relationship between their families. *This goes beyond me and you*, his grandfather had told Stefan as they had walked the garden path at home. *It goes to the very heart of trust and honor. Remember that he is Highborn and bound to his grandfather's promises. I want you to remember that you are bound to mine.*

"He only used that protection to attack me. He pushed and he pushed until I pushed back!"

"I know that," Jonthan said. He sighed and leaned against one of the room's several document cabinets. "So do the Malyrdeons. So does *he*. That may be the only thing that does save your life. It doesn't hurt, believe me, that the King is your grandfather."

But it did hurt. It hurt because more was expected, because Stefan was bound by promises Marc Frederick had made to safeguard an enemy's life. A Highborn life. All because of the stupid Rill and a bunch of old myths. "It's not fair," Stefan protested. The extent of his transgression set in, at long last. It was easier to deny the difference between his station and that of the youth he had attacked when he was angry. "Dorilian can just say anything he wants, do anything he wants—"

"Stop it, Stefan. Don't even try to justify your actions. There was nothing fair about what you did. You knew Dorilian would be alone and unarmed. You went with friends, and you went with a purpose." Jonthan looked upon his nephew with contempt. "And what of your friends? You enlisted them in a deed that may cost them their lives, a deed that proves to the world Khelds are violent, vicious, and not to be trusted! They are your *people*, Stefan. They look to you. Is this the kind of leadership you are going to provide them—should you live to rule them?"

"No, of course not! It's just that—" Why was this so hard to explain? Because he didn't understand it himself? Because he was frustrated at his inability to handle a situation with which his grandfather and family had entrusted him? "Grandfather warned me. He said it might be hard to be around Dorilian, that he had bad feelings toward our family. But Jonthan, it's not like he stopped at me. Cullen, Neddig, and Reard—all of us with Kheld blood—had to put up with his filth. We're not damn Staubauns, you know. We don't believe the Leur folk created the world from their own bodies or that the Highborn are gods. We don't have to put up with it."

Nothing he said mattered. His uncle's hazel eyes, eyes that had never looked harshly on him before, did so now. Jonthan's words fell like heavy stones between them. "You forget that you are a Kheld only in blood, Stefan—politically, you are Marc Frederick's grandson and by his grace a prince of this realm. He is the one to whom you must answer for this—he and he alone."

"I shouldn't have done it. Is that what you want me to say?"

"I want you to realize that what you did today was a coward's deed unbefitting of our family. You don't even grasp how badly you have damaged yourself or us. Someday, Stefan, you are going to want to look Dorilian Sordaneon in the eye—maybe you will even *need* to—and you won't be able to do it because of this day."

*Oh, yes, I will.* Stefan fumed, resenting that his uncle dared to tell him what he should feel. *I'll look him in the eye, and I'll tell him to go to hell.* But he couldn't tell Jonthan that.

Jonthan walked to one of the room's two imposing desks, where he sorted through drawers until he had retrieved paper, a fine pen and ink bottle, and a jar of sealant sand. He laid these on the table in front of his nephew. "You will extend apologies, Stefan. One to Dorilian. One to the Malyrdeons for having assaulted their kinsman. One to your grandfather for having blackened his honor. Start drafting at once—and choose your words well. Your life and those of your three friends depend on them."

# 4

Dorilian sat on a stool in the center of a high-ceilinged salon furnished with cushioned couches and low polished tables. Statuary occupied golden alcoves from which discreetly placed waterglobes reflected light like stars in the obsidian floor. The undraped windows displayed the winking lights of surrounding towers. Under other circumstances, the room might hold a hundred guests without seeming full.

Meeting with his Malyrdeon relatives had never been part of Dorilian's plan, and he resented Stefan as much for thrusting his Esseran kinsmen upon him as he did for his broken teeth and bones. Blood spattered his student garments of quilted blue-gray silks and silver leather belting. Though his stained cloak hung open, he had not removed it. He glanced up when men entered, then looked away. Elhanan again—and another man, tall and pale and older. For all that they shared a bloodline, Dorilian looked nothing like them. He was small for his years, and his hair was not silver blond but the color of caramel, barely bright enough to pass as Staubaun here in vainglorious Essera. Even his skin was browner, tanned by Sordan's stronger sun. Instead of being amber or brown like those of any other wellborn royal, his eyes were gray like his mother's. Stefan had likened his eyes to fish scales, prompting other boys to do so also. And it had gotten uglier from there.

The Stauberg-Randolph prince had made his biggest mistake when he had called Dorilian's brother Fish Eyes, too, and compared his movements to the flopping of a trout, just because Levyathan sometimes twitched and had trouble walking.

Having Levyathan here at Permephedon with him was the one thing that made the enforced stay bearable.

Dorilian hoped his ordeal would end soon. He had missed dinner, and it was now well into the middle of the night. Elhanan had already talked to him for hours, relentless in trying to get his promise to say nothing about the insult he had suffered.

He didn't see why he should not shout it to the heavens.

"Well, young Sordaneon." The new arrival eyed him unhappily. "Prince Elhanan tells me you refuse to have your injuries treated."

Dorilian eyed him narrowly. "Did he tell you why?"

The words slurred more than he would have liked. His jaw was stiff, his lips were swollen, and his tongue moved over broken teeth. The stumps had already sealed, so he no longer felt pain, but it would take a day yet for the crowns to regrow. The man's gaze dropped to the blood-covered hand Dorilian held clenched in his lap.

"You do not need to do this."

Did they think him that much of a fool? "I know what you are doing. You're just keeping me here until I heal. Until the proof goes away. Until it's what I say against what he says."

The man gestured for Elhanan to pull over a chair for him. He faced Dorilian across a table of polished jade, its squat legs carved with the figures of ancestral heroes engaged in battle with winged beasts. "Do you know who I am?"

"Austell Malyrdeon, Prince of Stauberg. You are the current Wall Lord." Dorilian had studied his oppressors.

All knew how Marc Frederick had gained his throne. The barbarian had made a mysterious bargain with the last Malyrdeon King and gotten himself named as Heir. And then, on the day of his coronation at Permephedon, the Malyrdeons—Austell and his brothers—had stood aside, allowing the new Esseran King and his soldiers to seize Labran Sordaneon and, with that, control of the Rill. Thirty-five years of occupation for Sordan and its people had followed. To this day, Labran remained imprisoned, held captive in the Esseran capital of Stauberg—a city to which the Rill did not run.

"We are interceding in this matter," Austell informed him. "What Stefan did to you cannot be condoned—and it will not be."

"In Sordan, he would be dead already."

"That is not going to happen. No prince of the Kheld people is going to die because of you. We will give them no reason to seek your life out of a desire to avenge his. That path is already slippery with our blood."

"Only because you and your King have allowed the fur-faced Khelds to spill it with impunity."

He watched both men for their reactions. Elhanan's pained wince told him much. Good, they realized the strength of his position. They could not will away what Stefan had done, neither could they make a Sordaneon heir vanish. They could only attempt to make him give up his accusation.

Austell continued his effort to sound reasonable. "the King sent me to talk with you. He wants a peaceful—and just—resolution."

"How? By tossing me in a cell?" He locked eyes with Austell. "Is he going to salvage his throne in the same way he took it—by silencing me as he has my grandfather Labran?"

This time it was Austell who sighed. The man looked away, trading glances with Elhanan. Their emotions reached Dorilian, prickling beneath his skull just under the hairline and behind his eyes—frustration, helplessness, and a tinge of alarm. He was making their lives difficult.

Good.

"Don't think Stefan will not be punished for his offense. He will be, and severely." Austell's face hardened. "*You* are a different matter. You are a projective empath, something you know very well. Stefan hates you? Well, you hated him first. For weeks you goaded, insulted, defamed, and baited him until he did as you hoped and lashed out at you. Perhaps it was your plan all along to bring about his death this way."

Dorilian did not deny it. He had hoped to provoke Stefan into striking him—only for Stefan to happily elevate the seriousness of the offense by spilling his blood. His nostrils inhaled the sharp, bright air of this place, clean of every extraneous scent but the nervousness of the men and the dangerous, sweet smell pooling hot in his hand.

"Do you know what price they will pay, all four of those boys?" Austell persisted. "Do you care?"

"Whatever it is, I hope they suffer."

"Stefan will no longer be a threat to you." Austell sank back in the chair. "He is to be pulled from the school to demonstrate the King's displeasure."

Dorilian shot a look from Austell to Elhanan and back again. Were they serious? "That's *it*? He's pulled from *school*?"

"He failed the first duty of a prince." Austell's clear, resolute gaze never left his. "It's wrong to lead to ruin those who put full faith in your orders. It's even more wrong when you know they will suffer in your place. The three boys who held you will be executed. Stefan will be sent into exile."

Exile sounded fair enough. Not as good as death, but whether Stefan lived or died was unimportant. Dorilian's real goal was to get out from under Essera's control. He frowned, then opened his hand, showing the sticky red mass webbing his fingers. Austell stared at the pale lumps of two teeth. "Stefan did this," Dorilian said before closing his hand again. "Stefan, not your damned King. Send me back to Sordan, and I will agree to say nothing about his grandson's offense."

"You cannot leave except upon the King's express order."

"Then have him so order." He could leave as soon as the permission was given. The first article of the Rill Covenant was that a Sordaneon be granted passage immediately at any time he demanded it. All he needed was the King's permission to step foot in the Rill sanctuary.

"No." Austell rose, his body straight and movements tense. "This farce has already gone as far as it will go. Three deaths are enough even for your bloody taste, I should think. Hatred makes a poor meal, Sordaneon. It nourishes only itself. That is a lesson I pray you learn before it is too late." He signaled to Elhanan.

Dorilian waited until the two men were almost at the door before he spoke again. "I can pardon them."

As he'd expected them to, the words commanded his kinsmen's attention. Austell stopped but did not turn. "A pardon?" A Highborn pardon could only be extended by the wronged individual—and it must be given freely. An act manifest in the Mind of Leur could not be otherwise.

"If your King allows me to leave, I will pardon them. All but Stefan. Your King can exile him for all I care."

"But you leave—and your brother too?"

"No, my brother stays." That point mattered more than his leaving.

"Are you certain that is what you wish to do?"

"It is what I am *willing* to do."

After a long moment, the other man nodded. Dorilian tried to read Austell's face but could not. Even Austell's emotions felt distant, protected by hidden power. "I will tell him. Go to your brother, and in the morning, be ready to go back to Sordan."

"Hold her still."

The falcon screeched, captive in Levyathan's small hands as Dorilian adjusted the strap on the bird's jessed leg. Morning sun blazed directly into Dorilian's eyes, making it hard for him to see. Just beyond the smooth blue wall of the terrace, Permephedon's central towers rose in dawn-gilded spires and thrusts, creating shadowed canyons. A handful of guards waited outside the manse's courtyard, assigned to escort him to the Rill station.

"There," Dorilian announced, satisfied. "She's banded." He rocked back on his heels out of the sun's glare and smiled at his brother.

*Fly?*

"Not yet," he said, then caught himself. Lev struggled with spoken words. *Not yet. You need to train with her. When you can call her back, then she can fly.*

Levyathan averted his gaze, turning his face. His shoulder twitched as his curious fingers stroked the black-flecked golden feathers more beautiful than a courtier's gown, softer even than his lynx kitten's fur. He adored textures, and his fingers coaxed happiness from the feathers. *Then I will see?*

*Through her eyes. When she flies, you will see the city in other ways. You will soar.*

*Alone.*

Dorilian frowned. He could not stay in Permephedon, especially not now. There was nothing for him here—but there was for Lev. In just a few months, Lev had shown more improvement than he had in years.

His brother had been the only reason Dorilian had gone along with this whole Esseran scheme. When he had first heard that his country's enemies wanted to subject him to their ways, teachers, and princes, he had rebelled. Nothing could force him to leave his brother behind. But then Marenthro, the immortal who called this place home, had consented to see Lev and use his extraordinary gifts to help the boy. After that, Dorilian had agreed.

Because Lev needed help—lots of it. He heard human voices but did not always understand words; he saw living things as shifting masses of light, color, and movement. He barely saw other things at all. Only under Marenthro's tutelage had Lev devised ways to navigate rooms independently, but he still risked wandering into danger. His thoughts linked oddly, played out as sequences of feelings, impressions, and symbols. Logic eluded him. And he struggled with speech, barely able to fashion simple sentences. It was one of Dorilian's great frustrations because he could hear his brother's thoughts clearly and knew his mind to be intact, alive. But different. Very different.

Dorilian had finally accepted that he was suited for the world in which they lived—while Levyathan was not. His brother's world would always be one in which Dorilian could never be more than a visitor.

*Keep?* Lev meant the bird. His young governess was not fond of animals. An image entered Dorilian's mind of a sun-filled shape as pretty in its own way as Noemi herself.

*Of course. Noemi let you keep the kitten, didn't she? Besides, I already hired a falcon keeper.*

Levyathan threw back his head and laughed. He cawed like a bird. His foot stamped happily on the ground. He mimicked the falcon keeper, who had a club foot.

Dorilian grinned, petting the bird until his brother looked away again. "I will tell Gorl that you are to fly her whenever you wish," he said, naming the falconer.

"I sp… speak, he… hides." Levyathan abandoned his stammer to continue in thought. *I embarrass… everyone. Speak shapes none see. Colors spin, dissolve my ears to noise.* He pressed his cheek to the gyrfalcon's wing. The bird made no attempt to turn on him but accepted his handling—as did all creatures.

*You don't embarrass me.*

*I touch you—I see, I hear. Without you, I am blind, silent… my world dark unmoving.*

Together they inhaled the strange cool air of this land, so far removed from the sweet sun-warmed smells of Teremar or Sordan's fragrant breezes. Here in this northern, Esseran place, they could not pretend they were anything but set apart and different.

*I'll take you back to Teremar after I get the Rill to see me.*

Levyathan shook his head. *No. You are small. If it sees you, it will seek you. If you seek it, it will find you. Blind you! Crush you!*

*I do not seek it.*

*Untruth, untruth. I know you yearn.*

Dorilian could lie to himself more readily than to his brother. And he found it hard, very hard, to lie to himself. He did seek the

Rill. He sought it with every fiber of his being. As one, he and Lev looked across the city at the silver supporting stalks that curved above the steep amethyst and blue edifices housing the College of Epoptes, the elite mages trained to bespeak and direct the Rill. Only the soaring spires of Permephedon's bone-white Citadel stood taller.

Something brilliant caught his eye, the shining extrusion of a Rill transport *charys*—a sudden mad glitter that appeared for a moment, streaking toward distant Dazunor, then was gone. The reverberation of its passage thrilled him.

*Twice twelve for passage, twelve on a hill.* Levyathan recited the ring configuration of Rill nodes. He turned his head sharply to the side, eyes closed, typical of when he was listening... or thinking. *At Askorras twelve fallen, broken. Like me.*

*Not like you.*

*Yes. I am broken. But why a broken god?*

Dorilian wasn't sure. According to his tutors, the living structure of the Rill could adjust for even unanticipated stresses within its own matrix and adapt in ways that should have prevented it from breaking. It was, in its own way, self healing, as Leur things were. As Dorilian was himself. But his Highborn kin could be killed or, as Levyathan had so painfully noted, damaged—so it was possible that the Rill, although itself immortal, could be broken. Such thoughts unsettled him. *It was before*, he decided, repeating what the aged tutor with whom he had studied at Askorras had said. *Before Derlon entered the machine, and the Rill awakened to its godhood.* That explanation satisfied him, at least as to why the Rill had allowed parts of its sacred corpus to fall into ruin. But that did not answer the other great question: why the Rill did not run where parts of its corpus still stood intact.

Like at Stauberg. Or at Hestya.

Dorilian turned away and leaned his elbows on the wall, staring at the Rill as though he could force it to give up its secrets, for surely it had some, having lived for so long. What did it know about the world it and its brother Entity, the Wall, had created?

Levyathan twitched again and curled against him. Dorilian reached to steady him. *You, me... like our gods*, the boy fretted. *Far apart.*

"Yes," Dorilian said. He liked how sometimes his voice seemed to fasten words onto the fabric of the world.

Lev's small body shivered. *Cold men surround us. I know them by their shadows.*

Dorilian felt them too, the shapes of other minds, many and toxic. But how much he saw through his own mind and how much through Levyathan's when they were together, even he could not be sure. *Why do they hate us?* Lev's question pressed into his thoughts. *Because they fear us.*

*But why do they fear us?*

Dorilian sighed and pointed across the city at the soaring shapes of Rill structure rising above so many buildings and so many lives. *Because of that. They fear a Sordaneon will awaken their machine.*

The chair in the Rill station's private waiting room overlooked the city. Dorilian didn't mind being alone in the room. He envisioned Epoptes closely attending banks of screens and devices and attempting to discern if his physical proximity had any effect, however minor or subtle, upon the Entity's functions. Before his and Lev's journey north two months ago, they hadn't had a Sordaneon so near the Rill in decades.

He touched his finger to his nose and traced the familiar straight shape of it. The bones, like those in his jaw, had knitted cleanly, the swelling vanished along with any lingering discoloration. While not altogether glad he now lacked proofs of the assault, at least his appearance would not raise questions when he reached Sordan. Anything but physical damage could be explained away, covered up, especially as he had not told anyone, not even the governess, Noemi, that he had been attacked. He still had not heard what Essera's King and his Highborn kin would do in return for his concession in pardoning the Khelds. That he was here, isolated in a room at Permephedon's Rill station and not sequestered in some tower, seemed like a hopeful turn.

*Why did they put me in a room looking out at the city?*

There were other rooms in the Rill building, some looking out over the vast white plain, others overlooking the Rill platforms and loading docks. Some rooms had no windows at all. This window, however, faced the glittering, glassy towers of the Citadel. Why? To remind him of where he had been—and that he could be returned there if he did not give them the promises they sought?

No Highborn promise had ever been broken. Sebbord, his

grandfather, had enforced the priceless value of this fact. Dorilian was very careful about the promises he made.

He looked again out the window. He must always remember that Essera was a Malyrdeon stronghold, ruled by the Wall. That Entity possessed powers utterly separate from the Rill, linked in mysterious ways to both the past and the future. No one knew just what a Malyrdeon saw when he communed with the Wall. *Be wary*, Sebbord had warned him before sending him here. *Only the Malyrdeons can construct a future by which to place you where they wish you to be.* The Malyrdeons had applied the pressure that had seen him brought to Essera. Had they also known what would happen, that he and Stefan would become enemies? That Stefan would attack him? He doubted it, but the thought continued to niggle at him.

*Stefan deserves everything he gets*, Dorilian reminded himself. *Everything.*

A whisper like a hiss alerted him when the room's only bare wall manifested a door, allowing two saffron-robed Epoptes to enter. Both men bowed, but not because they revered him. They feared punishment if he reported they had not.

Dorilian rose and braced himself for the physical sensations he would experience when he entered the Rill's powerful aurora. The invisible field could not be detected by most, but he always did. Secrets, Sebbord had told him, sheathed swords—and Dorilian had learned to conceal the secret of his Rill affinity so well the Malyrdeons themselves had pronounced him ungifted.

Seeing Austell on the platform caught him by surprise. He had expected Elhanan. Austell's presence bestowed far more importance on his departure. In a way it made sense, because he *was* important, but Austell was the current Wall Lord—and Wall Lords seldom came this near the Rill. Pairing the Entities was risky.

Austell gestured for the Epoptes to withdraw, and they retreated out of earshot. "I thought you should have these." He extended an envelope of heavy vellum, its royal blue seal stamped with gold.

"Are these from your King? Or Stefan?"

"Both."

Dorilian took the envelope without comment.

"I will be sending tutors to Sordan to oversee your education. You understand the condition, I hope."

"Sordan is not a backwater."

"Hardly, but your needs are different from any other student in Sordan."

Because he was the *only* Highborn student in Sordan, Dorilian accepted that his Esseran kin might have a valid interest in his progress. "I do not deny my heritage, *fra'don.*" He used the kin word for the first time and hoped that would placate Austell. "Nor, I think, should you." He sighed. "It will be better anyway. The other students here... they shun me as it is."

Austell lifted his head to stare at him. Something pricked lightly behind Dorilian's eyes, and he quickly tugged his thoughts back from the touch. He resisted the urge to stare back. What was Austell doing? What was he *trying?*

"Go." Even the Wall Lord's voice sounded far away, as if he spoke to someone else.

Dorilian looked at him sharply.

"I will," he said. He drew himself straighter. He might as well make the same pronouncement to this man that he had planned for Elhanan. That he spoke the words to Austell made the gesture even grander. "I believe you were to secure my pardons, *fra'don.* Well, then, I pardon Cullen Brodheson's assault upon me. I pardon Neddig Daronson. I pardon Reard Argllson. No harm shall come to them for the harm they did me."

He had said all along that he would not pardon Stefan, and he didn't. Even he felt how his words, those he spoke and those he did not, crystallized upon some fabric he could not see—but that Austell did. A gasp rattled in the Wall Lord's throat, his eyes strange and wide, pupils so dilated barely any gold iris showed at all.

Something shifted. Energy—a phantom otherness—snaked around them, lifting the hairs on his skin and dancing across the clear surface of his eyes. It was as if some veil had been torn to reveal the firmament within which they both stood. Dorilian sensed the Rill, an immense presence to him even ordinarily, pulling something else into its stream—something originating in Austell. The sensation snatched at his breath. Off to the side of the platform, the two Epoptes conversed normally. Other people walked along the colonnade as if they noticed nothing at all.

"Help me," Austell whispered. Abruptly, he dropped to his knees. Dorilian knew then what the Wall Lord had done... what he was *doing*.

"You're wearing it, aren't you?" he demanded. Could any Malyrdeon be so foolish as to wear a Wall artifact while in close proximity with the Rill?

Dropping to one knee in front of the collapsing man, Dorilian thrust his fingers into Austell's clothing, tugging aside the velvet jacket and plunging his hand under the silk of the man's shirt. He found what he sought—the polished oval of the Wall Stone—smooth, cold, the size of his palm.

Power slammed into his skull. His vision went dark as the world shattered into shards. He saw himself as boy and man, but never old... wearing Sordan's crown... fallen in red-stained snow... standing with a man he did not know atop a moonlit tor. He saw others too. Stefan laughing, haunted, proud, an adult in coronation robes, a sword across his neck. A hand, feeding chickens. A beautiful woman cowering beneath a wall of flames... himself again, sword clutched in his hand as he faced a man wearing a diadem of blood-filled crystals. The Rill at his back... again and again. Through Austell's mind, the Wall Stone revealed Dorilian a thousandfold, multiplied, surrounded, futures spreading outward from his body like wings.

Austell was trying to see *him*. Trying to *predict* him.

Wall force pulled at Dorilian, too, sought to suck him away from just this one existence into its many—a sundering that remained whole—except something massive stood in its way. The Rill. His affinity to it anchored him somehow, while Austell, far from his Wall, was not.

Closing his fingers around the Wall Stone's chain, Dorilian yanked the artifact away from Austell's skin, breaking the contact. The world reasserted, the stream of images vanished. Austell's convulsing body toppled, and he breathed again. Dorilian staggered to his feet, the Wall Stone in his hand, and stared at the Rill.

It loomed before him, revealed fully by his retreating contact with the Wall. Rings and rivers of pale half light vaulted the sky above the city—shifting, beautiful, and hideous. It had a body. A maw filled with stars. Even as he watched, his senses retreated to solely human, and the Rill Entity shrank again to the hard, diminished shape he knew.

"Get him out of here!" Dorilian shouted to the Epoptes already running toward them.

"Did you see?" Austell gasped, struggling as the Epoptes tried to pull him out of the Rill stream toward the safety of the terminal building. His wild gaze devoured Dorilian. When the men sought to drag Austell from the platform, he screamed at them in tongues they did not understand. That perhaps even he did not. Dorilian recognized none of them. Spectral light still gleamed from the Wall Stone clutched in Dorilian's hand, dangling from its broken chain. "Did you see?" Austell cried, twisting, keeping Dorilian in sight. "*What did you see?*"

But Dorilian only clutched the artifact tighter and did not answer.

The only thing he'd truly seen was that he needed to learn more, a lot more, about the Wall.

# 5

Another year passed before he made the journey. He needed time to plan his moves.

Dorilian felt the kiss of Wall power as soon as his Teremari ship's prow passed through Ergeiron's Eye. No ship could enter Stauberg's harbor except through the Eye, a broad opening in that portion of the Wall enclosing the sea out to the harbor islands. Though he had returned the Wall Stone to Elhanan before leaving Permephedon, Dorilian's body remembered its contact with the Malyrdeon Entity and answered its touch. Wall matter, like Rill matrix, existed on planes apart from those it shared with mortals. He shivered as the Wall's invisible stranding passed delicately over his skin with an icy tingle of recognition. The Wall sensed not only who and what he was but all that he had been and would be in futures yet to harden.

*Ergeiron, Time Binder.* He invoked the Wall by its other names. *Rift Mender, Keeper of the Keys.*

Once they had passed, he turned to look back and up at the light-filled shape rearing high above his ship's golden sails. Like the Rill Entity to which it was related, the Wall was not static. Its translucent shape shifted and flowed. Dorilian marked its monumental presence: nearly transparent where it bestrode the harbor like white silk sails in the sun, shining and tall where it lifted edifices upon land, rising above the clifftop city, spanning gorges and guarding Stauberg against any enemy. He had not expected it to be beautiful.

"The Wall truly is the Rill's brother," he said to his cousin Tiflan Morevyen, who stood on the deck beside him.

Now forty years of age and easily taller and broader than any other man Dorilian knew, Tiflan smiled with the ease of the worldly. He had also traveled more than any other man Dorilian had yet met.

"Now you know why they keep Labran prisoner here and not in one of their other cities."

Because the Wall shielded Stauberg from outside attacks and remote magic, its nature allowed it to know visitors by their intentions. "Does it prevent men from entering if their purpose is to free him?" Dorilian asked.

Tiflan shrugged his broad shoulders. "It might, if Labran as a free man is not among the futures it protects. But your grandfather's captors have other reasons for keeping him here. No Highborn prince has ever been slain within the Wall's shadow. It protects Stauberg so well that storms never lift so much as a shingle from any roof, and the sea is always moderate within the harbor." Tiflan acknowledged the Entity with a smile. "The Malyrdeons take pride in Ergeiron. A most reliable god."

Dorilian scowled. While he could hardly begrudge the Malyrdeons their pride, the Rill extended further and affected more lives. It powered diverse economies that allowed the human parasites that lived upon its largesse to eat, drink, travel, amass wealth, and extend their rule over their less fortunate neighbors. It even allowed those men to rule over the Rill's own progeny. They used their Entity to further his family's humiliation. Was he supposed to honor them for that? But as he looked upon the Wall, he could not quite bring himself to hate it.

"Remember why you're here," Tiflan warned.

"I do."

"You can still change your mind. None but Tutto and I know you're here. Only I need appear at the King's banquet. You can stay at the manse where the servants will think you are part of my entourage, and we can leave in a few days with none of your enemies the wiser."

"They don't frighten me. Neither they nor their fur-faced King. I will do what I came here to do."

"Then you face two bad outcomes. One is that they will not allow it. The other is that you should succeed."

"And what will I be if they succeed where I do not?" Inhaling salt spray as the ship cleaved water, Dorilian looked across the blue expanse of Stauberg's fabled harbor to its only island, a rocky mount barren of trees, crowned by the static rings and white monoliths of a dormant Rill node. He had seen many such mounts in his sixteen years. Rill-bereft edifices rose above the dusty houses of Hestya and beside the sea at Ilmar. Similar, uncrowned mounds stood at Ben-Aranath and Ogarth and Amroset. All waiting in silence.

*What will I be?* It was a question to which the Wall itself, not even a year before, had given no clear answer.

Tall as it was, the Wall did not impede the sun and the next day boasted a bright dawn. In the light-filled courtyard of the town manse belonging to the Prince of Teremar, two brown-garbed retainers bowed deep, though not deep enough. The man to whom they bowed—giant, laughing Tiflan—did not mind the lapse, but Dorilian did. Tiflan might not be Highborn, but he was Dorilian's cousin and Regent-Designate to Teremar, and that was rank enough for them to press their foreheads to the flagstones. The slight annoyed him.

"Here, young fella, hold this one for the sword master." The shorter of the men shoved the reins of Tutto's horse into Dorilian's hand. The sword master himself was nowhere yet to be seen.

"Why don't you hold it?" Dorilian asked. "That *is* your job."

"Which is one job more than you have, looks like." The man smirked before ambling away. Dorilian's gaze stayed on him as he rejoined his companion and the two men broke out laughing.

It was all Dorilian could do to not physically bite his tongue. Keeping his identity hidden was not in his nature. Clearly, people spoke and behaved differently when they didn't know who he was. Not only did they lob snide insults his way, but passed off their work. *I should do this more often.*

While waiting for Tiflan, Dorilian adjusted the pouch strapped to his side and concealed beneath a summer-weight cape. Everything so far had gone as planned. The ship had arrived on time and the retainers also, with horses waiting. They had ridden to the manse where he had spent the morning in preparation. The rich garments hidden beneath the cape suited his station and the occasion: Marc Frederick Stauberg-Randolph's thirty-fifth jubilee.

The name made Dorilian frown. A foreign name for a foreign usurper. Just the crude sound of it made him want to unsheathe his sword.

The manse occupied one of the hills of the city and provided a good view of the Malyrdeon stronghold that housed his captive grandfather Labran. Dorilian could tell which tower by the banner atop it: Sordan's Silver Eagle, the emblem raised wherever Sordan's Hierarch was present. That his family's flag had flown for thirty-five years above Stauberg and not Sordan, and that he had never even seen it before this day, brought fresh thoughts of vengeance. Of the hundred ways Dorilian might challenge Essera, only one would set Sordan free.

Though Sebbord had taught Dorilian patience, he found that lesson difficult to master.

Sebbord's sword master, Tutto Estol-Rhunnard, sauntered forward, his rich emerald silks embellished with gold in the shape of Teremar's heraldic sheaves of grain. "They'll take that from you." Tutto indicated Dorilian's sword, which showed beneath his cape. Brown and stocky, his thinning hair fast going gray, Tutto seldom approved of anything.

"They'll do nothing once I speak my name."

"Sure of that, are you?"

"Only one man among them would dare try." Even so, Dorilian knew he would not be allowed to approach their King armed. "I will hand my sword to you when the time is right. But I will not give anything of mine over to common men."

"I'm a common man. Never forget that."

"I don't."

Tutto hauled himself onto the broad body of the horse and gathered the reins Dorilian gave him. "Someday, you'll learn that your fate is bound up with that of common men, same as ours is bound up with yours."

The ride to the Aesa Eranos palace took them through the heart of the city. Revelers lined the close, winding streets and open squares with stalls, and the air was ripe with laughter, shouts, and rich scents from foods being grilled behind storefronts. The handful of soldiers Tiflan was allowed for protection barely served to clear the way. Not for the first time that day, Dorilian regretted that he, like Tiflan and Tutto, had only a gray horse to ride. The nobility favored gray horses of every breed, which merely meant they were so numerous they caused barely a stir. He usually rode ivory horses of the green-eyed, blue-hoofed breed reserved for Highborn and Staubaun royalty and for which crowds parted readily.

It was entirely possible Dorilian was the first Sordaneon in history to ride a common horse.

Tiflan presented Sebbord's invitation—gold leaf on vellum, enclosed in a jeweled cylinder—to the guards at the outer gate, who let them pass. They dismounted inside the next gate and gave over their horses to boys wearing shiny gold boots and livery of Stauberg-Randolph blue. As soon as the lads left, they ascended the grand staircase leading into the palace. Slender portals allowed streams of light to filter in through golden glass. Seven massive corridors, each a different color and wide enough to allow several men to walk abreast, led away from a domed sea-blue rotunda. The center of the floor was inscribed by sections with the names and stories of the Malyrdeon kings who had ruled here.

*They let that barbarian rule from this seat!* Dorilian fought down a surge of indignation at yet another sign of how far his northern kindred had fallen. Marc Frederick was not even a native to this land, yet he sat upon Essera's throne. A throne that, if the Malyrdeons did not want it, should rightly have gone to the Sordaneons.

Dorilian held those thoughts. How did he hope to control an Entity if he could not control himself?

A short walk later, down a corridor lined with festive banners and uniformed guards, they arrived at an open archway leading to where the celebration was being held. An armed man whose insignia informed them he was a captain of the Third Triemperal Guard approached. Tiflan—the only one who had actually been invited—and Tutto presented both the invitation and a letter bearing the seal and identifying ribbons of the Highborn Prince of Teremar.

"You are allowed one man to stand in your service, Lord Morevyen, not two." The captain scrutinized the papers, which bore Sebbord Teremareon's signature and official seal along with the precisely penned words stating he had sent his grandson in his place.

While the guards focused on Tiflan and the document, Dorilian reached into the pouch under his cape and pulled forth the royal circlet he had carried there. It was the last item of his ensemble and a necessary one. He placed the brilliant circle encrusted with green gems on his head before speaking.

"Lord Tiflan is traveling alone. The man is in *my* service."

"Yours?"

"Yes, mine." Dorilian lifted his gaze. He knew why the captain hesitated. He was well aware of his less than pureblood looks. "Ask *him* who I am." He stared past the man's right shoulder toward the blue-caped Dragoon Cadets. The corps of young officers stood as an honor guard leading into the Jubilee Court. "Ask Stefan. He knows."

Stefan Stauberg-Randolph, older now and more handsome, even with his blue eyes and dark hair, wore gold-edged officer's bands as he stood white-faced at the head of the brilliantly uniformed Dragoons.

"Cadet?" the officer demanded.

"Dorilian Sordaneon, Sir," Stefan replied. "His name is Dorilian Sordaneon." He spoke as if each syllable pained his mouth.

The gasps that followed pleased Dorilian immensely. Even in proud Essera, men knew of his family's history. The raising of the Rill. The throwing down of many-towered Iddolea. The shattering of Bynum's frozen lake during the Winter War. In their lifetimes, Delos Sordaneon—Dorilian's uncle and his father's twin—had assisted Ral of Leseos against the Kheld rebels at Gignastha, sending god's fire to sever the great Vermillion Aqueduct and quickly ending that city's siege. The Sordaneon name could not be spoken without evoking a legacy of power and sublime privilege.

The captain blinked. "If you will but wait here, Thrice Royal—"

"There's no need to announce me. I'm sure your King will figure it out." Dorilian released the throat clasps of his cape, which he tossed aside. He stood before them wearing a tunic of emerald green silk emblazoned with Sordan's Silver Eagle, over which he wore a coat glittering with enough precious gold and gemstones to purchase estates for all their families. He walked toward the door.

"He's armed! Stop him!" Stefan shouted at the captain.

The man spread his hands. "How?"

Nothing in the captain's rank permitted him to accost one of the Entity-bound Highborn. Even the other soldiers of the Guard dared not draw their swords. In Stauberg, as in every land of the Triempery, to bare steel at the Highborn was punishable by death.

With a smirk at Tutto that said he'd made his point, Dorilian led the way into the hall, leaving the captain with no course of action but to rush after them.

# 6

The guest list for the King's Jubilee covered seven long pages in tiny script. Several hundred guests filled the great hall that had been built eight hundred years before by Emrysen Malyrdeon for the wedding of his son to the Queen of the Pitiless Isles, that harsh archipelago in the north seas. Laughter floated lightly atop undercurrents of conversation and blended with music played by musicians in the gallery. Servants carried golden platters, attending the whims of noble palates. The hall swarmed with color and gaiety.

Marc Frederick was thoroughly enjoying Endelarin Nemenor's tale of how he'd acquired two recent wives, each maiden a jewel beyond compare by the Ardaenan King's account. Marc Frederick didn't know anyone who had actually *seen* any of Endelarin's one hundred or so wives, a number that varied in the telling and depended on how far removed the teller was from Endelarin himself. In any event, the man's marital exploits left Marc Frederick envious. His own queen, after delivering the Stauberg-Randolph heir desired and required by all parties involved, considered the sexual aspects of their marriage contract to have been fulfilled. Marc Frederick had for many years discreetly found companionship elsewhere.

He looked up as the room's conversational buzz faltered. Three newcomers had entered unannounced and now crossed the floor as his captain of the guard followed in evident agitation. Endelarin, shorter than Marc Frederick by nearly a foot and not often called handsome, having a large nose and even larger mouth, roared with laughter from his seat at the royal left hand.

"Remarkable!"

Marc Frederick wondered at that and looked more closely. He had been expecting Tiflan Morevyen, whose impressive height and broad presence now commanded nearly every eye in the hall. And the stalwart man stomping alongside Tiflan was a man he'd often seen in Sebbord's company. Though somewhat unexpected, Tutto Estol-Rhunnard was Sebbord's sword master and a suitable traveling companion. The third person, however, he had never seen before.

"By the many-named gods! You never cease to surprise!" Endelarin lifted an eyebrow arch with congratulation. "You did not tell me you had snagged a Sordaneon to grace your soiree."

There. That piece of information revealed whom he looked upon.

"Dorilian." Marc Frederick tested the name upon his teeth. He heard it often, primarily from the acid tongues of his advisors. It had only been a matter of time before he and this particular problem met, but he'd never dreamed the occasion would be public.

"Why yes, the same. Deben's unruly heir," Endelarin confirmed. He was related to the Sordaneons and, therefore, a frequent visitor to Sordan's court, at which few Esseran nobles were welcome. "Sixteen years of Highborn arrogance and the adolescent source of every one of his father's silver hairs—of which Deben has a head full. Dorilian would drain the seas if doing so would make his point. It's the Nemenor blood that makes him so restless. He has it on both sides."

Marc Frederick doubted being a Nemenor relation had much to do with that.

Tempering annoyance with elation, he remained seated. He knew a thing or two about making statements. He'd devoted hours of thought to the proper time and place, the optimal situation, for meeting this latest in a long line of enemies.

At the back of the hall, a handful of Dragoon Cadets tramped into the room beside a contingent of soldiers. Stefan stood at the head and center of the colorful corps, his face a florid, staring mask. Marc Frederick made a mental note to talk with his grandson in private later.

"Prince Dorilian Derlon Sordaneon ê Nemenor." Marc Frederick's bold announcement alerted the entire hall at last to the youth's identity. "Welcome. Had I known you wished to attend this occasion, I would have sent an invitation—and alerted my guard to your arrival."

Dorilian approached a few steps further, his companions and the King's soldiers arrayed behind him like an honor guard.

"I haven't come here to attend your celebration. I do not celebrate your rule." His voice was surprisingly clear and poised for one so young. Already it commanded an entire room with ease. "I have come to see my grandfather, Sordan's Hierarch, Labran Sordaneon. You keep him imprisoned in this castle."

Marc Frederick noted the provocation—and corrected it. "The Hierarch is our guest."

"Why do you think I would believe that—when none of *these people* do?"

The hall itself inhaled with one breath. Dorilian had just called him a liar in front of his court. Marc Frederick, however, recognized the embroidery of that verbal gauntlet. The youth had planned that remark. No spur-of-the-moment rejoinder could have been uttered with such splendid contempt.

"The distinction has its purposes, Cousin." He stressed the kin word because he could properly claim it: his mother had been the daughter of a Highborn prince. He owned the same degree of relation to holy blood as Tiflan Morevyen. He locked his gaze onto Dorilian's steel-cold one. "I will demonstrate our goodwill and turn this occasion into a welcome. Join me at my table."

The youth drew taut. The response had caught him by surprise. "I have come to see my grandfather, not dine at your table."

The chill that had overtaken the Jubilee Court had many sources. Marc Frederick could separate them one by one. His courtiers' disapproval of Dorilian's defiance and their fear of what he represented. Dorilian's own burning desire to perpetuate hostilities. Stauberg's Prince Enreddon, seated not far away, unhappy that his courtship of the Prince of Lacenedon's daughter, Palaistea, now must take second seat to the meeting unfolding before the King. Essera's other Highborn princes, alarmed at the prospect of having to choose between protecting their King and intervening on behalf of one of their own kind. Regelon of Merrydn, frozen at a table with his daughter, Ionais, and Marc Frederick's son Jonthan, whose betrothal they were to announce this night, their merriment now soured. And his Queen, Apollonia, who had risen at her table and now stood looking upon the rebellious youth with regal rage. Above all remained the soldiers' confusion and fear, terrified that they might be commanded to seize the boy and dreading all the bloodshed that would follow. Seventy men had died upon the Rill platform at Permephedon defending Labran Sordaneon. Marc Frederick did not know how many men among the hundreds present in this room might come to the defense of Dorilian Sordaneon. *More than I would want*, he realized, *and less than should.*

Marc Frederick cloaked his response in tones far colder than before. "If this company offends you, Sordaneon, you are free to leave it." His gaze never relinquished the other. "If you can see fit to tolerate us for the sake of a visit with your grandfather later, we insist you do so in a manner that will not disgrace the House of Derlon."

For a moment, he thought Dorilian would turn his back on him and walk from the room. He half expected this sixteen-year-old Sordaneon heir would reject, utterly and for all time to come, Stauberg and Essera and all he represented. Austell had warned him that any meeting with Dorilian would have to be pitch perfect. Dorilian's silver eyes flicked once to where tall Tiflan Morevyen stood silently nearby, then darkened with thought. What manner of bluff had been called, whether he had passed a test or survived a challenge of wills, Marc Frederick could not know for certain. But Dorilian Sordaneon unbuckled his sword and handed it to Tutto.

"Then we shall stay and share Your Majesty's hospitality."

Marc Frederick nodded. He released Dorilian from his gaze and looked past the boy to Tiflan. He indicated the empty chair to his right. "Lord Morevyen, I had intended for you to be seated beside me in Sebbord's place. That place is still yours, if you choose."

"I will yield to my Sordaneon cousin, Majesty," Tiflan replied. "I would not see him in other than a place of honor."

The steward made a place for Tiflan at the table's end, beside the Elector of Trongor, who looked happy with the company. The Elector's only other option for dinner conversation, a dour potentate of a client kingdom, looked unhappy at being seated among the lower born.

"And you, Tutto Rhunnard, will be allowed to stand in guard of your prince." Marc Frederick overruled his captain, who stared in horror of his decision. The danger of allowing an armed Sordani soldier to stand within striking distance of the King probably terrified most of the guests. There was undoubtedly an element of risk. But Marc Frederick understood that if he was to honor his guest properly, he must extend not only diplomacy but privilege. However much the men and women in this room—even his own grandson and his queen—wanted this brazen prince to be an enemy, Dorilian Sordaneon was not one. Not yet. And Marc Frederick was not about to treat him as one. He had enough of those already. *This boy is not like his father; he cannot be bound by fear. And Sordan cannot be won by force. Let other men make that mistake.*

The meal resumed under a cloud of feigned merriment. Dorilian sat at Marc Frederick's right hand with tense formality. Anyone watching him could see how the situation—the dinner, the people in whose company he found himself—constituted a form of torture. He pointedly concentrated on the dinner plates set before him, from which he ate not a morsel, and his wine glass, from which he drank not so much as a drop. He ignored every attempt at conversation. And through all of it—the whole painful, stilted charade—Marc Frederick waited. Thankfully, Endelarin Nemenor kept up a steady verbal patter, which allowed the King to nod and appear engaged in something other than taking the political pulse of the silent boy to his right. Something other than the only person in that vast hall who mattered.

Here, clothed in human shape, he saw at last his key to unlocking Sordan. Unlocking the Highborn future. Unlocking the Rill. Now that he met Dorilian, he believed it possible. He knew that he looked upon old Sebbord's most outstanding achievement: a Sordaneon heir in whose body and life were fused the coldest calculations and fiercest passions of a succession of powerful men. Marc Frederick thought that he should see Deben somewhere in the boy, but he did not. He did see Labran, the boy's grandfather—and alongside the resemblance to his enemy he saw the breathtaking legacy of Valyane, Sebbord's beautiful daughter, dead these nine years and almost forgotten.

A simple nudge, meant to seem by chance, pulled his attention back to Endelarin. "You just agreed to a new trade treaty," the Ardaenan ruler informed him. "All shipping rights to the next ten years of Narlassian corn tributes. I'm thinking of holding you to it."

"I'll say I was drunk or distracted—that there were no witnesses and you are making it up."

"And you'll have your Highborn friends to back you up, truthtellers all. I have not a leg to stand on." Endelarin chuckled, then leaned nearer. "Our young friend has the family looks, to be sure, and more than the usual burden of family pride. Far too high for his own good and too hard for anyone else's. Less wealth and more adversity, I say, would do him good."

"He has adversity enough already in men who wish to rid him of both his wealth and his birthright." His nobles had been plundering Sordan's rich estates, farms, mines, and industry for decades. The Rill itself, the greatest prize of all, stood chained to a burgeoning Esseran commerce glutted on the spoils of Marc Frederick's victory thirty-five years before. Dorilian had inherited his mother's vast dowry holdings, assets surpassing those of most Malyrdeons, at the age of seven. Sebbord had seized the boy to protect that estate. Looters circled the Sordaneon heir like sharks.

So why was Dorilian here, walking unarmed with only two men to protect him, into the very jaws of Essera? *He's practically daring me to seize him on the spot.*

Having satisfied Endelarin's amusement, Marc Frederick returned his attention to his young guest, only to find that he had become the object of study himself. He was too cognizant of the opening to be affronted. "What have you decided?"

"That it's true," Dorilian said. "You *do* look like a Kheld."

The blunt observation made Marc Frederick laugh. It had been years since anyone but Apollonia had made a point of his looks. Though he went to the effort of being cleanshaven so as to present as Staubaun a face as possible to his subjects, no amount of grooming concealed his dark hair or his Kheld blue eyes. "Is that all you've been told? Isn't there more to it? Horns or the like?"

"No. Just that."

The dinner was winding down. Dorilian still had not eaten, even though Tutto had dutifully sampled every morsel on every platter presented to him. He had, however, given at least the appearance of politeness by pushing the food about with his fork.

As the musicians paused between sets, Marc Frederick turned again to Dorilian. "I'm surprised your father consented to this visit—if he even knows of it."

"He thinks I am in Ilmar, studying under the care of dusty old philosophers."

"I should send you back to him under guard."

"But you won't."

That was accurate. Marc Frederick wouldn't give Deben the satisfaction. It was little wonder Deben couldn't control his strong-willed heir. He was himself controlled by administrators and palace interests. "Why did you come here? You couldn't have known how I would receive this visit. I could have ordered you seized or slain. For all you know, I might still do so." He leaned back in his chair so his steward might set a glass of blackberry cordial before him, and indicated that he wished the same for his guests.

"You cannot afford to do other than welcome me." Dorilian balanced the glass for a moment before setting it aside. "Another captive would gain you nothing more than you already have. And daggers would earn you a civil war."

"Neither of which interests me—captives or wars."

The answer earned him a sharp look. "You have perpetuated both."

"Yes, I have. Sometimes events command the man, not the other way around."

Dorilian looked unconvinced. Hate rose from him in waves that permeated the entire hall. Throughout the rest of the evening, though he tried to ignore the way his skin sent pricks of warning to his spine, Marc Frederick felt Dorilian's gaze upon him, harder than sword steel and colder than an enemy's hand. The look chilled him to the bone.

Once before, he had battled a Sordaneon—and won. Now that the battle was engaged anew, he hoped he would have the strength to finish it.

# 7

"Marc, don't do this. The matter requires discussion." Enreddon Malyrdeon had been his friend for forty-five years. He was also the most powerful scion of a powerful family. He had joined Marc Frederick in the private library, where his worry amplified already abraded nerves. Dorilian wasn't the only empath in Stauberg.

Marc Frederick resumed his preparations.

"We've had thirty-five years to discuss ramifications, Redd. We've always known that if we did not destroy the Sordaneons, we would need to eventually reconcile—or be destroyed."

Far from being dismayed, Marc Frederick felt invigorated. His uninvited guest had comported himself without further incident. Though Dorilian undoubtedly wanted to think of the evening as a public slap to the face of his host, the truth was otherwise.

"Labran inspired an insurrection, Marc. He stopped the Rill, however briefly, and threw the entire Triempery into a chaos from which we have never fully recovered. But for Labran, we would never have needed to subdue Sordan. But for Labran, you might have prevented Mormantalorus from seceding. And since then, even from behind prison walls, he has sought to bring all you have done to ruin. Why do you think Austell risked using the Wall to see this child through Time? It is because the designs of so many men converge upon him!"

"We still don't know what Austell saw."

"Only because the Wall broke his mind. He should never have used a Rill field to amplify Wall contact. Now my brother doesn't know when—or even who—he is... and until another of us, perhaps Elhanan, learns to use the Wall Stone, we have no Wall vision at all."

Austell no longer dwelt at Stauberg. For his own safety, he

could no longer use the Wall Stone or be near the Wall. Whatever he had seen that day, the Malyrdeons guarded it so well that Marc Frederick had never learned the content of that encounter.

He plucked a gem-encrusted clasp bearing his family crest from the tray in his desk. He never went before Labran looking less than completely royal. Never.

"Then who's to say I don't have the right of it? We deserve confrontation, Redd. We need it, and we need Dorilian to be willing to engage us. I *want* him to fight for his birthright. What I can't afford is to have him cast me in his mind as his *enemy*."

"Oh, that's happened already. What occurred at Permephedon between him and Stefan made certain of it."

"Read his actions, not his words."

"Dorilian's actions are rebellious. He may not be Deben's heir in paranoia, but neither is he Sebbord's image in conciliation. Coming here, demanding to see his grandfather, is not an act of friendship."

"An act of hostility?" Marc Frederick fastened the clasp at the throat of his royal blue jacket. "Of course, it is. It can be nothing else. That boy is perfectly aware of the messages he's sending. He *wants* us to distrust and fear him."

"Have you considered this might be some plan of Deben's?"

Marc Frederick adjusted the fit of the leather padding across his shoulders. Dorilian's father might be ineffectual, but he was no less malignant for that. "It crossed my mind: that and other things. No, Dorilian is here on his own, taking our measure and letting us take his. He knows what he's doing, you can be sure of it." Tugging on his cuffs, he walked to the door and prepared to join his young guest. "I promised him a visit with his grandfather in return for his being a *willing* guest at my table. He delivered—indeed, he delivered far more than he knows, and so, therefore, will I. Let him visit the source of his old family quarrel. The last thing I need is another *unwilling* Sordaneon on my hands. They're enormous trouble, and I can no longer afford the luxury of having them oppose my every course of action."

"I fear you underestimate him."

Marc Frederick paused at the door and flashed a confident smile at his old friend. The crown upon his head, with its seven broad points chased with bright silver, felt especially heavy tonight. "No. But he, I am sure, will underestimate me."

Dorilian marveled that his plan had gone so well.

He had expected the Esseran king to reject his demand. He had deliberately framed it for rejection, the better to build a platform upon which he might launch a barrage of grievances. Marc Frederick's response had circumvented that path. Maybe it worked better this way. He had never really believed Marc Frederick would seize him, but now he could lay those contingencies aside and focus on the meeting he had come to Stauberg to effect.

The man he was going to see was not merely his grandfather but the head of his Highborn House. The Hierarch of Sordan, titular ruler of seven domains. A man some called Rill Lord. Labran was the last of his family to have been visible to their ancestor-god. While the King kept him waiting in an antechamber, Dorilian spent some time on his appearance.

*To never see the Rill again or be seen by it. That is the sentence they placed upon him to ensure the Entity never acts other than as they will.*

A chill touched his spine at the cruelty of that sentence and that it might extend to any of his line, himself included.

Marc Frederick emerged from the room in which he'd been meeting advisors. The man had changed some items and now looked dressed for a state visit. His royal blue shirt contrasted with the brown of a soft suede jacket stamped with a pattern of tiny gilt winged horses. A heavy gold clasp carried over the design, a winged horse against a field of sapphire, encircled by a spiked border of diamonds and pearls.

"Shall we?" Marc Frederick said.

He nodded.

They passed from the center tower to another by way of a walkway that skimmed the tall trees planted in the outer courtyards. Spires of flowers released spicy perfume onto the breeze that wafted through open arches. Above, velvet night hosted stars and moonlit wisps of cloud. Below, Stauberg spread in patches of light. Weak light. Nothing like Sordan's incandescent glory.

Guards manned the doors at the end of the walkway. They also secured the chamber at the other end. Strong, broad men who looked to be neither Kheld nor Estol, but something else. Staubaun aristocracy had no hold here; neither did Staubaun beliefs. Given a chance, these men would treat him as a captive also.

Tasting heresy, Dorilian caught the eye of the man nearest him and held that dark gaze until the man looked away.

The chamber within would have seemed luxurious even to an emperor. Warm parquet floors of golden wood gleamed beneath rich carpets. Chairs and chaises upholstered in muted greens and golds formed intimate sitting areas before two hearths at either end. A spectacular chandelier clustered with waterglobes bathed the room in soft, pure light, and a fluted archway led out into what looked to be a courtyard—a courtyard only flying things might visit, but at least the Hierarch enjoyed fresh air and sunlight. Crickets chirped in its shadows. Dorilian followed the King through a different archway, through more rooms, coming at last to the bedchamber. From within, a woman's low voice stopped speaking.

An immense bed with lion's-head feet and sumptuous silk-damask drapery commanded the center of the room.

"Labran?" Marc Frederick said, his voice calm and free of nuance. "I have brought someone to visit you."

The old man sat propped upright in bed, bolstered by pillows and warmed by a silken coverlet. Hair raven black in his last paintings was now pure white, so Labran in his one-hundred and twenty-first year almost looked like he could be Staubaun. He also looked frail, his skin like weathered paper.

From a chair beside the aged man's bed, a matronly woman wearing a widow's cap and stole laid aside the book she had been reading aloud. With a demure nod to the King and his guest, she discreetly left the room. Labran cocked his head to peer more closely at Marc Frederick and gave his rival a weak smile.

"A visitor for me?" His voice cracked, barely more than a wheeze. "If Sebbord could not come himself, I wish not to see that baseborn mule he sends in his place."

Dorilian stiffened. He had heard his father refer to Tiflan that way but never any other.

"Not Lord Morevyen, old friend—not this time," Marc Frederick assured him. "I have brought one of your grandsons." He moved to put his hand on Dorilian's shoulder, but Dorilian stepped forward to avoid the unwelcome touch.

Labran's face hardened. His gray eyes, faded and rheumy, studied Dorilian's face. "Is this some sport you mean to pass off as mine? Or did old Enreddon finally sire something that lived?"

Heat flooded Dorilian's cheekbones. It had not occurred to him that his lineage might be questioned.

"You misunderstand, Labran." The King interceded before Dorilian could recover enough to utter a retort. "This young man is legitimate. He is Deben's son by Valyane. He sought me out for the sole purpose of visiting you. He came to Stauberg on his own and surprised the hell out of me by appearing this evening at my Jubilee celebration."

The Hierarch tilted his head, squinting for better light. "Then I think I look upon a fool—or two."

Dorilian met and held that dismissive gaze. To think he had come all the way to Stauberg to see this miserable old man!

"Come nearer, Boy, I need to see you better. Closer. Yes, yes, you have your mother's eyes. All agree on that. I have it, too, the Nemenor taint. Touch me." Labran extended his right hand.

Marc Frederick made no move to stop Dorilian from taking the gnarled fingers into his own. Labran's hand could have been five sticks wrapped in old cloth, so frail were they. Dorilian blinked as he felt a prickle on the surface of his mind, the scurrying of an ant upon his psychic skin before he brushed it aside, asserting mental barriers. Glancing to the King, Dorilian noticed how Marc Frederick closely watched Labran's face as the Hierarch released Dorilian's hand and sank back into his pillows.

"Which of Deben's sons are you?" Labran asked finally.

"Dorilian, Sire."

"The oldest?"

"Yes, Sire."

Labran's dry lips stretched in a thin smile. "I can see you won't be as weak-willed as your father." He turned to the King. "I wish to speak alone with my grandson."

Marc Frederick shook his head. "No. If you disagree with having me privy to your conversation tonight, then I will arrange for Enreddon to sit in with the two of you tomorrow morning."

Dorilian snapped around in disbelief. "You do not even let him speak to others except in your presence?"

"My presence or that of one of your Malyrdeon kindred. I trust no others."

"Always in the presence of those who betrayed him!" Dorilian had known Labran was a captive but not that his captors deprived him so completely of privacy. "But Sebbord, my *other* grandfather, led me to believe he was allowed to visit without hindrance."

"So he has been, and may again upon his next visit," Marc Frederick confirmed. As he spoke, he looked full at the captive. Dorilian was about to protest when he noticed his grandfather's smile. Labran was enjoying this.

Marc Frederick continued to explain with regal calm. "I have Sebbord's promise, his most solemn vow, that he will countenance no discussion on such topics as I consider off limits." That he valued that promise, and honored it, vibrated within those words.

Dorilian glanced at his bedridden grandfather, whose crooked smile bade him continue his questions. "And my grandfather, the Hierarch's, promise... does that not satisfy you as well?"

"He has not made, and has told me he will never make, that promise."

Labran's unblinking and amused regard confirmed the statement.

"And what of *my* promise?" Dorilian demanded. He was prepared to offer it.

Though he looked regretful, the King shook his head. "You do not know the substance of my limitations. And there is not enough time in the remainder of this evening for me to properly convey them. Perhaps... tomorrow."

"Yes, tomorrow." Labran lay back on the pillows, hands folding weakly upon his chest. "Tomorrow would be... better."

That night everyone in Marc Frederick's orbit saw fit to advise him on how to manage his unexpected guest. Immediately upon reaching his private rooms, he endured an hour-long tirade from Apollonia, whose criticisms of how he had handled the banquet were bearable only because he barely listened to her. He put off scores of high-ranking dignitaries, nobles, ambassadors, and guild representatives, all of whom petitioned for explanations or reassurances. He was most attentive to Stefan, mindful of the greater potential for damage from that quarter. Now that he had met Dorilian for himself, he found more reason than ever to be disturbed by his grandson's insistence on perpetuating their youthful conflict.

"He's pure poison!"

"He'll be Sordan's ruler one day." Marc Frederick gestured toward the couch opposite his. If nothing else, he would get his grandson to stop pacing. Stefan sighed but plopped heavily onto the upholstered cushions. "I'm not going to dethrone the Sordaneons. That is that. Dorilian is a fact. And we will all have to learn ways to coexist with him."

Stefan snorted. "Not me!"

"Oh? Have you decided to retreat into some Cibulitan redoubt, there to study obscure philosophies or resurrect forgotten lore? Or head off to explore the lands beyond the Pillars of the Sky?" If any men had ever crossed that mountain range, which formed the eastern boundary of the known lands that comprised the Triempery, they had never returned.

Stefan glared at him in reproach. "You know my plans. How can I promise the Khelds full citizenship in this land as long as I have the likes of him putting down everything I do? I can't even get Kheld merchants into the customhouses at Dazunor-Rannuli or Leseos because the Sordaneons hog all the Rill slots."

"That's not the reason." Marc Frederick regretted Stefan's pigheaded simplification. "The Seven Houses will never allow Khelds to compete in the Dazun markets, and the rulers of Leseos don't want to see their city become a base for Kheld mercantile operations."

"Are you saying that the Sordaneons have no hand in it?"

"No." Seeing his valet, Gareth, approach with a snifter of brandy in hand, Marc Frederick paused long enough to accept the glass. He treasured his rituals; they infused serenity into the tumultuous politics of his life. "I'm saying there is a bigger picture."

"You always say that."

"Then you might start anticipating me and stop bringing to the table the same arguments in our every conversation."

Stefan shook his head, curls dark about his ears. Marc Frederick marked the family likeness, though Stefan looked less like his Emyli and more resembled his late Kheld father. Erwan's dark good looks had made his rebelliousness that much more attractive to those who had followed him into disaster.

"Grandfather, you don't understand," the young man continued earnestly. "You don't understand *him*. Dorilian thinks everyone is beneath him. Everyone. Even you. Everyone in Essera. He's the biggest showoff in the world!"

Marc Frederick used the curved rim of his glass to hide a smile. "A showoff?" he prodded, finding the comment just shy of the mark. The Highborn seldom flaunted their gifts.

"His fortune. His name. His precious Rill. Like they even own it anymore."

So that was how the young saw it. "Don't mistake the asset for the commodity, Stefan. People only own access, not the Rill itself."

"Same thing."

Perhaps it was. Didn't those who controlled access to a thing for all practical purposes own it? Marc Frederick recognized a paradigm when he saw one. He also recognized the trap it presented.

"Besides, he thinks he's smarter than we are." Stefan's frown darkened along with his tone. He picked a book up from the table and flipped through it absently. "He did it in class one day in front of everyone. Took on a sequence puzzle no one had gotten right after an hour of trying—just walked over to the table and set every tile in order. One, two, three. It was done. He'd gotten bored watching us and wanted to move on. He's so damn smug."

Marc Frederick wished he could pursue the observation. It struck him as unfortunate that Stefan didn't find Dorilian worth getting to know. "How are your studies going?" he asked instead, seizing the opportunity for redirection. "Your tutor has mentioned you have a talent for metallurgy."

"I find it interesting. Which metals coexist in which kinds of post-Devastation seams and pockets. Where those can be found. And then the extraction processes, of course. There's money to be made in Amallar, I think." Stefan's face brightened with excitement. "The Staubauns went after the city cores first, which makes sense, but the outer cities weren't metal-poor. There are almost certainly rich deposits in Amallar, as there are in Neuberland. They're just harder to get to because of the hilly terrain and the forests."

"And the fact that Khelds aren't a folk given to mining." Khelds maintained a primarily agrarian economy and relied upon imported ores for their metalmaking.

"They're changing about that. They have their own mines now, in Neuberland. What they're not as good at is distilling or refining ores. They can't build units that get hot enough."

"They don't have the technology."

"They don't have money. If they had money, they could buy the technology."

Marc Frederick had noted Stefan's investment in one such venture, furnishing metal to shops that in turn crafted tools and farm implements for Khelds in the Brennan valley. The high profits to be made by separating rare metals, however, remained outside Kheld reach.

"Khelds are a clever people and stubborn once they decide what they want. In time, I'm sure, they'll be smelting the inner bowels of the Orqho hills." He named the ore source that most merited exploitation.

Stefan snorted. "Sure. Casting bars of bastard ore they'll have no choice but to sell dirt cheap to Staubaun merchants or cartel agents because Khelds still won't have a single damn Rill slot in Leseos."

Marc Frederick sighed, recognizing the resumption of an argument. Much as he wished to counsel more patience, he had none left himself. The hour was late and a full schedule awaited in the morning. "Stefan," he said, "We will have years to work out a solution to that problem. Tonight may well be a part of it. So let me now make the transition from your grandfather to your king. What I want from you—what I *require* from you—is something you have struggled to deliver in the past: princely restraint."

Startled by the firm tone, Stefan leaned forward, prepared to protest. "Grandfather—"

Marc Frederick held up a hand, silencing him. "For the duration of Dorilian Sordaneon's visit here, for however long he is here, I do not want trouble. If you do not trust him not to cause it, then remember my trust in *you*."

As far as he was concerned, Stefan had lost all right to claim the high ground in his conflict two years ago, the day he'd kicked in the right side of Dorilian's face. Marc Frederick had sent Stefan away from not only Permephedon but from the civilized world. Stefan had been shipped off to the frozen isles of Maskos off the coast of Cjtala, where he had been put to work farming giant slugs that thrived in steam vents beneath those icy northern seas. The slugs' harvested bodies were rendered for *krimoil*, a vital lubricant. After a year spent up to his knees in slime and covered in stink, Stefan had returned, expressing nothing but willingness to toe the royal line.

The King did not think his grandson would fail him a second time.

# 8

Morning light bathed the terrace of the palace garden, bright and crisp, the air ripe with portents of late summer just beneath faint hints of sulfur left over from the fireworks display the night before. Marc Frederick had missed them. Dorilian, after leaving his grandfather's bedside, had been uninterested in watching the display and had departed too quickly, intent on spending the night elsewhere. Stefan had left Marc with more worries than hope. Now, in the cool and clarity of another day, the King pondered how best to contain the uncontainable.

He looked up from his thoughts when Gareth ushered two men into the garden. The steward directed Dorilian to the breakfast table while Tutto hung back and sought a place apart from the other guards.

"Join me." Marc Frederick indicated the chair opposite his.

Dorilian paused a moment before he sat. Everything about him shouted rebellion. He had dressed for meeting with Labran: rich tan *challeth* skin hemmed and detailed with Sordan's green and silver. Indeed, with Sordaneon silver. The priceless metal, incorruptible and supple as silk itself, fused gloriously to the fabric of his shirt in sweeping eagle wings, evoking a device so fabled it was the subject of awe.

*Derlon's armor. He forces us to recall his family's history.*

Dorilian pulled the chair around and sat without acknowledging his host. He did acknowledge the food, reaching for one of the sweet rolls. Marc Frederick marked his lack of fear. Last night's display of caution had been for show. It would be ruinous now for Marc Frederick to poison a Sordaneon heir at his own table.

"It looks old." The youth gazed at the sprawl of the city below them. A few ships, keeping early schedules, raised sail in the harbor. Other ships dropped sail as they moved into the waiting quays.

"Stauberg *is* old," Marc Frederick agreed.

"Not that old."

"You're fortunate to live in Sordan. Sordan always looks new." The point being inarguable, Dorilian looked over his shoulder at the palace. Pale stone walls and windows fronted with sweeping screens of colored glass opened to admit sun and air. Colors danced from those windows as if from jewels. "I don't really live in Sordan," he offered. "That's where my father lives, surrounded by his courtiers and your administrators. My real home is in Askorras."

A telling remark. One of the easternmost strongholds of the Triempery, guarding the Far Passage of the Telarkans, Askorras commanded sweeping steppes and expansive views. Marc Frederick quietly applauded Sebbord's choice of locations to raise his grandsons. "A beautiful place. The rising sun turns Tulamanta's pillars to rose, and every night they shine silver with starlight."

Dorilian tipped his head to one side. "Yes. It's just like that. When I was a boy," he continued, as though boyhood were long behind him, "my brother and I would sit before the Stone Door to watch the passage of the sun."

"What did you see?" Local legend said it was possible to see doors open in the firmament. Doors to other places, other times.

"Nothing." Dorilian shrugged. "We did it often enough. Dawn, white day, noon shadow, hot afternoon, orange sunset and blue twilight, then night itself. Only the stars ever peeked through." He frowned. "Maybe others of my kind can see things in time or space. I cannot."

"Not everyone is sure of that."

"Permephedon? I gave the Wall Stone back to the Malyrdeons, to Elhanan. I had no use for it." He met Marc Frederick's gaze. "You know that."

"Your brother is at Permephedon still, I hear." Levyathan Sordaneon was widely rumored to be a damaged child with but half a mind, but Marc Frederick knew Dorilian loved the boy fiercely.

"Marenthro seems to be able to... help him." Dorilian's expression hardened. "Before I left, I taught him how to throw a punch and said if any Khelds tried to approach him, he was to strike the first blow."

"Well-meant advice, I'm sure, but wasted. Levyathan won't meet any Khelds during his stay. Khelds are no longer allowed to be educated there."

Dorilian surely knew this because he simply grasped the glass pitcher and poured himself a cup of the clear juice that filled it. Heavy and sweet, it was the sort of drink the Highborn preferred, one of Marc Frederick's concessions to what he thought might be his guest's tastes. To fill the silence, he raised another curiosity.

"I'm surprised your father never ordered Levyathan to return to Sordan. Given your experience, I mean."

"I kept my word. I never fully informed my father of my reasons for leaving, and he was too preoccupied to notice I was being vague. Besides" —he leaned forward to pick at some nuts— "I prefer Lev to be elsewhere."

"Why?"

"Reasons of my own."

Those were reasons Marc Frederick dearly wanted to know. Did Dorilian, too, have reservations about the company his father was keeping? Well-placed spies in the Sordaneon Serat claimed the Mormantaloran Regent, Nammuor, had made a secret visit to Deben. While talks between the two rulers might have been innocuous, dealing with Sordan's autonomous trade agreements or disputes along the Hierarchate's border in Suddekar, no meeting with Mormantalorus was inconsequential.

Dorilian, unfortunately, was already accomplished at the royal art of ambiguity.

Marc Frederick backed away from his thoughts to find Dorilian watching him, eyes narrowed with suspicion.

"I'm not going to befriend you or any of your bastard kin." Dorilian set down his cup. "Throw me in prison for saying that if you want to."

"Prison?" Marc Frederick laughed. At last, they had cut to the chase. He settled back in his chair and wished the morning sun were hotter. "You can provoke me until the Three Worlds collide, and I will not do that."

Dorilian sank back into his chair. The wooden frame creaked in the silence between them.

The pleasant interlude, such as it had been, was over. Whatever Dorilian had learned from the scant pleasantries of their meeting, he would take back with him to Sordan. There was no harm now in making a statement of policy.

"I honor your family more than you believe," Marc Frederick said to the brooding young man before him. "If you ever become open to explanations, I will explain all I have done. If you ever become open to friendship, I will offer it. If you ever become my enemy, I will show you what that means as well. But know this: I will not let you fall into any hands but my own."

"You think you can rule me?"

Marc Frederick signaled to Gareth that breakfast had ended. It was time for Dorilian to meet with his grandfather again. "No. But someone will, because you are still a very long way from ruling yourself."

Labran Sordaneon's prison seemed less like one in daylight. The extraordinary precautions initially designed to prevent the escape of a physically powerful and aggressive man now served more to protect a frail and valuable elder. Dorilian had learned from Enreddon on the walk over that even the servants assigned to Labran were drawn from Marc Frederick's fanatically devoted householders, descended from the handful of servants who had come with him as a young man. The only orders they took were delivered in a language spoken nowhere else in this world.

"Learn his language, if you get the opportunity." Labran spoke to Dorilian, who sat on the bed beside him. Enreddon sat in a chair nearby, watching and listening. The Hierarch clearly did not care about being overheard.

Dorilian cared, however. He resented it enormously; an emotion Enreddon did not mind throwing back his way by means of knowing looks.

"I mean it, Boy," the old man continued. "A wonderful advantage. We cannot duplicate it. Aryati is a more elegant language, but the Epoptes and scholars speak it as well as we."

"I know, Grandfather," Dorilian said.

Eyes rheumy with age fixed on him. "You don't trust them. You shouldn't."

"I don't trust anyone."

"Your father's weakness. Too little trust makes for paralysis. He who does not trust the ground on which he walks goes nowhere."

Dorilian would have said he did trust a few people. It was distrust of Enreddon that held his tongue, a deep reluctance to reveal anything useful to an enemy. He trusted his brother. He trusted

Tiflan and Tutto and his friend Legon Rebiran, whom he had left behind in Teremar. And he trusted his grandfather, Sebbord Teremareon, whose training he now put into practice. The designs he traced as if absently on the embroidered coverlet were saying more than Enreddon knew. *I see where I am going*, he told his grandfather. *I am strong. The way within lies clear.* He used the old Kituy symbol set—now extinct but for this singular application by the Sordaneons. His grandfather, of course, could not respond as openly. His captors had watched Labran's habits for decades and might detect even subtle alterations in non-verbal patterns. His fingers formed only the occasional glyph in reply, well hidden within a gesture.

The Rill Stone ring caught the late morning light during one such gesture, and the marvelous device blazed brilliant green. Labran kept his left hand, and therefore the ring, in plain sight, and Dorilian had been instructed to sit opposite. Though Dorilian knew why Labran still had the device in his keeping, he was surprised to see it on his grandfather's hand. Renderings had been faithful. A deceptively plain band of Sordaneon silver held fast a glowing emerald shard clasped by a filigree of metal beads and tiny, burning gems. From his studies, he knew that the Rill Stone's lambent details revealed themselves only when the matrix was in contact with living Sordaneon flesh. The single green gem bore an eagle image, elegant and agleam with silver, upon its surface. *Derlon's Sign.* Just as a living piece of the Wall had gone into the making of the Wall Stone, an enduring part of the Rill itself encircled Labran's finger. That immortal lifeforce, Derlon's own, communicated with the larger Entity and bound Sordan's Hierarch to it. By summoning bits of Derlon's latent power, a Sordaneon could imprint an indelible eagle image into documents, hides, or even stone, a silver signature famed throughout the Triempery. A small silver eagle aglow upon a human forehead signified a person who belonged to the High Order of Epoptes in the Rill's service. Labran, however, had dignified only a handful of Arch-Epoptes since his incarceration.

"It's the Rill, of course, that interests them." Labran lifted his chin in the direction of the seated Enreddon, whose attention predictably sharpened. "The Malyrdeons are our brothers in blood, our brothers in name and history, but they are not our brothers in kind. They fear what I might do with our legacy, that I might take it from them and reduce all they have built to ruin."

"You stopped the Rill. For a full day, it did not run." Dorilian admired any deed feared in Essera.

"A simple task," Labran demurred. He slid a sly smile to Enreddon, who watched him with golden reserve. "An Epopte could have done it. Sebbord could have. But I did it, yes, and we now pay the price for that. They won't let Sebbord within leagues of it and extracted his promise, didn't they? And your father, holed in the Serat like a beast—"

"That is his choice, Labran," Enreddon countered in a light, calm voice. "We've placed no restrictions on Deben's modes of travel."

"Only on his mind. Injected him with fear, seeing what you were willing to do, to whom you were willing to sell us! When the Epoptes betrayed us, whose hand was in that?" Labran turned again to his grandson. "Coming here was foolish. You see the kind of men they are, envious of our wealth, seeking to take from us the source of it. What they cannot seize by force, they would gain by breeding it from us! Promise me you will marry no Esseran woman."

Taken off guard, Dorilian resorted to deflection. "Maybe I shall marry several women as the Ardaenans do!"

Enreddon laughed, but Labran marked the evasion. He lent a chuckle of his own. "Too much a promise for you to make, eh, Boy?" He speared the Malyrdeon prince with a glare. "You know he'll have no say in it. No more than Deben did."

"And you know he's young for that," Enreddon intervened. "Leave him be."

Dorilian kept his eyes on the coverlet and continued his pretense of sullen preoccupation. This meeting seemed little more than an excuse for his grandfather to air old grievances. Deben, he now saw, had not come by his paranoia solely because of ill treatment at the hands of Essera. Labran also lived in a world reduced to enemies and those who plotted with his enemies, a narrow place into which his mind had been driven not just by his captors but also by his own nature. Sebbord had often said the source of information might surpass the surface value of the information itself. Surfaces, Dorilian knew, could be misleading. *The Rill... is greater than we can see. We must penetrate it to know what it is. We must know what it is if we are to use it.* But Labran, in his current frame of mind, did not seem like someone who could help him penetrate that mystery. The man was mired in the past, unable to move.

Despite his intentions, Dorilian's mind kept returning to his breakfast with Marc Frederick. The Esseran king had proved to be nothing at all as he had expected. He wondered now why Sebbord had said so little about Marc Frederick. It seemed unlikely the lapse was due to indifference. For all that the man looked like a barbarian, with a Kheld's blue eyes and dark hair, nothing about Marc Frederick's intellect or conduct supported what he knew of the breed. Last night the Esseran ruler had been courteous, even gracious, in the face of provocation. And this morning, he had been interested and pleasant—at least until the end. Only then had the famed Stauberg-Randolph steel shown through.

"You're not going to be compelled to marry." Enreddon was speaking now. Dorilian forced himself to look over at the man, wishing he would just drop the topic. "But you do understand, I hope, that a suitable marriage is in Sordan's best interest."

"Your King's best interest, you mean. You're not interested in benefitting my domain—or me. Don't pretend that." Turning to his grandfather again, meeting those old eyes, he added, "I thank Leur daily their King has no suitable daughter." He did not think even the Malyrdeons would advocate forcing him to marry Stefan's mother, a woman eighteen years his senior.

Whether because he caught the errant afterthought or because the main sentiment echoed his own, Labran burst out into laughter. The tired sound fluttered forth, at first sharp, then interrupted. A wheeze was born in his throat, breaking into a fit of coughing. Labran lurched forward, and Dorilian reached by reflex to grasp him. He was surprised at how light and fragile his grandfather was, little more than a cage of bones beneath thin summer bedclothes.

"Water!" Labran waved a desperate hand. Coughs continued to wrack his frame.

"You heard him!" Dorilian snapped at the matron. Labran had asked for her to remain at hand. The woman at once poured a cup from the silver ewer on a bedside stand and took a seat at the Hierarch's side opposite Dorilian. Together they held Labran while she fed him sips between coughs.

It was then that Dorilian felt the Rill Stone touch his skin, the eagle on the stone burning as it found his cells to be the mirror of its own. The point of contact, upon which Labran in secret focused every bit of power still in him, burned white-hot. Dorilian sensed that spot of flesh acutely, the sharp violation of his dermis, deep penetration into muscle followed by the sensation of hot shapes coiling and uncoiling in new patterns beneath his skin... and knew he would only later learn what it meant. *Derlon discarded human flesh. What remains... is not human.* Part of his flesh must change if he was ever to host his Entity.

"What are you doing?" Enreddon walked to the bedside.

"He gets this way more often now, Thrice Royal." The matron looked up as she withdrew the cup.

Labran coughed again, feebly, and tightened his arm across his ribs, bracing his efforts. The movement broke the Rill Stone's contact with Dorilian's skin, and the burning sensation dulled with the departure of the stimulus that caused it. Steeling himself as Tutto had taught him, with techniques designed to prepare mind and body for integration with a god, Dorilian made no movement at all except to turn his head the better to look Enreddon angrily in the eye. Already, he knew, the mark on his skin was fading as his Sordaneon cells absorbed the Entity's signature.

"Am I also to be forbidden from lending comfort?" He resorted to the expected pattern of hostility.

"You are fortunate to be allowed a visit at all. I am merely making certain all is well."

"I am as well cared for as a babe." Labran closed his eyes and sank back again into his pillows. "Do not berate old Enreddon. He is not bad company and has been a welcome visitor these many years. We discuss horses and the writings of Cibulitus, in particular the dialogues on political rhetoric and the ethics of divinity. Wall sight gives his family a different perspective on the histories. He and his brother Malyrdeons cannot understand why we don't simply follow their exalted lead."

"Because if we did, there would be a contradiction in our Entity." Dorilian snapped the words impatiently and rose from the bed. The pain in his arm, far from vanishing, was growing more intense.

"What contradiction?" For once, Enreddon looked genuinely interested in what Dorilian had to say. Labran, too, turned in anticipation of the answer.

"We can't follow you because we follow *it*."

"What do you follow?" the Malyrdeon prince persisted. "An idea? A physical manifestation? Or simply stagnation? The Rill is silent. Maybe it is true after all that Derlon has succumbed to his form and the Rill is now purely machine."

Dorilian shot him a look of disdain. "You don't believe that, or you would not take such pains to keep us from actively engaging it. The Epoptes in Sordan, you know, refuse to allow me to so much as gaze upon the corpus. I'm not allowed *inside* any station. I can use the Rill for transport but cannot use it to send my own communications, even though I have tested as a first-level Epopte. What are they afraid I might contact—a machine?"

"Perhaps, if what you possess is an inherent ability to take command of that machine."

"How small your little minds would make us."

Enreddon's regard did not waver. "Stay small, young Sordaneon, while you wish to avoid your enemies. There's time enough for you to grow large. And you do not need your Rill to do that. You have what is needed much nearer at hand."

The man was warning him. Dorilian needed to master his native gifts if he wanted to survive among men who had ceased to revere their kind. Many no longer believed the Highborn were descended from gods. But he had no intention of remaining small. With that thought, Dorilian walked away from the bed and its burden of history, from the two men who watched him, each palpably bright with emotions he feared to unravel. Everything seemed bright to him now. Indirect sun illuminated each deep-set window like a blazing portal, reflected in rainbows off panes of colored glass in the opened screens. Even the carpets danced with colors. And the air itself was rich with smells he had never known, of female blood and ancient skin, cold metal, and orchids in a jar by the door.

"You have business to attend to." Labran was speaking. Each word crashed into Dorilian's skull.

"Yes." He used that to explain his distraction. His arm throbbed, but he did nothing to draw attention to it. "A grain broker here in Stauberg buys the annual production of my Teremar estates. I wish to renegotiate our contract."

"Surely you have agents to do that for you." Enreddon must have sensed the meeting was drawing to a conclusion, because he left the bedside.

"I do. But they're not as persuasive as I am." He did not doubt for a moment that he would be followed, both to verify his story and ascertain the merchant's identity.

"Of course."

Dorilian returned to the bed and sat facing his grandfather, taking up a pale right hand. Those old fingers squeezed his, and Labran's face hardened in a smile. "We shall not meet again," he said. "But you'll remember. They have begun building your prison, but you may prove to be more than their flimsy bars can hold."

Those old eyes, so like his own and all the more disturbing for that, scoured his face, seeking signals he would not give. Enreddon was too sharp an observer for Dorilian to risk detection in the name of useless sentiment. All Labran wanted to see now was a sign that his last act of insurrection had succeeded, that the Rill Stone had begun its work on his grandson's Sordaneon body. Dorilian gave him nothing. Just a squeeze of the hand and a dutiful kiss on one cheek. *You think I will stop the Rill, old man. After all these years, that's the only revenge you can envision and the only one our enemies will expect. That is why I will succeed where you did not.*

Secrets sheathed swords. And the Rill, whatever it might prove to be for him, was wrapped in secrets.

# 9

Marc Frederick rode at the head of twenty men to the Tower Quay at Stauberg's harbor. Twenty was a good number, enough for show and not so many as to constitute a threat. The harbor district hummed with activity beneath a high midday sun, the heat of which was relieved somewhat by the breeze that lifted royal ensigns and toyed with regimental tassels on his escorts' caparisoned horses. Of the several ships still docked at that hour, Dorilian's square-rigged windclipper was not the largest, but it boasted swift lines and masts of the finest hardwood, every plank joined and sheathed with telltale gleams of Sordaneon silver. It was also, Marc Frederick knew from having commissioned a similar vessel, worth more than a merchant's entire fleet.

Other activity swarmed about the pier, in particular the noisy loading of Endelarin Nemenor's two nearby vessels. Dorilian's ship looked ready to sail and was probably waiting for the Ardaenan ships. Though the Sordaneon prince had arrived without an escort, his presence in the city was now well known. An escort would be wise for the remainder of his voyage.

Whatever work the vessel's crew had been engaged in stopped when Marc Frederick's party reined to a halt. He marked the wary looks from the sailors, their unconcealed distrust. Though occupied by Esseran forces, Sordan was still a sovereign state. Marc Frederick noted, too, the direction of their glances. The lively music someone had been playing ceased, and he looked to the stern of the ship where the ship's noble passengers had gathered. He watched Dorilian hand a long-necked instrument to Tiflan to set aside. The youth made a decisive descent and crossed to the pier.

"What is this?" Dorilian wore a simple seaman's tunic of pale gray cloth over loose trousers the blue color of the sea. He would have looked like a deck boy but for an impressive weapons belt and a heavy bracelet that conveyed his high birth.

"A proper farewell. I will not let it be said that I let a royal guest set sail without a parting gift." He reached down into the saddlebag before him and pulled out a silk-wrapped bundle which he extended. Warily, Dorilian took the offering. After a moment of hesitation, he folded back the wrapping. A book. He glanced at the cover and the title embossed in gold. Marc Frederick harbored no delusion that the youth would appreciate his latest literary effort.

"My grandfather, Sebbord, says that you write too much." Dorilian covered the book again. "I may not have time to read it."

"Ah, but if you did, you could tell me all that is wrong with it. Perhaps next year, your grandfather will resume his visits, and I shall enjoy some genuine discourse." To Tiflan, Marc Frederick handed a sealed and ribboned packet. "Lord Morevyen, if you would deliver these to the hand of your liege and adoptive father, then might our business of these last two days be truly done. Convey also my regrets that he did not make the journey. Enreddon is a less able opponent in chess."

Accepting the letters, Tiflan bowed his head. "A game few play, Majesty, although Prince Sebbord has introduced it to his court. Many in our land play it quite well, though none so well as he."

"This humble student of his method included." Marc Frederick had never encountered a better player. The man won every contest. It was their custom to write out games in advance, anticipating each other's moves and sealing them in separate envelopes. Almost always, Sebbord correctly scripted the entire sequence of their game before even the first move had been made. "I missed him." He settled back in the saddle, looking past Tiflan to the deck of the ship and the fierce protectiveness of the men standing at ready there. "Tell him that. That I missed our talks."

"I will, Majesty. And that we were treated well."

Dorilian cast an impatient look at Tiflan now. Marc Frederick found it interesting that the young man let slide this opportunity to make some biting remark.

"Did you get what you came for, Prince Dorilian?" he asked directly.

The boy nodded. His gaze strayed past Marc Frederick to Stauberg's prosperous clutter of buildings and the Wall rising white and splendid above all. Perhaps he lingered a moment on the tower from which, even now, Labran might be watching them speak. But Marc Frederick doubted it. Dorilian's visit with Labran had been nearly as cold as the old man's glee in it. The Sordaneon prince had spent as much time visiting a local grain broker.

"I thank Your Majesty for making possible my visit with my grandfather. And I thank you also for your parting gift." Tucking the book under one arm, Dorilian moved his hands to his belt, from which he unbuckled a dagger. The King's guards stiffened alertly, and a few of the horses moved, their hoofs landing loudly on the wooden planks. Dorilian took the sheathed dagger in hand, his fingers gripping the covered blade portion of the weapon, and leaned forward, extending it hilt first. "From me," he said. "A gift in remembrance of our meeting."

Marc Frederick accepted the offering. Closing his left hand about the scabbard, he took the polished hilt in his right and drew the blade. Grip, guard, and blade were of one piece, milky green, and so smooth the surfaces glowed with inner depths, the outer curves traced with rare metals. A *tullun* dagger, fashioned from a single vertebral process of an immense creature from another star. Or so the legend went. Such blades were rare because all that existed had been crafted from that one creature's skeleton before the Devastation. A *tullun* blade possessed an edge so sharp it could easily cut any other material, even stone or steel. The weapon's scabbard was of that material also, for no other could house it without being ruined. Giving one was extravagant—the kind of gesture only a Highborn prince could make.

"A princely gift indeed." He sheathed the blade again and tucked it with a flourish into his belt. He smiled at the young man but did not extend his hand. The meeting had gone too well for him to see it end with a public snubbing. "Godspeed, young Sordaneon." Marc Frederick signaled to his guard and took up his horse's reins, pulling it around. "For we will meet again."

He left as a King should—first and with the last word.

"Ionais is furious as only a bride can be. Even her father is avoiding her." Jonthan turned the *tullun* dagger in his hands, admiring the craftsmanship of the scabbard. "This is really very fine," he judged. "I'm surprised he had it on him."

"He's accustomed to fine things." Marc Frederick continued to sort through the slips of paper Gareth had given him before leaving the room. Not every message interested him equally and he picked three out for immediate response before returning his full attention to his son. "Just as Ionais is accustomed to getting her way. I don't blame her one bit for feeling cheated. She should have been the star of the evening, not have to take second seat to an upstart cousin coming in unannounced from a country her family would rather stay downtrodden."

Setting the dagger back onto the table, Jonthan gave his father an indulgent smile. "Oh, it's not as bad as all that between Merrydn and Sordan. Regelon despises Deben, of course, as they all do, but the Malyrdeons as a whole think the island is a fine vacation spot. They do, after all, own some of the most splendid villas—and, I might add, did not have to selectively murder native lords in order to get them."

Despite himself, Marc Frederick laughed; his son spoke a bitter truth. He walked to the window and looked out into the rain. The morning had dawned dark with clouds and now at noonday was little better. "What can we do to make Ionais happy again?"

"Nothing. Unless, that is, we can find some way to attend Dorilian's next birthday celebration, so she can make our wedding announcement then."

"I'd rather not do that."

"Neither would I. The Feast of Imenos is in three months. Regelon has proposed that as a suitable occasion... and I think she will soon agree."

"Wonderful. I want you two wed and happy. Children would be nice. Emyli got too quick a start on that, and you not quick enough."

Laughing aloud, Jonthan leaned against the polished onyx panel beside the window. "Did I hear you rightly? All those nights I withdrew from the finish because I feared your royal wrath?"

Marc Frederick regarded his son warmly. At twenty-eight, Jonthan was every inch a prince. Tall, with light brown hair and handsome looks taken from his Highborn-sired mother, he showed only a little of his father's Kheldish roots. His easy manner came naturally, and he was well liked even by his father's Staubaun subjects. "You know what I mean," he said. "A man properly wed is a wonderful thing. If you love your lady and she you, then do the world a favor and beget."

Jonthan pondered him more closely. "This is about more than Ionais and my wedding," he read, accurately. "You're worried about the Sordaneons again."

"And how not? We've just met their candidate for my throne."

"You don't really think they still hope—"

"Sordaneons don't hope, Son. Their kindred is an active force. Even Deben—don't let him fool you." Marc Frederick sighed and turned back to his desk. He enjoyed the work of the empire and was most often to be found in his study. He searched for a document and, finding it, offered it to his son. "Read this."

Jonthan walked over to sit on the opposite side of his desk. He held the paper lightly and looked up after reading but a few lines. "Mormantalorus?"

"Their resumption of relations with Sordan is not coincidental. Nammuor knows Sordan is our weak underbelly. The Archhalia and the Seven Houses have all but destroyed Sordan's noble class. We restrict Sordan's trade and allow the Hierarchate to field only a minimal army and fleet, just enough to patrol their own waters and secure the border with Suddekar. Thank whatever gods you will that the domain is guarded on one side by desert."

"And by Teremar on the other."

Marc Frederick nodded. "I had good reason to leave Sebbord in place, with or without his grandsons."

"I remember Nammuor from the border negotiations three years ago. Camas of Voret's adopted son." Jonthan frowned as he recalled the Mormantaloran Regent. "Very good-looking, cool-headed, charming. Delivered threats with a smile and followed through on most of them. The village of Kurrukam is now inhabited only by dead bones." His hazel eyes darkened with another thought. "Mormantalorus safeguards a substantial hoard of pre-Devastation crystals and possesses the means to make more. Rumors credit Nammuor's mages with using these crystals to produce crude spatial arrays in matrices similar to those once employed by the Aryati."

Marc Frederick had read that report before holding a series of intense and somber joint meetings with the Epoptes and their Psilant, Quirin. "Read on."

Jonthan glanced at him in puzzlement but resumed reading. His face paled as he did so, the paper rustling sharply as he flipped it to continue. "Lights off the coast of Xebbeth? Ten thousand dead... in a cove sealed with slime?"

"It boiled, Jonthan. The sea *boiled*."

Royal advisors had suspected for months that Nammuor might have achieved some means of generating large energy differentials. Jonthan shook his head. "Even with a device—even with one of the primary enhancers—Nammuor could not do something like this."

"Then we can ascribe the event to natural causes—or we can surmise that Nammuor used something stronger than a primary enhancer."

Jonthan sighed. "Witnesses say he was there, that he commanded it. They do not call it natural." He looked up bleakly. "Is it possible he used a core array—or one of the Entities?" Core arrays were fixed devices: massive, elaborate matrices holding minute amounts of star matter. Even if activated, they could not be moved. Unshielded, one might have boiled the water in that cove... except no core array was known to be located anywhere near the site. And the Entities could only be commanded by the Highborn.

"We don't know what it is. But the greater enhancers were not the only devices used by the Aryati before the Devastation."

"A Pre-Devastation device greater than the known enhancers? I suppose it's possible, but—" Jonthan turned the paper over, perusing it again as if its back might hold the answer. "The only one I know of is the Undying Crown, the unholy artifact Leur stole from Vllyr." According to the histories, careless use of the Undying Crown had opened the earth, swallowing the Aryati city of Mulsor beneath the sea—a cataclysm that had unleashed the Devastation. The crown had emerged again in Exile as the Diadem of the Devaryati. Jonthan rightly looked skeptical. "But it was destroyed by the Three."

Marc Frederick frowned grimly. "Ah, but what if *that* was the great secret the Three never told? What if it wasn't destroyed?"

"It wasn't?"

"The Wall... knew it all along. Endurin told me. It simply did not know *when*."

When the thing would be rediscovered. When the Diadem would be wielded again. The future created itself at an inconstant rate, in broken patterns.

Jonthan sank onto the nearest chair. "Gods," he whispered.

"They were not strong enough, the Three. One of them was not strong enough, or even all of them were not. So they hid it until they would be."

"But mortals, like Nammuor... Can a mortal wield so fell a thing?" The Devaryati had been nearly a god himself.

"Yes." Marc Frederick picked up a nearby golden globe and held it, turning the thing in his hands. "But mortal bodies are fragile. Nammuor is most certainly being creative by tapping external power sources." He frowned as he reflected on the revelations coming out of Xebbeth. That Nammuor could channel even small amounts of power was worrisome. "He is at least partly Aryati himself and may have found ways to amplify the Diadem with other devices. If not a sorcerer already, he is becoming one. When he feels he is powerful enough to make his move, I don't want to have to fight him with my domains in disarray."

Jonthan looked out the window. "But the Wall—"

Marc Frederick shook his head. "The Wall as currently configured protects only Stauberg. If we could raise up a Wall Lord powerful enough to assume its mantle, we could attempt to expand it as a means of defense. Austell's mind is now too fragile, of course, but I have great hope for Elhanan... or perhaps Enreddon's son." His friend was making progress in his wooing of Palaistea, leading the Malyrdeons to hope he might yet sire a living child. "But if we want to actively fight this thing, if we want to destroy it, we need a more active Entity."

"The Rill." Jonthan stared at him. "You're trying to awaken the Rill."

"Perhaps I am." Rain splashed against the windows, gusts rattling the multicolored panes of the shutters. Marc Frederick wished the rain would stop, the day turn to sun. The Diadem of the Devaryati had destroyed Mulsor, one of the Five Cities, as mighty as Mormantalorus or Sordan or Permephedon itself. It had plunged the very World into the Devastation—and could do so again. He set the golden globe back onto its jeweled bracket. "Only a Sordaneon can ever assume the mantle of that god, which is why I am going to make very certain that kindred survive its enemies."

"And you're trying to secure that hope by befriending Dorilian?"

Marc Frederick nodded. "His potential is blinding. Sebbord knows this. He saw to it that our paths would cross."

"Do you know why?"

"Oh, yes."

Jonthan waited upon the answer, but Marc Frederick was not

ready to tell him. The best way to abort any future was to reveal it. The machinations of the Malyrdeons could encompass generations. "And what about Mormantalorus?" his son asked. "Nammuor... and the Diadem?"

"He does not know we're watching him. Using it in Xebbeth had to have drained him. Drained him badly. He's not Highborn and doesn't have that rare blood of theirs. He may be years from using it again."

"But when he does—"

Marc Frederick looked over to the windows as rain pelted the panes. "We must be ready."

# 10

Courtiers and functionaries bowed low and backed out of Dorilian's path as he strode through the vaulted halls of the Sordaneon Serat. The guards at the gateway into the Regent's private apartment admitted him without question. Dorilian had gone first to his own quarters to change into clothing suited to his rank and his father's court: a knee-length, sleeveless tunic of deepest green on green silk, heavy and lustrous; a broad belt of excellent Rebiran leather with a ram horn buckle embellished with silver; and armlets of Sordaneon silver and gold in the shape of Rill emblems, such as only his family was permitted to wear. The lightweight, silk-lined cape clasped across his back and one shoulder, a formal touch, belied a casual visit. From the day of Dorilian's birth, every visit with his father had been an audience. He left his escort outside and entered his father's hall alone.

Deben waited in a chamber of solitude and darkness, a room with a floor of pure black obsidian reflecting walls of deepest green jade. At the room's far end, waterglobes floated serenely to each side of a single throne upon steps of midnight. A handsome man of eighty years—of which he looked to be only forty—the Archregent Deben was draped with princely splendor in fabric of palest silver gray upon his pale skin, his fair hair brilliant against the deep green panels at his back. The Sordaneon Silver Eagle appeared to frame the resplendent ruler with guardian wings. Two other men in the room remained standing, one beside the throne and one in the room's far corner. Dorilian recognized the man beside his father: old Mezentius Suddekeon, currently Prime of Sordan's Dodecai and one of the Archregent's longtime counselors, was both Highborn and a kinsman. The other man he did not know. A brief glance told him only that the visitor was Staubaun, tall and fair-haired. Dorilian thought he had seen the face before, but he could not place the man. "Father." He bent to one knee upon the second broad step and bowed his head. He had not been nearly so formal with Labran, and the contrast struck him. Raising his head, he extended the letter in his hand: an unopened document sealed with Esseran blue and ribboned with Stauberg-Randolph colors.

Deben frowned but took it. "How dare you consort with my enemies."

Dorilian stood at the acknowledgment. "I wasn't consorting. I visited *your* father." He emphasized the word deliberately. "My grandfather." He bowed his head to Mezentius with more than mere acknowledgment. The old man had sired Deben's mother and was his great-grandfather.

"You visited their captive. Which means you needed *their* permission. Where was your pride? You hurl it at me often enough."

"I made certain they could not pretend my visit was an affirmation." He glanced to his left, at the man standing just on the edge of the light and watching with acute interest. Who was this? A Triemperal official assigned to listen to and report upon this meeting? "I presented myself as a concerned kinsman, the Hierarch's grandson, not on Sordan's behalf. Or yours."

"Which raises a not insignificant point—you were not in a position to present yourself at all! What does it matter *how* you present yourself if you place yourself so your enemy can dictate to you—for all to see! Worse, you put my legacy before them without my consent." The veins in Deben's neck swelled as rage began to spew forth. "You can be sure they enjoyed the spectacle. A Sordaneon come to *beg favors*! Just as Sebbord has amused them all these years, bowing and scraping for the scraps they deign to give him—a few hours with his Hierarch by the grace of the very men who strive to bring us to ruin!"

Mindful they were not alone, Dorilian clenched his teeth and opted for propriety. "The Hierarch sends his regards to his son and his wishes for your continued health and wellbeing."

"I get reports," Deben reminded him. "I know his health better than anyone. He's not entirely well. He's aging more quickly than they would like. Once he's dead, they'll lose their greatest hold on us. Once my father's dead, Sordan can move and breathe again." He leaned forward with a glance at Mezentius. "Labran's death would end at least one Esseran hypocrisy, that of insisting he remains Hierarch. Dead men cannot hold that office." He again fixed his gaze on Dorilian. "My father knows the value of his life. He knows he has been reduced to a symbol, captive to a title—and a place—they fear to relinquish."

Perhaps. But Dorilian didn't think Labran's keepers truly feared Deben even should he become Hierarch. He studied his father's left hand where it rested upon the carved stone arm of the throne: a pale, languid shape, bones and flesh molded by a life of ease. The Rill Stone would someday grace that hand, powerless though it was. Deben had learned to use a sword in his youth and still liked to think he could wield one, but he seldom practiced with a weapon anymore. He relied on cohorts of skilled guards to preserve his life. Even the storied lineage in his flesh, the legacy those soldiers so dutifully promised to preserve, was barely detectable, no more than a flicker of power.

"I don't suppose they allowed you to be with your grandfather alone or speak with him unattended." Deben seemed determined to break Dorilian's silence.

"No. Their King was with me at the first meeting, which was short, and we said very little. Enreddon Malyrdeon sat in on the meeting the next day."

Deben turned toward the man standing near the wall. "They manipulate every meeting, every situation. They seek access into our private lives, our most intimate communications. Two years ago, they maneuvered Sebbord into sending Dorilian to Permephedon under the guise of furthering his education. Education! They placed him among barbarians, and he learned nothing there at all—except what louts they could be." Deben put his chin in his hand and leaned upon his elbow while studying his son again, still disapproving. "Yet he returned for more. Perhaps it's true that some things love their masters."

Blood rushed to his face. "I have no masters!"

"You cannot be your own when you sup at the tables of thieves and play lapdog to beast-blooded usurpers—"

Dorilian often hated his father, especially when, as now, Deben delivered petty attacks sheathed in insults. He had long ago ceased to think anything he did would earn approval. Deben was too filled with fear, and among the things he feared most was his son's impending adulthood. The only thing Dorilian truly feared was that he might become like his father.

"You have made your displeasure clear. Is my punishment to be made to stand here and listen, or may I be allowed to go about my business?"

"What is it this time? Grain contracts? Shipbuilding commissions? The discovery of new ore lodes in Rand-Chulpara?"

"I'm renegotiating contracts—of all kinds. They were made by my estate administrators when I was a minor. I am of age now and feel I can command better terms. Too much of my gold goes into Esseran pockets and does not benefit Sordan."

"All for Sordan's benefit?"

"What benefits me benefits Sordan."

Deben nodded, then inclined his head to Mezentius. "See that my Heir has updated lists. The Sheave Houses and Shiplords have made numerous reassignments. He can assist the new holders with their looting."

Biting his tongue, Dorilian consoled himself by thinking that Marc Frederick would not have dismissed his activities so lightly. No, *that* man was probably already looking into the reason behind his visits to the Stauberg grain brokers. Nor was Dorilian convinced that the transference of Rill legacy had gone completely undetected. During his sea voyage, he'd begun to wonder why the Malyrdeons had not done more to *prevent* it. Enreddon had given in to his demand to sit upon the bed only after a heated argument, but the man could just as easily have not allowed him within arm's reach of his grandfather. He could not discuss such inconsistencies with his father, however. There was something else going on here.

He focused his attention on the unknown observer. A Staubaun of the purest caste, with pale silver hair and handsome features so perfect that arrogance seemed part of nature's rightful expression. This man was not an underling. It was then that Dorilian knew who this man must be and why his father was posturing. Mormantalorus had a great deal to offer the embittered Archregent, including alliance against their mutual enemy.

"I think you had better introduce yourself," he said to Nammuor Varehos, "and also state your business if it has to do with me."

Nammuor's dark eyes narrowed. "You're right, Thrice Royal. He does require thick gloves."

Sensing the remnants of dialogues about him, but from which he had been excluded, Dorilian stepped down from the dais. "I see.

This man talks about me but only to you, and you prefer not to talk to me at all, but clearly discuss me with him. Both of you, enjoy your game."

"Dorilian, stay!" Deben's voice was calm, controlled.

"I'm not *your* dog, either!"

"You are my son! My Heir. And the time has come for you to attend Sordan's business above your own."

Dorilian had already reached the door, but he stopped to look back. "I do attend Sordan's business. I rebuilt the harbor out of my inheritance so no Esseran bankers or Lords could dictate its design or capacity, levy usage fees, or place looters in majority ownership of the warehouses. I provide generous stipends to artists who can now freely express Sordan's heart and soul, thereby lifting the spirits of our people. I have built granaries for our hungry and houses for our healers. Sordan is my enterprise, Father, and it will lack for nothing I am able to give."

"I will hold you to that statement. We will talk again in the morning after breaking the fast."

Another breakfast. Dorilian had planned on touring the new harbor, but could do it just as well later that day. Nodding to his father, Dorilian left. His mind raced far ahead of his footsteps, dissecting the meeting's layers of concealment, who was present and who was not. Only his most immediate family patriarchs, save Sebbord. And Nammuor. Why Nammuor?

He knew that answer even before he reached his room.

"I don't want to marry your sister. I don't care if I meet with your approval or not; I won't do it."

Dorilian confronted Nammuor beside the Well of Birds at the center of the Cloister Garden. Bounded on all sides by the Serat, the garden offered privacy and quiet to the privileged guests of the Sordaneons. The Mormantaloran ruler was not officially in residence, his visit unannounced outside the Archregent's most intimate circle. Dorilian had spent the first hour of the morning with Deben, hearing from his father's lips the yoke being placed upon him. Now, just returned from a ceremonial tour of the harbor reconstruction he had funded, he was in little mood for forced pleasantries.

Tall and elegantly dressed in a chiton of purple hemmed with black and red, Nammuor made no attempt to conceal his irritation. "You weren't my first choice," he told Dorilian bluntly. "It was your father I sought for alliance, but he has persuaded me you are the better match."

"He's wrong."

"I agree."

As if that made it better. On the one hand, Dorilian understood it. Deben would become Hierarch upon Labran's death, which all believed would be soon. Deben had also already proven himself a sire of sons—that qualification perhaps being the most important to a dynastic marriage. Only male children inherited the Leur traits that defined the Highborn race, and not every Highborn male sired sons. Some, like Sebbord, sired only daughters, their Highborn line thereby terminating. Dorilian's reproductive potential would remain unknown until the conception of his first offspring, an occasion that— for one of his race—would not be possible for years. Only rarely did a Highborn prince sire a child before he was twenty-five. What irked him was not that fact but the trace of contempt he detected within Nammuor's analysis. Dorilian's mother's mixed race showed in him. Moreover, Nammuor undoubtedly knew he had been tested for Rill ability with ambiguous results—unlike Deben, whose potential had been proclaimed long before the Stauberg-Randolph usurpation.

"Then seek another husband for her." He prepared to go.

Nammuor's jaw visibly clenched. "No. This is between Sordan and Mormantalorus. This is about alliance, not your childish preferences. Your father is right to think Esseran princes, in particular the Seven Houses and the Stauberg-Randolph barbarians who pretend to rule them, would be unduly alarmed by his marriage to my sister. He's right to point out they would almost certainly counter that alliance by demanding you be married to one of their princesses. Resign yourself. You are going to be getting a wife whether you want one or not. My sister is the better option. Sordan gains alliance with my domains, and the Sordaneons will become heirs to Mormantalorus."

Dorilian little cared who ruled Mormantalorus. But he couldn't deny that Sordan stood to gain by an alliance with its renegade neighbor: stable borders with Othgol and Kundallga, expanded commerce, and greater economic and social independence from hated Essera. The Hierarchate could also lose by it if Morman-talorus placed too many foreign advisors in the Sordaneon sphere or sought to exercise too much influence. Such prospects gave Essera more reason to be nervous and extend their oppression.

"There will be no wedding if I am not part of it." Dorilian felt confident saying it. His father had never yet forced him to do anything. And Deben, he was sure, had no intention of taking another wife.

Nammuor smiled, but there was no warmth in it. "You Highborn," he sneered. "So proud, and so useless, mere figureheads now. Another generation and you will be no different from any other noble clan, fighting for a toehold in a changing world, humankind tossing you aside as it charges toward new ways and new glories." He walked toward Dorilian, coming nearer than most would have dared. "Look at you. You're a diminution, a baser being. Your looks are attractive enough in a common way, but there's not enough Staubaun in your features for beauty and not enough Staubaun in your blood for power. It's what Essera wants, don't you see? They've been weakening the Sordaneons for three generations. And every time someone—Labran or Deben—attempts to change that direction, they enforce their design. Don't believe me?" The man laughed at the distrust in Dorilian's narrowed gaze. "Ask Sebbord why he took his third wife. Ask why they forced Deben to take your mother."

"You're lying."

"You see? You can't say even that with certainty. You're a far cry from your ancestors."

*Not that far.* Dorilian had met men like this before. Nammuor was no better than Stefan, telling him he was nothing. He forced a smile. "But I'm not so far removed from them as to be unsuitable for your sister. So, let me repeat my position: I don't want to marry her. I *will not* marry her. Perhaps you should spend your remaining time here convincing my father to wed." He knew all the many reasons Deben would not. His father was brave with other people's lives but never his own.

Nammuor seated himself on the fountain edge, the tiny birds that lived in the well's honeycombed nests flying up in whistling rainbow streamers. His eyes looked like black pits as they hardened. "You're an impudent young man. Deben warned me, but I now see he said too little. So let *me* warn you. You are diving into waters over your head, young Sordaneon. The affairs of nations are not yet yours to order—indeed, they will order *you*. Therefore, choose very carefully. I see your father has not told you all that has gone into his decision. No matter. You are stubborn and smart, so I know you'll find out what you need to know: who your enemies are and who are your friends."

Though Nammuor patted the ledge beside him, indicating he should sit, Dorilian declined the invitation. This man was not his equal, though he clearly wished to be.

"It may be that we want the same things, Southerner." The flock of birds, none bigger than one of his fingers, swirled in the sun. Colors danced—red, green, and blue—against the pale, smooth architecture enclosing the garden. Every day the birds rose from the well in musical swirls, and every evening they returned to the nests clinging to the deep tunnel's dry, cool walls, where they had been given refuge by the Sordaneons for two thousand years. "We, too, want to see Essera diminished, its threat to Sordan removed, the looters driven from this land and further from your own. We want Sordan restored to its proper place. And we want the Rill returned to us."

"The Rill, yes." The real reason for this alliance now clearly revealed itself in Nammuor's heated gaze. It was always thus when the Rill entered conversation—an acquisitive glint, knowing the wealth and power generated by the god-thing. "They stole it from you, or at least the operation of it. They can't truly steal the god, of course. It simply *is*. But the god's work, its enterprise, the wealth it generates—*that* they have taken."

Just as Nammuor would do were he able. Dorilian wondered at the way men often talked to him as if he possessed only a rudimentary understanding of the Rill, the same sense a foot soldier or a Kheld might have. "We'll take it back."

"When Deben becomes Hierarch?"

"When we're ready."

Nammuor continued to study him with an intensity Dorilian disliked. "Let Mormantalorus help you restore the god and return your family to its rightful place."

The answer bore a sincere spine. But there was muscle to it, an entire skeleton of other purposes sheathed in cunning ambitions. A viable thing. Dorilian fought a sudden urge to recoil from this man's presence. There was more to his interest than mere alliance, more even than the Rill. He now remembered where he had seen Nammuor before. He'd seen him in one of the Wall visions... wearing a blood-red diadem upon his brow, dagger in hand while stooped over a dead man. Dorilian carefully stepped back and prepared to leave. It was now more important than ever that he plot a way to make his father dismiss him from this court and send him to Teremar.

"If you would be a friend of mine or my father's," he warned, "do not seek a path into our affairs. Do not seek to wed your sister into our House. If you do, you will find me to be much more of a problem for you than you ever dreamed possible."

He left Nammuor sitting on the well's broad ledge, the birds long flown, only silence surrounding him. But he did feel those eyes, black and hard, burning into his back as he walked away.

"Insubordination!"

Deben hurled the word as if it were a weapon itself. Dorilian steeled himself against it—not just the piercing tone of his angry father's voice but the emotional texture of that volley, slicing into his brain like a heated knife. At his father's side, clutched by one arm, Levyathan let out an anguished scream, his thin childish legs stomping as he tried to pull away.

"Let him go!" Dorilian snapped. "You're hurting him!"

But Deben wasn't hurting Levyathan nearly as much as the boy's direct experience of empathic rage and pain. Dorilian knew this and still was powerless.

"No, *you* are hurting him," his father seethed. "*You* are hurting him because you would rather anger and disappoint me than shoulder your responsibilities as my Heir!"

Levyathan, keening, laid his head against Deben's arm. With a look of disgust, Deben cupped his free hand over the child's head to quiet him.

"I don't want a wife!"

"And I don't care if you want her or not. You will wed Daimonaeris to make this alliance with Mormantalorus."

"No!"

At the violence of that rejection, Levyathan howled again. Dorilian stared helplessly in horror at what his own emotions were doing. *Lev, it's not you. It's him. I don't want to marry.* But Levyathan didn't fully grasp concepts such as marriage or the causes of

Dorilian's distress. Deben shook the boy until Levyathan stopped making noise, his sobs dying to broken whimpers.

"You forget how you came to be here," Deben reminded him coldly. Dorilian's fingers curled into fists at what he knew was coming. "Do you think I wanted to wed *your* mother? That choice was made for me by others. But I honored it for Sordan. For Sordan! I wedded Sebbord's domain to ours by blood and ensured that the Teremareon inheritance remained Sordaneon, that foreign princes would not plunder it. The only reason you parade around with your wealth and your insubordinate pride is because I wed your fat, unworthy mother!"

Dorilian stiffened as Deben's bitter emotions crashed against his own. He remembered his mother as beautiful, tender, and smiling. Not as Deben did, with loathing at her figure and relishing the fear in her wide gray eyes. He turned away, not just physically, but to keep his memories unviolated.

"Why now?" he demanded. "You were over sixty years when you wed our mother. I'm sixteen! I can't even sire a child yet!"

"Marriage doesn't demand a child, only a ceremony. A child can come later, at your choosing." Deben sighed, his expression no longer entirely unsympathetic. "I want our house aligned strategically with Mormantalorus. Doing so... protects our interests."

But Dorilian understood that only Deben's interests were being protected. With his heir tied by marriage to Mormantalorus, Deben could be confident that his enemies in Essera would want him to remain alive—and in power. Esseran princes would approach him then for marriages, they would think twice before moving against him, and more of them would curry his favor. The only person in danger was Dorilian himself.

"You're ruining everything!" Was his father so blinded by self-absorption that he would put both son and nation in peril? Dorilian's position was about to become untenable. "I hate Essera as much as you do. More!" he vowed, remembering Stefan. "I will fight harder than any soldier to remove their minions from our lands! Their ships from our waters! I want them gone! Every moment of my life, I've devoted—" He caught himself, deep habits of secrecy well placed in advance. "Father" —he confronted the proud man regarding him so resentfully— "we can be free of Essera without this alliance. Derlon's blood runs in our veins. The Rill is what we must throw in the face of our oppressors. Remind them of our power, not hide behind alliances that merely add to our enemies."

"Enemies that already exist, standing at hand waiting to feast upon this corpse we call a Hierarchate. Enemies I expect you to help me battle by honoring your obligations as my Heir."

Now that Dorilian had resumed control of his emotions, Levyathan, too, had calmed. His shoulders ceased to shake, and his face grew quiet. His eyes stared into a private space, but he was listening. That morning he had been at Permephedon, immersed in lessons. He had come home at once when summoned, brought by his caretakers. His father and his brother ruled his very world.

Deben noticed the boy's growing calm. "Perhaps we can now proceed rationally." He indicated a nearby chair.

Dorilian took the seat angrily, dropping into the chair and kicking his feet out in front of him. He folded his arms across his chest as if that could restrain the blood pounding hot through his veins. Deben took the throne, carved of black stone, placed in the center of this interrogation cell beneath the Hierarchal quarters. Sometimes the Highborn had need of such rooms and of conversations no others would ever hear. Coaxing Levyathan to stay seated on the stone dais, Deben gripped the boy's thin arm less tightly. Whatever bruises he had caused would be gone before they left the room. Wide-eyed and breathing hard, the child huddled at his feet, his rich garments contrasting with the throne's hard midnight gleam.

"So here is what I expect of you." Deben's clipped words broke the silence. "You will wed Daimonaeris. You will provide her with property sufficient to maintain her as befits your wife, to be inherited by any children she eventually gives you. Following the ceremony, you will perform your public duties as a husband without rebellion. Handle your private life as you wish, within the bounds of respect for her person."

"I will not consider myself wed. I'll live apart from her. And she'll never have any children," Dorilian vowed. But the trap was set. The only way to escape his father's plans for him would be to leave Sordan and all its domains, forsake his position as Deben's Heir—and renounce forever his right to rule. And that he would not do. He would not step out of the way for any man, not even his own father. A new thought blazed into his brain—that his father might even be seeking that result.

"The wedding will take place in two weeks." Deben managed

a grim smile. "You are of sufficient rank that the event requires a formal celebration."

Two weeks! Stunned, Dorilian stared hard at his father, further enraged by what he now knew. "She's *here*?" Even a fast ship would be hard pressed to make the long journey from Mormantalorus in two weeks.

"Yes, she is. A beautiful girl, just twenty-one years. Pure Staubaun matrilineage, elegantly educated and entirely suitable. She's a virgin, of course." Deben brushed his fingers across Levyathan's fair hair, blonder than Dorilian's and finer. Just touching Lev made their father scowl. Dorilian knew Deben did not believe Lev to be his son. Had Levyathan died during the Blood Rite shortly following his birth, Deben would have rejoiced. Instead, the infant had survived the ritual Sebbord had conducted, proving that some Highborn prince, though not necessarily Deben, had sired him. "Your brother will stay here—indeed, in my company— until you have complied satisfactorily with every aspect of your wedding."

And so the trap closed tighter, the bite of iron in its teeth. Staying with Deben would be torture for Levyathan. "You can let him go." Dorilian forced the words through tight lips. "You know he isn't strong. Send him back to Permephedon, where at least Marenthro can help him. Being around me will only—"

"Will only what?" His father seized upon the opening. "Punish you for your foul temper and rebellious moods which inflict such pain upon him? Hinder your plans for sabotaging this alliance? Make you think a second time before you launch into willful histrionics? Those are the very reasons I insist upon keeping your pathetic excuse of a brother near at hand. If you have neither respect for my authority nor feelings of duty toward Sordan or me, maybe you will at least respect how your actions will bring your brother pain."

"I'll give you my word that I'll go through with it. I won't dishonor you or Sordan. Just let Levyathan return."

"After the ceremony. Until then, he stays." Deben rose, hauling Levyathan up with him, causing the boy to stagger to his feet. "Look at him. A waste of Permephedon's effort. Even Marenthro cannot unlock a shred of potential from his quivering, dimwitted skin." He shoved the boy toward Dorilian, who leapt forward as soon as he saw the movement. Freed, Levyathan dashed headlong into his brother's arms as their father rose. Pressing the inside lockstone, Deben left the chamber. The door closed with a whisper.

Dorilian drew Levyathan to him as the boy clenched his bruised arms about his ribs and burrowed close, his tear-streaked face crushed against Dorilian's chest. For the first time since coming to this room, Dorilian dared relax his mental barriers. His body tensed, anticipating the contact, eyes closing against the brilliance of it even as his brother's thoughts slid happily alongside his own. Levyathan relaxed in his arms.

"Safe," the boy whispered. *I tasted power. Yours and his. Thunder inside a room.*

*It was me he sought to frighten.*

*Fear for me.*

Dorilian nodded, brushing back a few strands of silk-fine hair from Lev's face. His brother opened his eyes, his face lively now, no longer gripped by confusion. "Struggle still," Levyathan told him. *My mind opens new paths, some gleaming long, some hollow thick. Except with you, except with Marenthro, I do not know which paths to question, which sense to use.*

*I'll always be here to help you.*

*Don't promise that.*

*I can. I do.* Dorilian had made that promise long ago.

Levyathan raised a hand and ran his fingers over Dorilian's left arm. It had hard muscles thick beneath sun-kissed skin—so unlike Lev's pale, weak flesh. *I taste the Rill change, like music and blood. Derlon's self, remembering. He will see you?*

*Maybe. I think so. But I must wait to find out.*

*Our father's ancestor memory tastes different... spoiled and sour.*

Deben had undergone the transference long before either of them had been born. *I don't think he can do anything with it. He's too weak, his mind undisciplined. The Rill would rule him. He fears it most of all.*

Sagging against Dorilian's more substantial body, Levyathan closed his eyes and pressed his cheek closer. *I am a knife in his hand. He stabs you. They all will.*

*That's not why I did it. Not why I agreed to go along with him.*

A pause, then Levyathan whispered aloud: "Sordan."

*Sordan, yes. I will be Hierarch one day.* He had seen it, one of the hundred Wall images forced into his mind the day he had lifted the

Wall Stone away from Austell Malyrdeon's convulsing body. He had gazed at his reflection since, trying to discern the young man he'd seen crowned, resplendent in Hierarchal ensigns upon Sordan's Eagle Throne. A *young* man, with Tiflan and Legon and Tutto arrayed at his back.

*I won't be there.*

*You'll be there!*

But all the fierce confidence of which Dorilian was so capable could not make that assertion. Levyathan had not been in that image.

Lev's thought firmed alongside his. *Only you must be there.*

Dorilian laid his head against his brother's, giving himself completely to Lev's outpouring of love and belief. When he and Lev were together, he could let down every barrier, abandon every facade. At such times it seemed the world itself opened to him, obstacles crumbling to reveal endless horizons. In Levyathan's eyes, there was nothing he could not do. Only one threshold did he refuse to cross, though he knew Lev looked straight into that place, deep in his cells where Rill stuff shimmered along the sheathing of his nerves.

*They cannot keep me from the Rill. They cannot stop me. None of them can.*

# 11

Rill arches crowned the top of the great hill at Simelon. Two of those arches, one broken into a giant's sharp stake and one half fallen at an angle so totally wrong as to be discordant, made the sight as jarring as it was glorious. Even had the Rill run there on its way to Stauberg, it could not have stopped. Scholars through the ages had debated whether enough of the fallen corporeal matrix along the way had been repaired for the Rill to run to Stauberg at all. In the first five hundred years following Derlon's habitation of the artifact, generations of talented Epoptes had worked in conjunction with the most gifted Sordaneons to raise the fallen structures littering the countryside. Restored Rill rings and arches dotted the landscape between Stauberg and Permephedon, but the Rill remained tethered to its single course. Even so, the sight of the broken mount lifted Simelon above other towns in that region. It at least *had* Rill potential.

Marc Frederick set the message cylinder on end, arranging it alongside other cylinders. They were of different sizes according to the documents they'd held.

"Married." He took some satisfaction in his company's stunned expressions. "Or, rather, betrothed. The wedding is in ten days." News of Dorilian Sordaneon's impending nuptials had taken two days to reach Simelon. Marc Frederick contemplated how best to alter his plans now that he must return to Stauberg. He alone would tell Labran.

Phellan Illarion, Bas of Serrain and host to the royal party, signaled to his steward that stronger drink was required.

Ostemun, Dannuth's ruling Prince and father to Phellan's wife, heaved a sigh. "Will you intercede?"

Marc Frederick shook his head. "The Sordaneon right to wed

without outside interference is protected by the First Law of the Triempery—a law I promised Sebbord I would uphold. Even were that not the case, half the population still hopes to restore Mormantalorus to the fold. You need only listen to the word on the street. People believe Sordan so firmly ours that the marriage might as well be to a prince of Essera. No, I lost my chance at intervention when my daughter refused to marry Deben." Had Emyli wed Deben as she was supposed to have done...

"We might have forced a more suitable match," Ostemun said, "had we known Deben's mind ahead of the matter." He reached for one of the messages written on thin, nearly translucent paper. "Mormantalorus! Does this not strike anyone else as strange? Under Nammuor, that land is all but cleansed of any who are not of pure Staubaun birth. In his first few years of rule, families not pure enough to meet his standards fled those lands and settled in places like Ilmar and Teremar. Those of lesser blood he keeps only as slaves to serve the better born. Deben's boy would carry a chamber pot in Nammuor's court!"

From beside the window, Ostemun's brother Rheger grimaced but said nothing. The Malyrdeons were well informed of Mormantaloran practices, all instituted since the demise of the last Highborn ruler of that land. It was doubtful the girl's father would have chosen one of the Sordaneons, with their mixed blood and diminished power, for his impeccably bred daughter.

"Nammuor gets more in exchange than he surrenders," Marc Frederick noted. "Sordan's next heir will be his sister's son."

Ostemun raised an index finger upon that point. "If Dorilian sires a son. More don't than do. Unless Austell saw otherwise and told you something we do not yet know."

Which Austell had not. "No," Marc Frederick said, "he hasn't."

"I am most surprised Nammuor did not seek Deben himself." Ostemun set aside the paper he had been reading, exchanging it for another. "That's where the purer bloodline lies. Deben's mother, the Gracious Hierarchessa, is herself of Mormantaloran lineage."

"Be surprised if you wish, Brother, but I am not." Rheger stepped away from the window and walked toward the table. "Deben is pliable and indecisive. What has Nammuor to fear from that quarter? It is Dorilian he needs to contain. No one wants a renegade heir in a position to make conflicting alliances. With the son, he gets the father anyway—and he places claim on Dorilian's inheritance, which is a treasury far greater than his father's. Nammuor gets everything from the son that the father would have given him, and more." He stalked to a map laid upon the table and traced the domains in question upon it. "Labran never renounced his claim to Essera's throne. Neither did Deben." He looked over with a thin smile. "And I doubt Dorilian has done so."

"Not that I ever heard," Marc Frederick acknowledged, though Dorilian's intentions concerned him less at the moment than those of the other men in question. He sighed. "Politics aside, Deben is a monster. Sixteen years is much too young for one of your kind to marry."

Rheger shrugged. "Only in that he cannot produce immediate complications."

The next few years, at least, would be free of dangerous new Sordaneon heirs.

"Will you be attending the wedding, Sire?" Phellan asked. His steward had brought refreshments, cups of summer cider, and was offering the many-hued vessels to his guests.

"No." Marc Frederick smiled thanks for the cup and recalled that one of Phellan's grandsons had just joined Stauberg's Dragoon Guard, serving under Stefan in his new appointment as a captain. "I have decided to send Apollonia. She will revel in the proceedings. And Jonthan also." He wished his son well. As soon as Ionais heard this news, she would be enraged anew, certain the Sordaneons were timing the event to upstage her impending betrothal. It was as good an occasion as any, however, for rubbing shoulders with the Sordaneons. They seldom opened their palaces to outsiders, particularly under Deben's paranoid regime.

Phellan returned his ruler's smile. "The most difficult aspect may well be the timely pursuit of an appropriate gift!"

Both Rheger and Ostemun lifted eyebrows to concede the point. Gifts upon the rare weddings of Highborn princes were generally spectacular, involving either prodigious amounts of precious gems and metals or elegantly penned deeds to vast tracts of land or property. Such gifts took time to create or arrange.

Marc Frederick spent the rest of the afternoon deep in thought.

Stefan arrived from the Dragoon Cadet barracks wearing an officer's dress uniform, carrying his half-helm tucked beneath his arm. Just turned eighteen, he already had attained the stature and appearance of a man.

"You have heard, I assume, why I have returned to Stauberg?" Marc Frederick asked. He had chosen to meet Stefan just prior to going to Labran.

"Because damn Dorilian Sordaneon is stabbing you in the back by taking a Mormantaloran wife?" The young man was making no secret of his feelings. The announcement had arrived in the city ahead of the King, conveyed by means of the Stauberg array.

"Because *Sordan* is allying with Mormantalorus, using that marriage as the bond, yes. Don't be so obtuse as to fail to see the maneuvering. This is Nammuor's work and Deben's. I doubt the boy had much choice in the matter. I can promise you'll have more choice in yours." Marc Frederick leafed through the letters his secretary had given to him upon arrival. "I will not be attending the wedding. Your uncle will represent our family. That is not to say you escape the need to make a statement. I want you to send a gift."

"A *gift*?"

Undeterred by the rebellious tone, Marc Frederick made his position clearer. "Now is not the time to deliver cold shoulders. We will observe proper form and comport ourselves with the very honor and goodwill we will expect from them when the time arrives for that behavior to be returned. This is how civilized people act. As I wish you to be part of my government, I expect you to behave the part. You will send a gift." He laid down the letters and looked his grandson in the eye. "It need not be extravagant."

"What, just a diamond mine? He's *Highborn*!" Stefan set his helm down on a nearby chair, his face rosy with rage. "And don't you think it's wrong that all he has to do is take a wife to get *richer*?"

"Someday, you, too, will get richer, especially if you choose your bride wisely."

With a sigh, Marc Frederick drew his grandson over to the nearest of the room's several windows. This one overlooked the harbor, the golden dome of the Harborhouse brilliant as it rose above a patchwork of warehouses and dwellings. He pointed over that landmark to the island at the harbor's center and its crown of splendid white structures.

"That is what everyone wants, including the man who will be

placing his sister in that boy's bed. We can't let ourselves be fooled into thinking it's about anything else. But we can make certain Mormantalorus is not the only option Dorilian sees when it comes time for him to choose his friends."

"Don't put me in that category."

"I only wish I could. It may be the best I can do is see that you do not fall into the deathtrap of being his enemy. I have battled them," Marc Frederick sternly reminded his grandson, "but I did so very carefully. The risks were enormous. We need the Sordaneons, Stefan, just as we need the Malyrdeons. The Malyrdeons are a defense, but the Sordaneons have been—and can again be—a weapon."

"I know about that. Don't think I, or the Khelds, have forgotten the fucking Sordaneon who did Ral's dirty work at Gignastha, who blasted the Vermillion Aqueduct and opened the gates."

Opened the gates so that Lord Ral of Leseos could enter the besieged city and avenge the murders of his Highborn uncle and cousin. Stefan's father had been killed that day. And among the living, held captive by Ral until Marc Frederick had come with an army to force his hand, had been Stefan's mother. Marc Frederick had to look away, so powerful was that memory. His lovely daughter in the hands of that man. Stefan, at least, had been away at school in Trulo, far from the unholy mess.

"Then don't provoke this one," the King said. He moved away from the windows again. Away from the sight of those surreal arches and the unrealized potential they embodied.

Stefan snorted. "He's untalented. I overheard Elhanan talking about it."

"Never count too much on what someone is not. Be more concerned with learning what they are." Marc Frederick heard the light tone announcing that his steward wished to intrude, and he went to his desk, where he pressed the lockstone. Gareth entered and bowed to his monarch, then to the young prince.

"Prince Enreddon has arrived, Sire."

"Splendid." When Gareth had again departed, Marc Frederick speared his grandson with another look. "You have heart, Stefan, and vision that can help this land. I need those qualities. But you need to learn that we do not rule in isolation. A people at war will always have a purpose, though it be a bloody one, but a people at peace—that is the more difficult path. This land would weep blood if it could. I have devoted my life to seeing that it does not."

"People are being killed anyway."

"I can't stop all misfortunes. Only those in reach. Help me see that Sordan remains in reach. Send the Sordaneon boy a damn gift."

Ministers and politics chose the seventh full moon of the year, the seventh week of Dorilian's sixteenth summer, as an appropriate date for the wedding.

Dorilian went through the motions his father had dictated. He allowed garment-makers to fit him with heavy robes of silk and velvet, guaranteed to be too hot for the season but which met the standard of a Highborn occasion. He chose costly ornaments he did not even like and accepted even costlier gifts he did not want. One, a golden chalice from Stefan, he would have tossed into the lake had Levyathan not lit up with a smile upon tracing its intricate Kheldish decoration with his fingers.

"Honor and truth," Levyathan said, awkwardly groping for words. He then finished as he was best able. *God-spear. The sign of our god as they see him.*

"They see nothing," Dorilian said.

At least there were no Khelds on the guest list, to which he gave only a token glance.

Two days before his wedding, he met his bride-to-be at the place and hour sacred for his kindred to first see the women they would take to wife. Twilight, as it had been when Derlon had first seen Neryllia as she danced upon the shore. Seized by passion, the son of Amynas and Leur had swept up an armful of the red lilies that grew in the shallows and offered them to her. As Dorilian recalled the story, she had run away. In a pavilion built upon the spot, about which reeds rustled with music created by the wind off Sordan's encircling lake, overseen by the tall white structures of the City and Rill, he stood as his forefather had with his arms laden with blood-red lilies. Nammuor's sister arrived, willowy and pale, draped with veils of rose silk, her hair gilded with the fading rays of the sun. Daimonaeris was taller than he. And there was very little chance of her running away.

He caught just a flash of golden eyes in a self-assured, beautiful face. As he presented the lilies, his hand touched hers and she jerked it away. The momentary contact shocked him because through it he felt her revulsion. He flinched from the unwelcome knowledge that Daimonaeris did not want a boy for a husband, that she found him inadequate, physically unappealing, and not her choice.

He thrust the lilies at her and silently vowed to never give her another gift.

Beneath a canopy of silk erected against Sordan's bright sun, the light of which gave fire to every hue and brought forth the Silver Eagle woven into its design, Dorilian exchanged vows with his bride. He felt the surety of his word the moment he gave it. He saw it, too, in Nammuor's smugness, his father's relaxation, the way the Stauberg-Randolph prince, Jonthan, closed his eyes as at some final, undesired act. The rest was a blur of processions and feasting, of insincerity so thick that it might have choked him had he not numbed his own senses. Dorilian moved through the day and then the night in a dull haze. Even when Nammuor prompted gasps from the audience by bestowing the new couple with the domain of Janu-Separ, Dorilian barely felt anything at all. The man's smiles, and his calculated attempts at goodwill, mattered for nothing.

Later that night, Dorilian lay on a silken, ceremonially curtained bed, with Daimonaeris beside him and guards outside the door. No one expected the couple to consummate their union that night, if only because of the bridegroom's youth, though his bride's distaste of him was a greater impediment. Dorilian was not immune to the desires of the flesh, and the Mormantaloran princess was female perfection itself, even if she did lie beside him fully clothed and awake, waiting only for morning to come.

"How many hours?" she asked, not bothering to whisper.

"Two." He was himself counting the hours until dawn. When it mercifully arrived, his bride would be free to move into her own quarters in the Serat or retire to the luxurious estate he had given her.

Daimonaeris turned to him, her wide golden eyes shining in the reflected moonlight that filled the room. "I can feel you. I grew up around it, with my father. Your moods cut like glass."

"You won't have to put up with me. I won't inflict myself upon you often. We will go to parties together."

"We'll create children."

He looked at her coldly and was pleased when she quickly looked away. He despised the reminder that his common looks disturbed her. "No, my pretty wife, not that. That is one thing they cannot make me give you."

"You'll change your mind." Her profile, serene and lovely as if sculpted from marble, shone pale against the shadows beyond their bed. Her lips softly smiled. "You'll feel differently when you become a man."

"You don't even want my children," he snapped.

"Of course I do." She at least made an effort to sound affronted.

The lie trickled like oil into his ear, seeping to his nerves and brain. It lay heavily atop truth, refusing to mix with his perceptions. As Dorilian lay there in silence, he discerned the ebb and flow of Rill pulses emanating from the node, the god's subtle, textured presence like a skin overlaying his own. His left arm throbbed. In the last few days, something new—sensations of being stretched or pulled—had begun to tickle along his spine. His awareness of the Rill, always at the edge of his senses, had become ever-present. Before, it had only been so when he had stood upon a Rill platform, near to the shining structures and the energy that pulsed through them, unseen but vital, the lifeblood of an empire.

Among the gifts in the outer room was one that penetrated his dull anger: a marvelous sculpture that drank every ray of light, a single block of midnight stone carved in the shape of Derlon's Eagle soaring above the arching arms of the Rill, living things the artist had managed, somehow, to convey as if in motion. Labran had commissioned the work during the last year of Endurin Malyrdeon's reign, and the artist hadn't been paid after the Hierarch's capture. The sculptor had refused several times to sell the piece, saying he would not betray the intent of its creation, until Marc Frederick had somehow persuaded the man, now old, to part with it so that he might present it as a wedding gift. When Dorilian learned its history, he knew the work had been meant for him all along.

As he waited for dawn, he decided it was time he read Marc Frederick's book. He needed to learn more about an enemy who already saw him in ways he had only begun to see himself.

More majestic even than Highborn weddings, the funerals of the god-born interred the dead side by side with legends. Labran Sordaneon's corpse left Stauberg in secret and was conveyed to Permephedon draped with black and emerald.

Labran's long captivity had neither diminished his stature in Highborn eyes nor reduced the importance of his bloodline. The kindred turned out in royal numbers. The only notable absence was Deben Sordaneon, Labran's Heir and now Hierarch, whose distrust of Essera was so great he would not leave Sordan even to see his father's earthly remains one last time. Dorilian traveled to Permephedon in Deben's stead, as Sordan's Heir. As nearest kin in blood, he spoke the words which sealed Labran's passage from the World, eloquently invoking Derlon Sordaneon's promise to Amynas that his line would uphold the Creation. *For only strength can wield the sword of change, and I am the thews of the World.*

At the Sordaneon Heir's side stood the tall, silent figure of Sebbord Teremareon, who had been already in Stauberg and indeed at Labran's bedside, at the time of his old friend's passing. Prescient as always, he had immediately left the weeklong festivities surrounding his grandson's wedding to board a ship built only for speed. He had sailed to Stauberg and spent the final weeks there. Marc Frederick accompanied the funeral procession from the capital but, being not Highborn himself, did not enter Permephedon's Vault. He stood outside the doors of silver among the lesser born and waited in a show of respect until the service ended. All his life in this world seemed to have revolved around—and been defined—by the man he had just watched leave it.

"He fought me to the last." A day had passed, and he faced Sebbord across a board of blue and green tiles upon which, from time to time, they would move one of the few remaining pieces. The ruins of a hearty breakfast lay strewn on a nearby table. "Labran never gave any quarter. He forced me to always be at my sharpest if I was to best him." Not unlike Sebbord himself, Marc Frederick might have added, contemplating his situation on the board.

"He approved of you—more than you know." At long last, Sebbord revealed the inner thoughts of a man whose private moments he had honored. "You also hardened him, sharpened his mind. He had little else at the end."

"Pure stubbornness."

"A trait not far removed from its source."

Marc Frederick took his hand from his rook, rethinking that move. His game was at that delicate stage where whatever move he chose would decide his next three. From long experience, he knew Sebbord favored misdirection, strategies concealed several moves deep. Marc Frederick spared a momentary glance at his companion. Sebbord's age showed more this morning than it had even a few years before. Hair of purest silver receded further above that broad brow, his nose looked a little larger, and the lines about his mouth were deeper. Without knowing his lineage, one would never have guessed his age, however. *One hundred fifty-six years*, Marc Frederick marveled, knowing he would never see so many.

"Deben lacks Labran's will. He'll never master his fears. He's already subject to a legion of them." Deciding his move, Marc Frederick shifted a pawn. He watched concentration sharpen Sebbord's features, the passage of intelligence as the man assessed the board. "I cannot believe you find nothing alarming in your grandson's marriage."

Sebbord glanced up. "She's a suitable bride. A political bride. You have one, and I have had three. I would be surprised, however, if he ever sleeps with her." The Prince resumed attending his game.

Marc Frederick was surprised, then less so as he thought about it. "And that doesn't bother you?"

Sebbord shifted his knight to block his opponent's diagonal, thereby thwarting two series of planned moves. "When you imprisoned Labran, you knew the dangers. Isolating Sordan spared Essera from Labran's ambitions, but it opened wounds that bleed still. Is it so surprising that Mormantalorus would come to lap at the sweet stuff of it? You are only surprised in that Deben made his move before his father's death."

"I thought I'd have more time."

"Ah, Time. An unreliable ally." Sebbord tapped the board. He looked to the windows and the vistas of greens and golds beyond. "The hour has come." He rose to his feet. "I think I shall leave our game unfinished. Then we may ever think we will take it up again. Our lives are too brief for this World. Only Leur ever lived in it fully."

"Leur lives in it still."

"A platitude. Men no longer hope to manifest the divine. Maybe someday we shall do so again." Sebbord's proud, aged face relented somewhat. "I kept my promise to you."

Marc Frederick sensed the shift in the World. Sebbord's promise had run its course and so, by association, had his own. He had thought long upon this moment, the choice he must make. What he wanted now, he could not gain unless he set this man free.

"I conferred with the Order of Epoptes. Despite the petitions of the Seven Houses, you are restored your privilege of Rill travel." He watched Sebbord's eyes close, the telltale bowing of that silver head. "You may do so today, if you wish."

But no gratitude looked back at him when those eyes opened again, no burying of the past. "That was never yours to deny me, nor theirs. Access to my god was the jewel I handed over to preserve a legacy. Had I ever sought the thing, not all your power or that of the Seven Houses could have kept me from its sanctum. Rill-kind cannot be ruled by men... not truly. All you can hope is that we rule ourselves."

Marc Frederick understood. Sebbord had just informed him of the new status of their relationship. A wiser man, or a more fearful one, would have ordered the Teremareon prince taken into custody—if indeed it could be done without others of his mage-gifted kind at hand. Thirty-six years before, only the sight of men holding swords to Labran's neck had rendered this man powerless.

"Godspeed to you, Sebbord, and to your grandsons also. It is for us to create the World in which we will live. You have my word as Stauberg-Randolph and as King of this land that no harm will come to you or your family by my word or my hand."

"I know the value of your word. I have long placed more trust in it than others would have had me do." Sebbord strode for the door. He paused at the threshold, turning back for a last word. "Deben is Hierarch... for now. But I have not forgotten, nor forgiven, how he forsook my daughter. Your Emyli might have disobeyed your royal will, but she is alive."

"What will you do?" Marc Frederick saw in Sebbord's face a look he had seen before. Prior to his exile from the Order of Epoptes, Sebbord had been a scholar, a prince, and a mage—but none had ever doubted he could also be a warrior.

"Take my grandsons to Askorras for the harvests, the wine festivals. The last month has been upsetting for Levyathan, and Dorilian wishes to be away from Sordan while his father consolidates his power. The people need to look to their new Hierarch, not his

Heir." Sebbord pondered a distance not contained by stone walls and human questions. "I will do what needs to be done."

"I cannot protect you if you engage the Seven Houses. And if you seek to stop the Rill—"

Those solemn eyes, glowing with the golden light of afternoon, locked onto his. "Is that what you think of me? Does Labran's memory still have so much power over you all? I have no intention of stopping the Rill. Not now, not ever. Let the Seven Houses cease their vigil, and the Order exhale its bureaucratic breath. I will not be their god's executioner. That terrible deed will be done by men who are godless already."

It was said among the Malyrdeons that Sebbord Teremareon possessed an intellect so penetrating that he needed no Wall to foresee the course of events. Marc Frederick felt the chill of truth within Sebbord's pronouncement.

"Rule carefully from your stolen throne, Marc Frederick," Sebbord warned as he turned away. The power of the Highborn Lords of old, of men who had directed Entities to their bidding, echoed within his aged calm. "Your surety has passed. But remember this: those who wish to set a living thing in stone must first kill it. And though they adorn it with praise and worship it for all the ages to come, they will nevermore be able to summon forth its benefits, because stone gods do not hear the pleas of living lips. I will not help the Seven Houses reduce their god to a stone giant nor shackle the world to the designs of its priests. I am a descendant of Derlon the Rill-Giver, dedicated to the guardianship of a god, and the time has long since come for me to exercise that office."

# 12

The hills of Tulamanta blazed gold with wheat just beginning to ripen upon tall stalks. Dorilian sat, legs crossed, upon a carpet at Levyathan's side and watched his grandfather like a hawk. Tiflan had joined them on the portico, a colonnade open to the west and east, through which a strong ruddy sunset painted full-bellied columns with fire.

"At Permephedon, I learned... many things." Though his words halted, Levyathan conversed with his grandfather for the first time in complete sentences. "I learned to scry people the way you, I think, see them. When I see, I cannot hear. When I hear, I cannot see. Those things I touch, I know are real. Dor would help me when I was younger. He helps me now. He shows me words my pathways struggle to create. Through him, my noise becomes clear, my meaning true."

"Born empaths. Both of them." Tiflan looked smug. He had long championed Levyathan's ability and had first suggested sending the boy to Marenthro, believing the immortal might unlock a mind only Dorilian seemed able to reach.

"He couldn't converse before," Dorilian said, "because I didn't show him how. I didn't know I *had* to show him how."

Sebbord said nothing but listened intently as Levyathan continued.

"People are shape and color. Some sharp, some soft, some bright, some dark. Marenthro is bright, enormous. He outshines the sun. You are bright. Dor is... getting brighter, larger. My father is small; he cannot stay bright. Nammuor is... dark. Where he walks, light dies." Levyathan's right hand rhythmically tapped the stone floor beside his knee. When he spoke, he looked to one side, never at his listeners. "At Permephedon, I see the Rill, deep below and vast above, folding the skin of the world. Sordan, too, grows bright from the ground and shines beneath the water."

Sebbord nodded. Dorilian wondered if their grandfather understood what Lev was seeing.

"I help Lev's thoughts find words." It was important for Sebbord to understand the words were Lev's, not his.

"Are you doing it now?"

"Yes."

"You're in contact with his mind?"

"Of course."

"And can you block him from your mind?" When Dorilian nodded, Sebbord said gently, "Do it."

Levyathan twitched his head to the side. "Dark. Hurts."

Sebbord studied them with his hands clasped in front of his mouth, his nose resting on the fingers. To Dorilian, he said, "Your gift is stronger than I suspected—or hoped. To channel another intelligence but maintain distinct thoughts... and you are yet unschooled. I thought you too young to awaken to the sharing of minds."

"He has been doing it since his seventh year," Tiflan put in.

Sebbord extended his hand. "Touch me, Dor."

Dorilian put his left palm against his grandfather's. A sudden surge of power tingled across the barrier of flesh between them. He fought the urge to resist the probe, instead tracking the invasion of energy up his arm and into his spine. What did his grandfather seek? Power flowed along his nerves, into his limbs, building beneath his breastbone, and the sensation thrilled him. When something delicate and cold sought the base of his skull, seeking to hook into his back brain, he wrenched his hand free, breaking contact. Like an exhalation, the power dissipated.

Sebbord had trained him to this. The old man smiled.

The first gongs of dusk sounded from the town below, summoning herders from the fields. The richly colored rugs upon which they sat repeated the dying colors of the sky.

Sebbord gazed into that distance and sighed. "I was never chosen to be gifted. The Entity manifests through but one mortal at a time, and it has been the destiny of the Hierarchs and their Heirs to bear that burden. So it has fallen to you. Labran believed Deben could not wield the gift, and so he consented that you might bear it. Your father's will, he said, would prove too small. He feared your father would be too untrusting to bestow the gift on another."

"On me," Dorilian translated.

"On any other."

Dorilian had barely spoken about his experiences at Stauberg, though in large part that had been out of caution. Esseran agents infested Sordan's royal court. Kneeling before the Eagle Throne to plant a filial kiss upon the Rill Stone that now graced his father's hand had reminded Dorilian that his position would henceforth be glaringly public, his activities more than ever subject to scrutiny. His family's enemies were active and influential, intent on eradicating the Sordaneons from power. Some even hoped to remove them from Sordan to safekeeping in Essera. He needed to move covertly.

Levyathan, averting his gaze, pointed to the red orb of the setting sun. "It moves; we move not."

Dorilian sighed. A breeze teased the loose silk of his sleeves against his arms. "I don't know what to do. But I must do something."

"Just for the sake of doing it?" Tiflan asked.

"Better something than nothing." Dorilian met his formidable cousin's gaze with pride of his own. "The Rill must become an active force again—not for Esseran grain merchants or looting nobles, but for us. For the Sordaneons. My enemies must learn that I cannot be controlled like my father."

"They will learn that in any case, by other means. What do you hope to gain by attempting this too soon?"

"The time is right. Sordan has a new ruler. The people are hungry for change and prosperity. If we do this" —Dorilian paused for a moment, crafting his argument— "if we show them the Rill can grow and change, show them it can open to new places, we will have something Essera wants even more than wealth or contracts. Something they fear. We will have revived a god."

"Or just the hope of one."

Sebbord remained silent, his face grave. Dorilian looked to him, asking what he thought. The old man knew the dangers better than they. What Dorilian proposed, the very plan toward which Sebbord had steered him, would give true power, of a kind even wise men might think several times before seeking.

"I do not fear your failure." Sebbord spoke slowly. "Failure here brings only disappointment, and what means disappointment

in the scheme of this world? Nothing. If you fail, none but a few—
we few—need ever know what you have tried, and you will be free
to try again. But what of success? Contact with the godhead is not
well understood. Derlon has overwhelmed much older and more
seasoned men than you. You may be able... but are you ready?"

"I do not seek to host the god. I know I'm too young for that.
I need an adult body before I can channel Derlon's being or power.
All I want is for the Rill to see a single node... Hestya."

"See *you*. You want Derlon to become aware of you. Only then
will the Rill see Hestya."

"As I hear, as I see," Levyathan reasoned.

"Very dangerous," was Tiflan's assessment. He sat with his
chin cupped firmly in hand, his visage like that of an ancestral
statue. "Your comparison is flawed, little cousin," he said to
Levyathan. "You are not even close to being the Rill. You are very
small compared to that. Very small and very weak, even in comparison to *him*" —he pointed to Dorilian— "much less the Entity. And
when you are in contact with Dor, he *knows* you and he are distinct
beings. We cannot assume how the Rill might perceive him, in
what form it envisions itself, or wherein its identity lies. It ceased
to be human long ago." He frowned a warning to Sebbord. "It may
detect Dor and think him an invader and destroy him. Or it may see
him and not distinguish him from itself, and in that way, swallow
him whole. It may simply not allow him to retreat. We do not know
what its reaction might be."

"True," said Sebbord. "Tarlon was the last to touch the Derlon
mind, albeit briefly. Four hundred years ago, he proved that the Rill
recognizes the Sordaneon bloodline as contiguous with its corpus.
The danger is that the Rill lives within a long dream. Not every
mind to enter its dream possesses the discipline—or the will—to
return to the world outside that dream."

"He's a *boy*," Tiflan persisted.

"Why do you keep saying that?" Dorilian had counted on
greater support. "I'm old enough. Just because my body is still
growing—"

"Your body and also your mind," Tiflan countered calmly.
"And your judgment too, if you mistake caution for criticism."

The two cousins glared at each other. Sebbord, however,
watched Levyathan. Noticing this, Dorilian looked too. His brother
held his head bent at an angle, his right hand and fingers moving in

patterns like a dance, alternately gesturing toward Dorilian and lifting them to his own head. His left hand twitched, thumb jerking up. A quick link to Lev's mind touched both confusion and hard points of clarity, but the contact informed him that Levyathan believed Dorilian could do what was needed. Grateful, Dorilian reached to pull the boy near. Lev's belief in him meant more than anyone's. Well, almost anyone's.

"Believe in me," he entreated his grandfather.

He detected the hubris of that moment, and he also thought that it might not be hubris at all. *Rill Lord.* He all but trembled at the road he had chosen.

To his relief, Sebbord nodded. Behind him, the sun was yet a fiery rim upon the horizon. "I do," the old man said. The words themselves created truth. "I believe you can open the Entity's eye. We will return to Sordan for the winter—by way of Hestya."

# 13

Stefan emptied his water bag into the trough and fumed. He and his three companions had left Dazunor-Rannuli several days ago, traveling by horse across the river into Amallar. From there, they had endured a long, sloppy ride to this outpost, Bellan Toregh. They still faced a good four days of travel before they would reach the Orqho Hills. It would have shortened the journey by half if they could have traveled by Rill to Leseos—except Khelds were forbidden to ride the Rill, and Stefan refused to travel without his friends.

And so there it was. The hill towering above Bellan Toregh's buildings mocked him with a crown of intact, though dormant, Rill arches.

"Tonnhal tomorrow, if we're lucky." Cullen named their next destination. He gazed up longingly at the darkened structures. "Too bad that thing doesn't work."

"Never will," Stefan said. He led the way to the hopefully named inn, the Cock and Kits, where he had arranged ahead for beds. Inside, Cullen and the others joined Stefan on benches to either side of one of the common room's long tables.

Stefan glanced around the tavern, assessing it as a stopping place. Perhaps due to the rainy night, guests were few. Most of the other patrons gathered near the center hearth's roaring fire, where they might share in the cheap communal meal: baskets of bread crusts and a kettle of vegetable-rich stew. Judging by the crowd around the pot, the cook was probably a good one, and Stefan hoped the man hadn't yet taken off his apron for the night. Summoning a bob, he found that they were in luck.

"Pork and potatoes!" He placed his order to the approving smiles of his friends. "Ale for all! And an extra copper if the bread was baked this morning!" The grinning bob hurried off as fast as his small feet would carry him.

"Bribing the young ones, eh?" Neddig Daronson remarked while unsnapping his cloak collar.

"I'd as soon give him reason to treat us well and none to treat us badly." Stefan rubbed a mud spot off his wrist. A Staubaun would have washed up before his meal, but Stefan took pride in not following Staubaun ways.

"He'd do it for nothing if he knew who you were," the third boy of the party said. Round-faced with tan freckles across his nose, Mahon Gormladson had only recently joined Stefan's crowd. His father served as Marc Frederick's new administrator in charge of official couriers. Though communication in the larger cities was largely by means of the Rill and arrays, couriers linked the rest of the far-flung Triempery.

"I don't want him to serve us well because of who I am," Stefan said. "I want him to serve us well because it's the right thing to do. Getting people to bow and scrape because you wave your ancestry in their faces is the way Staubauns do it—getting treated special because of who they want folk to think they are, not because they deserve it."

"You're not going to stop it mattering." Cullen blocked his frown with a shrug.

"I'm not talking about the way things are. I'm talking about the way things should be. It shouldn't matter that a person is Staubaun or Kheld. It shouldn't matter if someone is rich or poor, just that they treat everyone decently. And it shouldn't matter that just because someone like Dorilian Sordaneon gets himself married to a fancy-ass Staubaun princess, my grandfather orders me to send him a fucking present!"

"Madrock, that's a slap! After... well, you know." Neddig had been with Stefan at Permephedon and to this day wouldn't speak Dorilian's name. "What did you send him?"

"A fricking gold chalice made by Rhodhur's best craftsmen that he'll never use anyway, because I'll take bets he tossed it in his stupid lake the very heartbeat he saw it was from me." Stefan blew out his breath between tense lips. "I spent a year's stipend on it, too!" His grandfather had insisted the gift come out of his own funds—further punishment, he knew, for his original transgression against the Sordaneon Heir.

Mohan snickered. "Seems to me the princess got the worse of that deal... seeing as he's such a princess himself."

Cullen looked away and clicked his tongue, but Stefan ignored the warning. "They're all like that, the Highborn." He wrinkled his nose. "They consider women beneath them and cleave to their own kind. It's why there aren't very many of them anymore. You should have seen him at Permephedon, always hanging at that Legon kid's shoulder, giving him looks. And spending all that time in 'sword practice' with Elhanan. We kept hearing how he was so good with one, but if you ask me, he never got up a sword in his life."

The inn door swung open and more men entered the hall, accompanied by gusts of cold air and bellows for ale. Because the town served as a major crossroads between Amallar and Kheld settlements in Neuberland and Leseos, Bellan Toregh saw people of all kinds and occupations. Most of the townspeople were tradesmen who made their living off the steady stream of travelers passing through the town. Wagonwrights, coppers, smiths, and warehousers all prospered here. So did folk who thrived by the town's river. The men who had just entered, however, were clearly not tradesmen. They had a rougher look—and fiercer.

The head man of the group of five slammed a handful of coins onto a table. "Ale, I said! And quickly! Ten mugs to start. We're stuck in this pisshole for the night and wish to get drunk!" The innkeeper hurried over, eyed the assorted coins, and then pocketed them before he set about filling the order.

"Neuberlanders," Cullen warned.

Stefan studied the arrivals with new interest. He had met with Khelds from Neuberland before, of course. Their chieftains traveled to Rhodhur often and sometimes to Gustan, seeking the ear of the King. Neuberland had been deprived of a formal voice in the Archhalia ever since the death of the domain's ruler, the Prince of Gignastha, and a subsequent inability to compromise on a new government. The Sordaneons held some ancient rights over the Gignastha principality, which made the Staubaun ruling class nervous. That might change now that Labran was dead, but so far, it had not. It didn't help that local lords still hoped the Sordaneons might be able to restore the Vermillion Aqueduct and with it the fallen glory of that broken, water-lit city.

"Maybe I should talk with them," Stefan said.

"Maybe you shouldn't!" Mohan's round eyes grew wider. "You don't know what kind of men they might be."

"And I'll never know if I don't talk to them." Stefan climbed off the bench and to his feet, pulling back his shoulders before making his way to the other table.

Across the room, the innkeeper had plunked down a pitcher and large wooden mugs brimming with golden ale, liquid splashing on the table to guffaws from the men. Bearded and weathered, only one man possibly in his thirties, the others at least a decade older, they wore the skins of men who earned livelihoods out of doors. Their knives, which they'd laid on the table, showed blades of bone as well as steel. Noting Stefan's approach, they exchanged wary glances.

"You'll find no goodwill mugs of ale here, boy." The leader lowered his drink and wiped the back of his hand across dripping whiskers. "Go buy your own and leave us be."

"You'd do yourselves better to buy my ear," Stefan retorted. It was a well-known practice for a Kheld to 'buy the ear' of a man by putting a filled mug or a meal before him.

All five men laughed, and the leader flashed an unfriendly smile marred by two missing teeth and one bad replacement. "Your ear? I doubt it's worth my piss in your cup." Each man spit into his brew, their message clear. They wanted neither his ear nor his company.

"For that," Stefan said, "if you want my ear, you'll have to buy rounds for my friends as well." He pointed to the corner where Cullen and the others sat alertly, watching his every move. "We're over there, should you change your mind about the company." With that, he showed them his back and returned to his companions.

"Sharga, Stefan," Neddig said. He eyed the other men as if fearing they'd launch an attack. "Why'd you go do that?"

He shrugged and picked up a hunk of bread from the basket the bob had placed on the table. Judging by the warm dense crust and rich, yeasty smell, the bread was fresh out of the oven. Stefan set a newly minted copper on the table. "I told you. I wanted to find out what kind of men they are."

"Mean ones, if you ask me," said Mahon. He had already eaten one piece of bread and reached for another.

"Nah. Mean ones would have spit *on* him," Cullen reasoned.

The bob arrived, four trenchers on his arms, neatly setting them before the four hungry youths. Stefan used his fingers to rip away a pork rib from the rack on his trencher, the better to get at the dripping, sweet meat. His laughing friends did the same.

Near the hearth, a small knot of men clearly deep in their mugs began to sing about the dangers of drink. A nudge at his knee made Stefan look up to see Cullen give a quick nod to the left. The men at the other table had called the innkeeper over and, apparently, had been asking questions. The innkeeper knew little, but enough. The four soldiers of Stefan's escort were eating in his kitchen. When the innkeeper left, the headman of the group got to his feet. Two of his fellows joined him in making their way over.

"He told us who you are, Prince Stefan." He looked to his fellows before continuing. "It fits with your words. My name is Trahoc Caddenson, and these are my men, Krigan and Lorn. We're in town to buy hardware, and other things, for our settlement."

"Hardware? Including weapons?" Stefan asked.

"I know nothing of your business here. I'm not telling you mine."

"Then I will tell you that I am here on the King's business, which if it goes well will improve the prosperity of this land and its people."

Grimly, the man nodded. "Aye, we've heard that your blood follows your father's. A good Kheldman he was and faithful, a follower of Alm the Clear-Sighted. We mourn his death to this day." Having observed the Kheld tradition of mealtime pleasantry, Trahoc cleared his throat before proceeding. "I wouldn't disturb your meal, *keldanes*," he said, "but if your ears are open, my men and I would be honored to buy your ale. We could talk, if you would hear us, about our homes and learn what you have to say of the King's business and the lands beyond this one."

It was a polite offer, so Stefan accepted. Barely a good swallow later, the five Neuberlanders had butted a table against theirs. The bob, informed ahead by the innkeeper of a round in the offing, brought a tray heavy with pitchers of ale. He found his palm heavy with coin, not only the price of the round but also the buyer's display of generosity. Khelds seldom stinted on show. The men were not yet drunk, however, and the mood remained cautious.

"I fought alongside your grandfather," Trahoc recalled. All of the men at the table had just completed toasts to their new tablemates. "I led a company of men from Saemoregh that helped him retake Gignastha."

"Three days of battle." Stefan knew this from accounts he'd heard. He had been twelve years old at the time. "I wanted to come, but my grandfather wouldn't allow it. Kept me like a prisoner at Trulo, then Permephedon." The man shook his head. "He did right. It was no place for a boy. Especially one with a father there. We smelled death from outside the walls, and inside was something no man should ever see." His blue gaze weighed on Stefan in a way that felt new and dangerous. The Neuberlander was assessing him as a man. "We lost the city, and we lost good men. Your father moved too soon."

*It wasn't my father.* Erwan Cedrecson had made only rare appearances at court before being taken captive during a raid on Gignastha when Stefan was five years old. Seven years later, Kheld rebels led by his mother Emyli had entered the Waterglit Palace during celebrations for the prince's daughter's wedding. They had taken the entire wedding party and royal guests by surprise and ordered the captives freed. After releasing the wedding guests, a man named Howys had killed the three Highborn princes still in his hands and seized Gignastha, declaring it a Kheldish domain.

"My father lost his life when Staubauns recaptured the city," Stefan said. "Ral of Leseos drowned him in urine and burned him in a common pit."

"I was there," Trahoc grated. "I saw what was left of them. I knew my son by a healed collarbone and a scrap of cloth his mother had woven. I knew my brother by the gap of his front teeth. My daughter's husband we never found, but she... gave birth eight months later to one of their gold-haired brats. They tainted our very kindred."

Stefan tightened his fingers about the grip of his mug.

Trahoc seemed to sense that he had reached untreadable ground, but he plunged forward nonetheless using the custom of open speech at a Kheld table. "Is it true, what we hear, that your brother has blue eyes... like yours?"

"Listen—" Cullen spoke up, already offended.

The man held up his open hand, signaling no ill intent. "I'd heard it was so, and we know the way of Staubaun blood and ours. Their brats have their eyes. We have a rightful interest in the King and his kin—an interest dearly bought!"

"Hans' eyes are exactly like mine," Stefan said tightly. "Blue as his father's—as *our* father's. Blue as Amallar's blue skies and the azure runes of a Rappeleye witch. Come to Rhodhur in the summer, and you could see for yourselves instead of hiding insults behind mugs of good ale."

"Then we are glad of it." Again, the man looked to his fellows for support and received it in the form of nods and calls for another round of ale. "Need us more Khelds with a say in the northlands. You have a place, and your brother will, too. Your grandfather's line is a bold one even for the Thegnkeld, of which your father was the very thorn." Clearing his throat, Trahoc continued to hold court with the ear he'd purchased. "We're your father's people. You know that. It's why you came over to us, told us we might have your ear."

Other men entered the dining hall, local men wearing town clothes, quiet about their own business as they settled at tables near the hearth. Stefan nodded at Trahoc's words, albeit with a glare. "I can listen, but I can't help your war. Staubauns haven't forgotten how Khelds killed those Highborn lords—unarmed men, attending a wedding."

Trahoc held Stefan's gaze. "Unarmed, so they say. Sorcerers say we. There's witch blood in that breed."

"Did that excuse the butchery?" At least one man had been dismembered, another disemboweled. All three of the Highborn had been impaled alive—only to suffer for days while their tormentors watched in growing horror as their victims would not die. They had died only when someone, no one knew who, had taken up a sword and cut off their heads.

"No worse than how the Staubauns sport with us," Trahoc persisted. "Their troops rape and burn and kill, and the Highborn don't lift one hand to stop them."

"Cold breed," Neddig agreed. He reached past Stefan so that the bob could pour him another mug of brew. "Bastards gave the city over to Ral. They blasted the Vermilion Aqueduct."

"He died of what he did, the Sordaneon that did it." Krigan, who until then had remained silent, found his voice. "Blasted, folk say, with his own lightnings."

*Because he summoned too much power through an enhancer. A greater diadem. The one he used at Gignastha belonged to the Prince of Lacenedon.* Stefan doubted these rustic Khelds understood much about Highborn powers or that those powers depended on enhancement by Aryati devices. To Khelds, all sorcerers were cut from one cloth.

"They can be beaten; we've proven that," Trahoc said. "We showed they can be killed, and we've shown we're willing to do it. We don't need 'em and don't want 'em in our lands, not as the Staubauns do, thinking them holy. We honor land and kin, not men."

"The Way of Alm." Cullen acknowledged by lifting his ale before drinking.

"The Way of Alm." The other men repeated the credo, some a few times, then followed suit.

"Are you more afraid now?" Stefan asked. "Now that Labran Sordaneon is dead and Deben is Hierarch?"

The men exchanged glances and shrugs.

"The King's soldiers still occupy their land," Trahoc said. "A man thirty years beneath that boot will not rise overnight, even should the foot be lifted from his neck. We don't fear that man. We showed the Sordaneons what we do to those who spill our blood."

"If I were you, I'd be more afraid of Deben's Heir." Stefan drew another deep draught on his mug.

"That one? He's just a boy. The Sordaneons raised him away from their Rill—and their enemies—in Teremar. What will he care about us?"

"He's vicious, and he's rich—richer than any Seven House Lord, richer than my grandfather. And he hates Khelds." Stefan ignored Cullen's look of warning. He wasn't saying anything but the truth. "He calls my grandfather a usurper—and my mother worse things. I won't even start on what he calls me." He took another drink of his ale, savoring the heavy flavor of the dark brew. Wiping his mouth on his sleeve, he added, "He's probably a sorcerer, too."

"Aw, Stefan," Cullen protested.

"Well, who's to say he isn't?" Stefan snapped. Drink was loosening his tongue, but nothing he said was news to anyone. "They all are, you know."

"Pups grow to be dogs," Trahoc agreed. He scowled through his beard. "And you say this one will bite?"

Stefan considered briefly how his grandfather would regard what he was doing, consorting with possible rebels from Neuberland and raising their suspicions. Except these men distrusted Sordan already.

"I'm saying he has teeth. You'll see for yourselves when he shows them."

Cullen broke in with a question about Saemoregh, where his branch of the Thegnkeld had kin. All were soon engaged in talk of kin-ties, uncovering many. Every Kheld could recite their lineage and happily counted much of the population as cousins. Before the night was out, two of the Neuberlanders soon established their own distant kinbonds to the young men, though not before they'd consumed three more pitchers of ale and two trenchers of pig meat and potatoes among them.

As they parted ways upon leaving the common room, headed for bunks they had rented, Trahoc slung an arm across Stefan's shoulders. It was only partly to draw him near against eavesdropping; he also needed help staying upright. "You have our swords if you need them. 'Member that. They don't sell us swords, see, not of good steel. We make our own, of slag ore. But our blades cut as deep and spill as much blood. We've crossed the Gero, and the Staubauns don't like it. They want us to starve in the poisoned hills, see? Keep the good land for themselves. They wait 'til we clear it, then they take it, then we take it back. They'd make us slaves if they could."

"I won't let them. I'll fight them, too."

"That's why I wanted your ear. And it's why you wanted mine. You've had enough of friends and kin trying to talk you out of what you know is right. A man needs warriors, not women or children, if he's to march to battle."

# 14

"Hestya." Dorilian pointed, and Sebbord smiled in answer. Before them spread a land of farms and pastures, above which rose a singular hill clothed in late summer green and crowned by arching pylons.

They had sent their escort ahead and switched horses to disguise their arrival. Seated in front of Dorilian, secure between his brother and the saddle pommel, Levyathan turned his head. While the remaining horsemen separated into smaller units before approaching the town, he listened intently.

"Slow time and dust," Levyathan said. Dorilian experienced thoughts alongside words. "Sluggish water. Gray creatures, no shadow."

"These are simple folk," Sebbord concurred. "They struggle just to feed their children and themselves."

A river port four days from Bartulu, Hestya subsisted on grain traffic. Lands on both sides of the river were rich and fertile, the breadbasket of Teremar and its Highborn-ruled neighbor, Suddekar. A generation before, Sebbord had wisely married his eldest daughter to Suddekar's Heir, thereby aligning all three of Sordan's autonomous domains to a single bloodline. He had done so with an eye to Hestya and its dormant Rill node.

Sebbord dispersed the guard in groups of three. With their identifying insignia removed, riding from different directions at different times, the men would attract little notice. Dorilian and his brother, wearing attire that any prosperous grain merchant's sons might wear, accompanied Sebbord to a farm outside of town.

"A fine property." Sebbord's assessment approved the large stone dwelling and outbuildings. The land, still being farmed, was well tended. "How much did you pay?"

Dorilian told him the price. He had been quietly purchasing farms and other property around Hestya for two years, ever since Sebbord and he had first spoken of the town's potential. He had even made purchases in the names of his friends. Legon owned three sizeable properties, for purchase of which his friend had borrowed against his inheritance. Tutto and Tiflan had also acquired estates nearby, and Dorilian's cousin Deleus, son of Suddekar's Heir, had purchased lands across the river. The activity had not gone unnoticed. Several properties had recently gone to other buyers.

Once inside the house, Sebbord swept Levyathan up into his arms and walked to the main room's eye-level window. Much of the residence was built below ground level, with windows set high in the wall. This particular vista, looking out toward the town, framed the broad, low hill of Hestya and its crown of lifeless Rill structures. A trickle of river traffic floated through the town : silos being filled, barges being loaded.

"Your birthright, lad," Sebbord said to Levyathan. The boy closed his eyes and turned his head to better attend to him. Sebbord had spent the last few weeks establishing a rapport of his own and could now direct his grandson's visual pathways. So long as they were not conversing, he could help Levyathan see. "Had the world been saner, you would have ruled Teremar."

Dorilian squelched a faint twinge of resentment at his brother's new closeness to their grandfather. He knew why Sebbord was doing it. Dorilian had to keep himself detached for what they must do tonight. With a sigh of impatience, he sank onto a nest of pillows before a low table of golden wood polished to the sheen of sunlit water.

"All things come soon enough. Gods, especially, cannot be hurried." Sebbord set Levyathan onto his feet, and the boy immediately felt his way across the room to Dorilian and settled beside him.

"We've already waited too long." Dorilian frowned. "We should have done this before I was ever born."

Dorilian would have felt better had he seen something of the deed he now contemplated in any of the fractured Wall visions in his head. Part of him wanted to tell his grandfather about those visions, while part of him held fast to the secret. He did not want Sebbord to change his mind based on fragments that so far had amounted to little.

"Men older and wiser than you or I have tried to summon the god. They tried and failed." Sebbord signaled to Tutto, who spread a map upon the table. "They became convinced it could not be done. But I believe they tried too soon. It took time—an age—for Derlon's cells to completely permeate the god-thing. Legend tells how the Aryati and their Dog Men filled Peleor, Derlon's son, with poison and threw him, mortally wounded, into the corpus at Simelon. Derlon absorbed his son's cells. Derlon survived their poison, but it crippled the Entity's early growth and also our perception. What we do now will challenge everything men think they know about the Rill."

Dorilian had studied every level of the seven disciplines, including biology and mechanics, and already knew the Rill, like the Wall, fit uncomfortably within the parameters of science. The analogies his studies evoked, only Epoptes spoke of with authority. "The world we see tells us the Rill is a machine."

Sebbord nodded. "What men see, they believe—and what they believe, they see. Though Derlon's human and Leur origins give him vitality—his corpus lives, grows, responds to stimuli, and repairs wounds such as he suffers—these things they ascribe to a divine *machine*."

Rill disruptions never occurred due to breakdown; the offending element was always human. Misloaded cargoes. Improperly assigned slips. Whenever an inept Chantor directed a loading arm along a wrong path, causing an adjacent transport arm to break, the damage healed instantly—healed, and then continued to function just as before.

"Our enemies believe Derlon's body extends no further than it did upon his assumption of the godhead because the machine's limitation has become binding." Sebbord's hand smoothed the map as he traced a line down the heart of the continent. "But this shape is ingrained in *them*—not the Entity. The Rill's perceived limitation has defined their politics, their economy, their world for so long that they erected even their power structures upon its unchanging foundation." He tapped the cities served by the Rill: Permephedon. Dazunor-Rannuli. Leseos. Randpory Crossing. Sordan.

Five cities—*only* five cities.

Dorilian recalled the chronology of Rill service. It had Awakened originally between Permephedon and Sordan. Stations had opened between those points since: Dazunor-Rannuli by Derlon himself soon after the Awakening... then Leseos by Deben I, two hundred years after that. Last had been Randpory Crossing, by his great ancestor Tarlon Sordaneon, four hundred years ago.

"The plan," said Sebbord, "as Derlon conceived it, was to extend the Rill next to Stauberg, then Mormantalorus. Our ancestors sought to complete that vision. Rings all along the Stauberg route have been restored, but for a few. That hope was abandoned along with others when it became clear Derlon would not complete the plan."

"Or could not."

"That was the interpretation they chose at the time. That he could not." Sebbord hunched forward. His white eyebrows lowered. "The years since have not refuted them. The Rill has not altered its path in any way, and men have taken this to mean it cannot."

"So now we get to prove them wrong." Dorilian studied the map, its many-colored lines designating lost routes and nodes, critical passes or attendant structures, and current scheduling and secondary grid stations throughout the known lands. He touched his finger to a line that led from Sordan to Hestya and beyond. The line connected Sordan to Janukar and the Southernmost Sea. But he knew the Rill would not ever go that far, at least not yet. The rings beyond Hestya were toppled and lost and, for all he knew, might never be restored.

Sebbord had sent Dorilian to Labran to fulfill a shared vision for the god. All the world knew about Stauberg and its holy, failed promise, but the Sordaneons alone knew that the third Deben had reinstated the rings at Hestya. *To Stauberg's heart, and Sordan's belly* read that notation.

"Soon it will be dark." Sebbord rolled up the map. They had planned for a moonless night with no illumination to betray them. "We will enter the dead station then."

In the late hours of the night, Dorilian heard someone arrive at the farmhouse. He rose from the table where he had been studying encryptions with Legon. For the second time since summer, the Seven Houses had altered their codes. He followed every word of the cartel's communications with the Epoptes, intercepted by Sebbord's efficient network of shadow connections. Dorilian recognized the value of those contacts at every turn, and attended to every subtle shift of the cartel's alliances, every new contract and Rill partnership. Only the Stauberg-Randolphs merited as close a study.

Despite his wish to believe otherwise, Dorilian grudgingly concluded that Marc Frederick ruled Essera ably. Every intercepted communication pointed to a man utterly devoted to advancing his nation and people. They also demonstrated a man intent on keeping Sordan firmly under Esseran control. Despite Labran's death and Deben's ascension as Hierarch, the most recent missives from Essera conveyed that the King planned to continue administering Sordan by means of an "interim" military presence.

"Smug about it." Legon had disliked the translation of the Seven Houses' message.

"They brought him to power for this." Dorilian was grateful to have his friend with him. He'd brought only his most loyal men. "He knows he's a match for my father, but he's wrong if he thinks I will allow him to rule over me."

Silence fell upon the room as the sounds of the guard outside gave way, and the outer door opened. The Highborn presence in Hestya was secret so far. Dorilian was not completely surprised to see Tiflan enter. His cousin had gone ahead to Sordan weeks ago on Sebbord's business with the understanding that he would rejoin them.

Sebbord left the window beside which he had been standing, looking out into the night. "Did you get it?"

Tiflan reached into his hip pouch and drew forth a small, gilded box. It glinted in the low light as Sebbord took it from him. "You are not without friends, Sire."

Sebbord took the box in his hand. "My enemies overshadow my friends. I had this one followed for months to be certain he was to be trusted."

"He asks that you may now believe him."

They did not speak the man's name. Only when Sebbord opened the box did Dorilian understand why. Within the box nestled a pointed crystal of lambent green set within a ring of silver. He recognized it from his studies: a Ring of Order, one of only five keyed to the Rill Stone at Derlon's Transformation and now given to Epoptes who reached the rank of Arch-Mage. Sebbord had once worn such a ring but had surrendered it upon his removal from that office. Sebbord lifted the device and slid it upon his finger. The crystal abruptly glowed, its matrix shot through with brilliant light.

They left in deep dark. Hours ago, Sebbord's men had secured the way from prying eyes. The farm had been chosen for having woods that abutted the hill. Once they left those woods, they moved quickly up the slope. At the top, which Tutto signaled to be clear, the party walked onto a barren surface, dusty and smooth, bisected by twin deep and perfectly straight hollows. Tiflan's tall body and Sebbord's thicker one loomed among phantoms taller still. Pylons arched above them, glowing with a ghostly sheen. All about them, the flat land spread away to every side, the town little more than a smudge on either bank of a river crossed by ferries. A dusty land, poor and forgotten.

"If I succeed, these people will prosper," Dorilian said.

"They will indeed, when their grain can bypass Bartulu." Tiflan's concurrence was filled with pride. Shortly after Marc Frederick's seizure of the Triemperal throne, the Seven Houses had aligned with a handful of Esseran families to seize control of Bartulu's shipping and warehouses. Dozens of noble Sordani families had been arrested or put to the sword, their lands and holdings confiscated, then redistributed to Esseran merchants. After more than thirty years, they would be avenged.

Dorilian thought around the edges of this plan and found no flaw. He and his companions were undetected, aided by men fervent in their belief in the Sordaneons; the path forward lay clear. The only flaw would be if he failed to summon the god.

Footsteps sounded sharply, running toward them. Dorilian barely extended his arms in time to stop Levyathan's forward motion.

*You glow. They glow.* Lev waved his hand toward the structures that rose all around them, then he pointed to the station building. *It does not.*

*It sleeps.*

*Sleep breathes. It withholds.*

Dorilian looked up at his grandfather. "Are we ready?"

"Are you?"

He nodded, stepping away from Lev and breaking their joined thoughts. All day he had fought mental distractions, and he kicked himself for having allowed it now.

They approached the south face of the building, searching among the bas-relief designs of the vast wall. Near the center, Sebbord stopped and moved his hand over the flawless surface.

"Ah, here. This is the spot." He arched his fingers upon it.

He turned the Ring of Order upon his finger so the crystal jutted from the flat of his hand, then pressed it to the wall. The crystal penetrated the surface, and at once, the faint outline of a door appeared on the wall. "Stand back." Sebbord directed the men away from where the door would open. "Leur purged the nodes long ago, and men have died from standing too near the opening of them. Though records say this one was opened before, we would be prudent to take no chances." When all had lined up along the building, well away from the door, he turned his hand, the crystal contacting new set points. Levyathan cringed against Sebbord, held fast as something in the wall released and an inhalation, barely more than a sigh, announced some barrier had been breached. The station had indeed been opened, long before the memory of men now living. One by one, they walked to stand before the yawning door framed by white planes and black shadows.

"That is one obstacle overcome." Sebbord glanced at Dorilian. "Now we summon destiny. But no god ever does only what men command. The price for this awakening may well be higher than we imagine."

"And still be less than the price of not doing it," Dorilian answered.

"We will see if your pride is enough. Don't forget the god also seeks you."

Only twelve entered. Dorilian, Levyathan, and Tutto accompanied Sebbord along with eight of the burliest guards. Tiflan remained outside with Legon and the rest of the men, charged to keep away any who might stray near. As they entered the pitch dark of the interior, Dorilian was glad of Tutto stalking at his side. Light flared in Sebbord's hand, and Dorilian breathed deeply of the still, dead air as he held out his own sweat-cold palm.

Closing his eyes for but a moment, Dorilian focused energy from his body into his open hand. Like most of his race, he had practiced this skill even as a child, spinning a glowing ball of useful light. His *orbus*, with Sebbord's, illuminated the walls and painted the ceilings with light. Gold gleamed in shadowed recesses, metals reflected along voluptuous structures and fantastic curves slashed by angled interruptions. Long asleep, having last known footsteps a thousand years before any of them had been born, the Hestya node gave no indication of knowing it hosted men now. Wonders winked within shapes and shadows.

"We must first empower the core," Sebbord directed. Because he alone was familiar with the layout of such a place, he led the way. None but Epoptes and the occasional Highborn prince ever looked upon the Rill's innermost sanctums—and ever since Labran had so briefly stopped the Rill thirty-six years before, no Sordaneon had been allowed beyond the sanctum doors.

The corridor coiled, colored like coral, arched and spined with deeper hues leading downward. Dark crystals glittered in sculpted walls and flowed beneath their feet. Sebbord halted before a wall adorned with strange symbols. The fiery glyphs bespoke a power even those who did not understand them could grasp. Something of import awaited here.

Dorilian watched Sebbord pull an ornate pin from his cloak and prick one aged fingertip. He touched the large drop that formed there to the center symbol. The wet spot gleamed brilliant and red, then turned blue just prior to vanishing.

*Leur blood.* Dorilian had seen such bloodlocks before. Purely human blood, he knew, would have turned green. The Leur race that had built the living system had safeguarded its secrets with race-specific locks. Again, they stood back, bodies flat to the walls, as the leaves spiraled open. Air rushed from the open corridor to fill the vast room beyond. They walked into a chamber like none of them but Sebbord had ever seen. The *orbus* light in Sebbord's hand blazed and still did not fill its cavernous blackness. Dorilian turned, trying to shine his own light into that vast place.

"What is it?" Sparks danced in blue traces and glitters upon the surface of a dangling chrysalis of spires and reflections.

The men under Sebbord's command fanned out across the room. They soon located what they sought, a ladder leading down into the open pit beneath the thing. Levyathan's thin hands clutched Dorilian's arm, and the boy ducked his head, eyes closed the better to see.

*Size beyond size... it is bigger than this place.*

"Is this the Rill?" Dorilian asked. If so, what had his ancestor become?

"No." Sebbord gazed upward and held his *orbus* higher to reveal an array of black, many-faceted spires. Dorilian could not tell if he had heard Levyathan's thought. "This is something else. Vllyr technology, which we no longer understand. It holds a piece of a star, or something like a star. It must be handled... very carefully. Stay here." When his grandsons nodded that they would obey, he descended into the pit along with the men he had brought.

"Held small." *It surpasses this place.* Levyathan's eyes were now open, shining and clear.

"Can you see it?"

"Yes." *Under all, deep beneath... blackness swallows its light...*

The power source, it had to be. Core arrays, they were called. Dorilian had learned every node sat atop one. Only now did he actually look upon what that meant. "You mean it is below us?" With Levyathan following his every step, Dorilian moved to the edge of the pit. Looking over, he detected descending stories of metallic structures, circles of patterns, something concave and silver at the center. Shielded. Shadowed. Eight men upon a platform grasped rings of metal, hauling downward. Sebbord stood nearby, watching, his *orbus* providing light. The thing suspended above them moved ever so slightly. They were bringing it down.

"Whatever you do, don't touch it!" Sebbord shouted, not just to the men but also to the boys standing several levels above. But there was no danger of Dorilian or Levyathan touching the device, which glided far from their reach.

Mere mechanics, Dorilian recognized. This was the easy part.

Levyathan's thought nudged his. *Power the locks, open the gate. Create the path to the god.*

The eight grunting men who had taken turns hauling down the outer casing let go as the device achieved its own momentum and glided smoothly down those dark shining rods. Without a sound, faceted surfaces slid into the silver base. Only in the fraction of a moment before the seals locked into place did light appear. Dorilian covered his eyes against the sudden white blaze. And then the world again went dark.

*It awakens.* Levyathan's reassurance put that fear to rest. *Shining beneath.*

*The power?*

*Yes. But Derlon dreams.*

A dream in which Hestya did not exist.

Hearing men climb the ladder, Dorilian moved to the opening and helped Sebbord to the top. Though breathing hard, his grandfather looked victorious. Pride shone upon those aged features—pride and things unknown. He had done something only his most fabled ancestors had ever done before him. "The core burns again," he said. "This node is empowered. We can revive it if we can awaken the god and let Derlon know it is here."

"Levyathan says that Derlon dreams."

Sebbord nodded. "He dreams of being the Rill. His body gives life to all Rill stuff. Leur created living systems, organisms, not machines. Their creation melded with Aryati engineering. The platform, the rings, the power that now suffuses this node—all are part of Derlon's living corpus. But life does not presume perception. There are cells in your body of which you are not aware. If while you slept a hair grew from your ass, would you know it? So with this place. Though we have empowered this node, the Rill will not know it is here unless we awaken its awareness."

Signaling Tutto to come over, Sebbord took Levyathan by the shoulder. The boy closed his eyes as Sebbord knelt before him. "Lev," he said, "I want you to stay with Tutto. The Rill Mind, the Derlon mind, is very powerful. It can seize other minds if they are too near. Do you understand?"

"Lost." Levyathan twitched at whatever image or impression had evoked that word.

"Yes, they can be lost." Worried, Sebbord's golden gaze sought Dorilian's. "He is an unknown, but I think he can help."

"Promise no harm will come to him."

"That will be up to you."

*I should not leave him,* Dorilian thought as he followed Sebbord from the room. *Grandfather is wrong. Lev will try to find me.* But he could not have Levyathan with him when he stood before the god. If he did, Lev would be vulnerable and, worse, a distraction.

Sebbord guided Dorilian by *orbus* to another corridor, this one curved and vaulted, its rose-hued ceiling laced with shadowy ribs. From there, they descended into another chamber, even more hidden, by way of a passage lined with rings. Upon reaching the bottom, they stepped onto a floor that reflected light even as water did, ripples of stray illumination, except that it was solid underfoot. Before them rose a wall of gold, smooth and curved.

"Place your left hand on it," Sebbord instructed.

Steeling himself, Dorilian did so. His fingers met a substance warm and unyielding, so smooth that his nerves tingled. He felt nothing else. Disappointed, he looked back over his shoulder at his grandfather.

"Look again," Sebbord said.

He did. Faint symbols, traced in a color between saffron and violet, flowed from his fingertips and scrolled across the wall where nothing had shown before. He recognized the script: Aryata.

"Touch those I taught you."

Using the fingers of his left hand, Dorilian did as his grandfather had taught. He remembered the sequence perfectly, had burned it in egocentric recesses of his consciousness where the memory could not be discovered even in dreams or under the spell of drugs. The door opened to blue light. The chamber within held an immense shielded pillar, itself encircled by a suspended disk sectioned into six floating segments. Curved overlapping metal plates completely sheathed the monolith and suspended parts.

"Lockdown shields," Sebbord explained. "One of the Leur's last acts before the Devastation was to protect the living being that was and is the Rill. Every node was locked down in the hope that the core mechanics would survive the destruction. Although it was badly damaged, the Rill's base systems survived intact enough for Derlon's immortal life to heal it."

Sebbord strode between the two nearest suspended segments to the column. Closing his eyes, he pressed the fingers of both hands to raised points upon one of the plates. A blue glow accompanied his application of focused power. The plates on both the column and the disk sections flew seamlessly apart, silently folding and retreating into hidden housings. The pillar stood revealed: undulating, blue, veined, and knotted. Glancing down, Dorilian saw he stood upon a floor of translucent strands that glowed and coiled in thick ropes.

Sebbord pointed to the blue pillar. "What you see is a rudimentary vesicle upon an Entity's vast skin. A gateway into an immortal. The Entity is vast, bigger than you can imagine. I do not exaggerate when I say such a thing. Its body is as immense as the world, self creating, both energy and flesh. It is more Leur now than human. The Rill exists in dimensions we do not see and in some that we do. It has ceased all humanity but its memories—and Tarlon, they say, was the last to touch those."

"But it is the Rill?"

"A minute bit of naked nerve. Most of what makes up a node is a kind of shell. We look upon but pieces of it. There are chambers below this one which would show you more, but still, only a window. Men who look upon Derlon in his unclothed shape go mad—all but a few."

Dorilian thought he had already seen the god in its true form, but he could not be sure. He must become much stronger before he could command the thing he had glimpsed in his Wall contact and now saw snaking in ghostly streams beneath the floor. Today his only goal was to get its attention. Though fear made his heart race, he nodded to his grandfather. "I remember what to do."

A rim the waxy color of a honeycomb encircled the glowing well. The luminous pillar beckoned, yet Dorilian tensed at its cold promise of power. *Soul-sucker*, his father had called the Rill, seeking to warn him of its dangers. *Mind-sapper, destroyer of ambitious fools.* Many had sought to do what he would now attempt—had tried and failed.

*I am Sordaneon. I can endure the full gaze of the Father of all my fathers. I have prepared for this encounter. Only I may attempt this. Only I.*

Tracing the raised symbols on the rim's cold surface, he sent a thought forward. He could do it if he focused hard enough. There was an intelligence in the ring, faintly mechanical, the interface that governed node operations. A machine, for now, dormant and waiting.

Hestya.

The Rill could not see Hestya. It slumbered beneath barriers that time could not breach and imagined itself whole. Only another mind might draw it from its dream and alert the Rill to its new appendage, force it to see the Hestya node as part of its body. *Itself.*

Dorilian exhaled and tried to focus, but he found Levyathan there, a pinpoint of distant distress, sharp and piercing. He brushed that voice aside along with the tingle of Sebbord's immediate anxiety. This wasn't working. Too many distractions.

Trying again, Dorilian raised his left hand, the Rill hand, and placed it upon the glowing pillar in front of him. More than simply warm, it was also slick, and its surface yielded. As his fingers penetrated the Rill skin, blue light flowed up his arm in searing patterns. They burned to the bone. He bit back a scream, followed the pain, and let down the barriers that kept his mind from experiencing every emotion and life force around him.

What he touched then was like nothing he had ever known.

# 15

Everything moved... except him.

The promontory on which he stood was a mote upon a grain of sand surrounded by a dream. So small. Dorilian only now realized how tiny he was, how insignificant. Above, below, and to every side of him glowed currents neither hot nor cold that thrummed along his nerves until they too vibrated with music. All pain vanished. He extended his left arm, and light flowed over his skin, power hooking his nerves. Incandescence webbed his body, penetrated his veins, and filled them. New eyes opened within his eyes, allowing him to see immense forces at work upon invisible looms. Power unimagined. To one side of him, Sordan's white towers pierced a great blue dome of sky and sliced open the moon... to the other, rock flows of glowing crimson spilled over cliffs into the sea... while in front of his eyes, moonlight skimmed sapphire lakes and kissed mountains clothed in ice... voices called and somewhere an Epopte chanted archaic code into the machine they thought he was...

Permephedon reached out to touch Sordan, and the matrix around him rippled.

The displacement happened effortlessly. For him, it was nothing. He could go to any of those places. Go *now*. He could because he *was*...

*Inside a dream*, the deep core of his mind asserted. He was inside the Rill's dream of itself, populated by places it knew. A dream with only *five* cities. The Rill had no memories of lesser places like those Dorilian walked sheathed in skin, on stilts of bone...

He looked down at his feet to witness his mooring crumbling. His body was crumbling. Particles fine as stardust streamed from his extended fingers into the Rill. *Stop*, he willed and curled his

fingers back into his palm, but though the flow slowed, it continued. *No!* This time his will was stronger, and he broke free. Seizing
that moment, he extended his hand again to seize a thread of Rill
stuff, closed his fingers about it. *Here. I am here.* The currents
sweeping past him swirled into an uncontrollable vortex. He was
only a small being, impossibly small, pinching an immortal's skin.
Something vast, curious, and avaricious limned his lips, his eyes,
and then his nakedness with a taste of eternity, clear and bright—
nothing like the dust, shadows, and mud of the lightless town at the
heart of which he stood.

*Hestya. I am Hestya.*

The Rill pushed into his mind, sought to enfold him. The
World spread to every side, his to take as the promontory beneath
his feet broke away.

*Dor!*

The name triggered memory. He breathed mortal air and
struggled to remember who breathed it.

*Dor! Find me!* Such a small voice, so far away. So much smaller
than the other voice whispering seduction into his brain.

He tasted sunlight on his skin and bathed in the molten rock
of a volcano. He could stand upon both the sea and the moon. He
touched ice and starlight. And it went on forever.

*There is no other side!*

That other presence tugged at him, insistent as a needle,
nagging as an itch. It clawed at the edges of his vast being. He could
silence it forever. Except that it mattered, that one point of noise,
reminding him that he was not Rill. He was but a strand of mortal
stuff... and the place to which he clung was but a grain of sand in a
bottomless sea. If he let go, he would be lost.

*Dor! Brother, don't leave me!*

Levyathan. But Lev couldn't see what he saw, be the thing he
could become... and there was more, so much more... sunlight and
water light and secrets hidden deep in the earth...

*It consumes you, takes you. If you go, who will see me?*

*I see you, Lev...*

*Blind! Blind! It takes your eyes!*

*Here. I am here. Lev... here they are...*

Deserts and mountaintops fell away, Sordan and the sea and
the moon. And then he fell. The power streaming through him
ripped free, and colors burst apart.

Dorilian tumbled, something else hard and cold slicing at his dreams and against his mortal skin. He opened his eyes to a high ceiling of shadows above shadows, all converging upon a gold-laced eye of soft brilliant blue, translucent as water, crowning a lapis pillar. He lay on his back while the world reasserted. Turning his head, he saw glowing filaments, webs of vivid blue, twining up his left arm from his fingers to his shoulder. All that remained of power, singular and promised.

*Lev*, he reached for his brother's mind.

*Here, here... solid, real...*

But the Rill and its power had also been real. Now the contact had broken. He felt bereft, only half a being. The Rill lingered within him, and the part that remained ached to be made whole.

Other voices intruded. Sharp. Immediate.

"I could not stop the lad, Sire!" Tutto's voice rasped his nerves like sand. "He's a demon! Bit me all to hell! He would have fallen had I not grabbed him by the neck of his coat like a cat."

Sebbord's voice intruded. "No matter. No, don't take him away. Leave them be."

Dorilian felt Lev's urgent fingers stroke his cheek. Weight pressed his body from all sides, thick within his lungs. Mortal stuff, cumbersome and transient. Something wet penetrated the thin fabric of his shirt where his jacket had been opened. Lev's tears, sharp with terror. Blinking, full awareness returning, Dorilian looked past his sobbing brother's shoulder to where Sebbord stared down at him with pale alarm.

"I have grandfathered a reckless fool," the old man said.

"But Derlon saw."

"He did more than that. You lit a bonfire when a candle would have served. Nothing I did could bring you back. Without Lev, I do not think you would have returned."

Dorilian said nothing to the scolding. He knew his grandfather was right.

"Do you know where you are?" Sebbord asked, less harshly.

"Hestya."

"Good. Perhaps Derlon knows that, too. Now let us find out if our gamble was for naught. Whatever you do, don't touch it again!"

Sebbord pushed himself to his feet and approached the disk sections of the console, pressing illumined symbols and unseen artifacts. His training as an Epopte guided his hands so that his fingers wove over the smooth surface. Almost instantly, light flooded the corridors above. Intent, wearing a grim smile, Sebbord continued, his hands moving in crisp patterns, summoning a succession of complex schematics onto the chamber walls.

"Did I do it?" Dorilian had succeeded in sitting up, wrestling free of his brother's embrace, though Levyathan continued to cling to his hand. When he attempted to rise, his head swam and he had to use the edge of the console to steady himself. The blue tracery had faded from his left arm, but his flesh still hurt terribly from the contact he had made. "Well, did I?"

"Yes. The Rill acknowledges Hestya."

Dorilian knew it. He had seen Hestya in the Rillstream. But it still thrilled him to hear his success spoken. Not since his ancestor Tarlon had any Sordaneon awakened a Rill node! Triumphant, he sank to the floor again and cradled his aching head in his arms. Sudden nausea seized him and he lurched over, violently retching. Bile splashed upon the floor. Levyathan hunkered next to his side and reached for him with small, worried hands.

"Sire." Tutto moved forward.

Sebbord glanced over for a moment, his face unreadable. He nodded sharply to his sword master before returning his attention to the console.

Retrieving a large, jeweled flask from the gear he always carried strapped to his hip, Tutto stomped to Dorilian and squatted beside him. He pulled the ornate stopper. "Drink this," he ordered.

Dorilian hesitated, then drank—and abruptly spat it out. The golden liquid splashed on the floor and his trouser leg. "No!"

"Yes!" Tutto growled. He forced the flask back against Dorilian's lips. "And twice as much if you spit it out again!" He grunted on seeing that Levyathan patted his brother's neck. "See there? Even your brother knows."

Dorilian grasped the flask and pushed it back. "It tastes like gangrene juice!"

"And you'd drink that, too, if it were as good for you. Restorative sugars. Fluids. You need this. You'll drink the whole bottle if I tell you. Builds up your blood."

"I can—"

"Don't be proud." Tutto forced the flask into his hand. "Even the least of Leur gifts drains mortal flesh, and you just touched an Entity. You were warned this would happen. Wise princes carry ambrosia with them, always."

Tutto squatted nearby until Dorilian had downed enough of the brew to satisfy him.

Dorilian glared at the Estol swordsman as he handed back the flask. Much as he hated the taste of the stuff, it had cleared his mind somewhat. He felt stronger now. Feeling Levyathan nudge his shoulder, he wrapped a hand about his brother's head, pulling him closer. He still detected traces of Lev's desperation, his brother's terrible clawing fear, and knew that it had saved him from worse. He quieted Lev's fear for him, smoothing out those tattered emotions until Levyathan grew calm. It helped him to keep from reliving how effortlessly the Rill had swamped his defenses. Squashed like a worm. No, less than a worm.

But he had succeeded. *They* had.

For the first time since Derlon had awakened the Rill as his gift to humankind, the Entity was going to exceed their expectations.

# 16

Villas and gardens clung to the cliffsides overlooking the port at Tiris. With Sordan dominating the island, the towers of its shining Citadel rising above the mountain behind the town like a crown, the harbor attracted only small boats and the pleasure yachts of wealthy residents. From a terrace high on a jutting spur of rock between the town and a private beach, Daimonaeris lounged at the water's edge of her swimming pool and watched those boats bobbing far below. Though she missed Mormantalorus, she enjoyed her privileged new life. As wife to the Sordaneon Hierarch's Heir, she lived in perfect luxury—much as she had in her brother's household—surrounded by servants she had brought with her and unfettered even by a husband's presence. Dorilian had kept his word and never bothered her, not so much as an inquiry. For her part, she never knew for sure where he was, nor did she care. Turning over in the water, she swam to the other side and rose, water spilling from her hair and body as she stepped out of the pool. Two maidservants dashed forward with gauzy sheets to cover her nakedness.

Daimonaeris did not fear prying eyes. The estate was situated on high ground and approached on three sides by sheer cliffs and open lake. Only a towering Rill limb, soaring above the cliff face, was higher. Far out into the lake, another white limb raised above the water, but so distant as to be shrouded in haze, a faint blue suggestion.

After donning a robe, Daimonaeris took a glass of orange nectar from her maid and began to mentally organize her evening. She had brought a troupe of players from Mormantalorus to perform the latest work of a favorite playwright and had invited several of the local nobility to join her for the performance. There would be a lavish feast beforehand, as suited the occasion, and more feasting after. And games, of course, upon the lawn. She had heard of a man who owned a string of enormous two-legged lizards from the wastelands of Sansordan. He had trained them to carry people on their backs, and racing the creatures had become one of the island's latest rages. She knew the man had arrived at the estate, because from time to time the distressed squeals of strange animals trumpeted nearby.

Though she had initially resisted her brother's choice of a husband for her—having hoped for a man like Nammuor himself, handsome and tall, a man she might admire and love— Daimonaeris had come to terms with her lot. She might not like her juvenile husband, but she found much to like in being his wife. Dorilian put no limits on her expenses. Though he did not open his finances to her and she had been unable to ascertain the precise extent of his wealth, she could tell it might indeed be nearly as limitless as Nammuor had promised. *The greatest fortune in the Triempery*, her brother had said, *and you will be in a position to spend it however you choose.*

Her brother had left two days after her wedding, sailing back to Mormantalorus and his responsibilities as ruler of their homeland. Her heart ached sometimes, missing him and the protection he represented. Since childhood, he had been her guardian, her strong, golden champion upon whose broad shoulders she had been princess and queen. Nammuor was her only chosen partner for every dance, her consort for every state occasion. His throne child, he called her, for though but a child, she provided the legitimacy for his rule. Her country had not wished to see her wed to a foreign prince, but such was Nammuor's command, and none dared oppose his plans. *Sordan's rulers are weak*, he'd whispered to her one night in their private grotto, a cavern carved by a volcano and fed by the sea. Its dome was encrusted with glowing, omnivorous ferns, ones that feasted on tiny life forms lifted by air currents from hot, luminescent pools below. His eyes had glowed with the golden future he described to her. *The Highborn Princes of Sordan have degenerated, bred with half-men to become half-men themselves. All we need do is plant the seed we wish to flower.*

And so she was among them now, among half-men. Among people of bloodlines so tangled and confused that they lacked identity or even true history, whereas she could claim descent from the god Amynas through his son Ergeiron. Her Highborn forefathers had wrested the Citadel of Fire from the volcano that had claimed its lower levels, had made the City habitable and reclaimed Mormantalorus from the sea. Her people alone had kept their bloodlines pure: through isolation, through need, and through pride. Not for them the thoughtless coupling of animals, degenerate and indulgent. They were the Pure, the uncontaminated. Only sterilized slaves were allowed into the Citadel to serve their pleasure, and any child of a slave was a slave itself. Slaves were educated, well-treated, well-used—and they belonged to the god-sired rulers of the land. But here in Sordan, even the god-born had become half-men and coupled with lesser blood.

A woman ran up from the house, her fair hair shining beneath a servant's snood. "My Lady Archessa." She dropped to both knees before her. "Your husband has arrived."

"My *husband?*"

Daimonaeris, at first, could not believe she had heard correctly. The word was not one generally heard in her household. At her back, her three young maidservants froze in confusion, perhaps similarly stunned.

"Prince Dorilian and several companions," the woman said. "Six, including the Heir of Teremar and the younger heir of Suddekar. He says he will be here for the night."

*Not if I have anything to say about it!* Gathering the long draping of her robe over one arm, she swept from the terrace in search of her boy spouse. He was easily found. Dorilian waited in the entrance hall, still wearing travel clothes, his companions but for Legon having already dispersed to rooms the chamberlain had provided.

"What are you doing here?" she demanded.

"I'd forgotten how pleasant this villa is." He walked past her and ignored the implication that his arrival required explanation. He stopped at gold-crowned pillars leading toward a broad terrace looking over the town. The blue sky and lake framed him with disturbing clarity.

She noted something different about him, something new—or unveiled. He held himself taller. But he was still shorter than she, still as common, and still looked upon her with a half-man's base-colored eyes.

"I won't have you and your friends ruining my party."

Dorilian smiled. "A party? I said we would go to parties together."

She blanched. The last thing she wanted was for her husband to start playing the part. "It's a play, by a writer you wouldn't like."

"I will sleep through it. As for your guests, believe me when I say that I shall be your crowning achievement—unless you prefer I not announce my presence, so that they might treat me like the stable boy you think I should be."

"Don't be crass."

He stared at her coldly. "Don't you be stupid. I know you're not."

Tossing her wet hair back from her shoulders, she stared at her irate husband. She hated him for reminding her she could not deny him that status. It was also true that once her guests knew he was in residence, she would be inundated with requests for his appearance. The greater humiliation would be if she could not produce him.

*I hope he behaves himself.* Dorilian's reputation for not observing social proprieties was legendary. But worse than that was the way he looked at her, his gaze approving the way her filmy robe clung to her body's curves. She had seen that gaze in men before, but never in him. *Please don't let him want to sleep with me*, she prayed. She was a virgin still, a condition Nammuor had warned her to preserve until the time was right. Just the thought of Dorilian's hands on her body made her stomach turn. As she angled away from him to hide her reaction, she glimpsed the abrupt way his facial muscles clenched, betraying that he had noted it.

"I need to get ready." She left him there, framed by pillars and sky, his coldness pouring over her as if it could douse the same fire that hers had doused in him. Her feet flew across the floor as she ran to the safety of her handmaidens and the labyrinthine corridors of an estate that no longer felt fully hers.

The garden of the villa at Tiris had not yet divested itself of lingering traces of sweetgrass torch smoke and the aroma of lizard droppings wafting up from the lawn below. If Dorilian had not already resolved that he would leave the place after but one night, the stench would have persuaded him. He couldn't decide which had been worse:

accompanying Daimonaeris to the villa's banquet hall to play the part of her husband when they both knew he would never be one in other than name, or the drama he'd been forced to watch—about a virtuous Staubaun woman who chose to die rather than wed the powerful chieftain of a primitive people who had conquered her city. That woman had arranged for her servants and Staubaun lover to sacrifice their lives also, thus following her into virtue. He had turned to Daimonaeris without smiling and whispered, "There is your other option."

Unfortunately, he had little hope she would take up the suggestion. She'd ultimately been pleased because his appearance greatly enhanced her event. Even the noblest residents of Tiris could not have hoped to meet Sordan's Heir—or any of their Highborn rulers—under any other circumstance, and they had been suitably awed the entire evening. Though Tiflan and Deleus had later engaged in some lively discussion of the play, bestowing it with the pretense of respectability, Dorilian resented having his name attached to it. He was even less happy when Daimonaeris insisted he accompany her to the lawn for games. Appalled by the sight of giant lizards cavorting across the grass of his villa, human jockeys clinging to the creatures' necks as guests bet upon the beasts, he had stayed only long enough to let it be said that he had been there. Though Daimonaeris, wearing a gown of indigo silk and a necklace of firestones about her lovely throat, had hissed for him to stay, he refused.

"I'll be embarrassed!" She stood fists tight at her sides, her beautiful eyes hot with rage at the attention they were drawing.

"I already am!" He fervently wished that he had not given her *this* estate. Just steps away, Tiflan and Legon were exchanging a spate of lizard jokes, with more certain to come.

"You're a horrible husband—"

"Good! I never wanted to be an admirable one—or one at all, for that matter!" He left her to her happily shrieking guests and tables piled high with delicacies cooled by ice statues, each more extravagant than the next.

Now, in the gray light of morning, those statues were only memories, the lumps of their glory melting among the shrubbery where servants had thrown them. Only two servants had risen to attend the Heir and his friends as they broke the fast at a small table set near the terrace edge, looking out over the lake. Legon sipped from a cup of strong tea, his attitude watchful. Only Tiflan and Tutto knew for certain why they were there or why they had come to Tiris instead of riding directly to Rhondda.

"I know we didn't come prepared to find a party, but it was fun." Deleus was the first to break the silence they shared. Of course, half of the Suddekan prince's fun had come from being mistaken for Dorilian, whom he resembled. Though he and his cousin had been dressed very differently, the evening was sure to result in rumors that Dorilian had placed bets upon the lizards.

Tiflan and Legon, in fact, considered the creatures the high point of the visit.

"I took my biggest winning when the green-nosed beast crapped in the lily-pool." Tiflan had only to point to the evidence.

"A low-risk wager," Legon countered. "The creatures crap indiscriminately. The blue-toed one I bet on crapped on a lady's lap."

"Did I ever tell you how lizards lose weight?"

Legon met Tiflan's broad grin without a smile. "They shed their scales."

Dorilian sighed.

All of them wore travel clothes now, plain tan cotton and leathers for the road. Dorilian had earlier ordered the bodyguard out of bed and their horses readied.

The sun rose above the horizon and spilled rosy light across the lake like a carpet down an aisle. Brilliant sparks danced along the stream of tea the pretty servant girl was pouring. The young men smiled at her, and she shyly smiled back before realizing her error and ducking her head, flustered at the Highborn presence, perhaps mistaking which one was her mistress's husband. Light now gilded all their faces. Dorilian rose from the table. His friends rose with him, their gazes following his inland, toward the heather-shrouded hills where mist still clung to the gorges and sunlight painted the single Rill structure with blue and rose.

They heard it first, a deep low thrum, followed quickly by another slightly higher pitched, then another higher still. Spacial displacement, contained. A sound familiar to many, but one which this town had never heard. The last note, a gentle whine, pierced the morning as a brilliant spear of light, massive beyond most human experience of such things, erupted within the pylon ring before vanishing into pinpoint nothingness across the lake, faster than the eye could see. The Mormantaloran serving girl dropped her pot and it shattered, splashing hot liquid across the flagstones and the boots of the young men.

"Rill!" Her cry alerted the other servants, who, bleary-eyed from staying up through the night, stumbled out from the villa in confusion. In the town below, people could be seen running from their houses, turning and pointing.

The Entity had spoken.

# 17

"Take them all and imprison them wherever you choose, so long as it is deep and inescapable. Remand them to Rhodhur, for all I care."

Even for Chyralane, Denizen of Phaer, the statement was venomous. By wishing the Sordaneons into the custody of Khelds, she was as much as consigning them to death. Her audience, assembled over the course of a full day from those domains with access to the Rill, filled the audience chamber of Permephedon's Archhalia.

Marc Frederick refused to answer the provocation. He had just journeyed for hours, was wet and disheveled, and had not bothered to change from the elegant clothing he had worn to his son's betrothal celebration in Merath. A regal crown glinted in bright points on his dark, bedraggled head. He simply sat on the throne, chin in hand, and listened as the detritus of thirty-five years of his nobles' freehandedness in the Sordan domains came crashing to an end on the Archhalia's floor.

The ambassador from Trongor rolled his eyes at Chyralane's demand. "Imprisoning your Sordaneons would be easy, if they could be taken, but of course they can't be. They are in *Sordan*."

A noteworthy reminder. The island city had never truly been invaded. Marc Frederick had captured Labran at Permephedon and then pressured Deben into allowing Esseran troops to occupy his domain in exchange for his father's life. Expanding that presence would be precarious if the populace perceived that Essera was trying to unseat or kill their Highborn rulers.

*We cannot let it come to an invasion. That would create too deep a breach, an insurmountable wall. And the risk of losing the Sordaneons in the ensuing conflict would be unacceptable.*

The Leur's Ring burned on his finger, alerting him to dangerous swells in the emotional sea of nobles and dignitaries: the dominating currents were vengeful, self interested, with little hope of being turned.

From beside Marc Frederick, the Epoptean Psilant Quirin raised his hands, exhorting the group's attention. He wore his stately robes of office, symbols evocative of the Rill's rings and arches embroidered across the breast of his white mantle.

"Sordan is as stunned as we are here." Quirin drew upon the dense information to which his Order was privileged. "I have just come from there. Let me assure you that Sordan is at peace! The Hierarch Deben summoned me immediately, even before I could demand a meeting with him. I'm convinced he did not know of this in advance. He will be examining his options—and I suggest we move carefully regarding him. He presently is cooperating with the King's provisional commanders in controlling the public there."

Chyralane was not mollified. Tall as any man, dressed in black robes that gave her the look of an angry oracle, she was willing to say the things others would not. "Who cares about Deben? The man is a fool. It is Sebbord who roosts upon that mount, taunting us all. Your Order oversees the nodes. Well, Hestya's node is not needed. Get rid of it."

Quirin eyed her with the narrow-lidded disdain of a thwarted toad. "Do you think the Order did not try that first? The Rill recognizes Hestya as part of its body, and it does not honor our requests that it ignore or dispose of it. Shall I illustrate the problem?" He looked at her and issued a command. "Cut off your arm!"

Marc Frederick lifted an eyebrow at the analogy.

Those in the chamber watched the woman's bitter smile. "You know I will not."

"And the Rill will not cut off Hestya. It does not want to. And it does not hear our reasons as to why it should."

Because humankind could not talk to the Rill, it heard no mortal voices at all. All human communication with the Rill consisted of signals which to it were no different from animal nerves triggering lungs to breathe air or guts to digest food. Because the Rill did not, on any concrete level, even know that those who thought they commanded it were there.

But someone or something had told the Rill to extend that arm to Hestya.

Marc Frederick rose.

"So it is," he said. "If we are to slice off that limb, we must pick up the sword ourselves!" Let that give them pause.

"Majesty." The Sordani ambassador, embattled and heretofore silent, stepped forward. "My Thrice Royal Hierarch Deben does not himself yet understand this event, which occurred without warning. All accusation that it is of his doing is false. We do not know how it came to happen that the Rill now goes to Teremar."

"I think Sebbord Teremareon's army securing the mount pretty much explains that," Marc Frederick said. Upon his arrival not a half hour before in Dazunor-Rannuli, he had received a full accounting from the Epoptes there. They had communicated with every Rill port, including Sordan and Permephedon. For all the fear and confusion it was creating elsewhere, the Rill continued to perform as flawlessly as ever, and had conveyed him at once to Permephedon.

"The people expect you to deal severely with this rebellion." Chyralane stood front and center of a group of her cartel peers, including two lesser Denizens. The other four Denizens had been caught unawares like Marc Frederick himself, attending the betrothal. Chyralane only attended functions located in a Rill port.

"I'm not convinced this is a rebellion." Before arriving in Dazunor-Rannuli, Marc Frederick had spent several hours aboard a fast river yacht in conferences with Enreddon and other men he could trust, fashioning a full understanding of what had occurred. Sebbord was too deliberate, too intelligent a man not to have known what would happen in Essera in the event of a Rill alteration—or to have set in place the means to prevail against it. The fact that Hestya was in Teremar and not in the occupied domains of the Hierarchate presented an enormous problem. Essera had no legal jurisdiction there.

He noted Chyralane's furious glare at his dismissal of her demand for retaliation—but there was an intriguing nod from the Denizen of the Haralambdos, and a few glances exchanged among his companions. The Seven Houses, then, were not all of one mind. From other points throughout the chamber, voices ceased responding as one, sorting into factions, each pleading cause for alarm.

"Let me be clear." Marc Frederick raised his voice to quiet the crowd. "The Rill is vital to this empire's wellbeing. But the Rill has not ceased to serve our needs. Its presence in our lands, its service to our cities and our economy, has not been altered. Passengers and goods still travel, communications are being sent and delivered just as before. *Exactly* as before. No direct threat has been presented to us. Indeed, we need to look more closely as to what has truly happened here."

"The ruin of our economy!" shouted another Lord of the Seven Houses, a member of the House of Koillos. In partnership with the House of Phaer, House Koillos controlled the Teremari port of Bartulu, gaining substantial revenues from ferrying grain shipments to Sordan and then by Rill to Essera.

"We have yet to assess the real extent of disruption," Marc Frederick countered. "The Rill still runs. Goods still travel. Indeed, many of our merchants might see their markets expanded. Some, I dare say, will consider this an opportunity."

"What if Sebbord orders that contracts go only to Sordani merchants or nobles—or to those from Teremar?" A third man, member of the Guild of Grain Brokers, put forth that important question. The entire grain transport and brokering system in Suddekar and Teremar had been rendered obsolete the moment the Rill had sent that first *charys* to Hestya.

Marc Frederick answered. "That is an issue I believe can be negotiated."

He turned his gaze upon the Psilant, confronting the smoldering anger there. He needed Quirin's Order on his side or, at the very least, unopposed to him. The Epoptes, who served the Entity, would not advocate acting against it. "There is no reason to think Sebbord means to overthrow the Covenant," Marc Frederick said. "Unless it can be integrated economically as well as functionally with the rest of the Rill system, Hestya will be useless to him. I am prepared to send an emissary to Sebbord, in conjunction with the Order of Epoptes, to determine what has happened here and what Sebbord hopes to achieve."

Having established his position, Marc Frederick continued. "We will soon know a great deal more than we do now. Until then, I do not want to hear any threats against Sebbord or the Sordaneons. Such threats will do nothing to make him—or them—more cooperative." To Sordan's ambassador, he said, "Tell your Hierarch I am confident his hands are blameless in this matter and that we will discuss things further in the morning. I'm sure he has his own concerns about how to deal with his kinsman." The man bowed deeply before hurrying out of the room. To the rest of the gathering, Marc Frederick announced, "We will all discuss this further in the morning."

"But Majesty," an elderly woman, the Gracious Dowager of Leseos, spoke up, her voice carrying high and light above mutters of resignation and dissent. "How did the Rill *go* to Hestya? It has only ever gone to points between Sordan and Permephedon. How is it possible, and what does it mean?"

In the cold silence that descended over the room, Marc Frederick saw that realization had set in at last. The Dowager had laid her finger on the real source of their fear—and the only question he truly needed to answer. For once, he welcomed Quirin's magisterial stamp of approval.

"That is what His Majesty and the Order are going to find out," Quirin promised, locking his dark eyes with Marc Frederick's. "We stand fully behind his efforts to seek the truth about the Entity's emergence and to contain any damage that may be caused by transgressors who seek to use the Rill for ends of their own."

"Thank Leur you came when you did." Rheger spoke the moment Marc Frederick closed the door behind him. They were now alone in the King's private chamber just off the meeting room. "I thought my skull would split." With a grimace, he grasped the heavy crown he wore by its rim of glowing blue stones, lifted it from his head, and sank onto the nearest couch.

By the way Rheger let his sweat-plastered head fall back against the cushions, Marc Frederick had no doubt that long hours of holding lords and emissaries at bay had drained him. Rheger had arrived at Permephedon immediately upon hearing the news and had spent nearly a day performing as the King's surrogate: conferring with generals, gathering information, contacting allies. He'd probably worn the crown the whole while. Marc Frederick looked up as the door opened again, and Enreddon entered the room. The Stauberg prince walked over to join them, lifting an eyebrow in inquiry as he spied Rheger stretched out, eyes closed, not even acknowledging his arrival.

"Enhancer debilitation," Marc Frederick explained.

From the couch, Rheger lifted his right hand to display his

brother Ostemun's crown, then let it drop again. Opening his fingers, he let the thing fall to the floor. The priceless object landed with a gentle thud on the deep carpet. "He arrived in time to keep at least some order until I could get here."

"A pity Merath's Rill node is crownless and dormant," Enreddon noted.

Marc Frederick nodded. Even with use of enhancers, only a handful of his Malyrdeon kindred had ever been able to fold the world sufficiently to transport themselves bodily from place to place. Rheger had agreed to do so only because of the extraordinary situation.

"Yes, a pity." Marc Frederick slumped into a chair and ran a hand over his jaw, feeling the day's growth of beard there. Everyone had to have seen it, of course. "What is Sebbord doing? Reminding the whole world of what the Sordaneons are?"

Enreddon perched on the edge of the carved stone desk that dominated the center of the room. "Of course. What else could it be but that? But I'm more interested in who than why."

"Who was able to contact the Entity—that is the question," Marc Frederick acknowledged. He could be sure he wasn't the only one asking it.

"I don't think it was Sebbord. If Labran had bestowed power on him, he would not have waited this long."

"And it wasn't Deben," Rheger contributed from the couch. "He never left Sordan. People have placed him in the Serat every single day. He's always home."

Marc Frederick never broke gaze with Enreddon. "Dorilian."

The other man sighed. He had parted ways with Marc Frederick at Dazunor-Rannuli and taken the Rill to Hestya instead. He had just returned from that visit and, like his King, still wore the same garments he had worn to Jonthan and Ionais' betrothal feast. "I spoke with Sebbord. In an outer chamber only, for he would not allow me inside. Sebbord admits nothing. Yet we know the Rill does not spontaneously rearrange itself. He said only that the rings were revivified centuries ago. Apparently, one of the former Hierarchs died shortly after completing the work but left that detail out of the histories." Both men immediately thought of Tarlon, the Rill Lord who had opened the station at Randpory not long after denying a request by a Bas of Serrain to attempt repair of the structures at Simelon. But had he repaired those at Hestya?

Enreddon leaned nearer and lowered his voice, forcing a

disgruntled Rheger to open his eyes and turn his head to catch what he said. "Let them believe it was Sebbord. It's what he wants them to believe."

"Then Dorilian was there?"

Enreddon smiled. "Sebbord wouldn't say—but he did not say no."

Marc Frederick laughed softly. He rested his arms upon those of the chair. "We did it. Labran bestowed the gift on an heir besides Deben. Deben must be furious."

"I'm sure he is. Word in Sordan has it that Dorilian is at Rhondda, his estate south of the City. But he was at Tiris this morning."

*So he could see the Rill leave Sordan for Hestya.* Bit by bit, Marc Frederick perceived the pieces of that young puzzle falling into place. The visit to Labran. Seeking out grain brokers at Stauberg. The visit three days ago to someone in Dazunor-Rannuli... Who had he met? A merchant with ties to House Haralambdos, perhaps? Chyralane's instincts had not been mistaken.

Dorilian clearly was Sebbord's pupil in playing chess.

The birth of a new Rill node fueled a firestorm of speculation in Essera and beyond. The Rill would soon run to Stauberg, one rumor said, followed just as quickly by another that the Sordaneons would launch their campaign to destroy Essera by stopping the Rill altogether. A third rumor flew throughout both nations that the Rill would go next to Mormantalorus. None of these proved true. As weeks passed and then months, people realized the Rill, at least for the near future, would go no further than Hestya.

Secure within a ring of his soldiers and cloaked in the Rill mystique that attended his lineage, Sebbord negotiated his terms. In return for his formal acknowledgment of their guardian status and agreement to turn over physical possession of Hestya's Rill facility for governance under the articles of the Covenant, Sebbord obtained clemency from the Order of Epoptes. The Epoptes promptly accorded the Hestya node full and immediate operational standing, assigning a portion of future Rill revenues to pay for the infrastructure necessary to make Hestya a viable Rill port. With the Order on his side and administering its allotment of slots for the public good—

as set out in the Covenant—Sebbord undertook apportioning the slots that fell under his jurisdiction as Bas of Teremar. Keeping the majority in trust for the Sordaneons, he leased the remaining shares to a wide representation of interests, not all of them Sordani. House Haralambdos, which lobbied two other of the Seven Houses to jump to their side and completely muddle cartel attempts to create a unified opposition, quietly walked away with a princely percentage.

Sebbord then negotiated his personal freedom. After face-to-face talks with Marc Frederick, he was issued a pardon stating he had committed no treason. Stymied by the King and his allies on one side and the Order on the other, not to mention faced with absolute opposition from Sordan and its allied domains, the Archhalia could deliver no censure stronger than a reprimand. Opponents nonetheless mounted their own assaults. Sebbord could not get withdrawn or dismissed motions by three of the Seven Houses and other Esseran parties that he or Teremar owed them reparations for the business they had lost or would lose, and for properties rendered worthless. He shrugged off those battles, knowing they would drag out in courts and arbitrations for years.

When Sebbord left the node building on a bright, cold day a bare two months after he had summoned the Rill to Hestya, he found himself being cheered by more than his waiting army. Thousands had come from Sordan and all around to acknowledge him. With a bow of his head, Sebbord saluted them all before mounting his ivory horse and riding away. He had done all that he had set out to do.

Land around Hestya immediately exploded in value, with town properties in particular selling for exorbitant sums. Marc Frederick, who had months before noted Dorilian's visit to a Stauberg grain broker and checked into the young man's grain holdings, had also taken note of the Sordani prince's land purchases around that region. Uncertain as to what was afoot but possessing a keen sense of business, the King had secretively begun buying up prime river frontage in town. Far from impoverishing him, the Rill's establishment at Hestya enriched him beyond even what he had hoped. Any diminution in the value of Marc Frederick's Esseran Rill holdings was more than offset by spectacular profits in Hestya.

The King smiled to himself when he sent a message to Stefan approving purchase of whatever was needed to build the mining operation at Orqho.

# 18

The wide turf lane opened out of the curve, cutting in front of vacant stands. Sordan's empty hippodrome enclosed the course. Dorilian barely noticed the structure. He fixed his gaze on the green distance between the white head of his surging mount and the three horses pounding in the lead—horses belonging to men foolish enough to have bet against him. He would catch them around the next curve. Leaning lower over his horse's neck, his knees pressed just behind its shoulders and his chest hugging the rise and fall of its withers, he relaxed his grip on the reins. "Go!" he hissed.

The stallion leaped forward; motion translated into speed. Sural had never lost a race. Indeed, it was said he did not know how to lose—a trait he and Dorilian shared.

The stadium, already a blur, dissolved into a white suggestion as Sural flew down the straight course. Keeping the reins in hand, Dorilian clutched a handful of mane. Brisk morning air slashed across his cheeks, his face and arms flecked with foam from the stallion's exertion. Wind tore at his hair and hands.

Speed. Only the Rill compared to this, to riding pure power. The animal resisted his every attempt at guidance; Sural wanted his head, but Dorilian knew that to give up control would invite disaster.

Sural had already left one horse far behind. Now he passed another as if the hard-running beast were standing still. Dorilian tightened his thighs and shifted his weight ever so slightly, guiding the stallion inside again, saving ground.

Ahead, the churning hindquarters of the two remaining horses kicked up clods of turf. Muscles bunched beneath white hides, legs flying, hoofs digging deep into the grass. They streaked toward the pole. The leader, an experienced racer with leg wraps boasting Tollech's red and blue, pulled away and gained over the other horse. Flattening his body, nudging Sural with his knees as well as his hands, Dorilian guided him past the flagging second horse so quickly that he entered the curve too fast. Sural ran wide, but not so much as to leave him hung out. Leaning inward and hauling on the inside rein, Dorilian turned Sural to see the remaining horse, still a good five lengths in front, just coming out of the curve.

*Now.* Sural bore down upon the leader. Dorilian clung to the stallion as his neck stretched toward victory, legs driving into the turf. Clods thrown up by the other horse flew at him, and Dorilian ducked his face into Sural's slick neck. The stallion didn't seem to mind the flying dirt and plunged straight ahead.

Was the finish near? Dorilian glanced up, gauging the pole. But Sural lunged for the lead even before he gave rein. Dorilian did not look at the other horse as he flashed past and thundered into the lead. He grinned. Sural was still pulling away as they passed the finish pole.

Sitting up in the saddle, Dorilian pulled on the reins firmly, though Sural fought him for control. The stallion didn't want to stop running. They continued to gallop until they were nearly half around the course again before Dorilian could turn him around. He kept a tight seat, his thighs and calves gripping the horse's body, as Sural spun and reared in protest.

"Assist him!" Tiflan shouted to the handlers.

Dorilian had just brought Sural back on all fours. He looked up to see Legon reining in at the head of the handlers.

"Get a line on him!" Legon barked. Sural snaked his head toward the men, teeth bared.

Dorilian gave Sural free rein for a moment, then sawed the reins, pulled the stallion's tossing head down and to the side, guiding the massive body into a choppy prance. He held that control until Legon, urging his horse close, reached over and succeeded in snapping a line onto the beast's bridle as another man managed to secure a second line.

"Get off!"

Dorilian glared at his friend. "I will not! Not until we return to the others."

"You can ride with me."

"I said no."

"This was a damn fool idea."

With Legon riding at his side and nervous handlers trotting alongside, lines in hand, Dorilian headed Sural back toward the gathered watchers.

"Magnificent!" A blond young man, one of the grandsons of the Bas of Tollech, cheered as Dorilian swung down off the horse. "He is as swift as the stories of him have said."

"What he is is dangerous," was Legon's opinion. "A worse-natured beast was never born."

"The fastest horse anyone has ever ridden," Dorilian said proudly. He patted the muscular white neck but kept his hands away from the swiveling head with its blue-skinned nose and bared, snapping teeth. "Felarro himself was not as swift."

"I would not lay my gold on that," said Tiflan. Felarro, the great ivory horse Amynas the god had chased across the plains of Thossa, had been the fleetest of Sural's breed. "But he does have Felarro's temper."

They watched the handlers lead Sural away.

A man wearing a servant's cap approached the guard and pointed to the lowest level of the stadium's white marble seats. Dorilian looked over and frowned at the figure standing on the steps. "He can wait," he said. Ignoring the questioning glances from his friends, he continued talking with his distant kinsman, the young man from Tollech.

A short time later, Dorilian summoned Legon to accompany him and made his way to the stands.

"I heard you were in Sordan." He stopped several paces away. "But I did not think I was on your itinerary."

Nammuor had arrived two days before on a ship disguised as a Mercedan merchanter. The Mormantaloran ruler had met first with Deben and then spent time with Daimonaeris. Though Dorilian knew his wife had been in Sordan for two weeks, he had not attempted to see her. Their paths had crossed only once since Tiris—at a reception where they had arrived and departed separately.

"You will ever be on my itinerary, *Brother*, as long as my sister calls you husband." Nammuor's gaze raked the field, the horses, and the men. "So, this is how you spend your time."

Dorilian wished he could pierce him with a dagger instead of just a look. "Do not call me 'Brother,'" he said. "You succeeded in marrying your sister to me, but don't expect me to honor you for it."

Nammuor frowned. The morning sun cleared the arena, brushing his head with golden fire. "You are as in need of breaking as that horse you ride, just as disdainful of the rein. Your father knows he cannot control you, and so he does not try, hoping to preserve what little dignity he still possesses. But I do not have to care about appearances." He ceased studying the field and locked gazes with Dorilian. "My sister will be living in Sordan from now on. I expect you to pay more attention to her."

"You *expect*?" Dorilian didn't know if he should laugh or simply turn his back on such presumption.

"It shames her when your only attention to her comes in the form of appearing unexpectedly at a party and proceeding to behave like an ass."

So that was it. Daimonaeris had complained to her brother about what a boor he had been. This time Dorilian did laugh. "If she continues to treat me like an ass, I shall behave like one. A *royal* ass. I was willing to be good company until she made it obvious that she did not want me there. I will tell you what that party was—a collection of useless, empty-headed, self-inflated nobles without a single worthwhile thought among them. Most of them were damned Esseran sycophants. And there were lizards running about the lawn! She's lucky I didn't order them roasted! If I had, the food would have been better."

Nammuor shook his head. "You have much to learn about being a husband. Even more than she does about being a wife."

Dorilian looked about for Legon and signaled him over. The tall youth started toward them at a run.

"Send your minion away," Nammuor said. "You won't need him for this."

"I will decide that. You didn't seek me out to offer advice on my marriage."

The Mormantaloran smiled. Something subterranean lurked behind the unpleasant caress of those pitch-dark eyes. "You should try to make yourself a little more useful to me."

"To what end? Your sister would still despise me. And you have what you wanted."

"Do I? Naturally, I'm interested in what happened at Hestya."

Dorilian sighed, but he waved Legon back. The other youth took a seat on one of the stone rows, and Dorilian resumed his attention to Nammuor.

"Hestya is Sordaneon business, not yours," Dorilian told him.

"My sister is wed to Sordaneon business."

"Your sister is wed to *me*. She has fine estates and pretty dresses and all the worthless friends my gold can buy. She never cared about me before Hestya."

"No one cared about you before Hestya," Nammuor reminded him bluntly. "Before Hestya, the Sordaneons were one of Marc Frederick's great conquests. But now look: Marc Frederick wonders if Sebbord has power he never guessed at or if it is in the hands of another. Essera's masses clamor for Sebbord to open the Rill to Stauberg, and its nobles clamor just as loudly that he must not be allowed to do it. They both want the Rill and fear it. They fear Deben and Sebbord alike! And everyone wonders about you." Nammuor looked about and, seeing only the men standing on the racing field and Legon seated out of earshot, leaned nearer. "Sebbord testified to the Order of Epoptes and to the Archhalia that he served as an Epopte only. That he empowered the core array. That when he touched the console to bespeak the machine, the god already knew the station—and responded as at any other station. But the Epoptes questioned him too long to have been satisfied with that answer. Someone awakened the Entity to Hestya, and they think it was him. Or that it was you. Or maybe even your odd little brother."

Nammuor was fishing. The Epoptes, Dorilian knew from having followed the proceedings closely, had never seriously considered Lev as a gift bearer.

"Tell me what you want." It irritated him that he must listen to this man.

"The same things you do. Essera driven out of Sordan and her lands, and her people—her future—placed again as they should be: in Sordaneon hands."

"Pretty words. You have troops massed upriver of Hestya, in Mokkosa. You also have troops garrisoned at Ruphay and Jatar. Pull back those men, and I will be more inclined to believe in fair intentions."

Nammuor smiled crookedly. "Think. Have we not ourselves been beset by this plague out of Essera? These half-men and their degraded lords? When Endurin announced that Marc Frederick would be his Heir, we broke with the Malyrdeons. We broke with them first, before Marc Frederick ever stole that throne. When

Camas Ciennoreon died, Essera came at us, thinking I would be weak. They did not guess what I had learned, the strength I commanded, the power—" he looked into his own distance, leaving Dorilian to wonder what thoughts caused that handsome face to grow so cold. "Labran should have joined us from the first. Then might we have broken them. But he kept his faith with the Malyrdeons. He couldn't conceive that they would support the usurper against his Highborn blood, but he was wrong." He sighed. "My troops are deployed on your border because Essera has troops in Suddekar, threatening my domains of Othgol and Nalapar."

Little as Dorilian liked hearing it, the explanation made sense. Jonthan Stauberg-Randolph had until recently commanded Essera's army in Suddekar, ostensibly against Mormantaloran incursions. Frustrated that he could not dismiss Nammuor's argument, he simply averted his gaze and wished he could get back to his horses.

Nammuor watched him closely. "The Rill... could help us."

"The Rill goes where it wishes, not where men command it."

"So men say. So some want us to believe. But if it could wake up one morning and see Hestya, why not wake up another and see Stauberg? Why not Mormantalorus? Or are you also convinced of the machine nature of the thing?"

Dorilian scoffed. "What do I know? The Epoptes won't let me near it."

"Sebbord would."

Dorilian refused to look at him. A direct gaze would reveal too much, in particular that the question was one he could answer.

Nammuor cursed under his breath. "You deny me even consideration. Don't forget what I can give to you. Essera is careful now, but for how long? How long until they seek to seize the Rill from you, the way they did once before when they took Labran captive and placed Sordan in chains? Chains Sordan still wears! Look at your father, what they made of him! They will do the same to you. Drive fear into your brain, deprive you of all trust. They will cripple you as they did him, they'll cage you like some fancy beast, and you'll be like that horse you rode just now"—Dorilian stared at him then, and Nammuor's gaze bored into his with a piercing truth—"a bad-tempered creature they tolerate because of the power they can enjoy when riding your back. You will think you're running free, but they will control you."

"Leave me!"

"Gladly." Nammuor rose, and on the periphery of his vision Dorilian saw Legon rise also. The Mormantaloran's gaze remained locked onto his. "Daimonaeris resides in Sordan now because doing so ties her more closely to you. I would take great—and formal—offense if you do not live together and maintain a joint household. Maybe you are content to let Sordan remain in Essera's filthy hands, Brother. I am not. Sebbord accomplished his end, but at a cost to mine. Do not think the Stauberg-Randolphs find this station inconvenient or that they will not want to control it. Hestya is within a few days' march of Mokkosa, strategically near my border with Suddekar."

Dorilian welcomed Legon's proximity, the other youth's whip-quick presence on the edge of striking distance. Even though he did not fear an attack, he did not appreciate Nammuor's attempts at intimidation.

"Maybe we thought of that." He spoke in a whisper, directing his answer to Nammuor's retreating back as the Mormantaloran left the hippodrome. "I did."

# 19

The Crescent Palace of the Merrydeons crowned the second tallest hill in the city of Merath and was in every way a perfect Highborn dwelling. It possessed breathtaking beauty, blue stone walls, and a serene aspect. For three of four seasons, candleberry trees spread blossom-laden limbs to scent and shade the palace's broad terraces and garden paths. Each of the guest suites was suited to royal occupancy, having its own reception, sleeping, and bathing alcoves as well as servant quarters. Marc Frederick and his family arrived earlier than other guests and laid claim to rooms overlooking the city. He liked to see activity and bustle, and Merath was above all else a bustling town as it prepared for the wedding of its ruler's daughter.

Marc Frederick was happy to see all his family gathered in the royal suite, preparing Jonthan for the day. He was especially pleased to see Emyli and her sons there. Stefan had his young brother Hans on the great carpet in the center of the receiving room and was showing him how to wrestle someone much larger. The smaller lad had no chance at success, but Stefan allowed him some minor escapes that yielded shouts of victory. Emy herself looked more beautiful than ever, her rich brown hair pulled back to display her lovely profile, gems dangling at her ears and in the modest coronet she wore. It saddened him, knowing why she had not sought another man in her life. But that past did not shadow her features, and her thoughts only rested with her brother as she tugged and tucked at his neckline, trying as ever to make him more perfect.

"You shall never wear a collar correctly!" she despaired.

"Say nothing to Ionais, then." Jonthan twisted his neck so Emyli might fasten the jeweled clasps that closed the elaborate, embroidered ruff. "She means to lock one about my neck tomorrow morning."

"One you deserve," Emy scolded, "for having made her wait all these years." She gave up on the ruff. "We shall have to get the tailor to adjust this, or Jon will strangle before he even sees the bride."

Apollonia swept in from the corridor, her fittings finished and found satisfactory. "How handsome you are," she said to her son. "Tell those boys to stop cavorting," she bid Emyli. "They can act like barbarians elsewhere."

Marc Frederick benignly regarded his queen. She was at her most regal with subjects she could bring into line. Emyli at once set to chiding young Hans, who did not want to cease his game the way Stefan immediately did.

"We're due at midday meal later," Apollonia said. "More guests are arriving every hour."

"Any word on the Sordaneons?" He could count on her for the most current information.

"Their barge passed the customhouse this midmorning and by now should have docked upriver." Many royal guests from Dazunor-Rannuli preferred to disembark at the Merrydeon summer palace outside of the city rather than use the teeming public piers. "I'm sure they will ride in shortly, disrupting us all."

"Excellent." He noticed Jonthan's grin at his enthusiasm. The Queen, for her part, frowned.

"I'm still vexed that Dorilian's bride is not with him. I wished to see her again. I tell you, Marc, Daimonaeris is the very pearl of beauty, exquisitely bred. A jewel at the center of any court. Can you believe she said her brother would not approve?" Apollonia disdained any woman who was controlled by a man.

"You may be sure of it." Jonthan shrugged out of his ill-fitting shirt. Emyli took it from him and gave it to a servant to await the tailor. "Nammuor rules her as he rules all Mormantalorus. None live or speak or act but as he has approved. His sister could not be otherwise."

"Then he has married her into the wrong family, because the Sordaneons never do what anyone says." Having no desire to talk about Nammuor, Apollonia turned to her husband. "It will be good to see Sebbord again. We need to talk with him... about a great many things."

Marc Frederick did not envy Sebbord. Half the guests at the wedding would wish to "speak" with him about those same things. "I'm sure I can get at least an hour of his time. In fact, I'm counting on it. I brought my chessboard." He had set up the game table in his room, in front of a window looking out upon the confluence of the Dazun and Rannul rivers, the playing pieces already situated as they had been at their last meeting. "We have an unfinished game to decide."

"The better to discuss politics, I'm sure. I see how you tend your infatuation with that man, and with his grandson also. My father is the same way. All the Malyrdeons are. Even Wall Lords dream of Rill movement and power. You're one of us, you know." His wife accorded him a smile. "But don't be fooled into thinking a Sordaneon will ever grant you an inch of that ground. Coming to a wedding is not a concession; it is a policy."

"Then we need more weddings," he said. "More celebration and less battle. More policy. I want this year to be less trying than the last."

"It will be," Emyli assured him, ever spirited. "You'll see."

He only wished he could believe her.

"It really *is* blue," Dorilian said.

The Crescent Palace's azure towers stood in ordered ranks above Merath's clutter of walls and peaked roofs. Behind the palace rose a green-draped hill gilded here and there with meadows of golden lilies, the domain's heraldic symbol. The whole aspect appeared regal and well suited for a wedding. The barge rocked as it bumped the dock. The amiable Rannul River swarmed with boats, skirting a portion of the city's sprawling harbor and stands of steep-roofed, walled villas. Like so many town dwellings, they proclaimed wealth through the hiding of it. Only the Crescent Palace was ostentatious, a brilliant splash of line and color.

"Poor planning, if you ask me," Tiflan said. "The Merrydeons built their palace on the hill, but should the Rill ever awaken, every bit of land between it and the Dazun River will be given to warehouses."

"I doubt they're worried, given that nothing's happened in a thousand years."

"And it's your goal, I suppose, that they continue to believe it cannot?"

Dorilian shot his cousin a warning look. Since the opening of the Hestya node, he'd conversed at length with Sebbord and Tiflan about the danger he faced if he attempted another Rill contact. His physical contact with the Entity had marked him somehow. Rill awareness tingled along his nerves like spider silk and try as he might, he could not break those strands or brush them away. Just this morning, riding the Rill and placing himself even in shielded proximity to the Entity had made his spine ache, and his nerves crawl. He glanced at his left arm, fearing he would see snaking tendrils of blue. Fortunately, his Rill affinity remained invisible.

Prying his mind from thoughts of the Rill, Dorilian joined Sebbord on the dock. He and his grandfather, representing the Sordaneons, would enter Merath with an entourage. Two grooms led Sebbord's favorite charger from the barge, caparisoned for the ride through the city. The ivory horse charged down the weathered planks, and it took both men to calm the beast. Dorilian's own mount—its neck, breast, and flanks draped with silk finery in Sordan's hierarchal emerald and silver colors—jittered a few steps when he swung into the saddle. A groom bent to cup Sebbord's boot, assisting him. The journey upriver from Dazunor-Rannuli had tired the old man.

Legon rode in from the direction of the road. His flaxen hair gleamed almost as brightly as the golden buttons and clasps on his garments.

"An honor guard will greet us outside the Horned Gate," he reported. "Many important people, including two Denizens of the Seven Houses."

Sebbord scowled. "Ride to the gate and get rid of those jackals. I will meet no cartel looters."

Legon shifted and looked to Dorilian. "One is Harrun Haralambdos."

A transparent maneuver, seeking to parlay usefulness into acquaintance. Dorilian noted that Sebbord left him with the decision, and he made it crisply. "Send them away."

Legon turned his horse and set off at a gallop down the road.

The Sordaneon entourage rode out soon after, following a color guard past the expansive royal villa to which the dock belonged. Riding through a gate framed and hidden by smoothly trimmed yews, they entered the lane that would take them by way of a short ride to the city. Tiflan and Tutto fell into line behind the two royals. Dorilian was glad Sebbord had elected to use this dock instead of the main port in the city. Common folk lined the road, of course, waving scarves and rough leather hats, but they were fewer than would have jammed Merath's streets, overflowing already with folk come to attend the royal wedding. Dorilian's feelings about that union were mixed. The bride's lineage was impeccable, of course; he and Ionais were cousins through Sebbord's mother, reason enough for him to attend. Prince Jonthan, on the other hand...

*His mother is a Halasseon,* Dorilian reminded himself. An outstanding family, second among the Malyrdeons only to that of Stauberg itself. At least three Wall Lords had come from that line before it had failed. He experienced a flush of regret at what had happened with Austell. No Wall Lord sat at Stauberg now.

And no Rill Lord in Sordan. Expectations settled upon him like a cloak, dulling his pleasure in the sunny day.

"Cheer up, lad." Sebbord's voice carried above the clacking of harness and hoofs. Dorilian edged his mount closer. Ahead, the color guard's ranks narrowed to ride two abreast through the city's gold-horned north gate. Guards wearing Merrydni blue and purple stood to hold back the crowd. "Sordan's grievances today are few. The Merrydeons are my close kin, and we are very welcome here."

"Regelon could have been a better friend to you. Your mothers were sisters. Yet when the barbarian's men seized you at Permephedon, he stood by."

"As did all that kindred. I learned long ago never to second-guess a Malyrdeon. Regelon pled my case that day, and I was set free, though there was little freedom in it." With a sigh, Sebbord lifted his head and looked toward the city before them, with its shaded, moss-velvet walls and sunlit blue towers. "There is still much work to do to restore what we lost."

"What they stole, you mean."

Sebbord cocked a smile. "An act Labran made possible because he forgot the lesson Marc Frederick remembered: that men follow the path of greatest reward. Remember the lesson of Hestya. What Essera looted has ensnared them, more than ever, and provides our greatest advantage."

Yes, that lesson stood clearly above the rest. The aftermath of

Hestya's awakening had shown how many Esseran fortunes were tied to the Rill. It had demonstrated, too, how quickly the King's forces moved to use its speed and capacity. Marc Frederick had deployed six thousand troops around Hestya within a day. An exercise, Dorilian recognized, in more than Rill operations. He returned his grandfather's smile.

Morning sunlight glinted off the curved horns at the corners of the city gate and crowned the central coat of arms, a golden bear on a black shield bordered by gilded lilies. When Sebbord and Dorilian drew near, white rose petals drifted down like snow, flung by girls holding baskets. Boys shook wands topped by silver platens, creating a constant, merry noise. A wave of rich emotions—hope and joy, seasoned by traces of wonder and awe—looped over Dorilian like dancers' rings at Sordan's summer festivals, bright and beckoning. The smiling faces surprised him, as did the cheers. He had not known such at Stauberg or in Dazunor-Rannuli. Despite himself, he smiled back. He relaxed, letting the crowd's emotion flow over him, brushing his nerves the way a breeze might, warm and intoxicating. A royal wedding might not, after all, be so bad. People would be happy. To his right, Sebbord lifted a hand to wave. The grandeur of that gesture, the way it included those watching, acknowledging their welcome, encouraged Dorilian to follow suit.

They'd arrived at a place where a large building intruded on the road so that the procession had to turn to the left, into a paved triangle surrounded by shops, the outlet from which was yet another banner-hung stone gate. The Old City, Dorilian guessed, recalling the map he had studied before arriving and on which he had traced their route.

The procession slowed to funnel through the gate, Merrydni soldiers lining the way against incursions from the crowd. Dorilian glimpsed Legon among them and had no doubt that his friend had herded the merchant princes through the portal just in time to miss them.

The shadow surprised him. It fell. Movement followed, then screams. Something landed beside him, on Sebbord—landed hard. Sebbord fell back. The big ivory horse stumbled sideways, slamming Dorilian's in the withers.

Startled, his horse tried to bolt, but Dorilian pulled hard to turn the beast, ducking as Sebbord's mount reared, then staggered. He looked toward his grandfather.

A man had landed behind Sebbord and now grappled with him, legs around his torso and one hand tangling in his hair. Green flashed in an upraised hand.

"For Gignastha!" The words, harsh and guttural, slashed the air. Sebbord bellowed before the hand plunged down, slicing hard and cutting off the sound. Sebbord's head tilted unnaturally.

A gout of crimson sprayed outward, hitting Dorilian full in the face. Red splattered his vision as Sebbord's head toppled, and Dorilian looked straight into the crazed blue eyes of the man straddling the headless body, covered by blood that still pumped in fountains. Holding high a blade of polished green, the man hesitated. Hate emanated from him. Dorilian felt it, breathed it, cold as the underworld. His hand found the hilt of his weapon and closed over it. Then his horse reared again as another horse charged between his and Sebbord's. Tiflan. As both horses staggered, his giant cousin grabbed his horse by the bridle and spurred forward. Alarmed shouts split the crowd surrounding them.

Not now. Dorilian had a murder to avenge… a man to kill…

"No!" he cried. "Stop!"

Tiflan didn't. He ripped the reins from Dorilian's hand.

Because being unhorsed would be the greater peril, Dorilian grabbed his mount's ribboned mane and clung to the beast. Robbed of other action, Dorilian plunged into the Mind, the collective consciousness of his kind, and sought Sebbord's presence the way he did Lev's or his father's. Always he had felt his grandfather's presence as solid and steady; now he found only agony and the terrible, thrashing anguish of a dying thing. It was untouchable, the pain inescapable. Gasping, he sagged forward and saw his hand covered in blood, the same blood now sticky and warm on his cheeks, lips, and eyes. The skin of his left arm burned as though licked by flame.

The crowd ahead of them screamed. Legon and a blur of soldiers, some Sordaneon, some Merrydni, cleared a path to the gate and through it. Dozens of mounted soldiers surged, swords bared, into the crowded streets beyond, forcing their way through celebrating throngs and the entourages of Denizens.

Only a *tullun* blade could have done it—could have plunged into a man's flesh so easily that it cleanly separated the spine in one neat movement. Sebbord's face still looked surprised when Marc Frederick saw the severed head, placed respectfully in its proper position atop the rest of the Highborn Prince's blood-soaked body. Someone had closed the eyes. Marc Frederick hoped Sebbord had been rendered unconscious, that he had not fully realized what had been done to him, but he doubted it. Highborn bodies died hard, and the severed head had certainly survived long enough to suffer.

*An atrocity*, he pronounced the deed, and an atrocity it was, aimed at destroying a legacy, a bloodline, and a future. He knew at once who was responsible, though accounts quickly laid the blame elsewhere. A Kheldman, witnesses were certain, pointing to the dark-bearded, blue-eyed killer and reporting the words the man had said. *For Gignastha!* he had cried. They differed on who had taken the assassin's life. The Sordaneon guards, some claimed, while others said the man had taken the blade to himself. There would be more knowing later. The blade had been recovered.

Dorilian had witnessed it all. He had been riding at Sebbord's side through the city. The assassin had known which Sordaneon he wanted: he had targeted the old man instead of the youth. Tiflan had spurred his horse between Sebbord and the Heir, perhaps sparing Dorilian from the next blow, and had taken a deep wound in the upper arm.

Merath reeled, its merriment silenced. The stunned populace could not believe that a Highborn prince had been murdered in their midst. Or that the murder had occurred on the eve of another Highborn wedding. All knew Sebbord was blood kin to the Merrydeons, son of a Merrydeon princess, and had come at the personal invitation of their Prince, his cousin. The city's anguish was heartfelt and enormous. Though Sebbord had not been loved, his person had been revered. *Rill Lord*, some called him, though he had refused that title. He had testified before the Archhalia that he possessed only an Epopte's ability to organize existing Rill functions—to order a machine, not bespeak a god. The full tale of how the Rill had awakened to Hestya might now never be learned.

Regelon had not been seen for hours as he attended to consoling his devastated daughter and guests. The surviving Sordaneon was now sequestered in a wing of the Crescent Palace, though neither quietly nor comfortably.

"How is he?" Marc Frederick asked dully, not referring to the corpse in front of him. *My old friend. What have they done?*

"Enraged. A wall of emotions. He wants to leave." Enreddon had left Elhanan with Dorilian but expressed little hope of controlling the damage.

"Let me talk to him."

"You can't handle this." Enreddon's voice was weary.

"I can handle him."

"He's a projective empath. A powerful one. They... it's too brutal. Dorilian hates us all at the moment. I fear even letting him go back to Sordan. He'll be like a cancer."

"I'm not going to imprison him... even if it does lead to that."

"He thinks Khelds did it. Why wouldn't he? He saw the murder with his own eyes, heard with his own ears. His reality is fixed."

"He's smarter than that. When his emotions settle—"

"Which they have not yet. Marc, he is not listening."

"Have you considered that I might be better at this than you would be? Than any of you?" Marc Frederick had lived among the Highborn for decades and knew what he was asking. "I'm not an empath at all. He won't get through to me nearly as much, and I know how to contain it if he does. Don't you think I learned a thing or two from Labran in all those years? Believe me when I say I can handle him."

"No one can handle him. But you're welcome to try," Enreddon said. Someone had found a Teremari flag among the Crescent Palace's collection and brought it to the room. Gently he pulled the banner across the body, concealing the horror.

Elhanan looked surprised when he saw Marc Frederick come into the room. He had obviously expected one of his kindred to relieve him, not the King. Among other things, as Enreddon had aptly warned, Marc Frederick's looks were sure to be a provocation to Dorilian, who had seen so clearly the Kheld man who had attacked his grandfather. But Marc Frederick looked determined, and Dorilian said nothing, so Elhanan merely bowed and left the room.

Regelon had seen to his guest's comfort as well as his security. The suite of rooms was splendid, one of the palace's best. Food graced the long table alongside ewers of water and wine, none of which appeared to have been touched. Servants waited in the service hall should their attentions be wanted. Dorilian had been given every freedom but that of leaving. The young Sordaneon Heir had bathed and changed, and he no longer wore the blood-soaked clothing in which he had arrived. His elegant garments, dark blue over apricot silk, looked too bright for mourning. He had not brought anything more suitable. He stood near windows looking out over the town below, above which festive banners still floated, vivid colors in the afternoon sun.

It had been a year since Marc Frederick had seen him. That year had changed him. Dorilian's body was just entering a period of physical growth, his bones lengthening and his facial features quickly losing their juvenile softness. Grief sat heavily upon him, loss haunting the child still visible within those changes. His eyes, wet with tears or the remains of tears, turned murderously upon Marc Frederick.

"I don't want to talk with you."

That voice was anything but young. It had begun to deepen, and it now slid into Marc Frederick's mind like silk. He accepted the hostility. "It is I who want to talk with *you*."

"Why? So you can explain my grandfather's blood on your hands?"

The hardness of Dorilian's belief in that accusation slammed into the webbing of his nerves so heavily he recoiled. "That's not true," he said, "I would give anything to have him back."

"Even your throne? Even your *life*?"

He nodded. "Yes."

Dorilian turned a feral look on him. "How can you lie like that?"

"Like what?"

"Like *that*! Like you *mean* it." He stepped away as if seeking escape, his body knotted with more feeling than mere words could ever convey. "Gods! If they had not taken my weapons, I would slay you now—"

"Why haven't you? Slain me?" Such a dangerous question, to this man-child, in this circumstance. "You don't need weapons. You have hands. You have more."

The chill of defenses slammed into place. A Malyrdeon would have felt it more acutely, but Marc Frederick felt it well enough. In the presence of someone not of his own kindred, Dorilian had left his base responses unguarded.

"I don't have more." The well-placed parry had cooled Dorilian, if only slightly, and had forced his mind to erect a layer of discipline. No pupil of Sebbord's would have been without at least that.

Having accomplished his goal, Marc Frederick abandoned that direction. If he succeeded now, there would be other times. "I'm going to find out who killed him."

"A Kheld killed him! A filthy, bearded animal!"

"We have the assassin's body. We'll find out who he is and who ordered the deed." Marc Frederick was finding it difficult to keep his body's basal responses under control. He harbored no special immunity to Dorilian's hatred and rage. Projective empathy struck deep. His body wanted to answer the Highborn assault upon his emotions and pumped adrenaline into his bloodstream, causing his heart to pound and his breathing to quicken, heightening his own impulse to aggression. The very thing his body wanted to do most—to fight this young attacker, to defend himself whether with weapons or words—was what he must *not* do. He must not play into his opponent's emotion. "I'll find out who really killed him."

"It doesn't matter!" Dorilian's tear-filled eyes glowered darkly silver across the several feet still between. "The deed is done! It doesn't matter who did it. Only the consequences matter."

"That is why I need the truth."

"Truth? *He* gave you truth. He showed you the face of something great! And do you know what killed him? Truth and trust. All the hate in the world could not have destroyed him as surely as his trust in *you*!"

The words sliced deep. Deep as bedrock. Marc Frederick let that anger-tempered steel sink to the heart, Dorilian lodging the truth right where it would hurt the most. "In me?"

"We were told the city would be safe!"

*Safe.* That word, too, echoed through corridors of betrayal and pain. Sebbord had died because he had believed Marc Frederick's promises that Merath would be secure and its guests protected. All of his promises to Sebbord lay broken. All of them. *No harm will come to you. No harm to you or your family.* Could he ever speak those words again—any words, to anyone—and hope to be believed? He bowed his head, trying to think of what he could reasonably say.

"You are worse than the murdering Khelds." Having been pushed to speak, Dorilian did so with a vengeance. "All of you! He died because he stood up to you. Because he was strong. He died because he dared to show you that Sordan can fight back!"

"You're right," Marc Frederick said.

"If you think you have destroyed us, think again."

Others might have done better to hear those words. Through his own deep sorrow, Marc Frederick felt a flicker of hope. He tried to penetrate those layers of grief and rage to the foundations of that speech. *Think again.* Was there continuance here? Dorilian was a fighter, that was certain. Intelligent and proud, willful by nature. But was this mere fight, or was there substance behind it? Marc Frederick dared to hope not only that the Sordaneons would survive this mortal hurt, but that Sebbord's legacy continued.

"I will do that," he promised. He saw that Dorilian's anger was not defused. Only time, he decided, could do that. But he had succeeded in planting the seeds of confusion. He sensed that his restraint had set the boy aback. It was the best he could hope for.

"I just wanted to extend my personal condolences. And to ask what I can do... to help you."

"Help me?"

"If there is anything you need—"

"I need to leave."

Dorilian had made the one request he could not honor. "There are arrangements to be made. For Sebbord's body. For your safety." He did not blame the young man for turning away in pure contempt at that. "There is no array here at Merath by which to send messages to Sordan directly, but I have sent messages ahead in confidence to Dazunor-Rannuli, to be conveyed to your father. Enreddon told me you refused to send anything."

"Do you think I am an idiot? Just leave me."

It was what he truly wanted. Marc Frederick nodded. He would be leaving but not just yet. "My son is getting married in the morning. We've canceled the public celebration, of course, but there will be a private ceremony. Afterward, you and I will talk again."

It was Dorilian's turn to look surprised. "I am not attending your ceremony!"

"Of course not. No one expects you to. Attend your grief and your people." He wished he could say more, but saying less favored his situation. "I understand that Lord Morevyen took a wound?" he asked, not releasing those rage-filled eyes. Labran's eyes. He wondered what his great-grandfather would have thought of them, if Endurin would recognize in them his own hidden designs.

"The Kheld was going for me next," Dorilian said. "Tiflan got in the way."

"So I heard. But he is mending?"

"As well as common flesh can."

Marc Frederick was glad to hear it. He far preferred having Tiflan Morevyen as Teremar's next Bas to the battles that would erupt were there need to seek another heir. Reluctant to leave just yet, he glanced at the table with its platters of food and vessels of drink.

"Don't invite me to share food or drink with you," Dorilian warned. "I won't. Not ever again."

Marc Frederick shot him a glance. "Don't be so sure of that."

To his surprise, Dorilian abruptly averted his gaze. He stalked away from the windows and the sun. Marc Frederick marked his movements, the youthful energy. He could see signs of the youth's reported prowess as a swordsman in the way he walked, the smooth coordination of foot and hand. Dorilian was a more physical being than Sebbord had been even in youth: a rider, swimmer, and good with blades. A fearless inhabitant of his own body. He wondered if that, too, had been of Sebbord's design.

Having gained the upper hand, he walked to the door and rapped softly upon it. "Tomorrow," he said.

The door had not even closed before he heard something shatter against it.

# 20

The sun had passed noon when Dorilian agreed to be escorted to Marc Frederick's suite within the Crescent Palace. He recognized at once how the power in their positions had shifted. Yesterday, the upper hand had been his because the King had come to him; today, the advantage belonged to Marc Frederick. He wondered what it would take to get it back, or if he even could. The situation had undergone subtle changes. At least the clothes he wore now conveyed a proper state of mourning. The Merrydeons had provided a black tunic and breeches with deep purple hemming and gusseted armbands indicating kinship, and they had found black footwear to fit him as well. The black velvet mourning cap crowning his hair was rich enough, embroidered with beads of jet coral. The clothing oppressed him, further darkening his already turbulent emotions.

Though he had slept little, an entire day had passed and had worked to separate the tangled emotions of his loss. Alongside his personal pain and the horror of what he had experienced, he recognized that this event, like all events, must go forward. His grief remained unabated, as did his hatred for his grandfather's killers, but his desire for vengeance had hardened into something distinct. He could afford to be patient. His survival—and his freedom—mattered more. Gareth, the King's steward, led him through a royal apartment mercifully free of other members of that hated family. Dorilian tried to convince himself that the Stauberg-Randolphs could not afford the scandal of *two* Highborn deaths.

Marc Frederick stood beside a desk. He still wore ceremonial leathers and silks, including his crown, and was just removing his state sword when they entered. He made a point of taking a few moments to hang the weapon out of reach. Dorilian had to admit the gesture was nicely staged.

"Thank you, Gareth. As we discussed."

"Yes, Sire." The steward bowed his head and left at once.

Dorilian stood quietly but observed every detail of the room and of the man. Marc Frederick appeared at once grave and determined, showing little of the weariness the last day should have placed upon him. He possessed remarkable stamina for a man of his years. Sorrow and care lined his face, and there was something angry about him, too. But he never failed at being civil.

"You look better." He fixed Dorilian with those dark blue eyes. "Did you eat?"

"Nothing."

"That's not good. Young men should eat. So should old ones." He tapped his fingers on the wooden surface of the desk. The Leur's Ring upon his finger blazed with a bright blue shimmer, laced with oranges and golds. When Dorilian said nothing in answer, he pointed at a chair. "Sit down."

Dorilian refused. "When do I get to leave here?"

"After you sit down."

He thought about not obeying, then decided it wasn't worth it. He did, however, choose a different chair. He was not surprised when Marc Frederick did not sit.

"You deserve to know what I have learned about your grandfather's assassination. The man who killed him was indeed a Kheld."

"Everyone knows that." Dorilian would never forget that hideous, bearded face or the way the man had jumped on Sebbord's back and pulled a blade across the old man's helpless throat. "I also know it was a *tullun* blade."

"And that doesn't raise questions in your mind?"

"A few."

Marc Frederick went to a drawer and removed a long and slim box from it. Even before the metal box was opened, Dorilian knew what was within. He watched as the King lifted the object and laid the thing upon the desk, where the blade's flawless surface glowed like water. "This is the weapon. Have you ever seen it before yesterday?"

"No." He added, more pointedly, "Have you?"

"No." Marc Frederick continued to study the thing. "The only one I own, personally, is the one you gave me. They are very rare. So rare and so valuable, no one ever uses them."

"Well, a Kheld wouldn't know that, would he?"

"Some would. But you're quite right that most would not. I don't think this one did. But you might ask yourself how he got his hands on it." Again, those blue eyes considered his and would not let him look away. "No Kheld, not even the wealthiest of them, not even the cleverest, is in a position to get his hands on a blade like this."

"I don't need to sit here to listen to you defend your fur-faced kin—"

"You're too intelligent not to see that the pieces don't fit. What reason would a Kheld have to seek out Sebbord for the sole purpose of killing him? Sebbord was not involved at all in the Gignastha overthrow. He stayed well clear of any politics north of the Telarkans for over thirty-five years. Khelds barely knew his name until recently, but even that would hardly explain it. The Khelds don't have the Rill. They didn't take part in the plundering of Sordan. They lost *nothing* by the opening of Hestya. But other people did."

Dorilian looked away, the barrage of points hitting too accurately for comfort. He did not want to believe what he was hearing, even if he knew all of it to be true. A Kheld had killed his grandfather, and that fact could not be explained away. *Just like at Gignastha, all over again. They think nothing of killing us.*

"You can be manipulated by the face of this murder if that is what you want." Marc Frederick placed the blade back into the box. He walked the box back to the drawer and tucked it inside before closing it firmly. Dorilian heard the click of a lock being set. "I cannot dictate what you believe, only what I believe. And I do not believe that Khelds are behind Sebbord's death."

The man's sincerity was as powerful as any Dorilian had ever felt, as powerful as Sebbord's had been. What this man felt, he felt to the soul. "You really believe that," he wondered, the same way he wondered at savage men who believed the sun died every night and was born again each morning.

Marc Frederick sighed, then nodded. He leaned against the desk, resting one thigh upon the polished wood. He moved like a warrior. Dorilian recalled that Sebbord had described him as having been one. "I do. Many might feel their grievances great enough to justify removing the cause of their pain. Hestya ruined men. Powerful men. Entire families, even."

"You mean the Seven Houses."

Marc Frederick's gaze sharpened upon him. "What do you know of that?"

The question could be answered a thousand ways. Dorilian chose the least revealing. "Two Houses were ruined at Bartulu." He did not say that those Houses had been implicated somehow in his mother's death and Levyathan's premature birth, or that Sebbord had taken great pleasure in targeting cartel holdings specifically. That he knew these things did not make rejecting Marc Frederick's arguments any easier. He shored up his anger by remembering that those who had ordered his mother's poisoning had never been identified or punished.

"At the end of your grandfather's life, he didn't care about making more enemies." Marc Frederick rose and went to a table near the room's massive hearth. Picking up an ornate vessel, he filled a waiting glass with golden fluid. Glancing over, he pointed to a second glass. Dorilian shook his head. He would keep his vow about not eating or drinking with this man so long as he suspected his hand in Sebbord's death. "You think I ordered it," Marc Frederick said, responding to the rebuff. "You could not be more wrong. Sebbord and I were friends. Not close, but we shared visions such as men seldom do. We lived in times such as few men ever live in. He wanted stability, and I wanted change. But in the end, look what happened: he brought more changes in a fortnight than I ever could, and I am striving for stability." He took a sip from his glass. "I will learn who killed him."

Dorilian watched him, studying a man he sensed he had only begun to see. Sebbord had never said enough. *Do not mistake him*, his grandfather had said. *His gifts are not as yours and mine, but they are no less powerful.* Whatever those gifts were, they were also quite invisible. What about this man had seduced the Malyrdeons into giving over their throne? An entire nation had followed him rather than accept Labran as their King.

"You're not talking," Marc Frederick observed.

"You said you wanted me to listen."

"You are bound and determined to hate me. Well, I deserve that. For a hundred reasons, I deserve it. Your nation. Your family. But not for this." He sighed and settled on the desk again, the glass cradled in his fingers. He gestured across the room to a small table set before the windows. "I valued Sebbord. He was a brilliant man."

Utterly brilliant. We used to play chess." There was no mistaking the wistfulness in the man's voice at the loss of that pastime. "I never beat him. We would stalemate as often as not, or he would beat me. But *I* never beat *him*." He said it as if losing were something he did not often experience. "It hurts, knowing I will not see him again."

The honesty of that sentiment could not be turned into anything but what it was. Unwilling to accept that the Esseran King should have so much feeling for his grandfather, Dorilian sought a distraction. He rose and wandered to the windows where the small table waited. He looked down upon the chessboard and saw that the pieces were in play. Footsteps told him Marc Frederick was near, and he gave the man a look warning him not to come closer. He did not like—had never liked—people to be too near to him. Respecting his wishes, the man crossed to the other side of the table.

"Our last game, begun at Permephedon after Labran's funeral. He told me then that he did not think we would ever finish it. I was more hopeful."

But Dorilian saw far more on the board than an old man's last game with a friend. Sebbord had taught him this game. The configuration of the defense, especially, was notable. "He is gold; you are blue," he judged.

Marc Frederick looked over, curious. "You recognize his strategy?"

"He's defending with your rook." When the King glanced up from studying the board, his expression curious, Dorilian added, "You have to sacrifice it... or it will control your next three moves."

Marc Frederick took a seat and resumed his study of the board. "He's diabolical."

Dorilian noted the present tense. He, too, found it difficult to accept that Sebbord was truly gone. Blinking, he touched one of the pieces, his fingers tracing the carving of it, the elegant inlays of jade and gold. "Whose move is it?"

"His." Marc Frederick sighed and looked out the window. Below, the city of Merath was a sea of gray slate roofs jutting between two wide rivers. A soft knock at the door brought his attention around, and he rose to receive a message.

Dorilian considered several options before taking up Sebbord's Sorcerer and moving it directly in front of Marc Frederick's King. He left it in that place, Sebbord's next move completed. He didn't doubt it was what his grandfather would have done.

"There," he said upon realizing that Marc Frederick had noticed and was watching him intently. He walked across the room, no longer content with games. "I listened. Now I expect to be allowed to leave."

This time Marc Frederick did not contest him. "Of course. We can leave at once. Your barge has joined mine at the Summer Palace, but I have decided you will travel on my flagship with me. I will accompany you as far as Dazunor-Rannuli and see that you and your people are escorted safely to the Rill platform there."

The arrangement, while offensive, was reasonable. Of course, the King would want to see the murdered man's heirs safely out of Essera. Dorilian fished in his mind for a way to refuse without seeming unreasonable himself. His primary worry was that Marc Frederick might yet choose to hold him as a precaution against unrest in Sordan and Teremar.

"Why should we not travel with the Malyrdeons?" His Esseran Highborn kindred were a more suitable escort.

"They, too, mourn—but they will not be leaving Merath until tomorrow. I was sure you would want to leave today."

"I wanted to leave yesterday."

The sooner he put this wretched city behind him, the better. The thought of traveling downriver with Sebbord's body sobered him, however. Bright as the fire for vengeance burned in him, he would not dishonor Sebbord by striking out blindly or ignobly. He was not yet confident of Stauberg-Randolph participation in the deed. He had not forgotten his conversation with Nammuor and did not need Marc Frederick to remind him of the Seven Houses.

He stopped cold as soon as he exited the room to see other people standing, looking very much at home, in the room beyond. Just by the look of them, he knew who they must be. The damn Stauberg-Randolphs. Dorilian glimpsed Stefan staring at him, dark-haired and more Kheld-looking than the King, and his blood immediately began to boil anew. If he moved quickly, he might escape having to talk with any of them. It was all Dorilian could do to not strike out with his fist when Stefan stepped up to him. Only Marc Frederick's presence restrained it.

"I'm sorry about your grandfather." Stefan's voice sounded awkward, strained, and older. It also sounded sincere.

Dorilian paused and acknowledged him, wishing he did not have to. He hated the look on Stefan's face, the stupid blue-eyed pity. He thought he should say something, but there was nothing to say. Someone else mercifully stepped between them—a woman, tall and golden-haired—who began speaking to him. He barely heard any of it. He was too focused on holding back his feelings and wishing they would just leave him alone.

Marc Frederick watched Dorilian very carefully. The young man was a mass of conflict: convinced Khelds had murdered his grandfather and forced to exchange pleasantries with a family openly trying to bring Khelds into more power. For the moment, anyway, Dorilian was at least trying to appear as if he were listening to Apollonia. Marc Frederick could reasonably count on him behaving himself with the Queen, whose Highborn father had prepared her for handling these kinds of situations with delicacy. It was at such times as these that Marc Frederick realized the value of having her for his wife.

When Emyli came over and reached for her father's hand, he took it. He smiled thankfully at Stefan. "I'm glad you said that."

Stefan looked happy with his approval, but Marc Frederick knew that was not why the young man had said what he had. Dorilian's anger and pain clawed into the minds of everyone in the room. All the more noteworthy, then, that Stefan had put aside his old hostility long enough to express sympathy. He was growing up.

Emyli glanced over to where Apollonia was gently conversing. They were waiting only upon the arrival of the guard. "He's so young!"

"Far too young to have to deal with something like this. It's not just the death; it's the aftermath. I don't know yet what he'll do." There were too many possibilities, too many courses of action, to sort out the likely outcomes. Only a Wall Lord could have done so. Nammuor, to be sure, would attempt to seize this opportunity to push Sordan toward an open break with the Triempery.

"Stay a few more days," she suggested. "Perhaps a little more time—"

"No. He needs to get away from here. He needs the Rill and Sordan and things that are real to him. We're not, except as killers." He lifted his head, mercifully hearing the guards. He doubted Dorilian could take much more of Apollonia.

They reached the royal barge without incident and boarded the massive vessel, which set sail immediately. Already aboard were the other members of the Sordaneon party and the somber wooden box containing Sebbord's remains. Dorilian immediately rejoined his countrymen, spurning the King's offer of a stateroom.

In the cold morning hours before dawn, as the barge drew near the sprawling piers and canals of Dazunor-Rannuli, Marc Frederick still had not slept. He kept his own counsel on the upper deck, from which he could look down onto the chairs below where Dorilian huddled in talk with Legon Rebiran and Deleus of Suddekar. Whatever the young people said, none of it reached him. He turned when he heard steps on the stairs leading to his lonely post and was surprised to see the tall, bright-haired figure of Tiflan Morevyen. The big man nodded to him.

"You will be Bas of Teremar now," Marc Frederick said, thinking that was perhaps the reason the man had come. There would be some petitions, undoubtedly, imploring Essera to extend its occupation into that domain. He knew already that he would deny them all.

"Indeed, Majesty, though I would have preferred not to inherit. I go home to tell my people that the man who has ruled them for seven decades is no more." Tiflan leaned upon the rail at his side. He was a massive presence, much like his grandsire. "But you should know if you do not understand already—my first loyalty will always be to *him*." He nodded to where Dorilian held informal court below. "Sordan is a sovereign nation, its god a sovereign god. Sebbord never let go of that, and neither will *he*."

"I pray he never does." The barge rocked when one of the escort ships, moving forward as they neared the bustling Rill port, passed to starboard. "I don't want war."

Tiflan's thoughtful gaze recalled Sebbord's soulful calm. The white bandage on his left arm was the only suggestion of violence. "That will be difficult to avoid now... but not impossible. Do you seek my counsel, Majesty? Appease Deben. If you do not, Nammuor stands at his back, whispering of another course."

Marc Frederick knew the process of appeasing Sordan would be protracted and delicate. Staubaun anger against Khelds living both within and outside of Amallar would now burn hotter than it had in a decade. He cursed the Seven Houses for having embroiled him, again, in their acquisitive plots. He knew what he had to do but not how to do it.

"Give me something, Lord Morevyen." He sighed. "Anything. But do not tell me I can never reach that boy."

The man was silent for a spell of heartbeats before speaking. "The Highborn know only those realities to which they are exposed; all others are like dreams to them, potentials and might-becomes. Look at the world to which he has been exposed. If you wish to change him, you must change that which he knows."

"How?"

Tiflan shook his head. "That, I cannot say. Sebbord used to speak of it. But look at what happened when he tried."

*Rill awakening and death, the forging of new chains.* "Did he tell you how he did it? How he got the Rill to see Hestya?" There was no harm in asking. As studiously as he had kept from broaching that topic with Dorilian, Marc Frederick now feared he might never get another opportunity to ask someone who might have been there.

"What are you asking, Majesty?" The big man's voice blended with the night, privacy wrapped in shadow. "If it can be done again? Even Sebbord did not know if that could be. It was not he who touched the god, nor stood within its eye so that it might see Hestya. Knowing that, you know as much as I." He stood again, his huge right hand rubbing the bandage on his arm, and jutted his chin toward the deck below. "Dorilian will not come to you. And the day he seeks you out will be either the world's death or its salvation."

# 21

"We warned you. You should have heeded our advice when you arrived in Dazunor-Rannuli after the murder." Chyralane Rannuleonis settled with watchful grace into one of the chairs arrayed around a conference table that punctuated the meeting room like a radiant pool. Located in Dazunor-Rannuli's Rill station, two of the room's walls served as windows: one looking out onto the station's busy platforms, the other presenting a vista of the mercantile city, its rooftops dominated by alabaster towers and golden cupolas. The nearby Sordaneon palace called the Rillhome, a fortress of golden stone crowned with silver, dominated the waterways.

"I did not know then that you would attempt to make your deed look like the work of my grandson."

Marc Frederick had chosen the Rill station for this meeting because he no longer welcomed Chyralane at any of his palaces. Nor would he meet with her at any dwelling she controlled.

"Is that what you call it?"

"That is what I call this, yes."

A month had passed since his arrival here with Sebbord's body. Two weeks since Sebbord had been interred in Permephedon with his ancestors. A month of anguish and outcry, of Deben's icy threats and even more disturbing reports from Neuberland, where several Kheldish towns had been put to the sword by local Staubauns bent on vengeance. He could not be sure if the attacks were due to cartel provocation. He was convinced, however, that the Seven Houses had engineered the conflict that had led to them.

Chyralane tapped elegant fingertips on the table's shining surface. "You demanded to be told what we knew. There it is."

He looked at the documents. He had already read them, already knew what they revealed: the assassin, his name, his kin, and a catalog of his recent activities. The man's brothers and son had died at Gignastha, his daughter raped and impregnated. The man had vowed to exact revenge. And a report from witnesses who said the man and four companions had met with Stefan several months ago at an inn in Bellan Toregh.

"Your agents excelled this time," he said. "Did you arrange the meeting, too? Or was it simply fortuitous?"

She shrugged. "Our connections among the region's merchants are extensive. We've known for months about this man's contact with your grandson. The Khelds think Stefan will be important someday, that he will be a new Alm who will lead them to glory and riches."

On the Rill platform outside the window, passengers queued for the journey to points south: Leseos, Randpory, Sordan—and now Hestya. Tens of thousands traveled thus daily, paying the tribute demanded by the Epoptes, who relied on that revenue to support station staff and maintain the port. To judge by their clothing, most of the passengers were prosperous. There was also not a Kheld among them.

"And you want to be sure he never leads them."

A wave of the hand dismissed that statement. "What do we care who leads that rabble? That he put himself in contact with rebels... that caught our attention." Those topaz eyes gloated over what she knew. "If Stefan claims he's had no dealings with the rebels, he lies. He directs sympathizers to them. He directs funds. He told the man who killed Sebbord Teremareon that the Sordaneons still had designs on Neuberland because of their continued interest in Gignastha. He accused them of sorcery. He put himself in this situation. No one will see your hand in it."

"Because my hand was never in it." Only Stefan's hand was there, for all to see should this information become known. Marc Frederick's blood pumped slow and cold. Though Stefan's contact with this man had not been about murdering Sebbord, the association was damning. That plan had come later, a plot hatched within the halls of the Seven Houses. A plan directed not only at removing Sebbord but also at hobbling Marc Frederick's ability to deal with the consequences. "What do you want?"

Chyralane looked pleased as she settled back into her seat. "Nothing onerous. No compromise with Deben. Sordan to remain as a client state, and Teremar added as one. We also want Deben's Heir, Dorilian, brought before the Archhalia for questioning as to any role he might have played in opening Hestya."

"Deben will never allow that."

"Force the issue."

She knew that he could. He had a garrison in Sordan and influential men in position to bring pressure to bear upon the Hierarch—if he wished it. But he had always chosen his battles with Deben carefully, mindful he could push even that man too far. And now, with Nammuor waiting in the wings and Mormantalorus amassing troops along the Suddekar borders...

"No. Not about that. Deben rules a nation of kindling, just awaiting the spark of rebellion. I will not provide that spark by seizing his Heir."

She turned her head away, glaring disgust at the golden gleam of the Rillhome below. "It could have been done so easily two weeks ago! I told you then the wisdom of it. You already had the boy in your hands. You could have insisted on cloistering him for his own protection. Now see your folly? You have made the job more difficult."

"Be reasonable." The woman all but ruled in this city, and she was being petulant. "What can you possibly prove with Deben's Heir? That he has Derlon's gift? What if he does? Is that reason to imprison him?"

"Yes! Because if the Rill *does* see him, he's a catastrophe! Who is to say what he might someday do! You cannot convince me Sebbord was not shaping him toward our ruin. Even you can see that."

"Of course, he was. You ordered his daughter's murder. Maybe I should give to Dorilian the proof I never gave Sebbord."

Chyralane laughed. The Seven Houses had played such games of blackmail for centuries. "You will not do it. You fear that half-grown boy might strike out at us. Perhaps you already know that he would. He is not like the Malyrdeons, is he? No. He's rash, impatient. You know what we could do to him." She tapped the document on the table between them. "All we have to do, if we want him, is give him this."

If the cartel gave over those papers... what would Dorilian do with this compilation of half lies and truths? His grievances against Stefan and the witness of his own eyes would predispose him to believe it. Dorilian's retaliation, if Marc Frederick read the young man correctly, would bring Sordan into open war. And if that happened... Marc Frederick recognized a masterstroke when he saw one.

"You want your hands on him that badly?"

"Any hostilities on his part would give the Archhalia ample reason to secure the peace, even if that means seizing him."

"And for what? To be sure the Rill never deviates from the paralysis you've created? You know the Entity better than any. The corporeal arches at Hestya are ancient. Knowledge of a Rill node there has shadowed Bartulu since its founding. Sebbord opened an already viable station—he created nothing that did not already exist."

Chyralane's body coiled beneath the elegant knotting and brocade of her layered robe. "He caused the Rill to awaken where it previously lay dormant! There are arches at Stauberg, a nearly intact route to which the Rill was never awakened. The Hierarch Tarlon was able but refused to attempt it. Do you know why?" Her eyes glittered with purpose. "Can you imagine the riches, the possibilities, if the Rill would run to Stauberg? Hestya is nothing compared to that! A route directly to the sea! Essera, not just its economy, would change forever. So would Sordan. Immense changes. Such an alteration must be undertaken carefully, every facet negotiated—"

"You're talking about a dream, not a reality."

"A dream well-rooted in what that godling can possibly do someday!"

Pushing away from the table, Marc Frederick stood and paced over to the window. Though there appeared to be no barrier, nothing but air from ceiling to floor, he could not have walked through the substrate that let light in but not out. No one looking at the featureless wall of the station from the platform could see him standing before it, watching them. The Aryati technology mimicked that of the Leur-built Cities, the walls and windows of which were fashioned from magic.

The Seven Houses wanted the Rill to run to Stauberg even less than they wanted it to run to Mormantalorus. If the Rill ran to Stauberg, Dazunor-Rannuli would cease to be Essera's primary port for trade with other lands. Power would flow away from this city, not into it. The cartel would do anything to keep that from happening. They would ruin him, his family... create a war.

Whether or not he allowed this coercion, they were set on this murderous game.

*If I give in to this threat, she will own my family and me. Stefan, most of all. This battle was inevitable.*

"Do it yourselves, if you dare," he said. "See how long you can contain your god. I will not do it again. Not for you." He turned and walked for the door. On the platform, a *charys* shimmered into the proximal run, its shining surface reflecting nothing, not even sky.

"Majesty!" Chyralane demanded, imperious now. "Think again. Think of the consequences—"

"I have." The door opened to reveal his bodyguard standing ready in the corridor. "And I welcome every one of them."

# 22

Stefan paled as he read the message from his grandfather. Rain streamed from the tarp covering the window of this shelter on the edge of the mining colony. The tiny hut itself already felt like a cell.

He had left Merath two days after Marc Frederick, though he had rejoined him at Dazunor-Rannuli. His mother and Hans had continued to Gustan by way of the royal barge. Still, for once, Stefan had felt important, assisting Marc Frederick in meetings with the Amallaran ambassador to the Archhalia and other Kheld leaders in Essera. There had been no time to summon Kheld chieftains from Amallar or Neuberland, and so Stefan had taken part in speaking for the Khelds, in wording official condolences to the Sordaneons along with even more sensitive documents vowing that Amallar neither condoned nor would harbor any person found to have conspired in the Prince of Teremar's murder. The death represented a political disaster for the Khelds. Ever since the siege of Gignastha, the people of Amallar and the Kheld enclaves in Neuberland had struggled against Staubaun perceptions of them as Highborn killers.

Stefan, to be sure, had never wished Sebbord's death. He'd barely considered the man at all except, vaguely, as Dorilian Sordaneon's grandfather. That Dorilian was taking Sebbord's death hard had been clear the moment their eyes met in Merath. The tears, although unspilled, had been real, and Stefan had found himself suddenly inside that grief, seeing it as if it were his own—as if Marc Frederick had died like that, right in front of him. Stefan had been telling the truth when he said he was sorry.

Since then, however, he'd grown angry again. Everywhere he went, Khelds were still being blamed for the murder. The crazy

Sordaneons, who thought Khelds were good only as slaves in their mines or on Randpor's river barges, were again demanding that Neuberland's Khelds be driven off newly settled lands along the Gero River.

And now *this*.

"Damn them!" He kicked at the doorframe. "Of all the damned, blind, stupid—"

"What now?" Cullen had come in with Stefan from the rain, fresh from running a successful first baking of ore from the mine. The distillation unit had been hell to bring to the site. It had taken weeks to float and drag the machine upstream, building dams and locks along the way.

"The man who killed Sebbord Teremareon—we met him! At Bellan Toregh, our first visit here. And again, two months later."

Cullen sank on the nearest cot, his eyebrows lifted in surprise. "*Those* men? The ones we got drunk with? Those Neuberlanders at the inn?"

"We saw them again at Saemoregh. Trahoc Caddenson." Stefan thought he was going to be sick. "The body at Merath was all hacked up when I saw it. I—"

"Stefan, you didn't know. None of us did." Water dripped from Cullen's dark curls as he shook his head in dismay. "I knew he was hot about Gignastha, but I never thought—I mean, it's not our way to kill a man who had nothing to do with it."

"Marc Frederick doesn't think it was his idea. Someone got to him and paid him, even gave him the knife." Stefan continued to hold the letter as he looked out into the muddy rivulets running past the door. His whole life seemed to be dissolving just like the very hills. "He wrote to warn me. There are people—Staubauns— who have witnesses and documents that I met this man."

"How?"

"I don't know. My grandfather won't tell me who because it hasn't happened yet, but he says they're threatening to go with this information to the Sordaneons."

"Aw, hell, Stefan." Cullen went pale. "If that happens, they'll be after you!"

"Dorilian will be after me. Dorilian! That gods-damned crazy Highborn bastard will want my ass! He's already out for blood because I beat him up in school. If someone gives him reason to think I arranged a man to kill his fucking grandfather, do you think for one moment he'll ever listen to reason? I won't even get a chance to defend myself!" Stefan crumpled the letter in his fist, wanting to throw it away. Only knowing he might need it later stopped him.

"Someone set you the hell up for it."

"I know." Stefan's mind raced as to who might have done it. Dorilian himself, for all he knew. But he doubted even Dorilian would stoop so low as to use his grandfather's murder as a pretext to settle that old score. One thing was for certain, though—this letter was days old. Because they had the fucking Rill and he didn't, the Sordaneons might already have this information—and if they did, Dorilian knew where to find him. "Pack your stuff!" Stefan snapped to Cullen. He dove for his saddlebag and began shoving his clothing and personal items into it. "Then get the horses!"

"What—?"

"We're riding for Rhodhur."

"*Rhodhur?*"

"We'll be safer there. We already know someone has been spying on me, right? After that, we'll ride for Gustan."

"You should go to your grandfather, tell him all you know, and find out what's happening." Cullen rolled up his spare shirt and stuffed it into his sack halfheartedly. "He's King. Kings know what to do, and he has armies besides."

"I don't trust the Staubauns not to be watching the roads. Half my father's nobles want me gone anyway—if they can get Dorilian to get rid of me, all the better." He cursed the day he had ever lashed out at his Sordaneon tormentor. Dorilian was rich and mean and had reasons by the bushel to want Stefan out of the way. Marc Frederick had been right about one thing: Stefan could not have chosen a more dangerous enemy if he had tried. He grabbed his shaving kit and shoved that also into the bag.

"Stefan, what about the mine?" Cullen had stopped packing and now leaned against the cot.

Stefan rocked back on his heels. Alongside everything else, he had been thinking of that. "Gruff can manage things." He named the Kheld who oversaw the miners. "And Lohar Neddil runs the distillation unit. No one needs us for that."

"But men are coming up from Leseos to discuss contracts. It isn't enough to get this metal out of the ground, Stefan; we've got to *sell* it."

He'd forgotten about the merchants due to arrive from Leseos.

Not one ore broker in Essera had been interested in the Amallaran mine. No transport, they said. An undependable workforce. Only a third-rate consortium out of Trongor had been willing to come at Stefan's expense to examine the mine's production. Stefan cursed and pushed down on his pack. The flap barely buckled, but it would have to do. He would have someone bring the rest later, if he even bothered. "What do you want me to do, Cullen? Just stay here and hope Dorilian hasn't already sent someone to kill me?"

"Maybe," the other youth argued. "Maybe that's the way it's going to be for you—for all of us—the rest of our lives. But we can't just *dump* the mine. Those men come and find only a few Khelds chopping the basin and a half-breed Staubaun minding a distiller; that won't mean chicken shit. You're the one who knows what's in the ground, who has the royal grandfather. Hey, don't think that doesn't mean something." Cullen rolled his eyes at the look Stefan gave him. "It's the King's gold that will keep this mine running. They need to know you're rock solid behind it, or else it's just another gamble—and I don't think our boys out there can sell it."

He was right. Cullen was always right. Ever since their tenth year, Stefan had known he could rely on Cullen's advice. Not every Kheld had his friend's good common sense, the kind that cut through confusion like a knife to lay open the bones of the matter. If he had listened to Cullen four years ago, he wouldn't be looking death in the eye today. He couldn't abandon his people, not now when they were on the cusp of this thing. The heavy pack landed with a thud at his feet. "We have to arm them, then. All the men. Just in case."

"We can hold our own; you know that."

"Hells, Cullen, this is Lud's own madness." He slumped down onto the cot, resigned. They had to stay if this venture was to have a chance at all.

"I know it is. The whole thing, I mean. You'd never order a man to death. Would you?"

Stefan thought about it. "I don't think so. I mean, I might want to. But if I were to order a death, the man would have to have done something awful, something to deserve it. Rape a person or kill one. Burn a village, at least. Something. Not just because he belongs to the wrong family. Not just because he can order the Rill about and make it do things." He stared bleakly at the raindrops puddling on the crude wooden floor. The next funds he got, he would put a portion toward an actual door and better sleeping quarters, not just for himself but for the whole camp. "My grandfather told me, back a while, that anything to do with the Sordaneons all connected to the Rill. I'll bet this does, too."

"Maybe someone wanted to make sure it didn't go anywhere new."

"Maybe." It made sense, in a Staubaun way. But not a Kheld way. Khelds didn't care where the Rill went or did not go. *Staubauns did this. They killed the Teremar Lord, and they set me up.* Could he trust Dorilian to see through it? Nothing in their history gave him much hope of that.

"Can they do that, the Sordaneons? I mean, they can blast aqueducts, right? We know that. But the Rill—" Since becoming Stefan's companion, Cullen had seen more of the Rill than most Khelds.

Stefan shook his head, plagued by those same images. The Rill... was just too huge, its impact too far-reaching. The idea that the Sordaneons could somehow make the thing change or move was ludicrous—except just enough people believed it for him to wonder.

"Staubauns already know a Kheld delivered the blow. If they think a Kheld ordered it, too—" Even as he spoke the words, he realized he had just counted himself as a Kheld, not as an Esseran prince, not even as Marc Frederick's grandson. The disjunction brought his thoughts to bear on something else. "It's not just me. Whoever is doing this is also using me to get at my grandfather, to cast doubt on him." His fear swelled anew. The real target was the Stauberg-Randolph kingship. "I can't let that happen."

"What can you do?"

"I have influence here. I can help my grandfather find out who got to Trahoc, who was talking to him and seeing him." He had known for some time that the Staubauns had agents among the merchants who did business in Amallar. It was to his advantage, and that of the Khelds as well, to ferret out those agents.

It might also be the only way to save his life.

# 23

"You wish to marry?"

Dorilian smiled at Noemi's broad Estol face. He had been taller than his brother's governess for several months, and he liked that. He also liked that she had become pretty in the last few years since Levyathan had been at school at Permephedon. The young woman now wore her dark hair loose, more like a girl, not the aspiring matron she had been during the early years in Askorras. Her warm nut-brown eyes sparkled. Her gown clung softly to curves she had always had, but which he now appreciated anew. An Esseran Staubaun, he knew, would have called her garish, but he appreciated her warm voice and the bright colors she wore. She'd come from Permephedon to see him.

"I was going to ask the Hierarch's blessing." She looked upon him with a smile. "I should, given Lord Deben is Lev's father and his proper guardian, but I also know who makes the decisions about who takes care of him."

The smile dropped off his face. Levyathan did not cope well with changes. And he would never find anyone who loved Lev the way Noemi did. "He needs you."

"And who's to say I don't need him?" Noemi's hands reached for his, and he allowed her to take them. She was one of the very few people whose touch he did not find unpleasant. "Why, young Lord, I would do anything for him, and that's the god's truth! I don't mean I want to *leave* him. I just want to marry. I can still run his household and have a husband, now can't I?"

"I suppose." He decided to address the other potential complication. "Who is the man?"

"Heran Albos." Just saying the name brought the smile back to her face and that marvelous glow to her eyes. "He's a man in your service. Wonderful handsome, and with a quick tongue besides. We've been seeing each other since you were but a bad-tempered lad. He was your groom then. When you left Askorras to assume your rank, the old Lord released him so he could serve under your House Warden."

"I know Heran," Dorilian said, though that was stretching it somewhat. He knew *of* the man. Heran administered non-household attendants and functions—gardeners, woodworkers, pipe smiths, and masons—at Dorilian's estate of Rhondda. That the estate operated smoothly testified to the man's ability, as did Noemi's apparent happiness. It struck him that she was only nine years older than he. It had seemed so much greater a difference when he was seven.

"Please, young Lord," she said, noting his hesitation. "Heran would ask you himself, he was all ready to do it, but I wanted to ask first."

"By all means, wed." He had no firm objection so long as Levyathan's needs were met. He would promote Heran to his Sordan household and issue a Rill pass that would enable the couple to be together as conveniently as if they lived in opposite ends of the Serat. "No reason I should be the only one."

Noemi laid her hand on his arm. "They were wrong, forcing you to it. Royal or not royal, I told the old Lord, turning up the heat but burns the bread. A woman should choose her own man, and she'll choose one that's willing. It's better that way."

*I wouldn't know.* Nonetheless, Dorilian smiled at her attempt to counsel him. More true warmth was cast his way by earthy Noemi than he ever found in the gazes or smiles of other women he met. None of them ever seemed quite real. Not like Noemi, who really looked at him and saw him, whom he had subjected to tantrums and who had fought back, and who understood why he had done it. "Be happy," he said, feeling that was appropriate.

But when she left, and the door closed behind her, he felt vaguely dissatisfied.

"Your royal father wishes to speak with you." He looked up. Daimonaeris stood in the antechamber, obviously having waited for Noemi to depart. "You were with your nurse, so I waited."

Dorilian wished he could sew her mouth shut and send her back to her brother. "Noemi was never *my* nurse. She nursed Levyathan."

"Look how the color rises in your cheeks. One would think you were actually interested in women."

"No, Daimonaeris, I am *not* interested in *you*." It was truth and easy to say. Easy, even though she stood before him wearing a garment so simply perfect that it outlined her figure, flaunting her divine proportions. Easy, even though her skin was as fair and smooth as that of a goddess, her eyes wide and lovely, and her mouth full and smiling. The smile vanished as he walked up to her, the mockery in her gaze changing to alarm as she backed into the table behind her.

"What's this? You don't wish your husband to touch you?"

"No! If you do, my brother—"

"Nammuor? Last I heard, he is in Mormantalorus, but then he does spend a lot of time in Sordan of late. Is that to be with you? Or to be sure of my father?" He closed his hand about her wrist.

"Unhand me, or you will regret it."

"I was told to spend more time being a husband to you. Lucky for you, I don't often do as I am told." He released her arm.

Slipping around the table, she made certain she was out of reach before she spoke again. "I will tell your royal father you will be along whenever you *do* decide to do as you're told."

He watched her go and resolved to take his time.

It wasn't as if Deben could do anything to him. Dorilian's support among Sordan's noble class was high—and his popularity with the Hierarchate's citizens had never been higher. People on the street, manning the docks and barges, gathering about tables in taverns or cloistered back gardens, saw no accident in that Dorilian had achieved his adulthood in the same span in which Labran had died and the Rill now ran to Teremar. He, not Deben, embodied the hope that the Sordaneons would regain their old power—would raise up Derlon's Sword and break Essera's hated hold on their land. He had even vowed to do so, often within earshot of those very men. If Essera heard of it, he did not care. He cared less than ever now that Sebbord had been murdered. At least one of Nammuor's warnings struck him as truth: his enemies would try to rule him as they had his father, through intimidation and fear.

Deben was not alone when Dorilian arrived. Several men sat with him in the sparely furnished throne room. Daimonaeris was also there, perched tensely on a gilded chair. Dorilian took note of the company: Mezentius, his great-grandfather, seated as always near Deben's right hand; the Triemperal administrator, Sinon Kouranos, rising respectfully at his approach; Iachon of the Sordan Halia, also rising; and Jonthan Stauberg-Randolph, an important surprise. He must have come straight off his nuptial month. Elhanan Dannutheon was with him, his blue garments hemmed with funereal black. Tiflan was there, too, looking thoughtful and wary, wearing mourning black and purple. All watched Dorilian with an intensity portending bad news.

"What?" he demanded when no one spoke.

Deben merely frowned. Dorilian couldn't tell if he was angry or simply muzzled. It fell to another man to step forward. The Triemperal administrator bore two heavy envelopes in his hands.

"Two reports, Thrice Royal, on your grandsire the Prince of Teremar's death in Merath five weeks past. Lord Morevyen, as the other blood kin present, has said he yields to you as to the veracities of conclusions reached." Sinon extended both documents, which Dorilian took.

"Veracities?"

"The reports... differ."

Now thoroughly annoyed, Dorilian turned to the Stauberg-Randolph prince. "You couldn't even *agree*?"

Jonthan held his gaze, but Dorilian could tell it was difficult for him. The prince's expression told him the answer would be unsatisfactory. "Those who ordered Sebbord's death made that impossible," Jonthan said. "The first report was given to Sordan's ambassador just hours ago. When we learned the contents, my father immediately sent the second report."

A report important enough to command Marc Frederick's Heir as a messenger and demand the presence of Esseran representatives. Dorilian looked to his father. "Have you read these?"

"His Majesty," Deben snapped, "specifically requested that you should also read them." His gaze upon Jonthan bore only rage and disgust.

Dorilian piled one report atop the other and walked toward the throne. He wanted the symbolism of standing beside Sordan's Eagle as he read.

It only made sense to read the one report before the other. The Esseran King had gone to some trouble, apparently, to respond to whatever the first document said. After only a few paragraphs, he realized that what he held was more than just a damning document: it was a provocation, a rationale, an excuse. A weapon, even. *Stefan.* Something about the document's insinuations rose like an acid aftertaste in his throat, but the bitter facts went down easily. As easily as water. Stefan and the Khelds, men the young Stauberg-Randolph prince had met, twice visited... mining and arms. He had known about the mining and also about Neuberland and rebels and Kheld interest in colonizing parts of Gignastha.

As his rage mounted, other instincts warned him to be careful. He was in a city closely held by a tentative Hierarch and Marc Frederick's soldiers, in a room wherein Triemperal lackeys stood ready to carry out whatever order their King or Archhalia had placed upon them.

Knowing they expected a reaction to the damning news, he gave it to them. He lifted his gaze from the paper, bypassing Tiflan's look of warning to meet instead the equally silent, heartfelt desperation of Jonthan Stauberg-Randolph.

"We all know assassins, don't we?" he said.

The surprised men clearly expected him to say more, but he sank onto the step of the dais upon which the throne was raised. Sitting there, he leafed through the document a second time, this time imprinting the details into his memory, from which he would exhume them later. He made them wait, all of them, while he opened the second envelope and read those contents as deliberately, as thoroughly, as he had read the other.

*...reason to believe the facts but must condemn the conclusion as a construction and a lie... consider the source... the Seven Houses, fearing loss of Rill dominance... have already secretly proposed amending the Hestya articles... ultimate goal of testing the Sordaneon heirs for giftedness... an artful blackmail aimed at concealing their own designs...*

The King indicated to Deben that he was willing to meet, to talk. He wanted a chance to plead his case that Stefan was also a victim. Of course, he would say so. One had only to look deeper into the lie to see Marc Frederick himself. The Stauberg-Randolphs had not taken the Esseran throne without blood on their hands. That the cartel sought to damage Marc Frederick, Dorilian did not doubt. But neither had they concocted evidence where none existed. Stefan had met with Sebbord's killer not once but twice more; had passed gold to the man and his associates; Stefan also had gone secretly into Neuberland. And the Khelds... were a canker, had always been and always would be a boil inflamed to spew poison at every touch. Naturally, Marc Frederick wanted to talk. The same way the Stauberg-Randolphs always talked—after the deed was done.

Why then did these papers sting him so? Because he had believed Marc Frederick that day in Merath, when he had declared Sebbord his friend?

Dorilian looked up from the pages. "Are you saying you know *who* killed my grandfather—but that the killer was a puppet and there is disagreement about who ordered the deed?"

"That is true, Thrice Royal." Jonthan appropriately accorded Dorilian the higher status.

Dorilian folded the documents again and thrust them back into their respective envelopes before rising. The less he said, the less they would know about his conclusions. He walked to Sinon Kouranos, who had remained standing all the while, and handed the documents over.

"Then we know nothing more than before. A Kheldman's name... a handful of syllables pointing to his situation among other animals just like him. I expected answers."

The Triemperal administrator appeared taken aback. He had been prepared for some other response. So too, apparently, had others in the room, including Daimonaeris, who sat up straighter in her chair and shot a wide look toward Deben and Mezentius. Jonthan Stauberg-Randolph, for his part, looked unconvinced. Only Tiflan found reason for comfort, his great body subtly relaxing as he realized Dorilian was not going to do anything rash.

"We assure you," Jonthan pressed home the point he'd been sent to make, "the King assures you and all Prince Sebbord's kin, as well as his Hierarch, that our inquiry is not finished. We are intent on pursuing the hand behind this deed."

Dorilian didn't see how they would get anywhere. Essera was helpless within its own coils. It could and would do nothing, and so too, for now, he would mirror that stance. He was especially aware of how closely Elhanan watched his reactions. Dorilian was thankful for Sebbord's lessons in creating psychic structures to contain his emotions. He was a projective empath—but he could, if he worked at it, project a blank. Only raw grief had prevented him from doing it at Merath.

"I have nothing to say. Do what you must."

"Grandson," white-haired Mezentius began, "Prince Sebbord—"

Dorilian lifted a hand. "—is dead. Still dead." Without saying another word, he left the room.

Marc Frederick tapped the chessboard as he listened to his son's account of the meeting with Deben and Dorilian. Deben had reacted as expected, impotent in his certain rage that Essera's rulers had once again attacked his domain and alliances. But Dorilian...

Jonthan paced from door to window then back again, speaking his thoughts aloud, trying to force sense from the confrontation. "He was too compliant," he said for the eighth time that afternoon. "Dorilian is not a compliant person. He doesn't accept platitudes and poor resolutions. I barely know him, and I know that."

The board's pale blue and green marble tiles cooled Marc Frederick's fingertips as he traced patterns upon them. All three accounts he had heard of the meeting—Jonthan's, Elhanan's, and that of Sinon Kouranos—disturbed him.

"He said nothing else?"

"Just what I told you."

He sighed and closed his eyes, knowing that Dorilian had not believed him. Perhaps did not believe any of them. But he would believe the facts, and the facts laid a terrible trap. He damned the Seven Houses and their reckless disregard for their own god.

"I'm going to lose him. After all this time, my hard work, and that of men already dead." Not only Sebbord, but his great-grand-father Endurin as well, whose prescience had set the recent course of the World in motion.

"Maybe not," Jonthan said. "Dorilian's terribly smart. And I don't use either word lightly. He may blame Stefan, but he won't do anything stupid. He never has."

"No. But he takes chances. It's a quality that sets him apart from his father—from most of the Highborn, really—but we don't yet know where it might lead."

Marc Frederick picked up a chess piece, his King. It and its counterpart were the two largest pieces on the board, impressive effigies of rulers so secure in their roles that they stood with but scepters and orbs in their hands. In this case, the miniature orbs glowed with inner white fire, true to the sorcerous *orbi* Highborn princes created in their cupped hands. He could himself do so, courtesy of the ring he wore and Endurin Malyrdeon's blood in the finger it encircled. Distractedly, he put the King down and picked up the Sorcerer attacking it. The pieces were still set as they had been in Merath. He found it interesting that Dorilian had chosen to attack rather than proceed with Sebbord's strategy of defense. What to do about it was quite the question. If he removed his opponent's Sorcerer, he gained a key piece, perhaps a pivotal piece— but he would sacrifice his Rill and open his Wall to attack. If he chose to escape, he could last far longer but would have little chance of penetrating his opponent's screening emplacements.

"Look at this." He complained to Jonthan about his situation. "The boy is at least as clever as his grandfather."

"Deben doesn't know his own son." Jonthan ceased pacing and joined him at the chess table, taking the opposite chair. "I don't think the Hierarch even sees him most of the time. He's too busy plotting inconsequential personal victories over your administrators."

"I've always been glad for Deben. He allows me to concentrate on other things." Marc Frederick picked up Dorilian's Sorcerer and put his King in its place. *I have you now.* But he knew he did not.

"So, what will you concentrate on now?"

"Preventing the cartel from spreading more lies. They've discovered the Khelds can be useful. I had hoped Stefan could be established there as a stabilizing influence, a progressive leader for them, but..." He sighed. "If those statements in the cartel's report can be documented—as to what Stefan said to those Neuberlanders—his presence in Amallar only makes matters worse."

"I never thought he would speak so. Not with the Sordaneons under control."

"Something they never really were. The best we could hope for was to keep the peace. That won't happen now. Dorilian is not going to sit quietly on this information. This situation is going to take on dimensions all of us will regret." He moved the piece he had taken to the side of the board, wondering when he would ever get back to it. The next move did not belong to him. "Sebbord, at least, knew how to govern Dorilian and keep him from getting in over his head."

"Is anything truly over his head?"

"Oh yes. Even if he might someday command the extraordinary powers of his ancestors, the Rill is entirely over his head. Yet he may be our last chance with it. But that won't happen if the Seven Houses find a way to seize him... or the Khelds to kill him."

Jonthan looked up in surprise. "The Khelds? I know Dorilian has recently become a topic of conversation among them, but what reason would they have to kill him?"

"Whatever reason he gives them."

# 24

"Their war must come home to them," Dorilian said. "That's the only way to get answers—or justice."

"Wars spill a great deal of blood," Tutto said, "but little justice."

"Then let them see what their war has brought to us."

Dorilian looked toward the mountain passes. Clouds pressed from the north, crowding the peaks and layering stony crags with white. If he waited longer, the passes would fill with snow. He planned to move in the morning, whether Tutto approved of his plan or not.

He had delayed a full month before putting his scheme in motion. A political visit to an aged Sordaneon cousin, the Bas of Tollech, provided his excuse to travel. After a stay of several days, Dorilian had departed from Tollech under cover of darkness, taking with him his bodyguard and Legon. They'd headed for the mountains of Anit-Rebir, where an old friend, Bas Terveryen, had received them with great honor. The old Bas had married three times and sired several sons and as many daughters, all as comely, dark-eyed, and golden-haired as Legon, who was sixth in line for his father's seat. That Legon was settled in Dorilian's service and seldom visited home pleased his father, whose elder five sons constantly plotted against him. Terveryen graciously helped fulfill Dorilian's wish to retreat to a Cibulitan redoubt high in the Damarose Mountains. Legon had, of course, accompanied him, and Tutto had joined them a few days later, after a circuitous ride from Askorras.

Situated on a plateau and poised against snow-capped mountains, the redoubt's stone building presented four gates to the four corners of the World. Like Dorilian before him, Tutto had arrived at the Gate of Rain, where he had been admitted by yellow-robed scholars and taken to pray. Now, hours later, he sat cross-legged upon cold stone, facing Dorilian and Legon on a ledge above a waterfall. Mist drenched their garments.

Three sheathed swords lay like slashes between them.

Tutto looked at peace with having his weapon lying on the ground and not at his hip. "I cannot stop you, my Prince; this I know. All your life, you have not listened to reason, and I am not the man to teach it to you. Follow your godborn heart and I will follow *you*, because that is the way I have chosen. But know this: if you strike at that man, he will strike back. Don't complain to me when he does."

"I know what I'm doing."

"No, you don't."

Dorilian had eaten his fill of warnings. Tiflan had also warned him, even more passionately, before he and Legon had left Sordan. "I must do this. The Esseran bastards do whatever they want—imprison, kill, or rape Sordan's land and people—and they trust we will do nothing. We give them no reason to think otherwise. It's time we do."

"They have reason now, after what your grandsire did at Hestya."

*After what I did. It was not Sebbord.* Dorilian studied the mists rising wraithlike from the gorge. He remembered something Marc Frederick had said. "The Khelds don't care what happened at Hestya. And because of that, they don't see how I use the Rill to punish them."

"Let that be enough."

But it wasn't. It wasn't enough to covertly send contraband to Dazunor-Rannuli, to men who loaded it into boats and carried his revenge upriver to be delivered by the Staubaun Lords of Annech and Gobba. He sent gold for horses. He sent volatile chemicals and sword steel and glass. But all his aid to the Neuberland Lords was invisible to the Khelds—and also to Stefan. He wanted to send a message the idiot would understand.

"A Kheld spilled my grandfather's blood. They're wrong if they think I will not make them pay for that."

"Farmers tending their fields did not spill that blood."

"No, they only raised the creature that did. They reared him, tolerated him, nourished his poison, and then armed him with rebellion and lies!" Dorilian frowned at his sword's immobile shape. Without his hand to move it, that sword could do nothing. It was but an object, a length of steel honed to an edge and sheathed in polished leather; it possessed nothing in itself of politics or purpose. In that sense, it resembled the Rill. Its purpose resided in *his*.

"They celebrated the murders at Gignastha." He continued to list his grievances. "They attacked slag miners in Rand. They squat on the lands of Neuberland and claim those to be their own! And what price have Khelds paid for any of these things? Nothing! They point to their farms."

"You have too much of other men's anger. Sebbord did not raise you to fight for other men's gain, not when they are not fighting for yours. You're moving too soon."

Was it possible? He did not think so. A god moved when a god must. Except he was not a god—not yet. He was only the promise of one. Dorilian didn't doubt Tutto's loyalty. He never had. Knowing Tutto's every word addressed his wellbeing made at least one decision easier. Turning to Legon, he said, "I'm putting Tutto in charge of my guard. Wherever I am, there he will be."

Legon answered with a thin smile. In his shoulder pack lay the battle plans he and Dorilian had drawn up over three nights in the redoubt, during which they had studied the scholars' collection of maps dating to antiquity. "We leave in the morning? As you planned?"

Dorilian nodded. For every drop of Sebbord's blood, the Khelds would pay a hundred men.

# 25

Stefan was glad he had chosen to stay with the mine. The Trongorian traders, hungry for opportunities that wealthier Staubaun and Esseran ore brokers had overlooked, had agreed to a fair contract. The Khelds would assume the cost of transportation, which meant their profit would be small, but Stefan knew that, in time, the mine would surpass older Staubaun mines in production. Even with the distillation unit now running full bore, the Orqho Hills had barely been tapped.

In the three weeks since he'd signed the contracts, the town near the mine had grown fivefold. A stand of nearby forest had been cut down for sheds and housing as the population swelled with arriving miners and the crude industry attached to them: farriers and wagon makers, carpenters and smiths, cooks and launderers. Stefan hired a man in Leseos to oversee the town and another, a half-Kheld come up from Randpory with long experience working ore basins, to oversee the mines. Even so, his days passed quickly in the thrill of working hands-on with discovery, of finding unexpected pockets of a new ore, or by dealing with launderers unhappy with the flow of water into their facility from the dammed river. Building that dam had been crucial to maintaining adequate water supplies.

The camp was asleep when the klaxon sounded. Stefan immediately sat up in bed and grabbed for his sword. Two months ago, he had taken to sleeping with the weapon within reach. "Cullen!" he shouted.

Stefan and Cullen pulled on their boots and ran from the headquarters in their nightshirts just as the shed's pine thatch roof burst into flame over their heads. Fiery globes flew overhead, blue and orange, crashing in sprays of blazing liquid and spreading fire throughout the camp. In the hellish light and confusion, miners scattered. Several writhed in flames, screaming. Through the smoke, Stefan glimpsed armed men pouring into camp along the line of the sluices leading back toward the river. The shadowy shapes moved with precision: two units, one toward the distillation unit—and one toward the shacks.

"Stefan!" Cullen dragged him toward darkness and safety. If they could join the surge of miners running up the valley toward the dam, there would be no telling one Kheld from another. At least they would not be targets.

"No! The distiller!" Stefan yanked his arm away.

"You can't save it! Those men are soldiers!"

"Where are ours?" Marc Frederick had sent troops for protection, but Stefan couldn't see them in the smoke, which reduced the camp to shadows and nightmares. As he ran with Cullen toward the dam, screams and the ringing of metal filled the air, but he saw no enemies. His sword went unblooded. When he slipped in mud, he knew he was near the stream.

He realized a man was chasing him when he felt something sharp bite into his side. He threw himself as he had been trained, rolling away. Water soaked cold into his garments as he sank to his elbows in the stream. Lurching backward, he caught a glimpse of black armor and pale Staubaun features, of bright metal coming down toward his head.

"It's all right, Stefan. Don't fight now. They're gone."

"Cullen?" Stefan had never felt so much pain. His back was propped against something hard, and he shivered. He forced his eyes open.

"Still here." Cullen grinned weakly. There was just enough pale light by which to see his face. Stefan wondered if it were near dawn. He touched his hand to the hurt in his right side and found a bulky dressing.

"You're wet. That's why you're cold. Our soldiers won the camp back and drove them off."

"He got me—"

"Not bad. Not as bad as I got him."

"You?"

"How strange is that? Bad as I am with a blade." He assisted Stefan in pulling aside the bandage to look at the wound. A hand-long crescent of mottled flesh crusted with blood showed just under Stefan's ribs. "See, he got a good slice, but it's mostly skin. I just folded back the flap—" he laid the cloth over it again. "If it doesn't fester, it'll heal all right."

Last Stefan remembered, he had been in the water, but he now rested on a rock bank above the dam. Small orange fires glowed against the dimming night. As he looked about, he saw several other men nearby, some injured, some not.

"They're gone?"

"We don't know who the hells they were, just that they're damn good at killing. I talked with the Captain. By the weapons, he thinks maybe they might be mercenaries armed by some Lord in Neuberland or Gignastha."

But Stefan knew better. He shook his head and drew himself up to a sitting position. "Dorilian." He hated that he even had to say the name. "He sent them." His shivering increased. His every breath hurt, and he'd lost blood... and that crazy Highborn bastard had just tried to kill him!

Heavy boots crushed stones underfoot, and Stefan looked up at a towering man in armor, his helm bearing a reassuring crest of command. Jormar Staubaun-Gebren, the captain in command of the soldiers guarding the camp, knelt down to give his report. "Are you well, Prince Stefan?"

"Well enough to hear what you have to say."

"They were clever, no mere band of brigands. Sophisticated strategy with low-grade weapons. From hillside positions, they used sling catapults to launch glass shells filled with ignitable oil. They set the shells aflame, then lobbed them. Nasty stuff. They started with the housing to create panic, then went for groups and equipment. We killed a dozen of them, but none carried any item telling who might have sent them. The man we captured has not talked yet."

"Just one? Why couldn't we capture more?"

"They killed their own rather than leave them."

"Motherless monsters," Cullen whispered. Though Stefan agreed, he said nothing.

"We have a lot of injured ourselves, mostly miners. Twenty dead and counting. The facility... took a lot of damage."

"How bad?" he asked, his heart sinking.

"Your distiller. I do not know enough about the things to tell if it can be salvaged. The mill wheel, the buildings—some of the fires are not yet out."

Stefan turned and winced, kicking out his leg in pain. He extended the hand on his good side to Cullen. "Help me up."

"Stefan, that's not a good idea."

"I said, help me up!" He accepted Jormar's assistance when that man offered it. "I want to see."

He walked stiffly along the path to where it headed downhill. From there, he looked out across the smoking basin. Charred timbers marked where the mine headquarters had been. The mill wheel lay in the stream. Many corpses lay about, some still smoking. Blue-white smoke poured from the building housing the distiller, but he could not tell if it was from the fires or the machine. But it didn't matter. He already knew the machine had been rendered inoperative. Dorilian's mercenaries had made sure of that.

The mine would never meet the contract now.

# 26

*He tried to kill my grandson!*
The first reports from Neuberland arrived by Rill at the same time as news of the attack on the Orqho mines. Contrary to his custom, Marc Frederick had not gone to Stauberg for the season but had continued his presence in Dazunor-Rannuli. He had done so knowing the adversary he faced.

No proof existed as to who had done the deeds, but Marc Frederick knew. He recognized the signature of a volatile and brilliant eighteen-year-old hellbent on revenge. A Sordaneon, mercifully too young for his immature body, incapable of generating the powers already being ascribed to him. A subsequent report from Jormar had verified Marc Frederick's suspicion about the true nature of the fire attacks at the other locations.

Native oils and accelerants, chemical fire. Dorilian deliberately evoked powers others already feared. But not Highborn gifts. Not yet.

He did not doubt Dorilian had overseen parts of the attacks personally. Just as Dorilian had wanted to see the Rill fly from Sordan to Hestya due to his involvement, he would also want to see the results of the terror he'd unleashed. Marc Frederick had been keeping track of the youth's movements, but his agents had lost the trail in Anit-Rebir. Marc Frederick picked it up again in Neuberland. He alerted his garrisons at Leseos and Gignastha to immediately seal the mountain passes back into Rand and Tollech; then he called in every favor he had in the region, including the Seven Houses. *I will capture him,* he told Chyralane, watching as the woman's lined face betrayed her avarice. *I will take him prisoner, but you must promise I can do with him as I please.* Knowing what had happened to his grandson at Orqho and counting on his history of imprisoning and occupying the lands of his enemies, the cartel had agreed. The Epoptes and the Malyrdeons wanted only promises that the Sordaneon prince would not be put to death. They all wanted Dorilian contained. The network of spies available to Marc Frederick expanded tenfold.

Within days, he knew what he needed to know.

When he met with Rheger Dannutheon in his private chamber in the Emrysen Palace, Marc Frederick dressed for combat. Light armor of impenetrable Sordaneon silver clad his torso and limbs. The sword that rested against the table was not ceremonial but most definitely meant for battle. He would need it. Already talk gripped the streets of Dazunor-Rannuli the way wolves harried prey, fear chasing rumors. Whispers flew about violence upon or from the Khelds, speculating whether Sordan or Teremar might be behind the attacks. Stefan's name drifted ominously through conversations rife with news of war. The city fretted, its inhabitants gazing nervously across the river to Amallar. None knew what the Khelds would do now that the attacks on their settlements had become so bold—or if Neuberland's warlike Lords would strike again.

If Marc Frederick moved quickly enough, he could silence them all.

"I need a favor, Rheger. A great one. The greatest you or your kindred will ever do me."

Summoning a Malyrdeon bordered on insolence, even for a King. Even for Marc Frederick, who had fought those battles the Wall Lords had wished to avoid.

"I have never denied you such, Majesty." Rheger did not remove his cloak, though he did divest his hands of their heavy, studded gloves.

"You might deny me this. I wish you to use the Dazunor Crown." Marc Frederick named the state crown of the domain Jonthan ruled. To Rheger's lifted eyebrow, Marc Frederick continued. "I need to catch unawares, and take captive, one of your own. And I want you to do it for me."

"Dorilian Sordaneon?" Rheger looked wary, distrustful.

"His actions cannot go unanswered. Success will but fuel his insurgency and lead to further rebellion on his part—he will become unmanageable."

"Some say he already is."

"Do you?"

Rheger hesitated, then nodded. "Yes."

"I can manage him. But I cannot do it from afar. I need to get my hands on him first."

Something very close to horror passed over Rheger's handsome face. Highborn kind had never betrayed one of their own into common hands. Never. Collectively, and with the blessing of their Wall Lord and King, the Malyrdeons had allowed Marc Frederick on his coronation day to seize Labran Sordaneon, even to do so upon the very platform of the Rill itself. They had *allowed* it. Marc Frederick and his soldiers had done the seizing. Rheger turned aside, hand raised in objection.

Marc Frederick cut off his denial before he could speak it. "Please understand. I am not asking this lightly, Rheger. If you don't help me, if I do not do this, Dorilian will plunge both our lands into war. You know this. And it will be his death. I will be forced to try to take him by other means, and soldiers make mistakes. If I fail, he will continue this course and his enemies will grow by the thousands. If the Khelds don't kill him, the Seven Houses will— they already see him as a threat to the Rill. And you know what lies in wait back in Sordan, should that boy think himself his nation's avenger and that Mormantaloran monster take hold of his mind."

"Nammuor does not attract him." Rheger's kindred was watching that pairing very carefully.

"Does not attract him *yet*. Do not deny the potential. Men who want war also want allies, and some will accept terrible ones."

"But *this*, Sire." It surprised him to hear Rheger use the more familiar address. Their relationship had always been respectful but distant. "You are asking me to betray one of my own. A son of Leur and Amynas, an empath—the hope of his country—to take him bodily, by force. That is a profound violation. You are asking me to betray a *Sordaneon*." He said that name with the reverence it deserved. The risks to him were not inconsiderable. If there was a chance, even a small one, that Dorilian possessed the powers of his ancestor...

"Who else could get close enough to him? He's too well guarded." Marc Frederick paced to the window, looking out into the night. "I know where he is tonight. But only tonight. I cannot get there myself—not soon enough. We need to do this quickly, before word is out that he is even at that place. Before I can no longer deny it."

"Sire, I—"

"Once these Neuberland attacks are pinned on Dorilian, should anyone be able to prove that he ordered or participated in hostile actions in Neuberland and Essera—should it become known he was there when blood was spilled and towns put to torch—it will be out of my hands. It will go before the Archhalia, where the Seven Houses hold sway. You know what their demands will be. Once that proof is out, their designs on him will find the support they seek. I won't be able to circumvent things then. I won't be able to save him... from himself." He turned, no longer willing to bottle his strong feelings about what he meant to do. "They've already killed Sebbord. Now they're after Dorilian, too. Rheger, if you won't help me, for the love of your gods, will you at least help *him*?"

"But Sire, if it is true that he did these things, he nearly killed your grandson."

"And next time, he might well succeed. Or Stefan will succeed. Or Dorilian will kill me. He wants to, you know. And we will all of us regret the day we let this opportunity slip through our fingers." He sighed, trying to explain convictions he found difficult to put into words. "He's angry. He is gifted, his family has been murdered, and he thinks everyone he meets is against him. He trusts no one. What he has done is terrible, but it is nothing compared to what he might do—or what might be done to him—if he is not stopped. If your kind tries to stop him, the Archhalia and the Khelds will not support it. His enemies will say you are protecting him, and they would be right. But if I do it—that, they will believe. They have seen it before."

Rheger looked troubled, his will clearly wavering. What more would it take to convince him?

"Your kindred will not be implicated. I won't tell anyone else what you do tonight," Marc Frederick vowed, in case that should be Rheger's concern. Enreddon had said it would be. "If you can do it so he does not know, I will not even tell him."

"You mean take him asleep or by surprise?"

He smiled thinly. "We must hope it is by surprise, because he will be better than you with a sword."

Rheger sighed. "Perhaps I can catch him without one."

Had he just agreed? Marc Frederick slumped to the desk. He locked his gaze onto those gold-hued eyes and mouthed his thanks. "I trust you consulted with the kindred," Rheger said, conceding a tight smile, "before you ever asked this of me."

He nodded. "I did. I talked with Enreddon, and—the cylinders are on the desk before you. You can see they have not been opened."

Three message cylinders stood on end upon the table. Rheger triggered the resonant locks with his signet ring and opened them one by one, prying forth the papers within to read each missive. Every ruling Malyrdeon agreed the youth had to be stopped. All agreed to allow Marc Frederick to handle the situation. They agreed once again to distance themselves. For all the effort at sounding reasonable, an inescapable hypocrisy accompanied the words. Only the Sordaneons themselves had never set a hand against their own kind. Dorilian would utterly reject the very deed Rheger contemplated.

Resolved, Marc Frederick walked across the room to a smooth stone wall. He pressed the stone of the Leur's Ring against the surface. The wall opened, allowing him to extract a wooden box, which he carried to the table and set down before Rheger. After opening the lid, Rheger lifted free a circlet of brilliant white stones that blazed with the inner glow evinced by all Aryati devices of power. The Dazunor Crown, like several other crowns belonging to rulers of domains, was a lesser device than the state coronals of Stauberg and Sordan—but it was still an impressive enhancer of those abilities its creators had once wielded.

"I do not suppose you have a flask of ambrosia at hand?" Rheger inquired.

Marc Frederick opened a drawer and retrieved a silver flask set with garnets. It had belonged to the last Highborn King, his great-grandfather Endurin. "You will also need this." He handed Rheger another cylinder, larger than the others. This one bore mage seals.

Briefly setting the circlet aside, Rheger picked up the cylinder with care. Pressing the pearl-set code ring, he unlocked the chamber and retrieved a small box and letter from within. He smiled morosely as he read the letter. "This answers my remaining question." He opened the box to reveal a rare device. "A *shabba* fang." He held up the tiny object briefly before placing it over the tip of his second right finger, where its wickedly curved tip glittered with blue-green menace. The transparent chamber of the claw-like appendage held an amber liquid. "Enreddon assures me the drug is nonlethal."

Marc Frederick tensed his jaw. "I don't want him harmed any more than you do. Not a hair."

"You already know the risks."

Marc Frederick nodded. There was no turning aside now. He handed Rheger a cylinder of brass filigreed with gold. "Dorilian is at a lodge outside Gignastha. I have soldiers already in position and will put them at your command." Rheger would have to translocate first to a known place or one with Highborn resonances in the firmament, such as the former Waterglit royal palace in Gignastha. Marc Frederick gave the Malyrdeon prince a second cylinder. "This has orders for my commander. Read them if you wish. He will follow them precisely. I will join you in two days." It would take that long for him to ride from Leseos, for which he would leave by Rill within the hour.

Rheger nodded, then smiled grimly. He lifted the Dazunor Crown and settled its glittering circle above his eyes. The next moment, he was gone.

# 27

Nights in Gignastha were deeply cold. Though winter had not yet descended on the land, the frowning mountains to the south lifted heavy white caps above the Silver Lake. The lodge overlooked the lake from atop rock cliffs, also well hidden. Soldiers ringed the lodge and the access points below. Any fight to take it would be bloody.

Dorilian felt safe.

*I am protected. By a ring of stone. By a ring of men.*

The room he had chosen to sleep in looked out over a gorge. At the bottom, shallow water rushed over boulders and slithered over beds of gravel. He could pick out the low thunder of a waterfall on the other side of the building. A single track served as the only approach on this side to the lodge.

"I have posted sentries there"—Legon indicated a stand of tall pines, then shifted, bringing his hand nearly across Dorilian's body—"and there, beside that rock that looks like a ship's prow. No one will approach unseen or uncontested." They'd just arrived, after a hard ride around the lake to avoid Gignastha.

"Then I should get a good night's sleep at least. It may be my last bed for a while."

Dorilian had ordered the company to prepare for a morning departure. Though his location was well hidden and defended, he had already stayed longer than intended because the weather had been good. The day before, one of the mountain passes had snowed in, and he did not wish to press his luck with the others. He had caused damage enough to make a statement, though he had yet to hear if he had gotten Stefan. To stay any longer would be dangerous. The pass into Myrmida was still open, and he could return to Sordan by way of Tollech.

"I'll fetch you a plate from the kitchen," Legon said.

"Only if the hunters brought something back. I'm sick of provisions." He would rather eat nothing at all than more salted beef.

"I think we all are. At least this place has a store of good wine, so we can wash the fare down with better than boiled water." His friend left, closing the door behind him. Legon's footsteps retreated across the common area for the bedchambers and lightly descended the wooden stairs.

One of the first men in—Tutto most likely—had laid a fire, making the room nicely warm. Dorilian shrugged out of his coat and tossed the heavy thing onto a chair. From levels below came the sounds of men and horses, the rattle of soldiers running to their stations, the scrape and drag of furniture being moved. Much as he enjoyed the bustle of soldiering, there was also a sameness to it that irked him. An army, though it was a living thing, was also a machine... but this one he had assembled. It had done his bidding, did his bidding even now, and he felt gratified knowing he could excel at the business of slaughter. Though not a pleasant occupation, it was a necessary and useful one. He harbored no hope at all of freeing Sordan without spilling more blood.

He had just unbuttoned his jacket, wishing his trunk would arrive so he could change out of travel clothes, when the faint prickle of another of his race alerted him. He spun, hand already reaching for the sword he still wore. A man stood behind him... sun-haired, handsome, wearing a crown of stars.

He recognized the face from funerals and weddings. *Rheger? Here? How?*

Stunned, he obeyed the old prohibition not to draw steel against his own kind—until the man reached for him with fingers bared save for one of gold, and then it was too late. He drew his blade but not before Rheger's right hand clamped hard over the back of his neck and his left grasped Dorilian's right wrist. Something cold and evil penetrated the skin between his neck bones, delivering a sharp, stabbing pain. Before he could even gasp, ice flooded his very spine and poured into his veins, spreading to his limbs. His sword slipped from numb fingers, clattering to the floor, and his knees buckled. From below, an alarm sounded. Shouts and the clash of fighting rang out, frantic and violent.

*Just like Labran... betrayed by the thrice-cursed Malyrdeons!*

Rheger released his grip, wrapped his arm around Dorilian's ribs, and eased him to the floor. "Shhhh, *fra'don*. Don't fight it. It will be all right." The sounds of fighting were very near now, on the stairs. "I have my sword." Rheger's voice penetrated the blur. "I'll die myself before anything or anyone harms you." The man's damned fingers stroked his hair as though calming a sick child. Dorilian gasped, trying to fight the growing darkness, but the chill had spread into his gut and throat. It pulled him under until even gray gave way to black.

# 28

Marc Frederick unfolded the heavy parchment for the hundredth time, glancing at its neatly written contents but not reading them. There was no need. He already knew the damning words by heart. He had purchased every one of them. He looked out into the rain—autumn rain, gray as a wet veil. A good rain for growing things, for farmers and children, for this verdant, war-torn land. At least little fighting would get done. Soldiers hated wet feet only half as much as did their commanders. He refolded the damp papers and walked over to the room's massive table—a beautiful thing carved from a single block of stone—where he threw the documents down. After a moment, he reconsidered and moved them purposefully to the center, where they would be immediately seen as significant. Their business was important, however little he relished it.

Two nights before, his soldiers had overrun the cliffside lodge in which Dorilian had quartered. The place had been in their hands since. To judge by the trophies displayed on the walls, the lodge's owner, Lord Eskeros, was a fisherman, a detail which saddened Marc Frederick. The man's old friendships, not his choice of pastimes, had proven his undoing. The room displayed much of Eskeros's temperament: stone floors covered by dense, red and blue rugs enlivened by designs in gold or russet, heavy furnishings carved of dark woods, and a massive stone hearth fitted with cooking grates in which a steady fire had been burning for hours. Warm light reflected off stone walls from the orange glow of a single lantern agleam on the polished table. In the deepening cold of a biting late autumn, that warmth barely penetrated Marc Frederick's steely resolve.

*Dorilian, Dorilian,* he sighed to the silent walls. *I have the goods on you now. All it took was time and more of my currency than I cared to spend. And for what? To prove what I and everyone already know?* Though he had divested himself of his wet cloak upon arrival, he still wore traveling clothes. His dark-hued woolens and leathers were damp and stained from the day-long rain, but he did not have the luxury of time in which to change them. He had already been here two hours too long and would leave again as soon as possible.

He had taken time only to shave and meet with Rheger, a strange brief meeting during which Rheger had let him know, with a warning well taken, that Dorilian had seen and recognized his attacker. "He will never trust us again," the man had said, his regret piercing. "Not even his own kind." What price the Malyrdeons would pay for breaking that trust remained to be seen.

What he had done today already sickened Marc Frederick— would sicken him forever—deeds redeemable only if he succeeded in salvaging Dorilian Sordaneon's soul. He alone seemed to believe the boy to have one, though there had been something in Rheger's haunted eyes that suggested maybe he now believed it, too. Having done the deed and then protected Dorilian as far as possible, Rheger had left for Dazunor-Rannuli by the same means as he had come. Another favor called upon, another favor owed.

Hearing footsteps at the door, Marc Frederick braced himself. Though kept in isolation, Dorilian had been conscious for several hours. Gagged, hooded, and guarded by men under strict orders not to speak with him even if he attempted, the youth had communicated with no one. Rheger's presence in the room had made certain of that. The men did not know who they guarded and had been told only that the prisoner was dangerous, deluded, a liar. Almost certainly, Dorilian had boiled in rage. When the door opened and the six-man guard entered, Dorilian with them, Marc Frederick bid the men leave. They did so at once.

He removed the hood and gag himself. The Sordaneon prince stood before him, unharmed in any way, as promised. The garments, creams and tans, wool and leather, were of royal cut and richness but plain and now rumpled, downplaying the youth's sweat-darkened good looks.

Dorilian's surprise at seeing him—so brutally evident in the first moment—quickly gave way to an attempt to seize the initiative. "Where's Rheger?"

"He was never here." Marc Frederick placed the hood on the table.

"But he was! A faithless, prideless—"

Marc Frederick just watched, assessing the nuances. The young man was himself all pride and thwarted ambition—but not without a touch, for the first time, of uncertainty. He had to be wondering if Rheger's actions meant that the Malyrdeons were now willing to look the other way. If so, he had no access to any succor at all from others of his kind. It was an interpretation Marc Frederick was willing to leave dangling.

"He was never here. Neither, for that matter, will you or I have been by the time we are finished. Sit down, Prince Dorilian." Marc Frederick indicated a chair opposite his at the stone table, ignoring the hatred that blazed at him from those stormy gray eyes. "You have gotten taller than me, and it impairs my majesty."

If Dorilian took any satisfaction in his new physical stature, he gave no indication of it. "Just tell me what you mean to do, you fur-faced bastard."

"I mean to save your life. It's what I have been doing all along. Sit down." He waited, eyes locked on those others, until the young man gave in and did as told. Marc Frederick picked up the documents already on the table and slid them across the smooth, dark surface. "Read them."

He settled into his armchair, ignoring the padded backrest and placing his elbows wearily upon the table to watch the young man's face as he read—the downcast eyes and eyelash-shadowed cheeks, as well as the young hard mouth, untouched by response. Controlled. A steely discipline had emerged since Sebbord's death, yet another layer covering Dorilian's emotions. The Sordaneon youth's enemies had succeeded in driving his energy inward, to be released only as destruction. When Dorilian looked up from the papers, Marc Frederick got no more reaction than he had expected.

"In what market did you buy these lies?"

"Why did you attack the miners at Orqho? To kill Stefan?"

"He's not dead!" The young man threw the papers that had told him this fact down upon the table.

"But you tried."

The look that answered him showed pure Highborn disdain. "Think about it. If I had tried, I would have succeeded."

"Then you ordered it."

"If I had ordered it, it would have been done."

Marc Frederick noted that he neither took credit nor denied it. "Next time, be sure you hire better soldiers." He reached over to pick up the documents, then slid them back into the leather envelope from which he had initially taken them. "However, there will not be a next time. The originals of these documents will be forwarded to the Archhalia. That pack of wolves will be thrilled to have proof of your willful rebellion and criminal activities in the royal protectorates of Neuberland and Gignastha—activities and interference which you and any of your family are forbidden by law to so much as foster in word. They will have evidence enough to convict you. The usual punishment would be death—but you, of course, cannot be put to death." He looked up, pleased to note the fine tension about the young man's mouth and the tight line of his jaw. "Prison, I think, would serve as well."

*There, let him mull on that.* Dorilian was young and had just begun to live his long Highborn life. He would not want to measure out his remaining days—well over a century—behind high walls with but three visitors. How would he rule Sordan then?

"Do that, and you will have war in any case," Dorilian warned, eyes narrowing. It was no empty threat. "Sordan will not sit still twice."

Marc Frederick steepled his fingers and looked thoughtfully above them. "And who would lead the revolt? Your father? Perhaps, with Nammuor at his back. Oh, yes, I have considered that. And that Sebbord left Teremar with a formidable army. Nor have I overlooked that I would most certainly have problems with Ardaen. You"—he gestured to the young man—"are a nest of troubles for me. No one is unhappier than I that you have put me in such a position that I can no longer let you be free." He lifted other documents, these penned within the last few hours by his own hand, and pushed them across the table. "But at least you will not be dead. Unlike these five men, who will pay the price you do not."

Dorilian read each name, shuffling the documents. His face had gone white. Marc Frederick had memorized the names in order. Alban Eskeros. Legon Rebiran. Tutto Estol-Rhunnard. Philemon Leander. Tiflan Morevyen.

"Lord Eskeros was taken in Gignastha. Legon and Tutto, we of course captured here. Both took wounds on your behalf, although you may not yet know that. Lord Leander and Bas Tiflan

were placed in custody just hours before I left Dazunor-Rannuli."
Tiflan Morevyen had, in fact, been in Permephedon for his first
Archhalia since becoming Bas of Teremar, a circumstance of which
Dorilian had probably been unaware. Marc Frederick carefully
watched the play of emotions upon the young man's face, the
unguarded blanching as he comprehended what he was reading.
Dorilian knew the validity of the evidence against each man.

Those gray eyes turned dark as storms.

"I won't have it!" Dorilian slammed his hand upon the table
and pushed back so he could rise from his chair. The lantern on the
table, its oil-filled globe unsettled by the vibration, sent rings of
light dancing across the polished surface. "You cannot do this!"

"I can, and I have!" Marc Frederick answered, himself rising,
his voice edged with steel. "You have no idea what I will do. Do you
want to know everything? Tiflan and Leander are in cells in
Dazunor-Rannuli, but the men you brought here, all save Legon
and Tutto, are already dead. Two hours ago, I ordered my soldiers
to kill them."

"What?" Dorilian sank into the chair again. His stare was
disbelieving. Two hundred men had been at the lodge, with scores
more defending its approaches.

"You heard me."

"I do not believe you."

"Why not? Because you think I am soft? Think again. I am
every bit your match. How many have you killed? Three hundred
dead only scratches the surface of what you were willing to do. You
put just as many to the sword... women, children, babes cut from
the womb..."

"I did not do it!"

*"You unleashed it!"*

Dorilian did not contest the accusation because he could not.
He had brought those deaths to those people. His men had
committed atrocities. In no small part, they had done so because of
the anger inside him. And he knew it. In the deep, godborn core of
his Highborn being, where no truth could ever be denied, he knew.
How he justified his actions could only be monstrous. As monstrous,
perhaps, as what Marc Frederick was willing to do to stop him.

"You have a second force, the one that attacked Orqho, which
you planned to rejoin in two days. I have sent an elite wing of men
to intercept them. They will be killed, to the last man."

"No, I—"

"You have nothing to say about it. It's too late to call my troops back. If you did not accept responsibility for your men's possible fates, you should never have led them against me." Marc Frederick braced his hands on the table. "I hate what I am doing now. Those are *good men*, loyal men—loyal to you!—and they are dying for no other reason than they followed you here—because if that force is captured, its very existence can be used against you! I am removing evidence, you fool!"

Dorilian looked at him hard, stricken, his mind visibly racing. "Why remove evidence? Considering the trouble you've gone through to get it?"

Marc Frederick tapped the papers in front of him. He made sure he used his left hand, upon which the Leur's Ring glowed with fateful promises. "I do not want to subject *these* men, your friends—noblemen—to trial or execution. I do not want to divest you of your contact with House Haralambdos. I do not want to place Teremar under a ruler chosen by the Archhalia. I do not even want to slay your men in Neuberland, but I will. Five hundred is too many to leave alive." He walked over to the fire, where a pot of water had been set to boiling on the grate. He had brought along an elaborate old-fashioned tea set of which he was fond and had brewed some of his treasured native tea. Lifting the pot, he poured a cup for himself and one for his visitor. Dorilian stared at the rugged cup and brew. "You can drink it," Marc Frederick said. "I won't drug or poison you. I will never do that. I will never lay a hand on you or do you bodily harm. But I will do everything in my power to keep you from destroying yourself—and me with you."

"By killing my friends!" Venom dripped from the words.

"Kill? Far from it. I am offering you their lives." He put a sugar bowl upon the table and slid it and a spoon to the wary young man. At least he now had his full attention. "No one need ever know you were in Neuberland or that you attacked the mines at Orqho. I can claim that my soldiers slew the perpetrators, say they were rogues acting on their own. I can and will deny your participation. All evidence against you and these men"—he retrieved the papers, holding them in emphasis—"will vanish. Lord Eskeros, Legon Rebiran, and Tutto Rhunnard will be kept under house arrest at locations satisfactory to me, for a time also satisfactory to me. Bas Tiflan and Lord Leander will be released and allowed to go about their business after they give me their promises never to divulge what they know."

Dorilian stared at him silently, seeking a way out. There would be none, not this time. He was being offered five men's lives... but at what price? Marc Frederick never took his eyes from his adversary's face, seeing a pale mask behind which thoughts hammered against a reality that tightened like a slaver's chain. Dorilian had never been fettered—not in flesh and not in his ambitions—and he did not like the feel of it. But he did respect the power he faced and knew that it was he who had no recourse. Marc Frederick saw the moment of acknowledgment when the young man looked away and, with his spoon, lifted a star-shaped wafer of sugar and dropped it into his cup, nudging it until it dissolved.

"What about me?" he finally asked.

"Having you brought up on a charge of treason doesn't suit me, but neither does holding you as a prisoner. I have already had one Sordaneon prisoner and know I do not want another." Sharp new questions sought him in the young man's gaze. "Still, I cannot merely release you. So here is the final article of my proposal. If you accept, your freedom will not be impaired in any way—save one. You are to write your father and your wife, informing them that you have decided to be a guest at my court for a period of one year."

"A *year!*" Dorilian's protest registered his dismay at so interminable a length of time.

Marc Frederick laughed out loud, thoroughly amused. "I'm being lenient. It could be much more. And it will pass quickly... much more quickly than you think." He lifted his teacup and took a long drink of the delicate brew, savoring its sweetness. He had made better pots but never one more satisfying. "Think well, Cousin," he urged. "Legon and Tutto, and your hapless host Eskeros, one year in house arrest, yourself my guest—it is not so bad an exchange."

"You say I will be free in every way—but that I must stay with you?" Dorilian regarded him suspiciously. He tasted the tea, made a face, and put it down. "I cannot drink this."

"You will learn how," Marc Frederick said, completely confident. At this critical juncture, he must show no weakness, no hesitation. "You stay with me, reside where I reside. For the most part, it will be at my house in Gustan. I will place no restrictions upon your correspondence or visitors. None. Your own horses, your own servants—your own cook if you insist on one. We will, however, take meals together, you and me. I will not accept that you become a recluse. In return for this freedom, you will promise that you will not use your time to plot against me or my family in any way. I place full faith in your integrity, for I know what a Highborn promise is worth."

"I have not yet given it. What if I do not agree to these terms?"

"Then my protection vanishes. You and your companions will be remanded to the Archhalia, to be convicted of the crimes you have committed against its citizens, upon these proofs I have shown and my own word against you." He left no doubt as to that he would. "You have powerful enemies already. I would be but one more."

It was blackmail, plain and simple. Marc Frederick had gone too many rounds with the Seven Houses not to understand the many ways to play that game, too many rounds not to have manipulated the situation the better to entrap his opponent's mind and heart. Dorilian wanted to rule in Sordan—a goal that would be significantly imperiled if he fell into the Archhalia's clutches. More immediate and more compelling, however, were the lives hanging in the balance. The loss of his army had yet to sink in fully. Did he place so little value on human lives that he would throw away those of his friends?

"I would need to go to Permephedon sometimes to see my brother."

He had considered that relationship. "By all means, do so. If I have your promise, you have but to time your visits to coincide with my residence in Dazunor-Rannuli. You may also have your wife with you if you wish."

Dorilian shot him a pained look. The marriage was hardly in good order, then. But he still had not said what he would do. Perhaps he would not yield, too proud to keep company with his family's mortal enemy, too filled with hate not to fling himself with reckless disregard into the jaws of the Archhalia, little realizing how desperately they longed to get him into their hands. Perhaps Essera's insults to his family had left damage too far gone, scars too deep, a mind too poisoned for there to ever be more between them than hard words and battle. If so, there was nothing left, not even hope.

Marc Frederick calmed his nerves by quietly walking to the cabinet where Lord Eskeros had stored a few prized flasks. He had noted them in his initial exploration of the room and now had an idea. Make the rapprochement formal. Make it adult and honest and true. The young rebel needed affirmation even more than he needed a heavy hand upon his reins. A mentor, not a master. Choosing *ucajha* liqueur, with its overtones of sincerity, he took up two crystal goblets and filled each halfway.

Back at the table, he handed one glass to Dorilian. "Give me your word that you will remain with me for one full year, and I will burn these documents in a moment."

"You have copies." Dorilian shot him a glare of distrust, but he took the glass.

"I will burn those, too. Everything. Just as surely as I killed so many men this day."

Dorilian looked like he wanted to slay him still. But he was royal enough—and cunning enough—to know what mattered most. Revenge, for him, would remain an option long after he had served his punishment.

It was not his friendship Marc Frederick so wanted to gain at this moment—little chance of that—but he craved gaining the chance to earn it.

"Done, then." The young man at last accorded a grudging acceptance that would nonetheless hold him as fast as any he gave with a whole heart. "I agree. In return for the lives of Legon, Tiflan, Tutto, Lord Eskeros, and Lord Leander—and my own—you have my word that I will stay with you for one full year. And my word that I will not during that time plot against you or your family or do anything I know will cause you harm. But I want to have the papers."

Marc Frederick shook his head. He no longer bothered trying to conceal his triumph. Dorilian seemed to know he was feeling it.

"No. You would use them to discover my sources, and that I cannot allow. Let your betrayers worry about their anonymity. It will do them good, and they will tread lightly where either of us is concerned. As for the papers, I did indeed say I would burn them."

He removed the lantern cover and held the letters over the flame until they ignited, then lifted them for Dorilian to watch as the several papers burned down until he could hold them no more, at which point he dropped them onto the stone table. Within moments they were but useless black ash. He glanced across the lantern light at the sullen youth he had gained by artifice and savored a secret elation. "They have served their purpose."

# 29

Gustan in the fall was glorious. Emyli loved the place at any season but autumn most of all. She had only to look out from the terrace to see landscapes enrobed in coronation colors. Reds marched along the hills; golds carpeted the fields. Jonthan had arrived the night before. She spied him now on the west road fronting the vineyard, returning from a morning ride with Stefan at his side. As a boy, Stefan had idolized his uncle, and the two often rode on the same team in *pelekys*, a rough game on horseback that Emyli dreaded to watch. Stefan had not played since his return to Gustan just a few days before. He still nursed the wound he had taken in Amallar three weeks past.

She greeted them at the terrace edge to which they had ridden upon seeing her. Jonthan looked unusually sober, but the darkness on Stefan's face drove the smile from her own.

"What's the matter?" She reached for her son's arm as he dismounted.

"Everything!" he snarled. He tossed the reins to the groom and stomped up the steps, leaving her to stare after him.

"Jon! What's going on?"

Her brother also handed his reins to the groom. He put his arm around her shoulder and guided her to the terrace. Russet grape leaves draped the arbors as he pulled her aside, keeping her from following Stefan into the house. "Father is coming today." When her face brightened with delight, he added, "He's bringing a guest."

A guest Stefan clearly did not want to see. A guest so hated that Jonthan had traveled ahead to talk to the young man first. Fast as Emyli's mind raced, her brother's lay in wait.

"He is bringing Dorilian Sordaneon. The situation is very... political. And exceedingly tender."

"Oh, no, Jon." Emyli walked away, unable to accept this. "Not that monster—"

"He's not a monster. He's a problem. A problem Father has gone to a great deal of trouble to get into this position. He'll be with us for a while."

"How can he do this?" Emyli couldn't believe her father could be so blind, so unfeeling. "How *can* he? That Sordaneon beast tried to kill Stefan! *Kill* him!"

Jonthan's level gaze seized hers. "He could not have, as he was never there—neither he nor any men of his."

She stared at her brother, dismay taking root alongside disbelief at what their father was doing. "And so the lies begin—"

"Emy—"

"You know it's a lie! You know! And so does he... and Stefan! What's to stop him from trying again? What is Father thinking?" She turned with a mind to run after her son, only to find Jonthan's heavy hand on her arm, bringing her back around to face him.

"I'll tell you what Father is thinking. He is saving his country from war! And he is saving Sordan from breaking completely from us. Mormantalorus is eyeing that throne... and we can neither hold Sordan by force nor afford to lose it. Emy, Dorilian does not want to be here. Father went to extraordinary measures to lay hands on him." Seeing the look on his face, she did not want to know what those measures had been.

Tears sprang to her eyes, tears she hated because they marked her as weak. "I know why he could not kill him, but why bring him *here*? Why not imprison him as he did that horrible Hierarch of theirs, at Stauberg or Permephedon? The Malyrdeons would let him."

"The Malyrdeons want no part of it. Emy, this is Father's plan to *not* repeat the past, to give us a fresh start with Sordan. Dorilian is not a prisoner."

"Not a prisoner?" Now indeed, she saw the insult that had so angered Stefan. "How could he not be a prisoner?"

"He gave Father his promise to be his guest for a year. He is our *guest*, Emy. And he is to be treated as such."

"And what about Stefan?" This was Stefan's home. To welcome his enemy into it was a slap in the face. "How is he supposed to feel? Did anyone think of talking with him first?"

"There was no time for it. Father moved very quickly. Dorilian nearly got away."

"Stefan counts himself lucky to be *alive*," Emyli seethed. "Not all the lies in the world will remove Dorilian from that deed! I certainly am not going to be all smiles in his presence."

"So long as you are not all swords and needles."

It was now clear that Marc Frederick had sent Jonthan ahead to smooth a path he knew would be strewn with stones. Stefan could not stay here! How could he, with the enemy who had attempted his murder sleeping under the same roof? Her father's insensitivity appalled her. *Stefan will go to Amallar*, she decided. *He will be safest there.* Hans, too, would go... must go, before Dorilian could immerse him also in a bottomless well of hate.

"Emy," Jonthan urged. "Relent, for the good of us all. We seldom have Highborn guests. They live in seclusion because they affect us and we affect them. Dorilian's presence will be especially difficult because he is so powerful."

"Powerful?" Why did her heart chill so at those words?

"He's a manifested empath."

All the Highborn were empaths to lesser or greater degrees—but the Sordaneons were adept at energy manipulation, and some of them could fold space or send bolts against aqueducts. Emyli had witnessed the latter with her own eyes. "I don't want him here."

"That is not your decision. Father wants him away from the cities and especially the Seven Houses—someplace where he can control access. Gustan is perfect. Don't be hostile, Emy, please."

What Jonthan said was only truth. The manor was their father's most private residence. Here he could control every aspect of every day. That she lived here and considered it her home, and the home of her children, had barely entered his decision.

"I can't do it, Jon," she said. "To be always on guard, watching every word, is hardly natural. I must think of my children, and Hans especially. He's so young! To subject him to that, not to mention Stefan's anger—he won't understand what's going on. And how can I ask Stefan to stay here? How can I ask him to eat at the same table? Dorilian destroyed more than a few villages! He destroyed lives. He destroyed Kheld lives, men Stefan knew. Stefan is not going to forgive what was done to him or them!"

Jonthan looked at her with deep regret. "Don't you see, Emy? That kind of thinking is what led to those deaths in the first place—and will lead to more if it continues. Father has the right of it. We have to let go. So does Dorilian, but he's as far away from that as

Stefan is, even as you are. Father wants Stefan to stay because he wants to reach them *both*."

Emyli shook her head and laughed as bright and cold as the day had dawned. "Then he is the fool! No one has ever reached Sordan's heart, and no one ever will! It is sheathed in Rill stuff and drugged with Rill dreams, and it has no more human feelings than the beautiful towers of its undying city! What does Dorilian care if he kills thousands? The Rill kills all things that stand in its path—"

"That boy is not the Rill!"

"Look again. He thinks he is."

Horns sounded from the river, deep and booming, announcing the arrival of the royal barge as it approached the landing. Children and staff not on duty ran from the cottages and gardens toward the road and the river. Emyli watched how Jonthan lifted his head, the resignation in his bearing. He had left behind his new wife, his own pursuits. Clearly, he'd agreed to work with their father on swaying this young Sordaneon. She wondered if they had put as much effort into Stefan.

A child's voice ringing through the clear air snatched her abruptly out of such thoughts.

"Grandfather's coming! Grandfather's coming!"

Looking up, she saw young Hans already running far down the path toward the road, his dark-skirted governess in pursuit.

"Oh, my goddess!" With a furious glare at her suddenly laughing brother, Emyli swirled and dashed toward the steps again, thinking only about intercepting her youngest before any damage could be done.

Dorilian tested Marc Frederick's promises immediately. He insisted on seeing Legon and Tutto within the hour, and that permission was granted. True to his own promise, Dorilian revealed to his friends only that he would be accompanying Marc Frederick to Essera and that he would be spending a year as the King's guest. Tutto, gravely wounded in the left arm and side, alive only because the King had commanded he be taken captive, read the nature of the situation and brooded upon it. Legon, too, realized his life had been dearly bought. The Esseran King's soldiers had felled him from behind with a stiff bludgeon to the head. Both, however, swore the oaths Marc Frederick required. No word of their prince's presence in Neuberland would ever escape their lips. Dorilian had not seen his friends since, though Marc Frederick had informed him that Tutto would be held in Merath and Legon at Simelon. Alban Eskeros would remain in Gignastha under the guard of the region's new administrator, Sinon Kouranos.

After a journey to Leseos during which he was hooded and silent, and a subsequent arrival in Dazunor-Rannuli during which he looked at the cold face of the Rillhome palace for the first time with longing, Dorilian gradually realized the enormity of his concession. A year of his time was not inconsequential. Neither would it pass unnoticed. Despite the great care with which he worded his letter, he could be sure Deben would take his association with the Esseran King—indeed, his very promise—as defiance. And while Daimonaeris would no doubt rejoice at his absence, it flew in the face of Nammuor's threats. The latter fact pleased him inordinately, and it dawned on him that he might welcome the respite from his father and his marriage. The fact that Marc Frederick made no attempt in Dazunor-Rannuli to stop him from going to visit Levyathan merely sealed the realization that his word meant more to Essera's King than his very being did to his father or wife.

"I will see you as often as I'm able." He made the commitment to Lev in the evening garden of the Sordaneon Tower overlooking the High Citadel. "He has to be in Dazunor-Rannuli during Archhalia meetings." Lev leaned against him, his weight barely that of a much younger child. Noemi sat with them, neither passive nor quiet. Her face passed from frowns to suspicion to frowns again.

"The King himself?" Her eyes narrowed with distrust. "He has been no friend of ours!"

"No shadows, no fear." Levyathan's fingertips traced his brother's face and throat, seeking the vibrations of Dorilian's voice.

"No fear." Dorilian could not have explained why. Though he had good reason to distrust the man whose threats had led to this arrangement, he did not feel in any way endangered.

"Well, it's true he never killed the old Hierarch, though he had reason." Noemi folded her arms across her ample bosom. She recalled something else. "And the old Lord always said Essera's King wasn't the enemy Sordan most needed to fear."

"Did he?" Dorilian found the statement interesting. Sebbord hadn't said it to him.

"Well, Lord Sebbord was hard against the Stauberg-Randolphs when your lady mother died. Scared me, he did, he was so hard. Cursed Marc Frederick, then, and carried you boys away from Sordan before Essera could get you. But his heart softened when the King took his side against your father. 'That man understands the real matter,' he said. Overheard him saying it to Lord Tiflan one night in the nursery. Said what Sordan should fear most was the day that man died."

*Too many deaths. I touch them here... and here.* Levyathan probed places Dorilian did not want to be laid open. There had been deaths—so many deaths—because of him and the Rill. Their mother. Sebbord. And now, thanks to Marc Frederick, a phantom army of men no one would ever acknowledge had existed. A knowledge as walled off as tombs, as filled with corpses. He had failed those men, failed their belief in him. And he had ordered the deaths of children... of *mothers*...

*Stop. I hurt.*

He slammed Lev's thoughts aside, blocking the pain.

*Don't say anything to Noemi. She knows nothing of this, must never know where I have been or what I have done.*

*Silence. But no more, Dor... no more... death kills your brightness.*

Whatever brightness Lev referred to, he did not want to kill it. Only the pain.

"You two," Noemi said sternly, "talk too much."

Dorilian returned from Permephedon confused. Lev's disapproval had been for the deaths he had caused, deaths Dorilian himself attributed to failure. His failure. Tiflan, and Tutto also, had warned him. He'd let himself be blinded by anger and a thirst for revenge. He needed truth, but the truths he needed were locked away.

Upon reaching Permephedon's Rill platform, he faced an active choice and took it. He disembarked at Dazunor-Rannuli and rode down from the Rill Mount to his waiting barge, which he directed to convey him to the Emrysen Palace. There was brightness to a promise kept, smooth as silver in the hand. But his dinner with Marc Frederick that evening felt strained and taut. As happened so often after his visits with Levyathan, he craved solitude, not company. Later that night, he rose and stood at the window of a room in which he had never been, in a palace into which he had sworn never to set foot. He gazed out at the lights of a city that housed only enemies. If he lowered his barriers enough, he would detect whispers of the webs they wove. He wondered who the greater fool was, him or the King.

*Because my friends' lives have bought him a year of my time, he thinks I will be his friend.*

That Marc Frederick could think so should have made him laugh. Instead, the sheer presumption of the King's ambition rubbed at nerves still frayed from Sebbord's death. Bastard Stefan's grandfather. A fur-faced Kheld. A man who twice a day without fail took pains to scrape hair from his cheek and lip. A half-man, Daimonaeris would have called him, and it bothered Dorilian only a little to appropriate the term.

Dorilian was no happier the next morning. Soon after leaving Dazunor-Rannuli, Marc Frederick's barge entered lands no Sordaneon had visited since Labran's youth. Dorilian owned estates in this region—a palace in Trulo, a villa in the Glainoi currently leased to one of the princes of Gweroyen—but he had never visited these properties. He added doing so to a list of tasks to be completed during his stay.

Staring over the railing, he gazed upon Amallar, a country he had never walked and hoped he never would. He had not lied when he told Marc Frederick he had not been at Orqho. He had been mindful of the promise of a long-dead King, Erydon, who had sworn the Highborn would never assail the Khelds in the land he had given them to be their own. That promise, however, had not included Neuberland. Now Amallar passed before his eyes like a blood-soaked dream, crimson trees and villages of earthen houses. At times the dark-haired inhabitants infested the river like flies, men converging upon the water in crude boats or women with baskets of clothing to wash, balanced on their heads as they walked, bodies swaying, along the shore. Gustan, he began to think, would be such a place, and he wasn't sure he could stand it.

He became aware of Marc Frederick's renewed scrutiny from the moment the barge docked. Dorilian had ordered two of his own horses delivered by Rill that first night in Dazunor-Rannuli along with a selection of personal belongings. He had also ordered a groom to accompany the beasts. That man had saddled one of the animals for him, and he mounted it on the landing, the white charger so glad to have solid ground beneath its feet that Dorilian needed a moment to control it. The King's horse, in contrast, had been brought from the house, the top floors of which could be seen over the rise.

"It will only be my household and my family," Marc Frederick said.

He could guess why. "I know how to behave."

"Yes. But they will need to learn how to behave with you."

Dorilian cursed under his breath. He had been told Stefan was in residence and might be at hand, though he doubted Stefan would be stupid enough ever to strike him again. At Dazunor-Rannuli, Marc Frederick had handed over to Dorilian new evidence in Sebbord's murder, pointing to the killer's recruitment by agents of the Seven Houses... evidence gathered by Stefan. Dorilian no longer knew what to believe on that count. His last encounter with Stefan in Merath—how stunned Stefan had been—haunted Dorilian. Would someone guilty of the crime have been so surprised? That singular doubt prompted him to put his own agents on the new information. *Find out if these be truth or lies.* His life had become messy, his world littered with corpses, and he now questioned having targeted the mines at Orqho. But for that misadventure, he would not be in this situation.

Gustan Manor resembled no dwelling he had ever seen. The structure itself was of stone and wood, not surrounded at all by walls to guard it. The place had enough gardens, outbuildings, and paths to constitute a small town. The party drew to a halt in an open courtyard in which clusters of pale blue *lethe* blossoms glowed against somber stone walls covered in red leaves. Grooms and household staff, most of them dark-haired and plainly garbed, pressed forward as Dorilian chose to remain seated on his large ivory horse, above the rabble. He scanned those present, looking for Stefan, only to find his gaze arrested by the clear face of a young boy.

The child, fair-haired and no more than seven years of age, stood rooted to the courtyard floor, lips parted in wonder as he gazed up at both horse and rider. Dorilian glared back, hating that he was here at all, much less being openly stared at by a blue-eyed brat. In Sordan and his own domains—indeed, in Staubaun places where people at least attempted to be civilized—he was not subjected to such impertinence. But there was something unusual about this boy, something more than his apparent mixed birth. Something almost... recognizable. He narrowed his gaze, focusing. The boy's face lost its smile and changed, tinged by fear of him, just before a woman wearing a fine dress and rich cape swooped in to pull him back. He had seen her before, in Merath. He looked again at the boy, this time seeing the resemblance.

Emyli Stauberg-Randolph's blue eyes stabbed at him, but she was royal enough to hold back the words on her tongue. He refused to dignify her warning with any response whatsoever. The suggestion that he was a danger to her child merited none.

The surrounding servants were now staring also, many not having been aware of the identity of their master's guest until the whispers reached their ears. All at least had the sense to drop their eyes when he looked back. He swung down from his horse and allowed the groom to lead it away.

"Emy! Hans!" Marc Frederick happily greeted his daughter and grandson, ruffling the smiling boy's hair before lifting him in his arms and laughing as the youngster hugged him about the neck. Emyli, too, wrapped her arms about her father and smiled. Dorilian, however, continued to watch the child, Handurin, of whom he had heard remarkably little.

Dorilian wasn't surprised when he learned in the morning that Emyli was departing for Amallar along with her sons. A long-planned visit to relations there, he was told, even though they should have known he would see it for a lie. From the window of the south-facing suite of rooms Marc Frederick had set aside for him—strange rooms with furnishings that had nothing about them of any place he had ever called home—Dorilian watched the royal family say their goodbyes at the pier. Marc Frederick stood with his son on the landing as the barge departed and waved to Emyli and her golden-haired child. The barge pulled away into the river, moving toward a shore the color of blood.

Dorilian saw Stefan only once, the Kheld youth standing on the deck of the barge, his raven hair dark against the water as he looked back at all he was leaving behind.

*Good*, Dorilian thought. Yet, he knew the sentiment was misplaced. He wanted Stefan here, within sight, within reach. He had not put his finger on it yet, but an urge to seek Stefan out and see him bend to his will beat within him like a second heart.

# 30

If Dorilian had known he would chafe so much at another man's control, he would never have agreed to a year of it. But he had, and his promise bound him surer than iron. When, after one week, Jonthan invited Dorilian to accompany him to Penrhu, the nearby estate of a man who had dedicated his long life to the breeding of fine horses, Dorilian leapt at the chance. He despised Gustan Manor and would have accompanied Jonthan to Gsch itself, or even Amallar, just to get out from under Marc Frederick's thumb.

The Manor housed dozens of people, and dozens more might come through on any given day. Dorilian ignored them all. Those men who sought him out—overweening local nobles and ambitious merchants—he turned away. Instead, he spent hours perusing books in libraries or wandering the Manor's seemingly endless gardens or collections. Alone. His Malyrdeon kin, he quickly noted, stayed away, leaving him no companions aside from Jonthan or the King— and he dreaded the day he should become desperate enough to seek that man out for company.

As promised, Dorilian spent an hour or two a day with the King and found that to be all he could stomach. He joined Marc Frederick for most meals, during which he endured not only the monarch's barbaric foods and wines but also his discordant Esseran accent and broad humor. Marc Frederick liked to tell jokes and hear them, even from his servants, who fed quips to him as readily as they did bread and meat. Dorilian had not seen this same casualness toward the King at Dazunor-Rannuli or Stauberg. It was peculiar to this place, to this house and these servants who were different from all other servants he had known. Dorilian dismissed them, of course, but he could not dismiss their King. The man compelled him to talk by sheer force of personality, though their conversation mired in formality and they more often resorted to chess, facing each other across the board in silence. It was not that Marc Frederick was uninteresting, only that Dorilian wanted him to be. The effort of feigning disinterest in his host was becoming a strain. The King would make observations to which Dorilian wanted to respond, and he found himself fighting his impulse to engage the point. Passivity did not suit his temperament, and his own restrictions on interaction proved more galling than the empty freedoms the King granted.

Jonthan's invitation to get out of the Manor could not have found more fertile soil.

It had been Jonthan's idea to exploit Dorilian's interest in horses. For one thing, it was an interest Jonthan shared. For another, it would get his father's guest out of the house. After barely a week, the battle of wills was already so tense that it made the staff nervous. Making Dorilian feel less like a prisoner was critical and, fortunately, Marc Frederick agreed.

Machon, Archon of Penrhu, looked a lot like his horses: white-maned and a bit long of face. His family was an old one living off ancient wealth, of which his estate was a fabled portion. For hundreds of years, the green, rolling land had served as a breeding ground for equine royalty. The finest racing blood coursed through the veins of Machon's horses, and also the finest war stock. The resulting animals were without peer: clever, sound, beautiful, and fast as the wind. Felarro of myth might well have sprung from Penrhu's herd. Machon greeted his guests amiably and, if he felt intimidated by the company, he hid it well. He personally oversaw showing a brace of brood mares in which Dorilian took interest.

"He rides marvelously." Machon's gaze followed Dorilian as the Sordaneon Heir put the second of the horses through her paces. She was an unusual choice, not as immediately impressive as the other, but she moved like silk unfurling in the wind.

"He does everything marvelously." Jonthan had become nearly as much a student of the young prince as his father. "Everything, that is, except obey."

"Ah. Well, we wouldn't want that." The old man cocked his head with a smile. "I understand he owns excellent horses. Old bloodlines. Posani dams and Dinsura sires—very fast."

"Talk with him. He's not always as difficult as people say. And he does love horses."

"Yes, I can see that. See how she moves for him, the way her neck bows, and her strides are soft and even. There's no tension in her. He has her completely at ease."

Dorilian rode the mare up to the waiting men and dismounted, staying with the horse and stroking her neck until the groom arrived. They watched as she walked away, observing the splendid sway of her hind end with its fall of white tail.

"I wish to buy her," he told Machon. "My stable could use new bloodlines. I plan to breed her to my top racer, Sural."

Machon immediately stiffened. "If that is to be the case, I will not sell her to you. That horse is a demon. He savaged two mares brought to him to cover."

"There are ways to make sure—"

"He's also savaged several men—handlers and riders. He's a killer."

"I've ridden him myself."

The breeder's mouth firmed. "You can ride anything. The horse savages other horses. He tears the flesh from men's bones, tramples them when he can. You want to breed *that* into my mare line?"

"He outruns everything on four legs. I want the speed."

"And for what? A line of fiends that cannot be mastered or ridden hardly betters the breed."

"That's your goal, not mine. I breed horses to win."

Jonthan noted the way Dorilian answered Machon's challenges simply and directly. In one narrow matter—horse breeding—Dorilian conceded the other man to be an equal.

"Bring your stallion up here," Jonthan suggested. He jumped at a way to extend the breach, however small, the day had made in Dorilian's self-imposed isolation. By the ensuing lack of refusal, he could tell Dorilian would agree. He addressed Machon's doubtful look. "Why not see him for yourself, Machon? Sural can stand at stud at Gustan. Perhaps Prince Dorilian would let you oversee the breeding should you choose to sell the mare. I know how attached you get to your horses."

Machon waved him off, though the statement was too true to deny. "I tell you, the beast is savage. But it is true I would like to see him. Would you be willing to bring him to Essera, Thrice

Royal?" For the first time, he referred to his visitor formally. "Better yet, perhaps you would agree to run him in a race? One of your kinsmen in Kyrbasillon swears he has the horse to beat him."

"Truly?" Dorilian smiled ever so slightly.

"Indeed. A splendid beast of similar distance and running style to your own. The horses share sire blood in the broodmare lines. In fact, they share common dams two generations back in the sire line also—"

The youth nodded, though something about that controlled Sordaneon smile told Jonthan that Dorilian was interested in things other than the fine points of his horse's pedigree.

Daimonaeris received her brother on a stone barge in the Viridian River, so called because of its clear green waters. Contained entirely within the Serat, the river was born in the Temple of Falls and wandered past gardens and princely residences before emptying into a lagoon from which it spilled spectacularly over the Serat's towering wall. The lagoon's restful banks offered plantings of rare lilies, hyacinths, and orchids, as well as stands of fragrant shrubbery. The Eagle Barge, itself a sculpture of highest fantasy, bore the shape of an eagle skimming the water, carrying a pavilion upon its back. Its stone wings spanned a lily pool poised on the edge of the sky. Fish of every color flitted through the shallow water and leaped in brilliant rainbows at the eagle's talons. Daimonaeris enjoyed the Barge's privacy, which she had first discovered as Deben's guest. Months ago, he had given her leave to use it to entertain her visitors.

"You can see everything from here—the entire City." She drew Nammuor along one wing to the narrow place at the tip where they could look out across the glorious buildings of the City's heart. A series of deep thrums drew their gazes toward the center, where a Rill *charys* glided into the collecting arms of the immense white terminal. Throngs of people moved about the steps and landings of that structure like so many ants. Nammuor watched them with more than passing interest.

"This can be yours—all of it—if you wish for it to be," he said.

"I want only Mormantalorus, the warm stone of the Fire Vales, and the Grotto of Ferns. I want none of this sunbaked beauty so far from the sea." Just the thought made her wistful.

"What if I tell you I want it? All this sunbaked beauty?"

"Take it, then, if you wish, and welcome to it. This country's men are burned brown and fixated on gold, and the women watch me as if I were some strange, fragile bird whose habits they do not understand." She gazed unhappily at the white jewel of a city within its crescent of lake, despising everything about it. "You could have found me a better husband, or at least one who was a man. Dorilian is a foul-tempered, willful, self-indulgent *child*."

"You may not have to endure him much longer." To the hopeful swing of her eyes, he said, "Your unfortunate husband is nothing short of a captive to his Stauberg-Randolph hosts. Who knows but they may come to prefer him that way. Marc Frederick has made good use of captives before."

"Don't you dare protest it," she warned.

"Not protest? Why, I would be remiss if I did not. My sister's husband? Of course, I am outraged. Just as Deben is. However, neither of us will bring any real pressure to bear. I spoke with Deben earlier. He expressed little urgency to get his son back."

Daimonaeris and Nammuor exchanged knowing smiles. They, and she especially, had been much closer to Deben in the last few years than his often-absent son. Indeed, Deben seemed to forget whose wife she was. He engaged her ear often in lengthy complaints about being cursed with an ambitious, ungrateful Heir. He bemoaned how Dorilian trumpeted his own exploits, freely threw gold to the winds, and dangerously provoked other nations at every opportunity, leaving his father to smooth ruffled feathers and silence rattling swords. Recognizing another who disliked Dorilian as much as she, Daimonaeris had engaged the Hierarch as an ally.

"I hope Dorilian stays there. I hope they put him in chains." She meant it with all that was in her.

"I somewhat doubt Marc Frederick is going to do that. There is Malyrdeon plotting in this, or I do not know the breed. And believe me, sweet sister, I do know the breed—very well. Did I not understand your father's plans for me?" Nammuor placed a foot on the low wall and leaned over it, looking out again at the Rill. She wondered what he was thinking as those flowing structures caught the bright light of midday. More deep thrums sounded as this time a *charys* sped south, toward Hestya. "We can use this interlude. Turn Deben even more against his son."

"You think I have not been doing that?"

"Not as I now intend it. Dorilian has nearly outlived his usefulness to us."

"He was never of use to me."

Again, Nammuor laughed. She loved the sound of her brother's laughter, the way it folded the very World around his purposes. "Ah, but Deben still needs him. He needs his Heir to keep his enemies at bay, and for many reasons that young man serves his purposes well. Since Hestya, even more so. Essera has only to look upon Dorilian to wish Deben a long and secure reign. They fear Dorilian's warlike tendencies, his impetus to battle. So let us make him truly superfluous—and then get rid of him."

She laughed. It was the height of hubris, of sacrilege and the flouting of gods, to talk about killing one of the Sordaneons in the very palace that was their ancestral home. To speak such words within sight of the mighty Rill itself!

"How?" It was all she really wanted to know. Over the past several months, she had imagined dozens of ways Dorilian might die, all humiliating and well-deserved.

"Patience, little fire jewel. We have our spies in place, do we not? We will be able to move when the time is right. Just remember the prize." Placing his hands upon her shoulders, Nammuor turned her so she looked out upon the same sights as he. Standing at her back, he leaned his head alongside hers, his voice caressing her ear as he showed her Deben's domain and the Rill structures at its heart. "That is what we want, and what we shall have. But there is only one way to get it. Not the way of the Seven Houses, those clumsy gluttons, trying to force their gods into servitude by constructing prisons within palaces—but the way of the Highborn themselves."

She tasted fear, then, knowing his meaning and gazing upon a destiny for which she had steeled herself. "Our blood, with theirs."

"Their blood, to be ours."

Her lips parted the better to taste the clear, bright air. "You want his child?"

"I want his heir. I want his inheritance. I want Teremar's gold and Sordan's glory—and *that*." He fixed her eyes upon the Rill. "My power grows, Daimonaeris. It grows, and it hungers. There is power in the Sordaneons, Sister, great and ancient power even *they* dare not awaken. They fear their god more than they fear their enemies. They fear being inhuman. I do not."

He released her, and she stumbled two steps away from him, struck by the longing she saw in his gaze. She had seen that look before in the glow of the fire caves, watching as his mages filled *lr* crystals with energy from the molten core. She had seen him gazing out to sea while sheets of lightning raced across the waves at his command. Her brother's hunger for power and that of the Diadem he sometimes wore were indistinguishable, as was the godlike sway he held over their people.

"I have to wait." For once, she was glad of her husband's youth. "I have to wait until Dorilian is old enough. Maybe he'll be interested in women then."

"You could seduce any man, even one of stone."

Of her sexual powers, Daimonaeris had no doubt. Of her ability to seduce Dorilian, on the other hand, she had many. How often had she flinched from the spikes of his personality? For now, at least, she need not put herself to that test. Unnerved by the way her brother's heated gaze followed her every move, she walked back along the curve of the stone wing, back to the shaded pavilion and its comforts. The servants had spread a repast for them.

"You are thinking too narrowly, Sister." Nammuor lowered his tall body onto the silken cushions and stretched there with all the golden, feline control of a predator. Luxury suited him. "I want Dorilian's *heir*. The child need not be *his* son."

Her heart beat faster as she saw the working of his mind. "He would never—"

"Naturally, we will have to be clever. We will need an accomplice, of course. Deben already believes his son is too ambitious, willful, and dangerous. He is right. Dorilian has humiliated his father by falling into Marc Frederick's hands, indeed by consenting to play lapdog at the barbarian's feet. It eats at Deben's pride to know Sordan's Heir is an ornament at his enemy's court." Nammuor plucked a sugar feather from a sweetmeat fowl and popped it onto his tongue. "Deben resents everything about Dorilian: his inheritance, his popularity, his successes, and his freedom. He would think it a sweet victory indeed to see his son divested of all these things. It might be sweeter yet if Deben could snatch away the young fool's very legacy."

"Dare we attempt it?"

"Deben finds you alluring, does he not? Whenever you're near, his eyes follow your every move. He invents occasions simply that he might enjoy your company."

She could hardly deny it. Lifting her goblet, she smiled across it. "He gets wistful when he notes I am so often alone, and my husband does not keep me company."

"He would probably set afire the walls with jealousy if ever Dorilian took you for his wife in earnest."

The very thought made her shudder. "I would not put those fires out."

Nammuor studied her with amusement. "Your husband is not hideous, fire jewel. Shadowed by lesser blood, yes, but not ugly. He's growing into his looks. Women will eventually find his appearance as appealing as his lineage. Be wary."

She eyed him venomously. "I will not have to—if we are rid of him."

He laughed and reached for another sugar feather, this time choosing a different color and flavor. "A year he has promised, so a year shall we have. Let us work on the father, then, and attend to the timing. Deben's single vice in women is that he prefers young virgins. And thanks in part to your reluctant husband, sweet Sister, you have done a splendid job of keeping your temple pristine."

# 31

Sounds of steel clanging against steel drifted from the training hall of the Manor barracks. The soldiers guarding the King held weekly contests in the hall, a series of demonstrations and displays of prowess with various weapons. This week was to be swords, the next to be the bow. Marc Frederick acknowledged the men who greeted him and took a seat with Gareth Morgen at his customary place on the end of the benches, seeking not to disturb the contests in progress. He never missed Jonthan's matches.

Jonthan, not he, had informed Dorilian of the contest. As Marc Frederick had hoped, the Sordaneon prince sat on the sidelines to watch Jonthan compete. The two young men spent some of each day together, mostly riding. According to Jonthan, Dorilian rode superbly and for the last week had been helping him practice at *pelekys*. Every year at this season, Jonthan hosted games between his team and those of local Glainoi Lords.

Marc Frederick wasn't surprised that his son was having more success at bonding with their reluctant guest. The two younger men had much in common. Not only had they each been born to rule their nations someday, but they also issued from lineages thick with non-Staubaun ancestors and neither would ever pass as pure Staubaun. Though twelve years separated their births, both bore the same royal burden of expectations, questions, and hopes. However fervently Marc Frederick wished he could get Dorilian to open up to him—to get to know this young enemy in whose still-growing body and latent abilities resided so much promise and hope—he could not force the youth to accept him.

Each pair of combatants vied for a set time governed by a sand clock. The arms master filled a bucket with sand and placed it on a stand, allowing the grains to pour onto a scale through the bucket's bottom. When the scale tipped, a banner dropped down to signal the match was ended. The fighter delivering the most touches in that time period was the victor. Men could ask for a half bucket or full. So far, the matches had gone well. Jonthan, after taking his first opponent, lost to a guardsman of twenty years' service who welcomed the chance to move on and win the gold purse. Although more skilled than most men, Jonthan had not honed his mastery of weapons to the same extent as his father had. He had not needed such skill and had never served in the front line of battle. Rising, Marc Frederick went to join his son near the racks, where he stood divesting himself of the protective armor each combatant wore. Another contest was already underway.

Seeing Dorilian standing alone to one side, Marc Frederick placed himself at his shoulder. "What do you think?" he asked.

Dorilian showed no surprise at his being there. "About what?"

"My son's swordsmanship."

"That? Tutto would dismiss him for incompetence. He reacts slowly and falls into set patterns."

At last, an honest answer. They watched while Jonthan, who was laughing with one of his friends, slipped one arm and then the other into his velvet shirt and coat.

"I tell him that. If he doesn't concentrate, he resumes the same position. Any competent swordsman would knock him off his legs." Marc Frederick nodded to the practice floor. "Why don't you get out there? Demonstrate some of your technique?"

"I'm not a trained animal. I don't put on shows."

"I'm not talking about a show." Marc Frederick picked up the demonstration weapon Jonthan had set aside and tossed it to the young man. By reflex, Dorilian caught it neatly, his hand closing about the hide-wrapped hilt. "Just be less of a spectator."

"You know why I cannot!" He glared back in disgust. "Are you going to force one of these men to raise a weapon against me—knowing he will face death if he does?"

Jonthan and his companions were now attending the royal contention. Jonthan had told Marc Frederick that morning about Dorilian's dilemma in finding a sparring partner.

"Hardly. No man will lift a weapon against you here—no man but me." It would be reckless to allow any man to think a Highborn prince was fair game. Not even Jonthan could be allowed to demonstrate such disregard. As King, however, wearer of the Leur's

Ring and Ergeiron's Crown, anointed ruler of the Malyrdeons and the Royal North, Marc Frederick dared. "Humor me. It's been ages since I've had a good fight."

"You want me to fight *you*?" Dorilian looked as if he could not believe he was getting the opportunity. Already the youth was assessing him, seeing an older man, a slower man... a barbarian and an enemy. It would not have surprised him to hear Dorilian call for real battle swords.

"Yes, me." Pleased at how his suggestion had been received so far, Marc Frederick shrugged out of his heavy jacket of velvet and leather. He had come prepared. His shirt was of wool, and his pants the same leather pair he often wore out of doors. He wore ordinary but splendidly crafted boots and a sturdy belt of rich brown leather. Dorilian was dressed comfortably but more formally, the studied elegance of a prince for whom appearances always mattered. Gesturing to Gareth, whom he had cued to his plan, Marc Frederick caught the practice weapon the man tossed to him. "Shall we?" he prompted and hoisted the sword, testing its weight and balance. It was his practice weapon, mimicking the qualities of the sword he used for battle, and he used it often. He could only pray that his familiarity with it would offset the younger man's agility and speed.

Dorilian hesitated, eyes narrowed and glinting. "You think you can best me?"

"Full bucket or half?" Marc Frederick asked, granting his opponent the choice.

"Full."

Noting that they were between bouts, Marc Frederick indicated for Gareth to alert the arms master. Already the onlookers exchanged gawps. Men watching on the benches and the combatants who had just finished their match now took notice of their King and his Highborn guest. Marc Frederick even heard laughter, his soldiers chuckling that the young Sordaneon was about to be bested. He knew better. Spies had kept him abreast of Dorilian's abilities as a fighter. The youth would be agile, skilled, and driven. Marc Frederick lifted his arms as Gareth, ever helpful, belted the padded chest armor about his upper torso.

*If we cannot talk, then we will vie bodily. One way or another, I must become more than the bloodless construct in his mind—flesh and bone, not some vague outline. Only challenges will change his definitions.*

Dorilian, too, had removed his jacket and strapped on protective pads. His body was slim and young, not yet warrior hard but lithe and fit. Even untrained, the Highborn were dangerous foes—and the Sordaneons, with nerves and reflexes so superbly attuned to movement, so at home with trajectories and lines, balance and position, were the most dangerous of all. Marc Frederick had learned this from having had Sebbord as a teacher. But Dorilian might not know that.

A hush fell over the practice arena as they moved onto the floor. Soldiers quieted at more than just seeing their ruler take the stage. They'd seen him do so before. It was common for Marc Frederick to match blades with his son or one of his old friends, men who merited the honor or whose skills he wished to test. But to see one of the Highborn engage in combat, even for practice, was something none of them save Jonthan had ever seen. The arms master hung the bucket onto the stand with a heavy thunk, immediately spilling the first grains of precious time onto the plate beneath. Some wagers were placed early on the King, but that activity came to a halt the moment the combatants made first blow.

Heeding the convention that the fighter of higher rank initiate combat, Dorilian swung first. Men murmured at the perceived affront... then noted the delivery. Sharp, quick, and clean. Expecting as much, Marc Frederick parried. The youth swept the parry upward and off, feigned a break, then swung again. The movement was liquid, flawless, and would have been deadly against a less seasoned foe. Dorilian did not fight to display but to win.

Marc Frederick had battled opponents like him before, men who moved so fast they could strike two blows to his one. He countered by using his own blade as a barrier between himself and his young foe while still engaging in forward presses, circling for position. Steel rang upon steel, again then again. All the while, Marc Frederick studied his opponent. Though Dorilian moved aggressively, he was not impulsive. The youth's movements conveyed the warrior discipline instilled by Sebbord, who had known what he was raising. He presented no openings in his stances, no opportunities, no weaknesses. In combat, he would be well able to fend for himself.

Having ascertained what he needed to know, Marc Frederick adjusted. He was glad for the Leur's Ring upon his finger and the properties it lent him. He would never be other than an ordinary man, but the device bestowed some Highborn qualities upon his flesh. Though he could not equal the younger man in speed, he saw already that he was faster—his reflexes quicker—than Dorilian had expected. Furthermore, his main disadvantage, that his body was broader and heavier, also worked to his advantage: when his blows landed, they had more weight behind them. He marked each new blow as he parried it, allowing for give and then, without warning, giving too much. Dorilian's blade slipped early off the aborted parry, missing its mark, and Marc Frederick brought his sword sharply up, missing the touch only because the cat-quick youth leaped back. The hawkish look Dorilian shot his way reflected appreciation more than surprise. He, too, was enjoying the test.

*The Sordaneons are physical opponents. Not power alone, but action. Derlon's nature.* Feint. Thrust. Point and turn. They met, and they parted, struck and parried. Men in the arena, at first silent, grasped what they were watching. Cheers rang out on the heels of shouts of encouragement, soldiers rallying to their King. At the same time, they knew that he was also being tested. They remained sure that Marc Frederick would win because he had always won before. He had killed hundreds in battle and had never lost a contest. They groaned at every near miss, Dorilian dodging blow upon blow, and gasped at every thrust with which the youth answered, athletic flurries of steel even they could see were leaving Marc Frederick hard-pressed, his arms giving ever so slightly beneath the assault, his lungs sucking for air.

Dorilian was breathing hard as well. Sweat glistened on his face and darkened the back of his shirt. He moved faster, changing direction like the slicing of cards, but he had yet to land a strike. Marc Frederick's hard counterstrokes and devious parries were taking a toll. As sword met sword, Dorilian's arm took the force of each hit. Stroke after stroke pounded at muscle and bone. Lifting, heaving, and thrusting, the blades growing heavier with every heartbeat. They covered the floor with lunges and flashes of steel, locking blades just long enough to take the measure of the other's pulse pounding in his throat before breaking, circling, determining the next best course of attack.

*Now,* Marc Frederick thought. He had long since ceased to hear the hoarsely shouting soldiers but was relying instead on an innate sense of timing, his long experience at knowing how quickly the bucket emptied. He would not let this hellion of a Sordaneon get the winning blow. For it had come down to that. One hit. Just one. One blow was all he needed. A blow Dorilian, also, was fighting with all his determination and cunning to deliver.

Ignoring the sweat that nearly blinded him, the red-hot tearing of breath from his lungs as the younger man continued to press him, Marc Frederick put all his strength into a parry, a feint, and then the sudden cut that turned Dorilian's sword aside. It was there, just that moment—just that opening. Swinging his weapon swiftly, he struck hard. Something just as hard slammed into his chest, hammering the breath from his lungs so that his knees nearly buckled even as his sword arm encountered resistance. The scale clunked, the banner fluttered down, red as blood but for its ensign of Stauberg-Randolph blue. Both men froze. The soldiers cheered when they saw Marc Frederick's sword rested against Dorilian's neck. Only when the King nodded and moved did they see Dorilian's sword cleanly pressed into Marc Frederick's ribs.

The two locked eyes.

"Even for your kind, mine would be a killing blow." Marc Frederick stepped back, leaving his sword only for a moment on the youth's shoulder, then withdrawing the blade with a warning smile. Even with his neck guard having taken most of the force, Dorilian would have one hell of a bruise to show for the adventure.

"And mine would cut open your heart." Dorilian, too, pulled back his sword.

To the arms master's cautious inquiry, Marc Frederick acknowledged the only possible outcome. "A draw," he declared. He handed his weapon to Gareth, whose look of concern he waved aside. On the benches about the arena, men were settling their bets. Jonthan rushed over, but Marc Frederick indicated that he would say no more until he had caught his breath. He accepted a towel his son handed him and used it to mop his face and neck. He had not had so hard a test since his days on the battlefield. He nourished a deep sense of satisfaction alongside relief that the bout had ended.

For his part, Jonthan turned in wonder to Dorilian, who had simply tossed his weapon in disgust at the arms master's feet. Seeing Dorilian bathed in sweat, his hair out of place, and his breathing quickened was something new. "Where did you learn to fight like that? Amynas himself never wielded a sword so well! I cannot go half the time with my father and not get touched at least twice!"

The youth rubbed where his left shoulder met his neck. Now that he had removed his light armor, all could see the reddened mark the King's sword had left. "That's because he goes easy on you."

"Which you... certainly... did not go on me." Marc Frederick had gotten at least the fight he expected, and more. "I shall feel this for a week." He walked over to the benches to retrieve his jacket. Already he felt the bruise forming over his ribs. Dorilian had spared nothing from that blow. But then neither had he held back in any way from his. He granted the young man a cautious smile. "You're a hell of a swordsman. These men lost their wages betting against you. They won't make that mistake again."

Which had been part of his reasoning all along, and Dorilian now knew it. The King had made his interest clear, as well as his stake.

*This Sordaneon throws himself full measure into anything he undertakes. Other men will follow such a man. I saw it in my soldiers' eyes.*

Dorilian Sordaneon would prove to be an ally worth having—if only he would stop being an enemy.

A man awaited Dorilian at the Manor. A thin brass cylinder locked with Sordaneon codes declared his purpose, and Dorilian received him in the garden beside the pool, an open area where he could be observed and yet conduct his business in personal privacy. He took the courier's package and carefully read the contents of the three sealed cylinders within, each bearing documents and coded correspondence. While the courier waited with statue-like stillness nearby, Dorilian pondered the reports his agents had provided. Nearly two years before, the Seven Houses had indeed received a merchant from Neuberland, from whom they had learned that Stefan Randolph-Erwanson had met by chance with Kheld rebels. They had fostered a relationship with this merchant and, through him, with these same rebels. They had directed the merchant to manipulate the rebels into resuming contact with Stefan at his mines and also at Leseos. Each meeting was carefully documented, for purposes the informants could not ascertain. Dorilian outlined the shadow of the hand pulling that string. Just months prior to Sebbord's murder, two Kheld rebels had gone to Merath, meeting an unidentified Seven Houses contact posing as an arms seller. The day preceding the Sordaneon arrival at the Merrydni city, a barge laden with arms had crossed the Dazun, where Neuberland rebels received its cargo. The gold trail pointed to Stefan only in that he had given them gold. The shadow trail, by far more hidden and intriguing, told quite a different tale.

The Seven Houses had many more reasons than the Khelds to want Sebbord dead. He had presented an obstacle to them and, more than that, a threat. The Khelds were simply crude opportunists. Definitive proof and getting harder evidence on precisely where the killer had gotten the *tullun* blade would take more time and more gold. Dorilian had both and would authorize that expenditure before the courier left again in the morning.

Discovering that Stefan had played an unsuspecting role in Sebbord's murder failed to surprise Dorilian only because he had already reached that conclusion on his own. The Stauberg-Randolphs were... *bewildering* was the only word for it. They were a strange mix of honor and single-minded purpose ruled by diverse ambitions. Although Stefan was hostile and divisive, Marc Frederick was different: strong-willed, a formidable personality, but not a cold one. And while Dorilian knew Emyli thought him dangerous, it was just as clear that Jonthan did not. Not once had the King or his son indicated anything but total confidence in him. His word held him all the faster for their belief in it. He had even wondered, a few times, if he would be able to act against them once his year was up.

Dismissing the courier, Dorilian rolled the papers into one cylinder, which he tucked into his belt. He had to be careful now. The full scope of the cartel's plan had meant to ensnare not only him, by prompting him to seek vengeance, but also the Stauberg-Randolphs and the Khelds. Learning the whys of *that* would be fascinating.

He did think of one thing he could do to redress the destruction he had caused by acting upon the cartel's lies: he would order his mining agents in Randpory to close one of his striated ore mines in Lower Tollech, with the mine's distiller to be made available discreetly and without his name mentioned to Stefan Stauberg-Randolph. He needed neither the mine nor its equipment—and the distiller would keep Stefan gainfully occupied in Orqho's hills.

He looked up at the strange, foreign house with its hundreds of windows and as many eyes. Day by day, it became more apparent that Marc Frederick was taking extraordinary care never to lie to him. Every answer, to any question, was the unvarnished truth. Either that or the King would refuse to answer, or say he did not know. It was, Dorilian reflected, a standard to which he himself adhered but which few outside his race cared to maintain. The bizarre fact remained that he could, so far, trust any answer Marc Frederick gave him.

But did he really want to start asking the Stauberg-Randolph King more and better questions?

# 32

Stefan and Cullen rode up the lane to shouts of greeting and surprise. There had been no announcement of their coming, but their reception was festive. Garlands decked the Manor, and evergreen branches twined with winter flowers hung in swags over doors and scalloped lintels. Even the magnificent oaken banisters of the house's many staircases were festooned with greenery. Marc Frederick loved celebrating the Winter Solstice, and so did the scores of Manor-born staff whose holiday this also was. Kheld and Staubaun celebrations of the Solstice were far more solemn affairs. Only at Gustan Manor did the reborn year find such a happy welcome.

"Prince Stefan! Cullen Thegn! What a joy to see you." Gareth acknowledged them with one of his rare broad smiles. "Your grandfather and uncle are in residence, Sir, and I shall notify them at once. Is your Lady Mother coming also?"

"Not this time, Gareth," Stefan said. He'd spent two days at Rhodhur with his mother and brother. Emyli was holding to her plan of spending the year in Amallar, although she had sent gifts and warm greetings to her father and Jonthan. "She's giving Hans a Kheldish Solstice this year."

"A shadow on our days, then, because we will miss the lad." Gareth waved away the curious, most of whom were household staff peering around doors. "Sir." He acknowledged Jonthan and then excused himself as the Prince gave Stefan a sturdy clap on the shoulder.

"Stefan! And Cullen too! I thought you both were still in the field."

Stefan handed his gloves and outerwear to the maid standing by to take them. Cullen also gave over his cloak. "I would have been, but I had the most amazing luck. You heard that I found a distiller?"

"In Leseos. We got your message. Father and I couldn't be more pleased. A bit of a surprise, finding one so quickly."

"A *good* one! I have to get it to Orqho and run tests. We can be up and running as soon as I get enough men. I've got folk working on that. But Jonthan, I must talk with you. The potential of the mine is double now."

"Double?"

"You think I'm exaggerating—I'm not. It's a higher capacity distiller, and it can refine out some of the trace metals." Stefan followed Jonthan into the library, wishing he did not need to exchange useless pleasantries. Things were happening, and he wanted to cut to the chase. But Cullen was standing right here beside him. No matter how much his uncle or grandfather might consider Cullen *almost* family, he wasn't—and raising issues of family finances with Cullen in the room would be a sure way to lose Jonthan's much needed ear. He decided to address a different problem. "I suppose Dorilian is still hanging around the place?"

"It's only been two months. Do I need to keep the two of you apart?"

"Probably," Cullen said under breath. He shrugged as Stefan shot him a warning look and settled onto one of the deep, upholstered sofas, where he picked up a slight tome resting on the nearby table.

"I'm not going to be here long," Stefan assured his uncle. He wasn't planning to stay more than a day or two.

"Long enough to ride a game of *pelekys*, I hope," Jonthan said. "I've scheduled a match two days from now."

Across the room, Cullen raised his head eagerly.

"I don't know." Stefan hadn't planned on staying past the gift giving.

Jonthan clapped Stefan again on the shoulder. "We'll talk. Ionais is here for the festivities, and I promised her a private evening, which I must deliver or be called a sorry excuse for a husband. Let's go riding in the morning, just you and I."

Stefan dined with Cullen in Emyli's suite of rooms, in which he still kept a bedchamber. The two young men flirted ardently with a couple of the younger maids, only to have that pleasant pastime interrupted by a knock on the door. The maids blushed and bowed and nearly ran out the service door when Marc Frederick entered the room.

"Must I ask Gareth to issue a warning about you two?" The King embraced Stefan and exchanged a hand clasp with Cullen, then looked them over, his gaze warm. "You look good. Both of you."

"It's easy to stay healthy when we're not under attack."

"Yes. It so happens I have good news on that front. Sit, both of you." They all took seats on sofas arranged near the carved hearth and its crackling fire. "My new governor in Neuberland tells me the local lords have agreed to accept an annual tithe from unchartered Kheld villages in return for allowing them to settle their lands. They have also agreed to help fight incursions by outlaws intent on killing or trafficking in Kheld settlers. It's a fragile arrangement, but for now, the region is peaceful."

"For now."

"Now is the only moment over which any of us have much control. I aim for tomorrow as well, however."

"Is the governor here?" Stefan wished his grandfather had chosen a Kheld to serve in Neuberland instead of yet another Staubaun aristocrat like Sinon Kouranos.

"Oh, yes. He arrived just this afternoon. I had a most illuminating dinner with him and Sordan's hasty prince."

"Dorilian? You let him sit in on your meeting? He'll take anything he learned and use it against you! Or haven't you noticed he's part of the problem?"

Marc Frederick answered crisply. "That's why he must be part of the solution."

The rest of their conversation was strained. Even telling his grandfather about his success in finding a new distiller failed to bring Stefan joy. After that, nothing felt right, and he slept poorly. Although he knew what his grandfather was trying to accomplish in Neuberland, he didn't see how Dorilian was being punished in any way for his misdeeds. Being forced to live in luxury and enjoy meat and wine while taking part in critical discussions did not strike Stefan as anywhere near harsh enough for the things he knew Dorilian to have done.

*These Highborn are part of the problem, too. All of them. If they do something wrong, they can't be punished. They're above the law.*

The next morning, still brooding over his grandfather's weak solutions, he walked to the stables to join Jonthan for an early ride.

Jonthan, at least, seemed to have his mind on other things—on horses and tack and the *pelekys* game to be played the next day. They rode out from the Manor along the river, following familiar trails past the estate's fallow fields. When they stopped just above the millpond to water their horses, Stefan broached the subject of his need to borrow gold for the Amallar mines.

He had always known that his uncle was Prince of Dazunor and also Heir, through Queen Apollonia, to the Principate of Tahlwent, but Stefan had never before looked to Jonthan as a separate economic resource. Stefan outlined his reasons for not approaching his mother again, or his grandfather, following up with hard numbers of the mine's startup expenses and projected output. He would be able to pay back the loan once he had met the first contract and secured an advance on the next.

Jonthan listened intently, asked a few questions, and then agreed to lend him the monies.

"I want to see this venture succeed as much as you do," he told Stefan. "Khelds argue that they should have the right to simply settle open land, but they have not yet made the most of the land they already have. I would love to point to the Orqho mines the next time any fat-mouthed Lord says Khelds are worthless except as field workers."

On the way back to the Manor, Jonthan took him by the horse breeding sheds. In one of the stallion barns—a square building with four large stalls, each opening onto its own sturdily fenced paddock—Jonthan stopped to admire a horse Stefan had not seen before. The stallion tossed its shapely head and moved nervously about the immense stall, its muscled, powerful body gleaming whiter than moonlight.

"Beautiful, isn't he?" Jonthan spoke with as much pure longing in his voice as Stefan had ever heard there.

Stefan leaned against the stall's outside doorpost and warily eyed the horse. It looked bad-tempered. "He's put together nicely."

"He's put together *perfectly*. Look at his knees, how deep his chest is, how wide his nostrils. He's built for nothing but speed."

He smiled at his uncle's obsession, his worship of the beasts. Jonthan owned many outstanding horses but none that had ever commanded such admiration. "Is he yours?"

Jonthan shook his head. "No."

Stefan knew then to whom the horse belonged. He fought not

to roll his eyes. Dorilian owned everything. Even the horse his uncle wanted.

"Sural," Jonthan said. The word flowed from his tongue as if it were something rare and wonderful. "That's his name. I rode him once, on the track in training. He's a demon's ride, has a mind of his own, but the wind itself cannot outrace him."

What could Stefan say? That it stood to reason that Dorilian Sordaneon would own a vicious, beautiful, and nearly unrideable horse? Stefan, for his part, preferred less high-tempered horses, the kind he could count on to give what he asked them to give. He kept two very good *pelekys* mounts stabled at the Manor and used them only for the game.

Without warning, the stallion charged the stall door. Sural's huge white body slammed into the wooden lower panel where Stefan stood. Startled, Stefan stumbled and fell to the plank floor. Jonthan, too, retreated. Head snaking, Sural trumpeted and reared, his deep-blue hoofs slashing at the wooden posts. Having driven back the humans, he returned to all fours and quickstepped away from the door again, lowering his head to noisily drink from a suspended water trough in one corner.

"Madrock!" Stefan swore, breathing hard. His heart pounded against his ribs. "What the hells—!"

"Are you all right?" Jonthan offered a hand. He pulled Stefan off the floor.

"The beast attacked me!"

"We must have looked too comfortable. Sural fights everything and everyone, including his own groom. Even the stable dog won't go near him."

"And you rode that monster?" Stefan looked upon his uncle with disbelief and new respect.

"Once. I tell you, he runs like lightning. It was like riding wild fire—or maybe a waterfall, white water, just holding on and flowing along with his power." Together they left the barn, abandoning the now-calm stallion to the solitude he preferred. "If you and Cullen would stay for the game tomorrow, it would give our team the edge. I barely have five horsemen."

Leading their horses quietly behind them, they walked back toward the main stable, enjoying the last quiet of morning. The Manor would soon be alive with bustle.

"Then I'll do it, on one condition—that nobody rides *that*

thing!" A game of *pelekys* was dangerous enough without having to play alongside an unreliable horse.

Stefan felt good about his decision. He had not ridden a game in months, and his body needed this. He wanted to throw himself totally into the milling fray, to fight for the ax, and to ride like hell to the post.

Marc Frederick noticed tension expand in the Manor following his remarkable dinner with Sinon Kouranos. The most surprising thing about it was that Dorilian had been a somewhat talkative dinner guest. Caught off guard—because the young man had previously endured their daily meals in near silence—Marc Frederick had decided to see where it led and exercised little censorship over what he allowed his governor to discuss. It helped that Sinon laced the conversation with anecdotes and dry humor, never once talking around Dorilian. Sinon had been forewarned of his monarch's interest in fostering a dialogue. When he'd asked directly for the Sordaneon prince's opinion on Kheld settlement rights, Dorilian had just as directly stated his own perception of the underlying conflict.

"That they seize land and think it theirs is not inconsistent with the example of their rulers," he said.

The condemnation made Marc Frederick wince. Dorilian aimed his barbs with masterful precision. But he had also found the comment revealing: Dorilian's dislike of Khelds was rooted in specific actions, not their race. His stance mirrored his grievances against Essera in general and its rulers in particular—the betrayal and imprisonment of Labran, Essera's plundering of Sordan and the Rill, then Essera's silence at the murders of his mother, grandfather, and his Highborn kin at Gignastha—and a disdain that people who committed such deeds should presume to think they deserved his goodwill.

And of course, Gareth had then come in to announce that Stefan had arrived. The look which had stolen over Dorilian's face— the closure—had spoken volumes.

*He will never forgive Stefan for that day, for kicking him in the face. If I cannot mend that animosity, at least I can keep them apart.*

But Marc Frederick would not keep them apart in his own

house. The place was filled with guests for the holiday. In addition to Sinon, there was Jonthan's wife Ionais and her ladies, and his old friend Kathanos, come just the day before from Gweroyen. Some of Jonthan's friends were visiting, also. There would be activities and diversion enough, and if worse came to worst, he could master two headstrong young men.

"Dorilian pretends I don't exist!" Stefan complained to Jonthan the next day as they harnessed their horses for the match. The *pelekys* saddle—with low horn, grab straps, open cantle, and simple stirrups—afforded riders optimum mobility astride a galloping horse. He cinched the wide girth strap tightly about his horse's broad bay body.

"Let him," Jonthan advised. "Once it gets ridiculous, he'll come around." He kept looking out across the yard, waiting for the rest of his team to arrive. Two of his friends, Myron and Penalus, both spending the week at the Manor, saddled their horses in the next barn. Stefan and Cullen would be the only Khelds. Though dozens could play on a side in *pelekys*, the minimum number of players was five. Royals usually played the minimum to reduce injuries, with reserve riders ready in case a man was lost to the side.

Nearby, Cullen finished saddling a spare horse for Jonthan and a mount for himself. Because *pelekys* horses required years of training and a good mount might cost as much as a fine Glainoi farm, the Kheld youth would be riding one of Stefan's. The other team waited across the field. Beyond the brightly attired riders, spectators gathered on a grassy bank in a wall of movement and color. Jonthan swung onto his horse and cantered across to where his father waited to make his entrance. Ionais, resplendent in fox furs and russet velvet at his father's side, smiled at his approach. Even Dorilian stopped looking bored for a moment.

Jonthan reined in before the royal party and leaned down to speak. "Keralas and Skeron are late. I have five but no reserve. If one of them does not come soon, I may have to forfeit the match."

Marc Frederick looked disappointed. The onlookers included not just the Manor's guests, but visitors from surrounding towns and estates. *Pelekys* games afforded vigorous entertainment, and crowds followed their favorites. All knew the rules, however, and the game demanded that each side field a complete team and a reserve as insurance against forfeited matches. The other team had eight mounted men.

Dorilian stepped forward. "I have a horse trained for this game stabled here, and I know how to play." He spoke with complete confidence.

"You?" Ionais snickered. "Why would you do that? So you can get your hands on an ax?"

Jonthan interceded before Dorilian could bite her head off. "This isn't practice," he said. "And you might not get to play at all. You would stand in reserve."

The young man shrugged. "The rules require that you have a rider *ready* to play, not *that* he plays."

Jonthan hesitated. It was not only that he had never seen Dorilian ride in a game; it was a matter of *who* he was. And yet... this game mattered. The other riders were longtime rivals who matched their boasts with hefty wagers. They called themselves the Golds, not because their uniforms were so colored, but because gold was what they won. To lose by forfeiture would cost him far more than his pride, especially when the other team need never learn the identity of his sixth rider. As Dorilian correctly pointed out, his presence alone would qualify the team.

Tempted, Jonthan looked to his father, who also attended their young guest closely, assessing the offer. With only five other men at hand and injuries not uncommon, there remained a chance that Dorilian might find himself called into the game or the game thrown in any event if Jonthan would not allow him to enter. *Pelekys* was a far less controlled situation—horses, men, the heavy flying mass of the ax—than a fight with practice swords. And with Stefan also riding in the game—

"Go," Marc Frederick decided. "In reserve."

Dorilian simply nodded and ran toward the stable.

Heartened to have this chance to play, Jonthan grinned thanks to his father and turned, spurring his mount across the field to let the other team know he had found a rider and could field a team. He then rode to inform his teammates. Though prepared for their responses, the alarm that met his decision surprised him. "He's standing in reserve," he assured them. "Just that, so the other side will see we have someone who can ride. He won't be on the field unless one of you boneheads gets hurt."

"He's not riding that crazy horse, is he?" Stefan wanted to know.

"No. He'll be riding a trained horse, one of his own. They play *pelekys* in Teremar, you know. I've ridden with him in practice. It's not like he doesn't know how to play."

"But a Sordaneon?" Myron, who would be riding point beside Jonthan, blew a breath from behind his teeth. "The Highborn are not fair targets, Jon. That kindred will have our damn heads if he gets hurt!" He inclined his head toward the other team. "Do they know?"

"No. I didn't tell them. I didn't want them to demand we forfeit just because they would be afraid to hit him if he got in the game. The way I look at it, he won't get in the game."

"Jon—"

"Do you want to play, or don't you? Our other option is to forfeit."

Penalus grumbled that his wagers were too hefty to lose. Stefan looked worried and Cullen even more so. But none wished to just hand the match to the other team, and they all wanted the Glainoi team to play the game as it was meant to be played, full out.

Jonthan set his jaw and picked up the reins. Over on the far side of the field, Dorilian approached wearing the *pelekys* jacket and quilted trousers he kept in the stable for practices. His sturdy, plains-bred mare pricked her ears and quickened her powerful legs, restively sensing the game about to take place, unsuspecting that she would never get to run.

As soon as the reserve rider reined in at the designated side, Jonthan took his team onto the field.

Dorilian lifted his head at the hoarse yells that signaled the start of the game. To the thunder of hoofs and a resounding roar from the crowd, both teams charged for the ax that hung from the post at the blue end of the field. He had dismounted upon reaching the side and donned a tabard with the Prince's colors. He now stood beside his horse, his attention fixed on the moving mass of horses and men. Jonthan reached the post first and grabbed the ax, or *pelek*, before turning his horse about the wooden post and spurring it to charge upfield.

The *pelek* consisted of a shining double blade and heavy red leather-wrapped shaft, its end widened and lightly weighted for balance. Although a *pelek* could be deadly, dull blade edges ensured that no player in recent memory had suffered an amputation. A blow from the ax could, however, break a bone or crack a skull. After getting hold of it, a rider's main goal was to outrace all pursuers and crack the ax against the other team's pole, or *herm*. The first team to score three cracks against the opposing team's *herm* won the match.

The match might last hours, Dorilian decided soon after the first exchange. The other team, wearing gold, their horses decked with sturdy leather trappings and high-backed saddles, played hard and quickly recovered the *pelek*. Jonthan's blue team, quicker and able to harry the opponent's larger horses and riders like bees, rode the Golds around the post. Jonthan's riders kept the *pelek*-bearer from passing off midfield. Dorilian frowned. Though fast and agile, the Prince's side did not match up physically with the other team. Furthermore, it was overmatched for experience. Stefan and Cullen rode wing, running interference for the three more experienced players. Whenever the other team snatched the ax, crowding Jonthan and his nose men close, the young Khelds pounded the sides, herding the ax-wielder back toward the core riders.

And every time, a gold rider would anticipate the move, lurking just outside the fray.

Not everything pointed to failure. What Jonthan lacked in swordsmanship, he more than made up in horsemanship. Dorilian noted how the Prince's long legs assured both his balance and steering astride his quick, dodging horse, while freeing his hands to grapple for or carry the ax. And Stefan also had solid riding skills. He kept his seat even when his horse turned on a knife's edge.

"Ride!" Shouts from the sidelines burst over the field in a roar whenever a rider broke free, the ax clutched in his hand.

"Eye on the side, not the *pelek*!" One of the King's grooms, standing with Dorilian's horse, yelled at the heedless riders. Together they watched Jonthan's side execute a flawless screen, the Prince and one of his flankers getting their horses between their ax-bearing comrade and the opposing riders. The gold riders crowded close, and one knocked a defender's horse nearly to its knees.

"He's a bully," the groom said. Dorilian had also been studying the man in question, a big, hard-riding Staubaun who repeatedly ran his dapple-gray gelding into his opponents. "Name's Aleistes.

Terrifying good stealer. But he favors running left, you see. Watch next time he gets the ax."

Dorilian watched the blue team score, Jonthan swinging the ax against the other team's herm. The first crack of the game resounded through the crisp cold air.

The gold team got the ax with the remaining horses waiting at midfield, and the contest was on again. A few charges and tangles later, Aleistes outraced Cullen's defense to slam sidelong against the blue team's ranger, from whom he wrested the ax. Then, using the other man's horse as a screen, the stealer turned for a clean run up the field. Though Jonthan and Stefan both emerged from the pack to harry him, he pushed through for a clean crack at the herm.

The crowd chanted support as Aleistes handed off the *pelek* then rode his horse in a prance onto the field.

But Dorilian now knew his weakness. He plotted out the next two courses, following the action closely—not for possession of the ax but movement of the sides. Both sides favored the midfield, although the surface nearest the stands was firmer and faster. He noted, too, that the bully's horse was not the only one that turned more quickly and powerfully to the left than it did to the right, a lazy habit of riders who carried the *pelek* in their right hands. Both teams relied on muscle over speed, under-utilizing the wings. Stefan's horse, though its top speed was less than those ridden by the rangers and stealers, accelerated more quickly. The Kheld youth weighed less and rode down nearer his horse. Both Khelds did, but Cullen looked clumsy compared to Stefan, who crouched tight over his mount's shoulder. When several horses pressed together, Stefan got free sooner than the others.

*If I were riding, I would drive the gold team off the side.*

Dorilian's mare tensed and pulled on the rein, head tossing impatiently when the sides thundered past, hoofs throwing up clods of turf and grit.

Jonthan's team scored again to cheers from the crowd. Taking the *pelek*, all five gold riders charged to the right from the midfield and tried to clear a path, but the defenders cut the screen and trapped the point rider in a swirl of horseflesh and shoving men. Whips brandished as weapons slashed above men's heads. Though friends off the field, they were not above elbows and blows when on. Penalus, the largest man on Jonthan's side, yanked the *pelek* from the trapped man's hand and urged his horse into the open, only to be caught between two of the other team's riders. Back and forth the riders waged, Penalus unable to escape the press of gold defenders. The crowd roared when Aleistes emerged, the *pelek* in his grasp.

Yells and curses broke from the field as the horses moved in a line again, this time toward the blue *herm*. The bully's gray horse dodged free of the churning pack. Cullen spurred to cut him off. Onlookers heard the sound of the horses colliding amid shouts and squeals. Aleistes charged toward the *herm*, and Cullen followed at top speed, leading the pursuit. The Kheld slammed his mount into the gray horse again as they reached the post, bumping it away from the post, but the bully held ground. Aleistes' gray horse reared and twisted, coming up high over the Kheld's shoulder and landing hard against the smaller horse's side. The beast pitched to its knees. Cullen clung to his falling horse's neck. Aleistes urged his mount forward to the post and swung, the ax cracking against heavy wood.

Whoever made the next point took the game.

"Take it!" one of the blue riders shouted. Cullen's horse had regained its footing, and it was Cullen's job to take the *pelek* back into play.

"I can't!" The shout held a desperate note.

Dorilian snapped to attention as Jonthan turned his horse and joined his Kheld teammate, who was now bent over in the saddle, clutching at his leg. Cullen kept one foot in the stirrup but the other, the left, dangled. A moment later, the scorekeeper summoned a mounted groom from the blue side to lead the injured rider from the field. The scorekeeper then signaled to the side that the reserve rider come in.

Dorilian grasped the saddle and swung onto his horse. The groom dropped his hand, freeing the reins to Dorilian as Jonthan rode up, pulling up sharply.

"Cullen's hurt."

"I saw."

"You don't have to do this. I appreciate—"

"You want to win, don't you? Well, I'm a better rider than he is."

"But you have to ride the *pelek* in—"

"I know how to do that."

"I know you do. It's just that—" Jonthan glanced over his shoulder toward the scorekeeper, who was waving them in. The gold side had taken position on the field and looked impatient. "My men know you're Highborn; the others don't. They'll be aiming their horses at you—and whips and elbows, too."

But Dorilian had already considered that. Lifting his head with excitement, he gazed out at the field. "It's just a game, right? They act without malice. I pardon them all in advance, including the horses." He hefted the ax in his hand. Its weight commanded action. "You need only one score. I will make this painless."

"Painless?"

"Leave it to me."

The roar from the spectators, at first jubilant as Dorilian rode out onto the field, grew strangely quiet as rumor rippled through the stands. Marc Frederick could have stopped the game, perhaps had even thought of doing so, but by the time Dorilian's horse reached the blue post, the Sordaneon Heir knew the King would not deny him this chance to play. He grinned. All he owed Jonthan was a win.

*Pelek* in his right hand, Dorilian waited at the post only until Jonthan had reached the midline. He then held his arm straight out before him, just above his head, the ax displayed with its broad blades glinting. The gesture caught all eyes—and captured those of the other riders as well. Those eyes followed the gleaming arc as Dorilian brought the *pelek* down and dug his heels hard into his horse's flank.

His sturdy mare drove in a straight line at the center, Dorilian crouched flat over her neck and shoulders. His unexpected break ahead of the screen caught them nearly as much by surprise as his horse's speed—and nearly as much as the beast's sudden cut to the right. Ears flattened to her head, the compact mare skimmed past the startled first riders and raced toward the side. The bully's gray horse charged to cut him off. Muscular legs pounding, hoofs throwing up grass, the horses converged. Just before they collided, Dorilian tugged the rein. His horse eased a step—just barely that—and passed to the outside. The defender was now on his left. Stefan, he knew, was on his right.

Stefan was the *only* man on his right.

He caught the dark-haired youth's look of surprise, then grim determination. Stefan dug his feet into the stirrups and swung down with the whip, his bay giving him more speed. As Dorilian had planned, Stefan was no longer positioned to run interference: he was in line to ride straight to post. And he knew it.

"Give it to me!" Stefan shouted.

Aleistes' gray charged to Dorilian's left, matching him for speed. It would take only a nudge from the big man to slow his mare, allowing the others to catch him. For his plan to work, he needed to get the *pelek* to Stefan before the bully's horse tangled his.

A pass was safer than a throw—and there was only one way to do it that would keep Aleistes from the *pelek* and not cause Stefan to lose ground.

Dropping the reins, he wrapped his left hand securely in the padded grip ring of his saddle and jammed his right foot deep in the stirrup. Shifting his weight fully to the right, Dorilian dropped sideways in the saddle. He grabbed the mare's breast collar with his left hand, crooked his left knee against the saddle's pommel and angled his body outward from the beast's rippling white side and shoulder. So balanced, his extended body flying above the field, he held the ax out toward Stefan.

The crowd roared, on its feet.

Seeing the ax hanging in easy reach beside him, Stefan leaned over and grabbed it. Dorilian watched Stefan's hand close about the wooden shaft behind the blades just before the *pelek* left his fingers. He glimpsed Stefan's heel dig into the bay's laboring side. The horse leaped forward. Done. Dorilian lurched back into the saddle, picked up the reins, and slid his left foot back into the stirrup. Shifting his body's weight again, he signaled his horse to bear hard to the left. Aleistes bellowed as their two horses collided while Stefan spurted past both into open field.

Somewhere on the perimeter, human voices cheered. Dorilian ignored them. He jammed the toe of his boot against the other horse's ribs and eased his tight grip on the reins, giving his mount its head. The mare recovered ground, then ran at the gray again. Aleistes, now furious, swung his whip and tried to break free of the harrying. The whip found Dorilian's face, whistling and then stinging as it sliced across his cheek and jaw. *The bastard!* He shot Aleistes a glare as blood welled and dripped down his face.

The big man laughed. "Wear that, pretty boy!"

But Dorilian refused to get out of the way. He urged his mount forward as his opponent tried to get past—keeping himself between Aleistes and Stefan. When two other gold riders converged, charging toward Stefan and the *pelek*, Dorilian turned his plunging mount sharply to the left, driving the hard-running mare shoulder first into Aleistes' struggling gray, knocking it into the others. All three horses—Aleistes, another gold rider, and Myron, who had been riding hard to ward the second man off—tangled, the bodies of beasts and men colliding and screaming, each jostling to be the one to break first from their collision. At the edge of that knot, Dorilian turned his winded horse upfield.

There was only one man now between Stefan and the post. *Damn you, Kheld, this is your chance. Don't be stupid. Use your horse!*

With nothing left for him to do, Dorilian watched, heart pounding, as Stefan waited until he saw the opposing rider tense—committing to impact—and sharply whipped, asking his horse for more. The experienced beast drove its legs hard and leaped for the finish. Though the defending horse bumped the bay's hindquarters, causing a stumble, Stefan's horse recovered and lunged forward. The crack of the ax sounded above the crowd's roar.

The match was over.

Breathing hard, Dorilian wiped the back of his hand across his jaw and grimaced at the bright red streaks. Curse that Esseran rider! He'd be damned if he would join the others now and let that man gloat at having landed a blow. Nor would he bring censure upon Jonthan by allowing them and the King to see his injury. Riding with Jonthan's side, however briefly, had given him greater pleasure than he'd enjoyed in months. Resolved, Dorilian cantered his horse toward the opposite side of the field, where the blue team's grooms waited.

Two other blue riders, the missing men, had just left their horses and could be seen running across the field to join the Prince's triumphant group.

"Pair of idiots." The groom took hold of Dorilian's horse to help him dismount. "Got themselves tied to their beds by some wenches. Fluff bought off by the Golds, most like. Prince told 'em to sleep in at the Manor, but no... had to take a dip in the other men's pond." The fellow squinted at his face. "Nasty cut, Thrice Royal, Sir. Should get that looked at. Healer's set up at the groundskeeper's."

The man didn't even wait to be dismissed before walking away with his horse. Dorilian watched for a few seconds to be sure the mare was not lame. As for the groom's suggestion that he seek a healer... in a more civilized part of the World, the man would have known he didn't need one. But Dorilian was too worn down by being among barbarians to be offended anymore. And the healer might not be a bad place for him to go. He found the groundskeeper's hovel tucked behind the tool house. Though in good repair, the weathered logs and stone chinking promised few comforts. The door opened to a touch, and he entered. The one unshuttered window, the tarp usually covering it caught back on a nail, let good light and air into the tiny room. A man wearing a thick wool coat over a white healer's tunic sat on a three-legged stool beside a plank bed topped with straw and covered by coarse ticking. Cullen lay there, his trouser leg cut from ankle to hip, leaving his left leg exposed. Bruises bloomed the entire hairy length of it, swelling over the shin, leading to a mottled, badly turned foot. One look at Cullen's cut boot showed why: no reinforcing steel or even wood sewn into the leather.

"I'm busy." The healer barely spared a glance at Dorilian's cut. "Someone in the kitchen can clean that for you." He put a cup back on the room's single table, now laden with vials and pouches.

Dorilian ignored him and walked to the end of the bed, the better to see its occupant. Strands of Cullen's dark hair clung and curled with sweat. Pain glazed the Kheld's blue eyes and paled his lips. "Your leg appears broken."

"It is," the healer confirmed before Cullen could speak. "Now get along and let me tend it."

Dorilian continued to ignore him. To Cullen he said, "Your sacrifice was not in vain. Your team won the match."

"I saw, from the side." Cullen gave him a weak smile. "Where'd you learn to ride like that?"

"Teremar."

"Well, you sure made them sorry they hurt me out."

"They deserve their losses. I hope you wagered on the outcome."

Cullen's eyes widened for a moment. "Sure. Didn't you?"

Dorilian looked out the window. A steady stream of colorfully garbed noblemen and women trekked along the main path back to the Manor. He could still make it back ahead of them, avoiding stares and speculations. "No," he said. "The last time I gambled, I lost."

Stefan poured another cup of wine and stabbed his third slice of boar, the meat dripping clear juices onto the table before he slapped it on his plate. The lodge's silvery, roughhewn walls framed a brace of stone hearths, in front of which the men who had ridden that day shared platters of venison, pheasant, boar, and hare, and ewers filled with rich red wine. The room vibrated with conversation and laughter. None of it was directed at him.

Everyone wanted to talk to the Highborn prince.

He couldn't even make a winning score without Dorilian being the center of attention. Sordaneon this and Sordaneon that, like he was some kind of god. Why? Because a distant ancestor in some long-forgotten past had convinced people that he had a special connection to a *machine*? To the Rill... the fucking world revolved around the Rill. But the Rill did not play *pelekys*... the Rill did not help anyone with anything, except to enrich the same damn Staubaun hierarchy it had kept in power for a thousand years. The more Stefan thought about Dorilian, and the more he drank, the more he felt slighted.

*Dorilian's horse was too slow. If I hadn't demanded he hand me the pelek, we would not have scored. He would've lost it to Aleistes. Then we would be celebrating their victory, not ours.*

So what if Dorilian had taken a cut on the face? The bastard *healed*. Only a few hours later, the cut was not even a shadow on his smug Highborn face. But not one of the Staubaun players had thought to ask about Cullen.

As the night wound on and people rose from the tables to find other conversations, Stefan staggered to his feet and sought Dorilian out. He approached him on the covered walkway leading to the rear of the lodge.

"They think they need you, but I don't," Stefan said. For the first time in five years, he stood in striking distance.

Dorilian dismissed him with a look. "Then don't talk to me."

Stefan grinned, though the expression took more effort than he would have liked. Dorilian was taller now than he was. Muscle layered broader shoulders and longer limbs than those of the boy he'd attacked years ago. This Dorilian looked and moved like a man.

"I got the mines running again." It needed saying—because Dorilian needed to know that his attacks hadn't succeeded. "You couldn't kill me then, and you can't stop me now. I bought another distiller, a better one, and I hired more men. We're refining ore again."

"Good." But when Dorilian tried to move past Stefan, he stepped in front of him.

"You won't stop me from completing my plans."

He wanted Dorilian to back down, to show surprise or even anger. Instead, the other youth stepped closer until Stefan could smell the lingering scent of wood smoke his clothing had picked up indoors and detected the heat radiating off his smooth Highborn skin. Dorilian's body pressed so close that Stefan feared they would touch. Some errant ray of light skimmed the curved surfaces of Dorilian's eyes as they bore into his.

"Is this to be the way of it, Stefan? Then start by realizing that I'm not a fool. I'm not one of your Kheld followers to whom you can tell whatever you would have them believe. I know what you did and did not do in Neuberland. I know where your gold went. It didn't all go to buy seed and wagons and horses: some went to purchase arms, and some of those arms went to the hands of Kheld rebels, even if not the one who killed my grandfather. Don't expect me to believe all your protestations of innocence."

"Fair enough, because I don't believe even one of yours."

"The scales balance. Now leave me alone."

"That's easy enough." He stepped out of Dorilian's way. He tried not to show how powerfully Dorilian's presence disturbed him or how stunned he was that Dorilian no longer held him to blame for old Sebbord's death. "I will be leaving again in the morning. But Cullen is staying because that Staubaun bastard broke his leg. I don't want to hear about you giving him trouble."

"Why would I do that? Five years ago, he was the only one of your gang who didn't kick me."

Stefan controlled a flinch as he remembered the way Dorilian's face had looked after he'd kicked it twice with a metal-toed boot:

jaw distorted, skin torn over one cheek and eye, broken teeth showing white through a mouthful of blood. Nothing remained of those injuries but the smoldering remnants of hatred that burned in Dorilian's eyes. At least that hatred was for him, not Cullen.

"You don't fool me." This was Stefan's family's house, his family's domain, and he was determined to have the last word. "You hate Essera's aristocracy even more than I do. You despise every man with whom you ate bread tonight, every man who toasted you with a goblet of wine. Even my grandfather—though he saved your life—and my uncle, and all the men you rode with today. You would bring this land to ruin if you could and rejoice over the corpses. But I won't let you do that. I'm going to stand in your way, because I care what happens to all of them. Remember that."

"What if I care, too, Stefan—what will you do then? What will any of you do, if I decide to bring the World to ruin... or save it? Because men like you are so filled with fear, you deal with phantoms of your own making, not even with reality. Which means someday, I am sure of it, you are going to create exactly what you fear most."

He watched Dorilian walk away. The bastard never looked back. Within moments all that remained was that fear, filling Stefan's heart and constricting his lungs and making him pull his hands into fists. Every time he was with Dorilian, he felt like he was being attacked. That was why he knew what he would do when the day finally came.

He would attack first.

# 33

The day after Stefan left for Dazunor-Rannuli, heavy snow moved in. White drifts pushed up against the Manor walls and blocked roads, while tree limbs cracked in the wind and crashed beneath the weight of snowy burdens. Like the snow, the Manor's guests settled in. Dorilian, no longer subjected to Stefan or the comings and goings of Esseran courtiers, relaxed in ways he had not done before. He accepted Jonthan and Ionais' invitations to games of cards, and could even be found on occasion having conversations with Marc Frederick in one or another of the Manor's many libraries.

"He's winning you over." Ionais smothered a laugh as she and Dorilian played cards in the Red Library, where the King kept his collection of historical books and maps.

She had chanced upon Dorilian in conversation with Marc Frederick, disputing the reliability of the historian Meles. The King had taken the opportunity to excuse himself, but she had seized her Highborn cousin for a game of bluff and princes. They sat at a table before expansive windows, where there was good light despite white veils of falling snow.

"Marc Frederick does that," she blithely continued. "People are intimidated by him at first because they don't know what to expect. But then he starts to talk to them, and they listen and gaze into his eyes and realize he's ever so interested in what they have to say, and they start to like him."

"He's well learned—for a barbarian."

"Oh yes, very." Ionais laid down four crowns, forcing him to match count.

"I thought he would be more of one. A barbarian." Scowling because his cards were not good, Dorilian laid down four cards in a strong suit, causing her to snicker in delight as she gathered her bounty of cards.

She flipped through her hand, selecting another suit to play. "Why? Because he is dark haired? Because he has blue eyes?"

"Because he is Stauberg-Randolph."

She laid out two pairs of swords. Dorilian had to match swords or shields and knew she was banking he could not. As he pondered how to play the bid, she continued her relentless provocations. "And what is this with you and your wife not living together?"

"Daimonaeris likes snow even less than I do."

Her golden eyes narrowed like those of the vicious little dogs she favored. "You know what I mean."

"And so do you, Cousin." It meant she was not to ask about his personal affairs. He placed shields atop two of the swords and overmatched the other pair with three swords of his own, taking the set.

With a delicate flourish of her bejeweled hand, Ionais played two princesses. "My handmaidens say you have no way at all with women. You frighten them so badly that they run the other way."

"I can tell when people find me appalling." He covered the princesses with two crowns, raising the suit.

"And why is that? I don't know why you must radiate hostility. You're not ugly, you know." She smirked as she laid out the last of her swords, sealing the suit. "It's your manner. Your manner says you aren't interested in them. Maybe you like boys more."

"What I like is intelligence. I don't lack for female companionship. If I wanted it, I would have it." He laid out his remaining cards. "I believe I have sufficient ships to overmatch you."

She threw down her hand in disgust. "Had I played princes, I would have had you! I should have heeded what my ladies say."

Marc Frederick would have uncovered his strong suit, Dorilian knew. Essera's King was a much more challenging opponent. Ionais had been distracted by her attempt to probe his private life. He resented the intrusion and her suggestion that his sexual preferences or habits were the subject of so much talk. That he didn't share his wife's bed was a poorly kept secret because he did not care who knew it. Far fewer knew he had never had a romance with any woman nor known one sexually.

This latest speculation that he might prefer men, however... that was new. The inference rankled because he could not imagine why people would think it, unless it was because of his race. Highborn princes often formed intimate bonds with each other, because being around their own kind was... easier. And if there were few women in his immediate circle, it was because he did not know many.

Ionais had delivered another jab at what was becoming a nagging, nasty itch. Why did his bedmates, if any, even matter? His enemies probably hoped he did prefer men, so they could ridicule him more. Or maybe they hoped he would never sire children. Now he would have to sire a few heirs just to spite them.

Returning to his room, restless and unhappy, Dorilian snarled at the chamber boy more for being a boy than for not having lit the fire. He despised northern frigidity and wished he could simply flee the country for Sordan's more temperate climate.

Once the fire was fat in the grate, Dorilian stood in the center of his bedchamber and pondered how to release his wrath. All he needed was a target. Marc Frederick's most grievous insult had been leaving him alone with Ionais—not enough cause for a rage worthy of his pique. It would have been easier to be angry at Marc Frederick if the man would just once employ coercion. Save for that night at the lodge outside Gignastha, he had not. Finding reasons to be angry with him was becoming a chore.

Faint sounds filtered through the walls, that of a door opening and closing in the chamber next to his. Though he knew Cullen was staying in one of the bedchambers, Emyli remained at Rhodhur—and the adjoining room was her personal bedchamber, not one even a maid would sleep in.

When he had first arrived and learned Emyli and her Kheld brood were to be his neighbors, Dorilian had spent hours examining his three-room suite and discovered a hidden, connecting passage between the two apartments. Most royal houses had such passageways. He had felt safer that first night once he had jammed a hearth iron into the latch to ensure the door could not be opened from the other side. Now he went to the wall panel concealing the door and eased it open to expose the short passageway. Once he ducked within, he could hear sounds even more interesting: whispers interwoven with giggles, a series of thumps and the rustling of fabric, followed by laughter, then silence. Quietly removing the hearth iron he had wedged into the mechanism at the far end, Dorilian opened the door to the other room. Enough faded daylight penetrated the tall windows for him to see clearly.

As he had suspected, someone had found Princess Emyli's high, silken bed to their liking. Cullen's dark hair fanned out in waves across silver-pink pillows, his face framed by silk and flounces. His mouth eagerly kissed the pearly skin of a girl's bared breast as she bent her body over his. Bright hair spilled like a curtain of sunlight about her white shoulders and the young Kheld's broader ones, where her hand wandered freely. They had not bothered to undress fully, they had merely opened their shirts, and the girl's heavy velvet skirts mounded and tangled with Cullen's coarsely trousered legs.

Dorilian stared, both at the arresting sight of the two young people upon the bed—particularly the beauty of their bodies—and at the jarring inappropriateness of the pairing. It never occurred to him not to speak.

"Shouldn't you be coupling with milkmaids, Cullen, instead of seducing my cousin's handmaiden?"

Cullen bolted upright, propped on his free arm. The girl, wide-eyed with alarm, tugged frantically at her bodice to hide her state of undress. Dorilian placed a name on her: Asphalladra, youngest daughter of the recently landed and vastly ambitious Enlad of Chennor. Just last week the man had dared to suggest a marriage between Asphalladra's older sister and Dorilian's cousin Deleus, Heir to Suddekar. He'd made his disapproval so clear that the man avoided him still.

"Dear Lady, I don't believe your father would approve."

"Leave her alone." Awkwardly, hampered by his heavily splinted leg, Cullen moved his body to block Dorilian's view of the girl. That didn't help matters. Cullen's kiss-swollen lips and dark-lashed eyes were no less arresting. "What are you doing here?"

"My rooms are on the other side of that wall"—Dorilian indicated the panels behind him, opposite the bed—"and the architects, not I, created the connecting door. It's well-concealed. No one yet knows I've found it." He regarded them both, appreciating the advantage he now held. "I heard movement in this room and, knowing it to be unoccupied, thought it best to investigate. My enemies are not above sending assassins."

"You'd have walked right in on them, then." Cullen no longer looked cowed, but defiant.

"Yes. But instead, I walked in on you."

Asphalladra, her bodice restored though her hair remained

unbound, slid from the bed to stand proudly before him. "Thrice Royal, I beg you please not to tell my Lady. My position is important to my family and to me. It was my idea to visit this chamber. My Lady charged me to assist Master Brodheson in reaching his room and"—even in the darkening light, a blush burned across her pale cheek—"once we reached here, I... I continued being playful and pulled him with me."

Dorilian continued to hold Cullen's gaze, which told him volumes more than the girl's ever would. Those blue eyes met his inquisition fiercely, though not without apprehension. Within that silent plea lay something they held in common. People despised Cullen because of what he was, too. Relinquishing the Kheld, he turned his attention to the distraught girl. "I don't think Princess Emyli would approve of noble handmaidens frolicking with common Kheld men in her bed—however often she herself has done so. A woman's bed should be her own, and only men of her choosing should ever visit it. Besides," he reasoned, more to the point, "I don't want to listen to the two of you thumping around."

She lowered her voice. Fear framed her words. "Please, Thrice Royal. I beg of you."

"I'm asking you, too," Cullen said. "It was me that invited her in."

"And you who find Staubaun girls to your liking?"

"She did nothing wrong."

"Only imperil her value to her family."

Asphalladra's eyelashes glistened with tears. If rumors flew about how she had entertained a Kheld man between her thighs— that Cullen's base lips had touched her lips, that his rough common hands had touched her soft skin or, horrors, that he had coupled with her—she would be ruined for a noble marriage. Her scandal would also taint her sisters and her brother.

"But I *like* him." Her voice barely broke above a whisper. "We cannot see each other any other way. I beg for myself, and also for him. Tell the world if you want to, though it would tear us apart."

"Phalla!" Cullen warned, horrified.

"They know truth; the Highborn always do." Her pretty chin lifted, her lips trembling as she drew her next breath. "He would know, whatever we say. It would be worse to lie."

"She's right," Dorilian said. Asphalladra's utter sincerity disarmed him. He could have ignored her request not to tell Ionais, but not her belief that the Highborn should not be lied to. Her simple faith honored him in a way Cullen, by the look on his face, distrusted. At least Cullen knew better than to attack him in some misguided attempt at defending her honor. That wisdom was probably enhanced by the bulky bindings hampering his leg. Dorilian studied Asphalladra with new interest. "You *want* to be with this Kheld?"

Without hesitating, she nodded. "I enjoy his company."

Dorilian shrugged. "Then be with him." He did not care particularly for either the Enlad of Chennor's honor or any presumption that Dorilian owed Essera an obligation to protect its noble virgins. The country allowed usurpers and barbarians to rule and so deserved whatever came of it. Cullen himself was a neutral factor in his eyes.

"Ionais will hear nothing from me," Dorilian said. "Neither will anyone else, as long as you use any room but this one for your liaisons. Go to another room and howl like mating merwhales if you want to."

"Thank you, Thrice Royal!" Asphalladra looked stunned, every fear on her face wiped clear by relief.

Cullen watched Dorilian suspiciously, as if unsure if he had heard correctly.

"You can even tell Ionais, when she uncovers your gutter-loving ways, that I knew of it. She will be furious that I did nothing to stop you." Dorilian smiled as he envisioned Ionais railing to the heavens that he was the very foreguard of society's downfall.

"She will learn nothing, Thrice Royal, I promise it!" Asphalladra vowed.

"Then you had best leave before she questions your absence and recalls where last she sent you."

The girl gave Cullen a rueful look as the Kheld reluctantly nodded. She bound up her hair again before leaving without another word. The sway of her skirts held them both entranced until the door closed behind her. Dorilian shook his head in admiration. "She's too high for you."

"But not for you."

"No. For me, she is too low."

Cullen's gaze narrowed.

The territorial spark of offense in the Kheld youth's eyes amused him. "Heed my advice, Cullen. I'm ideally situated to instruct you in these matters. Didn't anyone ever teach you why powerful men sport with women beneath their station? It's because wellborn women have powerful parents and siblings, and powerful people make for dangerous enemies."

Pushing off the bed onto his feet, Cullen reached for the walking stick he had rested against a side chair. Although the Manor's healer had constructed a brace to bear his weight, Cullen used the stick for balance. "You don't have to tell me about dangerous enemies."

"I think I do. Because Stefan doesn't." Dorilian shrugged at the resulting glare. "He doesn't know how to prevent them for himself. If he knew of your interest in Asphalladra, he would go to her father and demand that the man accept you."

"Look—"

Dorilian waved him off. "Do as you please. I am leaving. I will secure the way on my end, but you might want to block the panel with a piece of furniture to bar me from coming in again."

"I'm lucky I can haul my ass across the room right now— forget the furniture." Cullen shot him a weak grin. "Besides, I don't think you'd do anything after all this time. Hells, I might even come in handy should any assassins show up."

Dorilian doubted that. Cullen, he half suspected, would show them the passage. But as he closed the panel behind him, he could no longer be sure of it.

# 34

The Lower Canal had the patina of old silver, its turgid water moving languidly beneath a placid winter sky. Marc Frederick had arrived in Dazunor-Rannuli the previous evening after traveling upriver during a lull in the weather. He now looked forward to weeks of meetings and grand parties, of receiving ambassadors and digging deeply again into the business of the empire. Here at the Emrysen Palace, he could take the pulse of the Triempery. Permephedon to the north was a steady note and Stauberg a strong one, while Sordan throbbed like a dull, uneasy ache to the south. Farther away still, Mormantalorus slithered on the edges of his ability to detect it. Overriding all of them was Dazunor-Rannuli, with its Rill thrum and bustle, its palaces and waterways, and a heartbeat as dark as the Rill was bright.

"Behold." Marc Frederick sat at the broad table of polished white wood that had become his workplace. He held aloft several cards bearing invitations written in letters of gold. "A summons to the Customhouse. The cartel wishes my attendance at a dance celebrating the Heptacentennial of the Consignation."

At another table nearby, Jonthan looked up from his writing. "Dorilian received a similar invitation." To his father's lifted eyebrow of inquiry, he added more. "He sent his regrets this morning."

"That settles one fear. I want him kept well away from the coils of those vipers." Marc Frederick wished he could practice just a little of Dorilian's utter contempt for some of his subjects.

"Is it possible he now believes you? That you—that none of us—had a hand in killing his grandfather... and that the Seven Houses did?"

"Anything is possible with that young man."

"You were right about the approach to take. I think he can

resist almost any punishment. Pressure just makes him dig in his heels. You push, he shoves. You pull on the chain, he lunges for your throat. The man who engages a Sordaneon in a battle of wills is going to lose."

"Opportunity is a strange creature. One can search its very hairs and see it not."

Jonthan frowned. "Maybe he cannot recognize what he's never seen."

"Friendship? We've all seen that."

"I think we forget how impossibly isolated he's been. From his seventh year, Sebbord controlled all access to Dorilian. Before that, Valyane did. The men with whom Sebbord surrounded him surround him still: Tiflan, Tutto, Legon, the retainers of his Sordan household. He has protectors by the hundred—and subjects by the million—but very few *friends*."

"No loyalties outside himself." Marc Frederick found that insight illuminating. Sebbord had constructed the perfect Rill avatar, a being that would follow no mind but its own. He shook his head and sighed. "What have they done? That young man is human, and he needs to *be* human. He needs to feel a connection to humankind in his being, in his soul. All that potential—"

"He loves his brother. He protects him."

"Yes. That is where he keeps his heart." Marc Frederick threw down the invitations still in his hand. Unlike Dorilian, he could not hurl disdain at his enemies. His part was to meet them face to face and eye to eye, to exchange insincerities embroidered with purpose. "He knows he's stronger than the rest of us. What he loves, he'll defend. As matters still stand, all the rest of us can go to hell. He doesn't realize yet how strong he's going to have to be... or how terrible it is to be utterly alone."

Now that the King had moved his court to Dazunor-Rannuli for the last weeks of winter, Dorilian spent his afternoons at Perme-phedon. In the high and shining Sordaneon manse where Levy-athan lived in the security and isolation his condition required, the brothers exchanged their tales of mutual exile. Noemi fed them slabs of hegemon cake rich with nuts and dried fruits, washed down with the sweet juice of fruits native to their island. Her husband, Heran, often visited, prompting Dorilian to promote the man again, this time as his Steward of Household. Heran did his bidding excellently, not only performing courier duties but reporting on the latest gossip.

"Lies kill truth," Levyathan worried. They sat upon the highest of the manse's terraces overlooking the city. "The faces strangers weave conceal who we are." *We*, to Levyathan, meant the two of them and, possibly, Noemi.

"I prefer it that way."

"We are not enough." *Others must see you, know you. Someone besides us.*

"The Rill sees me."

"The Entity sees itself."

Dorilian wondered if being separated for longer periods had improved Levyathan's ability to communicate. Levyathan spoke more naturally now. He made abstract connections more nimbly. Much as Dorilian celebrated his brother's achievement, it took greater effort to keep their thoughts distinct.

Vocalizing those thoughts was one way of maintaining separation.

"Has Marenthro trained you to communicate with the Rill?" For the first time, Dorilian felt something akin to fear for his brother. His own brief contact with the Entity sometimes burned like tentacles moving within him.

Levyathan averted his gaze. A deep thrum reverberated through the towers. Together they watched a silver spindle move toward the city like a water drop across a plane of ice.

"I cannot ever let it see me." He turned toward Dorilian and grasped him by both wrists. Lev's large eyes returned to him, really looked at him. "It would find its way into my being and unravel all." White-faced, he rose and drew Dorilian after him toward the terrace edge, groping with his free hand until he found it. "Look," he said. Together they stared out at Permephedon's soaring spires. "Let me be your eyes, the way you are mine... let me show it to you."

Dorilian did not even have time to ask what Levyathan meant. The world around him suddenly turned inside out, its coverings torn away. Beneath a bruised, nightmarish sky, Permephedon's citadel blazed—towering and bright, a multihued wonder. He recognized the city only by its circles and spokes, patterns that he knew.

Beyond those shining rings unfolded a landscape such as he had never seen. An empty plain spread outward from Permephedon's bright edges. In the distance, wild sheets of malevolent green erupted between the dark land and purpled sky, illuminating fissured hills and plains pocked with sickly inflorescence. Dorilian gulped for air and found it true, cool and nourishing, the air he knew. But what he saw... was a white-boned giant. Spined with familiar architecture, it spread outward from the city, its body reaching in every direction toward the horizons. Immense vertebrae pulsed rings and waves of light—blue, purple, and aquamarine—into limbs that spanned the cracked floor of the World like those of a primordial beast emerging from the depths. The Rill, he knew, having glimpsed it before. Another creature, just as monstrous, hovered to the west. Luminescent, it reared above the distant mountains, moving with the terrible slow beating of immense wings, its many heads searching the night.

"Ergeiron." Levyathan's voice touched his reason, identifying the Entity. "He is moving through Time. And the other is Derlon, whose body spans the Creation and sustains the thin shell of the World that Is, the world that remains. We stand upon the third Entity, the Protector. Look." He turned his head to gaze to the east, where something glowed with incandescent fire beyond a horizon of silver. "There's something there. I don't know what it is. Marenthro won't tell me."

"Marenthro revealed these monsters to you?"

"No. He named them."

"Lev." Dorilian barely managed to speak. He feared sinking further into his brother's mind. Pulling back but still entangled, he rasped, "Is this the way you see?"

Only then did Lev look at him. "Yes."

Dorilian saw himself. What he saw possessed terrible power. He appeared human but somehow liquid and strange. His own eyes gazed back at him, pupils spilling light. Azure filaments fine as spider silk radiated from his left arm. They coalesced in ghostly tethers that snaked through Permephedon's luminous towers to connect his body to the Rill's rearranging form. His left arm itself looked hollow, like a limb spun from blue light.

"No!" He turned to run but the world had changed. Darkened. This, he knew, must be what Levyathan saw—blackness and distortion and danger. Paralyzed by blindness, Dorilian dropped to the ground, to his knees, confirming through touch that he was still anchored to the world he knew. "That's not *me!*"

With all his will, he tore his mind away from his brother's, slammed down every shield Sebbord had ever taught him.

"Dor, don't leave me! Don't go away!"

The distress in Levyathan's cry was as terrible as anything he had ever heard.

Dorilian rocked back and sank down with a groan until his buttocks rested on the welcome terrace surface. Only then did he open his eyes. Blue sky arched overhead, and Permephedon's pinnacles glittered in the bright sun of day. His legs stretched out before him, normal again. His left arm was solid once more... no snaking filaments defined his limbs, no light shone beneath his skin. Staring at Levyathan's tortured, worried face, he understood for the first time what his brother's world *was*. That knowledge filled him with dismay. Even standing within the Rill had not been like this. "Lev, how can you stand it?"

"I see what I have always seen. I see you. Only you."

"That wasn't me. Not all of me."

Levyathan gazed upon him, unafraid. "I see but half the world, Dor—the hidden half. I see what human eyes do not. Now you know why I cannot navigate the World as you do. I cannot be the mortal face of *that*. I am already too much like it. But I think it sees you... as I do."

Was the Rill even of *this* World? For that matter, was *he*?

Shaking his head, Dorilian pushed away and got to his feet again. "I did not need to see that."

"The Entities are being lost completely to their otherness. Derlon longs for his lost humanity. Without us, he will never find it again. We are his progeny, his regeneration. He cannot see other mortals at all. I can hardly see our father, Dor. He is tethered to the Rill as you are, but his umbilici are withered and thin, barely visible. He is lost in shadows. The Rill does not see him or any other man. It sees only *you*."

Dorilian pondered his brother anew. "What do you see when you see other men? Not me or Father, but men who are not Sordaneon?"

"Shadows, only shadows—except for others of our kind. And Marenthro. He... shines, as you do."

"More than me, I would think."

Ducking his head, Levyathan laughed. "Much more."

"Godsblood, Lev." Dorilian rejoined his brother on the ground. His heart raced, a very human hammer in his chest. Trembling, he settled himself onto the winter-chilled stone. "What will it take for me to command that monster?"

Lev took his hand and clutched it tightly. "We do not know. I think Grandfather knew, but he is gone."

Yes, the Seven Houses had seen to that. Someday, Dorilian hoped, he could turn their captive god against them. He felt powerful when he thought of doing that. But he was not powerful, not yet—not really. Other men commanded his life. He stared at Lev with a new understanding of his purpose. "You're warning me. You think I might try to command it too soon."

"Not too soon—too late. It fades, and darkness grows."

Dorilian felt the pull on his flagging strength. He pried his fingers from Lev's grip. "I have to leave again. I'll be back soon," he promised. "Just not tomorrow. I'm leaving. But I do not want to see the Rill again. Not ever again—not like that."

Lev's gaze, filled with the only authentic, perfect love Dorilian had ever known, turned on him again. "Some evil thing hunts us even now across the plains of darkness. I see its shadow sometimes beyond the mountains of the south. Others stand in its path, so it might tear them to pieces first." Levyathan clutched at him again. "Grow strong, Dor, before it does."

Marc Frederick's yacht hugged the quay at the base of the Rill Mount. Though not the biggest ship on the Dazun River, it dwarfed the usual Lower Canal traffic of flat-bottom barges and trading schooners. Out on the Canal's green-gray waters, other boats big and small slowed so people could stare at the royal transport. Sleek Staubaun ladies caped with fur reclined in a passing *gond*, from which they pointed gloved hands at the horses being led onto the yacht's high deck. Marc Frederick merited less attention, dressed plainly and standing on the dock near a load of bales destined for some other ship.

He waited on the loading of the horses... and for Dorilian, who had paid a visit to his brother in Permephedon.

As for Marc Frederick himself, the last months had been an unceasing parade of royal business. Not a day had passed without addressing grievances from the Seven Houses, entertaining client Lords, or settling his far-flung financial interests. Marc Frederick disliked Dazunor-Rannuli for that very reason. Matters that functioned very nicely in his absence for some reason demanded his personal attention when he was in residence. His days were never less than full.

He looked forward to visiting Kyrbasillon, where his court would be celebrating Jonthan's birthday. Because of a horse race.

When Jonthan had proposed matching Sural against Rheger's prize racer, Caillepern, Dorilian had agreed with a ferocity only Marc Frederick and Rheger understood. Rheger's role in Dorilian's capture at Gignastha had not been forgotten. Distance and social mores were flimsy protection against an angry Sordaneon. It didn't matter to the youth that Rheger's horse had won every race it had ever run or that Rheger extracted a host of conditions. Dorilian promptly and uncharacteristically agreed to each stipulation without complaint. As rumor of the race spread throughout Essera and beyond, it took on the force of inevitability—until eventually Rheger, unwilling to concede that his horse was not the better, finally set the date. It had been Apollonia, with her fine sense of royal timing, who insisted the festivities coincide with Jonthan's birthday.

*Thrum.* A deep reverberation sounded across the city, at a distance but imminent. Looking up, Marc Frederick watched a *charys* appear. The vessel's immense mass effortlessly glided between shape-shifting arches before it came to a stop, suspended above the city like a sword in mid thrust.

No matter how many times he saw the Rill in motion, he never quite got used to it. Its size, for one thing, obliterated human scale. He watched the rapid ascent of cargo elevators up the side of the mount, heading from the docks toward the platform.

One of his guards interrupted, indicating a visitor important enough to merit his attention. He bit back a curse. For three months, he had avoided Chyralane, talking with her only briefly the night of the cartel's Heptacentennial. Now she had pinned him, so any refusal on his part would be public.

"You've been elusive," she complained. Her cosmetician had done outstanding work, and her eyes glittered like topazes beneath amethyst-beaded brows. "I gave you information, and you gave me promises. So tell me why that boy is still free."

"I never agreed to deliver him to you—or anyone. And he has

not set foot out of Essera in five months." He was glad they were alone, with only bales and boxes and the Rill overhead, a silent witness.

"That's because he is running around the property as if he owns it." She looked down her long nose. "His father's mighty throne already his to inherit, and you invite him to cast his eye upon yours? Ha! You should run from the very breath of his nostrils!" Across the wide canal at her back, the palaces of the Seven Houses stood court with ornately tiled walls and fanciful landings. Larger and even more splendid was the gold-faced Rillhome palace of the Sordaneons. Its commanding domes and towers stood at the entrance to the Lago, the central lagoon across which could be seen the spires of other, more distant Highborn palaces.

"We want access," said Chyralane.

"To Dorilian? No. Absolutely not."

"You allow others. A horse breeder. Dangerous young men wielding axes."

He laughed despite his resolve to thwart her. "He wanted to play. He gets so few opportunities." Heaving a sigh, he addressed her real complaint. "I would prefer he face a hundred soldiers bearing axes to what you would do to him."

She dismissed his words with a wave of her hand. "Me? I worship the Sordaneons more than you do. All know the Rill would die and the Wall darken to mortal stone if the Highborn perish from this World."

"I'm not talking about death. Perpetual captives serve your purposes as well."

"Is that what you think?"

It was more than what he thought. It was what he knew. For centuries, already, the Staubauns of Essera had sought to secure their Wall god for their own purposes. Marriage ties to the Malyrdeons were so plentiful that every ruling family and most minor nobility felt their very existence predestined. Securing the Rill god had been less successful—but not for lack of trying.

"What do you hope to do with him, Chryalane? Entomb his paralyzed body in that room you built two hundred years ago beneath your Customhouse? Seduce him with one of your daughters, the way you've been throwing virgins for years at poor Deben? You'd do it yourself if you thought you would get a child of it. Are the Seven Houses really so terrified that this boy can unseat you? Bring you to ruin? You are much more terrified of that young man having his freedom than I am that he might want my throne. I stand in *his* path, Denizen, but he stands in *yours*. And I am not going to sit still while you demonize my family to trick the Sordaneons into exacting vengeance on me and mine instead of you."

As it always did when it detected his anger, the Leur's Ring constricted upon the flesh sheath of his finger—his muscles, his nerves, enrobing Endurin's living bone and nourished by immortal blood. Since the day of his coronation, when it had been placed upon that finger to seal his Kingship, the ring liked to remind him it was there. He did not overlook the power that resided in the device, though he had yet to invoke it.

The dock area resounded with a clatter of hoofs and shouts. The area around the ship became a nexus of movement. Dorilian had arrived. Chyralane turned, eyes bright in her pale face as she scanned the crowd, hoping to spy the youth. Marc Frederick wondered if, in her covetousness, she even remembered having ordered Valyane's murder.

He left her side, signaling to his guards he did not want her to follow. He would keep her from this Sordaneon a little longer. In time, he hoped, he could tell Dorilian what she was.

*There is your natural enemy,* he would say. *Not me, but her. You want the Rill to change? That woman will do everything in her power to make sure it never changes—that you never change it.*

*And I will do everything in mine to make sure you do.*

# 35

Kyrbasillon in spring rivaled Stauberg for splendor. The
Highborn had ruled the domain of Dannuth in benign
serenity for the twelve hundred years since its founding,
and had blessed the city with public places. Libraries nestled
alongside theaters, and the baths were second only to those of
Bynum for curing the ills of men. Ancient trees shaded narrow
streets and wide boulevards, some of which were restricted to foot
traffic only. It was all very quaint, but what Dorilian liked best
about Kyrbasillon was being among others of his own kind again.

His recent visits with Levyathan had given him a host of new
questions about his Essera-born kindred. More and more, he
pondered how completely the Malyrdeons had avoided him—first
as a child and now as he grew to manhood. He no longer believed
their absence to be solely the product of great distance or political
estrangement.

*To look into the future is to change it by that very act*, the Wall
Lords liked to say. Had they foreseen him as Rill Lord? And was
that a future they wished to secure—or prevent?

Prince Jonthan's thirty-second birthday celebration drew
revelers to the city from every corner of the Triempery. Among the
guests were Highborn princes from Stauberg and its adjacent
principalities, and even from more distant domains. Queen
Apollonia hosted a sumptuous banquet in her son's honor, counting
among the guests such luminaries as her father, Tahlwent's Prince
Elegiros Halasseon, and her cousin the Prince of Stauberg,
Enreddon Malyrdeon. Enreddon's presence was especially
celebrated because his new young wife Palaistea had given birth to
a living son just weeks before. All in Essera rejoiced that the child
thrived, a continuation of Enreddon's powerful lineage.

Dorilian thought rather less of Enreddon's feat, though he had married sooner and accomplished less. Siring a child with Daimonaeris appealed to him about as much as plunging his cock into a beehive. He was relieved beyond words that the Wall had not shown him copulating with his wife. Then again, it had not shown him copulating with anyone. Tearing his mind from such distracting thoughts, he scanned the banquet hall, looking for someone to engage in conversation. The answer appeared at his elbow.

"Pondering your wager?" To judge by his lopsided grin and the goblet in his hand, Jonthan was enjoying the eve of his birthday.

"Only a fool would enter into a wager against a Malyrdeon."

"Then you and I are both fools, for I have put a fair sum on your horse." Jonthan put down his cup. His smile had a wickedly self-indulgent edge. "Rheger's horses always beat mine, and Caillepern has three times outraced Machon's best. And here's the rot of it: Rheger breeds the beast only to his own mares. Claims the animal descends from Felarro."

"Felarro is in all the best bloodlines, including Sural's. Both swift *and* wild."

"Well, he did run away from the gods."

"He did worse. He ran away *with* one. Felarro was never broken—only the Leur could ride him." As children, they had learned the story. When the mad god called the Devaryati had sought to slay Amynas by chaining him before the beast, Amynas had tricked the horse into breaking his chains and then thrown himself upon Felarro's back. He tied himself to Felarro with the horse's own mane. The earth itself had shaken as the horse fought Amynas from the mountains to the sea. At last, the Leur found them on the ice plains, tamed the horse, and cut his friend free. "That's where the bad temper comes from. Two thousand years have not relieved Felarro's descendants of it."

Jonthan nodded. "I felt that when I rode him. The temper— and the power. I felt legends come true."

"That's why he will win tomorrow. All he knows how to do is run—that, and to throw down any who dare to challenge him."

"The descendant of a god cannot do otherwise." Jonthan slid a smile which Dorilian returned. "You identify with him; I can see that. As well you should. He's a pure force in the World—all motion, all power. He doesn't want direction, only to be left alone, to do as he was born and bred to do."

Dorilian stopped smiling.

"It's natural to want to be left alone." Jonthan picked up his cup again. Together they gazed out into the room, where Marc Frederick had just risen from his seat to begin what was sure to be a round of toasts. "All people want that for themselves. That's why they hate their gods. Who wants a god on their back? So they seek to throw off their gods, to get out from under them. They want to grasp power and truth, so they bind themselves to their deity and dig in their heels and forget that they are just men riding a god."

"And thinking they control it even though they don't."

"It just hasn't thrown them off yet—or maybe they've tied themselves to it so well that they cannot cut themselves free."

At the room's far end, the King raised his booming voice. More toasts were being made to each of the challengers and their riders and beasts. Dorilian joined in, even offering a crisp toast of his own to his honorable foe, praising Rheger for being deceptively modest for a man of so many gifts and the owner of so outstanding a horse. He enjoyed more than anything the dagger-edged look Rheger gave him. *I'll get it from him one of these days,* Dorilian vowed. *I'll learn the truth of how he traveled that night to catch me unaware. If there is any power at all in me, I will get these Malyrdeons to teach me what they know.*

Pleased at having yet another goal for the remainder of his internment, Dorilian fixed his attention on the royal table, where Jonthan had joined his father. Marc Frederick, robust and regal in purple velvets cut and trimmed with gilt leather, threw a strong arm about the shoulder of his even taller son, giving him an affectionate hug and shake that Jonthan returned and Dorilian immediately envied. He pushed down that feeling for the intruder it was, but it lingered like a stone in his boot. Marc Frederick lifted his goblet anew, and all his court followed, Dorilian with them.

"And this to my son, Jonthan, whose birthday it will be tomorrow. Son, your mother and I are proud of you and celebrate the man you have become. You bring to our people the very things they would most have for themselves: strength in arms, intelligence in adversity, courage in confrontation, and compassion in making decisions that affect others' lives. To all who have taught you, well done! And to you, Jonthan, for your first gift this year, I give you once more a King's gratitude... and a father's love."

Cheers resounded with adulation as Marc Frederick embraced

his son. Dorilian wanted to throw down his cup again but did not. He simply set it down on the table beside which he stood. The cold knot in the pit of his stomach was not hatred or anger, but a feeling he wanted to banish altogether from his life. *What is it like, Jonthan? How does it feel to have a father who loves you? Who thinks you are good and wonderful? How does that feel?*

Dorilian knew he would never know that feeling. Not in a hundred years. He would give almost anything to be the recipient of the beaming approval he saw on Marc Frederick's face when he looked upon his laughing, happy son.

The damn Stauberg-Randolphs were richer than gods. Stronger than armies. And they didn't even know it.

The day of the race dawned bright and dry. Among other applications of their gift, the Malyrdeons always managed to time their parties for good weather. Rheger, after showing exceptional skill in avoiding Dorilian until the prior night's toasts, had arrived ahead of him and now stood in the company of a dozen Malyrdeon kin on the King's festooned platform. The elevated stage overlooked the finish line and would afford an unencumbered view of the race. Jonthan stood there also, in company with his mother and wife. Dorilian did his best to mingle and betrayed his grudge against Rheger only once, following a comment by Enreddon about being surprised by Rheger's agreement to the match.

"He likes to catch people by surprise," Dorilian said. He caught the barest flicker of Enreddon's alarm in the way the man's gaze intercepted his. That look answered any question of whether he knew about his kinsman's complicity.

Dorilian turned to Jonthan. "Sural doesn't have to race another horse in his whole life. Not one. I just want him to show up Rheger."

People from all over had come to witness the race, even from Sordan and the south. Endelarin Nemenor, who had accompanied the Sordani nobles, approached Dorilian as he greeted Tiflan and Deleus.

"How are you, lad?" The Ardaenan King bestowed a toothy grin. "Still growing, I see! And not wearing chains. I was asked by your father to report on that point."

Dorilian scowled. "I have received every envoy my father ever sent my way. If he doubts my letters and the reports his flunkies give him, he could come to see for himself. He doesn't need to send *you*."

"A thousand reassurances would not settle the matter for a man of his temper. Speaking of which—" The short man, his blocky figure extravagantly attired in every possible shade of red and purple, leaned over the royal railing. His hand shaded his eyes as he gazed toward the starters. "—I think your horse is trampling some of the stable boys!"

Dorilian, who could see what was going on more clearly, sighed. "He is not. See? They got out of the way."

"So they did." Endelarin rocked back on his heels and puffed out his chest with pride. "I placed a wager on the beast, I'll have you know, in honor of your kinship to my royal house."

Dorilian wished the man would stop bringing that up. It was bad enough that Endelarin's mere presence allowed people to make comparisons, particularly as to the similar color of their eyes.

"A lovely girl, a stepdaughter to a noble house, has found me worthy." The sea-king's grin grew wider still as he reflected upon his wager. "Her scoundrel of a stepfather has agreed that I can have her as a wife if your horse wins."

His embarrassment complete, Dorilian turned on the Ardaenan King in outrage. "You wagered for a *wife*? You only have a hundred!"

"I'm allowed as many as I can support!" Endelarin justified his wager to the handful of onlookers who had overheard them. "A King, you know, has a duty to exercise his virility."

Marc Frederick smiled at the man. "One of the best of royal traditions."

Endelarin beamed at Dorilian tolerantly. "You are a young man still. One of these days, you will understand and realize the wisdom of your elders." He returned his attention to Marc Frederick before he continued. "My little Rannuli flower is willing, I assure you. Should I win, I will, of course, bow to your superior station in the matter. Indeed, I expect the man to attempt to cheat me."

"We will not allow that," Marc Frederick assured him. "And what shall the stepfather receive if you lose the bet?"

Endelarin sighed. "I will then wed all of *his* daughters. Every one of them. Seven scheming harpies in silk, each vainer and more demanding than the one that preceded her from the womb. Naturally, I only want their half-sister, for that girl is as clever as they are cruel and as sweet as any that could be found in a pail of pickles."

"'Tis nearly good enough to persuade me to have my horse lose," Dorilian muttered to Jonthan, who laughed at his discomfiture.

"Then let us pray your royal cousin's horse sees fit to deliver you from such a fate." Marc Frederick said to Endelarin over Dorilian's remark. The King gestured his son forward and nodded to the heralds. The horses could be seen being led to the distant post from which they would start their run.

Rheger had set the race at half a league, with each horse to carry identical weight. Caillepern's rider, a wiry young Kheld who was small even for his puny kind, weighed less than the short, muscular Estol riding Sural.

"A pity we cannot ride the beasts ourselves, *fra'don*." Rheger addressed Dorilian as the horses tossed their heads and pranced to the noise of the crowd. The riders were to ease their mounts forward apace to the post, where the starter would signal if he saw them as even. "It will irk you all the more when your animal falls short to a Kheld rider."

Dorilian wondered why Rheger thought he might have overlooked that nuance. "I think you put a fur-face on yours so you will have an excuse for when it loses."

After two near misses, the horses achieved a clean start. A deep, golden note from the starter's gong awakened the crowd's roar. Both horses leaped forward, their graceful bodies extending into bursts of speed. As expected, Caillepern went for the early lead, his dusky-blue hoofs striking deep into the lush and familiar turf of his home course. Dorilian had calculated his own horse's disadvantages. Sural had run only a few races in Essera before being purchased and brought to Sordan three years before. He had run every race since then on drier surfaces. He had, however, trained at Gustan for three months, and Dorilian was relieved to see the horse running well. Sural galloped just a horse length behind when they entered the first curve of the course, as it bent downhill and headed around a rush-hemmed, pretty green lake.

*Keep Sural behind.* The rider was obeying instruction so far. *If he gets in front, he will think the race is over.*

The predominantly Esseran crowd's noise rose to a roar as Caillepern's lead widened to several lengths. Rheger looked to Dorilian. Dorilian smiled back. A well-informed onlooker would know Sural ran best from behind. The white devil took pleasure not in leading his opponents but in *passing* them, letting his rivals know they could not match his stamina and speed.

"Which one is he?" Endelarin's loud voice rose above the buzz of speculation. Though the riders each wore the respective royal blue or emerald green colors of the owner's Highborn Houses, at a distance, it was hard to tell them apart.

"The one that's *behind*," Ionais took pleasure in saying.

"Not for long, I think." Endelarin noted how the distance between the two horses, which had grown to nearly ten lengths as Caillepern accelerated around the curve heading back to the stands, was rapidly shrinking.

Dorilian leaned forward, hands tense on the railing. Rheger's horse still held a commanding lead. The crowd's cheers, excited from the first, took on new urgency as Caillepern emerged around the curve with Sural charging hard. Sural drifted to the left to emerge between the leader and the stands. Caillepern stretched his neck, digging deeper. Hoofs sliced into the turf as the ground thundered with the horses' approach. Dorilian lifted his head as the Estol rider held Sural out just enough to create a lane between his mount and its rival. Once, twice, the rider brought down the whip. The horse unfurled his long body above the turf, forelegs extending and massive hindquarters gathering.

A thrill of satisfaction parted Dorilian's lips. He watched Caillepern notice a rival on his flank and falter. The horse's Kheld rider, who had never had to do more than urge his mount to victory, looked over his shoulder. Sural's white legs slashed as the horse gained ground. In every race Caillepern had ever run, no horse had been with him at the finish; now one was. With a burst of speed, Caillepern lunged forward, hoofs stabbing at the grass, opening a half length between his haunches and his pursuer's head.

It was then, as the horses charged down the straight course toward the stands, that Sural's fluid motion transformed into pure speed. Sural seemed to leave the earth. His legs moved so fast his hoofs blurred across the turf, and he gained on Caillepern again. The crowd screamed as Sural's head reached out to catch the fleet leader's flank, and then his shoulder. Dorilian added his voice, his arms lifted in victory. For a moment, the two horses raced neck and neck, pounding down the grassy green course as the crowd's cheering reached a gigantic roar that drowned out the thunder of hoofs. All eyes saw the moment when Caillepern, laboring but not yet defeated, met the eye of his rival. And then Sural surged into the lead by one length, by three—and finished nearly five ahead, running as strongly at the end as he had at the beginning of his unholy charge around the curve.

"I shall be wed but once tonight!" Endelarin thrust his arms high above his head. Before Dorilian could evade the maneuver, the man embraced him heartily about the ribs and nearly hauled him off his feet. "A fine race, lad! A fine race! Showed these fat-pursed Esserans a thing or two, now didn't we, Cousin? Aha! What a magnificent beast! If you ever have a mind to sell him—"

Dorilian stepped back and pushed Endelarin away. "I don't!" he snarled. Fortunately for the Ardaenan King, there were other well-wishers, some gleeful and some simply amazed, to intercede before Dorilian could express his displeasure more abundantly.

"A great race!" Jonthan declared. He looked happy: his own wager was secure. "Rheger," Jonthan said to the devastated man, already receiving condolences from those nearest. "I never thought any horse could catch Caillepern—until I saw this one run."

"Sural deserves his fame." Rheger did not bother to conceal his great disappointment. On the field, the horses, having both been slowed and turned, cantered back toward the stands. Exchanging a kinsman's arm clasp with Jonthan, he forced a smile. "Your wager on the beast was a good one, Cousin, for it appears your winnings shall be my first gift to you."

Jonthan smiled warmly. Before he could turn away or move on, Dorilian stepped forward. There was something he wanted to do—and he wanted to do it here on the royal stage with the others still at hand.

"I also have a gift for you." Dorilian opened the side vent of his jacket and pulled a scroll from within. A braid of emerald and silver ribbon looped around the smooth vellum and identified it as a formal document. He extended it to Jonthan. "For you, Cousin."

Essera's Heir had received numerous gifts already and would be given more during the festivities later that afternoon. The silence that fell upon this gathering stemmed only in part from his getting another.

Jonthan took the scroll in hand and, with an inquiring look that Dorilian declined to answer, slipped the ribbon and unrolled the document. His expression went from bemusement to utter amazement. "The horse? You're giving me Sural?" His astonishment repeated, every person in the box exclaiming it to their neighbor.

"I have already done so. The document transfers ownership." Dorilian grinned. "I keep today's winnings, however."

Laughing with pure joy, Jonthan showed the ownership scroll to his father. Marc Frederick appeared to be reading it carefully. But there was no trick in it. Dorilian had written the document himself and signed it, clearly identifying the bestowed horse: Sural, sired by Alezan on the dam Royal Dessura.

"A princely gift indeed," the King concurred.

The gift represented the first ever given personally to a Stauberg-Randolph by a Sordaneon. Dorilian had caught the King at a loss for words.

"Thank you, Cousin." Jonthan had the presence of mind to repeat Dorilian's acknowledgment of kinship. "This is the most marvelous gift I can imagine." Out on the grass below the royal viewing box, Sural reared and kicked against the lines the grooms had attached so his jockey could safely dismount. Though lathered from the race, his hoofs caked with grass and dirt, the horse looked magnificent.

At Jonthan's shoulder, Rheger glowered with grim understanding. Dorilian smirked, knowing he had just ensured that nobody would talk about anything else for the rest of the day, if not for weeks to follow. Catching Rheger's gaze, Dorilian held it, enjoying the flavor of having delivered a dual message.

*It meant nothing to me.* His look conveyed every word to Rheger. *Neither winning this race nor giving this gift. The only thing that meant anything was seeing you lose.*

"A worthy gift." Enreddon spoke on behalf of the Malyrdeon kindred. He nodded approval to Dorilian. "We have long held Prince Jonthan to be our cousin, but this is the first time we have heard you refer to him as such."

Dorilian had not expected to be asked to explain. The reasoning seemed obvious. He shrugged. "I merely acknowledge Prince Jonthan's royal breeding on his mother's side."

He noted immediately upon saying the words that Marc

Frederick was still watching him and had heard. The flicker of pain that crossed the man's features, covered over just as quickly with patient resignation, stung Dorilian in a way he could not explain. What did Marc Frederick expect from him? Approval? He surely knew that his bloodline was the lesser one.

But the sting stayed with Dorilian the rest of that day, under the skin of his awareness, to intrude into his thoughts like the bitter prick of an unexcised nettle.

# 36

After three months away, Marc Frederick returned with his household to Gustan Manor. He was glad to be home. Snow had melted from the countryside, and the surrounding fields and meadows stood clothed in early green. The Dazun River had topped its banks and filled the flood plain below the Manor with water and silt, in which the region's villagers farmed sedge and freshwater eels for as long as the marshes lasted. Indeed, eels were on the menu more often than any other meat. Marc Frederick noticed how Jonthan and Cullen laughed about it, because Khelds were accustomed to the tradition, but Dorilian raged at the fare.

"Eel on toast, eel with rice, eel stuffed with greens, and hot eel soup—it is all still *eel*, and I've eaten so many I would rather starve the remainder of my days before I eat another."

Cullen had stayed on at the Manor and healed well enough to have the cast removed from his leg. He slid a small clay pot across the table. "Eel jelly." He identified the purplish slime lurking inside. "Spread it on your scones. It's a delicacy."

"I thought it was used to seal festering wounds."

"That too." The young Kheld flashed a grin at Jonthan, who broke out laughing again. Marc Frederick watched the young men with satisfaction. Five months ago, Dorilian had rarely spoken with a Kheld. Now he did so at every meal. "You see, Your Thrice Royal Highness," Cullen continued, "we use this stuff for all what ails a body. Nothing else is as good for strengthening the heart and stimulating sluggish bowels."

"My bowels are not at issue. And *your* people all live to be fifty." Dorilian let the pot sit untouched between them.

Cullen refused to be baited. That Khelds did not live as many years as Staubauns was not due to eel consumption. "It's not how long we live that matters. It's how well."

"Dogs live well."

"Aw, we live better than most. Nothing fancy, but a Kheld in his own house eats better food and better-*tasting* food than any lord in Essera. Can't speak for your country as I've never been there, but I would match a Kheld cook against any. And I'll wager we laugh more often, and sing and dance because we want to, and have happier children." Cullen pulled back the pot of eel jelly and slathered some on a biscuit. "What I'm saying is maybe we don't live as long or get to put on the same airs, but I'm saying we enjoy it more."

"Considering the general misery in which Khelds live, I suppose the rest of us should be thankful they haven't noticed it yet."

"You're the one not noticing." Cullen caught himself and, looking sheepish, turned to Marc Frederick. "Sorry, Majesty. I'm not good at holding my tongue."

"Men at my table are not required to do so." Marc Frederick had been enjoying the exchange. He often hosted Khelds at his table and never forbade any from speaking as the conversation moved them. Most, like Cullen, spoke openly and honestly. It was part of his plan to expose Dorilian to the concept that people who were not his peers merited listening to.

Dorilian's gaze had narrowed. "Eels obviously lubricate the tongue even more than the gut."

Cullen shook his head. The Kheld youth and Dorilian got along better than Marc Frederick had ever expected, though he had yet to grasp the connection fully. He regretted that Cullen would be leaving soon to join Stefan in Amallar. Stefan had written that the mine was operating again and producing both raw and refined ores. With the arrival of good weather, it was necessary to transport the production quickly and safely to warehouses in Leseos so it could be sent by Rill to brokers in Randpory. Cullen had spent the last two months working to buy a fleet of wagons.

"Given my tongue is already loose, let me ask you something." Cullen leaned toward Dorilian and earned a gaze that flicked upward. "If I wanted to procure a Rill slot from Leseos to Randpory, how would I go about it?"

"Lease a portion from someone who owns one of the slots."

"No, I mean, how would I get a slot, a whole slot, so I could use it myself and lease the excess capacity."

Marc Frederick arched an eyebrow. Cullen had been studying up on how Rill slots worked.

Dorilian regarded the other lad as he might a slug with pretensions of godhood. "You don't get a slot. You *lease*. Like everyone else."

"Except you. You don't lease. And pardon my getting uppity, but I know His Majesty here and Prince Jonthan, they own slots too. So do most of the powerful noble families. What if I wanted to own one?"

"Marry into a noble family." Dorilian cast a sidelong glance at Marc Frederick. "He did."

Marc Frederick suppressed a frown. The young man still pinched his nerves on occasion. "My slots came to me from Endurin Malyrdeon—my great-grandfather and predecessor— whose ancestors gained their portions as do all the Highborn, by Right of Covenant. My son, however, owns a portion of his mother's dower entitlement as well as inheritance rights to the Halasseon slot portions." Having set the matter straight, he smirked at the glaring Sordaneon prince.

Dorilian shrugged. "Marry into a noble family—if you can," he reiterated to Cullen. "And make sure a slot or portions are part of her dowery." There was, to be sure, slight chance of either occurrence.

Jonthan provided a more detailed answer to the question. "Rill slots are hardly ever offered on the market, Cullen. All are owned— and have always been owned—by powerful families dependent on the income their slots generate and the alliances they build by leasing portions."

"Which is why Rill-dowered daughters are in high demand," Dorilian embellished. "Take the Enlad of Chennor, for example. He wed the only daughter of the Archon of Mureddal and got his hands on three Dazunor-Rannuli slots. A man would do well to consider *his* daughters."

Cullen shot the other young man an urgent look.

"Indeed," said Marc Frederick. The exchange of looks did not escape him. He'd known about Asphalladra's flirtation with Cullen but not that Dorilian might be aware of it. *How fascinating. Why would he be willing to keep a Kheld man's secret?* Perhaps it was true that all young men held an unspoken pact against their elders. "I've contemplated those well-dowered young women as possible wives for Stefan. But every time I put him in the same room with one of the Chennor daughters, nothing comes of it."

Fascinated by the remnants of food on his plate, Cullen shed no light on that complaint. Neither did Dorilian. If he had an opinion on anything pertaining to Stefan, he concealed it well, with a sudden renewal of interest in eating. But the dish was cold, and he pushed the plate of congealed egg aside.

Jonthan appeared not to notice the younger men's sudden preoccupation. "My father flung women at me until I had no choice but to marry." He chuckled and set aside his napkin. "Now, I must leave tomorrow for Aral to join my bride for the summer." Ionais was spending the season with Queen Apollonia in the Halasseon capital.

"You haven't spent enough time together." Marc Frederick regretted having been the reason for that.

"I will make it up to her in full measure." Jonthan's grin reassured his father that he had not lost sight of his wife's many attractions. Though as a royal couple they would necessarily spend a great deal of time apart, the pair genuinely enjoyed each other's company. Kicking back his chair, Jonthan turned to Cullen. "However, I am not gone yet. Shall we ride, lad? Work your leg back up to strength?"

"Aye, Sir!" Cullen rose eagerly from the table and looked as happy as a pup. His enthusiasm for riding had returned along with the soundness of his leg.

Dorilian was Jonthan's customary riding partner, but this morning he had plans to ride to Trulo. He had asked for, and received from Marc Frederick, permission to see for himself the restorations he had ordered on his grand villa in that town. The visit would require him to stay overnight.

After Jonthan led Cullen from the room, Marc Frederick enjoyed a bit more conversation with Dorilian. Six months had made them more comfortable with each other, and Dorilian no longer avoided him at every turn. That he'd called Jonthan his cousin and showed signs of accepting him were cause enough for celebration. Yet Marc Frederick wanted more.

He remained confident that Dorilian held the entire set of keys needed to unlock an endangered future. To that end, he contented himself with measuring progress in footsteps, not leaps, and found solace in knowing their conversations no longer resembled interrogations.

*You and I are going to understand each other, young man.* More than anything, he still wanted to believe he could make a difference. *I will do whatever it takes. I'll lock horns with you until both of us bleed—because only strength can satisfy your integrity. But what will it take to scale the walls of your pride?*

"He's a demon, sir." The groom rubbed his upper arm through the thick leather of his sleeve. He was not the first groom Sural had bitten. To a man, the handlers believed Dorilian had given the horse to Prince Jonthan solely to plague them. "Can't keep him in the pasture because he's wild to get out again. He jumps the fences to get at the mares, and those fences he can't jump, he breaks."

"That's what stallions do. Maybe he needs exercise." Sural was storming about his mammoth stall. Jonthan admired the horse's perfection: the powerful ripple of muscles beneath that white skin; the long, combed mane and sweeping tail so regally and precisely trimmed; the pure blue hoofs of his exalted breed. His heart swelled with the deep thrill of owning such an animal.

"That may be, Sir. The lads, you know, are afraid to ride him. We've been long-lining him."

Jonthan sighed and regretted not having retained the Estol rider while in Kyrbasillon. Sural needed someone to ride him on a regular basis. Dorilian had been doing so, but he had left that morning for Trulo and would not be back until late tomorrow, long after Jonthan would have departed for Aral.

"Saddle him," he instructed the groom.

The man eyed him dubiously. "We already had him out on lines this morning."

"I'll ride him myself." He looked about the stable yard. "Is Cullen still about? He can ride with me."

"He's tending his gear from this morning, Sir. Said it needed oiling."

The groom had managed to saddle the restless horse by the time Cullen hurried in from the other barn. He had saddled his sturdy horse again and led it behind him on the reins. Jonthan was glad to see the young Kheld was barely limping. In time, when his muscles returned to full strength, he might not limp at all.

Sural tugged and pranced as he was led from the barn into the yard. He whinnied and jerked his head on the rein, but Jonthan and the groom kept a tight hold on him. "Let's go, bull head." Jonthan swung up into the saddle.

Cullen stared. "You're riding *him*? I'll never keep up!"

But Jonthan had already turned the ivory horse toward the lane. Sural, full of energy, fought for control as he pulled on the reins. Jonthan felt the force of the horse's will on the leather straps, the strength of its massive neck vying with his hands and arms. Out of the corner of his eye, he saw the Manor's gamekeeper riding up the lane toward the barns, the gamekeeper's dog bounding forward in a black, barking blur, eagerly greeting familiar humans. Sural despised dogs as readily as he despised humans or other stallions. Baring his teeth and lowering his head, ears back, he charged the surprised dog, which wisely ran toward the nearest fence and leaped between the lower railings. Caught off-guard by the horse's sudden movement, Jonthan fell across the beast's neck, grabbing handfuls of mane as Sural bore straight at the fence.

Jonthan slipped from the saddle, one foot still in the stirrup. His mind grasped only one fact: *The animal knows I can't control him!* Just before reaching the wooden rails, the horse reared and twisted its body, driving his hoofs deep into the soft, spring-wet earth and throwing his rider's weight forward. Jonthan tumbled from the animal's neck and into the railings. He heard two cracks, the rail and then his body, as he fell to the ground.

"Sir!" The groom ran toward them.

The enraged horse reared again. Sural saw only a tormentor and attacked. Jonthan had just raised his arm, protecting his face, when the first flashing hoof struck and crushed his bones. To his horror, he realized his lower body would not move. He must have broken something in the fall, because he could neither roll nor drag himself beneath the fence. The next hoof shattered his jaw and tore open his throat. Blinding pain accompanied his last breath bubbling through ruined airways as the horse reared again and its hoofs crushed his ribs. Blood sprayed across the gleaming white arc of the stallion's leg. The last thing Jonthan heard was Cullen Brodheson's voice screaming, but he could not understand the words. Even his thoughts were fading.

*So this is how it happens.*

The blackness was perfect.

# 37

Restoration work on Dorilian's villa in Trulo had reduced the dwelling to a shamble. As did most Highborn palaces, the place had a magnificent aspect—high on a hill overlooking the Dazun River on one side, with a fine view of the town on the other. Unfortunately, the structure was crumbling, and the workmen were incompetent. Perhaps they thought Dorilian would never spend any time in the place and, therefore, never notice the shoddy workmanship—or that very little work had been done at all. Furious, Dorilian toyed with the idea of executing the overseer and his head men on the spot. His promise to Marc Frederick had been that he not harm the *King's* family and did not, in Dorilian's opinion, extend to his subjects. He relented only when the city magistrate, summoned by a guard, promised that the lot would be publicly whipped.

Soured on the villa and mourning the careless destruction of a fresco he had seen only in artist renditions, Dorilian dined alone. Every time he sought something to like about Essera, he ended up despising it. Even sleep proved challenging. He had barely fallen asleep when noise from the antechamber preceded men barging unannounced into his room.

"You are to come with us, Thrice Royal." The foremost man was Trevor, a swarthy officer who commanded the King's elite guard.

"Why?" His mind raced for a reason this man would be in Trulo.

"An order from the King. I am to bring you back to Gustan at once."

"For what reason?"

"That is the order, Thrice Royal."

He had nothing more to accomplish at the villa, but going back to Gustan like this felt all wrong. To reverse their hard-won accord without explanation did not fit what he knew of Marc Frederick. He dressed without a word and departed with the soldiers. The only thing he trusted about his situation was that they probably would not kill him.

The sun had just set again when Dorilian reached Gustan. His escort of soldiers had not stopped to rest, and they had changed horses several times along the way. Flying the Stauberg-Randolph banner overhead, the group had ridden along a Dazun Road from which all other travelers were forced to stand aside. Dorilian gave the soldiers no trouble. The fault was his own for having slipped into thinking his captivity was not captivity at all. He resented only the reminder.

When he saw the Manor, he was struck at once by its bleakness. The architecture looked the same, a now-familiar pattern of courtyards and stairs and roofs, but a pall had settled over every aspect. Light showed in only a few of the windows, too few—and none at all in the royal wing. Soldiers ringed the darkened court-yard, parting reluctantly to let them through. They looked at him with hard, thin mouths and murder written in their eyes. Inside the house, Trevor led him through empty rooms to Gareth Morgen.

"Thank you, Sir, for coming." The aged steward took over from Trevor, who nonetheless followed them into the next room and closed the door behind them.

They were in the grand gallery, which had become a place of shadows. Only faint traces of moonlight reflected off the suits of armor that Marc Frederick so cherished. A pair of oil lamps splashed gritty light high on the walls, illuminating Gareth's lined face and the black mourning garments he wore.

"What happened?" Dorilian didn't need a sinking of his gut to know something terrible had occurred. His fear compounded. Despite his unholy bargain with Marc Frederick, he did not want the man to be dead.

"Follow me, Sir."

He did. Trevor stayed at his back, an armed and deadly presence.

They walked past the great staircase, then around the corner into a wide, paneled passageway that led to the servant areas. A more modest stair of golden oak, carpeted for silence and well-lighted by lamps, led to the upper floors. A table stacked with trays of dishes and a few candles stood to one side. It was so unlikely a place for him to be taken that Dorilian stopped before he would go any further.

"I need to know what this is about."

Gareth glanced at Trevor before answering. "The young Prince, Sir—Prince Jonthan—has died."

"That's impossi—" To Dorilian's horror, he could not finish the word. He could not because the word was no longer valid. The truth was written in Gareth's tear-reddened eyes and Trevor's hooded stare. *How could I not know!* But Jonthan was not Highborn, so his death had not disturbed even one strand of the firmament through which the Highborn felt such things.

"How did it happen?" That, surely, would tell him much. But his mind reeled. *Not Jonthan!*

"It was the horse, Sir. A riding accident. The horse turned on him."

*Sural.* Dorilian's stomach lurched. But how? Jonthan was to have left for Aral. Only he hadn't left. He'd died. *I did this. I gave him the horse.* His throat thickened. "I'm sorry, Lord Morgen. I don't know what—"

"Are you sure of that?" Trevor asked harshly.

"What do you mean?"

Gareth stepped between them. "We need your help, Sir, but Commander Trevor is not convinced you can be trusted."

"Then we're even, because I don't trust him."

Trevor inhaled with a hiss and adjusted his grip on his sword. The skin on Dorilian's neck crawled. He had no weapon but his birth. Where was the King? Had he arranged for these men to kill him? He could not believe it.

"Is it true?"

Dorilian swung to the sound of the new voice and saw Cullen leaning against the wall. The Kheld looked tense, arms crossed and eyes haunted. "Gareth told us you can't lie. Is it true?"

Dorilian managed to bark out a laugh. "What do you think? If one of my race lies, the lie becomes truth. Shall I tell you why? Because in order to lie, we have to *believe* it."

The three men shared glances. After several long moments,

Trevor spoke. "Fine, then, Thrice Royal. Consider your answer. Do you mean our King harm?"

Dorilian never hesitated. "No."

"I'll hold you to that, with the Kheld here as my witness." Trevor turned to Gareth. "I obeyed my orders, Morgen. Do what you will with yours." Trevor signaled to Cullen, and the two of them left. Cullen held Dorilian's puzzled stare until he had turned the corner.

What in the name of Leur was going on?

"It is His Majesty, Sir," Gareth said. Dorilian held his breath, finally getting his answers. "He will not come from his room. He has given no orders, not for more than a day, save the one that sent Trevor to bring you back—and another that no one else leaves or enters this estate. He killed the horse with his own hands, Sir, cut at its throat with a sword as if it could be felled like a tree. The screams and the blood"—Gareth closed his eyes, pausing to draw a deep breath—"I had to drag him back, Sir, back to the house. Since then, he... he so grieves for the young Prince that he will let no one near the body, nor will he stir from it even for food or drink. I have beseeched him to allow me to send notices, and he has refused. He expressly forbade me from doing so. He is adamant that the house be sealed. Word will get out and... and he will see no one."

"I don't see what I can do."

"Talk to him, Sir. He ordered me directly to issue no notices and to admit no one to his room. I cannot break his trust, not in his time of need, but"—the steward blinked and his expression firmed—"he told me once, in Trevor's presence, that if ever *you*, Sir, wanted to see him, you were to be admitted without question. No matter how late, no matter the circumstance, he would see you."

"I don't think he had this circumstance in mind." But was there ever a more perfect conjunction of circumstance and need? The Manor's staff lurked like mice behind walls and doors. Their confusion bordered on panic, a taint in the very air. The soldiers outside were hardly in a better state. Someone needed to take things in hand before the emotional disintegration worsened—yet none of them, not Gareth, not even the soldiers, dared presume what their grieving king would want or allow.

"He believes in you, Thrice Royal. Not every person in this house does, but *his* faith never falters. Now, mine must follow his. I, too, know what a Highborn promise is worth."

To do no harm to the King or his family. Dorilian knew better than any other how solidly that vow held him. In a deep and as-yet-unexamined recess of his mind, he pondered that he no longer needed it.

"I will do what I can—or am allowed."

"Trevor will support me in this. And Cullen Thegn is our witness. Do what you will, if you can but help him."

"I will start with helping you."

Gareth's pale blue eyes closed with relief. The steward's gratitude washed over Dorilian, and he knew he'd chosen rightly.

"Send notices at once to Princess Emyli and Queen Apollonia. Do so in the King's name. Get me paper, and I will myself pen a note to Ionais. She must be told about her husband. Use the Trulo array to send word also to Prince Enreddon at Stauberg—he will know what to do." The next words were more difficult to speak, but necessary. "I will try to get him away from the body so that you may remove it. Wash the corpse and lay it out should he wish to view it later. You will do these things upon my command. Indeed, you risk my Thrice Royal rage if you do not." The last words would shield Gareth from blame later.

"Indeed, Sir, I understand." Gareth disappeared for only a short while, returning with sheets of fine ivory paper and a writing instrument. Dorilian found a clear space on the nearest table and wrote out a note neither Ionais nor his Highborn kin could possibly take amiss. He would trust Gareth to write appropriate messages to the others.

"Tell the household to go about its activities as normally as possible." Even pretending things were normal was better than what was happening. "Marc Frederick is still King; there is no change in rule. When he comes out of his room, he should not have to face other peoples' fears. His grief is heavy enough without having the sorrow of the entire house thrust upon him."

"Of course, Sir. If I may say, without being forward, thank you for taking on this burden."

Dorilian nodded. For better or worse, royal privilege was something he had exercised from birth. Rulers, even grieving ones, had obligations. Before Marc Frederick could take offense at what he was doing, the man would have to find out about it. Until then, at least some critical business would get done, and the appearance of the King's capacity to rule would be maintained.

*What am I doing? This is madness.* It didn't matter if things needed to be done or even if Gareth Morgen was willing to allow him to direct such matters—he had no right to intercede in Marc Frederick's affairs. Not even this much. He was a rival, not a kinsman. His family claimed Marc Frederick's throne to this day. Recalling Trevor's look of hate and the soldiers' hostility, Dorilian was certain he would become the next victim should Marc Frederick fail to recover. Those men out there would make sure of it. Even if they did not kill him, the whole of Essera could well collapse about his ears.

Just when he could really take advantage of a situation, he had no choice but to salvage it.

Gareth led the way to the King's apartment by way of the servant hall at the back of the bedchamber. Guiding Dorilian around the corner into the cavernous room, the steward pointed to the great curtain-hung bed upon which Jonthan's body lay, still clothed in riding attire. Another figure, half-hidden in shadows, huddled on the floor beside that bed, curled against it as if turning away from the world. The coals in the fireplace had long since died, and only a single oil-burning lamp on a table near this door gave the room a few flickers of low, golden light. Several broken objects that once had been vases or figurines littered the area around the hearth, evidence of how the servants had been driven off. Dorilian gestured that Gareth should leave, or at the very least place himself out of sight, before he took a deep breath and walked toward the bed.

The corpse's garments gleamed dark with blood. The room itself smelled of death. Marc Frederick sat on the floor, clutching his son's lifeless hand in his, pressing that dangling arm to his face. When Dorilian approached, the grieving man turned away.

"Why are you here?" The once regal voice was hoarse, ravaged by shouting and tears. "Go! You have my consent and my blessing. Go back to Sordan. Do whatever it is you were god-born to do."

"No."

"Will you always oppose me?" Marc Frederick shouted, his voice cracking. "Go, damn you! Isn't this what you wanted?"

Looking upon the broken man and his dead son, Dorilian could only shake his head. "No. Never this." It was true. He no longer remembered what it was he had wanted.

"He can't stop you now, if ever he could have. And I no longer have the strength to deal with you." The strangled sobs that came from the other man's throat barely sounded human. "I will pay the price... we will all pay the price. Just leave us... leave..."

"Not while you're like this." Dorilian knelt before Marc Frederick and reached out. He laid his hand on the stiff, blood-caked leather covering the King's shoulder, then turned his hand so his fingers pressed a tear-wetted cheek. The coarse hair there startled him, but he left his hand where it was, feeling the man's profound reality.

"Don't." Marc Frederick tried to pull away but could not. Sobs choked his voice. "Please go."

Dorilian knew he had caused this. He had given Jonthan the horse. His promise teetered at the edge of breaking and would break if he left. He could not bring back the dead, but he could keep faith with the living. If he could just draw away some of the burden, he might pull this man back from the brink of ruin.

"Let me help you," he whispered. Marc Frederick was too wracked with anguish to help himself.

"Stop feeling, stop helping! You don't understand. I need him... I need my son. My light, my life... you destroyed it all, you with your rage and your hate running wild through our lives! He should not even have *been* here but for you! And now I don't want him to go!"

More sobs shook his body. More tears spilled across Dorilian's fingers, leaving trails rich with pain. He welcomed the assault, invited it inside, his nerves drinking a palpable, heavy grief to which his own was but an echo. So many skeins of suffering, a tangle of hurt... the senseless loss, the sudden end that had claimed not just a man but all he had embodied. Hope, most of all, but love also, as rich and deep as the soul from which it had sprung. His feelings and Marc Frederick's swelled to fill the space between them. No longer held apart, their emotions melded.

Dorilian blinked as tears burned his eyes. It took all his strength to soak up the pain. That pain was not his, but he would carry it for all time.

"What do I tell his mother?" Marc Frederick mourned against the dusky skin of Jonthan's cold arm. "How do I tell her he is gone?"

*I'll tell her.*

*You can't... Her only son, her only child... Oh God, how do I tell her?*

*I'll tell her. She hates me already. Let her hate me for this also.*

*She will hate us both. Her grief will bind you and me in the same breath.*

Dorilian closed his eyes. One by one, he vacated his outer senses until he could sort through the layers of emotion, separating the other man's from his own. Until now, he had not realized what it meant to touch another mind the way he touched Lev's. Lev's mind was familiar, a contact shared from birth. The textures of Marc Frederick's thoughts were alien to him, fragile, mere strands of translucent emotion so drained of strength that he hesitated to break contact lest he tear the man's mind from its tenuous moorings. Instead, he assumed the full weight of their sharing, modulating his confused emotions, fearful of imposing a greater burden.

*My people, my wife...*

Dorilian absorbed the emotional morass surrounding the King's fear... Marc Frederick's certainty that his wife had never loved him... that without their son, there would be nothing between them... how he feared losing so much more than words could ever say. His alliances. His Kingship. The love of his people. All these he had tied in his mind to his son. As gently as he could, Dorilian stilled those turbulent currents. He shifted direction with every eddy, maintaining clear channels, evening out the flow.

*They won't hate you. How can they? Even I don't hate you. Every time I try to hate you, I fail. I am here. I will stay. I will do whatever you need of me. You won't be alone. But you cannot remain like this. You have frightened your servants and your soldiers. Let them help you. Let us help you.*

*I'm lost. I need him, not you. Help me find my son.*

*Jon isn't here. He's embarked on a path we cannot follow and from which he cannot return. You must not follow. He would not want that. He would want you to live forever. Stay. Others loved him, too. Let their love help heal you. Let your servants tend him now. His wife must not see him like this. You should not. Let me call Gareth; let him help you.*

The wracking sobs stilled. Ever so gradually, Marc Frederick's mind calmed to his touch, the tense body relaxing against his. The emotional quality between them shifted as Marc Frederick's scattered terrors quieted one by one, and deeper resources rose to the surface. Like a floundering swimmer brought to shore, the King found new strength by grasping truths that were solid and real. As Dorilian cleared the blocked pathways of that mind, he also divined its scope—its disciplined nature, emotional structure, intellectual breadth—resonances as brilliant and clear as vessels of light. In this deep empathic state, his barriers lowered and equilibrium quickly returning, they sensed each other. He was naked to the King's sight now. Shock... sadness... concern... fear for him... a steady presence intent on help. Nothing at all of a foe's hatred, triumph, or glee. He felt none of those things.

With a sudden, sharp inhalation, Marc Frederick moved his left hand, the better to look at it. The Leur's Ring glowed brilliant white upon his middle finger. Dorilian stared at the device, knowing what it detected. As with all Entity-bound devices, the ring's white glow indicated contact with another Entity.

But Marc Frederick merely let his hand drop to his lap. "Damn you."

The mental connection severed. Dorilian pulled away as the break became hard, barriers slamming into place. The light in the Leur's Ring faded and grayed to barely a flicker. But he sensed that Marc Frederick had, at the very least, gained a foothold of command of himself. "Let people help you," he repeated, speaking softly. "Let *me*."

Eyes closed, the dark head turned away from him. "You should not have been able to do that."

"I don't know how it happened. I felt your pain. I wanted to reach you, only that."

Now that his eyes had adjusted to the dark, Dorilian saw the man's face clearly. It looked waxen and pale, much older, with lines where none had been before. Marc Frederick had not washed or combed his hair, nor had he shaved in the day and a half since he had looked upon his son's broken body. Dark stubble thickly lined his strong jaw and cast a deep shadow upon his upper lip. Other shadows, more terrible, stained his elegant, gold-embossed jacket, face, and hands—the tell-tale smearings and black soaking of blood. Whether the blood was Jonthan's or Sural's, Dorilian could not tell. On the way up the stairs, Gareth had told him how Marc Frederick had held his dead son's body, futilely trying to put back the ruined shape of his face. Dorilian could imagine that scene and was all the sadder for it.

"I don't want anyone to see me like this."

No. Of course not. Gently, Dorilian wiped at the glistening trails wetting Marc Frederick's face, letting him know that he was not repulsed. "Let me help you. I will help you wash and get you some clean clothing. No one will see you until you have prepared yourself." He could not see over the bed, but he trusted that Gareth was nearby, prepared to take whatever steps were needed to preserve his monarch's dignity.

Those blue eyes, red-rimmed and puffy from weeping, met his. "Did they foresee this, the Wall Lords? They see everything. Why didn't they tell me?"

The question struck Dorilian to the heart. "I don't know. Maybe they didn't see him." None of the Wall images in his mind had shown Jonthan at all. None.

Marc Frederick's head fell back against the bed and the dull gleam of its silken coverlet rippled with failing light. The last oil lamp was dying. He stared up at the ceiling, long lost to shadow. "Do they ever tell us the half of it—or only what it takes to get us where they want us to be?"

Sebbord's old warning echoed in those words. Dorilian's last shreds of anger against this man vanished. Marc Frederick battled the same demons he battled himself. *I have at least seen in my own mind pieces of what the Wall has revealed. But he has relied on what others have told him. What if they told him falsely—or not enough?*

It was still possible for Marc Frederick to plummet back into the black depths of his sorrow. Dorilian knew he must get the King away from the bed and its burden of death, to allow others to remove Jonthan's body for the funerary rites.

"Majesty, we cannot know. But it doesn't matter what they see. All that matters, in the end, is what we do. You know what you must do. I saw that in your mind. You love your people more than I understood. It was never power you sought, but unity. You became Essera's ruler because you believed you could lead them justly. That hasn't changed. Essera still needs you, and you will need them. Here"—best that he initiate action—"let me take off your boots." The boots were blood-caked, and he did not want Marc Frederick to have to touch them.

The grieving man nodded. Dorilian removed the boots and set them aside. Marc Frederick curled against the bed, his hair coarse against the pale coverlet, his face more reminiscent of the barbarian they thought him than the man Dorilian knew him to be. The mind he had touched had been civilized, intelligent, untainted by vengeance or bitterness or resentment. It was the mind of a man who could have found purpose and joy in any calling, but who had given himself completely to the task of being a ruler. *I cannot hate this man. Not now. Not ever again.* Dorilian helped Marc Frederick to his feet. He deliberately placed his body to block the view of the bed and Jonthan's terrible wounds.

Once on his feet, Marc Frederick did not need help but walked on his own power across the room and through the door leading to the bathing chamber and wardrobe. Dorilian stationed himself outside the door, listening to the sounds within—of the King relieving himself, of running water—and watched while Gareth directed two male servants into the room to remove Jonthan's body. It was difficult to believe that the unmoving flesh they attended was all that remained of the man he had known. Just two days before, Jonthan had laughed at something he had said.

A young boy came in and lit a fresh fire in the grate to warm the room again. Two maids cleared the bed of its linens and remade it; another saw to the windows by loosening the cords holding back draperies so that they fell across those dark expanses, closing out the night. A third maid hurried to sweep up and pick the carpets clean of shards. Gareth refilled the room's other oil lamps and lit them. Before he left again, Gareth made a deep bow to Dorilian, gratitude in his eyes.

When Marc Frederick emerged, the servants had withdrawn. The King had washed his face and body, and the bloodied clothing was gone, replaced by a clean shirt and loose woolen leggings. He wore thick socks and no shoes. Dorilian had never seen him attired casually and marked how the plain garments brought out the Kheld in his looks. Still unshaven, he could have passed as one, and Dorilian found the resemblance uncomfortable.

"You conspired with them." Marc Frederick had noted the changes. The room was brighter, and there was now a roaring fire. He did not look at the bed.

"They did not know what to do."

"But you knew." Getting no answer, the King went to one of the chairs before the fire. "Why? My son is dead—my Heir—one less obstacle between you and a throne you think should properly be yours. Why do you care what happens to me?"

Dorilian stiffened at the remonstration, though he deserved it. He sighed and sat heavily on the long, upholstered sofa opposite the King. "I got tired of fighting you. Both of you." When the silence between them persisted, he added, "I liked Jonthan. He treated me like I was no different than he was. Human."

Marc Frederick nodded to himself, to the softly snapping fire into which he had stared since coming back into the room. "Then why in the name of all that is holy did you give him that horse?"

Dorilian had been asking the same question of himself. His bare understanding did not make it easier to answer the dead man's grieving father. "Because he wanted it. Because I wanted to do something shocking. I wanted to rub it in Rheger's nose that I could just give away the horse that had beaten his. I thought if I could do that and also make Jonthan happy—" His tears welled forth unexpectedly, before he could think what to do about them. He felt them thickening in his throat and spoke past them even as they spilled hot down his cheeks. "I liked him. I gave him the horse because I could, and I knew he wanted him. I wanted to make him happy, not... I didn't want him to... This. I didn't want this."

He had never sobbed before. Never. Until now.

Marc Frederick stared at him a long time, then closed his eyes. "He did want that horse. He told me... he told me it was the best gift he had ever received. I agreed... because it came from you."

"I'm sorry. He was a good man. I wanted to know him better."

Now they both spilled tears. "You are crueler than any blade to deliver hope only when hope is gone. He would have ruled this land in a way I never could, been truly just in a way I never could be. He would not have had to fight the way I did." When Dorilian looked away, Marc Frederick laughed hollowly in recognition of the reason. "Oh, you think I fought because I wanted to, don't you? You would think that, given your history. But think again—and take a good, long look at yourself when you do. Because you are less like him than you want to believe, and much—*much*—more like me. You fight because you can, because you are strong and tough and have the stomach for battle that others do not. Because others will look to you to fight their battles for them—and you will do it, because they will have convinced you that you must. You will fight until you have killed or enslaved or silenced them all, every perceived enemy, every people that does not speak and think and act as you think they should—and then you will step back one day and see what you have wrought. You will see that you are alone. You will have wanted to create a world for people like you, only to find that there *are* no others like you and never will be. But then it will be too late. You will have destroyed even hope."

"I never had hope to start with." Dorilian wondered at his own words. Seeking where they had come from, he discovered something unexpected: an emptiness he had not even known was there. He stared at Marc Frederick, his amazement renewed.

The King lifted his hand, pointing to him heavily. "That's where you are wrong. There's always hope."

Dorilian afforded him a brittle smile. "Now you're being inconsistent."

"I wonder." Marc Frederick sighed and tilted his head against the seat back, swallowing thickly and blinking at the ceiling. "I've never believed that our lives are predestined. Even Endurin did not believe that—which is how he was able to walk the Wall. He used precognition to free the future. He wanted it to vanish entirely and become a white void, a blank slate of possibility. If he had not done so, we would all of us be slaves."

The King was rambling, but Dorilian knew him well enough by now to think even his rambling held meaning. Endurin Malyrdeon, the last true Wall Lord, was also the last to have gazed clear-eyed into Time. This white void—perhaps that was why Jonthan's death had not been foreseen and why no images of Lev existed among those in his mind. And this talk of slaves... the Wall images he had gleaned had shown something of that. Kheld slaves, though not Staubaun ones. But there were Kheld slaves already, working the mines in Rand and Gignastha.

"They are going to say you did it."

Startled out of his thoughts by that comment, Dorilian looked at the King. "Did what?"

"That you killed him. That you murdered Jonthan. That you knew the horse was dangerous, and that is why you gave it to him."

Dorilian bowed his head in his arms and clasped his hands in the tangle of his hair. He had been a full day and two nights now without sleep—and Trevor had already broached that line of thought. This storm was not yet over.

"You know better." He looked up confidently. The sharing of minds had gone both ways. Marc Frederick had gleaned whatever he had needed during those deeply empathic moments before Dorilian had defended himself.

"I do. Others, however, do not. And many, like the Seven

Houses, are not above seizing the opportunity to put us all in a bad position."

*Just as they seized upon Sebbord's death—to direct my anger against this man and Stefan.* Dorilian recognized the pattern he would encounter. They would say he had trained the horse to attack, then given it to Jonthan knowing what would happen. Entire regions might turn against him at that accusation. *This is my fate, then: to be reviled in Essera.*

"Perhaps I should send you back to Sordan," Marc Frederick said.

"That would only weaken you." He managed a crooked smile at Marc Frederick's look of surprise. "I would become an even more viable rallying point for your opponents. Everyone knows my father will never leave Sordan—even to rule in Essera."

Despite himself, it seemed, Marc Frederick laughed. "You're right, of course." He sighed again and shook his head. "I cannot do this tonight. I am beginning to like you too well. Ah, poor Jon—I know he did not leave willingly, for he would never have abandoned me to these cares. It was always his place to hold out his light, to laugh and stand at my side that my enemies might forgive me for living." Those blue eyes, though the sadness in them had not dimmed, held his. "You know why I ordered you brought back, don't you?"

Dorilian nodded. "To protect my life."

The King looked again at the ceiling, eyes closing. "At last, he understands."

"I did think, in the first moment after hearing what had happened, that maybe you had brought me back with the thought of killing me."

"Did you? Well, I did kill the horse." The Leur's Ring glowed warm purples and blues as he rubbed his hand across eyes from which the tears had at long last dried. "The soldiers never suggested, I hope, that I meant the same for you."

"No. And, had I been there, I would have slain the horse myself."

"Yes. I think you would have."

"But I also realized that if you wanted to kill me, you would not have had me brought back so that you could do it *here.* You would not taint this place you love with such a deed."

He caught the appreciative glint in Marc Frederick's eyes just before they closed, and the grieving man succumbed to exhaustion.

It was the look of a man who felt understood. A man who grasped that though his world had shattered, he might also—somehow and against all hope—salvage something worthwhile.

*You have not won me yet, old man.* Dorilian tried but could not find any weight in those words. He could not say with any certainty just what would come to pass between himself and Marc Frederick Stauberg-Randolph. He only knew that he felt more accepted, more secure, in this man's presence than anywhere else he had ever known.

*You and I are not yet done with each other,* he realized as he was drifting into sleep himself. But too much of his life had shifted for him to guess at what lay ahead.

# 38

"Good morning, Sir." Gareth greeted Marc Frederick in his study, where he had gone upon waking some time before. The steward set the tray on a stand and proceeded to lay out a light breakfast. "I have told the staff that you will be observing your routine this morning. Will you be down to speak with them later?"

"Within the hour," he assured his longtime servant. For once, the formality was comforting. Except for such routines, his life felt unanchored, completely adrift.

He had awakened before dawn after sleeping only a few hours. The fire had still burned brightly, though someone—the house-keeper, no doubt— had turned down the lamps. He might have thought the last two days a bad dream but for seeing Dorilian sleeping on the sofa. The sight of the youth, his body sprawled and relaxed, his head cradled on his arm and half-hiding his striking non-Staubaun looks, had seemed a dream. Dorilian still wore the heavy, travel-stained garments in which he had ridden from Trulo, his jacket open and rumpled, trousers mud-streaked, dirt from his boots scuffing the silk upholstery. Something was astounding, too, about his willingness to fall asleep so unguarded in an enemy's presence.

*Because he no longer sees me as his enemy.* But what did that now mean? Marc Frederick wondered if he could find the energy to explore that development. With Jonthan dead, Dorilian Sordaneon was poised more than ever to complicate his throne and his dominion.

Gareth pulled back the study's heavy draperies one by one. Muted light filled the room, telling Marc Frederick that the day would be a sunny one. He resolved to dive into it.

"Tell me what you have done and what needs to be done," he said.

Gareth's spare body straightened with self-conscious composure.

"Upon His Thrice Royal Highness the Prince of Sordan's instructions, I sent out death notices in your name." He unfolded a list and handed it to Marc Frederick, who took it from his hand. The list named every person with a vital personal interest in Jonthan's passing. "This morning, I released official word to surrounding towns and the late Prince's secretary in Trulo, who will, of course, post the official announcement. Also, as ordered, the staff have washed and laid out the body. The carpenters will finish a fine casket for transportation by this evening."

"I want you to notify the stone masons. For a sarcophagus and crypt."

"I did not know one would be needed, Sire. Surely Prince Jonthan is to be interred at Permephedon—"

"A petition that will almost certainly be denied." His son, for all his royal blood and descent from two Highborn bloodlines, was not himself of Highborn birth. Marc Frederick would petition because he felt his family deserved that respect, but he held little hope of Jonthan being granted such honors. "In that event, I wish that he be buried here."

"I see, Sire. You will choose a location, of course." The only burials on Gustan's soil thus far had been those of departed staff and resident holders.

"When Emyli arrives, yes." He looked out at the view of Sonnen Hill, crowned at this season with the misty pastels of spring flowers. "Thank you, Gareth, for your attention to these matters."

"We wish only to ease your burden, Sire."

"I miss him."

"We all do, Sire. It is very hard."

He had hoped it would be easier, as if Jonthan were merely away. On one of his trips to Aral, perhaps, to see his mother, or when he had been courting Ionais at Merath. Away, only away. But his mind would not allow the lie. Jonthan was not away—he was gone, to a land from which there would be no return, no more joyous reunions or embraces of welcome. To ward off the thickness rising again in his throat, Marc Frederick resumed other things. He had another day, two at most, before the politics of his realm descended upon him, clamoring for their part of his legacy. He had to move quickly if he was to secure his family's hold on Essera.

"Is Prince Dorilian awake?" He took note of Gareth's response, marking the man's quiet approval of the association.

"Yes, Sire. I'm afraid my moving about disturbed him. He inquired about you and, when I assured him of your wellbeing and that I was bringing food, he went to his room to wash." Gareth lifted the ornate silver pot and poured a perfect cup of morning tea. He set the pot aside with nary a sound. "A most unusual young man, cool-headed and decisive. His presence is strangely comforting."

*A projective empath can have that effect… or its opposite.* Dorilian's identification with the situation—and his profound sense of royal duty—had injected calm and purpose, but he could just as easily have rendered the staff helpless with confusion, hate, and fear. Marc Frederick wondered how much of that calm had resulted from calculated deployment of empathetic effect. And what role it had played in Dorilian's ability to dampen his profound grief.

Nodding agreement to Gareth's observation, Marc Frederick lifted the cover on his breakfast plate, glad to feel a faint stirring of hunger. For what lay ahead, he would need his strength. "Yes, most unusual. After I have spoken with the staff, bring him to me."

"Last night, you said you wanted to help me," Marc Frederick said. "This morning, I am going to ask for that help."

"*My* help?" Had he not remembered making the offer, Dorilian would have laughed.

He had welcomed the summons to the King's private rooms. Before last night, he had never been in them. Marc Frederick had always kept their meetings in common rooms. Now that he had good light by which to see, he marked the monarch's signature style: solid, comfortable, and richly reminiscent of his family origins. There was always some hint of the exotic about Marc Frederick, whether a belt of ornately tooled Kheldish leather girding his garments or the artifacts he liked to collect and place about the house. Cabinets of polished woods with inlaid doors and handles of ivory lined the walls, while the floor boasted numerous trunks and cases. The room overflowed with objects and maps, its tables laden with elaborate fixtures. Before one of the three windows stood a table he had seen before, a chess game unfinished upon its blue and green tiles. Marc Frederick was not seated but standing at a cabinet in the center of the room, looking at something in his hands. Dorilian recognized the *tullun* blade the King had shown him in Merath. The blade that had killed Sebbord. He looked away.

"I wanted you to trust me after Sebbord died," Marc Frederick remembered. He set the blade upon the long table that dominated the room's center. "It was too soon; I know that now. Others took advantage of the fact that you could not. I am certain now that you know this too."

"What I did last night does not make me your friend, Majesty," Dorilian said, lest that be misunderstood. He walked to the window and looked out at the view.

"As you wish. I can see where my friendship would place you in a difficult position with your father, not to mention certain... alliances." Dorilian had no trouble reading Nammuor into the King's words. "You do have to return to Sordan, after all, and resume your path to leadership there. I very much want you to do that."

They had never talked about Marc Frederick's interest in his ambitions, though Dorilian had assumed it beneath every conversation. "I thought you were asking for my help. I am certainly not asking for yours."

"No, you would not. You have everything you need to achieve your goals. You were born to rule your people and, moreover, they *want* you to rule them. The people of Sordan were ever proud and loyal; now their hardships have made them tough and determined, and you are poised to shape them into a nation that will challenge everything Essera has believed for a thousand years. Sordan is going to rise again, more powerful than before—of *that*, I am sure."

Dorilian stared at him. Something had changed in Marc Frederick. The King was not being as careful with him as before.

"I've thought from the day we met that you were going to be a remarkable man," Marc Frederick continued. "I am now even more convinced of that. So much so, in fact, that I am more interested in gaining *your* cooperation than I am your father's."

It was unnecessary to read the wording on the document the King lifted from the table to know the subject it surely addressed. Dorilian had already given the matter much thought. "You need to name an heir... decide the succession."

"Yes, I must—or have one decided for me, which of course I will not—"

But Dorilian already knew, had long known, who would follow this man. "You're naming Stefan." Catching Marc Frederick by surprise was a rare event. Dorilian took only a moment to relish the look before he shrugged. "Maybe some things are inevitable."

"I expected you to oppose my choice."

Part of him wanted to. But at every turn, he encountered the Wall images that vividly showed himself wearing the regalia of the Hierarchate—and Stefan standing before him, wearing coronation robes. *I will become Hierarch... and Stefan will follow his grandfather as King.*

"No," he said. "I will not oppose it." Haunted by a knowledge he did not want, he refused to meet the eyes of the perplexed King. *I should tell him what I know...*

"If I name Stefan, you will support me? Or simply do nothing?"

"Do nothing. Maybe I can support you... I'm not sure."

"I see." Although puzzled, Marc Frederick was relieved enough to be pleased. "Then my request is answered. Your father will make a lot of noise but ultimately do nothing, of course, which pretty much settles the opposition from Sordan. You might as well know I'm making arrangements to adopt Stefan and young Handurin as well. That will satisfy customary laws of inheritance though not, strictly speaking, the articles of my political alliance with the Malyrdeons."

That matter, the King's tone suggested, would not be settled so easily.

"I'm not going to renounce my claim."

Marc Frederick looked over at him with regret. "It would be better if you would. Not everyone in Essera is going to believe the Sordaneons will do nothing when I name my daughter's sons as my heirs."

"They can make of it whatever they choose. That fact will speak for itself." It was sickening enough to think that Stefan would be named Marc Frederick's Heir. The Kheld-born fool was not even worthy of this man's name, for all that he would soon bear it. "The Sordaneon claim goes nowhere if there are none to support it."

To Dorilian's relief, the King did not press the matter. *He takes what I give him, even when he hopes for more.* It was a new experience to *want* to confer upon Marc Frederick some of what he sought, even if he could not hand over everything. The Sordaneon claim to Essera was a political asset, as useful as it was dangerous—certainly not something to be surrendered as a favor just because Stefan might regard that claim as a thorn in his side.

"I will not stand against you." Dorilian owed the monarch that much if they were to have any kind of new relationship. "Not in Essera, not in anything you choose to do in your own domains. As the Malyrdeons are content to let you rule them, so be it. If they will accept your Kheld-born grandsons as heirs, so shall I accept them—as *their* ruler. As Emyli's sons are your blood, so I will accord them that which their subjects will give them. But if they or you oppose me in Sordan, or as regards Sordan's subject domains, then we will come to odds."

Marc Frederick's dark-blue gaze never relented as he took a seat at the table. He moved slowly, wearily, weighed down by grief and the obligations attending his son's sudden death. "Your words mean a great deal to me. I know you will never consider me your peer. I'm not. But that you at least acknowledge my right to rule, that I will accept—and with respect for what it might yet cost you. I'm sure I will hear quite different words from your father."

Dorilian was sure of it too. He could well imagine the satisfaction that would seize Deben when he heard that the Stauberg-Randolph Heir had died. There would even be celebrating in certain quarters of Sordan's populace. At the very least, another petition would be presented to the Archhalia demanding that Derlon's descendants be upheld as Essera's rightful rulers. Dorilian doubted, though, that Esseran domains would be lured by the same promises Labran had once held out to them. In all these years, Deben had demonstrated no Rill talent at all. *And I am in Marc Frederick's hands.* All in all, then, the situation favored the King.

Refusing to discuss his father, Dorilian went to the gaming table near the other window and studied the pieces. It was the same game he had seen at Merath, but something had changed. Marc Frederick had countered his move. The gold Sorcerer had now stood to the side, the blue King firmly in its place. He frowned at the statement. A sidelong glance at Marc Frederick showed the man to be smiling. Smugly.

He took a seat before the board and began to study it. *Sebbord never lost a game to him, and I'm not going to give him this one!* He had more than expected the King to take the daring course, and Dorilian knew what paths Sebbord had laid for countering the move. It did not surprise him when Marc Frederick joined him.

"Sometimes it's more than just a game, isn't it?" Marc Frederick observed. He angled the other chair away from the sun.

"Sometimes."

"I never wanted the discord between our two nations. Never. Not even when I knew it had to be. My greatest hope has been that someday I might bridge our estrangement. Dare I hope for that? That Sordan and Essera be as one again?"

"Not soon." Dorilian refused to yield so much ground. "The only goodwill you have at the moment is mine—and that is for you only, not your nation." Deciding between two paths with high probabilities of success, he picked up one of the three screening pawns and advanced it, threatening the blue King. That piece must now retreat or set up an aggressive but risky counterattack.

Marc Frederick leaned forward. He studied the board. "You're setting me up. I will need to analyze this."

"Is that how you win your battles? You study your enemy— his moves, his plans—until he makes a mistake?"

"That strategy only works if my opponent *makes* a mistake."

*As I did. By not understanding what this man was willing—or able—to do against me.* The time had come to stop fighting blindly and to study Marc Frederick with the full attention he deserved. To assess all of them, these Stauberg-Randolphs. Even Stefan now merited close examination.

"I assure you," Marc Frederick continued, "that my goodwill is toward all of your people. I endorse your family's place and right to rule them. The situation I cannot, and will not, abide, is that of having an enemy on the Eagle Throne."

Which was the state at which Sordan currently stood for him— and his heirs. Dorilian was in a position to change that. But he understood the deeper request. "What do you want? My promise that I will not be Stefan's enemy? I cannot promise that. No trust will ever grow upon that ground."

"Your dispute was four years ago, nearly five years. You were boys. He was an angry adolescent who did something stupid."

*He is still that boy, still angry and stupid,* Dorilian thought. Whatever friendship he now felt toward Marc Frederick did not extend to Stefan. "Whether we get along well or not is up to him. Ideally, we would have no contact at all."

"I never intended to force you to endure each other, though I confess I rather hoped you would find a way to make peace." Marc Frederick looked unhappy to have to say it. "After the funeral, I will send him to Trulo to take up his new duties there." In addition to being adopted and named as Marc Frederick's Heir, Stefan would inherit the Principate of Dazunor. It was as good a domain as any for a young man to learn a future ruler's many responsibilities and duties. Marc Frederick looked to see what Dorilian's response would be. "He can rejoin me after you return to Sordan. You still have five months."

Dorilian nodded. Five months suddenly did not seem so great an imposition.

# 39

The first thing Emyli did upon reaching the Manor was to seek out her father. She found him on a rise overlooking the Dazun River, facing Sonnen Hill. The tall oak beneath which he stood was still in the early stages of leafing, and it cast pale, dancing shadows in the afternoon light. "This place gets morning sun," Marc Frederick told her, when she had finished pouring her heart out on his shoulder.

"So senseless. So pointless. That horrible horse!"

She could not believe Marc Frederick held no anger at all toward Dorilian. The Sordaneon Prince had known the horse was a killer. More than a few of the many grieving dignitaries and relations who swelled the guest rooms of the Manor suspected the gift had been bestowed with murderous purpose—a view supported by the grooms who relished relating Sural's man-killing ways.

Together, father and daughter walked to the chill storerooms where Jonthan's body lay, already in the fine wooden casket the carpenters had made for him. It was embellished, as the King had ordered, with oak leaves and acorns in circular motifs. Emyli recognized the Kheldish pattern and stared at it with mute pain. The Queen, she knew, would not approve. Not for the first time, she was glad Apollonia was not her mother, and that her mother had been Kheld. *Her* mother had loved Marc Frederick with all her heart.

She touched the smooth wood and traced a carved leaf's perfect curl, struggling to believe her brother was dead, that his body lay in this box, never to see the light of day. "It was wrong of them to deny Jon burial at Permephedon. After all you have done for them, and he was married to Ionais—"

"Jonthan wouldn't mind. He would approve the place I've chosen." Marc Frederick had received word that morning by way of the Trulo array, eloquently regretful, written in Enreddon's familiar hand, telling him the Highborn had denied his request.

"How can you be so calm?"

"Because I have already wept enough. I have a nation to rule and enemies who need to see that this does not destroy me." Gently, he led her from that dark place back into the light and the sweet smells of early summer lifting on a river-blown breeze. Leaves danced overhead as they walked back to the house.

"Apollonia's not coming, is she?"

"No. She's Highborn, and they—"

"She's his mother. Ostemun will be here, and Ionais and her father. Rheger is here already, and Elhanan is traveling with Stefan." She had just received word that Stefan would reach the Manor in two days by river. She had left Hans at Rhodhur rather than expose him to an unsettled situation. Dorilian was someone she did not trust to respect even the grave.

"I need to talk with you about Stefan."

Her heart picked up a solemn note in her father's voice that told her this was a matter of state and not just family. Part of her knew what he was about to propose—and was glad beyond words that she would not have to raise the question on her own before her son's arrival.

"He loved Jon, you know," she said. "Loved him wildly. Jon was so wonderful to my sons—" *Damn these tears.* The cloth she carried was so damp that it chafed her eyes.

Marc Frederick stopped beside the well house, where a young herb garden flourished. A border of purple-leafed sage perfumed the air as his boots and her skirt brushed against it. "Emy, I need to talk to you because I wish to adopt Stefan... and Handurin too. A King needs more than one heir. Apollonia will bear me no more children, and I will have no other wife."

"Your heirs." Though it was all she had hoped for, she would never have wished this knowing it would mean her brother's life. "Stefan... and Hans also?"

"It's a lot to ask. I could command it, but they are your sons. Grant me this, Emy. Let my family continue what I have begun."

She could not bear his sadness. "Of course, Father." She wound her arms about him and held him close, glad that she could give him the gift of her children. He had never lacked in love for her, but she had failed him so deeply. Someday, maybe, she could put those transgressions behind her. "But surely Apollonia, the Halasseons and the others, will protest."

"I don't care what they think of this. They can protest all they want—I will do no more of their bidding unless they pay the price I set upon it." He gave her a wolfish smile so masculine and confident it presaged victory before he had even entered battle.

"But the Sordaneons will never—"

"Do as the Malyrdeons do, Emy. Leave the Sordaneons to me."

Was it possible? Had he already reached an agreement with them? Dorilian was here at the house. Her mind raced to understand where her father's desperation might have led him. "But, Father—"

"Not a word." He drew her close to his side as they resumed their walk. "I need cooperation, not arguments."

Only with a sigh did she cease to plague him, though she ached to learn every detail of what he had done. For now, at least, that he wanted her sons as his heirs was enough. She shivered at the audacity of his plan. Stefan had few supporters among the aristocracy and, unlike Jon, not even a distant claim to Highborn blood. What Marc Frederick wanted to do would remove Essera's throne entirely from its former ruling dynasty—and place it firmly in his own.

*But the Khelds will have a place. They will have a champion. And Essera will have a Kheld as King.*

From the deck of the Malyrdeon yacht, Stefan watched the river go by in arrows of spray. They had passed Trulo two hours before and now followed the broad river bend leading toward Gustan.

Jonthan had been dead for eight days.

Stefan had learned of his uncle's death three days after it had happened. The news had reached him at Orqho, but none of the details. Nothing of how it had happened. He had learned more upon reaching Leseos after another two days of hard riding. That crazy horse. Dorilian Sordaneon's crazy, man-hating horse! Some of the soldiers said the deed could only be rooted in Sordaneon cunning, because the Highborn were known to ensorcell beasts. It took no stretch on his part to believe it.

He knew better, though, than to share such thoughts. Elhanan stood beside him on the deck, his moon-pale hair teased by the wind. With his fair skin and chiseled features, he looked as untouched and perfect as a work of art.

"I feel your pain, Stefan, and also your anger." Elhanan broached the silence only now that they neared the end of their voyage. "Jonthan's death is a senseless tragedy. Not all things that happen in the World can be laid blame to villains."

The thing Stefan hated most about the Highborn was that his emotions might as well be written on his forehead. "Don't try to tell me what I feel."

Elhanan sighed and looked away again toward the water.

"I'll muddle through," Stefan added to soften his words. "It just hurts—all of it. It hurts that he died, and it hurts *how* he died, and it hurts that my family gets none of the honor we should."

"None, Stefan? That is harsh, for your father has earned his place at our side. And so too did Prince Jonthan, who we deemed our cousin—"

"But you wouldn't bury him among you."

"Some of us would have."

"You only say that because you didn't have to slam the door yourselves. You left that to Deben Sordaneon." He had learned in Leseos that Deben, as Hierarch of Sordan, had cast the deciding vote to refuse Jonthan's internment in the Vault of Incorruption at Permephedon. Any corpse laid within that sacred place remained forever unchanged, so that a thousand years would not cause it to become corrupted. Deben had pointedly stated that Jonthan must be remanded to the elements, there to follow the way of all mortal flesh.

Deben wanted his enemies to rot.

Elhanan sighed. "We have never let any but our own kind be laid in Permephedon's Vault. No man in two thousand years but of our blood. No woman ever, not even the mothers or daughters of the Lords of Wall and Rill. Deben chose not to alter that tradition, and he was not alone in saying nay. It would be wrong to introduce discord into a place of final peace. It is no dishonor to your family that we did not open for your uncle doors we have never opened to others."

"Why? Only because your kind holds the keys to that crypt and will not share its secrets?"

"What secrets but those of the dead?" Elhanan looked at Stefan with wonder. "All those within that place are emptied. Though their shells have not corrupted, though they are surrounded by the riches of Kings and Hierarchs and the dusty remembrances of their dead deeds, they *are* no more. Therein lies our history, Stefan—ours, not his."

The Highborn would always defend their own and their ways, their exclusion of lesser men from their exalted lives and affairs. They would even defend Dorilian to the end. Arguing with Elhanan was pointless.

"Is it true? Are you going to be named Wall Lord at Stauberg?"

The first buildings of Gustan's village nudged into view around the bend. Late afternoon sunlight painted the bare crown of Sonnen Hill with fire.

"Wall Lord is not a title to which a man can be named." Elhanan looked removed again. "It is a stature few attain. My family prays that I will have the ability to communicate with our Entity."

Of course, they did. For the moment, the Malyrdeons were blind. Though rulers of domains, they no longer took firm stances in political matters. They had for so many centuries ruled through advance knowledge of what to do that they could barely function now when their prescience had flown. Maybe the Wall's silence was a good thing, Stefan mused. Anything that disadvantaged Staubaun rule and hampered them from preventing any change in their society would be to Kheld advantage.

The Malyrdeons, in Stefan's estimation, were in their own way at least as dangerous as the Sordaneons.

Jonthan Stauberg-Randolph was buried on a quiet morning in late spring at Gustan, in an aboveground crypt built into a hillside overlooking the Dazun River, which he had loved, and facing the forested Amallaran homeland of his Kheld forefathers. Descended from gods and barbarians, he found his final resting place among neither.

Stefan had only to look upon the knoll where his uncle's sepulcher stood in lonely splendor to feel a sense of foreboding.

"No one wants me to be King, Cullen." Stefan sat with his friend on the riverbank, not far from the landing where Marc

Frederick's barge sat waiting. In the morning, he was to ride with Emyli and a handful of advisors to Trulo, where he would undertake his first lessons in princely administration. In two months, he was to join Marc Frederick in Dazunor-Rannuli, then accompany the King to Permephedon, where his formal adoption and designation as Heir would take place.

Cullen looked neither surprised nor particularly worried. "No one wanted Marc Frederick to be King, either, and look where he is." He grinned at the glower he got in return. "You'll make a good King one day, Stefan—the best! A Kheld King, right? Just like in the old tales, what the Old Woman swore to Alm the day he sought her out and gave her Madrock's Eye."

"That was hundreds of years ago." Stefan was unimpressed by prophecy. Given time enough, anything could come to pass. Essera now boasted hundreds of prosperous Kheld merchants, adminis-trators, and craft guilders, where two generations ago there had been but a handful. Yet there were no Kheld nobles, no Khelds holding estates or titles. It was Stefan's destiny to change that.

"You know what's best about leaving tomorrow? Getting away from Grandfather." Stefan plucked several long, thick strands of new summer grass and launched the heavy stems one by one into the lapping water. "I have to sit with him for hours every day while he talks. I know I have a lot to learn, and I'm going to learn it. I am! Because there's no gain in him naming me his Heir if I can't hold the throne when he dies. But he's holding back on me, Cullen. There are things he's worried about that he's not telling me."

"Give him time. Maybe it's something he thinks he can tell you only when you're ready for it. Like my Bada only telling me about the way it is between men and women—two years after Bronwen taught me everything I needed to know."

Stefan grinned at his friend, and they laughed. Brodhe had disbelieved any girl would find his fifteen-year-old son useful—until Cullen had returned from school that summer boasting whiskers on his chin.

"You're likely right. I guess I have to show him."

Cullen nodded. He pried a flat, river-washed stone from the silty bank and rinsed it in the water.

"Can you believe Grandfather's still trying to convince me to be friends with Dorilian Sordaneon?"

"Do you know why?"

"No. Not really. But he keeps reminding me that Dorilian is going to be this person I must deal with. I mean, Dorilian is Sordan's Heir—but his father is only seventy or eighty, not old at all for a Highborn prince. Look at Enreddon; he's got to be a hundred twenty and counting. Some of them live to be two hundred years! Which means old Deben is going to rule almost forever. As long as I am going to be alive, at any rate. I need to learn how to deal with *him*. Not damn Dorilian."

Something deep and thoughtful crept into Cullen's gaze.

"But maybe you will, Stefan. I mean, Marc Frederick has a Malyrdeon eye, they say, and he sees things clear. Look at what happened just last year, when Lord Sebbord died and people tried to put it on you. Things happen. Dorilian, you know, he's not one to sit quiet. I saw that when I stayed here this winter—people coming and going—he's all about trade and politics, and from what I can tell, he's popular in his own country, even if everyone hates him here. And even people who hate him aren't in a hurry to cross him." Cullen tossed his stone and searched for another. "Your grandfather's smart, if you ask me, to keep him close. Besides, you can't say for sure that nothing will happen to Deben. Then Dorilian would be Hierarch and very dangerous to you if you two are still fighting. Hell, he's dangerous enough even without a throne."

"He thinks the world exists to serve him. I never met such a vindictive bastard."

If there was any lesson to be learned from the last year and its tragedies, it was that things could change and generally for the worse. Dorilian had already tried once to kill him, and Stefan didn't put him above trying again.

"I don't know, Stefan." Cullen stopped trying to find rocks. "He's hard to figure out. He's not always cold to people, and... even when Jonthan died, he kept to his word."

Stefan could only roll his eyes. Khelds often admired even their enemies if they saw traces of strength or honor. It was that tendency that had made them lay down their spears to the Highborn King Erydon in return for being given clear possession of Amallar instead of their original settlements in more fertile Tahlwent.

"The fact remains, I need to build support that can stand against him," Stefan stated flatly. "Grandfather's a start, but one egg doesn't get a farmer to market. I've invited some Staubauns I think I can trust to join me at Trulo." Stefan marked how Cullen looked up with interest. "Remember Erenor Tholeros, my Cadet Captain from Stauberg? He's of noble family and well-connected. His note of condolence to me was friendly, and I think he would make a good captain for my Prince's Guard."

"Good as any, I suppose." Cullen looked less than happy about it. Khelds had never placed many men into Essera's military, and none had advanced to become other than junior officers.

"Eudes Illarion has already offered to come to Dazunor-Rannuli in a few weeks to assist in arranging meetings with my fellow Basarchs and Princes. He's a good man—I met him once or twice. I like the Illarions, and their domain borders Dazunor."

"See that? You're going to be dropping all your Kheld friends soon."

"No. I'll never do that!" The suggestion bordered on offensive, even if Cullen was only teasing. "It's just that I have to start polishing up some Staubaun ones, so they don't get to thinking I'm not with them. I want to rule fairly. But I'm going to bring my friends along with me. Reard likes the military, so I'll make him Erenor's second in command. And you, Cullen—I'll put you in charge of Dazunor's trade office with Neddig to help you. You can expand my domain's trade with Amallar and run my mines, too."

"You need a Staubaun for your trade minister." Cullen rubbed the stone in his hand with his shirt. Together they gazed out at the wide river, where a merchant barge floated in the distance, a vast thing rendered small. "Dazunor's not some outpost or undeveloped province like Amallar or Neuberland. It's a major domain, a producer and buyer of goods, and it has a Rill port. A big one! You need someone who can handle the Seven Houses, and that kind don't even talk to Khelds. But even more, you need someone who can travel freely, and that means by Rill. If I or any Kheld were your man, it would take months to conduct any visits outside Essera."

Because Khelds couldn't ride the Rill.

"I'm going to change that."

"Not in your first week as Prince of Dazunor, you won't. Not in your first month. Hell, maybe you'll never change anything. If Marc Frederick couldn't do it, what makes you think you can?"

"I'm more determined than he is. He's only part Kheld, you know, and I don't think he cares about this the way I do. He Rill rides, and his family does as well. Don't you want to ride the Rill, Cullen?"

The other youth added his handful of dried stones to his shirt pocket. "I don't know, Stefan. I mean, I want our goods to ride it, Kheld goods—but I'm not that driven to ride it myself, to be honest. It's not quite a natural thing, you know. The Rill is powered by prayers, they say. Prayers—not wind, not current, not the four legs of a beast or the arms of a man. It's the invocation of a god, if you believe that, and I think I do. Because there's no better explanation for it. I've stood on Bellan Toregh and I've seen that thing coming, and I've felt it pass, and when it does, there's nothing *there*. Just tingle and magic. Sure, I've been at Dazunor-Rannuli and Leseos, and I've seen the Rill coaches, the way people walk in and walk out. I reckon they ride it, and it takes them places, and Lud bless them for their trust in it. But I fear for my life should I put my body at its mercy."

"I've ridden the Rill, Cullen. It's like riding in a fancy carriage. Just a very fast one is all." This Kheld superstition about the Rill needed to be abolished. Stefan found merit in the commonly held Staubaun perception of the Rill as an immense—and immensely powerful— machine. "It's the Sordaneons we have to convince to let Khelds ride. They let Estols ride, don't they? They let *horses*."

"I talked to an Epopte once who told me that the Rill remembers horses from when it was alive. It doesn't find them strange, nor Estols either, because Estols were bred from Staubauns. And your family has Staubaun blood, right? But the Rill never saw a pure Kheld or, if it did, reckons us as enemies. Until we can get the Rill to reckon us as human, Stefan, there's no way to change it."

Together, they started walking back to the Manor, grass brushing at their boots and sunlight skimming through the trees ahead.

"The Sordaneons refuse to acknowledge that their domain is now a client state and their days of Rill overlordship are over," Stefan fumed. "The Seven Houses and Essera control Sordan now—and we control the Rill, too. When I become King, we'll see then who can ride it."

# 40

Within a week of Jonthan's funeral, Emyli, Stefan, and Cullen boarded a royal barge to Trulo, where Stefan would take up the responsibilities of his new Principate. Ionais accompanied her father back to Merath, there to come to grips with her widowhood. Elhanan rode with Rheger and Enreddon to Dannuth. But for a handful of administrators, the Manor emptied. In another week, they too would be gone. The King had announced he was returning to Stauberg.

Dorilian had not enjoyed his first visit to Stauberg and did not look forward to seeing it again. Gustan had been isolated, but Essera's royal city would not be. He saw advantages as well as disadvantages. For one, he would have greater access to information, and Tiflan had written to say he would spend part of the summer there. For another, Marc Frederick had said they would journey by way of Simelon, where Dorilian would be free to visit Legon, whose letters had been infrequent and unsatisfying. Never verbose even in person, Legon's missives reported only on meals and impositions, occasionally deviating to relate news about family quarrels in Anit-Rebir. Two of his brothers had been executed the month before for having sought their father's death. Legon's refusal of Terveryen's request to return was sitting ill with the old man.

*He's as trapped by my promise as I am.* But maybe it was better this way, keeping Legon away from his brothers' plots and family quarrels.

Now, as he and Marc Frederick rode away from the Manor in the clear light of morning, Dorilian was glad to push such thoughts from his mind. No longer determined to be difficult, he enjoyed being with Marc Frederick. The man was intensely real and refused to let his feathers be ruffled. It was much more rewarding, therefore, to simply relax and enjoy that generous personality.

The weather being fair, the royal party made swift progress. Their escort was well-armed and drawn from Marc Frederick's most loyal troops—led by Trevor, although their numbers were few. Instead of riding into Trulo, Marc Frederick chose to stop for the night at a secluded villa belonging to the Enlad of Velsithae. Lord Eldonus was very old and ill and so often confined to bed and chair that his lower limbs no longer bore his weight. Even so, he welcomed his royal guests personally. Beside his chair stood his much younger wife, Palimia, whom he had wed two years before and whom the King greeted as warmly as he did his old friend.

"You look well, Eldonus, and happy." Marc Frederick assessed his friend after they'd finished a simple dinner of roasted meat and good bread.

"Then I surely look to be in better health than is upon me. As for being happy, however, that I am." The old man smiled at his wife.

"And I could not ask for a better husband," Palimia said.

Dorilian had been studying her since they arrived. He knew the woman was Sordani by birth, though her dress and manner told him that she had lived long enough in Essera to have adopted northern ways. As a girl, she had been forced to marry the Esseran lord who had ruined her father, and that man had later died. Eldonus was her second husband, wed after the first husband's family seized control of her dower properties. Why she had chosen this old man to facilitate her escape, however, eluded Dorilian. Eldonus Kastrion was only modestly rich, and his bloodline rather common. She could, he reasoned, have done much better.

When Marc Frederick and Eldonus retired from the table to exchange remembrances before the fire in the villa's library, Dorilian confronted the woman. "Why did you wed such an old man?"

She stiffened at his direct inquiry, though she dropped into a formal curtsey. "Not for his fortune, Thrice Royal, as many believe." She spoke with a directness he found disarming. "You see, I shall inherit nothing of his lands or wealth which, as you must already know, are not great. I wed Lord Kastrion because I wished to escape my late husband's family, and he was quite aware of that." She raised guileless brown eyes to his. "He has long admired me, and I found his offer of companionship incredibly alluring."

"Alluring?" Her choice of words intrigued him.

"He has a wonderful mind—complex, unexpected, and deep

delving. All things in the World inform him." She shrugged her lovely shoulders to indicate that if he did not understand her, she could do no more to enlighten him. "After one of His Majesty's parties in Dazunor-Rannuli, I encountered Eldonus in a hallway. He took one look at me and said, 'The birds of the south are not meant for cages. Come with me, and I will show you the sky again.' And I went with him."

"And you saw the sky?"

"At night, strung with stars above the lights of the city—and I have seen it thus every night since."

Dorilian smiled despite his doubt that love could be had for so small a price. He looked across the room at the two old friends by the fire. They were laughing, and it struck him that he had not seen Marc Frederick laugh in far too long a time.

"He could be so much to you, if you would but warm to him," Palimia said.

He turned a narrow stare on her. It was presumptuous in the extreme for anyone to offer him advice. "He would do better not to wait upon it."

"But he does, though it hurts him."

"You speak too familiarly. What is Marc Frederick to you?"

She was a woman of his domain and would have been one of his subjects, but for her first marriage. Pride lifted her chin as she answered. "He is my friend, as well as my husband's. Many times has he visited, and I have heard him speak his heart. He has ever been your advocate."

That last was something Dorilian no longer doubted. However, it was best not to offer false hopes. "Don't think me unobservant of his efforts on my behalf. But I am not a beast to be tamed to hand."

"Yet you oppose his friendship. To what end? So you can say to your ghosts, 'See, I remained distant and cold'?"

"You don't understand."

"I understand that the dead take no comfort from the things we do in their name if by doing so we become dead ourselves."

There seemed to be no end to her effrontery. Yet, far from being offended, Dorilian found himself charmed by her boldness. Most people showed him slavish and insincere politeness. Palimia showed him an independent and somewhat irreverent mind.

"Do you think me cold?" He was mildly surprised at wanting to know her opinion.

She held his gaze without the slightest hint of coyness. "No, Thrice Royal. Not in your heart. That, I believe, burns as hot as the fires beneath the mountains of ice in Cjta."

He smiled. He did not think of himself as passionless—however little he had yet acted upon his impulses. Sex for him offered too many pitfalls, as many as there were opportunities, but this lovely woman, although older than his wife or other women he had indulged with such thoughts, prompted him to assess her possibilities. "Be glad, Lady, that you are faithful to your husband."

Only then did a laugh break upon her open, perfect lips. "My dear prince," she replied, "he may be glad as well!"

Marc Frederick looked across his friend's gaming table toward the two people standing near the door, happy for the young man's smile and the woman's pleased laugh. "I had hoped he might warm to your wife," he said to Eldonus, who smiled. Though pain stretched those aged lips and clouded his eyes, Eldonus still had one of the clearest minds in Essera.

"Palimia is a balm to any man's mind. I bless the day you asked me to travel to Dazunor-Rannuli. I promise you, she will be gentle with him."

"I'm not afraid of that, but I fear he might not be gentle with her. My guest is often... abrasive."

"Such is the nature of his god. Cold. Controlling. Power makes men so."

"I should fear the day he has it, then," Marc Frederick responded. The fire felt good on his back, driving away the late summer chill.

"I have been watching from a distance, as you asked of me. Dorilian is a remarkable young man, and there is more to him than most see. His Malyrdeon kindred treat him with a reverence uncommon even to them; that they keep a distance hints at his importance to them. They take such great care so as not to taint his future with theirs."

"They know that he will someday have to live without them."

"Is that sure?"

Marc Frederick nodded. "It is. Such is the perversity of their gift, that they can spare him that. I wish they had told me I would have to live without my son."

Eldonus reached to him and gripped his hand. "Say not so. That knowledge would have torn you in two, and which would have prevailed—the parent or the King—we cannot know. Jonthan was a gift, even if he was but yours for a short time. His life is not worth less because its length did not live up to your hopes, nor is your love worth less because your dreams for him did not come to fruition. You are a better man because of him."

"And sadder."

"At least it is after the joy. How sad it would be if we shunned love rather than let it open us to the bitterness of loss. There, in the dark places of the soul, is where we find our humanity. You, my friend, have never been more completely alive than you are now as you struggle to make sense of what is left to you."

*My family. A mere handful of friends whom I can trust. An empire still unaware that it is already shattered or that I am making one last attempt to save it.* Marc Frederick lifted the silver chalice to his lips and drank deeply of Eldonus' rich red wine. His son's death had harrowed his soul, but it had not destroyed the will to go on.

"We camp close to the wild lands." Dorilian noted their surroundings as he and Marc Frederick dismounted. Several hours ago, they had left the main road without explanation, and now the guard was making camp early. He turned the reins of his horse over to a groom who came to lead the beasts away.

The hills of the Hyllorhose, north of Trulo, were beautiful and wild. Nothing in all the domains of Sordan approached the jagged, tumbled beauty of this land of hills and sudden, plunging gorges. Dangerous to roam, the region was thick with game—and lore. One of the great cities before the Devastation had stood here, and its death had resulted in metal flows that had left behind rich deposits on either side of an impassable land of gorges and steep hills known as the Kragh.

"We won't be staying here." Marc Frederick gestured for Trevor to approach. The man brought with him two horses, a chestnut and a bay. Swinging up into the saddle of the bay, Marc

Frederick directed Dorilian's attention to the tallest of the lumbering hills. "That is where we ride."

"We ride into a land where monsters dwell? At night?"

"We will have guides, and our safety is assured. Believe me when I say we could not be safer."

"And if I refuse to ride with you?"

"Then I will regret your choice and go without you. It might be easier in any event. I gave my word I would bring only myself, my kin, or men they have agreed to allow."

"And these—your hosts—they have agreed to allow me?"

"They do not know about you. But they would not turn you away. Your name would put them on their knees."

Dorilian considered. Autumn came early to these highlands, and the trees were tipped with flickers of orange. Stories abounded of men who entered these hills and never returned. Those who did babbled of having lost their way, hunted by horrific beasts. Yet Marc Frederick believed they were safe.

"So be it." Dorilian grasped the horn of the chestnut's saddle and swung astride, taking the reins. Once seated, he edged aside his cloak to show the weapon at his side. "But I remain battle armed. You will never have a surer bodyguard. If you fear not these beasts, then I will match your confidence."

"You need fear them not at all. Your blood is sacred, whereas mine is but red." To his remaining men, Marc Frederick said, "Look for us before sunset tomorrow."

# 41

The pool at the south end of the Sordaneon Serat had a mosaic roof upheld by lapis pillars with gilded lily crowns. It was Daimonaeris' favorite spot for bathing. She stood, holding her hair off her back as her maidservants poured urns of water drawn from the blue pool over her naked body. The action lifted her breasts to better show their perfect shape.

Deben was watching her. She knew he did so from behind the privacy screens of the gallery overlooking this secluded garden.

Several months ago, when she had first mentioned her love of water and bathing, he had made this pool available to her, saying it was the most beautiful and private to be had. It was certainly beautiful—hidden in the Hierarch's palace, surrounded by grounds which only he enjoyed and colonnades along which he alone walked—but it was not private. Deben enjoyed spying on her, and it amused him to learn that she did not object to his doing so. With her knowledge, Deben had seduced one of her maidens and deflowered the girl, an act the maid had reported he did with great delicacy and vigor.

Then, to the Hierarch's disappointment, Daimonaeris had taken her husband's prolonged absence as an opportunity to pay a lengthy visit to her brother. She had even twice extended her stay in Mormantalorus, though she had sent Deben playful letters describing in delicious detail how she and her maidens bathed in the grotto pools of volcano-sculpted caverns or beneath waterfalls of rose-hued wonder cascading from towers overlooking the sea. It had been a necessary separation, designed to whet Deben's appetite. *He never visits a girl but once*, Nammuor had advised her. They had studied the Hierarch's habits in depth. The only exception had been Deben's late wife, and those visits had been for purposes of dynasty.

So now she was again in Sordan, standing in the blue waters

of Deben's pretty pool, her hands skimming her breasts and trailing down her water-drenched skin to the curve of her hips and thighs. He would like what he saw. She was everything he desired in a woman, though he had given her to his son. Tonight, she decided, she would present him with another of her virgin maidens, another conquest to fan his fire.

At lunch, however, when she joined him for that meal, Deben was in a black temper, his anger aroused by a dispatch from his ambassador to the Triemperal Archhalia.

"They denied my petition." Fuming, he threw the letters to the floor. They dined in a room the pure white of pearls, in which waterglobes in skins of precious stones hovered overhead to even out the shadows with pearl soft light. "Instead, they nodded to the usurper's heirs, his bitch daughter's fur-faced bastards. The Malyrdeons would rather give their throne to Khelds than acknowledge me!"

"They know they have fallen." She cut her knife deep into the juicy flesh of a peach. "It matters not to them if they fall further still." How Marc Frederick could have been allowed to adopt his Kheld-born grandsons to be his heirs with so little opposition defied understanding. And making lowborn Stefan the Prince of Dazunor was nothing short of travesty.

Deben continued to scowl. "My son said nothing. He made no statement of opposition, uttered not so much as a word against it. The best my representatives could get him to do was affix his signature to my rejection of the Archhalia's demand that I withdraw my family's claim."

"He said nothing at all?"

"Nothing. And he refuses to explain himself."

"He is interested only in his own pursuits: his horses and his palaces. He is restoring one in Stauberg, I happen to know. And another in Trulo." As far as she was concerned, her husband's enforced stay at the Stauberg-Randolph King's court was an embarrassment.

"Marc Frederick is heirless—and my son is restoring palaces while I must rely on *spies* to tell me what he is doing! Half the nobles in Essera think Dorilian is a viable alternative to that miserable, baseborn upstart, yet he offers no more opposition to that man's plans than does a slave to the boot. Indeed, he now keeps the bastard good company, if my spies are to be believed!"

Daimonaeris nibbled thoughtfully on a crescent of fruit. Dorilian, for all his many faults, had never been particularly friendly to the Stauberg-Randolphs. Much less so, in fact, than Sebbord had been. Deben gave her a grimace reminiscent of Dorilian's wolfish snarl. There were times, she thought, that he almost—but never quite—looked like his son.

"You think him too willful for that?' Deben snorted. "So did I. But perhaps he found the man who could bring him to heel."

"I am quite embarrassed, really, to call him husband." She had never led Deben to believe that she loved his son.

"He was never the prize in your marriage."

"I know." She sighed and allowed her gaze to drift to the pretty view of the city outside the window. "I wed him to secure his inheritance, of course, and to see that his blood—your blood, dear Lord—be mated to a true, royal line worthy of a Sordaneon. Our children will carry your line forth." She allowed a worried look in his direction. "He has hinted in his letters that he will wish to claim his husbandly rights on his return."

"He thinks so? I should think he would still be rather infantile."

"Only in his behavior." She blushed. "Physically, he says, he has quite grown." She continued to watch Deben from beneath her lashes.

She could provide the letter, if asked. Having Heran, one of Nammuor's long-placed spies in Sebbord's household, pursue her husband's doughy little nurse had been one of her more masterful moves. The silly creature had even married him. Heran had been promoted rapidly and was now trusted with his prince's correspon-dence, into which she had begun to slip a few notes of her own.

The Hierarch frowned. Daimonaeris leaned nearer to the table, aware of how her skin glowed translucent in the fine light, her white-gold hair barely caught up and threatening to fall free of its combs. She had applied color artfully to her mouth, that it should look at once appetizing and innocent of such artifice.

"It seems so wrong, sometimes," she confided, "that I should find you so much worthier than your son."

The smile that greeted her overture sent a shiver down her spine. "What do you want, little minx?" Deben leaned toward her in turn. "I'm not going to forbid my Heir from claiming his wife."

"Only that you claim her first."

First. It was his one true perversion, his most sublime pleasure. To take a beautiful young woman or girl and bend her to his body's use. Nammuor had told her of Deben's weakness, how he believed placing any part of himself where a lesser man had gone before him was beneath his privilege. Deben envisioned the other man's remnants, his body fluids, his diseases, lurking within the female's infested chamber. His women were always perfect and pure, as befitted those who would couple with a god.

"Only that?"

She knew already how hotly he lusted for her beauty, breeding, and perfection—and the delectable wickedness he might find in penetrating his proud son's wife. But he, like she, knew such pleasures came with a price.

The time had come to reveal her thoughts. She did not feign the passion in her eyes or the fervent plea on her lips. "I do not want to bear Dorilian's children. I would feel no passion in coupling with him, not even desire. See how he abandons me! He will make it painful, and he will despise any son I give him. If, indeed, he can sire sons. Who knows but maybe he cannot? Then you would be called upon to take another wife and sire another son. I do not think you would wish for Levyathan to do so." She reached for his hand, and he did not move it to avoid her grasp. "I want *your* child! A son of Derlon's blood for Sordan and Mormantalorus. A son to stand tall against Essera and its half-men in *all* the ways Dorilian has proven he cannot. His mother and her father forsook you and turned him against you, Thrice Royal—why should a son of theirs sit upon your Throne when you have had to fight so hard to keep it? Let my body bear the son whom you deserve and Sordan must have."

He stared at her as at some beautiful, mad thing he had yet to identify but of which he was not afraid. "A son he would call his?"

"He would never know it was not."

What she offered was more than mere biological release, more than the simple satisfaction of sexual conquest. She offered Deben a banquet of revenge upon a son who had defied him at nearly every turn. That and the surety of another heir. Another heir to keep Essera and its marriage shackles away from his bedchamber door should risk-taking Dorilian somehow fall again into enemy hands. Another heir to perpetuate Rill kind should Dorilian prove *gynekos*, capable only of siring daughters, as happened with so many of Highborn kind. Should such circumstances befall his rebellious Heir, all Sordan would be glad of Deben's foresight while Essera could but howl and gnash its teeth.

He lifted her hand to his lips and kissed it.

# 42

Dorilian sensed something ancient in the waiting rider whose blue roan pawed the steep trail ahead of them. He didn't doubt that more watchers lurked in the dense forest. Great-limbed trees latticed the sky with branches through which weak, late-afternoon sunlight dappled the forest floor. Earth and decay hung in the air—old leaves and a rich scent of matter from the stream below the path, on the banks of which logs rotted and mosses grew. But there was another scent, just barely rank and reminiscent of beasts, pointing to things unseen.

"Greetings, Baran, Lord of Gloannech." Marc Frederick's strong voice boomed among the rocks. "I come as promised, to look upon that of which your correspondence told me." He used Low Aryati, seldom spoken outside the halls of scholars and a scattered handful of enclaves tucked among Gweroyen's inhospitable coastal mountains.

The rider, a hulking figure wearing a fur cloak that matched his horse in color, looked the visitors over through eyes of tawny gold. "Hail, King of Essera. My folk will guide you and keep you safe. None will disturb your work." The voice bore notes of gravel and growl.

Dorilian marked the russet color of the man's hair—not only on his head but also on his face and hands. It was an unusual color, seldom seen even among Khelds, who sometimes bore it. Ginger fur appeared to grow on every exposed body part.

Hairs rose on the back of his own neck. *Furred men.* He glanced hard at the King in warning but received no response. Marc Frederick might not know the old stories or understand the danger—but Dorilian did. He knew those stories in the core of his Highborn being, from images imprinted on ancestral cells. Those memories vied with other impressions, confused bits interspersed with his fragmented Wall visions.

More men, all similarly furred, some on horseback, some not, emerged from the forest to escort them. Not a few moved in ways that could never be called human.

"Do not go with these creatures." Dorilian drew his sword and showed it.

The leader, Baran, who had gone to the head of the party, twisted to glare at him. The King raised his hand but kept his horse with Dorilian's.

"You gave me your word, Lord Baran, and for me, it is enough," Marc Frederick said. "My companion, however, needs more proof of your goodwill than I."

Dorilian stared at him in disbelief.

"These creatures are Highborn killers! They are Dog Men, the breed of Hen that slew Telarion and his sons at Bynum ages ago—*and* they hunted down Peleor, son of Derlon, across the Eleutheron before they tore apart his body and heaped his bones about the arches at Simelon. Peleor's blood stains those structures to this day! Only the Dog Men have killed more of my people than your murderous Khelds. Why do you bring me among them, if you know what they are?"

"Because they will do you no harm. Lord Baran's people repented to King Emrysen long ago, when they were banished to this place. They swore upon the lives of all their race never to spill another drop of Highborn blood. They have fallen into legend since, hidden and forgotten by the world of Men, as they have wished to be."

Dorilian wanted to believe him. Few things tasted as sharp to his mind as Marc Frederick's sincerity. But these others... could he trust in the word of creatures bred by the Aryati of old for one purpose only: to slay his kind? He shook his head.

"I know what they are and that they cannot be trusted."

"You know what they *were*. You must see for yourself if you are to know what they *are*."

Although Marc Frederick did not possess Highborn memory or the ability to pluck truth from bones of words and skins of thought, the admonition was apt. Sebbord had often said as much. Framed by tall trees and ringed by silent half-men, Baran sat upon his rough steed, his rugged expression now deeply perplexed and disturbed.

"This young one is no kin of yours." Baran guided his horse nearer and leaned forward, inhaling through his large, impressive nose. Nostrils flared, testing the air. "He is not one of yours. He is none of any of your kind." Doubt gave way to revelation and wonder. "He wears a scent we have long since ceased to taste upon the winds. Why do you bring this youngling of the God-Kind among us?"

"You know why. You know why I am here—should he not be also? Or do you forget your ancient promise?"

Baran, still looking stunned, nodded. In a surprisingly fluid motion for so large a man, he leaped down from his horse and dropped at once to his knee, his great head bowed. "Breathe deep," he commanded his companions, "for we are doubly honored. We stand again in the presence of the God-Kind we wronged of old! Let this son of Leur see that his safety is promised!"

Each of their escort, who had been exchanging glances laced with trepidation and growing fear, tossed aside their weapons and dropped to their knees where they stood. Those who were mounted like Baran did the same, dismounting from their horses. All laid their bodies on the ground and bowed even lower than their lord. Their empty hands splayed upon dirt—hands that were in many cases bestial and clawed in testament to the cursed blood that was in them—and their foreheads kissed the damp, fragrant earth.

"*Sonq naneil, Hal-adon'i. Ichoryai na' Leur debelthenari.*" The ancient words, guttural and rough, rose as one voice. The woods went quiet save for the stamping of horses and calling of birds. None of those hugging the ground so much as stirred. *Take my life, High One. It is forfeit to the blood of Leur.*

Dorilian looked upon the circle of prostrate bodies and felt the force of their reverence, that he was in their eyes all that the King had earlier called him: sacred. What these Dog Men offered, they would freely give. They meant him no harm.

"Very well," he said, sheathing his sword. "I will accompany you."

Baran proved to be a man of few words. He rode ahead, broad and deliberate, and made no attempt to speak with either the King or any other man in his party. Though Dorilian remained tense and watched their every move, neither Baran nor his men said or did anything disrespectful. Nor did they show anything other than a desire to guide and protect. The path opened to a narrow road two hills later. As night fell, they rode through a town of permanent structures, wood and stone houses, some with plank roofs and some with thatch. Everything was built solid and low to the ground. Chimneys spouted smoke, lending a sharp, civilized tang to the air. Golden light shone through stiff, tanned skins covering tiny windows, hinting at warmth within. They did not stop but rode through the town, past doorways where shadowy figures stood or crouched in watch—not in fear, but with a resignation that had long ago yielded such things as hope.

The road rose again on the other side of the town, winding past crude homesteads, then scant pastures clinging to steep rock. Few trees grew upon this face of the great hill, known as the Maw, and those few were twisted and stunted by exposure. Wind blew in swirling gusts off the slope, ripping at the riders' cloaks. They slowed when the light grew too thin and dismounted, going the rest of the way on foot, leading their horses. When they reached the treeless summit, they spied a cluster of tents framed with wood and skin, all glowing from within. Above the largest tent flew the banner of the King.

Marc Frederick nodded to Baran, who backed away respectfully. "Have this dwelling made ready for two. My guest will stay with me." He then led the way within, ducking to clear the low doorway.

Dorilian followed. "Your host did not expect you to bring a guest." The tent was spacious and comfortably appointed. A single raised bed stood at the center, and there was a squat table with an array of drink and foodstuffs among lighted candles. He settled onto a sturdily made footstool—or possibly it was a chair—carved of heavy wood and cushioned with skins. "These are a rough folk."

"Don't disdain them for that. Rough folk may possess truer characters than civilized men."

Dorilian could hardly disagree. He had spent his life thus far among civilized men, very few of whom he could recall liking. "Even so, I shall not sleep tonight."

"Neither of us shall, if my excavators are correct in what they have found."

"Excavators?"

"This is not a diplomatic mission; it is an archeological one. For nearly a year now, at the request of the Hen Kyon and based on research conducted by my court historian, a crew has been digging into the bones of the Maw. Two weeks ago, I received a letter saying they had found something I believe will prove one of my theories correct." Marc Frederick laid his pack out on the bed and opened it, retrieving the makings of a huntsman's meal: a loaf of bread and wedge of cheese. Using his hunting knife, he carved out slices of both and handed them to his guest.

Dorilian took the bread covered with a slab of golden cheese. Biting into it, he tried to ignore his unease. Marc Frederick had not brought him here without purpose, though what the King might hope to unearth and what it might have to do with him, he could not fathom. It was not that he did not trust the King. He did—and hated it for blurring lines he preferred not to cross.

He crossed anyway. "What theory?"

"The location of the pre-Devastation city of Gyges. I believe the Dazun changed its course after the Devastation, something a generation of cartographers failed to consider, and later mapmakers never corrected. Not that it matters, of course. The Dazun's history doesn't change its current situation. Still, people make assumptions based on such things, which is why Trulo was built where it is."

"Trulo was built where it is because the river makes an excellent highway."

"True, though the ore fields nearest Trulo are neither large nor rich. Omadawn, on the other side of the Gap, sits on larger fields, but it lacks two things that Trulo possesses: a sustainable harbor and a rather impressive hill."

Dorilian shrugged. Dazunor's unfavorably located ore fields were not among his problems. He bit again into his food, this time with more enthusiasm. "This is good cheese."

Marc Frederick looked pleased. "I shall pass along the compliment to my cheesemaker. The cheese, and the bread also, were made at Gustan. Both are very close to the kinds of food I enjoyed as a boy. But that was another world, of course—another life entirely. It's a wonder I try still to keep some parts of it with me."

"We all do that. My mother rubbed *ucaja* petals on her skin." The scent had lingered on her death bed, sweet floral notes punctuating the sharp iron of mortal blood and tang of female fear. He glanced away again rather than meet the sudden look of concern Marc Frederick gave him. "I ordered a box of *ucaja* petals when I first arrived in Gustan last fall. I wanted—I needed—to smell them."

"Why?"

"To remind me that I was now among the people who killed her."

Marc Frederick sighed. "You have never been among those people. Never. I had hoped you would have realized that by now." He bent down, tucking away the emptied wrappers from his portion of bread and cheese. "It will soon be night. I must consult with Lord Baran."

"Lord?" The designation seemed discordant. "Who granted that lordship?"

"I did, twenty years ago. Baran came to me at a time of discord between his people and their neighbors, and I heard his case. Hen Kyon lands for several hundred years had enjoyed a de facto protectorate under the Princes of Dazunor, and he wanted to know if that protection was still in force. I enacted a treaty that granted the Hen Kyon their lands under force of their observance of the royal peace, with Baran as Lord to enforce it. Their neighbors fear them. They live ever on the edge of being hunted themselves." Marc Frederick inhaled wood-scented air warmed by a pair of braziers shielded within brass cages. "Are you sure you will not come with me?"

Dorilian shook his head. He had agreed to continue this ill-advised excursion, not to being companionable with Marc Frederick's accursed subjects. These bare accommodations hardly held the promise of a comfortable night. The sun must have set, as the tent walls no longer glowed with ruddy finery. "I trust this diversion will not long delay our departure to Stauberg."

"A day or two, no more."

Dorilian nodded his satisfaction at that, even though he was not satisfied at all.

Dorilian had tired of endlessly rereading the five letters he kept with him. For one thing, the light was terrible. Though brighter nearest the brazier, the fire's heat drove him off, and he settled for weaker light some feet away. For another, he knew the contents of each letter word for word. At least he was not cold, which said much of their furred hosts' ability to provide creature comforts. The occasional gusts that blew in under the tent wall let him know the temperature outside had plummeted. He marked off another day on the calendar he kept and counted just fifty days remaining until he had fulfilled his obligation. Then he could leave the miserable northlands for his native, sun-drenched, hospitable shores.

*Where is he? He is staying away long enough.*

Marc Frederick had become a surprising source of wellbeing in his life, and Dorilian didn't like that the King had not yet returned. Either the man had abandoned him or was ignoring him, neither of which seemed likely. *He is outlasting me*, Dorilian realized. Dorilian could outlast stones if needed, but he had learned from Sebbord and Marc Frederick both that it was best to pick his battles. There was something out there—among the barbarians and cursed, furred men—that Marc Frederick wanted him to see. Staying in the tent would provide nothing in the way of answers.

*Damn him!* Refastening his jacket's high collar and grabbing his cloak, Dorilian stomped out of the tent. Trevor, who had been seated on his bedroll outside, snapped to attention at his abrupt exit and quickly followed. Men and furred men nearby scattered; others dropped to their knees. Scanning the hilltop, Dorilian immediately saw where he must go. Dozens of Dog Men and some of the King's gathered in the open area where he had earlier seen a ramshackle hut that probably marked the excavation site. Light spilled softly about the feet and legs of the gathered crowd, a pale moonlight glow. He walked toward them. As he drew near, a head turned to mark his approach, and from that one movement, a path opened for him. One after the other, every person but one knelt, head bowed, to admit him. Marc Frederick remained standing below them upon a stone ramp that led into the pit. Beside him, the Hen Kyon leader Baran knelt with his hulking form painted in light and shadow.

"Thrice Royal." Other voices repeated their leader's greeting, the title falling softly from inhuman lips.

Dorilian did not look at them. He walked a short way down the ramp, then stopped. Framed by jagged edges of *skellai*—the brittle, flaking earth that characterized the site of a former city— rock, and debris, something smooth and white had been uncovered. It was that substance which shone with soft silver light. He tore his gaze from it, knowing what it was.

"It seems you were right." He looked accusingly at Marc Frederick. "Gyges of the Thousand Spires presided over a Rill node." He'd seen images purported to be of the vanished city, its Aryati-built towers soaring above other constructions no less vast and holding at its heart a corona of shining points. There was no denying what these beasts had unearthed. "You know what you have found. *Vasa'khar*. The Living Body of Leur, the Matrix of the Creation. This can be none other than Derlon's corpus, for there's no immortal City or Wall here." Dorilian looked upon red-haired Baran, wishing he did not have to endure those hope-filled yellow eyes or the terrible fear that resided behind them. "Cover what you've found," he said. "If any of your people should touch the Entity, they would be smitten by Derlon's anger against the race that slew his son."

Baran held his gaze. "Three already have given their lives. Only the ashes of their flesh remained upon its skin, and those were swept away by the winds. We called upon the King to send men who would not be punished."

Dorilian nodded. Although the Rill's deadliness to its enemies felt right to him, he didn't see the point of killing more of these poor creatures simply for performing their King's will.

"You cannot use it." Angry again, he faced Marc Frederick. What he read behind the King's involvement in this venture smacked of ambitions he understood only too well. "This godforsaken height is not Hestya. The Sordaneons who awakened those other hills never visited this one. Derlon's body strikes these men because of what they are, not because he knows this place exists. *Look around you.*" All about lay only empty night and the wind sweeping across the open hilltop, the people standing upon it the tallest things to be seen. "The Rill arches are *missing!*"

"Broken. Fallen," Baran said, "down the hillside. The few we found are lightless, and themselves buried."

"They are not fallen just here but for leagues around. Devastation shattered Gyges. It broke the Rill and buried it! There is no possibility at all of mere mortals ever raising them."

"I'm not asking you to awaken this station," Marc Frederick said.

"Good! Because I cannot." Dorilian stared into the pit again, then turned his back on it. He walked back up the ramp. "Cover it. What need have these wretches for a god they cannot invoke?"

He hurried through the still kneeling Dog Men, none of whom as much as lifted his head from the dirt. When they were well behind him, Dorilian walked to the edge of the hillside. There he sat upon a ledge and looked out at the moon that swelled heavy upon the horizon. Behind him, the Dog Men at last moved and began to follow his instruction to bury what they had found. The crunch of shovels digging into dirt, the shuffle of feet, and the dumping of grit became the only music he heard. When at long last he detected footsteps beside him, he knew who it was.

"How dare you bring me here." His lips were stiff with rage. He refused to look at Marc Frederick. "Do you think that I will become your footpath to my accursed birthright? Or that through me, you can purchase a god?"

"I would never think that. You would put up far too much of a fight."

"I would."

"And I am too old to think I could see such a battle to its end. No, I concede defeat ahead of the matter. The Rill is yours and ever will be. I desire only knowledge of it—and Leur's plan—before all is lost."

*Lost*. Dorilian turned to look at him then. He wasn't quite ready to forgive this latest maneuver, but he was curious again. What did Marc Frederick know of the Entities and the doom upon them? More than he did? Sebbord had not taught him everything.

"There was once a great city here." Marc Frederick lowered his body, joining Dorilian on the ledge of stone. Silver moonlight painted the familiar planes of his face and etched the prominent slope of his nose against the shadows. "It was a mighty metropolis, a place of beauty unsurpassed and joy unanswerable. It is written in the *historie* that the tower circles of Gyges reached so high into the sky that, for leagues around, the streets below them existed in perpetual night and the towers themselves in perpetual day. A hundred billion lives, all snuffed out in a moment. We ride our beasts across their bones, plant our crops upon their ashes. Leur gave us back the World and with it their agony—their ghosts. Most of us never think of that. We do not see or feel them. But the Highborn do. You see worlds others do not."

"I don't. I see this World and this World only."

"You know what I mean." Knowledge beyond that of other men peered back at Dorilian. "This World is more fragile than most men know. Because we live within Leur's Creation, we are blind to its foundations. We see but the moment—Leur's gift—and we think that is everything. We never see what lies beneath. We never see the blighted World."

Dorilian stared for a long moment and then could no longer meet that gaze. The night held less terror for him than the truth. He didn't need to know how Marc Frederick had learned these things; it was enough to know that they shared the same vision.

"Levyathan knows more than I... sees more than I," Dorilian revealed. "He showed me, one time he showed me, what he sees: a world stretched upon a rim of ruin. This land in which we live, which men believe to be the World, is but a skin of life covering a corpse. The rest... is a dark place, poisoned and withered." He gave the King a rueful grimace. "I would not want to live there."

"That was Leur's Gift to your kind, then, to make you as men so you might live within the Creation as men."

Dorilian nodded. He lived in the World as men did because of the way his flesh was fashioned. It was Levyathan's fate to live half in that other world. "The Rill would cease to exist in this World if my bloodline should fail. It would fall into darkness, cut off from the Creation."

"The Malyrdeons fear this fate as well, for the Wall. They are desperate to save it."

Few men not of his own kind understood these fears so well. "I try not to think about how close I am to my Entity or it to me. If I did, I would be terrified the way my father is." Dorilian looked out into the night, and it was brilliant next to the horror he'd seen. The inky expanses of the wildness were less empty. Here, there was still moonlight and hope. "Why did you bring me here? It was not to show me that."

"Look around. We are alone. You and I, the Rill and the World. This is what I wanted, I guess. An opportunity to talk."

Dorilian shook his head. This man... did he ever stop trying? "What do you want from me?"

"An open mind, if you can manage that. I didn't bring you here to pry answers. You will provide those when you are ready. I merely wanted to show you that I know more than you might guess. That there may *be* more than you might guess. I know what lies beneath this hill and others like it, scattered throughout the land. I know what beats at its heart: a piece of matter smaller than a ladybug, contained by a device so large that only the tip of it comprises this hill—the rest is buried deeper still. I know Derlon is powerful, immense, and resides not just in what we see but in places men have forgotten."

His face wore more than a look of wonder; it conveyed something deeper, akin to worship—a worship Dorilian seldom saw even in the faces of the Epoptes or others who purported to uphold the Entities. More than anything, Marc Frederick was a student. Few men had greater appreciation for history or love of science, and fewer still embraced as he did the deep, abiding symbiosis between societies and their institutions. The Rill was both. That love configured him, placed him at home in this place where legends pushed near the surface.

"This is how they found the World, your forefathers Amynas and Leur. This dark. This empty. This silent. Sordan, shining like a sword through the night. From that, they created the World as we know it. It was primitive but sustainable. Then came the Three, giving their immortal lives to extend their Fathers' Creation. Ergeiron guided men, but Derlon moved us, enriched us, and propelled us forward. Dazunor-Rannuli was once a settlement no different from the river town at the foot of Gustan's hill or the simple town of the Dog Men below this one. The Seven Houses then were but the children of former slaves to the Aryati. The World had no Kings or Hierarchs, and the gods had just been born. And look at us now—nations of petty princes warring over scraps when we should be creating empires."

"I will not help you create a new one." Though Marc Frederick's words had touched an infrequent empathy for the vagaries of history and his family's enduring role in the affairs of men, Dorilian heeded much more strongly the warnings they awakened. He feared what men might do to him if they knew of his ability. And he was beyond certain that he did not yet possess what it would take to control that power should others find a way to force him.

But Marc Frederick simply let the moment slide by, his gaze sadly touching the darkened land of this place into which the Rill might never awaken. "No," he said, "I fully expect you will do that on your own."

Baran hunkered in the tent when Marc Frederick returned. The brazier light rendered his red hair and beard orange as he knelt on the carpets beside a second bed that had been brought in, his large hands locking the boards of the upper frame into place. Like the first, the bed was a raised affair, the mattress placed above a heavy, iron-lined space into which Baran next stacked glowing bricks that would heat the sleeping platform. When done, he closed the door to keep in the heat.

"That should keep you warm, Majesty. Nights atop the Maw freeze even before the leaves fall."

"All the more reason to warm ourselves with drink. Be seated and talk with me."

The list of items he had requested had been met, and it was apparent the Hen Kyon had provided their best. The water pot was a voluptuous piece with curved handles and a spout figured with running stags beneath a thick, beautiful glaze. Generous cups made of the same blue clay graced a wooden tray with carvings that would not be out of place in a prince's palace. Marc Frederick rinsed the pot before taking pinches of tea from his bag and placing them within, then covering them with water already boiling in a copper pan.

"My grandson Stefan is now my Heir." He noted how Baran's expression acknowledged that he had heard this news, and it troubled him. "He will assume Prince Jonthan's place as ruler of Dazunor and will see to it that your neighbors honor our treaty."

"They will test him." Baran spoke warily, as well might a man who seldom socialized with royalty. "But I will make his acquaintance and remind him that while my people wish only to be left alone, we will not abide his subjects pasturing their beasts on our lands or hunting in our hills. Perhaps he will allow us, as the late Prince did, to sell our goods through the trade store."

"I don't doubt that he will. He is quite fond of trade, Stefan is."

"A Kheld man's child, they say, much given to their ways."

"True enough, but Khelds have never done your people harm."

"No more than others. The Khelds do not offend us, Majesty. They are mostly river folk and farmers and do not, as do Staubauns, band together to hunt. The local Lords and their tenants, Staubaun folk, murder us on sight where a Kheld will hold his arrow."

The brew having obtained full color and aroma, Marc

Frederick placed a ceramic strainer over the cups one by one and filled each half full. He then added a splash of hundred-year *brannach*, a Kheld liquor that blended well with good leaf tea. "Outside," he said to Baran. "I must keep an eye on him." On his instructions, Trevor placed the tent's two chairs just outside the tent, beneath the weather awning. Together they sat awhile in silence, listening to the muted distant sounds of workers shoveling *skellai* and dirt, filling in the months-old excavation. They would work through the night and well into the days to come, for the site was expansive.

"He is angry," Baran noted at last. His gaze, like Marc Frederick's, never strayed from the figure standing, traced by moonlight, at the Maw's sharp edge. Dorilian was watching the Hen Kyon workers—or, possibly, absorbing the hill's contours or the moon's elevation; anything but the King and his guest. "Is he angry at you?"

"At the World."

"Perhaps you erred to bring him here."

"Perhaps, but I don't think so. He'll get over it. Maybe, if I have succeeded at all, he will think about this night."

"About the Hen Kyon? Or about the Rill god?" Baran looked more perturbed than convinced.

"Both."

"That is a deity we fear to awaken. What if he had done so tonight, with so many of my kindred near and within its reach? It is I who should be angry, Majesty, that you did not warn us."

"And what would a warning have accomplished, Lord Baran? Would your folk have stayed away?"

"No," Baran growled. "More would have come just to catch a glimpse of him, even if only the soles of his boots. Their hearts would have beat with hope that he might lift the curse his kindred laid upon us."

Marc Frederick turned his attention upon Baran then, marking the robust features, the traces of otherness that lurked within the jut of that imposing nose and powerful jaw. And Baran was one of the more human-looking of his kind, with ordinary nails at the ends of his manlike fingers. That likeness to men allowed Baran to be an effective liaison with the world beyond these hills, but it also downplayed the extent to which the Dog Men were different. Dorilian, of course, had probably seen right through it. Like the

Dog Men, the Highborn possessed race memory extending back across centuries. Derlon's experience of his son Peleor's death might well lurk in a Sordaneon mind, just as other deaths had left in their wake a deep enmity against the Kheld folk. But even a god's opposition need not last forever.

Though Dorilian's possibly might.

"He will not lift your curse, Lord Baran. Do not ask that of him. He will not alter the doom his ancestors laid upon you, and his refusal would do more harm to your people than good."

Baran bowed his head. "Wisely you speak, for I see the coldness of his Entity in him, young though he is. Though our doom ties us to his, I now dread its coming even more."

Such words saddened Marc Frederick. He remembered the joy with which Baran had written him, telling him of what his folk had uncovered.

"In time, he will turn his eyes on the people of Hen again—of that, you may be sure. The day you prove yourself to him may be the day for which you have waited."

# 43

"Tell me one thing and one thing only: if I am headed in the right direction."

Marc Frederick stood upon one of the many terraces of his family's manse in the Tower of Jewels. All around him, Permephedon's surreal structures glittered in a ring of many-hued spires. One nearby tower—a deep blue-green traced with vivid turquoise lights, guarded by forgotten technology and the Rill power at its roots—belonged to the Sordaneons. Other towers, some smooth and some terraced, gathered at its feet. Unlike at Stauberg, the Sordaneons had never been diminished here. Yet he wished he were at Stauberg again, more time with Dorilian still before him, and not coming to an end.

The man standing to his back was less interested than he in the architecture of the High Citadel or its symbolic impositions. Permephedon was *his* City, after all, and he knew all its secrets.

"That would depend on where you want to go," Marenthro said.

Permephedon's resident immortal had his foot up on a ledge where sapphire-hued flowers, blue as the garments he wore, glowed against polished walls. No one looking at him would guess the years he had lived. Only his eyes—a copper hue reminiscent of another race and time—sometimes revealed that he had outlived a hundred generations of humankind. And only *once* during Marc Frederick's long knowledge of him had he interceded directly in mortal affairs.

"Don't tell me you do not understand what I'm asking." Marc Frederick was weary of riddles. "You brought me to this World."

He remembered that day vividly. A thunderstorm had swept across Lancashire, and the sky above Warding Hall was the color of lemons. Rain beaded the Triumph roadster parked on gravel next to the lane. He had ridden his Friesian gelding Percy—short for Percival Pompey—through the downpour, and his clothing was soaked. Hair plastered to his head and neck. He had tended to Percy and exited the stable to the sight of this man.

Anger welled up within him as if he were still in that day. "You owe me."

Marenthro was unperturbed by the reminder. "More than you know."

"I no longer care what you might mean by that. I just want to know how this will end."

"Even if I knew that—"

"—you would not tell me. You still treat me like some damned barbarian."

Marc Frederick understood what he was, even if no one else did. He had been born Marc Frederick Randolph, son of William Soames Randolph, landed gentry. He had studied at Oxford, earned degrees in Letters and Public Policy, and served as an officer in a dirty and unsatisfying war. He had driven cars and repaired them, even piloted aircraft. For a brief time, he had played keyboards for an enthusiastic but mediocre band.

All of that life, erased. This World held no trace of him, nothing at all—not one memory or scrap of evidence—before he had emerged within the Wall, captive and angry... to stand face to face with Endurin Malyrdeon. Marc Frederick had been twenty-nine, and nothing he had done from that moment forward had resembled the life he had left behind.

Nothing, that is, but battle and war.

Marenthro hadn't finished reminding him of their respective roles. "When I brought you here, I did so for another."

Yes. *Endurin.* Probably the most powerful Wall Lord ever to be born. Marc Frederick's great-grandfather. One of the more tremendous shocks of Marc Frederick's life had been learning that his late mother, philanthropist and toast of English society Arie Randolph, was, in fact, Ariande, a runaway Malyrdeon princess. Not only that, but her father was Estevan, Endurin's son and Essera's Heir. Discovering that his mother's royalty was one of Entity-gifted quasi-humans who ruled over a very different version of the world from that of Marc Frederick's birth had been... jarring. Not as terrible, though, as being told it would be impossible for him to go back.

He had known *nothing*. No language they or he could understand. Not the writing or numeric system. History. Geography. The people. Could his slate have been any blanker?

But Endurin had adopted Marc Frederick and given him a royal name. Trained him. Marc Frederick had learned it all. Everything. Every. Damn. Thing.

Except for those things Marenthro refused to tell.

"You knew that Jonthan would die, that my Kingdom would be heirless, and that my grandson would come to rule. You knew what would come of my efforts to befriend that boy."

"I knew what *could* come of it. I know what still can. But would you have me warn you of one event—and prevent ten others?"

What would allowing Jonthan to live have prevented? Marc Frederick didn't ask because he didn't want to know. He sighed and studied the horizon. Beyond this flawless City, the Triempery Marc Frederick had vowed to save was crumbling despite his every effort to shore up its foundations.

"So I am merely a mortal after all—a blind creature who finally understands that his world is just a cavern floor, who believes he has built an empire only to learn in the end that he has fashioned a thing of mud, to be crushed under the feet of giants."

"That sounds bitter."

"My son is dead."

"You are not."

"Not all of me, no."

Marenthro's intense attention warmed on him then. "Ask Emyli if your life means anything. Ask your grandsons. Ask Dorilian."

"I fear too much what he would tell me." Marc Frederick allowed a grim smile. "I know now why he resists the Malyrdeons so fiercely. He won't let them do to him what they have done to me."

"And what is that?"

"That I should have everything in this life but the freedom to decide its course."

What thoughts moved in those immortal eyes remained secret, although approving. "You admire Dorilian for that."

"I do. I admire his will. He saw me as part of a conspiracy to keep him from his Entity and his rightful place as Sordan's ruler, and so he fought me, however determined I was not to be his enemy. He craved enemies—but now, I think, he realizes that not every enemy needs remain one. That marvelous destiny of his is maturing. He's casting off the limitations others would place upon it."

Abandoning his view of the glittering city, Marc Frederick strolled back into the manse's interior. Walls of bluish substrate flowed from one open space to another, each chamber veined with crystal and glowing with wonder. This had been Endurin's residence upon a time, and there was something of a Wall Lord's affinity with stone things enlivening the rooms. The fossilized remains of ancient creatures lurked in the depths of some of those walls, shadows of what had been, while other walls bore bas-relief images of long-forgotten places and peoples. In the Malyrdean Hall of the Beginning and the End, renderings of the Five Cities of legend shone upon the curving walls. Two of those Cities had been lost, only their images remaining: sunken Mulsor and the even more mysterious Leur City of Îs. Even Marenthro, it was said, had never seen Îs, if it had even existed, though he had looked upon the face of Mulsor the Damned. Marc Frederick stood beneath a ceiling as elaborate as any jeweled brooch with a center glowing with light.

"It's a delicate task, undermining Highborn perceptions." Marenthro trailed his fingers upon a stone shelf. "Who has changed more, I wonder: he or you?"

"A good question." Marc Frederick walked to a table offering several selections of drinks, choosing one for himself and another for his companion. "Dorilian is powerful enough to alter the world around him. That he does it unknowingly merely makes the gift more elusive. I may well become a vessel for what *he* needs from the World, and if so, I welcome that purpose. What does he need, after all, but what all young people need: acceptance, understanding—and an open heart to show him that life has more to offer than cold purpose? Deben withholds these things from his own son. This last year I have seen for myself what that man has done to him. Jonthan, at least, knew I loved him. The sad thing is that Dorilian knows love exists. He understands it on some level—his brother has been his gateway to that gift. But I'm not sure how, or if, love moves him."

"He's not the only one who needs to find how far love will move him."

Marc Frederick rubbed his hand and the ring heavy on his

finger. "I love my daughter and my grandsons. I love this land. I love it more than those who were born into its bosom. How much more of it must die before I cut deep enough into the rootstock to make it grow again?"

"Be patient. Not every work shows its fruits in a single season."

But had he not been patient already? What did fifty years matter to an immortal? Not what they mattered to Marc Frederick, whose mortal days were numbered, and for whom the prospect of a lifetime without ever seeing the fruits of his labor suddenly seemed unbearable.

"I have prepared that field for forty years, yet Stefan will enjoy none of it. He doesn't have Jonthan's advantages. The Malyrdeons count themselves my kin, though barely, but they do not count themselves as his. Who will acknowledge Stefan as their King except for the Khelds? He is going to be too Kheldish for Essera—you know it, and I know it. He may well do them more harm by it than good."

"He would say you have been too slow to raise Khelds to power."

"He would be wrong. Power is a dangerous catalyst. Stefan thinks power is a finite mass to be divided—if one has more, another has less."

"Some power is like that."

Marc Frederick knew about that. The first power he had ever wielded upon becoming a prince of Essera had been as a commander in Endurin's military. He had instilled order by the judicious rationing of power and put down uprisings by the stern application of force. Stefan had served as an officer in the Dragoon Cadets. Power over other men was the definition to which Stefan retreated at every turn. The young man was already using the resources of his Principate to find ways through which Kheld chieftains might extend their influence. The positions created addressed river trade primarily and changes in leadership in some smaller towns, but there were already signs that, but for his grandfather, Stefan would not stop there.

"There's still time." Marc Frederick sipped his apricot-hued drink, appreciating the notes of brandy lacing its sweet essence. "Dorilian is leaving Essera. I will spend my time with Stefan now. I won't ask for your advice on that."

"You have had a good effect on Dorilian. He's less angry now, more accepting of things other than what he already knows."

"His world needed expanding. It still does. His Entity's worshipers would keep him in a box."

"They worship the box, and so must keep their god within it."

"I'm going to break the damn thing."

"Why? Is a freed god less destructive than a chained one?"

"No. Probably not. But men are better freed of those who control their god."

Marc Frederick went to one of the floating chairs, pushed it to a suitable place, then lowered his body into its embrace. These Aryati places, these Highborn dwellings, had the best furniture, though few pieces functioned quite so well beyond the great Cities. "Dorilian wants me to meet his brother."

Marenthro lifted his head with interest at that. "Levyathan? How unusual. You would be the first person since me whose visit he approved."

"I admit I'm curious. All I know about the boy is what others have told me." He looked at the wizard. "You, of course, have told me nothing."

"I think you will find him surprising."

"Yet another discovery I must make for myself."

"You unlocked that door the day you gained Dorilian's trust. He does not give it lightly."

Marc Frederick reflected on the time he had spent with his guest after leaving the Kragh. They had ridden to Stauberg, and the month and a half in his capital city had confirmed more than Dorilian's trust. Marc Frederick had seen firsthand the young man's energy and resolve, some of the scope of his dreams for Sordan. More than once, he had allowed Dorilian to persuade him to support petitions that removed troops or administrators from Hierarchate domains. Of course, Marc Frederick had intended to grant the measures all along, but he'd also wanted to engage the Sordani prince's participation. For similar reasons, he had several times taken Dorilian into his confidence and sought his opinion on matters of state. Minor situations, but Marc Frederick relished having access to that incisive mind. He craved it even more for no longer having Jonthan to steady his ship of state. Dorilian was more brilliant and more aggressive—everything about him was larger, whether his mind or his ambitions. Marc Frederick found the contact bracing in the same way a sea storm was bracing, not only because it was massive and terrifying but also because being so near such power reminded a man what it was to be alive.

*But he closes the door every time I try to talk about the Rill.*
*Everything about him descends toward silence, underground, as hidden*
*as the Entity itself. He doesn't want us to see it—*
*Or see it in him.*

While Marenthro watched him quietly, as only a man who
knew what lay ahead might, Marc Frederick ignored him as only a
man who created his own future could. He had already forgotten
the wizard as he gazed at the smooth, shining reliefs that marched
across his chamber wall. The Rill linked them all in a blazing silver
crown.

"Grandfather wants me to *what*?"

Stefan had not even finished removing his princely crown and
accessories after his morning of audiences. He despised audiences
in the Golden Palace. The meetings invariably were with Lords or
prosperous merchants presenting either petty grievances or
proposals designed to put more gold in their coffers. The only part
he *did* like was appearing before them with the white fire of the
Dazunor Crown on his head, and the heavy blue cape of state draped
upon his shoulders. He was glad for the wardrobe and also the
lessons in royal conduct provided by his first minister. That his
subjects talked behind his back about his unsuitability to be their
ruler was an unpleasant given.

Emyli extended the missive. "He wants you to marry. As a
means of securing your new status. A royal marriage—"

"He told me I could choose my own bride!" Snatching the
jewel-encrusted badge of office from its place at his throat, Stefan
dropped it into the velvet box where it resided between wearings.
He added the three golden chains of state but continued to wear the
massive Dazunor signet ring.

"That has not changed," Emyli assured her son. "He but
wants you to choose one now." Though she sympathized with
Stefan, she understood her father's command. "You know how he
wishes Jonthan had married sooner."

Married sooner—and fathered a child, preferably a son, who
could have stood where Stefan now did. He did not appreciate the
reminder: he had been second choice.

"Let me guess. He wants me to wed some woman of noble

blood. Some Staubaun heiress whose father has enough lands—maybe even a Highborn princess like stupid Dorilian has and doesn't even sleep with." He sat down and removed his boots of fine leather. "You know, Grandfather is a fine one to talk. His queen hasn't slept with him in how many years? Since Jonthan was born? Maybe if he had wed someone besides that Highborn bitch—someone who actually *wanted* him in her bed—he would have had more sons, and then he wouldn't be trying to stick me with some Staubaun cow."

"I can't believe you're saying these things." Emyli walked to the window and looked out across the city. Palaces and villas crowned the nearby hills.

"You know that's what he wants."

"He wants you to be secure, for your legacy to be founded on a good alliance."

He sighed, looked at her, and shook his head. "Mother, I'm not one of those Staubaun men who lusts to wed a domain or a fortune instead of a flesh-and-blood woman. I want someone I long to jump into bed with every night, a woman who will give me not just one child—one heir—but a house full of children. A woman for whom I would want to build a house."

When a Kheld man found a woman he wanted, the first order of marriage was to build a house for her. It was Kheld wisdom that a man who could build a fine house would make a fine husband.

"Are you telling me you want a Kheldish bride?" She sank onto the edge of a nearby chair.

After a long pause, he nodded, then resumed his undressing. "Maybe Cullen likes Staubaun women, but I don't. I like Kheld girls better. I like the way they laugh and move and the way they look at a man—as if they see him and not just his property. And I think they're prettier, too."

That would not be enough, of course. Marc Frederick wanted him to make a marriage the Archhalia would find suitable for Essera's future King. Khelds were not recognized as full citizens, far less as peers.

"Is there a woman you would choose?"

"No. But I won't marry a Staubaun girl. I don't care if her father owns all of Lacenedon."

Emyli laughed. "That one was taken when she wed Enreddon."

Stefan frowned. He had been proposed as a possible husband

for that girl, but her Highborn father had disdained him for being of lowly, Kheldish birth.

"I don't know what to tell Father," she said.

"Tell him I'm looking." Stefan had put on good day boots and stood again, then walked over to the rack that held his ordinary clothes, which were much finer now than those he'd worn before.

"That's what Jonthan always said."

Remembering his uncle and the woman he had married, Stefan was glad Ionais would not be Queen someday. "He should have looked longer."

"I miss him so. He was always my protector, even as a child, when he saw me being treated differently from him. He never accepted that I was in any way less royal than he or that my children were not as royal as someday his would be." She sighed. "I think Ionais loved him." With a wan smile at her son, she said, "However, I think you are right. You need not wed this very week. But you are now on notice to start looking."

"At Staubaun daughters."

"Surely, there must be one you might learn to love." Rising to leave, she passed near him and put her hand on his arm, pleading for his compliance. "Sometimes a prince does not do what he wants, but what he must."

Everything about Levyathan Sordaneon defied what Marc Frederick thought he knew about the boy, his brother, and Sordan's Highborn rulers. It was not that the Sordaneon Tower was other than he expected. He had been in it before, many times. No—it was the brightness, the joy, the utter ease with which the two young people greeted each other. From the moment the boy's dark-haired nurse welcomed Dorilian with open arms and a smile as warm as summer, then turned to regard Marc Frederick askance through narrowed nut-brown eyes, he knew he was in a world unlike any other.

No Staubaun gatekeepers guarded Levyathan Sordaneon's every contact or directed his every move. The ruling class did not care what happened to Deben's damaged son. Deemed useless even for dynastic purposes, Levyathan was consigned to obscurity. Marc Frederick could not imagine a happier state.

Levyathan's world consisted of bright, airy surroundings ruled over by a pretty, dark-haired woman who was herself with child. Cheerful, brown-skinned Teremari girls and an Ilmari cook as swarthy as old leather saw to the boy's every comfort. The soaring manse in which Levyathan lived boasted of spacious gardens, open rooms with few pieces of furniture, soft edges, and as much fresh air as vast windows and lofty passageways could allow. The nurse, Noemi, stayed at hand, included as family, while Dorilian guided his brother forward to make the introduction.

The likeness was there. The brothers shared the same color hair and eyes, though Levyathan often as not would turn his gaze aside the better to listen. They had the same handsome not-quite Staubaun features, but where Dorilian's were confident, often arrogant, young Levyathan's expressions sometimes were jarringly inappropriate. Levyathan had a child's proportions still, the distorted image of his athletic brother, and when he walked, his gait was jerking and tentative. But for all these deficiencies, he possessed striking poise upon his introduction.

"Majesty." There was nothing inappropriate in Levyathan's shy smile as his head, as if on its own, ducked to one side. He looked very young even for his twelve years. "I have wanted to meet you, to see you clearly."

So this meeting had not been entirely Dorilian's idea. Intrigued, Marc Frederick met his companion's resigned confession with a smile. "I have wanted to meet you also, Prince Levyathan, but you have formidable guardians."

The boy laughed and turned toward Noemi. "She is fearsome, is she not?" The woman glared at her ward fondly, and less fondly at the King.

"Not so fearsome as your brother."

They settled onto lushly cushioned couches facing each other across a glowing bed of green and gold, living crystal that flowed into new shapes much as dancers moved to music. Dorilian sat beside his brother, whose hand sought and found his either for reassurance or out of deep habit. Levyathan's long, slender fingers curled against Dorilian's browner skin.

Noemi took her place on the same couch as the King, putting the greatest possible distance between them, and folded her hands over her round belly. Marc Frederick found her nearly as fascinating as the young Sordaneons. *So this is the woman who raised them after Valyane died. She is one of few who will someday be able to say she knew Dorilian as a child. Almost all will only know or remember him as a man.* It intrigued him to see the inner world Sebbord had created for his grandsons: comfortable, woman ruled, and surrounded by competence. *This is something new. He rejected the Staubaun paradigm!*

Emboldened by what he had discovered, Marc Frederick saw no need to rest upon formality. "I will miss your brother when he leaves for Sordan." Dorilian was the one point of conversation they had in common. Levyathan lived apart from most of the world beyond these walls.

The boy looked at the ceiling. "Dor leaves only enemies behind. Friends he holds near."

"Then we shall see which it shall be with me."

Dorilian reproved him with a steady silver glower. Levyathan, for his part, smiled. Not all Highborn could share minds, but Marc Frederick knew already these two did. That gift had reached through his grief at Jonthan's death and located him in a wasteland of despair. Dorilian had employed the ability so easily, so well, because he had learned it with his brother.

Dorilian related to Noemi his visits with Tiflan at Stauberg and Legon at Simelon, describing each town in detail. She had never visited either place. Her eyes glowed at hearing about the vast, shining Wall and Stauberg's many-colored towers. The market-places. The wind wings. She was saddened to hear of the broken Rill pylons at Simelon, though she had seen similar structures, she soon told the King, on her travels with Lord Sebbord and the boys in Teremar. "But I would like to see such fine places in Essera for myself someday," she said wistfully.

"I think I shall take Lev on a sea voyage," Dorilian decided, his tone confident. "He has never seen the sea."

"Far." Levyathan grew agitated, his hand jerking away from his body. "Too far."

"A ship would be too dangerous for him, young Lord." Noemi put the idea to rest. "Too many ropes, too many rails, too many things he can't see properly and would trip over. Too many things for *me* to trip over!" It apparently never occurred to her that she might not be on the ship with them.

"He can handle it." Dorilian did not appear dissuaded.

"He might fall into the water. He might fall down the stairs."

"Would you like to go?" Marc Frederick asked the boy

directly. Levyathan sat next to Dorilian with his eyes closed and his head bobbing, his right hand tracing paths through the air between them.

"Meet Ergeiron," Levyathan said. "Touch his crown, look upon the water."

"He should know the Wall too," Dorilian said to Noemi.

"No, no," Levyathan protested. "Derlon does not go there. I must stay near. The sickness will come." Dorilian and Noemi stopped their conversation to listen to Levyathan instead of each other. "I cannot stray too far."

"Best you stay here," Noemi agreed, though she did not look particularly worried by this talk of sickness. "Near the Rill is best for you."

Dorilian did not refute her assessment, though Marc Frederick could see he had more to say. That he did not was noteworthy. Levyathan's remarks had strayed too near something which Dorilian wanted to remain unsaid.

"You are welcome to visit any part of my lands." Marc Frederick assured both young Sordaneons, though his mind was trying to grasp the precise import of Levyathan's comments about the Rill.

"What lies to the west?" Levyathan wanted to know.

"West of here? Great cities, many built by your kindred. Derlon set the foundations of Stauberg, you know, and of Bynum, Simelon, and Kyrbasillon as well. Simelon and Kyrbasillon were originally fortresses against the wilderness. It was the Rill that opened up the interior."

"Derlon's gift."

"Yes." Marc Frederick smiled, admiring that simple truth.

"Derlon's limbs cleave the darkness." The boy spoke slowly. Marc Frederick had heard that, for Levyathan, language was an awkward invention. "Darkness pushes at his light, but cannot diminish his dimensions. The destruction... cannot prevail, great though it is. So many small lights flicker out and cease to be... but Derlon and Ergeiron shine through the long night."

The men who had called Levyathan Sordaneon a simpleton had assessed a child yet to acquire linguistic tools. It had taken Levyathan more time, and much more effort, to learn to communicate. Marc Frederick accepted the milky beverage a servant offered to him. "Endurin once told me that if I could see the Wall—or the Rill—in their entirety that I would not be able to comprehend what they were. What we see, he told me this, is what we are capable of understanding. An earthly representation, if you will, of the Entity's nature. Ergeiron's purpose is protection—and so, a Wall. Men inherently understand it. The temporal aspects escape detection by ungifted minds—of which mine, I regret, is one."

"I see your brightness."

"Mine?"

"His gift to you cannot be hidden from us."

Holding out his hand, Marc Frederick displayed the Leur's Ring, glowing white within its shining setting. Even Noemi rolled to sit up straighter, the better to see it. "This is what you see. Endurin gifted me with some of his cells, some of his being. A mighty gift, for I could not wear this device without it or command the powers it allows. Yet I am bound neither to the Wall nor any Entity."

"You are bound to Leur."

"Yes, I suppose I am. To Leur."

Sitting at his brother's side, the boy having released his hand, Dorilian watched Marc Frederick with the intensity of an eagle spying on some creature it had allowed to climb the crags upon which it lived. One false move would destroy that fragile trust. But Marc Frederick had no fear of trespassing any boundaries. He extended his hand, allowed a touch of the Ring that blazed with its own life upon that altered finger. Let Levyathan Sordaneon divine the secrets of his wearing that Ring, if indeed he could. His only concern was that the child might be deeply Rill-linked, as some of the Sordaneons were—as Labran himself had been. If so, Marc Frederick would feel it, as he had those few times he had touched Dorilian unguarded. But Levyathan's touch had nothing of the crackle of Rill flow as it touched the Ring, then his hand; only the tentative warmth of fingertips, a touch as light as a butterfly dancing upon his finger, before that was also withdrawn. Levyathan slid his head around toward his brother. "Leur rejects shadow men. This is a Wall Lord's work."

"So he is not a shadow man." Dorilian's tone merely confirmed a conclusion he had himself reached. He smiled at Marc Frederick congenially.

"Not shadow. He shines true, different. Not our kind."

"Neither am I." Noemi bounced back onto her cushion and arranged her hands over her rotund belly. "Yet you say I shine like a kitchen fire."

Both young men laughed, Levyathan throwing his head back and kicking his leg against the floor. Kitchen fires were small but warm, seen only when near. Later, after sharing a small repast of nuts and fruit, as Dorilian and Noemi talked in another room and they were preparing to leave, Levyathan spoke to Marc Frederick again. "Many men shine darkly. Nammuor's dark garments breed shadows. He stands upon an abyss that swallows all brightness."

Later, when Marc Frederick asked Dorilian about his brother's words, the young man merely shook his head. "I know less about Nammuor than you do. Why should he know more?"

*Because I know what Levyathan's words mean; I know what it is he sees.* But their friendship was still tentative and new, and he could not bring himself to reveal to Dorilian the extent of the horror that awaited.

# 44

If Daimonaeris had hoped Dorilian's absence would diminish his popularity, she was mistaken. The sight of their prince's flag rising above the Gate of Wings brought Sordan's people out into the streets, their voices raised in joy. High on the battlements that soared over the City, Daimonaeris and Nammuor watched as thousands emerged from their dwellings to catch a glimpse of him. In contrast to the past, when Dorilian would depart from the harbor or the Rill in great haste and secrecy, this time he put himself on display. He rode his horse down the three staircases of broad steps that led from the Rill station to the Dekkora, an immense public square. Women held out coins for him to bless, children offered flowers, and old men presented words of welcome and thanksgiving—he even touched some people briefly, clasping their hands as they gasped with wonder.

"It seems they love him better than you do, my little Hierarchessa," Nammuor noted. "And certainly more than they like his father."

She drew away from his side. "Deben has not appeared in public in forty years. The City barely knows he's alive."

"Unlike Dorilian, who, apparently, they like that way. I'm sure the mourning at his passing will be profound." His gaze narrowed as he watched the street so far below. "A pity he could not be more useful. There are times I like what I see."

"Like?" Daimonaeris lifted the hem of her gown and trod the clipped herbs growing between paving stones. Every step crushed leaves underfoot and released sweet scent into the air. "That boy maltreats everyone. He regards both of us as a bad purchase he wishes would just go away."

"How ironic." Nammuor cocked his head, watching her move.

"Ah, well, he has a bit more time. After all, we *are* going to wait until you've made your virgin sacrifice. Now that the prodigal has returned, and can conceivably be the father, I trust you can get Deben to do his part."

"He's so eager, he can barely keep the secret." She laughed, knowing her beauty could make even a Sordaneon foolish. "He has been marinating for months in reasons to resent his son. After today's public display, it will take little more for Deben to burn with the desire to cuckold him. And you can be sure—oh, so sure— that Dorilian will give him more."

She had shown Nammuor the letters Dorilian had sent, not only his letters to her but those he had written to his father. These she saw even before Deben, thanks to Heran, who delivered them to her first. The letters announced concessions the young Heir had garnered from Essera's King, including restoration of the City's port to Sordaneon authority, and withdrawal of one-third of the occupying Triemperal garrison. In addition, Dorilian had laid out what he hoped to accomplish upon his return. The projects ranged from minor to massive: a granary complex to be built at Hestya; a new reservoir and system of irrigation dams at Ulguay in rain-parched Sansordan; a trade mission to Kyredon exploring a possible route to Essera's eastern provinces, bypassing the cartel-controlled Dazun River.

Nammuor crossed to his sister and put his arm around her shoulder, his fingers brushing the jeweled brooch of a lily that held together the two drapes of her gown. "And there, dear Sister, is the reason I like him. He is every bit as gifted as Deben is hopeless. I think it's charming the way he aspires to philanthropy, though it isn't quite in him. Dorilian is not truly philanthropic, no more than I am. No, he uses his people as an actor uses a chorus—the better to amplify his goals. His father is much less likely to engage in open conflict with a popular son."

Servants emerged onto the terrace and fanned a brilliant blue cloth in the air above a table being prepared for their meal. Dorilian would not be joining his wife for hours, as Deben had already commanded his appearance.

Nammuor bent his head, putting his lips near her ear. "He's an enigma, this boy husband of yours. I'm sure Sebbord taught him a great many useful things besides how to manage his inheritance. It's unfortunate that he's warmed to Essera. That was the whole purpose of this adventure, of course—Marc Frederick is no fool. His family's feud with the Sordaneons no longer serves any useful purpose. I dare say we have only a little time before Dorilian realizes what I am up to in Suddekar and undertakes to turn his father against me. At which juncture"—he smiled engagingly—"you will make a lovely young widow."

She toyed with the bracelet upon her wrist that marked her as a wedded woman. "The grieving Hierarch will console me, you may be sure." The bracelet of heavy gold, its surface colored with the Hierarchal crest of the Sordaneons, proclaimed her status as a member of the domain's ruling House. She enjoyed wearing the lofty symbol for the reverence it garnered.

"It would be best, of course, if you could seduce your husband."

Daimonaeris frowned. "After the fact, of course."

"Of course." Releasing her, Nammuor returned to the rampart and looked over it. Daimonaeris followed, and noticed that Dorilian had mounted his horse again, riding at the head of his soldiers toward the Gate of Wings.

Seeing Nammuor frown, she laid her hand upon his cheek. "Are you growing stronger again? After the last time?"

"Yes. I can wear the Diadem for longer periods. I can channel more power than before... but it drains my life force. The mages have built a healing chamber in which I might sleep, and it revives my energy, yet by each day's end, I flag again. I may have to resign myself to knowing that I can only use it sparingly—unless I can find a better energy source."

"You mean better than your body?"

"Much better. I've begun using new crystals—life force crystals."

Nammuor had discovered the Diadem several years ago, the day a fissure opened in Dzalarad, the Mountain of Fire, sending glowing plumes of lava streaming into the sea. The wound had exposed a previously hidden and mysterious artifact at the center of the volcano. It had cost ten mages and dozens of slaves their lives to create a path to the crypt, only to find it could not be opened, because it had no lock and no door.

Mages proclaimed it Leur work, which only the Highborn could penetrate. Daimonaeris had long ago found the secret passage that had allowed Nammuor to enter the Serpentine Palace where her father, Camas, lay on his deathbed. Nammuor had lifted his aged stepfather and carried him to the mountain, down into the foul, blistering pit and into the arms of slaves so desperate for their lives that they ignored the old man's cries. Camas had lived long enough for his blood to flow onto the surface of the crypt, which yielded entry at last. The slaves brought back both the cask within and the dead body of the Nuarch. Camas had later lain in state, accorded all the honors to which he was due. But Nammuor took possession of the terrifying cask, its surface bearing script so ancient that scholars could not fully translate its meaning, only that the warnings were dire.

Yet what power the crown within had given him! What energies it brought forth from the earth, the very seas and the air! A god-thing, his mages called it in whispers, for what they had seen convinced them that it surpassed even the greater enhancers possessed by the Highborn. Nammuor had used the Diadem to claim the throne, gathering his enemies and destroying them with a blast of flame from his outstretched hand. Since that day, Daimonaeris had watched her brother turn a mountainside to glass and boil the very sea until a pretty cove became a cauldron in which ships had burst into flame and men had died screaming.

But using the device hurt him, caused headaches and blindness. Boiling the sea had cost him so greatly, Daimonaeris had feared for his life. For three weeks following that day, she had stayed at his bedside, soothing him with cool water as he lingered in terrible dreams.

"When can you wear it again?" She was as eager as he for their war to begin. As before, she would deliver the first blow.

"Soon." He closed his eyes, lashes dark against his skin. "I need but a year. I need to perfect my crystals. I need more time."

Daimonaeris laughed, light and airy as the beautiful garden in which she stood, floating above a City of a million people, the dreams of which she would never know or feel compelled to address. "Then be patient, brother, for I shall give you your year. Then I shall rule Mormantalorus as you promised—and you shall rule all the rest."

# 45

The most important of Highborn holidays was celebrated annually at Sordan. For three days and as many nights, unrestrained merrymaking ushered the World into renewal by repeating the age-old mysteries of the Illumination. On the morning of the Third Day of the first month of summer, in the World's holiest hour, a miracle occurred. The first ray of the first sun of the Return shone through solid stone to illuminate the most revered spot of ground in the Triempery. According to myth, Amynas and Leur had brought forth the Three on that spot. Afterward, Amynas had come down from the mountainside to utter his famous invocation: *Go and bring the People home! For here in Sordan, to which my heart longed to Return, shall I make my City!*

For two millennia, Staubauns throughout the empire esteemed a yearly pilgrimage to the island city for noble and common folk alike, though the tradition of pilgrimage had suffered in the hostile aftermath of Marc Frederick's occupation of the City. But there was no diminishing Sordan's importance for properly observing the Illumination—the event occurred nowhere else.

Four months after they had parted ways in Permephedon, Marc Frederick accepted Dorilian's invitation to attend the Illumination. He fully appreciated the danger.

"I wish I could do as he did for my Jubilee and just show up unannounced at the party." Marc Frederick had traveled with Enreddon and Regelon to the island city. "What freedom it would be to see this City and its revels from the streets! I would love to get a better look at everything—explore the alleys, meet the people, drink the common wine."

They stood on the porch of the King's House. Before Essera's seizure of Labran—and Sordan's subsequent occupation—the grand building overlooking the Dekkora had served as a royal residence for the Malyrdeons. Now, once again, flags floated above the roof, and banners draped the balconies, announcing the presence of Essera's King and his Malyrdeon relations. After arriving by Rill, he had entered the City without fanfare by using the underground road called the Va Haira, bypassing the crowds that waited outside the palace's walls to curse his name and decry his presence in their city.

"At least you won't have to bear too much of Deben's company," Enreddon said by way of consolation.

"No. Just the Feast of Coming, I should think, and that incredibly long play the next day—you know the one—"

"The Tribulation of Amynas. It should be performed in the Dekkora, from the very steps upon which Amynas stood as the sun set, not in the courtyard of the Serat. Deben's fear-eaten mind robs our very rituals of beauty." Enreddon was disappointed that he would not see the sacred play performed in its proper context. He leaned upon the terrace wall. "What a magnificent City this is, pure beauty."

"Amynas chose it for a reason."

His Highborn friend flashed a grin. Marc Frederick should have said Lord Amynas or Holy Amynas. "Clearly, you have been among us too long. You think you are one of us."

Laughing, Marc Frederick turned his back on the view and retreated into the house with Enreddon following.

"Would it surprise you, Redd, if I said I feel as if I know this ancestor of yours? I know how Amynas felt about his City, his people, and his offspring."

"Ah, now that is blasphemy."

"He wanted to preserve something. I don't think we completely grasp what he was trying to do—we're too far removed from it now. But I'm fairly certain the World has not yet become what he wanted it to be."

"Or wants it to be. Some say he became the World itself, just as Derlon became the Rill. Some say he sleeps still under the Mountains of Ice. No one really knows what Amynas decided to do with his immortal life."

Marc Frederick had his own ideas about that. He and Enreddon had spent a summer once digging into the archives, trying to find out if Marenthro was Amynas. Ultimately, they had concluded he could not be, though he might be the last of the Three. "I think old Amynas just simply went away one day, and no one noticed."

"Perhaps that's true. By then, we had forgotten what our god looked like."

Just as the World was in the process of forgetting who and what the Highborn were.

At least Marc Frederick's relations with Sordan were not openly hostile for the first time since the day he had placed Ergeiron's heavy Crown upon his brow. Within grasp—indeed, barely out of reach— waited the ally he needed: a young man with whom he could finally accomplish the work for which he had been born. If only Jonthan stood at his side, that work might have filled him with more joy.

What if Sordan was not ally enough? Nammuor built up armies but did not use them. Why? Nammuor had left Sordan soon after Dorilian's return, and spies had yet to learn Nammuor's plans. Marc Frederick gleaned only rumors and pieces of rumors. Nammuor slept in a mage chamber... he had revived dangerous *Ir* technology to translocate matter... his shipbuilders had laid keels for a score of new ships. Just as a few stones did not make a wall, rumors did not create facts.

Nammuor moved about the edges of their lives like a creature in the dark.

When he arrived for the Feast of Coming, Marc Frederick noticed how Dorilian, now secure in his domain, adopted the role of a prince being civil to an enemy of his people. Though he still hoped the day would come when Dorilian would befriend him, for now, their relationship had merely thawed. Until then, Marc Frederick must accept the necessity of appearances. Among these were the chill formality of his hosts and the icy disdain with which Daimonaeris received him.

The young woman was every bit as beautiful as Apollonia had raved her to be, with passionate topaz eyes and smooth lips practiced at portraying innocence. She carried herself with the golden grace of a goddess. Dorilian was probably the only man in the Triempery who didn't entertain thoughts of taking her to his bed. Marc Frederick had joined that multitude upon first sight of the radiant young Archessa, unable to grasp how any man could turn away from such a wife. Taking the hand Daimonaeris had offered, he lifted her slender fingers as such a gesture entreated, only to have her withdraw them too quickly for politeness. The rejection did not go unnoticed and Enreddon, to whom she was presented after, greeted Daimonaeris as icily as she had greeted the King. If the rejection stung, she did not show it but proceeded to favor other men thereafter. Dorilian she ignored entirely, except for the once or twice she placed a possessive hand on his arm.

"Beautiful, isn't she?" Dorilian stopped to exchange a few words while others danced after the meal. "Everyone thinks the blessing of Imenos himself has fallen on me. They don't have to live with her."

Marc Frederick had enjoyed the ceremonial banquet, the best feast to be had in the Triempery. The gathering now dispersed onto the moon-white floor in pairs. Deben had asked that his Heir's wife grace his arm for the first dance, and Dorilian had dutifully yielded—not that he had wanted to dance with her anyway. "Are you finding the occasion bearable?"

"More than you are, I can see. I was surprised not to see Levyathan at your table." He'd heard the boy had rejoined his family for the three days of celebration.

Dorilian frowned. "He doesn't handle being in public well."

The real reason—that Deben found the boy embarrassing and feared his enemies would point to the Hierarch's half-witted son as reason to erode Sordaneon rule further—was not one Dorilian would say aloud. With an aristocrat's crisp acknowledgment that the time had come to move on, Dorilian noted a few more pleasant things and left. Marc Frederick watched him the way he should have watched Deben. He was not mistaken. Dorilian, not Deben, was the Sordaneon the other guests sought to corner. Powerful women and men, dignitaries and diplomats, all went to great lengths to introduce their companions to him, and he invariably allowed each a moment of his time. The young man was building his power base.

"He'll surpass Deben by summer's end." Endelarin had planted himself at Marc Frederick's right elbow. His wine cup never seemed to drain, however much he sipped from it. "Not a moment too soon, really, as Deben is well despised. He's too sour a man for this sunny country and provides too little action. See—even on the dance floor, he pretends more movement than he delivers."

Together they watched the Hierarch dance, how Deben made each step a stiff and formal exercise. Only Daimonaeris gave life to their movements, her graceful body promising delights that every man in the room could imagine. Endelarin sighed. "She would show even better with a livelier partner. Dorilian dances very well, of course, but his pretty wife would rather flirt with old men." The Ardaenan King chuckled. "A pity we don't qualify as men in her eyes, since we certainly count as old!" Marc Frederick could force a dance if he wished, though he also knew better than to do it. A complication such as the Heir to Sordan's wife, even for such polite incursions as an obligatory dance, was best left by the wayside. Plenty of other women would welcome his company. Indeed, he had earlier spied the delightful Palimia, his old friend Eldonus' Sordan-born widow. Eldonus had died not long after their last visit, and Palimia had taken up residence in Dazunor-Rannuli. Seeing her here was a pleasant surprise. When he'd met her eyes this evening, she'd rewarded him with a smile. He laughed as he realized that, for the first time in months, he was thinking about bedding a woman.

As it had been for the last thirty-eight years, the hours-long play of the Tribulation was performed in the courtyard of the Sordaneon Serat. Deben would not leave the safety of his dwelling, and the grand columned front of the imposing palace—with its steps and vast, open space—offered a secure setting from which he could grace the event with his god-born presence. From a golden sun-effigy throne on the landing of the Serat, with his Highborn kin arrayed beside him and the highest nobles of many lands seated beneath awnings of layered gauze against the blazing Sordani sun, Deben presided over the reenactment of his ancestors' Return. Marenthro, come from Permephedon as he had done every year since accounts of the event had been kept, sat in the place of honor at Deben's right hand, adding his immortal mystique to the event.

Although there was no denying the majesty inherent in the play's events, Marc Frederick soon agreed with Enreddon that the Dekkora would have been a better location. The main drawback of Deben's paranoia—being seated so high on the Serat steps—was that the action took place too far away to see or hear very well. The actors moved about like miniatures, their voices muted to faded strings of words. Unlike the Dekkora, which had been built for public purposes and was a marvel of acoustics, the Serat courtyard had never been intended for performances. Marc Frederick sat at Deben's left hand as a political statement, acknowledged as a Sordaneon guest, but he was otherwise ignored. Dorilian preferred to look bored, and Deben, when he spoke at all, spoke to Marenthro.

Afterward, following a greeting of the actors, Deben added a short speech consisting of vaguely drawn grievances against Essera and its King. Upon that note of ill-defined rebellion, the Hierarch concluded the presentation, and the crowd dispersed.

When they reached the King's House, Marc Frederick led Marenthro and Enreddon onto the high porch overlooking the square. Together, they watched the uncoiling of hundreds of thousands of people breaking into dance. They, at least, looked like they were having fun. Marc Frederick wasn't fooled, however; he knew just how serious the whole business was.

"Do they really think they will banish the Devastation?"

"They dance to see what demons they awaken—and then they seek to drive them away." Marenthro smiled as he watched the crowd, and the music swelled to fill the dense space enclosed by the Dekkora's glorious buildings. The Three Sisters, suspended orbs each the size of oak crowns, hung like immense globules of clear water above the Rill landing. The colorful awnings of aristocratic tents spread around and beneath them looked like laundry upon a sunny bank.

When Gareth interrupted to announce that Dorilian had arrived, all three men looked up in surprise. They were even more surprised when the young man walked into the room.

"I'm inviting you to accompany me to the Dekkora," Dorilian said. "I will be attending the public celebration this year."

He had changed his garments and stood before them wearing a close-fitting body suit of emerald cloth, upon which bold designs had been embroidered with gold thread and tinsel. Panels of felt encrusted with gems in intricate patterns formed a loincloth of sorts about his hips, and covered his shoulders and chest like armor. Boots of gilded leather encased his feet, hugging his legs with painted flames to midthigh. A cloak of silken ribbons hung from his broad shoulders, and he held under his arm a headpiece with curving, gilded horns and glaring, bejeweled eyes.

"The Sorcerer." Marc Frederick identified the deity whose guise the young man had assumed. Even saying it gave the words a sinister edge.

"That is not a perception we encourage." Enreddon looked to Marenthro, imploring support. But the immortal merely perched on the edge of the low wall, oblivious to the dangerous fall behind him.

Dorilian ignored both men. "Lev chose it. He wants to see and hear the dances—and I am his only way of doing that." Just to look at him was to know his mind was set. "It's his first year in the City during this celebration. It was always too much for him before."

"Your father—"

"Is unhappy. I saw him as I was leaving the Serat. He tried to stop me, but—" Dorilian shrugged at a matter of no importance, "—no one stops me in my own City. Not even you." He and Marc Frederick shared a smile. "Which is why I am asking you to attend."

Marenthro's lack of support did not prevent Enreddon from voicing his own concerns. "Do not encourage this travesty, Marc." The familiarity could not have been more blatant. "I stand with Deben on this. It is inappropriate for one of our blood to dance in the streets—particularly as *that* deity! The masses created it, not we, and we refuse to identify ourselves with it."

Dorilian turned on him. "It's not as if I will turn into a demon by the wearing of these rags!"

"You are an *empath*!" Enreddon snapped. "What will your mindless dancing draw forth from their hearts or create within them? You do not belong among them!"

"That's the big difference between us. I think we *do* belong among them."

When Enreddon strove to answer, Marenthro drew him aside and spoke to him. Then the two left together, going to some other place to continue their conversation.

Marc Frederick walked again to the overlook. In the streets below, the music had picked up its tempo. The sounds of laughter, merriment, and celebration carried even to these imposing heights. Dorilian joined him in his glittering costume, his presence as brightly powerful as the mystical entity he evoked.

"I did not bring a costume," Marc Frederick said. It was customary to appear masked in public on Second Day. What a man did on Second Day, he might well want to deny afterward.

"I will get you a mask. Dress in whatever else you believe will blend in."

Dorilian would see to his safety. In Sordan, he could hardly ask for a better guardian.

"I thank you for the invitation. I will join you."

Gareth intruded again, this time to announce the arrival of yet another royal guest. Endelarin sauntered into the room, his arms jingling with golden rings, his legs clad in purple barbs and hooks of crimson glitter. "I am the Demon of Darkness," he said ominously. He laughed and shook his dark head upon which a rack of horns gleamed with tassels of false blood and gore. He flipped his black cloak from his path and posed. Only then did he ascertain the identity of Marc Frederick's companion. "Dorilian! I heard your father was combing the town! They're arresting Sorcerers by the dozens when they can catch them, and now I see why. Can't have the Heir get himself into an unprotected situation; oh no, we can't! A Highborn prince running amuck with the masses—"

"The people need to see their future Hierarch."

"Then stand upon a battlement somewhere, as your father does. But of course, that is why everyone thinks your father is *this* big!" Endelarin showed two inches between his fingers, laughing at his own joke and bounding out of reach from his Sordaneon cousin just in case the royal temper ignited. "Has he invited you first?" the Ardaenan asked Marc Frederick. "Because I was going to offer you the comforts of my tent. Food and drink... all the very best and plenty of it. I'm going to dance a little with the crowd, but I don't think you ought to mingle. They consider me harmless, but they don't think that of you! Some might say good riddance and, well, especially with young Dorilian dancing around down there, we can't allow any beheadings or the like."

Dorilian walked around Marc Frederick, the better to get in reach of his annoying relation. "My soldiers will protect him!"

"I'm sure they will! I was just offering."

Marc Frederick laughed. "The Malyrdeons have commissioned a tent, and I will gladly watch the both of you from there. Send over some of your best mead, good Endelarin, if you would be so kind, for I have not tasted the milk of wisdom in more years than I care to remember."

Levyathan asked Noemi to lead him to the part of the Serat overlooking the Dekkora and Sordan's heart. The Rill's majestic Temple of the Inception, the Scroll Houses and Temple of Healing, the cliffside markets beneath the Colonnade Mercantile, and the King's House with its domes of blue—all these spread before him, patterns of color and light like an ever-shifting mosaic. Here at the center of the World That Is, there lurked no darkness. Noemi placed his hand upon the sun-warmed surface of the low wall and stood with him a while, answering his questions as best she could. She knew Sordan less well than she did the carved sandstone streets of Askorras or even Permephedon's majestic thoroughfares.

So many people, so many, too many... Levyathan couldn't sort through the confusion, and as he so often did when confronted by a jumble, he mentally sought his brother's orderly, disciplined mind. Less and less of that mind was available to him these days. As Dorilian grew into what he would be, he claimed more privacy for his own thoughts—but Levyathan slid into the parts he could inhabit and tapped that ever-familiar strength, insinuating himself into the open paths of his brother's senses.

He was astride a horse, dismounting... a thousand people, tens of thousands, cheered his jangling wands, because Dorilian played the Sorcerer that day. Levyathan smiled, because he had wanted to see the dances about which he had heard so many tales. He had helped Dor hide the Sorcerer costume beneath garments deep in a chest in his own rooms, where Serat servants did not go, and only Noemi ever thought to pry. Through Dorilian's eyes, he saw the two men who were with him. A short, blocky man dressed in purple and red, a horned laughing scarecrow with startlingly brilliant eyes. The second man was one he knew... Marc Frederick, warmly approving him with blue, smiling eyes. Levyathan had not realized before how very blue they were. At Permephedon, he had seen this man only as an ill-defined figure with a bright hand. Now he saw him as his brother did: dark-haired, older, and handsome, with a regal bearing quite apart from his lofty title.

A fleeting breeze touched Levyathan's face, teasing hair across his skin and eyes, and he absently brushed the offending strands back with his fingers. The momentary distraction wrenched him rudely back into his own body, and his distinct senses became aware of other things... shadowy Noemi leaving the rampart to talk to two servants who appeared to be arguing... something else as well, flickering in the Serat at their backs, the hint of something new and bright. It blazed like a new star in the heavens where none had ever been before, or a flower newly opened in a field where flowers never grew. A spot of color, so tiny that it was like a single white grain of sand upon a black sand beach, and yet he saw it clearly. Drawn to that speck, he felt along the rampart wall until he reached the broad steps leading to the Serat. At the top, he groped until he found a wall, wide and tall, and followed that until he came to an opening and entered the Serat's cool corridors.

Levyathan felt his way among the shadows, using densities to distinguish walls from openings. The thing that drew him was more substantial now, a steady pulse but not yet a heartbeat. Trying to identify it, he detected his father's life force vividly, his brother's even more so, distant but still the stronger, pounding like a drum... ancient Mezentius thin as water... the Malyrdeons a steady burn... Marenthro a blue-white blaze... but this other, so small and new, was so much nearer...

A wall blocked his way, but he felt along it with his fingers until it opened again. The terrace. Outside. He went there and kept his hands pressed to the building wall. He was afraid to stray too far from known paths. His feet pressed a new surface, seamless and smooth. Again he found an opening, heard the resonance of human voices, male and female, laughter and whispers and more laughter. Angling his head toward the vibrations, he felt something sheer and light caress the skin of his face, touch his lips. Not air but nearly so. A curtain. Through it, Levyathan could see them, one body clearly drawn and the other a shadow. Deben was above, his limbs impossibly intertwined with hers, her shadowy legs about his hips. But not all of her was in shadow. He saw the Highborn life within her, the spark of it barely more than a flicker but already bright. Then there was distortion and movement, his father suddenly standing. Levyathan recognized the woman with him.

Daimonaeris hissed in the confusion of sound that was human speech to him. Frantically, Levyathan picked out words and tried to arrange them. *Brother... tell... silence!*

"Father?" he pleaded as Deben grabbed him by the arm and twisted. His elbow exploded with pain. With a cry, Levyathan fell to his knees.

The deep voice, which had never said a word to him in kindness, spoke syllables both black and cold. Deben's fear tasted sharp while the other shrieked red desperation.

Deben ceased to hold him, and Levyathan tumbled free. Deben had Daimonaeris in his arms instead—a writhing, screaming shape.

Levyathan stumbled back, scrabbling at the surfaces around him. *Dor!* His mind sought more than a haven. *Dor!* He had to let his brother know there was now another like themselves, powerful and new... He pushed his feet against the floor. He fell backward, tumbling through the curtain into an open space leading onto the terrace. The curtain tangled his limbs as he landed on the hard surface. Knowing Deben would come after him, Levyathan rolled and kicked at the fabric about his legs. Groping along the floor until he found the wall, he stumbled to his feet. He followed the wall until his knee hit something hard. A step... a wall... another terrace, a ledge... he didn't know for certain, but he pulled himself up onto it and began to feel along the tall wall of the building again. *Dor! I am lost! Find me!*

"Noemi!" He screamed the name though he knew Noemi was no protection from his father. Only Dorilian could help him now—but his brother was not here. He was far away and far below, dancing with the demons.

The Sorcerer was a paradox. Part fool, part god, he was the incarnation of the creation myth in all its archetypes: he was Amynas Malyrdys, warrior prince and human father of the Three; he was Leur, sorcerer prophet and maker of destinies who was killed but could not die; he was the Devaryati, perverter of power, slayer of gods, killer of children. As all three, the Sorcerer evoked pent-up superstitions while driving off evil spirits from entering the reborn World.

The moment Dorilian dismounted from his horse in Sorcerer attire and placed the heavy headpiece of that entity over his head, settling it on his shoulders, he became far more than Sordan's Heir. He assumed the magical nature of the deity. The crowd cheered. They opened the Dekkora floor so he might dance among them, as the sun dropped lower and dipped into an inkwell of red clouds, to reemerge more brilliant than before. Dorilian danced, his face concealed by the mask, his every movement a rippling suggestion of supernatural power.

From the heights of the Dekkora where noble tents and awnings ringed the square in color, men and women rose to their feet and pointed. Word had reached those who had not seen him arrive. Drums crashed, and brassy horns summoned forth raucous laughter. People loudly clapped their hands and called to him. *Welcome! Welcome! Giver of Luck, Maker of Magic, Bringer of the New!*

Drunken excitement caught up citizens and pilgrims alike, and they began to move with the Sorcerer, disjointed at first and slow, then faster and faster as the music fed their cries. The Highborn blood of Amynas Malyrdys, of his son Derlon the Rill-Giver, the blood of gods and sorcerer-kings, ran true and purged itself along with them in the sacred madness of the Sorcerer's dance. As Marc Frederick observed what was happening, he saw what it meant to take a crowd into the palm of one's hand. Not his hand. His hand was empty here. Even the ring he wore paled in power so near the heart of the Rill, upon the very landing of that Entity's primary housing. In some way at once primitive and shatteringly imminent, the Rill itself seemed to infuse the Dekkora with the hum of its hidden potential. Dorilian-Sorcerer whirled and danced around the perimeter of the square with tens of thousands following in his footsteps, costumed women and men tossing foil coins and bits of colored cloth. In the deep bendings of the dance, he touched the ground to take up coins and tawdry trinkets in his hand, flinging them back over his head into the crowd again, dancing away in a shower of gold and silver and confetti. He circled the great Dekkora twice, and then again, twirling, spinning, sending children screaming as they darted out of the way of his bell-tipped club and whip when he charged in mock fury. Laughing, he jangled his scepters in defiance of the throng pressing from all sides as he transformed the dance into reality.

For it was real. There was sorcery here for all to feel. Marc Frederick detected the grip of mass empathy even as the ring on his finger blazed to warn him against it. But there was no evil in that surging energy—no coercion—only the pulse of a power that celebrated itself and drew upon the frenzy. The music rose to a crescendo, the laughter to a fever pitch. They would dance while there was daylight left. His legs must ache, his lungs protest... and still Dorilian danced, arms raised, head thrown back to show the gleaming teeth of his painted mask. *Deus Sordanaeyi! Amynas Sordanaeyi! Derlon... Dorilian...* The crowd called both names as Dorilian's feet stamped the beat of drums and cymbals, the wildly keening pipes following him into madness...

He was demented... he was divine... he was the god incarnate...

The dizzy tempo spiraled. Dorilian leaped and spun upon the rim of Sordan's fabled fountain, where the statue of Amynas lifted his sword to proclaim the World Re-Born. Water splashed crimson around Dorilian's feet as the sun died into Sarkuan Lake, and he swayed at the foot of his forefather's statue like the drunken, half-wild thing they all believed him to be. The scepters fell from his hands, only to be snatched up by those nearest him. The mask followed, revelers lifting it high and bearing it away as Dorilian slowly slid to his knees.

Marc Frederick leaped to his feet. Dorilian's guards had reached him first and chased the mob away. Now Legon also knelt beside his prince.

*He stopped dancing. Why?* The sun had not yet set. Turning so he could see where Dorilian was staring, Marc Frederick froze. Before Essera's King could move, Dorilian was already running toward the Gate of Wings at a speed to outpace even the guardsmen's horses.

Levyathan couldn't understand what his father was saying. "Dor!" he screamed. His throat released the first word it had ever spoken clearly. He saw Deben as a fragmented thing, not enough brightness to hold back the malignant shadow that crowded, bright-bellied, at his side. Music, however, filled his ears... drums... laughter...

*Dor—*

For some reason, Deben had stopped pursuing him and stayed where he was, as though blocked somehow, not walking nearer. Levyathan breathed relief but did not cease backing away.

*Levyathan!*

Not Dorilian, but another. He flinched at the awkward incursion, the crude touch of an unfamiliar mind. His father's will... seeking to latch onto his own.

*No! No!* He beat at that invader with his mind, with his hands. Mercifully, it retreated.

The cacophony surrounding him grew. Noemi. Dorilian, coming out of his immersion in the dance. For a moment, Levyathan saw blood-red water and the soaring pinnacles of the Citadel above the Serat's sprawl of soaring terraces... white figures against the white.

*Dor... Father... lay with her... Quickly! There is another...*

A hand reached out, sudden, strong, and quick. Deben, snatching at him. Desperate, Levyathan jumped back from his father's clawing, wanting only to get away.

There was nothing beneath his feet.

# 46

Marc Frederick ordered one of his guards to dismount and took the horse. Spurring past the stunned men stationed at the Gate of Wings, he rode the beast not only to the Serat but up the steps and into the open, high-ceilinged corridors. People already alerted to the disaster scattered from his path. He emerged again outdoors on the lower terrace that ran around the cliffside face of the complex. Anything that fell from the higher terraces would land here. Dismounting the horse, he ran toward a woman's screams.

Deben stood barefooted just within the nearest doorway, sagging against the wall and wearing a cloth about his hips, his shoulders covered by a hastily donned robe of peridot silk. Not far from where the Hierarch stood, the white marble floor of the terrace ran with red. The crumpled form from which it spread was barely recognizable.

Hardly a bone in Levyathan's body remained unbroken. One leg lay completely under his torso, the foot peeking out beneath his ribs, bones visible through holes in his red-stained garments. Noemi, her dark hair spilling across her face, knelt in the pool of blood. Dorilian slid to his knees beside her.

"Lev?" As Noemi lowered her head and buried her face in her hands, Dorilian touched the least broken parts of his brother's face, beside the nose and along his cheek.

Horror coursed through Marc Frederick as Levyathan's eyes fluttered open in blood-filled sockets. The boy had survived the fall. The pale gray irises focused, aware, followed by movement of the boy's distorted lips.

*He should not be alive; God no… not like that!*

"Don't be afraid, Lev. Stay with me," Dorilian said. "I won't let you go. I promise you."

Noemi sobbed. "Oh, no, Dor... don't!"

Footsteps, running, came up behind him. Marc Frederick turned to see Enreddon, breathing hard, stopping yet paces away. Marenthro also stood there, not quite in the shadows. How long had the immortal been there, watching? Enreddon took one glance and turned his horror-stricken face away before looking to Deben for answers. If the Hierarch had any to give, he did not speak them. A froth of blood and air bubbled from Levyathan's lips. Dorilian covered his brother's mouth with his own as if he could force breath to lift those shattered ribs.

Marenthro strode to Dorilian and placed a firm hand on the young man's shoulder. "There is nothing you can do." Marenthro tried to get Dorilian to look at him. "Now is the time. Let him go."

Dorilian glared at the wizard for attempting to stop him. His face was red with blood. "You don't know what I can do!"

"Don't I? You saved him the day he was born. But he was the size of your hand then and whole. I don't care how strong you are— your body cannot sustain his now. Not like this." He grasped Dorilian by the shoulders, intent on pulling him away by force.

"Don't touch me!" Dorilian's fist connected with Marenthro's jaw, sending him sprawling onto the floor at Deben's feet. The Hierarch made the first sound any had heard from him, a sharp bark of laughter strangled by pain.

"There is your reward, fool, for what you have done," Deben croaked to Marenthro. "You allowed all that led to this, and now we must suffer its conclusion."

Only Dorilian's soft, urgent pleas broke the silence that followed. Each word shattered against the mind like glass, shards ripping new pain. Marc Frederick ground his teeth against it.

"No, no... Lev, please... I'm here now. I won't let anything hurt you..." Cupping his hand around the boy's broken skull and blood-matted hair, Dorilian pulled his brother's body into his arms and cradled it fiercely. Blood ran freely in rivulets around the gaudy beads of his costume, shattered bones grinding audibly in the embrace as he buried his face in the boy's sodden hair. "Stay with me, Lev." The plaintive whisper could be heard only by those who stood nearest. "I can bear it... I can bear anything. Stay!" Those ragged words died to sobs even as the light in Levyathan's staring gray eyes slowly dimmed.

The boy died without speaking.

Marenthro, risen again to his feet, stood over the brothers, his stark face white with a look no man among them had ever seen upon it before. The silence now was more horrible than Dorilian's pleas had been. Even the pain that had been assailing them was gone.

"Dorilian, let him go." Marenthro dropped to his knees beside the huddled youth and his brother once more. This time his touch met no resistance. Gently, with Noemi's help, Marenthro pried Dorilian's fingers free of the body and, together, they eased Levyathan's corpse from his arms. Dorilian did not resist their efforts. Indeed, he appeared to have lost every fiber of will.

"Young Lord, speak to us now, please." Noemi touched Dorilian's face with her bloodied hands, stroking his blank features. "Oh, young Lord, don't be angry. He didn't mean it. Blame me! He wandered off and got out on the ledges. He didn't know. Young Lord, look at me, please look—" He neither answered nor looked at her—or anyone else. His open eyes reflected scattered shards of lamplight, nothing more. Despairing, Noemi turned to Marenthro, her face awash with tears. "He's not listening! He will not hear us! Oh, Highest, what will we do? What if he dies also? They were one mind, always together—what does that mean when one of them is gone?"

Alarmed at the scene unfolding before him, Marc Frederick strode to Deben, who would not meet his eyes. "There lie your sons! Help the one that has not died!"

Deben turned on him with a snarl. "What help have I for a weak-minded fool? He brought this on himself with his unnatural ways. *You* did, when you sent murderers among us and countenanced the monsters that slew their mother! Help him yourself if you can."

It was all Marc Frederick could do to hold back his fist. To not strike Deben. All he could do to keep himself from succumbing to the paralyzing pain of seeing another body as broken as Jon's had been. Though he had no help to offer, he went to Dorilian and knelt beside him. Noemi's cheek rested on Dorilian's blood-streaked hair, her hand stroking his face. The young man's open gaze acknowledged none of them. Even the breaths that from time to time passed Dorilian's lips were so shallow that it seemed he walked with the dead.

"He didn't know." Noemi sobbed repeatedly. She would not look at the bloodied remains of the younger boy. "Poor Lev, the poor boy... he didn't know. He couldn't see the danger. The Hierarch tried to grab him, to save him, but he stepped off."

Realizing that to touch Dorilian now might do more harm than good, Marc Frederick consoled the woman instead, placing his arm about her. Her heart was broken. Levyathan had been her nursling, as close as a son, the center of her life. Dorilian had hardly been less so. She had already lost one of her charges and now feared losing the other. When Marenthro lifted Dorilian, carrying him into the Serat and away from this place of blood and death, Marc Frederick gently held Noemi back from clinging to the young man. He embraced her when she turned, sobbing, into his arms. Though still soft, her body was no longer round, and he remembered that she had given birth to a daughter three weeks before.

"Go with them, mother." It was only right to acknowledge what she felt for both young men. "He will need your love now." A look of bright gratitude rewarded him.

"Stay with us, Majesty," Noemi entreated, "for you knew the poor boy, too. Lord Dorilian trusted you, or he would not have brought you to us."

"I will be near," he promised. "But go with him."

Only when they were gone, and Deben had also vanished, without a word, into the private places from which he never stirred, did Marc Frederick kneel again. He wanted to spend a few moments with the poor, broken boy before the servants would come for him. He touched the purpled eyelids, closing them over now dead eyes that only weeks before had reminded him, all too achingly, of Dorilian.

*He loved you.* He addressed Levyathan silently, though the boy would never hear his thoughts. *He loved you, and now see where he is. Look what's happened. Yours was the only love he never questioned. And now you're gone, and all you might have done together will never be.*

Horns sounded from the Dekkora below, announcing the setting of the last Sun of the year. Red light played upon the Serat walls and the Citadel of Sordan, the City of Light, burned bright as flame, illuminating the sky. A long shadow fell across the terrace floor, causing Marc Frederick to look up. He had forgotten that Enreddon was with them.

"Ah, Redd." He rose to his feet. Though tears washed his eyes, he did not wipe them away. "He is just a boy. Even his father is not here to stay with him. I cannot leave him like this."

"Leur, Marc. You don't know?"

"What do you mean?" His heart was too heavy for guessing games. Not with Levyathan's body lying mangled at his feet.

"This Sordaneon... this"—Enreddon stared at the gleaming blood, bright now in the last blaze of Second Day reflecting off the Serat—"this mortal shell has ceased its life upon our plane. It would take all the powers of Leur to regenerate something so broken. But Levyathan himself, his life force"—his voice dropped to a whisper of horror and revulsion—"it never released its hold on this plane. We still feel him in the Mind. That child may be dead, Marc, but he is not *gone*."

For two days, Dorilian wandered in a place no other man could find. Even Marenthro, skilled as he was in the ways of Highborn kind, knew no way to break into the trance that held the young man's mind. Dorilian's barriers proved insurmountable. He walled himself from the world and the pain it now held. Deben visited only once to verify that his Heir yet lived and, thereafter, stayed away. Marc Frederick thought the man looked ill at ease but decided Deben came by it naturally. Strangers had invaded his house.

"Deben reacts badly to crowds, even small ones. Three is more people than he can handle." Endelarin visited Marc Frederick daily after he insisted on staying at the Serat while Dorilian's fate remained uncertain. The Ardaenan had not sought to look in on his young cousin, not wanting to hinder his convalescence. "I've never been a favorite of Dorilian's, you know. Just the sight of my silly face would probably set him back. A pity about his brother, though. The entire City is in mourning."

Yes, Sordan was in mourning, yet barely knew what it mourned. Levyathan had been a hidden member of the Sordaneon royal house. Whereas Dorilian was loved by the people who placed so many hopes upon him, moving their hearts to pity him and pray for his recovery, they did not feel in themselves any great sorrow at Levyathan's passing. Just as Sordan's people had mourned Sebbord for weeks with funereal rites, inscribing devotions they immolated in public bonfires and tearing their clothes in tatters to symbolize the rending of their spirits, the Hierarch's subjects did the same for Levyathan—except the verses mourners wrote more often bore his brother's name as the flames carried the words to the heavens, and they tore their clothes more out of respect for Dorilian's grief than to demonstrate their own. Marc Frederick observed these displays ambivalently, sad that Sordan would never know the strange and beautiful gifts Levyathan Sordaneon might have given the World. He was heartened only by the domain's love for its surviving prince.

"They will follow him," he said to Enreddon. They walked the cranberry-tinged garden of the King's House and listened to a song of farewell wafting up from the Dekkora below, where mourners gathered in the dusk. "They know his worth far more than his father ever will."

Dorilian had never ceased to be aware. Voices penetrated his silence in much the same way as air filled and left his lungs, as blood flowed through his organs and limbs. His body tethered him to the World, and he never left it. Someone had closed his eyes, and when he opened them again, he recognized the men at his bedside because he had already known they would be there. His skin tasted each man's signature.

"How long?" Even to his own ears, his voice sounded broken.

"Three days," Marc Frederick answered. Welcome smiled from his eyes. Marenthro, silent and disapproving, stood behind the King.

Three days. The information was useful. Dorilian had had no awareness of passing time, and his body protested the prolonged inactivity through aches and twinges. He couldn't attend to its needs and maintain his equilibrium if he had to deal with distractions. Dorilian drew a deeper breath.

"Leave me. I want to be alone."

"Alone?" Marenthro's response sliced at his choice of words. "That is a state you dread above all others, seeing as you have never truly been alone. What have you done?"

"Leave me—or I will again leave you."

It was Marc Frederick who laid a warning hand on the wizard's arm, who enforced Dorilian's wish. Lying back on his pillow, Dorilian closed his eyes and listened to them leave.

Marenthro knew... but it did not matter. Though Dorilian would never again see life in his brother's eyes, hear his laughter, feel the texture of his hair—in other ways no less familiar, Levyathan was still with him. His waking mind flooded with the horrible last events of his brother's life—the blinding physical pain, so overwhelming, the desperate scattered thoughts that stayed with him like accusing shades. *There is another... lay with her... Father... tried...*

His own voice screaming at Lev not to let go, followed by his brother's encompassing final thought.

*You… so bright.*

Lev's untethered life lingered like a promise Dorilian must keep, captive because Dorilian had refused to let him go. Lev's lifeforce resonated within his flesh, jangled his nerves… an indelible refrain whose chords he must not lose, for it could never be reproduced—yet he heard that melody and knew by some strange, half-remembered instinct that his brother survived, if not in whole then certainly in sum. As the Highborn knew when their kind died, so too they might detect their own when they lived. His body had nourished his brother's as a fetus born too soon. For years, his mind had been Levyathan's portal to human experience. Now his body and his mind served as the repository of Lev's essence.

He recognized the danger. Sebbord had trained him for it—though Sebbord's goal had been the Rill Entity, of powerful Derlon's god-mind, not of young, unfinished Levyathan's mortal one. As now constituted, Levyathan possessed no ability to generate independent thought or focus emotions. He had no will. He existed only as a life force and memories, the purest form of yearning. Dorilian instinctively walled his mind from the invader, however beloved, and it had taken him uncounted hours to devise a means to contain the gift Levyathan had entrusted to his care. But that accommodation—so tenuous, so temporary—was little more than a cage. His body, linked already to an Entity, barely tolerated this third presence.

When Dorilian opened his eyes again to the world, he knew he had found at least a temporary means to sustain them both. Though his body's weakness frightened him, he dared not risk discovery. He trusted no one with his brother other than himself. One by one, he drove away all who came to his bedside or sought to offer help. All except Noemi, whose acceptance would extend to whatever he did. *Leave me alone; I'll be all right. I'm not sick, just tired. So very tired. Just leave me alone.* And because they feared his mercurial nature, they did leave him alone… time Dorilian seized to nurture the other life that coiled in the core of his flesh and clung to the architecture of his spine.

He didn't know what he must do, only what he must not. So he did not sleep, and he did not go near the Rill, not even for the funeral in Permephedon that entombed his brother's abandoned flesh. He did not allow the touch of minds or hands. He isolated himself from all other lives so that he might contain the precious remnant within him.

# 47

"We're very pleased with the town at Skairen. The Darms are fine fisherfolk and know how to handle matters on the river." The Kheld ambassador to the Archhalia, Cedrec Aelfricson, folded his hands across an ample belly. Like most Khelds, he enjoyed good eating and it showed. "The new docks encourage more traffic, but the market remains only half full. Mostly it is for locals and farmers. Craftsmen do well, but the most prosperous among us are still those who sell to Staubaun merchants who will take their goods across the river."

Stefan had come to Dazunor-Rannuli in part to escape Trulo's fetid summer. The town sat at the edge of a marsh, and no matter how high the Golden Palace was above the water, the heavy air held heat the way a towel held bath water. Besides, he needed to be in Essera's main Rill port should something befall Marc Frederick during his state visit to Sordan's Illumination festivities. As Heir, he would have needed to act swiftly in that event. The only bad news out of Sordan, however, had been the unfortunate death of Dorilian's half-witted brother. The boy had been only thirteen years old and Stefan, who dearly loved his own younger brother, sympathized with that loss. He'd lost one near kinsman in the past few years, but Dorilian had lost three. Sympathy did not lead to kinder thoughts, however.

"They have to stop selling to Staubaun traders, Grandfather." The title was appropriate: Cedrec's son, Erwan, had been Stefan's father. He looked upon the older man and hoped he would inherit the elder's full head of gray hairs. "Khelds need to start selling their goods in other markets. Staubaun merchants rob our craftsmen blind."

"They do. They do, I know. But our craftsmen have no luck selling in Staubaun towns. Staubauns want to buy from other

Staubauns. Estols want to buy from Staubauns. Their wives say they don't like to buy from Khelds because our beards alarm them. How are we to develop more distant markets? We have no serviceable seaport. The Dazun is our coastline."

"Cullen has been trying to find some way we can obtain a Rill slot." Stefan glanced over at his friend. The young man sat nearby, beside Cedrec's administrative clerk. In true Kheld tradition of employing kin wherever possible, Robdan was Cedrec's younger brother.

"Rill slots are hard to get. By the looks of it, I'll have to marry one. Rob here says I should get a Seven Houses girl, since they have the best slots." Cullen grinned at Robdan, who looked slightly sheepish at having his jibe revealed. The suggestion was, of course, ridiculous. The cartel had never accepted Khelds even as servants in their palaces, much less as marriage partners.

Stefan didn't laugh. "The damn Halasseons wouldn't let me take over Jonthan's Rill holdings. Ionais got those because it was part of the marriage contract."

He sighed, recalling his latest disagreement with Marc Frederick, who had insisted that the Crown slots also remained off limits. *Those are our family's surety*, his grandfather had said. *Do not mistake assets for access.* Stefan picked up the petition he had drafted and which Cedrec had returned to him upon reading.

"Are you telling me not to pursue the legislation of Kheld Rill ridership rights?"

"Such rights cannot be legislated. You are new to your office, *keldan*"—Cedrec used the familiar term for a member of his own kin group—"and you haven't learned these things. We've petitioned before, a hundred times, but the answer is ever the same: Khelds cannot ride the Rill. It will not *let* us. Even the Highborn cannot legislate what the Rill does."

Sunlight poured through the windows in brilliant streams. The Prince of Dazunor's residence looked out on the center of the city, over which the Seven Houses' Customhouse presided like a monument, outshining even the golden fortress of the Sordaneon Rillhome and the celebrated Illystri palace of the Malyrdeons that stood like a star at the center of the city's canals. Only the Rill itself, its white arms uplifted and enduring, overshadowed the grand statements of mortals warring over its spoils.

"But what if there were a station? Simply for moving goods?

That would be something." Stefan was thinking of Bellan Toregh, which he had seen so often on his treks to Orqho.

"But there are stations already which we cannot use and from which we cannot ride. Even if it could be done, why would we want to open a door into our land which only Staubauns could use?"

"They would be quick to set up shop." Cullen was quick to concur. He had spent two months examining the possible outcomes of Stefan's ideas. "Staubauns or Estols are the only ones that could ride with goods or documents. We couldn't even be our own couriers. Staubauns would step in because we'd need them. They'd start wanting to control the land about the station, too."

"So there's no advantage to it?"

"Oh, there would be an advantage, of course," Cedrec acknowledged. "Who could not find advantage in a Rill port? But we foresee as many opportunities for our competitors as for ourselves." He spread his aged hands. In them, Stefan saw a lifetime of pens and ink. "I have knowledge of these things. What you ask is impossible. Hestya inflamed many hearts, but Hestya was a living station, they say. Bellan Toregh is not. The Rill, apparently, doesn't see it. If it doesn't see it, it doesn't exist. If it does not exist, the Rill cannot go there." He politely indicated that he wished to rise, which Stefan gestured that he could do. Robdan followed, after quickly packing away his pens and the papers of scribbled notes. The man had beautiful pen strokes and was in great demand as a scribe at the Archhalia, which had just recessed.

Stefan heard noises of greeting from the antechamber beyond his closed door. He had adjusted to constant demands on his time and trusted his soldiers and secretaries to keep those demands to a minimum. All four men in the room were surprised when the door opened, and Stefan's chamberlain stepped through to announce that the King had arrived to see him. Stefan alone did not bow his head deeply when Marc Frederick entered.

"Just come from Sordan?" he greeted his grandfather, adding, "Cedrec's here." It was not often that both of his grandfathers were in the same room, and he took a moment to appreciate that conjunction.

"Ambassador." Marc Frederick bestowed a smile upon the man. "How is that bull working out on your farm?"

"My cows are already swelling fat. He's the strongest I have ever owned, and I had to build a stone fence between my farm and my neighbor's. But the calves, I swear to you, will be the envy of Amallar."

"Of that, I am sure. And what of you, Master Aelfricson? I see you survived your daughter's wedding."

"Yes, Sire. Though her husband has yet to build her a proper house."

"No brothers to set him right, eh?"

"Indeed, Sire." Robdan bobbed his head and respected the bounds of the monarch's time.

Cullen then led his countrymen to the door and exited with them, leaving the two royals within the again-quiet chamber.

"These Khelds are stubborn beyond words." Stefan guided Marc Frederick to a seating area of elegantly upholstered benches and slender stands intended for the placement of drinks. "I'm trying to get Amallar to petition for Rill ridership rights, but Cedrec refuses to endorse it. The Staubauns have them so cowed that they're afraid even to try! All Cedrec keeps saying is that they've tried before."

"They have."

"Not recently."

"That may be because nothing's changed."

"Then you belittle my efforts, too. You know what Rill service would mean to them."

"How could I not? But wanting something is not the same as getting it." He regarded his grandson regally. Stefan hoped he could someday master that expression. "You, for example."

"Me?"

"Yes. I made it known months ago that I want you to take a wellborn bride."

*Aw, hells...* "Grandfather," he began, then stopped when he saw Marc Frederick smile. He allowed a smile of his own as he grasped what the man was doing. "But you *could* force me."

"I could. But only because you're human. You want to remain my Heir and stay in my favor. More drastically, should we take the argument to the extreme, you would want to stay alive or not be subjected to pain or have your family subjected to hardship. You care about such things. But the Rill, you see—the Rill isn't human. Not even remotely; not anymore. What could you do to it that would force it to concede that Khelds should ride—when it doesn't even know they exist?"

"You sound like Cedrec, only you say it better. The same metaphysical nonsense."

"Is it? Nonsense?"

"Force the Sordaneons, then," Stefan proposed. "They talk to it, right?"

"Some do. Some have, in times past, just as some Malyrdeons have talked to the Wall. But now, alas, both Entities are having communication problems."

Sensing that he had reached the end of what his grandfather would say about his ambitions for Amallar, Stefan decided to proceed along more princely lines. "I heard about what happened in Sordan. I sent official condolences on behalf of Dazunor, of course."

Marc Frederick nodded to show he was pleased. A smile returned to his eyes. "You've done very well these last few months. It's not easy, you see, to rule the affairs of state. People start to expect their rulers will advance their own ambitions. That is a trap to be avoided at all costs."

"Tell me you did not advance the ambitions of your Staubaun subjects."

"I did. But I also didn't do enough to stop them from acting on those ambitions themselves. Things happened in ways I didn't foresee. I undertook the imprisonment of Labran Sordaneon for very different reasons than people suppose. Highborn reasons... Wall Lord reasons. Occupying Sordan and making it a captive state was never part of that design. It emerged as a necessary consequence, but it was not the objective."

At long last, Marc Frederick was starting to reveal some of the answers he had withheld. Stefan understood that these revelations were linked to other lessons, to political structures he was just learning to recognize. The King gazed upon him with the calm, decisive look of a gardener deciding when would be the time to transplant, to thrust Stefan from the sheltered spot in which he had nursed his understanding and into a world consisting of harder truths. Stefan thought he was ready. "What was the objective?"

"A chess move. A misdirection. My becoming King created a parallel potentiality."

Perhaps Marc Frederick realized the inadequacy of the explanation, because he leaned forward, trying again to explain.

"Ordinary language is not the right vehicle for these concepts.

One needs to speak Aryati for that—one of my reasons for having sent you to Permephedon as a youth. It was to have been part of your lessons. Aside from the Highborn, only the Cibulitans and the Epoptes, and a handful of other folk, speak it anymore."

"I had a month of it. I remember it as a mouthful." What Stefan most recalled about his class in Ancient Language was how Dorilian had not needed to attend—he already spoke the languages to be studied. The smug look on the Sordaneon's face when the instructor had informed the class had rankled Stefan to no end.

"A mouthful, yes. *Ilusm'yavvr umbri nas'yrrem.* Aryati is a language we of this age barely grasp. So many of its concepts refer to experiences into which we have never entered and reference technologies that no longer exist. But Aryati allows for other ways of framing the World in which we live—powerful ways. Endurin was a Wall Lord, and he spoke Aryati and the tongue of Creation, Leur. He foresaw a great many things. In time we will discuss them, but for now, it is enough to know that he saw the rise of new peoples and powers. He saw that these changes would decimate the Highborn. My Kingship is an attempt to save the race."

"Why, if they cannot save themselves?"

"They *are* saving themselves. I'm part of that plan, to be sure. Which means you are part of it. All of us are, to one degree or another. Once launched, all plans have an integrity—a life, if you will—all their own."

"More Highborn gibberish?"

"They have a word for it." Marc Frederick smiled. But Stefan sensed he was retreating again from the subject matter. *I'm not responding as he would have liked. Jonthan would have let him explain further, delved into his explanations.* But he didn't care about the Highborn as his grandfather did or as Jonthan had.

"Were Khelds one of those new peoples Endurin saw coming to power?" he asked instead, getting to the part he did understand.

The older man weighed him, his question, and his reasons for asking, then nodded slowly. "The Wall Lord Emrysen foresaw the coming of Alm. He may have seen more. Endurin revealed some, but not all, Malyrdeon lore about that foreseeing to me. Prescience, by its very nature, alters outcomes. Does foreknowledge cause an event or serve to prevent it? Even the Malyrdeons see their gift as a sword: not with two edges but a thousand, as capable of destruction as of guidance."

"They've used their gift to keep Khelds from power."

"Give me an instance in which they did so."

Stefan scoured his mind but could not. He cursed his lack of attention to history as his grandfather continued. "Only they could have given the Khelds a land grant such as Amallar. Only they could have given Khelds the protection of Erydon's Promise."

"And in the end, the Malyrdeons are useless because only Sordaneons can give them the Rill. You've made that clear enough." Stefan was tired of Highborn excuses. "I guess we have different definitions of power. Khelds will outnumber Staubauns someday. You know that, and so do I. And Khelds don't believe the Highborn are holy. Powerful, yes, and a little of the god-born part, but not the part that says they're perfect and their every word is law. Khelds look at the Highborn and see Staubauns."

"Because they are Staubaun, predominantly. They take the race of their mothers." From inside his jacket, Marc Frederick pulled out a thin, palm-sized book with a faded tan cover. "I want you to read this. Only a few copies exist. I found this one in the King's House library in Sordan, probably unread for years. You might find it revealing."

The volume felt light to Stefan's fingers. It was probably a hundred pages, the script purest Stauba. *Sordan's Heresy: The Labran Abomination.* He looked up with surprise. "Lepidros? The Seven Houses historian?" Though he had read some of the writer's works, he had not heard of this one.

"Very illuminating. It reveals everything."

Stefan walked over to his desk and placed the book there. "You haven't pointed me wrong yet. But I don't think I'm understanding all of the lessons."

"Lessons take time, even for one who learns quickly." His grandfather regarded him with warmth in his gaze. "I want you to understand why I am working so hard to end the enmity with Sordan. I need to remove the reasons others use to justify their destruction of that kindred."

"And you don't care that the damn Sordaneons have tried to destroy you? All of us? They've been at our throats for years."

"You would fight, too, if you thought you knew the enemy." Marc Frederick sighed. "It was a necessary detour. I knew what I did when I undertook Endurin's plan. I have never ordered or consented to the spilling of a drop of Highborn blood. Not one drop. I condemned the killings at Gignastha, refused every petition those murderers presented to me, and even refused to see their emissaries. When Ral slew every man, I said nothing. But I did retrieve my daughter." He looked unhappy.

"Khelds killed Ral for what he did."

"I said nothing then, either."

Stefan leaned forward, puzzled, his chin on his hands. He sensed that Marc Frederick was warning him. "Is that why the Rill won't recognize Khelds? Because of that?"

"No. It's possible the Rill doesn't know any of that happened. It is oblivious to almost every human event." Marc Frederick looked out at the vista beyond Stefan's window and absorbed the golden canals of the Rill city. "But the Sordaneons are not oblivious to these things. And if the Rill is ever to know anything at all about Khelds, or the World, it will know what the Sordaneons know. So read that book, think about what is happening, and ask yourself why the World is killing them."

Stefan didn't have his grandfather's Highborn-educated tolerance for pinning events back against the tapestry of Time. "Because they are unreasonable? Or worse, dangerous? Maybe the Sordaneons don't have power anymore, but they act as if they do. Sordan, too. Those people are getting too full of themselves again, trying to throw their weight around. I've been talking with the noble houses. They come to me because they know I have your ear. Sordan makes them nervous. They like Sordan better knowing that you have the Sordaneons in hand. Right now, they're not sure if you do."

"Is that what they think?"

Stefan gave a sharp look at his grandfather's nonchalance. Marc Frederick knew his people's minds. He had spent his lifetime setting Esseran fears to rest, but Stefan refused to be so mollified.

"This time, they're right. Dorilian is more dangerous than Deben. People say he reminds them of Labran."

"Nearly all of the people saying that never knew Labran."

And only old men would remember that Hierarch before captivity had removed him so completely from public experience.

"They know about him. They know what he tried to do. They're saying Dorilian will try it too."

"They don't know if he can," Marc Frederick pointed out.

"They don't want to find out." Unable to stay still, Stefan paced the room, the click of his boots muted on the soft blue carpet. "Some people don't know enough to stay down when they're beaten, and Dorilian is one of them. You think because you bested him in Neuberland, he's going to respect you... but what if he doesn't? And he's been talking you into doing things, like giving control over Sordan's harbor back to them and removing our troops."

"This kingdom has no overriding interest in Sordan's harbor. We do have an interest in a stable relationship with that domain and its rulers."

"You've got this crazy idea that he can be your friend!"

"He was Jonthan's friend. I wanted him to be yours."

Was the old man truly mad? Stefan sensed they had drifted from revelations again to secrets. What Erenor and others had been telling him, what he had gleaned from rumors of discontent and his new understanding of his grandfather's politics, Stefan now knew to be true: Marc Frederick had deeply entwined himself in Highborn schemes, so much so that he would rather court dangerous rivals than take the kind of decisive action needed to secure his people's interests and prosperity.

"Dorilian Sordaneon can't be my friend," Stefan declared. "He had a hand in Jonthan's death. He overstepped his bounds when you were grieving and, thanks to your 'friendship,' he is running roughshod over your administrators in Sordan. And you don't do anything about it."

Marc Frederick did not challenge him. He very calmly changed the subject to Emyli and Hans, who were situated back at Gustan and enjoying the new fishing pond he had built for them. Hans had named the new ducks. But as Marc Frederick left, Stefan caught wind of something sorrowful in his grandfather's goodbye.

# 48

"In order to seduce your husband, it works best if you can be in the same room with him," Nammuor said, further infuriating Daimonaeris.

Using the knowledge gained through his wielding of the Diadem, Nammuor's mages had fashioned a new form of *Ir* array, one that transported not message cylinders but flesh. Uncounted slaves had died in perfecting the technology before he had used one of the new devices himself. The innovation, still secret, was potentially devastating to their enemies, though at the moment Daimonaeris resented it for other reasons. Her brother used every visit to press her to sleep with her husband.

"He's still mourning his brother. There is ever a guard outside his door. He wishes to see no one—not even his father dares disturb his solitude. He will allow no one to be with him except his wretched nurse." She despised Noemi for having physically barred her way that morning. "That stupid, sniveling, half-minded boy! Why did he have to crawl out on that ledge and on that day? Deben almost fell himself trying to save him."

"What a pity that would have been," Nammuor said archly.

His sister glared at him. "I cannot be declared regent for my son if only Deben dies, not Dorilian."

"No. You would merely become your husband's Hierarchessa. Of course, in a few months, your visible pregnancy will become a bit difficult to explain to him—"

"Oh!" Stamping her foot, sending petals scattering from the delicate straps of her daisy-adorned sandals, she left him and headed along the winding, lakeside path. Deben's infatuation with her had diminished after their heated union and his younger son's death—so much that now he was nearly as cold to her as was her husband.

Currently in favor with neither Sordaneon, Daimonaeris distrusted even those places where she had formerly felt safe from eavesdropping. This stretch of common beach, secured by her handmaidens against other visitors, provided the privacy she sought.

Nammuor came up behind her and took her shoulders in his hands, staying her flight, and she settled back against his tall body.

"Dear Sister," he counseled, his breath warm against her hair. "Don't dismiss Dorilian too lightly. He's quite capable of violence. Men tend to get vengeful when they realize their wives will bear another man's seed. Should he learn the boy is his father's, he won't necessarily be more forgiving. Deben fears him with reason."

"So do I."

"Then sleep with him. When you prove to be with child, what can he do to you? You will be a sacred person, the mother-to-be of a Highborn heir. Even he would hesitate to harm you. We can simply let politics take its course. So long as he cannot deny the possibility, it will not matter what Dorilian believes or Deben claims—there is no way to prove which is the natural father. And you are, indisputably, his wife." He dropped his right hand to her belly. "Are you certain, little mother?"

She smiled, a tiny crescent of superior knowledge. "Yes. I am past my normal flow, and a *kanchi* petal turned green in my urine."

"So, we have secured the bloodline. Now we but seek the inheritance. Find a way, you clever girl. You have a spy in his household—find out where he will be. A man in grief might well welcome the solace of a woman."

She curled her nose at him. "You can actually call him a man?"

Nammuor's black eyes barely showed pupils even in the sun, but they did not hide the subtle flavor underlying his smile. "If he's not... then I suggest, dear Sister, that you *make* him one."

The Eagle Barge on the edge of the Serat, overlooking the City, suited Dorilian. No one came to this place who did not first pass through the Hierarch's apartments. Deben had shared a rare meal with him, then left, his preference being for enclosures. Dorilian, on the other hand, ached for open places.

Evening moonlight painted the eagle wingspans of the stone barge with silver and made stars of night-blooming lilies in the reflecting pool. He wore a Teremari tunic of cotton so fine it barely weighed upon his skin, as light as the breeze that stirred perfume from honey-scented night flowers. Had it only been three weeks ago that Levyathan had gathered an armload of lilies and presented them, dripping, into laughing Noemi's arms? Memories of his brother broke through the skin of his grief, and Dorilian felt the tug of that unmoored life against the fragile bindings he had placed upon it. He could not hold it much longer and despaired of the darkness, the emptiness that surely awaited when Lev's life finally slipped through his fingers.

When he saw Daimonaeris walking toward him across the stone lilypads, he made no move to stop her. He watched as a man entranced. Perhaps he was, afflicted by moonlight and struck by the beauty with which she moved, her sheer garment floating upon the night's light breeze. The most beautiful woman in all Sordan, men said, and for once, he understood what moved them. Moonlight painted her smooth thighs with silver and illuminated her high, perfect breasts as though no garment could hide them from view. Something bright and beckoning seemed to glow through her skin and within her golden eyes. When she came to him, she noted his silence and did not break it. Unspeaking, she lowered her body onto the couch where he rested. When he did move to speak, not yet knowing what he would say, she touched her finger to his lips. The touch was soft and lingering as his gaze sought hers.

Intrigued, leaden with grief and a weakness none but he understood, Dorilian allowed her to touch him, fascinated by this path she had chosen. She had never sought him thus before. Why now? The thing inside him, his brother's life so delicately bound to his own, leaped and pulsed to her touch. He continued to stare at his wife's lovely face as she leaned down and kissed him.

It was his first kiss, and he should have felt something other than her coldness. No tenderness for him moved Daimonaeris, none at all. It was ever the Highborn curse to know where passion existed and where it did not, and the passion on her lips bespoke nothing of desire. It touched his lips as might a snake's cold venom, imparting sight, allowing him to see her clearly by means he had not employed before then. Hers was a new attack upon him, no less deadly for being concealed.

Dorilian welcomed it with the abandon of one for whom death had become a companion.

Her body awakened his flesh. All the emergent yearnings that moved other men, also moved him and he yielded. The presence of a beautiful woman, her long legs straddling his, her mouth open and inviting his, had the power to inflame needs too overwhelming, too rooted in his very being, to deny. And yet her dislike of him caught like hooks in his skin, the calculation in her touch undermining the hot, sweet pull of her hands pushing his garment above his hips...

Sensing danger, Dorilian grasped Daimonaeris by the arms. He wanted her off him, gone—not commanding the clamoring urgency of his loins. Only there was something else. More than his body hungered for what she was doing. Something about her... her presence... not his arousal... strangely stirred the brother-life within him. Lev wanted this... craved her more than he ever could.

Caught upon such brilliant thorns, he could not drive from his mind his brother's last thoughts. *Lay with her... there is another... Father tried...* He no longer remembered the order, only the command.

*Lay with her.* He must do this.

Dorilian was now certain, he must... he *had to* penetrate his wife. But it would be, this time as always, on his terms. She was already astride him, having taken advantage of his listlessness, but he had not yet fulfilled her desire. There was yet victory to be had. He had matured in the years since she had married a mere boy. Grabbing Daimonaeris about the waist, he shifted his weight and easily pulled her under him as he rolled himself above her. Holding her down onto the couch, it was he whose knees held hers open and whose body would dictate their union. He felt her wonder as his flesh parted hers... her surprise that he knew what to do... that he was doing it... her joy hot and sharp as it flashed across his mind, followed by triumph tinged with distaste.

*So this is what it is like—this act for which men give their hearts and lives.*

For Dorilian it was disintegration. Eyes closed, repulsed by the cold energy of the woman beneath him—her lips pretending to kiss him, her body poised as a receptacle and nothing more—he sought solace in images of other partners... bodies as forbidden as his secret lusts, as untouchable as Time itself could make them... Noemi, loving and warm... lively Palimia's beautiful smile... myth-drenched Neryllia of the thousand portraits, dark-haired lady of the lilies...

Dorilian seized upon the last as being the most fitting and drove his body hard into that imagined one, envisioning her welcoming him. As he moved inside her, his excitement expanded, then crested. Within him, the webbing that contained his brother's life force released, but he felt no dispersal. Instead, that other life pooled with hot urgency in his loins. Helpless to stop it, he stared at Daimonaeris, certain she felt his imminence. All thought vanished from his mind, and there was neither pleasure nor pain, only release, the primal rushing of fluids and, with them, the fragile life he had so temporarily harbored fled his body into that of the woman. And still, Lev was not gone. Dorilian felt him upon the World's skin, as tenuously tethered to him as ever.

"Husband," Daimonaeris whispered against his lips, mocking him.

Dorilian angled away from her and sank back onto the silken cushions of the couch, drained but not exhausted. What the hell had he just done? He rolled from her body, felt the firm surface receive him, his wife's legs slip out neatly from under his. His garment, light though it was, now stuck as film to his skin. As Daimonaeris arranged her gown to leave him, he extended his senses to search for Lev within her and saw what he had not seen before.

There was a Highborn life within her. It glowed from her like a beacon, centered in her pelvis and burning many cells bright. Too many cells, though still barely detectable, to have been conceived mere moments ago. And it was there, nestled in her pink flesh, encasing and permeating a body the size of pea, that Levyathan's life force now resided.

Daimonaeris went to Dorilian a few days later to announce her pregnancy. It was not impossible that it should be detected so early, nor was he so minded as to contest his possible fatherhood. Though he missed Levyathan's closeness, and the new life had not yet developed enough to allow empathic contact, Dorilian knew his brother had been restored to him—in however bizarre a manner. He now understood what Lev's dying mind had attempted to communicate, and resolved not to let anyone around him suspect that he knew Deben to be the child's father. By accepting paternity, Dorilian hoped to protect the tiny life that was his brother twice over. He vowed, at the very least, to be a better father than Deben had been.

The next day he left Sordan, ostensibly to look in on his interests in Dazunor-Rannuli. He and Legon arrived at nightfall, an hour he now detested, and immediately descended the Mount to a waiting *gond*. From there, he sought the secure surroundings of the Rillhome. He dined with Legon and afterward spent two hours staring at the Rill Mount across the Lower Canal, a god encapsulated by rings of warehouses and glittering palaces.

*It cannot move.*

As a child, he had envisioned the god in motion, a force of transformation. But there was no transformation in what he saw before him. *It is static. They have fixed it; the better to serve them. They think the Rill is theirs and theirs alone.* How not, when this was what they saw? For all its massive structure and soaring strangeness, the Rill glowed less brightly than the brilliant domes of Dazunor-Rannuli's alabaster palaces, those gold-painted facades reflected in glittering carpets upon the waters of lacework canals. Perhaps all gods were ultimately ruled by their creations.

"Thrice Royal." The palace's secretary intruded softly. Dorilian turned to look at him. The man bowed. "If I may inquire as to your plans for the morrow?"

"I have no plans."

"Invitations have begun to arrive."

Dorilian gazed out at the watery city. "Decline them all. I have no plans that include the likes of them." He barely noticed the man backing away.

Wherever he looked, he saw only enemies clinging to the monuments his ancestor had erected, infesting the cities Derlon had founded. Infesting his bloodline. Infesting his life. Levyathan had lived in a world inhabited by shadow beings, and so, now, did he.

An hour later, accompanied only by Legon and using the palace's secret passageways to access the lagoon, he took a plain dark boat out into the black-watered city and headed unannounced to the Emrysen Palace.

# 49

"It is Prince Dorilian, Majesty. Dorilian Sordaneon. He wishes to see you."

Gareth stood in the doorway of Marc Frederick's bedroom, his expression providing no indication that the turn of events was in any way extraordinary. Marc Frederick stared at his steward in wonder. Upon Gareth's insistence, he had banished Palimia from his bed, sending her away gently but without explanation. The beautiful widow had in the past two months become his discreet companion.

Interruptions of his intimate activity seldom boded well, but Gareth's announcement fit into none of the scenarios Marc Frederick most feared. He belted a robe of dark-blue silk embroidered with his royal crest, concealing his decidedly unroyal nakedness.

"Dorilian? Here?" He was still getting his bearings on that news. "Why?"

"He did not say, Majesty. He arrived accompanied by a single man, Legon Rebiran, and asked for me by name. It was then that he revealed his identity and desire to see you, but not his purpose. He is, such as I can determine, unarmed. Do you wish to receive him, Sire?"

"Yes, of course. Receive and welcome. See also to his man's comfort and our privacy."

Marc Frederick looked briefly in the mirror and grimaced. He had not planned on guests that night, so he had not shaved before retiring. The shadow of facial hair was now damning. No matter. Dorilian had seen him in far worse state.

*He gazed into the caverns of my soul that night. He brought me back from a deeper grave than that of earth.*

When he entered his private audience chamber, he found a fire already lit and a tray of cakes set beside his chair. The room, adorned with sweeps of color, overflowed with beloved objects and books, and was one of Marc Frederick's favorites in any of his palaces. He called it the Royal Cave because it resembled one, with only sky openings for light. He could have illuminated the room using its resident waterglobes, but he preferred firelight for confidences. He readied two glasses and a flask of fine Kheldish brandy.

The door opened, and Dorilian entered. When Gareth asked if he needed anything more, Marc Frederick shook his head, and Gareth left the two men in seclusion. the King indicated a chair, taking a seat only after his guest had done so. Clothed in dark woolens such as any merchant might wear, Dorilian looked pale and subdued. It was evident that he still mourned his brother. It had been but two months for him, and Marc Frederick still, for his own part, felt Jonthan's loss keenly after more than a year. He watched his guest in silence until the young man felt ready to speak.

"Daimonaeris is pregnant." Dorilian's voice was dull, simply laying out a fact. "I am not the father," he added before Marc Frederick could express even a tentative congratulation. "Deben is. I will be claiming paternity, however. They think I do not know." He glanced over with pained eyes. "I slept with her. It was... strange."

"I don't know what to say." Marc Frederick's thoughts tumbled in too many directions to be coherent. By the awkward tenor of the confession, he knew that the act had been Dorilian's first time with a woman. He felt only sadness that the occasion had been soulless—another charade in a long chain of political acts.

Dorilian shrugged. He might as well have been discussing the weather. "It is Nammuor's doing, all of it: Daimonaeris, my father, and the ambitions that drive them. I figured it out. The child is male, of course. My father... the child is Highborn. And if I cannot contest paternity—which I cannot, as I did sleep with her—then her son inherits all that is mine, including my Teremari wealth and interests, my birthright, and my destiny... should something happen to me. Which it will."

Stunned, Marc Frederick realized the import of both of the plot and that Dorilian had ascertained it. His own throne was among the birthrights Dorilian claimed.

"What will you do?"

"Make sure their plan fails." The young man gave him an eagle look that Marc Frederick had learned to recognize, a look that said he would never concede any battle. "They need a live child to claim my inheritance, so I have at least that long. They will want to be sure. Besides"—his thin smile carried a note of icy resolve—"Nammuor is underestimating me. I intend to surprise him."

"That is something I'm certain you can do."

"You're the only person I could think of to entrust with this."

Marc Frederick bowed his head and closed his eyes. Those were words he had waited half a lifetime to hear. He looked up again. "What do you need of me?"

"The same thing you need of me. I need Sordan."

In those three words, Marc Frederick heard the echoes of their tenuous bond. His capture of Labran so long ago, his decades of hold over that nation, had shaped his and Dorilian's every interaction. Yet Sordan had never been his—either to take or to give.

"You have more of Sordan waiting upon your next word than I have had in forty years." He laid out the first stone—the cornerstone—upon which he would build his response.

"That is a political answer." Dorilian challenged the deflection. "Your troops command my City's garrisons and are stationed throughout my domains. Triempery soldiers guard the Rill Terminus; they patrol the Va Haira. My father is a captive in his own Serat, and when I am in the City, I am barely more than that. Why did I hate you all those years? Because of the power you wield over us! Your occupation is ever-present. My people would gladly trade one tyrant for another if Nammuor poses as a liberator, which you can be sure he will." Dorilian appeared to note he had touched a vein of truth. He leaned forward. "Let me be Sordan's liberator, not he."

"I believe with all my heart that you will be."

"Then let it be now. I cannot wait any longer. In return, I will give you the political tool you need to sway the cold hearts of your nobles and the greed of your people." Dorilian's glacial confidence acknowledged the questions embedded in Marc Frederick's silence. The fire crackled in the hearth, filling the void until Dorilian spoke again. "You've wondered, haven't you? All the time I have known you, I've seen the question in your eyes—unasked, unspoken. I've seen that same question burning behind the cold stares of the

Epoptes and lurking in the gazes of my Malyrdeon kin, and I have answered none of them. But I will answer *you*." He paused again, weighing something, or perhaps simply overcoming his long habit of keeping his every facet hidden. "I was present at Hestya. I stood at Sebbord's side the day the Rill turned its eye upon Teremar. And it was I—not he—who summoned the god."

Marc Frederick could not have taken his gaze from Dorilian had he wished to. After all the years of believing, hearing the truth, did nothing to rob the revelation of its power. "Derlon sees you?"

"Yes. I"—Dorilian cast his gaze aside for a moment, remembering—"I was Rill-gifted by Labran at Stauberg, four years ago."

"I believed as much." His heart still pounded, but Marc Frederick found it easier to encourage Dorilian than it had ever been to conceal his hopes. "I even expected it. Enreddon was not sure, although he was there. All we could do was pray that Labran had seen fit to awaken the gift... and that your flesh would not be too young to receive it."

"Labran saw fit. And Sebbord had prepared me well. He taught me what would be needed to host an Entity. However," again Dorilian raised that resolute gaze, "native talent and knowledge are not the same as experience—or the ability to command what is summoned. I have spent a lifetime in concealment, but now that I am coming into my adult talents, I have no teacher. I don't know how much I can do." He appeared to have doubts as well, and not only about his limitations. "Some part of my flesh is shared by the thing. Lev showed the Rill to me, how I am bound to it, so I know this is true. I saw it and myself through his eyes."

Levyathan had possessed the ability to *see* Dorilian as Entity-bound and gifted? Ancient writings suggested these structures might be visible to the Leur-gifted among the Highborn. Marc Frederick said nothing that might stop the flow of revelations.

"You know what I speak of." Dorilian leaned forward, no doubt sensing Marc Frederick's belief in him. "You, who have studied us so near and so well... Endurin would have told you what we are."

"He did."

"Then you also know that Derlon's gift predicates potential but not ability. I don't know for certain if I can integrate with the Entity. I think it's too soon for me to try. But I do know I possess what is needed to turn the Rill's eye, and I don't intend to sit upon this gift and hold it useless. In the changes I might bring or the power I might command, I will be at least the equal of my predecessor Tarlon or possibly the Three Debens. Surely that is worth something to you."

That ability was worth more than armies, more than succession. More than the towering cities which men had built upon the Rill's footprints. There was no telling what forces Dorilian might awaken, if not tomorrow, then in all the days to come. There was no telling what changes he might command, what new empires he might raise, or old ones destroy. Dorilian knew this, too. Yet the dream remained a dream. Its rewards were but conjecture and rested upon a stature Dorilian had yet to attain and a fate he might never embrace. But if he was willing to try... yes, that *was* worth something.

"But you want something of me in return." Marc Frederick read what lay behind that offer. His only fear was that Dorilian would ask too much, and the price be too high.

Dorilian nodded. "I want Sordan, Majesty. I want Sordan returned to autonomy—all Triemperal troops removed, and our army restored. I want a court set up to arbitrate reparations for wrongfully seized lands and estates. And I want to be its Hierarch."

The fire crackled and blazed, throwing orange light and shadows across the room's blue-traced walls. That same fire danced in bright flickers across Dorilian's eyes. What he wanted, he no longer wished to wait upon. Neither yet was he ready to seize it. Marc Frederick drew a breath, looked toward the patterns on the ceiling. What a night this was proving to be!

"Hierarch, you say... of an autonomous state. And you think I can put you there. But why now; why like this? You could have come to me at any time and offered me your friendship—and in return, I would have set in motion the very things you ask. Have I not done so already? For months I've been withdrawing troops, returning control of administrative offices—you know I have, for what else did we spend all those nights in Stauberg plotting? And why? In preparation for *you*. Ultimately, we have the same goal, you and I. I want to see your nation restored in full to its rightful rulers and people no less than you do, and I know that, between us, we can find ways to set right the wrongs that were done. But Dorilian"—for the first time, he used that name familiarly—"however much I want to see you, not Deben, upon the Eagle Throne and ruling justly, I cannot—I will not—help you depose your father."

He had expected Dorilian to dispute his decision, so he was both surprised and relieved when the younger man did not. Instead, Dorilian closed his eyes and sank forward, resting his forehead on his hands, his elbows braced on his knees.

"Please understand my position." Marc Frederick measured each word. His politics with the Sordaneons lay riddled with opportunities that glittered like jewels, each designed to lure the Triempery—and him— toward disaster. "I hold my vows as sacred as any Highborn prince. You should know, if you do not already, that I made a promise to the Malyrdeons—to Endurin first, and then to the entire Highborn Council including Labran and Sebbord. I promised I would not interfere with Sordaneon rule. I will not break that promise now, not even if doing so would buy me your friendship. What kind of friend would I be if I could be purchased, or if I would agree to set a son against his father?"

"No," Dorilian agreed. "That is something you would not do."

"If you truly believed that, you wouldn't have asked. So why did you think I could be persuaded to serve as a mercenary to your ambition?"

The expression on Dorilian's face let Marc Frederick know he had struck wide of the truth yet close to the mark. "I need no mercenaries for my ambition! With or without you, I know where I will be. I have seen it. And if you vow you will have no part in placing me there, then your answer tells me one thing: that this is not how it happens."

*These are Malyrdeon words! To know where he will be... but not how it happens... to have seen it. There is foreknowledge behind his phrasing!* Sordaneons did not foresee events, however much they created them. Dorilian's outburst smacked of cognizance. Carefully, as carefully as he might approach a great beast that had leaped for a moment onto the window ledge of his room, Marc Frederick weighed this discovery. It didn't matter at that moment that the beast might flee at the sound of his voice or, if it chose to allow him near, might slash its claws across his throat. The beast was too marvelous and the possibilities too fascinating not to examine.

"How what happens? And how can you be so certain?"

"Because it is so clear. Never was anything clearer. I have seen myself—" Dorilian paused, but for clarity, not diversion. He knew what he was revealing. His recognition of the import showed in taut features, so human and young. His silver eyes shone with sincerity.

"I saw things, Wall things, when I touched Austell at Permephedon. I was trying to help him. But the Rill field... we were in it. It linked us somehow when I touched the Wall Stone."

Marc Frederick stared at his young visitor anew. "Austell's mind shattered."

"Maybe because I was there. I don't know. What I saw was so vivid, so real... flesh and blood real, and I knew it to be so... but only fragments. Nothing cohesive, more like paint thrown against a wall—or blood. There was no order to it, just agony. But in one of those visions, I saw myself clearly. I was wearing the full regalia of the Hierarchate, seated on the Eagle Throne, surrounded by my court. The Rill Stone was on my hand, and I was wearing Derlon's Crown and holding the Gweroyen Sword. And I was *not* an old man." Dorilian's look beseeched Marc Frederick's understanding of how compelling that vision still was. "Majesty, when I look in the mirror now, *that* is the face I see. This face"—he touched his nose and cheek—"but I don't know how I get to that place. I only know it awaits me and will happen soon. I thought... maybe you—" He sighed deeply, and with relief. "I'm glad it will be some other way."

*So am I.* Marc Frederick could barely believe this evening could become more surreal. This young man of Highborn blood had glimpsed, even if only in fragments, the visions for which Austell Malyrdeon had destroyed his very sanity. Except that Dorilian had survived those visions with his mind intact.

"All these years, you kept secret what you saw." He understood so many things now.

"I was young and angry. The Malyrdeons had betrayed my grandfather. They'd brought me to Permephedon against my will, and I did not want them to keep me there another hour. The Rill was standing by to take me to Sordan, so I told them nothing."

"Who did you tell?" Had Sebbord known?

Perhaps Dorilian read that thought. He shook his head. "I told Lev, no one else. He saw the images in my mind. He saw that he was not with me when I became Hierarch. He kept telling me he would not be there to see me, and I kept telling him he was mistaken, that the images could be wrong. But I was the one who was wrong. The Wall shows what will be." His gaze locked on Marc Frederick's harshly. "I never saw Jonthan in those images. The first time I met him, his face was new to me. But I have always seen you. So many images of *you*." Something haunted went unspoken behind that silver gaze. "I saw just we two sharing a meal—and later, at Gustan, we did. I saw you in a pit surrounded by furred, armed men, and then you took me to the Maw. I also see Stefan. I see him in coronation robes."

"Is that why you did not oppose my naming him as my Heir?"

Dorilian nodded. "I don't know how connected my being Hierarch is with his becoming King." He shook his head and allowed a brittle smile. "Does it mean I succeed in killing you—or that someone kills my father?"

Mark Frederick stared at Dorilian, wondering if this youth had seen those events also. Much as he wished to pursue the matter, he could see that Dorilian's secrecy, nourished on Deben's paranoia and Sebbord's well-founded fears, protected them both—and also the unformed future. For it was unformed... nothing of it was utterly certain.

*Let it be without warning. I don't want to know events ahead of time or how they will occur. How could I continue if I foresaw only failure—or death?* All he knew now was that Stefan would succeed him. And Dorilian had seen himself as Hierarch... but not Deben's death. Even so, he gave one bit of advice. "You should talk with Marenthro... or Elhanan."

"No." Dorilian's refusal could not be plainer. "We will do this without them—or not at all."

Dorilian distrusted even his own kindred. And yet the bond between the two of them was stronger than it had ever been. Marc Frederick sighed but nodded.

"I will work with you. I know something of Nammuor's designs upon Sordan. He will not stop there, so in helping you, I also help myself. Perhaps, together, we can defeat his plan."

As though a burden had been lifted from him, Dorilian relaxed. He raised his head and took a deep breath, as if he had at last encountered fresh air after having endured for too long an airless, poisoned place. "You have my deepest thanks and gratitude." It was, for him, a rare expression of indebtedness.

"Don't thank me too quickly." Marc Frederick successfully stifled a yawn. It was dutiful of his body to remind him of the hour. He had never kept late nights, though, for this meeting, he would have missed three nights of sleep. Something about Dorilian, too, spoke of having not slept. They both needed to spur their tired minds.

Mastering the minor stiffness in his joints, Marc Frederick rose and lifted the brandy he had earlier set out. Dorilian, for his part, had taken the cue to raid the tray of cakes. Displaying the bottle, Marc Frederick inquired if his guest would like a glass, pouring even before Dorilian had warily nodded.

"You have told me what you want from me and what you are willing to give in return. This direction is, of course, agreeable to me. But we haven't touched on what I will need from you."

"I had assumed my offer would meet your need." Dorilian took the proffered glass in hand and held it up to the firelight, the better to examine the contents.

"Your proposal promises much—most of all your good will, for which I give you my own in equal measure. But I need more than dreams if I am to divest Essera of its prize. My nobles—indeed all the Epoptes, the Seven Houses, every electorate of the Archhalia— have harbored visions of Rill expansion since the Triempery's founding. Hope that the Rill might run to Stauberg is not new. The Sordaneons dangle that dream every few hundred years." Having watched Dorilian's face carefully the whole while, he intercepted the hot flash of anger his words awakened. "Hear me out. This is not about your sincerity or integrity, not even about your ability. Of these, I have no question. Your belief in yourself cannot begin to match my belief in you. It is not I who needs convincing."

Dorilian's glower broadcast his mood well enough. "I told you already I cannot promise success. The Entity obliterates wills other than its own. Control of it requires that a man be in command of his own mind, his own will—and I'm not such a fool that I believe I have attained that mastery. Why do you think I've told no one? They would find a way to force me to attempt it. The price of their ambition could be my life!"

"I understand this. That is why what you have told me tonight will never leave this room. Nor will I ask you, ever, to test yourself against the Rill. Your life means more to me as you stand before me now than that of any Entity."

That avowal soothed Dorilian's opposition. He needed to know he could rely upon at least one other person to be steadfast and principled. His intellect could penetrate any situation, but his emotional connections were all the more powerful for being so few and well guarded. Only love would endure long enough to penetrate the walls he had built, and love was not something Dorilian stirred in those who met him. He was more likely to awaken envy, resentment, or fear. There was enormous danger that this empath—this man—might one day be so feared or despised, and so surrounded by the reflections of that revilement, that he would withdraw from human emotion and cease to feel altogether. Gods could function thus, but not men. *We will lose him, if that happens. Lose him and the Rill completely. He needs to determine the boundaries of his own humanity—not be forced into some useful shape.*

"Don't look at me like that," Dorilian said.

"Like what?"

"Like you wish you could fight my battles for me."

It was what he wished, what he felt. "I suppose I do wish that. You face so very many." Marc Frederick took a sip of his brandy and mulled his own battles.

"Then tell me what I must do to free my country."

Dorilian's urgency was understandable. But Sordan's freedom was not something Marc Frederick could grant simply by publishing a proclamation.

"Very well. Sordan's occupation was ordered by the Highborn Council in compliance with the founding documents of the Triemperal Concordance. That order is not one I can unilaterally revoke. It would take a new order from the Council to reverse it. I ask you again"—he addressed the newly resentful look in Dorilian's eyes—"to talk to them."

"When I'm ready."

Marc Frederick set his glass aside. "Unfortunately, even were the Highborn Council to grant my request to restore Sordan's sovereignty, I anticipate fierce opposition from my people, most especially from the Seven Houses. Their Rill holdings enable them to dictate policy in the Archhalia and, as they have ceased to find me useful to their purposes, any attempt on my part to end Sordan's occupation would bring them down upon me." He leaned forward. "If you want to help me, repeat your success at Hestya—but not at Stauberg, which would require too much. Many arches leading there are broken or missing, and it would be a massive endeavor, almost certain to entail early failures. And because Stauberg is a seaport, opening it to the Rill would threaten the Seven Houses far more than Hestya ever did. You need not risk so much when there's a better option at hand. I am speaking of the node at Trestethion."

Dorilian's head shot up, and his gaze widened into a brutal stare.

"You want me to open *that* node? In *Amallar*?"

"The rings and arches are already in place. The Rill already runs above that node, past it—through it. I can get you access to the notes—"

"I don't need ancestral notes!"

"Of course not." Marc Frederick steeled himself against the empathic surge of the young man's barely restrained fury. "You already know how to get the Rill to recognize a dormant node. You opened Hestya."

"Are you completely mad?" Dorilian raged. "I offer you a gift, and you turn it into... this insult!" With a frustrated growl, he rose to his feet and threw the glass in his hand against the blue stone wall within which the hearth burned like a great orange eye. Glass exploded in a glittering shower of shards. "How *dare* you ask this of me? To have the Rill run to Amallar would be a travesty! That tribe has slaughtered countless thousands and slain in unholy manner five of my kind. I watched a Kheld cut off my grandfather's head!"

"For which you destroyed three Kheld villages and sent hundreds of innocents to their deaths. Sebbord would not have asked for that."

"And you, it is clear, would have me forget the reasons they deserved it! I will not give that unwashed tribe the Rill. Why should I? They cannot even use it!"

"Then tell me whose interests you serve if you withhold it? Not your own. The greatest evil your enemies ever committed against the Sordaneons was to plant the seed of that hatred, knowing it would grow powerful enough to hem you in on every side. Because hate becomes fear—and fear allows others to assume control over your actions."

"I'm not afraid of the damned Khelds!"

"Aren't you? Ask yourself why the Seven Houses made it appear that a Kheld slew Sebbord at Merath!" Marc Frederick barely restrained a growl of his own as he hurled his still half-filled glass against the wall, punctuating his question with a spray of glass and brandy. As he had anticipated, his unexpected violence brought the startled young man's attention around to him again. "They *wanted* to shatter everything to hell! He was challenging their Rill preeminence, raising the possibility that the Sordaneons would reassert their birthright—open the Rill to Mormantalorus— open the Rill to Stauberg! They needed to have him removed. But why a Kheld assassin? Ask yourself that."

"Perhaps because one was easily found?"

"Don't give me disdain where I want answers."

"Very well, then: to recall Gignastha," Dorilian answered crisply. The pattern had not escaped him. "To make it look like Stefan's hand was in it—and yours, by association. They didn't want me to trust you."

"They don't want you to trust anyone."

"They want to immobilize me."

"They want to immobilize the Rill."

*Stasis.* Some might call it permanence, others stability. The perfect machine, the perfect god—untiring, unceasing, unquestioning—and permanently in the possession of the Seven Houses. Marc Frederick did not doubt for a moment that Dorilian fully grasped the permutations of his conclusion.

Marc Frederick approached where Dorilian stood before the room's centerpiece, a great globe of alabaster and lapis encrusted with gold.

"Marvelous, isn't it? I spend hours looking at it—the World *before* Exile." Every golden dot, grid, circle, and spire represented the cities of that lost time. Rill lines of glittering emerald webbed that fabulous sphere. "The wonders of an entire civilization—all the riches and inventions the starfarers discovered in the universe—poured into one shining World."

"Until they destroyed it."

Dorilian's finger rested atop a tiny peak in what was now Amallar. In the mists of memory, a great city had stood there: Trestethion, mysterious and storied, from which in ancient times the starfarers had set forth. The immediate area was metal-poor, but to the west and east... using the gilded point as a pivot, he measured with his thumb the distances to both Dazunor-Rannuli and Leseos.

"We are lesser men now than were living then," Dorilian said.

"Most, perhaps—but not *you*. The blood of Leur lives on in your veins."

He received a blistering look in answer. Marc Frederick held that gaze until, turning his back on the globe, Dorilian walked away.

"I will not raise up the Khelds for you."

"Not for me. Changing the World will not liberate me. But it might liberate you."

"Enemies—"

"A treaty will establish their role, and there would be Epoptes, administrators—administrators we can agree to have you appoint. I believe that much in your integrity. The Khelds would learn and evolve."

"I don't know what they might evolve into—and neither do you." Dorilian looked unconvinced but no longer completely at odds. He lifted an eyebrow of interest. "An exchange, then? Sordan's freedom, and mine, for giving you a new Rill colony uncontrolled by the Seven Houses?"

Marc Frederick was tempted to laugh. Dorilian had distilled his argument to its very kernel. "Yes. But I think you will find them useful as well."

# 50

The bird, bursting from cover into flight, flashed briefly gold in the sun before the arrow struck and it fell, dull and lifeless, to the ground. A reddish hound released by the huntsman bounded off into the meadow to find it. Marc Frederick lowered his bow and smiled at Rheger, whose count he had just surpassed.

"Four," he pronounced, as satisfied by Rheger's expression as he was by the kill. He handed the bow to the huntsman, and the two men walked back toward their companions. "Now tell me why you will not come with me to Trulo. You did so when Jonthan lived."

"Your son was our kinsman."

"And my grandson is not?"

"Not to the same degree." Rheger looked uncomfortable. "You know our stance. Why must you challenge it?"

"Because he resents it." Marc Frederick paused their walking while still out of earshot. Several more archers lurked at different points on this side of the field, shooting at targets being flushed from the thick grasses. "There is something in your kindred's refusal to deal with Stefan that points to things I have not been told. So be it. I swim in a quarry of such secrets. But Stefan does not have my patience with Highborn prescience."

"If prescience it is. It may be only intuition. Consider, Sire, that Stefan makes no secret of his hostility toward us."

"Neither does Dorilian Sordaneon, yet you would attend the cutting of his fingernails if he extended an invitation."

"That is because he is another matter."

"Yes, I know." Shouts broke from a group by the stand of oaks, pointing to another fallen bird.

Marc Frederick had stopped off at Rheger's estate in the Glainoi both as a resting point on his journey from Kyrbasillon and because he wanted to speak personally with the Highborn prince. His summer had been spent in such meetings, building a coalition of Highborn support for his activities in Sordan. He needed every Highborn voice. Opposition among Staubaun nobles ran high, and the Seven Houses were plotting to revoke his reforms. "Oddly enough, Dorilian is one of few people I trust these days *not* to be maneuvering against me."

"You trust him where others do not." Rheger sighed. The sun brushed his skin with the golden warmth of a summer day. "We know your reasons for it, and I, at least, applaud your success. Power must be shifted in Sordan if we are to keep Mormantalorus from deepening its hold there, not only of the domain and its resources but also of the Sordaneons themselves. Your actions have been masterful."

"I'm not plotting them alone."

"No, and that is even more brilliant. But neither has it gone unnoticed. The Seven Houses are as contentious as ever, protecting their interests, but Essera is rightly concerned that the Sordaneons will revert to old stances once they free their domain from our grasp. What surety have you of Dorilian's change of heart?"

"Only his word."

"Has he said more than you have revealed?"

Marc Frederick shook his head. "I look at what he has done. Dorilian has kept his every agreement with me. He neither flinches from command nor overreaches. He stands up to his father, but it is always in such ways that Deben cannot alter without seeming the villain to his own people. Every man and woman Dorilian has schemed into newly created Hierarchate ministries is learned, loyal, and able—so much so that often a merchant knows not if he is dealing with a Triemperal minister or one answering to the Sordaneons. You call me masterful, but it is Dorilian who is laying the groundwork for me. Not even your kindred know the degree to which Dorilian already rules in Sordan."

"More than you suspect, but we do not disapprove of it. Your nobles do, and what they do not know, they are not short of fearing." Rheger's frown deepened. Marc Frederick was struck by the resemblance to Enreddon, the likeness borne of having so many ancestral matriarchs in common. "The Seven Houses have approached us, as we have recently told you, seeking an alternative heir to the throne—"

"And I was also told that your kindred collectively refuse to entertain that petition."

"This is true, Sire. I stand with my brothers to the path the Wall foretold. The Creation will founder if the Entities fail. Indeed, all knowledge would be unwritten, and the World fall back into eternal ignorance of itself. Thus, we stand fast. But our kindred is not your concern. The attack will come from Mormantalorus—this we know, though we do not know how or when."

"My ships hold safe the seas, and my armies are strong. As for Sordan, Dorilian is no friend to Nammuor."

"No, he sees the design his father put upon him. That does not mean he can thwart it."

"Then make Dorilian too valuable to lose."

"He is already so."

"Not all would say that. Make Dorilian too valuable for Nammuor to lose."

Rheger's golden eyes, Highborn clear, sought the distant line of trees as if some answer might be found there. "I see no way to do that. I trust you have thought of one?"

"It already exists. Dangle the Rill, the possibility of it. Make Mormantalorus hesitate. Make Essera take pause, if only to wonder what Dorilian can do."

The boiling question—what Dorilian Sordaneon could do— had cooled in the three years since Sebbord's violent death. The young prince had never been brought before a Tribunal, had made no display of aptitude, and in matters of the Rill had been mostly silent.

"You would awaken dangerous speculation." The other hunting parties, having secured their kills and cleared the field, were looking their way. Rheger signaled that they should head back to the house. As the others went on ahead, he and Marc Frederick followed along a path of crushed grass and soft earth. The deep scents of late summer, warmed by the sun and trod by many feet, perfumed the air.

"Young Dorilian is Rill-gifted, Sire. I sensed it the night I assisted in his capture outside Gignastha. The channels I detected were too powerful to be mortal. He is bound to an Entity, and we can well guess which one."

Stunned, Marc Frederick stared. The Malyrdeons, then, already knew that Dorilian had succeeded—and had not told him.

"Who have you told?" He sought to clarify the extent of that dissemination.

"Only Enreddon, as highest of our kindred, and my brother Ostemun. And now you." Rheger smiled thinly. "Dannuth's improved relations with the Sordaneons have not been coincidental."

Why had Redd not revealed this valuable knowledge? He, too, had moderated his stance against the Sordaneon prince. Marc Frederick battled a leap to conclusions. He must wait upon that answer. But his anger at the exclusion rose to new heights. When his favorite hound, having retrieved the bird and delivered it to the gamekeeper, bounded up to him for its reward, Marc Frederick only absently petted its hard-broad head and sent the animal, barely satisfied, on its way. His full attention remained fixed on Rheger.

"Then you know that if Dorilian offered to deploy his Rill talent—whatever it might be—to the betterment of all our realms, that offer would not be an empty one."

"Empty, never. Even if he could but marginally access his Entity, it would be a gift beyond price." Now it was Rheger who looked at him with questions.

"But his agreement *would* come with a price. A very high price. And one the Malyrdeons hold the power to release."

Acknowledgment twitched at the drawn corners of Rheger's wry frown. "Sordan."

"Sordan."

"You have spoken with him about this, then—yes, I can see that you have. That would explain much, though it raises new alarms. Be wary, Sire, in dealing with this Sordaneon without our guidance."

"I am not standing here to exchange pleasantries. Your kind moves too slowly for me, Rheger. I do not have the time you have... or think you have. The noose grows tight about our necks; yours as well as mine." Marc Frederick shot the wary Highborn prince a warning look. "I imprisoned Labran when none other would do it. I committed a heinous insult against one god in the name of another—because I do not worship your gods, I merely honor them. I kept your hands clean of the deed. I salvaged Dorilian's life and lost my son as a consequence. I cannot blame Dorilian for being what he is—but I remember who set me upon the course that created him. I am done with secrets, and I am done with honor. I am calling back my favor."

"The Highborn Council doesn't meet again until spring."

"Soon enough. For Sordan, and for me."

"Strike him! Strike him! Get him down!"

The shouts—deep and roaring, high-pitched and shrieking—bounced back from the saffron-hued walls of the expansive courtyard. Emyli stood upon the terrace, shaded by a shimmering canopy and watching her son at play. The courtyard echoed with the sharp clack of sticks as Stefan swung his heavy staff at Cullen. The young Kheld just as enthusiastically countered the blow. Knocking Stefan's staff upward, Cullen shortened his grip and swung his pole in a long arc at the prince's feet. Nimbly, Stefan leapt aside. He laughed as he jabbed at Cullen's ribs, sending the young man sprawling onto his side.

"Get up, or I'll take your stick!" A man bellowed, and the surrounding Khelds, most of them men, laughed.

Cullen glared but scrambled to his feet, advancing on Stefan again.

Emyli jumped as a much louder crash sounded on the terrace, and one of her handmaidens cried out, "My dress!" Emyli turned to see young Hans standing red-cheeked near the table, a pitcher of citrus beverage shattered into pieces at his feet. He still held what appeared to be a broomstick in his hands. Lady Zoranna, eldest daughter of the Enlad of Chennor, brushed ruddy drops off her heavy silk skirt.

"Oh, Hans!" Emyli sighed. "I told you to be careful!"

"But I'm a warrior!" Hans had pleaded earlier to be allowed into the courtyard among the men. "There's not enough room here. And your ladies are no fun." He assessed the three young women critically.

"Put that down. And come here to watch Stefan." She was surprised a moment later to hear her father's unrehearsed boom of laughter.

"Nonsense, Emy. Boys need to play."

Marc Frederick strode onto the balcony as shouts erupted again from the courtyard below. Still wearing travel clothes, he looked dusty but otherwise hale as he brandished his sword, safely sheathed in its scabbard. "Here you go, Hans lad—I'll take you on. Hit me as hard as you please."

With a yell of triumph, Hans launched himself at his grandfather, who fended off the furious assault with ease. Emyli smiled at the sight of her eight-year-old wielding blow after well-timed blow, his blue eyes fierce with imagined battle. They went several rounds before Hans, having successfully blocked every one of the older man's blows, declared himself the victor. He accepted Marc Frederick's solemn request to deliver the sword to Gareth Morgen, who had been there two days already setting up the King's rooms.

Marc Frederick approached the balcony edge, coming to stand beside his daughter. "The boy moves well; he'll make a good fighter. Uncommonly quick for a youngster."

"He's growing so fast!"

"They always do." He smiled down upon her. "That one," he indicated Stefan, still engaging Cullen, "has grown quite a lot."

"He wants to be a good prince to his people. He wants you to approve of him. He works very hard for that." She turned, wishing she could mend every one of Stefan's problems. "Why won't you give it to him?"

"My approval? Perhaps because I don't approve of all that he does."

Emyli bowed her head. "He thinks you are obvious, taking a Staubaun mistress just because you want him to take a Staubaun wife."

"I don't believe my personal life needs his approval. I performed my duty in providing this land with an heir. Stefan has yet to do so."

"The status of your heir remains open. Some of your nobles—many, in fact—openly discuss their wish that you have another child."

"Another heir? Well, that will not happen. Stefan is my Heir and will succeed me." He looked sad, at once resigned and determined, before he cocked a more pensive look at Emyli. "You need not worry about Palimia. She has had two husbands and no children. I have known from the beginning that she cannot conceive."

She sighed. "You think I worry about that? I have given Palimia a chamber in my suite." She laid her head on his shoulder. "I know Apollonia goes into a rage over any woman you entertain, even though her role as your wife is now simply ceremonial. She wants to prevent heirs while others want you to provide them. I just want my father to be happy."

"Do you?" He bent to kiss her hair, and she inhaled the warm scent of horses and leather that wafted from his jacket. "Then perhaps you can do me one favor more and tell my grandson to cease voting against my proposals in the Archhalia."

"Stefan is just doing what's best as he sees it."

The contest in the courtyard was over, the crowd breaking up as news of the King's arrival filtered through to the Prince and his court. Trulo's midsummer festival had swelled the numbers of Khelds in residence at the Golden Palace, and the level of noise had grown commensurately. The place resounded with Kheldish brogues and hollers.

Emyli pulled away from her father's fond embrace so that he might escort her into the palace. Noise from the corridor outside preceded Stefan's entrance, accompanied by a score or more of his courtiers.

"Grandfather! Majesty!" Stefan bowed deeply as public protocol demanded, yet he looked anything but formal as he rose to offer an embrace. Confident and in charge, he turned to receive a quick hug from his mother.

They exchanged ample pleasantries, Stefan treating his grandsire to a list of his recent schemes and successes. A respectful circle of Kheld kin and Staubaun courtiers, standing back from the royal pair and mindful of their place, listened enthusiastically to every word, nodding affirmation and laughing at the right places. They beamed when Marc Frederick gave Stefan a sound clap on the shoulder, telling him he had done well.

Later, when the courtiers were gone and the Kheld kinsmen, having overstayed their welcome, had left with the promise of a good meal and singing in the courtyard, Marc Frederick retreated with Stefan to the east-facing library of Trulo's palace. Since it was summer, the twin hearths stood cold and empty, though filled with flowers gleaned from surrounding hills. Garlands of oak leaves draped the mantelpieces.

"I did not vote against *you*, Grandfather. I voted against allowing the Sordaneons to assume control of Sordan's trade ministries."

"When we spoke in Dazunor-Rannuli, you seemed to accept

my reasons for the proposal and said you didn't foresee it being a problem."

"It became more of a problem the more I studied it. We are rearming an enemy!"

"And as I see it, we are strengthening a nation that will be our strongest ally." Marc Frederick had long passed the point of patience.

"Against Mormantalorus?"

"Yes."

"But that country's done us no wrong!"

Marc Frederick could not believe his grandson could mouth such absurdity. Mormantalorus, unlike Sordan, had successfully separated from the Triempery rather than acknowledge a non-Highborn King. The new state had openly opposed not only Marc Frederick's right to rule but his family's very existence as well. Though there had been no assassination attempt from that quarter in many years, the first two decades of his rule had seen no fewer than ten.

"Then you do not know your own family's history. Morman-talorus swore at my ascension to destroy me—*and* all my family—because it galled them to see a 'descendant of beasts' upon the throne of their forefathers. A descendant of beasts! And Nammuor has not veered from that assessment."

"Times change."

"Yes, times change. So do enemies. Sordan, and the Sorda-neons, are not our enemy. They never really were, thanks to the Malyrdeons and their Wall. The bonds between the Highborn cannot be severed. They are partly Leur, and they feel kinship with each other in ways you or I never will. They do not war upon each other: remember that. Never. Neither must we." All his life, Marc Frederick had held fast to his belief that family was at once continuance and hope. Though he did not love Apollonia, nor she, him, Marc Frederick had never faltered in his love for his children or for the people he ruled through them. "You only encourage my enemies—*our* enemies—when you speak against my policies. More than that, you endanger your future alliances and support. Not all who support me are yet convinced of you, and your demonstrations of defiance concern them gravely."

"Why? Because for every noble who follows your lead, there are two who disagree with you?"

"Because the lords who support me want a stable monarchy. If they did not, they would seek another King." He studied the fierce pride in his grandson's look, remembering the many times he had encouraged it. "Ships of state are best turned slowly, Stefan, and ever into a favorable wind. Seek out storms only at your own peril and never generate your own if you can help it. I speak as a man who has done both. Do not throw away the support I have amassed over the years. It is worth more than the Stauberg treasury."

"You expect me to toe the line."

"I do. If you have concerns, come to me before you air them on the Archhalia floor."

"Fine, then. I don't trust the Sordaneons. You do. I don't think we will ever agree on that." Stefan rose and paced to the window, through which they could see the distant bend of the Dazun flanked by tall, forbidding hills. "It's not like I don't have supporters of my own to appease. The Khelds, you know, have a long list of grievances against Sordan and its rulers. There's this whole Rill issue, which you know the Sordaneons cannot be separated from. And there are mining cartels..."

"Personal. Don't let your personal involvement overshadow decisions to be made for the good of your people."

"I don't. I just have a different idea of what's good for my people."

*Not "our" people. His. Even without knowing it, he limits his concern to those with whom he sympathizes.* Marc Frederick went to stand beside him. In the distance, the misty heights of the formidable Kragh stood as reminder of a past long forgotten.

"Do you know who your people are, Stefan? Not just the Khelds, but *all* of them? You will reign over Staubaun lords, too, and Estol folk in whom many bloods mingle—and also the folk of yonder secret hills. You will have many subjects, all of whom will want different things, and you will only be able to chart one course by which to govern them. I can teach you how to chart such a course."

The young man's expression hardened. "The Malyrdeons don't approve of me as your Heir, do they?"

It was the first time Stefan had raised that observation openly. *Truth,* Marc Frederick told himself. If Stefan was to succeed him, he should not have to wade through a morass of falsehoods.

"They question your ability to serve as a fair and just ruler. Your antipathy toward the Sordaneons is a problem. And they are sensitive to accusations by some of your Staubaun subjects that you are disinterested in their troubles."

"If they dislike that I have opened river trade to the Khelds, that's not my concern. And some of those Staubauns apparently expected me to appoint them to certain offices—and are not happy that I put men in those offices whose attitudes I like better. Not all of my ministers are Khelds, either, whatever they say."

Not all, but many. Not that Marc Frederick particularly disapproved. He had himself appointed a considerable number of Khelds to important positions. Nor did he find fault with the men Stefan had chosen, all Khelds of good name and family and as qualified for their positions as Khelds could be—which was the crux of the problem, of course. Khelds were underrepresented among lower-ranking administrators, and most had minimal experience in the complexities of their posts. But he had not come to Trulo to critique his grandson's performance, which, overall, he found satisfactory.

"If Dazunor is prosperous and its people content, how can I not be happy with that?" the King said evenly. "But *my* support for your reforms will grow cold if you cast one more vote against me. Yes, *me*, Stefan. What I am trying to do will be my last gift to this land. The alliance I am proposing will anchor your reign in bedrock and ensure that our family continues to rule Essera in wisdom and justice—even after my passing. It is an alliance that Mormantalorus fears, and so might the Khelds, though it stands to bring them great rewards. It is an alliance nearly all will oppose because they will not understand it. But it is an alliance that will restore the very heart of the Triempery."

Stefan blanched. "You're going to make a pact with the damned Sordaneons!"

"Yes."

"With Dorilian!"

"Him most of all." Marc Frederick kept his tone even. "I had hoped—still hope—to include you as an architect of this treaty."

"An architect?"

"On the Kheld side. There will be numerous negotiations attendant upon the treaty of emancipation—"

"The Malyrdeons agree, of course."

"They do. The City and attendant domains of Sordan will be restored in full and unencumbered to the Sordaneons. But we will not come away emptyhanded, I assure you."

"And you expect me to support this treaty?" The blue eyes locked on his revealed Stefan's outrage, his feelings of betrayal. He would never forgive Dorilian for having tried to kill him. The Seven Houses had succeeded in that, if in nothing else.

"Yes." Marc Frederick sought to soften the blow by adding, "Only publicly, of course. You can argue with me all you want about it in private. The proposal is still in its infancy, its formative stages. These things take time."

"I don't know. I'm not sure how I feel about this. I'm not even sure I would want anything to do with it."

It was a Kheld answer, rooted in pride. If only... Marc Frederick had hoped Stefan would prove capable of surmounting old hurts. And he had hoped he could tell Stefan about Trestethion. He would have told Jonthan. Dazunor-Rannuli's Rill trade would be as affected by opening a new Rill node as would that of Leseos. Of course, he had not informed Leseos' Bas either. Secrecy remained paramount. It would be dangerous to give the Seven Houses any warning. Maybe next week would find Stefan more open to his ideas.

Leaving the young man to grapple in private with his thoughts, Marc Frederick turned his back on the window. "We will talk more about this later. I would like to rest before tonight's banquet."

"Of course. You should. I've invited dancers from the villages—and Amallar." The young man's dull voice revealed a mind besieged by strain and intense emotion.

"Excellent. I should travel there again... to Amallar. It has been a few years, which is far too long. Tobold keeps me abreast of any changes, of course, but I would like to see for myself. We can go together, you and I, and your mother and young Hans as well. Perhaps at harvest time." He clapped his now-quiet grandson again on the shoulder. "I won't ask more of you than you can give, Stefan."

"I think you already have."

"What? My singular belief that you and Dorilian Sordaneon might sit down to a civil discussion of trade matters?" Marc Frederick allowed Stefan's silence to answer that question for him. He gave one more bit of advice. "Don't fear him, Stefan. Never that. Never let him see it in you. The moment you do, you have already lost."

# 51

"It seems you forget who is Hierarch of this domain."

The summer day sweltered, and even the sounds of gulls had long since fallen silent in the midday heat. Dorilian approached his father across the bone-white stones of the river terrace. The Hierarch sat on the ledge of one of several artful ponds, feeding jewel-colored fish from a bowl in his lap. Wide mouths gaping, they flocked to his hand in splashes of blue, coral, and ivory.

"Not I, Father. Your people. You don't go out among them. I do."

"Twice this week, I have had to suspend the Halia to prevent your conspirators from enacting business in my name that I *forbade* you to pursue. You are provoking our enemies and making our friends nervous." A fat, rosy worm wriggled in Deben's fingers until a hungry fish rose, mouth wide as a fist, to accept it.

"Our enemies need provoking, and I differ as to whom we should consider friends."

"You are warlike and a fool. Don't you understand our enemies would place you—and your family and nation through you—in chains even heavier than those we now wear? They want only the Rill. They want the Rill such as *they* understand it. Let them have it. Let them have what they believe they possess: a mindless machine. If they cannot bespeak it, they cannot change it, and neither can they bring it to ruin."

"But what if *we* can change it?"

"What if we can? That doesn't mean we should." Deben picked through the tidbits in his bowl, coming up with a pink prawn. He used it to lure a particularly colorful fish to the side of the pool where he could better admire its markings. "There's a beauty. It's rare to see one with scarlet dorsal fins—very rare." He tossed a quartered orange into the water, and the fish attacked it ferociously, dislodging the pulp and ripping at the rind until they had torn it apart. "I will never wield the power of my forefathers, and if you are wise, neither will you."

"I will not crawl on my belly, hoping my posture will convince them I am harmless."

Deben laughed. "Too late for that. You can be sure they have noted your violent ways. Already they are wary of your maneuvers. Marc Frederick is not a stupid man, you say? Very well, I say this: He is using you."

"And I am using him. He is no longer young. He has lost his son and Heir, and he knows that Stefan will never command Essera's full allegiance. Marc Frederick wants to see Sordan stable and an ally before he dies."

"Then tell him to come to me. Because while I live, there will be no goodwill between the Eagle Throne and that unwashed, thin-blooded brigand who sits like a vulture on Stauberg's holy seat. He deserves it not—not after forty years does he deserve it! A *thousand* years will not make his descendants fit to rule the Creation! Tell him that, the next time he tries to plant his heresies in your simple mind. Tell him you cannot give him what he seeks, that you will not stand aside while he fixes his barbarian line upon the Star Throne of the Malyrdeons and pretends himself our equal! Then, perhaps, he will find you less useful and abandon his efforts to subvert this domain through my son."

Dorilian placed his foot upon the sculpted back of a stone serpent. The statue served to scare away any birds that might want to feast on Deben's precious fish. Dorilian disliked being ordered— but he did not wish his father to think him untrustworthy. Nor could Dorilian say for certain that Marc Frederick's intentions might not entail some of the very things Deben feared.

"Never accuse me, Father, of placing anyone before our family's honor. You have but to look upon my successes. We cannot rest upon Esseran might to secure our lands when so many of them want it for themselves. We need our own army. Give me ten thousand men, and there is not a power in any land that might take what I would hold!"

"You have no experience in military command."

"More than you might suspect. And more, I might add, than you."

"Then it's true," Deben looked up from feeding his fish. "You were behind the attacks in Neuberland. You ordered men to kill the Stauberg-Randolph bitch's brat."

He had sworn upon four men's lives that he would never own that act—and he did not break that trust now. Silence was answer enough, to judge by the hard edge of approval that tugged at Deben's lips.

"Marc Frederick had to have known," Deben mused. "Yet he flattered you somehow into staying at his court. But did he win the rebel over?"

"He won nothing. I have my own plans."

"Plans that mesh only too well with his." With a sigh, Deben tossed the last few orange segments and bits of prawn into the pond, then put the bowl aside for servants to retrieve later. He rose and adjusted the folds of his chiton. "I will not have my Heir usurping my place. I am sending you to Hestya." Dorilian's head shot up, protest cut off as his father continued. "I have instructed Tiflan Morevyen to appoint you governor of that region, and I am giving you command of the military garrison currently headed by the Triemperal Legate Proseno. Marc Frederick has released it, no doubt upon your instigation. I would have you oversee the final phases of the Lissam Palace construction. This assignment will, I trust, remove you sufficiently from the Hierarchate's affairs here in Sordan to afford me a clear grasp of my office."

It was enough work for three men.

Dorilian had not plotted with Marc Frederick to release Hestya from Triemperal administration; the King had concocted that plan on his own. Had he anticipated that Deben would give him the command? Perhaps. Doing so removed Dorilian from Sordan itself, away from the Rill hub and the convoluted politics of his City—and far away from his scheming wife and her brother.

Or did his father harbor a more devious reason for the order? *Levyathan.* Dorilian visited the unborn child daily. "You are sending me from my wife and my son!"

Deben grimly smiled at his belated grasp of the situation. "Your heir will be well-protected here. You saw no reason to play the husband to Daimonaeris before, so do not plead to play the part now. She desires not your companionship."

Of him, she desired no part at all. "I wish to stay near my wife while she is with child."

"The babe has no need of you. Her body, not yours, sustains

him." Deben exhaled sharply. "Have I not seen how you hound her, how you press until she allows your hand upon her belly? What do you seek? You know it lives."

"I seek to know him."

"As you knew your brother? What if it was your touch that twisted Levyathan and cast his mind strangely? The abilities of our kind are not to be deployed upon a whim. You will know him soon enough, in the hour of his birth, if she will allow you to be with her."

Which would not happen, if Daimonaeris had any voice to lend.

"I will go." Much as Dorilian hated it, his banishment afforded an opportunity. Sordan's army was in the first stages of being strengthened—and he would be ideally placed to make Hestya's command his own. Marc Frederick might not be so wrong to have schemed him into such a situation. The King had himself been a military man.

*First, he takes away my army, and now he gives one back.* If he had needed proof that Marc Frederick trusted him, he had just received it.

Nammuor tested him at Hestya, just as Dorilian had expected he would. Word had come that the Mormantaloran ruler's party had crossed the border, on his way to Sordan. The delegation had traveled by land to Hestya and would take the Rill the rest of the way. Indeed, they were to leave that very afternoon. Nammuor's banner arrogantly displayed the Crimson Flame of Cienorr, son of Ergeiron and realm-father of the City of Fire. In his tenth year since coming to the throne of the southernmost domains of the original Triempery, Nammuor had decided to adopt the crests and artifacts of its defunct Highborn rulers. He strode toward Dorilian across the dusty parade field as though he were descended from Cienorr himself. Nammuor's diadem, crafted of dark wire and filigrees of metals Dorilian could not identify, sat upon that presumptuous brow. The blood-red gem at its center looked strange also, overblown, like a compound eye. Disturbed by it, Dorilian focused on the flags and ordered the offending Highborn banners struck in his presence.

"Do not dream," he said to his wife's brother, "that her marriage to me has exalted you. Neither do these heirlooms you have usurped. You are not Highborn, nor will you ever be."

Dorilian had just returned from a long day of meetings during which he had wholly redesigned the outer courtyard of the palace complex being constructed within sight of Hestya's Rill mount. A Sordaneon palace presided over every Rill port. The walls of this palace, smooth and new, rose from the plain in sweeps of golden sandstone already being polished by the wind. Above the walls, seven gold-crowned towers could be seen for leagues, as powerful a summons to the town as the Rill pylons arching in shifting white wings upon the hill.

"I came to ask if you wish me to convey a message to your father." Nammuor managed to sound amiable in making the offer. "Every week, I hear more news of how Sordan's popular government is being resurrected." Nammuor cast a pointed look at Dorilian's princely vestments, which displayed his emblems of governorship. "Has old Marc Frederick, now that he lacks a son, grown weary of ruling your difficult land?"

"Maybe I convinced him that I intend to seize my nation back whatever his will. He knows my temper."

"Your temper, yes. I have myself often weighed its implications, not least toward my sister."

"I will not discuss my wife with you."

"Nor your child?"

The Mormantaloran's inquiry slid like a probe into a wound.

"Especially not that." Dorilian could not explain why he disliked the diadem the other man wore. Something about it kept drawing his attention to the deep inner fire of the gem. "She got what she wanted of me, and I of her. Our marriage was ever a contrivance to provide Sordan with an heir. Now she has her wish. At least she no longer pretends she wants my company."

"Her pregnancy is not the end of your husbandly duties."

"I am, for the moment, required to stay in Hestya. You cannot expect Daimonaeris to come to me."

"No. I expect you to go to her."

Because Hestya was a Rill port, Dorilian could have visited the site daily as needed and returned nightly to sleep in his luxurious rooms overlooking Sordan's splendid vistas. But for his father's wishes, he would have done so. After three years of Rill commerce,

Hestya had prospered and its wealth increased a thousandfold, but in comparison to Sordan the town remained provincial. Its unpaved streets swirled with the dust of the plains; its buildings bore evidence of hasty construction from materials at hand. A handful of fine buildings had sprung up at odd intervals, faced with imported stone and offering interiors that afforded a degree of elegance, but most structures were rustic. Even the palace he lived in was in various stages of construction. His father and his wife were about the only aspects of life in Sordan that he did not miss.

It was unfortunate he could not tell Nammuor his real thoughts.

"I'm respecting your sister's wishes by not imposing my unwanted attentions on her. It is not by my choice that I am not at her side."

"You force her to communicate with you through your former nurse."

"I trust Noemi. And I take the greatest care with any matter that has to do with my wife."

"The woman insults her. Daimonaeris tells me she is impertinent and bold. She has told you as much, yet you do nothing to alleviate the situation."

The complaint amused Dorilian. It told him that Deben must have refused to intervene. "I am not very experienced with women. One night your sister led me to believe she found me pleasing. But then, for no reason I can fathom, she closed her door to me again and grew colder than she had been before. Tiflan told me that sometimes a woman with child can become moody and difficult and find nothing to her satisfaction—especially not her husband. I can think of no other reason for her unhappiness."

Though Nammuor's gaze upon him did not falter, the man appeared satisfied with his position. "It would not hurt to cater to her mood. Men with pregnant wives have done so through the ages."

Dorilian accepted his horse's reins from Legon and swung lightly onto the saddle. "Such men have had to dwell with their wives. I do not."

Because the fastest way to rid himself of Nammuor was to assist him on his way to Sordan, Dorilian directed his guard in that direction. Nammuor had succeeded in acquiring a royal escort. The market-day crowds in the streets parted for the mounted men, pulling back under the awnings and against the mud walls of buildings that had not existed but a few years before. Many called to Dorilian with words of reverence, naming him Derlon's Heir and Rill Son, kin of Lord Sebbord the Rill-Bringer. The man riding with him earned glances also, but warily. Mormantalorus was a familiar yet uncertain neighbor.

"I have no message for my father," Dorilian told Nammuor once they had reached the Rill platform and stood alone upon a far corner of that white surface, a place bounded by tall white walls and shaded by the crisp shadows of overarching struts. A line of the Sordaneon Eagle Guard fronted by crimson-skirted Mormantalorans kept onlookers at a distance. "I send him detailed reports daily."

"Very well. Then let me pass one to you." With an abrupt twitch, Nammuor's hand stole to his temple, pressing where the metal of his splendid diadem rested. "Our domains are to be joined. I have taken no wife and sired no child. My sister bears not only your heir, but mine. Our enemies have noted this union, and they will seek to prevent our joining forces."

"Is that what my father contemplates? That our nations be joined, and you and he merge forces?"

"He contemplates his security and neutrality. No man is more immovable than he. But you, dear Brother, are another matter." In the distance, a high, bright tone announced activation of the first deceleration of an incoming transport. One of the two slips was sheathed in a delicate shimmer as overhead structures shifted to contain the energy stream. Nammuor winced, closing his eyes, but only for a moment before joining Dorilian in watching a *charys* materialize above the town and glide to the platform edge.

"How old are you?" Nammuor assessed Dorilian with a calculating grimace. "Twenty years? Surely you have ambitions by now. You are more than capable. I expect that within months you will have transformed this dusty backwater into a provincial capital worthy of a Sordaneon. Imagine what you could do with an entire domain of your own."

*How intriguing,* Dorilian thought. Nammuor was testing him out in the very way a prospector tested a vein of ore, applying heat to see what trace metals could be teased to the surface. If his response suited Nammuor's intent, he might this very evening find himself inheriting the Hierarchate—or denounced to his father as a traitor.

"Someday, I am sure I will find out."

The *charys* disgorged its passengers. Transfer mechanisms embedded in the mount performed the exchange of cargo. Among the newly unloaded containers were several of gold destined to embellish the walls of the new palace. A little more time, awkward and strained, passed before a bell signaled boarding to commence.

Nammuor smiled at the chance to depart. "As ever, Thrice Royal, it is a pleasure to leave you. I will be sure to give my sister your regards."

"Tell her that I trust she is attending to the wellbeing of our son."

"Yes." Those pitch-dark eyes fastened on him inquisitively. "You are proud of that, aren't you? Knowing that she carries a son?"

"Just tell her."

As a diplomatic mission, the Mormantalorans would be the only ones allowed to board. Any disgruntled passengers would have to wait some more for Sordan to generate and send a second *charys*. As Nammuor stepped down onto the hilltop proper, crossing the faint demarcation of the Rill's corporeal bounds, he abruptly bent over, clutching his head. He jerked upright again, his face twisted by pain as he swept the diadem from his brow and turned it in his hands, staring. Stumbling back a few steps, retreating onto the platform's apron, Nammuor never took his eyes from the fiery jewel at the diadem's center.

"Disembark!" he shouted to those who had entered the *charys* ahead of him. Thrusting the diadem beneath his robes, he shot a glare over at Dorilian, seeking to determine what he had seen. "We will not take the Rill today." His voice could not conceal a note of panic. "We ride to Bartulu." He hurried from the platform without looking back, either at the Rill or the astonished Sordaneon prince who stood there.

*The jewel in the diadem went dark.* Dorilian played the moment again in his mind as he stood upon the platform edge and watched the black Nalapari horses of the Mormantaloran company race swiftly along the trade road to the north. They would reach the port of Bartulu after three more days of riding. *It lost its fire.*

And Nammuor had, for a moment, looked as if he had lost something more.

# 52

Dorilian went to Essera in the first week of autumn. His real reason for going north was to visit Marc Frederick, although he publicly announced a desire to choose the facing materials for the state throne room of the Lissam Palace. He wanted nothing less costly than genuine *verlumnas*, mined from an ancient Serrain quarry famous for that sublime deep-green stone. The Illarions received him graciously, old Phellan giving him residence for the night in rooms overlooking the millennia-old palaces and courts of Simelon. Dorilian stared long out the window at the discordant sight of luminous, broken Rill arches rising above the white crescent shape of a useless platform and station.

An artifact. A ruin. A promise obscured by appearances. Dorilian had not seen such a sight in a long time, and the thought that these people might regard the Rill as an inert Entity struck him strangely. For all that they lived and worked in its shadow and could still see the blood of Peleor gleaming where it had been absorbed into the Entity's bones, for them the Rill was no more alive than it was for the Khelds.

By afternoon he had finished his tour of the quarry, from the stores of which he had handpicked fifty panels of sheer translucent mineral, each of exceptional clarity and color, which Lahgaelan artisans would shape into the walls of Hestya's unfinished throne room. The green stone depths shone with living hue, yet drank so much light as to promise power and hint at secrets. Dorilian returned to the Illarion palace to find a message from Marc Frederick asking that he join the King at a hunting lodge outside the city.

Trusting Marc Frederick came easily now. The King had kept his word: Sordan's Halia had taken control of the more mundane aspects of governing their City. Although Triemperal offices still oversaw Rill trade, sea and land trade administration had reverted to Hierarchate ministers. Sordan's military had grown from one thousand men assigned only to the Sordaneon personal guard to forty thousand men, ten thousand of that number manning the garrison at Hestya under Dorilian's command.

It was fall again. Everywhere he looked, the trees of Simelon's hills shimmered with hues of gold and flame. This day had been beautiful, and he knew that the following days would be, also. That utter optimism caught him by surprise. He had become so unaccustomed to it that the joy of small things now felt new again, as to a child.

"It might not have been our wisest move to have Deben send his son to Hestya." Nammuor practically growled that opinion.

Nammuor did not often frown at Daimonaeris, but he frowned at her now. She wondered if it was because her belly had begun to bulge quite visibly. Despite that, people now complimented her complexion, saying she had a lovely glow.

She waved a dismissive hand. "I could not be happier. Dorilian never fails to curdle my happiness, and his hands are forever upon me. He insists that I allow him to feel *his* son. His! The fool believes it! I'm glad Deben sent him away."

"Be glad that he does believe it. I don't want you facing his rage should he learn otherwise."

She laughed. "I'm not afraid of Dorilian."

"Neither is he afraid of you—or me. He is remarkably fearless for a son of Deben. He more resembles Labran... or Sebbord." Nammuor leaned forward from the blue cushions of the couch on which he was seated. "Do not provoke him, my little Hierarchessa. Indeed, I think you should maneuver to have Dorilian brought back to Sordan—and back to your bed."

"Are you mad?" She turned on him with narrowed eyes. "I will never allow him into my bed again! Being with him is like mating with an animal!"

"Calm down. I'm sure he was not so bad as all that. I have looked upon less comely men. I cannot believe you preferred Deben."

Daimonaeris stared at her brother, flustered. Not every aspect of her night with Dorilian had been unsatisfactory, and thoughts of her husband's forceful and hard-muscled young body had invaded her dreams recently. She resented him for those incursions as well. With a sigh, she seated herself at her brother's side. Nammuor had been at Sordan for nearly a month and was to depart on the morrow by ship.

"I like it best when Dorilian is away. You have not had to endure him as I have—his comments, his touch."

Something indulgent touched the laughter in Nammuor's gaze as it warmed upon her. "No, dear Sister, I have not, but then your husband has only recently intrigued me. I am convinced, where I was not before, that he needs to be closely watched. Dorilian has proven more adept than I thought he would be at turning a situation to his advantage. He obeys his father even less from Hestya than he did before."

"But when he is here, he is officious and in the way. The people of this wretched City adore him."

"Let them. They admire him because they see Marc Frederick conceding to him. They see Essera retreating from their land, and they credit Dorilian as the cause. He fancies himself Sordan's hero, building his nation anew and making it strong. That works in our favor."

She caught the direction of his thought and smiled. "Better to inherit a strong nation than one that is weak and easily reconquered."

"My brilliant sister." He chuckled. "Now you see why we must keep your husband close at hand. Even the smallest flame, if left unwatched, might leap to new kindling and cause a fire in some other quarter."

She wrinkled her nose. "That one is too like a stone for there to be much heat."

"Endure him but a little longer. Learn what you can of his ways. It may be that he is playing Marc Frederick's game to his gain, but it could be that *he* is the one being played. Marc Frederick has an agenda, we can be sure."

"The advancement of his half-men kind."

"Ah, but have we not taken the first steps toward reconquering Essera?" He placed his hand upon her belly.

"The Highborn have been poor guardians of their own destiny and that of our people. We will do better."

"Indeed we shall, little mother."

If there were hidden purposes behind his smile, she did not see them. The dream they pursued was one they both had shared: a dream of golden promises and an age of beauty, the restoration of power, and an order that had once made the World great. Half men could not even imagine such things as they dreamed.

Dorilian knelt alongside Marc Frederick, his body so still that even the trees moved more than he. He had cocked his bow, tensed for the shot. Together they watched the stag step into the clearing. The great head lifted, displaying its magnificent rack. Fourteen points, at least. His harem grazed in the clearing, unafraid, yet the stag maintained his vigilance. Gray light barely filtered between tree limbs still heavy with leaves not yet fallen to the forest floor. Dew clung like strands of jewels to bent elder branches and blades of grass. The stag stepped forward again. Dorilian waited.

Marc Frederick watched both hunter and prey. Dorilian had perfected his skill both with the bow and the more delicate challenge of awaiting opportunity. He held the curved wood and horn bow precisely, head still, arrow level. In the moment before he released, his breathing relaxed, then stopped, and his fingers parted. The arrow glittered through the half-light before it plunged deep into the stag's fully exposed rib cage. The beast bounded back into the woods, its does fleeing the clearing in a leaping flurry of raised tails. Dorilian jumped to his feet before the King could, notching another arrow even as he ran in pursuit of his prize. The stag would not go far.

Marc Frederick, forgoing the chase, gathered up his bow and loped after. Never built for speed even in youth, he made up for it in age by being able to keep a pace. He found Dorilian only yards into the trees, on his knees beside the fallen stag, the throat of which he had slit neatly. The animal's eyes had already dimmed. Hot blood steamed on the forest floor, darkly staining the leaves and the shining blade in the young man's hand.

"A fine kill." Marc Frederick knelt and laid his hand on the warm beast, admiring the placement of the arrow.

Dorilian looked over toward him. "We can now truly claim that we were hunting."

Marc Frederick unslung his quiver and opened a side packet, removing a rippled length of hollowed wood. Picking up a nearby stick, he ran it up and down the length so that it emitted a loud, resonant clacking. They had told their huntsmen to wait on the edge of the wood. The men would come to the signal and see to dressing and then carrying the carcass. "I will enjoy another chance at venison. My cook sees it less often now than he did before."

Dorilian studied him, breaking the look only to wipe the blood from his hunting blade. He had become quieter since Levyathan's death. Marc Frederick found it too much to bear.

"What do you see with your Highborn eyes?"

"Your pain," Dorilian said.

He probably did, in the way the Highborn saw so much of human emotion. Not through his human eyes, but with that ancillary Leur sense that detected hate and love, anger and compassion—and pain. An empath's power, but also by channeling such perceptions into and through his own loss, feeling it deeply. Marc Frederick nodded since there was neither way nor cause to deny it.

"I miss him still. I think I always will. We hunted together often, Jon and I." He stared at the stag and the blood on the ground, then abruptly felt ill and weak. Turning away, he walked from the woods into the less somber, open space of the clearing. Dawn's light there lessened the gloom.

"I was not thinking." Dorilian had followed on the King's heels. "I shouldn't have asked you to hunt with me."

"No, don't apologize. I'm glad you asked." Marc Frederick drew a deep breath, wondering that the tastes and scents of the hills should be so vivid today, so sharp. "I enjoyed this morning. A good hunt." He heard men approaching just beyond the trees on the other side of the clearing. "Let's do it again."

"Come to Teremar. We can hunt cats on horseback. That will remind you less of him and still be great sport."

"And I will think how he would have enjoyed it."

That gray gaze continued to search his. "It never goes away, does it?"

"No," Marc Frederick admitted. But this time, though the tears were close, he did not spill them. He found some sweet among the bitter. "It fades somewhat. I hear his voice less often now. I no longer catch myself thinking it is all a mistake, that I will see him again. I had to let go of so much... not just my son, but my hopes as a father and as ruler of this land. He was to follow me. Carrying human life forward is such an important business, and we so often leave it to happenstance and afterthoughts. Jon was never an afterthought. I had wanted him desperately; I wanted a son. I wanted to leave something better in my place—a legacy—however unfair it was to burden him with that."

Men emerged from the gray shapes of the trees across the dawn-traced clearing. Seeing the hunters they had been seeking, they broke into a run. Birds scattered from the grass as the men came through it. Pink laced the sky. Dorilian pointed to the trees nearest where the stag would be found. Together, he and Marc Frederick walked back toward the next hill and the gamekeeper's cottage where they had spent the night. From there, they would ride to the palatial lodge where courtiers waited like crows.

"Daimonaeris is starting to show," Dorilian noted. "We are not moving quickly enough."

"We have time still. I have laid the important groundwork. It may surprise you to learn that some of your Malyrdeon kindred already knew of your Rill affinity."

"Rheger." Dorilian swiped at a stand of high grass in frustration.

Marc Frederick said nothing to confirm that conclusion. He had never revealed all he knew regarding the events of that night. "Those who know have kept the secret. You have nothing to fear from them; you never did. But I think the time has come for you to present your case to them."

Though he hesitated, Dorilian nodded. At long last, his country's autonomy mattered more than his desire to exact retribution for old wrongs. Nammuor's designs on Sordan were deadly, and Dorilian would need allies beyond Sordan's borders.

"I will go to them," he said.

Later that night, before a slowly dying fire in the great hearth of the lodge, Dorilian put his signature on a series of documents, set them again in order, and handed them to Marc Frederick, who affixed his signature and seal before inserting the papers into a message cylinder to be carried by courier to Permephedon. There, the documents would be presented to the Archhalia. In them, the King and Sordan's Heir requested the establishment of a court of reparations to address longstanding disputes between Sordani property holders and Esseran nobles who had received those properties through illegal seizure or confiscation. It was a simple petition, one they both knew was certain to be voted down. It was only a first step, designed to create a dialogue that would reveal strategic alliances. Marc Frederick was surprised to see Dorilian place another cylinder—a much smaller one, used for personal correspondence—upon the table.

"What is this?"

"A message to Enreddon Malyrdeon, requesting a meeting. If your courier could take it to Permephedon, it can be sent by array to Stauberg, and he will receive it quickly."

Marc Frederick picked up the gleaming object. Distinctly Sordaneon, its emerald insignia and seals glinted upon the weighty brass surface. "What do you know of your kind's Leur gifts?"

For a moment, he thought the young man would not answer, but then he did. "I can generate an *orbus*."

It was a start, an admission. Thanks to centuries of peace and luxury, Highborn seldom resorted to using many of their native abilities. Some, like device affinity, were difficult to manage even when the gift was present.

"What else did Sebbord teach you? Did he teach you how to send?"

They were treading the tenderest of ground. Although Sebbord had been one of the most powerful and experienced of their race, Dorilian's youth would have limited his ability to incorporate those lessons.

"Yes. I used to send to Sebbord. I send to my father. But I cannot send to Enreddon. I'm not familiar with his resonance."

Flipping the cylinder in his left hand, Marc Frederick walked to the other side of the lofty room. They were alone. The servants, of which there were but two, had retired to their own quarters. Facing the bookcases that lined the far wall, Marc Frederick turned his back on his guest. "Catch!" he said, barely even a whisper. He had experienced Dorilian's resonance deeply that dark night after Jonthan's death and had refined his knowledge of the young man since. He now knew Dorilian so well he could have located him in a multitude, and while the powers the Leur's Ring gave him were not great—barely those of a Highborn with few gifts at all—he could do this much. The weight of the cylinder, so substantial before, departed from his hand. He closed his fingers inward upon the emptiness where it had been and turned to look across the room.

Standing framed before the fire, Dorilian held the cylinder in hand. He glared back at him then, eyes narrowed and focused. The cylinder vanished from his hand, and simultaneously Marc Frederick sensed the shift. He opened his left palm to receive it, closing his fingers about the weight as the cylinder returned.

"I will send it to Enreddon for you," he said. "This time." The cylinder vanished again, and both men knew it would not reappear.

Dorilian seethed. "We could have saved a lot of time between messages all these months, if you had shown me you could do this!"

"Or if *you* had shown me that you could. I am not ungifted, my young friend. My grandfather left me well prepared to rule alongside your kindred." He regarded the Leur's Ring upon his hand, where it glowed benignly. "It is mostly this Ring, of course. A device of sorts, very like the Rill Stone or the Wall Stone. I'm not sure what this is a piece of, but it is similarly talented. It extends life, which is a useful thing, and enables me to direct energy flows... though not powerful ones and only for a short time."

"You've been clever about concealing your ability to use it."

"You would understand that, wouldn't you? You have spent your life concealing greater secrets than I will ever hold." For a moment, he held the younger man's silent gaze. "My ability, to be sure, is more limited than yours. Perhaps I will yet be proved a fool for revealing it to you, but I think not. I just wanted you to know that I can do... some things that will be useful to us." With a sigh, he embraced having breached yet another barrier. "I believe that from now on, we should send our messages this way. No one needs know the extent to which we correspond. We can do so at night, at a certain time perhaps. That way, we will not provide the Seven Houses or other fools with fodder for conjecture."

He had settled on this means of introducing Dorilian to new concepts: just plunge him headfirst into them and let him figure out the parameters. Stefan, he knew, would have floundered in such a situation; indeed, Stefan should have been here with them. But his grandson's votes had been perfunctory, his heart not behind them. Perhaps when Stefan saw how the new union between

Sordan and Essera revitalized the Triempery, he would come around.

Going to his case of documents, Marc Frederick thumbed the brass locks and retrieved two pages of gossamer-thin paper, once tightly rolled and smuggled out of Mormantalorus in a shipment of spicebark. He handed these to Dorilian, allowing his young guest to read the spidery writing and drawing. Both were somewhat distorted for having been written blind in transparent ink. A code stone had had been rubbed across the lettering to reveal it.

"Nammuor has moved seven thousand more men into Othgol. He has also nearly finished the construction of two dozen warships. Ten of those ships are at Ossum. Seven others are being built in a hidden harbor at Neerba. I want to send Admiral Zepheron on a mission to destroy those ships. Any attempt to destroy ships in other locations would be too risky." Marc Frederick looked hard at his companion. They had just gone from being allied in a peaceful venture to restore Sordan's autonomy to discussing an act of war. Marc Frederick hoped he had not misjudged their alliance. "I want Sordan's fleet to patrol the Kolpos. That will free my ships to make the attack."

"War games. Black and red flags. Your fleet can slip out in the confusion. Sordan can, if necessary, later claim to have been misled. You bear the blame. In the meantime, our ships will guard the seaway."

Marc Frederick smiled. "Mind reader. Yes, that is what I want."

"You have it." To judge by Dorilian's expression, he relished the opportunity.

"Even had you not agreed, I wanted you to know. Your brother-by-marriage is going to be unhappy whether or not I succeed in destroying his warships."

"I will put the garrison at Hestya on alert—after I 'hear' about the dastardly deed. He won't be able then to seize this as an opportunity to attack your troops still in Suddekar. I will make sure my father does not position the Hierarchate militarily in condemnation, which should discourage Lahgael and Ardaen from taking punitive actions in appeasement."

*What a Hierarch he will be! Already he wields better political instincts than any man I have known in decades.*

"Good." Marc Frederick retrieved the documents and locked them away. He had accomplished even more than he had hoped. "I think we can present our case for the dissolution of Sordan's occupation to the Archhalia this spring. That will give us all winter to hammer out support, provided of course that you have by then reached agreement with the Malyrdeons and can persuade your father to attend a meeting of the Highborn Curia—or, alternatively, bestow upon you his vote."

"He will never do that."

"He also has not left Sordan in forty years," Marc Frederick pointed out. "You have your work cut out for you."

# 53

" We *what*?"
"We attacked Nammuor's ship construction projects in Mormantalorus. Our force destroyed twenty or so warships."

Turning his back for a moment on Stefan, Marc Frederick signaled Gareth to bring his impossibly heavy, gem-encrusted State Robe, the next-to-last item he would don before going into the Archhalia chamber. He had convened this special meeting of the Archhalia to preempt the necessity of answering a formal summons.

"Why did we do that?" Stefan had joined his grandfather because Marc Frederick wanted the two of them to enter together in a visible show of unity.

The King adjusted the set of his robe's fur-trimmed shoulders so that they sat perfectly before allowing Gareth to undertake the garment's cumbersome closures. "Because Nammuor was going to use those ships to attack us. No one needs to build a hundred new warships in secret unless they plan to do something with them. Our spies obtained evidence of plans involving those ships."

"I cannot believe even an idiot would think he could attack us with ships! Our fleet's too powerful! The coastal cities are well armed—"

"Not us. Sordan."

"That's absurd! They are his allies. Dorilian is married to his sister."

"Who is pregnant with his heir, who will also be the heir of the Sordaneons. After the babe is born, Nammuor will have achieved at least one of his goals with the Sordaneons—and he would have used those ships." Crooking his finger ever so slightly, Marc Frederick indicated that it was time for his royal crown. Though the Star

Crown of Ergeiron was by far the most symbolic of Essera's royal headgear, it was not at Permephedon. It sat in Stauberg. A good thing, as far as he was concerned. That crown was a greater enhancer and gave him unbearable headaches. He was just gifted enough to be sensitive and not gifted enough to use it properly. In the Star Crown's place, he wore the Second Crown of Elaemon, a piece nearly as storied and made of a ransom of gold and priceless gems. Possessed of the power to make even the least of men look kingly, it sat with blue and white fire upon his dark head and flawlessly performed that service.

Stefan still looked astounded, though not by his grandfather's regal appearance. "Did Dorilian tell you this tall story?"

"No, he did not." It was a question many among his nobles were sure to ask. Marc Frederick saw no harm in rehearsing his answer. "I have long known—and have long warned you and others—about Nammuor's hidden agenda regarding that alliance. The fact that it took this turn is no great surprise. I did, of course, discuss my plans with Dorilian before undertaking military action."

What he had not expected was the look that abruptly seized Stefan, the sudden hard hurt that came into his grandson's blue eyes. "You told *him* about it ahead of time? But you didn't tell *me*?"

"Nammuor is not your brother by marriage."

"And Dorilian is not your Heir! He's not even your friend!"

*There is my error.* Marc Frederick resisted his impulse to defend the Sordaneon prince. To do so would but drive the wedge deeper. "I feared, since you had openly doubted my warnings about Mormantalorus, that you would not appreciate my decision. Military ventures require silence, Stefan. They require secrecy. Nammuor has a thousand ears in Essera, and some of them may be nearer to you than you think. I told very few people—every one of them a person whose cooperation I needed for my plan to succeed."

"I am your Heir!" Stefan repeated.

"And I am your King. In this, I will not be second guessed. I did what was needed. The ships are destroyed. We will discuss at length later whether I should have told you—and I would have done so had I been certain I could trust you to be silent."

"Like you trusted Dorilian."

"Yes. His nation was at stake. Nammuor's anger could well fall upon them first now. You might notice that I did not tell Deben. It would not surprise me to learn that he has been in league with Nammuor."

"And you believe Dorilian is not? What are you doing, cozying up to him, believing everything he says? Don't you know you look like an old fool? And you know what else, you make me look like one, too! A fool. Now everyone will know you didn't tell me! They'll know you don't trust me!"

"How will they know I didn't tell you? No man I told can say who all the others were. Stay silent, and they will not know otherwise."

"And lie about it, should they ask me?"

"That, Stefan, is up to you." Was it only age, or something more, that made Marc Frederick's crown seem heavier than it ever had before? Yes, he should have trusted his Heir. Instead, he had trusted his instincts. What he could not know was whether those came from wisdom, or fear. "We want the same things for this land; remember that. Prosperity, equity, the wellbeing of our people, and peace with our neighbors—we want all these things." He met his grandson's tormented blue-eyed gaze. "Trust me, Stefan. For once, will you do that? I know what I am doing."

"I'm trying. I really am."

"We have to stand together, you know. We Stauberg-Randolphs cannot afford to be fighting each other."

The young man looked away, conceding that point. His dark hair stood out against the pale colors of the mural behind him, a vague landscape of winter and ice. "I just want you to trust *me* too. Is that so much to ask? There's a lot I don't understand, and why is that? Because I never know your thoughts. What is it you are trying to do?"

That was the crux of the matter, the bitter truth.

"I'm repairing the rift that I created, Stefan. I am making whole a fabric that was never meant to be sundered. Be patient just a little longer, and I will tell you the entirety of it."

He wished he could do so here in this room and wipe away the look in his grandson's eyes of being left out once again. But the Malyrdeons had not yet met with Dorilian. They were to do so this very afternoon. No agreement had been reached, nor had they secured Dorilian's assurances that the Sordaneons would enter negotiations to open the Rill station at Trestethion. Amallar had not consented to provide access to that station. Essera had yet to propose to end its occupation of Sordan. Until such accords were in place, it would be unwise to say too much. That kind of hope could, like fire itself, feed on dormant dreams and quickly flare out of control. He dared not endanger the process by speaking too soon.

"Great things are going to happen, Stefan. Great things. Things that will write our family's place in the history books for generations to come."

Dorilian presented his conditions to his Malyrdeon kindred without preamble. They knew as well as he did what was at stake. Only seven met with him—only the heads of the seven Malyrdeon kinlines that remained.

Did he have the Rill gift? Yes. They were welcome to touch his flesh if that was their wish. Everyone did. He endured it without outwardly flinching, only lashing out when Regelon crudely attempted a mind probe.

Had he been at Hestya? Yes. Was it him, or Sebbord, that the Rill saw then? Him. Did he recall the steps Sebbord had taken to awaken Hestya? Yes, clearly. Could he perform the same functions? Yes, he believed he could.

Could he enable the Rill to see the station at Trestethion? Probably.

The last provided a logical place for Dorilian to put forth his own requirements. His training by Sebbord had been cut short by the old man's murder. Paranoia demanded that Deben empower no rivals, so his father was unsuited to teaching. The few remaining Sordaneons were of no help to him: Mezentius was ungifted and the ancient Lord of Tollech, talented in his youth, was bedridden and incompetent. Therefore, Dorilian had no teachers. What was he to do, teach himself? He could see that the prospect made them nervous. Sordan's treasury contained a wealth of mage devices, most reputed to be powerful and some known to be. He informed them of what he had witnessed at Hestya a mere two months before, of Nammuor's device and the man's strange behavior on the Rill platform. Clearly, their enemy also owned a device. Dorilian reminded the gathered council of the assistance he had given Marc Frederick, not only in the recent matter of Nammuor's ships but also in not challenging the King's choice of heirs.

And then he told them why.

He had looked where none of them had looked. He had stood with Austell in a conjuncture of Rill flow and Wall space, and emerged intact with visions in his head—a handful of which had already come to pass.

And what of those not yet come to pass? He could not be sure. Not all things foretold by the Wall came to be. But he was willing to forge ahead and see which of them did. Were they?

What did you see? Even he could not put the vision-flow fully into words, and he would not let them into his mind to mine for the answers. Stefan in coronation robes. Himself as Hierarch. Images of blood, so many that he did not know which might be past, which had failed to become, or which might yet be.

The Malyrdeons stared at him and each other. Then they told him that he had revealed many portentous things and that they must think upon what he had proposed.

It remained to be seen if their fear of him proved greater than their fear of the future.

Enreddon lowered the brass cylinder he had just received from Marc Frederick's hand and frowned at him. "He is unbelievably dangerous. A wild talent—a wild *Sordaneon* talent—impetuous, secretive, and now, we find, unschooled!"

"Why are you surprised? Other adults of his kindred were murdered before he came of age, leaving only Deben to teach him. Who was supposed to take on the job?"

"Marenthro. Myself. We had him brought to Permephedon, I recall, just for that purpose. Now we can truly regret how that turned out." Enreddon sighed and paced to the glittering spires that dominated the center of the room. He ran a hand through his silver hair. "The strongest mind I have ever encountered. Even Austell said as much. That Sordaneon has willpower enough for all of us."

"Thank your god for that."

"Thank his. The Rill cannot be commanded by less. By the Father, Marc, what are we going to do about him?"

Marc Frederick didn't find the question difficult. "Give him what he asks."

"Just like that? Teach him to use devices and native gifts he has perhaps not yet tapped or into which he has not yet grown? I see no wisdom in your solution. Already he overreaches. What if it should prove that he is false after all and set against you? Against us? What defense would we have against him? Remember Delos, Deben's twin, and how he blasted the Vermillion Aqueduct? The Sordaneons were ever more powerful than we at wielding devices."

"A given, considering their Entity's nature. Really, Redd, you're being Wall-bound. You look at possibilities in the heights and the depths, but miss the step that's in front of you. Dorilian has had ample opportunities to eliminate me, if that were his wish. Yet every chance he has, he lets pass. I think he's as surprised as you that he no longer wants my head, but the facts remain: he does not wish me dead and gave me his word that he would not oppose Stefan as my Heir. It may not be a perfect situation, but it is one with which I am more than willing to work. He is worth that."

"That and more." Turning aside for a moment, Enreddon tapped one of the delicate fins of the twining blood-red sculpture before which he stood. The stone altered its color to a more calming hue, though the blue quickly returned to purple. "My kindred will agree, of course—you need not fear that. The possibilities are too astounding. But we will hold off on any teaching until after we have Sordan's official signatures upon a piece of paper. Deben's word, and Dorilian's too, uttered in our presence, that the Sordaneons acknowledge our common purpose and that they will honor the Wall's direction. This is our decision."

"A good one, as always." Marc Frederick had never doubted that his Highborn kin would come through for him. "He will surprise you, Redd. Mark my words; he will light up the World. I'm going to tell you something I did not tell you before. A year ago, I took him with me to the Kragh."

Enreddon spun on him in surprise. "The Hen Kyon?"

"The Dog Men, yes. He was gracious to them, though not so much to me. I angered him by showing him an excavation that revealed the Rill corpus atop the Maw. I wanted him to think, Redd, and he did—about his god and what the Rill means to people other than himself; about his place in the World. What it is, and what it could be. I think I opened his mind."

"I think you unnecessarily placed a Sordaneon in harm's way. Marc, what you did was madness!"

"I don't regret it. Not a moment."

The other man sighed. "Be careful, Marc. You are modeling uncommon clay. What alters *him* alters the Mind. What alters the Mind may alter… everything. You can create the perfect vessel—the best materials, the most pleasing shape, with hope itself gilding its surfaces—but what good will it be if it cannot withstand the fire?"

# 54

"I admit your wife's pregnancy surprised me, considering you and she are so seldom in the same city."

Palaistea Malyrdeonis smiled pleasantly at Dorilian, and he smiled back. He found smiling easy when looking upon so beautiful a woman. Her flawless skin glowed with health, and intelligence danced alongside the sparks of laughter in her eyes. At twenty-four years, only three years older than himself, Palaistea's loveliness outshone even that of Daimonaeris. He wished his father and Sebbord had worked harder on breaking down the Prince of Lacenedon's opposition to him as a bridegroom.

"I make the most of my opportunities, Cousin."

"You will ever have your way, I suspect." Her curves, for she was pregnant again, swelled delightfully beneath the beaded bodice of her gown as she made the requisite small bow before turning her shoulder toward him and directing her attention elsewhere. Enreddon, Dorilian decided, could not possibly deserve so delectable a wife.

The Illystri Palace stood on an island at the center of Dazunor-Rannuli's Lago, not far from the Rill Mount. The Highborn gathered in rare numbers that evening to celebrate the betrothal of Elhanan to the younger daughter of the Prince of Gweroyen. Margarid, a vision in blue, looked well pleased with the match, as did Elhanan, if the prince's smiles were any indication.

"Now there is a couple I expect to be happy."

Dorilian turned to gaze upon the woman who had boldly staked out a place at his side. "As you were, Ionais?"

Her gold eyes, flecked by bits of brown, flashed in remembrance of the husband she had loved. "Yes, I was happy with Jonthan. I will never forgive you for that horse."

There had always been a core of bitterness in Ionais. Now, in her husband's death, she had found a well of it from which she might draw freely for the remainder of her life.

"I would give you the beast to flog, were it not dead already. I won't give you me." He turned to leave, but she was not that easily put off.

"I hear the rumors about you. Didn't anyone ever tell you it is dangerous to dangle promises you cannot keep?"

"Name a promise I have not kept."

"It's coming, I am sure. You have made too many people too eager to see if you can prove your birthright. Them, especially."

Upon the main floor, a delegation from the Seven Houses greeted the Lords of Dannuth and Gweroyen, offering gifts in honor of the betrothal. Resplendent as princes, the men bowed, and the women—their skirts rivaling peacocks' feathers in their many hues—lowered into deep curtseys.

"They should fear the day I choose to prove my birthright." He never took his gaze from the spectacle unfolding below. This enemy was one he knew of but had never met.

Her smile grew cold. "You do not even say its name."

*The Rill.* Elsewhere the Entity hung like the moon, bright and sublime; here in Dazunor-Rannuli, it burned like the sun. Day and night reverberated with low, resonant thrums above warehouses by the thousand, a heartbeat driving the pulse of this city where trade flowed like blood and power emanated from the gold in merchant's coffers.

"I do not need to say its name," he said.

Ionais stiffened and tilted her head to look at something just over his shoulder. "You know what irks me more than seeing you still alive? Seeing Emyli's bastard wearing my husband's crown and believing it makes him a Prince."

Dorilian turned to see Stefan standing near one of the room's three immense frescoes and pretending to admire it. He was dressed finely and wearing a circlet rather than the crown Ionais had invoked, but there was no mistaking why Stefan was so painfully, obviously, alone. He looked like none of these people. Stefan was short and dark-haired, and even though his hands and cheekbones were elegant and his lips well shaped, his nose was a little too small and his eyes too brilliantly blue. A Kheld in masquerade.

Dorilian excused himself from Ionais, who rolled her eyes. A few steps brought him to Stefan's shoulder.

"The founding of Dazunor-Rannuli." He named the event depicted. It amused him to note how Stefan drew a slow, deep breath before speaking.

"A few mud houses... and no Rill."

"Not yet. But Derlon is there. See? There's a Silver Eagle on his cloak, and the sword in his hand is edged with white fire."

Stefan's jaw tightened. It seemed that Stefan hated even Dorilian's ancestors. Provoking Stefan was entirely too easy a game, making Dorilian question why he continued to do it. Maybe he just wanted Stefan to lash out again, to give himself sufficient cause to put him down. For a moment, Dorilian envisioned Stefan on his knees, and the image slammed him in the gut. He would like that far too well.

"I might as well tell you." Stefan's words pulled him back to his current situation. "I've made Cullen my trade minister."

"That's a mistake. He will be burdened with limitations."

"You mean the Rill?" The laugh Stefan attempted died between them.

"Yes. And the Seven Houses also. They will show him only closed doors."

Stefan glared. Now Dorilian knew at least one reason he baited the other young man: Stefan's blue eyes blazed brighter when angry—much like Marc Frederick's, but less controlled, as if at any moment the passion inside would escape. The same fire filled his words.

"I won't let my choice of the best person for the job be dictated by bastards determined to keep Khelds away from all avenues of prosperity and wellbeing."

Was that what Stefan thought? There was some truth to it, but that didn't change the fact that Stefan was hampering his Principate—and Cullen. He should give Cullen a job he could excel at, such as ambassador. Dorilian shrugged and decided to cease his game. "I don't suppose you want my advice."

"No." For once, though, Stefan looked confused. "People are staring at us."

Of course, they were. That Dorilian hated Khelds was one of the hard facts of the universe. So was the fact that Stefan feared and despised him. Half the hall either expected or hoped the two of them would kill each other.

"Good. Now you will have their ear when they come up to you afterward to ask what this was all about."

He had handed Stefan a gift, Dorilian thought as he walked away. It remained to be seen if Stefan would have the wit to use it.

Below the ice-sheathed terrace of the Illystri palace, the Lago looked like silver. Palaces and great houses rimmed it akin to jewels. Rill structures and rings shone above the city in a regal crown. Dorilian looked toward the Mount, white and encrusted with light. It was a place where work never ceased. The Rill Entity never rested, and neither did those who fed upon its bounty.

The Rillhome palace of the Sordaneons glowed at the Mount's base, and Dorilian felt an aching desire to be there, not here. The closer he came to his goals, to delivering on his promises, the more distance he wished to put between himself and other men. Once he agreed to open another node, once he actually tried… there would be no end to their demands.

And maybe no end to what he could do. What he had experienced at Hestya now preyed on his mind.

To go *anywhere*…

"Some say you are Rill-gifted."

He turned to see an old woman, taller than he, wearing a headdress of ruched silk checked with white and black beading. Moonlight did her face no kindnesses, revealing the seamed canvas of her skin. How had she gotten to him? A look behind her showed Tutto still standing watch at the door.

She waved a beringed hand. "I was willing to walk all the way around on garden paths to avoid your guard." Her intense gaze fixed on him. "You are difficult to get alone." Dropping her gaze, she sank into a deep curtsey that belied her incredible age. "A moment of your time, Thrice Royal, no more than that."

Dorilian assigned the woman a name: Chyralane, Denizen of Phaer.

"For what reason? Is not the Rill performing well enough on your behalf?"

She stiffly rose and looked across the Lago. "The Entity is wondrous, marvelous—a gift from the gods."

Her meaning slipped like a needle of ice between his ribs. *A gift, not a god.* "And yet you treat it like a beast."

Her lips curved ever so slightly. "It's true, then. You believe the poisoned words that man has fed you. It was he who did your family harm, not we. He is doing it still, turning you against your natural allies. The Seven Houses are the Entity's guardians, Thrice Royal. We hold the Rill higher and dearer than any have ever done before us."

She believed what she said. Here, on a terrace bathed in Rill-light, every word of her blasphemy let him know the degree to which the Seven Houses now claimed the Rill as their own.

She must have read his face, because she lifted her chin so she could regard him down the length of her nose. "You don't believe me? I tell you none defend your Entity better. We *honor* the Rill; we obey its rhythms and inhabit what it has created. We uphold the Covenant wherever we are and honor the charge laid upon the Epoptes. We serve the Rill by creating and distributing wealth, easing the lives of its dependents and believers, and condemning all who would interfere with its gifts. All that we do celebrates the Rill's being. Can your family say as much?"

Rill thrum boomed softly across the city. The shining spindle of a *charys* rippled as it reflected across the surface of the Lago.

Her false reverence played underneath that image like a familiar refrain, lies told a child, concealing adult truths. Maybe a child was what she thought him.

"Are you telling me to stop working in tandem with your King?"

She would never say it openly. But Dorilian knew he had surprised her when her eyes flashed with warning. "I am suggesting you honor the Entity, Thrice Royal—not pander it to a man whose power is waning and who would set your feet on the path to ruin."

"Ruin, Denizen?" Dorilian breathed the scent of old woman and nervous sweat. "What ruin do you foresee being visited on me? Or on him? A plague of Khelds to kill me as they did my grandfather? Let me tell you now: that is not the path by which I will die. Are you warning me that your King might fall from his Throne? Too late, for I know already that it will pass to his Heir. Let me advise *you* instead: make no move against me—or him—you are not certain will succeed. For you have no idea, none in the World, of the kind of enemy I would be."

# 55

Dorilian retrieved the ball the baby had thrown at him and held it out to the child until she grasped it in a pudgy hand. The child then threw the ball again. He had done this several times already, and Noemi's bright-eyed daughter *always* threw the ball right back at him. Her aim was poor, however. Again, it missed. The girl laughed, happy when he had to reach for it. Excited, she tried to lurch forward on her fat little legs, only to fall back on her padded bottom.

"Fahme!" Noemi clucked, swooping in to pick up the girl, who looked startled. Noemi had kept the roundness childbearing had added to her figure, and her already lush curves were now soft and maternal. She placed Fahme back on the floor and watched with pride as the girl scooted on hands and knees toward a blanket spread with toys. "How she moves! I never thought a child could move so quickly."

Levyathan, the only other infant with whom Dorilian had interacted to any notable degree, had been slow to creep and even slower to walk. It had been part of their play for Dorilian to teach his brother even ordinary means of movement, helping Lev traverse spaces he could only abstractly see. Fahme did not have such limitations. Pushing his memories aside and forgotten by Fahme for the moment, Dorilian got off the floor and joined Noemi on the room's long, padded bench. "Daimonaeris has informed me that she wants to care for our son herself."

"Your son?" Noemi snorted. "That child is no more yours than Fahme is!"

He shot her a stern look. They had gone over the child's paternity at great length several months ago, including that he did not wish to be reminded of it.

"Have it as you will," Noemi sighed. "None will ever hear it from me. Though what you tell me, that the young Lord never left this life and that he is now in the new child—well, that doesn't rest easily with me. You shouldn't have done it."

"I told you why." *He did not want to go.*

"Gods help us. What will it mean?"

"I don't suppose we'll know until it happens."

"Will he remember us, I wonder." Noemi and looked to be sure of her daughter.

They were in the fine apartment Dorilian had given over to Heran and Noemi upon the birth of their child. Not only did it afford the couple more room, but the residence was also located in a desirable part of the Serat. He had done so to put her closer to his own living quarters as well as his wife's. "Don't let Daimonaeris intimidate you into not visiting her. I want your thoughts on her pregnancy."

"Well, your father also makes her see me. Nearly warms my heart sometimes." Noemi regarded her former charge comfortably. "But she's caring well for herself. Has her own nurse, she does, a woman who tended her mother."

"Her mother *died.*" Dorilian pointed out a drawback Daimonaeris had chosen to overlook.

"Is it a wonder then that the lady is so careful? Her poor mother dying of the fever, and now she is herself bearing a Highborn babe, if what you say is true. One in three dies of that."

"One in five."

"Might as well be one in three, for all the difference. Bearing a child of your kind is a perilous undertaking for a woman. I wouldn't do it."

He studied her. "You would not? Not even for me?"

"Not even for you." She blushed then, realizing what he had suggested. "Handsome thing, you are wicked to ask that."

He *was* wicked. It had been a foolish thing to say—a childish thing—but he was glad he had done it, even if only to see Noemi blush and to hear her say that. It pleased him to prompt such responses. He would hear nothing nearly so fun from Daimonaeris.

The ceremonial guards standing outside the Hierarch of Sordan's audience chamber lowered their spears and bowed their heads as

Daimonaeris made her way into the grand hall. She hated when Deben would do this: demand her presence just to force her to spend an hour with her husband. *His son*, she reminded herself, just as this child was. She put her right hand on the swell of her belly, her condition now having progressed to where clever garments could no longer downplay it. She noticed how Dorilian's gaze immediately went to that part of her body and, for the first time, she wondered if he measured her state against the length of time since the night she had seduced him.

While in the corridor, she had heard the rise and fall of angry words. The two Sordaneons, father and son, quite possibly had never agreed on anything in their lives. Deben glowered from the throne that graced this audience chamber, his hands clasping the arms with barely suppressed frustration. Dorilian merely met her gaze with a mocking silver stare.

"My Heir has requested to see his wife. He wishes to ascertain if his child is thriving." Deben's voice had the cold flatness of a man who had lost the battle.

Daimonaeris no longer flinched at the pretense. Deben's disinterest in her and his unborn son was cutting. Dorilian better deserved to be its father. He at least *cared*. She held herself straight and met her husband's gaze.

"Let him look, then."

No longer the sullen sixteen-year-old she had married, Dorilian had grown into at least one of his more promising qualities. As he came to stand before her, it was now she who had to look up to him. When he moved his hand to place it upon her belly, Daimonaeris swung in protest to Deben.

"He is not to touch me."

"It is our way. The child's father has the right to feel the life within you."

Nammuor had instructed her to humor her husband. Daimonaeris steeled herself and allowed Dorilian's hand. His fingers slid over the fabric of her gown, his palm cupping the curve of her womb. She stared at his face, seeing it closed to her, tranquil, his long lashes shadowing his cheekbones. What did he feel... or sense? The babe within her turned, as it had begun to do more of late. But there was nothing unusual in that movement, only in the way a smile moved across Dorilian's face, his look of wonder when he glanced up at her. She smiled to let him know she had felt it too.

"Does my husband consider me fat enough?" She asked when he had touched her for as long as was needed. Immediately, she regretted being sharp. The smile died from his face, replaced by icy acknowledgment.

"Yes. Clearly, you have been feeding my son well." He looked back to the throne, where Deben sat in sullen silence. "Now, I will go and do as you have bid, Father."

He turned and left, his purposeful footfalls echoing in the otherwise empty chamber until the door shut behind him.

She whirled on Deben. "What did you bid him do?"

The Hierarch looked down upon her, colder even than his son. "You bear my son's Heir, woman—not permission to demand answers about my purposes for him."

Of late, the Hierarch had been increasingly closemouthed. Though he assured Nammuor that the ties between their nations still held fast and had filed a formal condemnation of the Stauberg-Randolph attack on the Mormantaloran fleet, no military consequence had followed, and Deben's command of Sordan weakened every day. Some of it might even be by design. He had never been comfortable making difficult decisions, something Dorilian embraced. One by one, Sordan's military commanders, guild masters, merchant lords, and influential nobles were handing allegiance to Deben's Heir.

"You give him too much authority. Do you think he will be content to let you rule in name when he rules in fact?"

"He will. I am his sire, a Sordaneon even as he is. We share a legacy lesser men cannot comprehend, and its laws are sealed with blood. Though I know his faults, and he mine, ours is a bond he will not dishonor. My place is far more secure than yours will ever be."

The Highborn never murdered each other or made war upon their brothers, and they seldom vied against each other for titles or land. Even the Malyrdeon betrayal of Labran had been done delicately, using a surrogate. Her heart sank as she suddenly realized she had mistaken the strength of the bond between Deben and his son: though vastly different in temper, at the core they remained the same, linked to a tradition and race memory more potent than anything other men might bring against it.

"I am to be the mother of your son," she reminded him. "It is in your interest to make my place secure."

"*My* son, you say? Not so. You will be mother to *his* heir, not mine. That was ever my purpose, to ensure the blood line. I sired this child for the very reason you and your brother plotted for it: to ensure Sordan's succession and the Rill's continuance." Deben rose from the throne, a pale man in pale robes, his every aspect as faded as the power he had once wielded. "Do you think I trusted you? A woman who would seduce her husband's father? Your child is Sordaneon, and that is the only thing that matters. You wish your place to be secure? Look to your husband. Should Dorilian discover that the child sprang from my seed, not his, he will hate me all the more—and you may believe that he will hate you and put you from his side—but he will not hate the child, and he will not overthrow its father."

The babe turned beneath her hand again. Every day, it seemed, the child pushed against her thoughts, terrifying her more and more with its unearthly presence, testing its powers upon her. It would order that she consume more sweets—though she wished them not because of her figure—or listen to Teremari music which she otherwise despised, or seek out the sun and bare her belly to it. Then, if her choices suited, it would grow still and peaceful.

She could not ask Deben, as she had meant to, what he knew of Dorilian's negotiations with the Malyrdeons or what he meant to do either at their behest or in response. She did not know whom she hated more: her infuriating spouse for his determination to overlook the myriad failings of Essera, or Essera's King who had somehow discerned what it would take to seduce him. For Marc Frederick *had* seduced Dorilian, of that she was certain—seduced him in ways she could never have thought.

As she left Deben's throne room, sweeping past guards who bowed low before her, she felt Sordan slipping through her hands where but months ago she had grasped it firmly. Now her only remaining grip on the domain was the child tumbling within her.

"I don't know what they are doing. Deben wouldn't tell me." Daimonaeris looked around the starkly beautiful room without pleasure. Even to spend the night here would be an impossible imposition. If Nammuor had not directed her to inspect the palace at Hestya, she would never visit at all. "I hate this place. It's dusty and colorless. Why did you ever ask me to meet you here?"

"Because it's no longer prudent for me to meet you in Sordan. People ask questions, dear Sister... such as how does your brother arrive in Sordan unannounced, only weeks apart, not by Rill and not by ship? I don't want to reveal my new inventions or powers too soon."

"Like these?" she asked. She reached to touch the crown on Nammuor's head, but he caught her wrist, preventing her. Where once there had been only one great red jewel, it was now surrounded by a glowing lattice of smaller ones. "You've succeeded in finding a way to feed it!"

"Blood crystals, yes." With a knowing smile, he reached into the loose robe he wore and pulled out a velvet bag, from which he retrieved a long, deep-red gem the size of her littlest finger. He placed it into the hand he had caught and let her go. "I can drain the life force of a slave—of any living thing—into a crystal. I need the creature's blood to bind it, but—"

The jewel felt warm in her palm, like a spot of blood itself. It looked like no crystal she had ever seen, odd and frilled. "And these allow you to use the Diadem again, for longer?"

"Yes. But not in Sordan." He frowned. "Not near the Rill."

She understood. Here in Hestya, the Rill field was narrow and did not extend to the new palace, whereas in Sordan the Rill's vital presence ran throughout the crowning complex that was the City of Light, including the Serat.

"I probably cannot use it in Stauberg, either, because of the Wall." He looked frustrated. "The Entities... obliterate other fields, other powers."

A complication. Daimonaeris huffed down onto a couch, though doing so made her belly balloon like a pillow.

"Well, we can't get rid of the Entities. We'll just have to work around them."

"People have for ages." He walked to the window and looked out at wheat fields as far as the horizon, dotted with farms. "At least Dorilian isn't here tonight. I find it interesting that he prefers to spend time with an old man instead of with his beautiful young wife."

"I met Marc Frederick once. He was fur-faced and ordinary, with hideous blue eyes. I could not bear to look at him, he was so ugly." She snorted, perplexed by her husband's willingness to entertain lesser men as part of his circle. Dorilian surrounded himself with such creatures. She cringed every time she saw his squat, brown-skinned sword master or his fat, dark-haired nurse. "There's to be a meeting of the Highborn soon," she said, telling what little she knew. "Even in the street, there is talk that Sordan will be remanded back to the Sordaneons and all Esseran presence withdrawn for good. Many, of course, do not believe it."

"Negotiations are never one sided. Why would Essera give up so much? Even if Marc Frederick is willing, his nobles and populace—all of them enriched from Sordan's spoils—would oppose such an extravagant gesture. What is Essera getting in return that would silence such opposition?"

"That the Sordaneons acknowledge the Stauberg-Randolph King's rule, I suppose."

"Oh, I believe there must be more to it than that."

"Deben's signature is required, as well as his oath. He's been asked to attend in person."

"Has he? Away from Sordan?" Her brother's pitch-dark gaze sharpened.

"Yes. Permephedon, I think, or maybe Dazunor-Rannuli. But he is terrified of the Rill. He won't even stray outside of the Serat except for once a year, and that on Third Day." She couldn't herself explain why anyone thought Deben would actually honor the Malyrdeon request.

"But Dorilian wants him to go?"

"Yes. He said something interesting—this according to his nurse's husband—that Deben should be on hand to witness the breaking of the Seven Houses."

Nammuor turned his back on the window and walked toward her, his attention suddenly hard and fast. "Breaking the cartel? Only one thing ties the Sordaneons to them, and that is the Rill."

The child within her startled her by moving, causing her to put her hand upon it. Seeing this, Nammuor walked over and placed his hand just below hers. She gasped, fighting sudden nausea and alarm.

"He moves strongly now," Nammuor noted. He removed his hand.

She exhaled with relief, then glared at him. "Don't touch me while you wear that device! I think it knows."

"The child?" His voice slithered into new thought. "That may be possible. All Sordaneons are linked to the Rill." But his dark stare lingered on her abdomen, approving how well their plan had progressed so far. "Someone opened the Rill to Hestya. I'm not convinced it was Sebbord alone. What if Deben, whom none suspect, played a part? Or Dorilian? What if they have *that* power to barter?"

"If they did have it, they would not spend it for Essera's benefit, whatever Essera did."

"No. But they might use it to benefit themselves in some way." Again Nammuor frowned. "It might be to our advantage if Deben would attend that meeting."

"Why, when his participation renders any outcome binding? Not attending would seem more prudent. If Dorilian agrees to anything, Deben can renounce it."

"Are you sure of that? I don't pretend to grasp the intricacies of Highborn oaths. Still, Deben might be more useful if he would attend. An autonomous Sordan by treaty is worth more than a state Essera might try to claim still theirs. Especially if some misfortune befell the adult rulers. We must examine the clauses with care."

"No one will overlook our interest in the outcome," she said. "No one is going to overlook who is the mother of this child."

"Trust me, little mother," he smiled down on her. Above his eyes, the great jewel of the Diadem glowed with crimson fire. "This treaty will cost us nothing—for I have no intention of it ever coming to fruition. And more than that, I will find a way to make it pay off royally."

Nammuor gave her a circlet set with jewels as golden as her eyes, linked by two of his new blood crystals. Each bore a slave's life within it, to serve him now even as they had in the flesh. It came as little surprise to Daimonaeris when he told her the casket found in the molten mountain had produced gifts other than the Diadem. This circlet had been within as well.

"When I found it, this array was keyed to a mountain in Gweroyen." Nammuor placed it over her hair so that its triad of *lr* jewels, each a pool of golden fire, rested upon her forehead. "But I have set it again so it will convey its wearer to my own chamber in Mormantalorus."

"You mean I could travel there, in an instant, as you do?" She had never used a *Ir* device, not enough to move so much as a stone, though she had seen him do so... and more.

He smiled. "Even as I do, but only there. And only once. It would need new blood crystals to be used again by any but a mage. Wear it always, Sister. Say you love it so well that you will not be parted from it. Give me your hand, and I will place your hand on the code jewels... see, here... here... and here." Beneath her fingers, Daimonaeris felt the slightly raised jewels, like tiny pearls, and repeated the sequence for him without pressing. "Now you have a means of escape should you fear for your life."

"Do what you say, and I will not need to."

"How eager you are to be rid of your promising young husband."

"And his quivering father as well." She turned from the mirror in which she had been admiring her appearance. "Both of them."

"Then you know your part, little mother." Returning to the velvet box from which he had taken the *Ir* array, Nammuor retrieved another object and came back to her with a small vial in his fingers. "Such a rare elixir, *melsajra*—distilled from such foul things as I will not tell you, things not of this World—for which I delved deep and long. From an ancient scroll I learned its secrets, and it took years to make. I have not yet, alas, had the chance to test it on other than slaves. But if this small amount does but half of what the Aryati devised it to do, then we need not fear."

Daimonaeris took the glass vial in her fingers and peered at the pale amber liquid within. How deadly could it be? She cared not. "It will kill them?"

"Yes, but slowly, in a way that will allow me to collect what I need. You and I, it would kill in moments. They will be paralyzed, unable to even breathe—yet such is this drug that their bodies will not be able to change or alter it, and so they cannot cast it off. A marvelous thing, to be so stable within such a being." He looked at his creation with wonder all his own. "The Aryati formulated it to kill an Immortal. Derlon, to be precise. They failed then, and the amount needed to kill Derlon now would be impossible to distill or deliver. But I'm not trying to kill a god this time, only mortal shells that house immortal blood." He smiled again at his sister. "The Sordaneons are to provide the wine for this momentous occasion, I understand?"

Her eyes glittered. "Yes."

"And the nurse's husband, whom you placed so cleverly, little fire jewel, will do whatever you ask?"

"The ambitious fool is besotted with me and believes my promises to raise him to a high title when I am Hierarchessa."

He curled her fingers over the vial. "When they make treaties, the Highborn drink wine drawn from a common bowl. Have the man wash the bowl with this before filling it. Use it all."

She blanched. "What if he cannot?"

"My part will be much harder."

# 56

Stefan welcomed the Kheld delegation when it reached Dazunor-Rannuli. Unable to use the Rill, they had to ride overland, and their journey to Permephedon would take several days. Had he not been encumbered with the demands of his Principate, Stefan would have liked to travel with them. As it was, the best he could offer the group was overnight accommodation in his palace.

"I understand this is a country of few inns." Old Tobold's lament was apt, though the problem was not the number of inns but that Khelds were not welcome in them. Even Tobold, who was Thegnard, acknowledged leader of all the clan chieftains, was certain to be refused lodging. "In a country with few inns, a man is happy to find kinsmen."

"I'll send an escort with you to clear the road and assure that you meet no trouble at way places."

They spent the night eating well and talked of many things, including hopes and dreams.

"It will be a good treaty. The King, your grandfather, assures us it will grant us prosperity and a stronger voice in the affairs of this land," Tobold said. "We are honored that the Highborn princes include us in their great plan. That has not happened since the sons of Alm bent knee in Tahlwent and accepted that we should settle instead in Amallar. What a gathering it will be!"

"It's not like anything they decide will be given on the spot." Stefan set aside his cup of ale. "Any petition would still need to find approval among Essera's noble houses, or it matters for naught."

"I have it from the King's own mouth that we shall be most pleased with our reward. Our presence is required because a portion of the new treaty touches upon the Oath of Erydon. Perhaps the

Highborn wish to amend their promise in some way. We were told that it is to clarify some point of our consent—consent for what, of course, we do not yet know. The meeting is most mysterious. Not all the details have yet been agreed to."

That the Malyrdeons would resume strong kinship ties with the Sordaneons struck most Khelds as a good thing. For the first time since Marc Frederick took the throne, there was a chance the deep wounds between the kindreds might be healed. It surprised no one, however, that the process was proving delicate. The Thegnard had brought his fellow clan chieftains with him to assist in the negotiations. Others in the party included robust elders from Rhodhur and Eastmeary Brenna, including Stefan's grandfather Cedrec and the renowned *faetha* Wyra Elhredda, Consecrated of Aurdollen, lending the support of Amallar's adherents to the Mother.

The next morning, Stefan rode with an honor guard to accompany the Khelds to the edge of the city. People lined the streets to watch the riders pass, though there was little cheering. The folk of Amallar in such number were a rare sight and a cause for interest but not celebration. Because it did not involve them, there was, as yet, little notice among the ordinary populace of the meeting at Permephedon, so it was not on their minds as it was on that of their Prince. Stefan parted with the delegation upon a stone bridge crossing the Cahad River where it emerged from the Arkan Hills.

Tobold clasped his hand warmly. "I would have liked for you to ride with us. You should be there, at the King's right hand."

Stefan nodded. It was hard for him to look upon the pride and hope that sat upon his kinsmen's rough Kheld features, the shining of their eyes, and not wish to be with them during the negotiations. Marc Frederick had hammered out difficult alliances before; why not again? For weeks Stefan had watched as, one by one, Essera's nobles retreated from their opposition, landed Lords stepping back to watch what unfolded, willing to see how the King's designs would affect their lives. Stefan had taken to doing the same. "May this meeting be all that you hope it to be, *keldan*," he said, and he meant it.

Tobold turned in the saddle to look upon the city now in the distance. Stefan followed that movement. Dazunor-Rannuli glittered with silver-threaded waterways and sun-tipped golden spires. Amallar could not even be seen across the broad, shining swath of the Dazun, but they knew it was there.

"We rule our own country and thank the Mother for that!" the old man said. "To listen to some men, you would think we were slaves, not the rightful holders of good land and water." He lost a stirrup and took a moment to fish for it with his boot. "I will not lust for Staubaun land or Staubaun gold. Nor will I lust for that"— Tobold pointed at the soaring Rill structures that loomed overhead, the majestic rings glimmering smoothly in the fading light—"for I fear the thing. Lud's Spear, we call it, for a reason. A spear is a sacred weapon, and Staubauns for centuries uncounted have killed to possess it. I would not have us do the same. Then would we be worse than they, fighting over a thing that does us no good." He settled his weight heavily back against the rear brace of his saddle and regarded Stefan from beneath bristling gray brows. "Until your grandfather can change that, not much changes at all."

"I hear he has agreed. Dorilian will attempt to awaken the Rill to the station at Trestethion."

Marc Frederick found it interesting that Marenthro had chosen to comment on the matter. The wizard watched from the doorway as Gareth delivered a leather envelope, and Marc Frederick took it in hand. The King had spent the morning in meetings, none of which the immortal had attended. Though Permephedon was Marenthro's City, he left the details of administration to his Sages.

"He insisted on stipulations, of course. A lot of them." Marc Frederick considered stipulations a kind of progress.

"What a very great risk to take, just to benefit the Kheld folk." Like most of Marenthro's pronouncements, this one probed other ground.

"The Khelds, to be truthful, are incidental. We have not told them that, of course. Their participation is solely a matter of location."

"What if they refuse to alter the promise Erydon made and decide they don't want the Highborn to set foot in their land?"

Marc Frederick leafed through some papers on his desk and thrust them into the leather envelope he would be carrying with him. "You play word games. The Promise was never that the Highborn *never* set foot in their lands, only that they not do so with hostile intent. We're establishing friendly intent ahead of the matter.

I believe they will agree once they see what they have to gain. Then, if Dorilian is successful, there will no longer be any doubt of his ability. We can next turn our energy toward Stauberg or Askorras."

"Dorilian is certain, then, that he will not succumb to the Rill?"

"No, he's not certain at all." Enreddon stood nearby, coding a set of message cylinders the King was to bear to Sordan in the morning. "By his own account, Dorilian is susceptible to Derlon and is powerfully bound to him. I feel it every time he is with me in a Rill field. The god... collects about him, an effect amplified when he is nearer the source. He needs to learn how to control and channel that affinity. He nearly succumbed at Hestya but for his brother somehow pulling him back." He gazed at Marc Frederick, frowning. "Sebbord was reckless to expose him to the Entity so young."

"The treaty doesn't demand that he attempt to open the station at once. It says only that he will agree to attempt it—and there are all kinds of terms and conditions upon when that might happen." Marc Frederick foresaw spending years building up warehouses and administrative offices, perhaps even a Sordaneon palace if the Khelds would be agreeable. "A more delicate issue is when, or whether, Khelds will be able to ride the Rill. All of the Epoptes, learned Cibulitans, and aged Sages in the World cannot agree on what is needed to make that possible."

"They should ask the Rill—or a Sordaneon." Marenthro appeared to think that obvious.

Marc Frederick nodded. "Dorilian contends that they will be able to ride the day he no longer believes they are his enemy."

"A belief that, in him, may be hard to eradicate." Enreddon packed the cylinders into the beautiful box in which they would be borne to Deben, conveying the assurances of every ruling Highborn prince that they would themselves be at the meeting. Deben had not yet announced his attendance.

Marc Frederick saw no reason for worry. "You do not know the Khelds as I do. They're an obstinate, impatient people. Remember, too; they do not live as long as Staubauns do and so will be in more of a hurry to see results. They will press for it, I'm sure. However, they will be satisfied in the interim, I think, by the Rill portions to be given them out of my own treasury and yours." Marc Frederick was backing this treaty with several of his Dazunor-Rannuli slots in tandem with portions to be contributed by the

Malyrdeons. "I find it interesting that Dorilian resisted assigning portions until I agreed to name Cullen Brodheson as one of the Khelds to administer them."

"Cullen Brodheson? Indeed?" Marenthro smiled, ever so slightly.

"Cullen and Dorilian got to know each other at Gustan."

"So your plan worked that far, at least."

"Dorilian is not unaware of the manipulation." Enreddon handed the sealed box to Marc Frederick, who took it and walked over to his travel packs, still open on a nearby table. "I think he admires Marc's stratagems. We may have underestimated our King's understanding of the Sordaneon paradigm."

Not that his grasp of it had come easily. In one manner or another, Marc Frederick had battled that kindred for nearly all his adult life. His one real gift was that he had been willing—as the Malyrdeons had not been—to confront his powerful opponents not by proxy or surrogate but in person. No Sordaneon could be brought to heel without direct interaction. There had to be a meeting of minds; otherwise, destruction would result. Such was the nature of men and their gods.

Enreddon, having finished with the message cylinders, bowed and left. Only Marenthro remained, a silent presence at once comforting and disturbing.

"Is this what we have worked toward?" Marc Frederick asked. "Is this where we change it—the way Endurin planned?"

Marenthro had been there that day so many years ago when Endurin had forcibly abducted his sole remaining descendant and brought him to this land. Marc Frederick still sometimes wondered if, in following Endurin's design, he had made the right choice. His becoming King had been the boldest in a series of bold moves, enacted that all foreseen futures might be erased, hoping they could be rewritten. Only time would tell if the Wall Lords had succeeded.

Marenthro slowly nodded. He met Marc Frederick's gaze and held it in his own.

"Yes, my friend. It is."

# 57

"Sordan will be ours again."

Dorilian had presented Deben with the terms of the treaty he had negotiated with the Malyrdeons and Essera's King. Only three of them were in the Hierarch's state audience chamber. For once, Deben was not seated on the plain marble throne but at a table in an adjoining alcove with expansive windows overlooking the City and harbor. The Hierarch presided at one end of the table, with Marc Frederick to his right hand and Dorilian to his left.

"Our enemies but give back that which they stole—and we should reward them?" Deben rifled through page after page of documents. His frown deepened with each term.

"Returning this domain fully to Sordaneon rule was ever our mission." Marc Frederick had assured the Hierarch as much several times throughout the day. "I offered it to you in the weeks following your father's rebellion for terms not much different from what I ask now. My kin and I needed only the assurances you and your Heir shall give us, that you acknowledge my rule over Essera and its traditional lands and territories—bar Gignastha, which will become a joint protectorate—and my heirs' right to rule unopposed after me. That these assurances were so long in forthcoming, I lay upon your family's pride."

"Is it pride to refuse to cast aside a thousand years? The Heirs of Derlon are the inheritors of the Scions of Ergeiron, and they the inheritors of Derlon should we fail—such was promised of old. When the Malyrdeons one and all stepped aside, it was our right to demand that we, not *you*, sit upon Essera's throne." Deben assessed him through narrow, pale eyes. "None has ever proved to Sordaneon satisfaction that you are of the lineage of Endurin, even though you claim to be born of Ariande. Where was she to claim she bore you? Who witnessed your birth?"

Deben was resurrecting arguments settled in decades past. Marc Frederick held out his left hand, the Leur's Ring aglint on his middle finger. "Could I wear this, if I were not the rightful Heir?"

The Hierarch regarded him coldly. "I know not how that sorcery was done, but I will own that it is Malyrdeon work and cannot be refuted. So be it. If my Heir cares to overlook your illegitimacy, his consent will suffice for this agreement, as all Sordaneon Heirs after him will also be bound by it. But our claim to Essera remains because it stems from oaths older and greater than these retractions."

"I withdrew it not, nor had I the last time you read these things." Dorilian had been cross with his sire for hours, since the morning's meeting had started. They were now in afternoon. Deben had already gone over every detail severalfold. "Tell me what it will take to get your signature on these documents."

"I will not be hurried." Deben continued to shuffle papers.

"You've had them for a week. Every point has been explained a dozen times over."

The Hierarch simply ignored him. "You see how he is," Deben said to Marc Frederick. "Ever proud and bent on getting his way. In time, it will irk him that he cannot be Hierarch, for I stand in his path."

Marc Frederick calmly held the narrow glare that burned in the younger man's eyes as they met his. He, at least, found Deben amusing, even if Dorilian did not.

"You should worry for yourself, Stauberg-Randolph." Deben continued when the response he sought was not forthcoming, "Be wary should my son ever wake up to find that it is you, not I, who impedes him."

"His intentions do not trouble me."

"Clearly not, or you wouldn't be pressing for this treaty." Deben at last laid down the papers and folded his hands upon them. He frowned at his son. "Are you mad? To even suggest that one of our blood should travel to Trestethion for the purpose of awakening that node—"

"I have decided." Dorilian refused to back down. "Trestethion's location is an advantage. So long as the Rill remains fixed at locations controlled by the Seven Houses, our hands are tied."

"Opening that station will not remove the Seven Houses from influence. Neither will it remove their enmity for us. No, *that* it will only make greater! The station will but enrich and embolden the barbarian Khelds, as this King of theirs wishes."

"They will profit only if they abide by the terms of the treaty— a treaty which Khelds will make not with the Seven Houses, Father, or even a treaty with the Staubaun domains of Essera, but a treaty they must make with *us*. Others will see this and know that *we*, not the Seven Houses, have the power to further their ends. They will see that we will neither sanction nor abide what some men have done, and continue to do, in the name of the Rill."

"Are *you* its guardian now? Is that not what the Epoptes call themselves? The Seven Houses? So claims every richly garbed slot-holder in Essera—that what they do is not travesty but devotion! They say they strive but to preserve the full and intended spirit of the Covenant! Is this how they have cajoled you into doing for them what my father refused to do? To pretend that we will have some voice in this mockery?" The Hierarch shoved the papers across the table, into the middle. "I will not put my name to this abomination."

Marc Frederick leaned back, sorry that it had come to this. He had hoped for more from Deben, after all these years, without ever honestly expecting it. The wounds of former betrayals ran too deep. Dorilian, less resigned and with far more he might yet bring to bear, leaned toward Deben.

"And if you do not, Father, I will turn this domain against you. Yes, you know that I can. I will stand upon my alliances. I will send away my wife."

"You would put her from you?" Deben stared, icily regal.

"Tomorrow. Before her child is ever born, I will tell the World it is not mine."

The Hierarch's lips grew still, barely moving around the words that came from them. "You would lie?"

"It is no lie."

"She will swear it is yours, and I will not refute her. I will put the child to the blood rite."

"That will not matter. Claim it yourself. I will disown it, even as you did Levyathan when he was born. Daimonaeris' son will inherit nothing of mine—not even the Hierarchate after me, should I take another wife and sire other heirs, and you may be sure that I will. I will do it within the month. But I will not leave you unimpeded, Father. I will stay in Sordan, at your side and in your sight, and be a thorn in your boot unless you disown and banish me—and *that* you will not do. Our people will know which Sordaneon has freed this domain and forced Essera's hand. They will know as well that it was *I* who opened Hestya, because I will shout it for all to hear."

"So that you might assume Sebbord's place in their hearts and in their hates? And for what—that you should be murdered as he was? Because that is what they will do should you attempt what this creature proposes!"

"What a Sordaneon does with the Rill must not be dictated by parasites!"

Deben pushed away from the table, though he did not yet rise from his chair. "Do you think you will be the one to finish what Derlon did not? That you can be Rill Lord, as Tarlon was?"

"I am already as Tarlon was. Look forward, Father: I shall be greater than he."

The words sounded clearly in a corner shaped for silence. Ashen, Deben turned to Marc Frederick. "And you encourage this, you monster?"

"I do not tell him what to do."

"The Rill will destroy him. Surely you know what it can do. It nearly consumed me, the time I tried it." The Hierarch laughed at the looks on their faces. "You did not know that, did you, barbarian? Long before this one was born, I stood with my father and brother within the Rill matrix, behind the shields. He wished that Derlon should see us—and He did. I felt us dissolving within that other Being. Only because there were two of us, and twins, were we solid enough to withstand it. It took Labran and Sebbord together to pull us out, still sane. The thing consumes minds, it consumes wills, and bodies also can it devour. It *is*, and it will ever *be*, but mere mortal flesh cannot contain that power." To his son, he said, "And if the Rill does not destroy you, men will. They would use you in such ways as you should fear."

For once, Dorilian didn't have an immediate answer. His father's words resounded in a part of him that had itself experienced something of what Deben feared. They both feared the Rill as only Sordaneons could fear it, with the deep race knowledge of others who had gone before them and failed.

"I will not let them use me," Dorilian said after long moments. "I, not they, will choose the time."

"And if that time never comes for you?"

"The treaty calls for opening Trestethion if possible, but it will remain in force even if that cannot be done," Marc Frederick said. "We have provided other incentives."

"For your Kheld barbarians, a share of Rill profits. At least those portions will be from your treasury, not ours." Deben continued to glare at his defiant son. If Dorilian followed through on his threat to divorce his wife and disown the child, Deben would have to deal not only with his rebellious Heir but also Nammuor. Between the two, Nammuor would be the lesser problem. Dorilian had correctly pointed out that he, not Deben, commanded the loyalty of Sordan's military—the very military his domain would need the moment Nammuor became enraged.

Marc Frederick watched the subtle traces of Deben's thoughts, seeing in them the struggles of a proud man capitulating not to reason but fate. Crippled by his father's captivity and his own deep burden of fears, saddled with a powerless title and an occupied domain, Deben had sought only to survive and exact a measure of revenge. How early had he recognized that his son would surpass him? So many things now looked like acts of desperation, including marrying his son to Daimonaeris—a vengeful man's futile hope to find satisfaction in shackling his son into an alliance with the enemy of his enemy. But he had not counted on Dorilian to prove so bold so soon or to move openly against his plans. Now, faced with rebellion by an Heir he could no longer coerce, he became again familiar with defeat.

"I will sign this travesty," Deben said at last, "but do not ever hold that I did so freely."

"Would you have done it?" Marc Frederick asked. Poised against Sordan's splendor, Dorilian looked very much a descendant of its builders. "Would you have sent Daimonaeris away... and the child?"

"Her? Yes, and good riddance! She has despised me since the day we wed and loves only her position. I will send her away whatever my father does. I wish no part of the alliance she creates with Nammuor." The young man frowned into the distance. "But the child... no, I could not do that. He is Sordaneon no less than I am. Though not my son, he is my brother, and I wish to be everything to him—all that a father should be."

"I think you will be a fine father."

Dorilian looked pleased by that assessment. "I have sensed him, you know, my Heir. Not just with my hand but in other ways." He looked away again, toward the silver shadows of the Serat. "He is happy when he feels me near."

Marc Frederick remembered what Enreddon had said months ago about how Levyathan had never really left the World. In what ways did that child's spirit linger? Dorilian had never said so much as a word about it. From here, they could see the terrace from which the boy had fallen. As they looked upon that fateful height, something fierce and victorious glowed in Dorilian's eyes.

*What have you done?* Marc Frederick wondered, though already he saw that Dorilian had retreated from his former willingness to be candid.

Marc Frederick had spent his life seeking to understand a race that was at times wonderfully human and at other times terrifying and strange. Because of his place among them, he had seen the Highborn wield powers other men had never witnessed. He had even been given the gift of some power himself. And still, always, there was something unseen and imminent, waiting in the wings.

"Did my brother not do as he promised and restore your family's accounts and estates in Orm?"

Daimonaeris noted that Dorilian's steward, Heran, looked happy with that portion of his anticipated reward. His family had left Mormantalorus during Nammuor's purge, disguised among the thousands of refugees, specifically to infiltrate advantageous positions such as the one he held today. He, of course, still hoped to be raised to the nobility.

"They will be happier when they can return to those estates and spend the accounts," he said. They spoke openly in one of the Serat galleries. Daimonaeris had insisted upon speaking with Heran about her cats, which Dorilian had demanded be declawed. No one stood near enough to know what they really talked about.

"Soon. I think you will be very pleased by your new title."

The avarice she counted on flitted across Heran's handsome features. He came from good blood, though noble only in bastard lines. His birth had been ordinary enough to qualify him for service in the less scrutinized lowly ranks, and his marriage had served to position him perfectly.

Heran looked toward the far end of the columned hall of benches and views across the residential palaces of the City. "What does my Lady require?"

"You will be attending my husband tomorrow at Permephedon. Are you performing the wine service?"

He nodded.

"If we attack them there, we can free Sordan of its baseborn rulers, and Essera as well. Those few who remain will be dependent on us. And there will be many estates—and Rill contracts also—to be granted those who serve my brother and me well." As she had counted it would, his interest deepened. Rill contracts meant wealth far beyond what he had already hoped for. "My brother has devised a poison."

His face hardened. "You ask my life? You know I am his taster."

"You are not Highborn, therefore not party to their treaty. You will taste the wine *before* it is put in the communal bowl." She extended her hand, the vial tucked discreetly within. "You have but to wash the bowl with this before it is filled."

Understanding flickered in his eyes.

# 58

"We need new blood and have needed it for too long." Enreddon spoke freely to Marc Frederick as they looked upon the gathering. At one time, the Highborn had numbered in the hundreds, and a gathering of ruling Princes and their Heirs would have filled the chamber. Now a mere forty gathered for the treaty signing, of which seventeen were so ancient that even their Heirs were old men. Only because Khelds too attended did the great Arcana of the High Citadel not appear empty.

Marc Frederick had just put the finishing touch on his regalia by adding the *tullun* blade—Dorilian's gift to him—upon his belt. He missed the weight of a sword at his side. The Highborn did not carry swords in Permephedon, their most holy City. For other men to carry one in their presence was a grave offense. Only the guards would be armed at this meeting. On the far side of the antechamber, Deben was being draped with his robe of state while Dorilian himself, steely with determination, stood at hand.

"We forgot too soon that the gifts of our kind can be bestowed upon any nation," Enreddon continued. "It was Endurin's plan to make us more like men, not less. He set Sordan upon the path we should ourselves have taken. Dorilian's mind is a fortress. Our every attempt to read the Wall visions he holds meet with only muddle and blur."

Marc Frederick fixed his old friend with a warning look. "He kept his part and told you what he knew. Now you keep yours. Teach him, Redd. Perhaps that will convince him to unlock his mind to your inquisitions. If this treaty is to mean anything at all, Dorilian must be given the means to attain his potential."

"As if we could keep him from it. He is Rill flesh and god stuff. He will command power no matter what we do. We could as soon ignore a child seated atop a keg of powder with a flint in his hands."

Marc Frederick laughed, though the image was apt. For a moment, he wished Marenthro would attend, if only to see how well that intervention fifty years ago had turned out. The immortal, however, declined at every turn to take a part in human affairs.

It was time to make a grand entrance. Together, Marc Frederick and Enreddon walked toward the golden door that would lead them into the Arcana Amphicura. Enreddon paused just before they reached it.

"You have succeeded, my friend. I don't know how you gained Dorilian's trust. I never thought you would win him over. I don't believe anybody thought it possible but you. There is a lesson in that for all of us."

Marc Frederick clapped his old friend on the shoulder. Enreddon's praise signaled the end of a protracted disagreement, and he looked forward to easing the strain that had existed between them.

"Ah, Redd. It was something Endurin taught me—his key to dealing with temporal paradigms. What is Time but a sequence of events and the shadows of events? Alter an event, and you alter its shadows." He smiled at how well that lesson had served him. "I suspected what Dorilian was the moment he walked into my court at Stauberg as if he owned it. Everyone else saw shadows, Redd. They saw grotesque distortions of Labran, of Deben, of anger and war, and their own fears—and they saw the Rill, always the Rill. They thought Dorilian a shadow, too, but they were wrong. He's greater than that." He looked upon the gathered Lords that filled the Arcana and prepared to greet them. "Dorilian Sordaneon is an event."

"Look at them. Barbarians." Deben's voice, strained and thin, betrayed his anxiety at being seated in the open. Even with Dorilian on one side and Mezentius on the other, the Hierarch felt exposed. Deben had barely spoken since they had left the Serat and made the journey by private Rill *charys*. "Self-satisfied and smug, all of them. They think they have our Rill upon their platter. Do they realize, I wonder, that you are simply playing a game?"

Was that what he was doing? Dorilian wondered. Chancing his freedom and Sordan's autonomy on a throw of Marc Frederick's dice as opposed to a hand of bluff and princes with Nammuor? What was today, after all, but a way of declaring the game of Esseran ambition finished and launching another, different game with rules he had himself devised? It was, Dorilian thought, a brilliant abandonment.

What was it Sebbord had told him? *Surround yourself with the highest you can find—the best, the brightest, and the least polluted by luxury and greed. Even as Amynas rejected the magnificence and beauty of the Aryati and sought refuge among the hardened folk of the wilderness, arm yourself with character and truth.*

Marc Frederick was the truest man he knew.

Ignoring his father for a moment, Dorilian looked at the center of the table where the King presided. Marc Frederick looked relaxed and happy. So many things that might have gone wrong had not. Opposition had not led to rebellion... the Kheld emissaries had agreed to present Sordaneon terms for the Rill at a meeting of their clans within the year... the barbarians were satisfied with a Malyrdeon promise that the offer was genuine and the treaty would be enforceable... this very afternoon, the King would present the signed treaty to the Archhalia for the first time, beginning a contentious process of review. Months of effort, distilled into a few more days.

For a moment, Marc Frederick looked his way, and the royal smile deepened. It was a look of accomplishment acknowledged, a victory shared, and Dorilian's heart pounded in a way he had never felt before. The Esseran King was proud of him, of what they had done, and of all they would yet do.

He returned the smile.

*I changed it,* Dorilian wanted to tell him. *I changed what I saw in the Wall's broken visions. See, there is no sword in my hand, and there will be no blood upon the floor. And, against every vision I ever had of you, I am your friend.*

Before turning over the vial Nammuor had given her, Daimonaeris filled a tiny injector with a single drop of the golden fluid, then capped it again. Now, as the sun passed its zenith, she retrieved her weapon. "Send for my husband's nurse," she told her favorite handmaiden. "Tell her I am in pain and vomiting."

What was the price of a Highborn child? Women throughout the ages had suffered as the pawns of men for whom ordinary power was not enough. Many perished in the quest to give birth to a god. Half-men could not grasp such glory. Highborn blood was too rich for animal veins, too rare, too strong—some element within it caused lesser blood to congeal and lesser flesh to mottle. Like the blood it nourished, the chorion enveloping a Highborn fetus was immortal and was placed, even as failed fetuses were, within a repository buried deep among their citadels. Such a place lined the deepest chamber in Mormantalorus—a room of tiny golden caskets. But the women who died in those births, though buried in honor, passed from memory unless their sons proved mighty.

As her son would be.

Her child would be Heir to Mormantalorus and ruler of Sordan. He would someday command the Rill, wear Nammuor's Diadem, and all the people in the World would bow before him.

*I will ensure your place and mine also*, she bespoke her son while setting the injector upon her finger. *You will not be twisted by base men, as your father was. You will live in full your glorious birthright.*

Noemi rushed in, a robe thrown about her shoulders, her dark hair wild and loose.

"Lady?" she called and headed toward the alcove and its curtained bed.

Hidden in the shadow of the door, Daimonaeris came up behind her. She smelled Noemi's scent of damp hair and *ucaja*, of clean human skin. As she had practiced for hours, she clapped her hand over her startled victim's plump arm and dug deep, her middle finger driving in the tip of the injector and pressing the fluid home. She then stepped away as Noemi, startled, stumbled forward, falling against the bed's white coverings as she dropped to her knees.

"Lady! What—?"

Nammuor's drug worked quickly. Daimonaeris stood within reach, the better to enjoy Noemi's wild-eyed terror as her body ceased to obey her. The stricken woman fell to the floor, her limbs twitching, her breath rasping into silence. Her mouth made a few more weak attempts at speech, then hung open. But her eyes... her eyes remained on Daimonaeris, staring and knowing, even as they dimmed.

"You stupid cow. You love your young lord so much, you may as well die with him. But you will never nurse my baby." Daimon-aeris removed the injector from her finger and placed it in a drawer where it could do her no accidental harm.

Summoning her handmaidens, she ordered the body hidden. She would dispose of it after her brother's triumph.

If his father did not soon choke to death on his own vitriol, Dorilian would do the honors for him. If ever Dorilian had been certain of anything in his life, he was certain of that. Deben looked angry and sour, his ocher gaze bitter. Despite his nation's imminent auton-omy, he preferred to hold on to his resentment at past hurts. Not surprisingly, the Hierarch's demeanor had prompted the Kheld delegates to ask for yet more reassurances, which only served to worsen Deben's mood. Dorilian, his temper stretched thin by two days of his father's intransigence and now faced with Kheldish distrust, simply wanted it to be over.

Only when his gaze met Marc Frederick's did he resolve to see the day through. There were yet promises to make.

Even when written, Highborn promises did not reside merely on paper. Dorilian felt the force of every Highborn oath ever spoken residing in his memory, permanent and unbreakable. Often sought but seldom granted, his race's oaths had created the Triempery, bestowed the Rill Covenant, outlawed the Dog Men, declared the Dazun River a royal protectorate and highway, and established Amallar for the Khelds. In each case, those promises had also been extended in writing, acknowledging that other memories were short and required proofs. This document, like its predecessors, required signatures. Starting from the least of those present—the Khelds, who signed it first—it made its way Lord by Lord to the highest.

Dorilian leaned to speak in a low voice to his father. "When the treaty is before you, sign it—or, by the Leur, you will have no throne come nightfall!"

"You would do it, too. Rob me of legacy and birthright, and for what? That *he* might fawn and smile upon you?" Deben spat back, keeping his voice low. "I should have smothered you at birth—"

"Sign it," Dorilian repeated. With an exasperated sigh, he

looked to Marc Frederick again. The treaty was currently under the pen of Ostemun Dannutheon, whose Heir, Estevan, would get it next. The Khelds watched each signature with anxious, hope-filled looks that both Sordaneons found disconcerting. Dorilian again felt a vague sense of unease. He had foreseen Khelds standing before the Rill... but none of *these* Khelds.

Marc Frederick rose again to speak. Enreddon, as Lord Chamberlain for the meeting, had brought out the golden wine bowl used at every gathering of their kind since the first. The King drew their attention to the communal act.

"You will notice the wine being poured into the bowl. I wish this to be a celebration, a marriage, as all true covenants should be." The look the King gave Dorilian at that moment invoked that union. Theirs was a joining of purpose—of minds, of domains, and of two families that had been at war.

As the youngest of his house, Dorilian drew three cups—for his father and Mezentius, then lastly for himself. The ceremonial vessels of fine alabaster and gold glowed ruby, the rich wine showing through their translucent shells.

"You won't drink wine with me, but you'll drink with him!" Deben continued to complain as he retook his seat. Dorilian had refused to drink with him the night before. Wine had been dipped into goblets for the Khelds and set before them also. Deben snatched a grape from the silver plate of sweets before him and placed it in his mouth, sucking the pulp and juice from it. He then flicked his fingers, discarding the skin, which landed in Dorilian's cup. Dorilian fought a hot rush of anger.

The act had been deliberate. Deben would stop at nothing to ruin this day for him.

"Let us drink to a Triempery renewed and reborn!" Marc Frederick raised his cup, and the gathered guests—Highborn and Kheld, Sordani and Esseran—followed suit. A host of voices repeated the libation. As one, they raised their cups to the rebirth.

Dorilian grasped his cup and lifted it high just as the others did. The beautiful chalice of metal and stone kissed his fingers with promise. Tense with rage and making a silent vow never to allow his father in public again, Dorilian lowered the cup. The grape skin bobbed on the wine's surface, a loathsome taunt. Determined to deprive his father the satisfaction of seeing him drink spit, he set the goblet aside. The metal base hit with a clear, bright note upon the table of blue glass.

"How unfair," Deben said in a gleeful aside. "'Tis your favorite vintage." He took a deep second drink.

*After this day, I am done with him. Done!* Dorilian now had a perfect idea of how he might come to sit on the Eagle Throne. He would force his father to abdicate. He would seize command of the army. The generals favored him, and all but a handful of nobles would come over. It could be done quickly, without bloodshed. Deben would capitulate, and if he did not... Marc Frederick could be made to accept the necessity. Only Nammuor might present an obstacle.

He saw Deben stiffen. The document had come to him and now rested on the table like a summons. The Hierarch sat white-faced and impotent as the stylus was placed beside his hand. The room grew silent again, its gathered celebrants frozen in place, as if even the slightest movement on their part would alarm him. One of the Khelds, leaning to another to whisper, was unceremoniously hushed. With a half turn of his head, Deben glared his resentment at Dorilian, who returned that gaze without fear. His father was too much of a coward to provoke him in front of the gathered princes.

"So be it!" Deben hissed. Taking up the stylus, he fiercely set it to the paper as if to attack it. For a moment, he hesitated, raising his left hand to his head, then he gathered himself. The pen scratched the paper in an upward stroke.

Enreddon Malyrdeon flinched. A Kheld sagged in his seat, drawing the alarm of the man beside him.

And then the stylus dropped.

# 59

"Father?"

Deben slumped upon the table, eyes staring at the light-filled window. Dorilian touched the warm skin of his throat. "Father?" he asked again. Though not breathing, Deben had a pulse. Life still flickered in his stark, terrified eyes. All around the room, other men called out in surprise, then fear and alarm. Then those voices, too, fell silent one by one amidst thumps of falling bodies.

*Paralysis.* Panic at being unable to move dripped like acid along Dorilian's nerves. And not Deben's panic only: the terror of being unable to move or breathe hammered Dorilian from every side. He looked around to see every other man in the chamber, Highborn and Kheld alike, slumped over in their chairs. Some who tried to rise fell to the floor. And then the screaming began, not aloud but silent... Highborn minds dying, terror-stricken, finding voice inside his head. Their thoughts jabbered madly about poison... treachery... Wall and Rill...

Shaking his head, Dorilian barricaded off the dying as best he could, silencing the voices in his mind. Only he and the King were standing now... and Marc Frederick was wobbling.

"Guard!" He ran to Marc Frederick and wrapped his right arm under the man's ribs, steadying that body against his own. Where were the guards? Triemperal legionnaires were supposed to be stationed outside the chamber doors—doors the Wall Lords themselves had warded with seals. *They cannot enter,* he realized.

Marc Frederick's eyes, shockingly blue in a face suddenly stricken and pale, fastened on his. On his hand, the Leur's Ring blazed: pulses of green laced with black. "You are not harmed?"

"No, thank Leur." A stench from released bowels stung his

nostrils. Death stalked the room. "Come with me!" Dorilian urged. He would have drawn a sword if he had one.

Supporting Marc Frederick's weight, he pulled the King along with him toward the central chamber doors.

A tingle of energy, alien and expanding, distorted the space in front of him. Though the golden doors stood unopened, four men simply walked into the room—four men cloaked not in Esseran or Sordani colors but in long robes of brilliant crimson. Not soldiers, but mages. Fire symbols sparked upon red armor and circlets blazing with rubies crowned each golden head. A transference field still shimmered about them. He would have known them as Morman-taloran even had he not recognized the foremost among them.

"Go! Now!" Marc Frederick tried to push him away.

Undeterred, Dorilian dragged him. They didn't get far before their assailants were upon them. Two men grasped Dorilian by the arms and wrenched them behind his back, hauling him aside. Marc Frederick, unsupported, fell to the floor.

"Nammuor!" Dorilian yelled. "You are thrice-damned to any hell I can reach!"

The Mormantaloran ruler smiled. He was dressed as Dorilian had never seen him, in flowing mage robes that harked back to a more ancient time and race. The diadem he had worn at Hestya, its strange matrix of metals intricate beyond any other device Dorilian knew, crowned Nammuor's pure white hair. Except it was different somehow. Other crystals, spikes aglow with crimson fire, ringed the blood-red monstrosity at its center.

"Do you like my work, Brother? It's but the first stroke of a masterpiece. Nay, the second, as it appears my dear sister did her part well."

Daimonaeris. All of this could be laid on the head of his misbegotten bitch of a wife? Dorilian fought his attackers, but they pushed him against one of the room's many columns, holding him fast. "Rhypos take you! May you drown in Mulsor's hell! And that whore with you!"

Nammuor's black gaze hardened. "Silence him!"

While one man held him, the other grasped his hair and yanked his head back, wedging a length of leather between his teeth, tying it so hard the rough edges cut into his tongue and the corners of his mouth. The man then slammed his head back against the pillar. Blood trickled into his mouth along with the rank taste of leather.

Nammuor turned his attention to Marc Frederick. "What is this? Lingerers?" He circled the chair where the King had somehow pulled his unsteady body upright. "Dorilian, I might have expected, since he has a way of being inconvenient. But you... surprise me. How are you still standing?"

"What foul—"

"The Leur's Ring, perhaps? Its powers are rumored to be life binding. Killing you, then, will be a pleasant bonus. But that must wait. Just watch this."

Unsheathing a sharp, bright dagger, Nammuor advanced to the man nearest him, Ostemun, and with a single stroke, cleaved the helpless man's throat. Red rapidly flowed across the table and spilled to splatter in plumes on the floor.

"Such a waste, isn't it? Immortal blood," Nammuor observed. "Fortunately, I don't need much." From his pocket, he produced a crystal. Like those in his crown, it was long and faceted but so black that it reflected no light at all. One end was twisted with wires and filigrees of oddly tarnished metals and pinpricks of golden, glowing gems. The black tip of the thing touched the spilled blood, and the crystal turned red in his hand.

*Lr* magery. The device end flashed. *Pain. Helplessness. An edge sharper than steel amputating a life from the Mind.* Dorilian flinched. The crystal in Nammuor's hand appeared to pull blood into its matrix, then blazed with crimson light. One of the voices crying out for help stopped. Ostemun's. But he was not gone. The same way Lev had not been gone, his lifeforce captive within a cage of bones. Kicking, Dorilian strained against the arms holding him, but they only tightened their grip.

Nammuor was not killing his enemies; he was harvesting them.

Nammuor placed the red crystal into a large pouch hanging at his belt. He found another victim, this time seeking one at the table's head. Jerking Enreddon's motionless body against the back of the chair, he exposed the pale throat.

"No!" Marc Frederick tried to lurch forward, but the poison had left him weak. He stumbled against the chair.

The blade in Nammuor's hand flashed again, and Enreddon's head dropped back as his blood spurted free. Pain ripped through Dorilian as another life was severed from the Mind, another voice silenced. A second black crystal drank immortal blood, shunting Enreddon's untethered life into a blood-filled prison. Nammuor yanked the Wall Stone from around the dead man's neck before turning to his two unoccupied mages. "I want them all."

Nammuor and the mages circled the room, stabbing each Highborn man as they went, collecting blood in crystals. Seven were silenced. Eight. The tables, the floors, flowed with red.

*Stop. Stop. Don't crowd my mind with your pain!* Dorilian pushed at the clamor, but it raged back at him, fracturing thought. *Murder.* That much was apparent—murder and something more. *The wine.* Wrenching his gaze from the sight of his dead and dying kinsmen, he looked at Marc Frederick. The blue eyes met his.

*He hasn't won yet. I'm alive… and so are you.*

Nammuor prowled to where Deben lay with his hand still upon the document he had been signing. "Alas, Deben. There's a fitting end. As usual, you have left the thing unfinished."

He would not watch. Not that. Eyes closed, Dorilian tried to block out every sense, but still he felt the phantom slice across his throat, the release of the lifeforce. His father wore the Rill Stone to which he was conjoined. He released a muffled groan through his gag and would have fallen to his knees had the man holding him allowed it.

"You should watch. You'll want to see this." Nammuor's voice penetrated Dorilian's blanket of death and pain. He looked up to see the sorcerer twist the Rill Stone from Deben's finger. Beneath his father's lifeless hand, the treaty lay blood-soaked and abandoned.

The device flashed purple as Nammuor held it up for him to see. "My Heir will need this." He placed the Rill Stone in the pouch along with the Wall Stone and hellish crystals, then crossed the room, uncaring that he walked in blood. "What is your story, Brother? How are you still here? The Rill, perhaps? Is it trying to *save* you? Or did you simply fail to drink your own sweet wine?" Dorilian flinched as the backs of Nammuor's fingers brushed just under his left eye, the thumb tracing the line of his cheekbone. "My opinion of you differs from my sister's. She's blind to your appeal, but I'm not. You have some value. The Seven Houses would pay a lot, so very much, to get their hands on *you*." He smiled. "And then there is another reason."

Nammuor's fist plowed into Dorilian's gut and forced his body to buckle. The taste of iron filled his mouth, mortality and blood, and he struggled for his next breath. Marc Frederick's cry came through thick black fog.

"Damn you! Don't hurt him!"

Through blurred eyes, Dorilian saw Nammuor confront the weakened King. "Oh, but I am going to hurt him, my usurping martyr. I am going to hurt him in ways no other man has ever dreamed. You see, I know how you are able to wear The Leur's Ring."

"No! What was done to me cannot be done again! That was Endurin's work!"

Nammuor signaled, and two of his mages wrestled Dorilian over to the table. "Do it."

As they dragged him forward, Dorilian focused on his footing, seeking balance, control. Sebbord's lessons, written in muscle and bone, spoke as loudly as the din of Highborn slaughter in his head. Any change—position, location, movement—might provide the opening he needed. The key to survival was to seize the opportunity... They splayed his left hand at the edge of the table, the first two fingers above, the others and the thumb below... and a sword was lifted.

He saw the blow, felt the slice of pain. He cried out as metal struck stone. The man released his hand, and Dorilian pulled it back, but both fingers remained on the table, along with part of the hand. Blood pumped from the cleaved flesh in a thick red flow.

Nammuor swooped upon the severed digits, cutting the forefinger away from the other, then dipping the severed end in a tin of melted wax that still sat atop a warmer, awaiting regal seals. "This should live for a good long while." He wrapped the digit in a white cloth and tucked it into a silver box which he then hid within his robe. "Seeing as you did not die, I'm going to take your body apart, again and again, until I get it right."

Dorilian hardly cared. He blinked, focusing on commanding his body, the key to all his options. Let Nammuor think him too stunned, too deeply in shock. Anything but the truth. Nammuor had tortured him, but he had also given him pain—and pain was an ally. It drove back the madness, held the voices at bay. Pain was his lifeline, and he clung to it.

"Now for you," the Mormantaloran said to Marc Frederick.

Marc Frederick knew what he stood within and that he would not survive it. The Wall Lords had foreseen the Demise and had sought to prevent it. However, when the Wall showed them no other way, they had put themselves squarely in its path. Something—only the Wall knew what—lay on the other side.

Marc Frederick met the dimming eyes of old Regelon, unmoving and dying but not yet dead, and saw his own fate written in that glimmering stare. *Yes, old friend, I now know what the Wall Lords would not tell me. I thank you. No man truly wants to know in advance what day he will die.*

Dorilian alone did not recognize the moment—Dorilian, bloodied and maimed but not yet finished. The young man's pain-bright gaze locked onto his, and hope surged into Marc Frederick's limbs. There was steel within that stare.

If Nammuor were not between them, they might have a chance.

Marc Frederick made no move until Nammuor was within reach, then summoned all his strength and lunged with the *tullun* blade in his left hand, thrusting at the madman's breast, aiming at his heart. Like a twig beneath a house, his right leg folded and his thrust went wide and low, slicing a long slash in the other man's robe. Enraged, the twisted crown on his head flaring, Nammuor raised his hand to deliver a bolt of blue fire. The fire engulfed the dagger, and Marc Frederick cried out, dropping the blade as his hand crackled with pain. Hot blood trickled where his skin had split open and the smell of burning flesh, his own, rose to his nostrils. He dropped, his knees hitting the floor as his weakened frame could not catch or support him. To his horror, Nammuor knelt beside him. In the next moment, Marc Frederick felt the agony of a toothed dagger sawing at his hand.

The Leur's Ring... he needed it still, but Nammuor held him in a crimson haze.

And then there was movement: clatter, the ringing of swords, and the curdling scream of battle. Colors erupted near the table, red silk and emerald, red falling to the floor. Nammuor released him, twisted, and found steel already swinging at his head. The Mormantaloran turned aside in time to avoid a mortal blow but did not escape the blade's edge. It cut his face across the left eye and cheek. Marc Frederick saw Nammuor's white face, blood spreading between his fingers as he cupped the wound. At that moment, Dorilian swung again.

Though Nammuor fled back several steps, this time, the sword tip struck his broad leather belt, cleaving the metal ring upon which he had hung his pouch of looted treasure. It fell to the floor, sliding toward the table. Dorilian dived for it and pinned it to the floor with his bloodied left hand.

The bloated gem on Nammuor's crown blazed with new light as the sorcerer stretched out his hand. The crimson malevolence spread again, directed at Dorilian.

But this time, Nammuor did not stand between them. Marc Frederick extended his hand.

"*Nas ancyarie!*"

The word Endurin had used to bind the Leur's Ring to Marc Frederick's hand rang forth. He let the syllables swell in his mouth and roll off his tongue. A Leur word, the sound of Creation with which the original wearer of his ring had fashioned its matrix and that of a restored World. The word Endurin had used to imbue the ring with one last spell. Power resonated across his teeth as Marc Frederick released it. His outstretched hand blazed white even as the sorcerer's erupted with red.

Power met power. Dorilian was barely inside Marc Frederick's circle, but it was enough to spare him the full force. An angry crackle of power split the air as the red bolt encountered the Leur shield and shattered, its force diverted instead to ceiling and floor. Jeweled surfaces on every side shattered and sheared. A mage caught in the surge burst into flame with a scream and just as quickly vanished. While the floor beneath his feet cracked and shifted, Dorilian tumbled, coming to rest against the gallery stair. Marc Frederick staggered but clutched at the draping near the window and kept his footing.

Though the spell held, the great tower had broken along its spine.

Within the shield, the floor was no longer level. Dorilian was on one side of the seam, Marc Frederick on the other. Dorilian dropped the sword he had taken from one of his captors and, using his good hand, ripped at the knot behind his head, releasing the gag and tossing it aside. He clambered to his feet and moved toward Marc Frederick, only to be thrown to his knees again as the floor shifted and the crack became a chasm. Energy still radiated outward from Marc Frederick's hand, shimmering in oscillations of white, blue, and purple between him and the invading Morman-talorans. One of the remaining mages now stood just on the other side of that veil, Nammuor railing for him to get the crystals.

*The crystals!*

The pouch lay nearby. Dorilian pounced on it, spilling its contents onto the floor. Seven blood-red crystals glowed before his eyes. He lifted his face and saw the black avarice in the maddened monster who had brought his race to ruin. The spinels bracketing the central red eye of Nammuor's crown looked darker now; three were black. Emptied. Dorilian now understood why Nammuor wanted *these* crystals.

Highborn lives, bound by immortal blood... his father's... Enreddon's... bound over for torture and foulness, and he had no means at hand to save them—only to spare them.

He turned, seeking the sword, but a glimmer of milky green rested nearer at hand. The *tullun* blade. Its rounded hilt felt cold in his palm as he hefted it, then stabbed downward onto the first blood-red gem. The crystal shattered in an eruption of black shards and a mist of blood. Like splinters into his skull, the howling resumed, lives begging their return to the Mind.

"No!" Nammuor's voice resounded.

Dorilian brought the *tullun* blade down again, destroying another crystal, then another, before the next red bolt slammed into the shimmering shield. When he looked up again, more of the crystals in Nammuor's crown had died. Only the huge gem in the center had not dimmed.

"You are their murderer!" Nammuor screamed.

He was. The remaining crystals lived still. But when he glanced at Marc Frederick, the wounded King—his power still bright—nodded his approval.

It did not matter if they forgave him. Their bodies were ruined, and he would be damned before he would let Nammuor enslave his kinsmen's power. Nammuor's screams rang in his ears as Dorilian broke every crystal, littering the floor with black needles and Highborn blood. Done, stabbed by pain and choking back tears, he threw down the *tullun* knife. He saw two objects, glimmering near the emptied pouch, and gathered the Rill Stone and the Wall Stone. Thrusting them back into the pouch, Dorilian tucked it into his belt, then rocked back onto his heels, clutching his bleeding and throbbing left hand.

Booms resounded at the door. Others now knew of their disaster and were trying to reach them. "Leave!" Nammuor shouted to his mages. "Take what you have!" He turned a snake's flat stare at the two men still living. "I'll finish here."

Another boom shook the door. The mages vanished, a flash of golden crowns and black inversion. All at once, the floor buckled again, stone tables and bodies lurching toward a yawning crack. The slab Dorilian sat on was still sound, anchored to the internal structure. He crawled to the broken edge. He looked down, and his breath stopped in his throat.

Far below, the ground lay littered with rubble and tiny trees and antlike specks that were people fleeing a rain of debris. And above... only sky. The piece of the room where Marc Frederick was standing had no attachments to the tower at all, but floated apart from it.

"Sire!" Dorilian shouted. "You must get to this side!" He extended his good hand across the chasm.

Marc Frederick shook his head. "No. I can still hold him a little longer. Run! Nothing you do here will save anything! Not me, not Sordan, not the Rill, and not the Creation—"

"Grab my hand!"

"When the Ring's power is spent, I am dead anyway: I drank the poison. I have only this to give you. Promise me—"

"Anything!" Dorilian thrust his arm out farther. "Just take... my... hand!"

Marc Frederick's fierce gaze locked hard onto his. "Look after my family."

"I will, I promise—my most solemn vow. Just take it—" He pushed his body further... just a little further...

"You are the only thing here worth saving. Finish what we tried to do here this day."

"I promise! Now try"—Dorilian had stretched as far as he could without falling into the abyss himself—"I can't reach you!"

Wind howled up from the city below. The Rill Stone throbbed against his belly and the Wall Stone vibrated through his viscera, both embers of power he did not know how to use. A section of the outer wall cracked and fell away. The shimmer holding Nammuor was fading along with the force of the Leur's Ring. The Diadem's unnatural energy would soon strike again.

"Leave me!" Marc Frederick's plea became a command.

"I can't!" *I need you. I love you. I will not let you go!* The air burned red, and Dorilian turned to see a scythe of energy sweep from the Diadem to slice into the white vault of the shield, fissuring all it touched. He inhaled hot gases and coughed.

"Run, damn you!" Marc Frederick screamed.

The shield from the Leur's Ring held a moment longer, then fractured, the Diadem's energy exploding outward. The force of the blast lifted Dorilian and threw him hard against the stair leading to the gallery. The outside wall near where Marc Frederick had been standing was gone, its windows and lattices streaming outward in a rain of debris. Wind howled through the breach.

"Marc!" The name vanished in the roar of destruction.

Nammuor turned to him, the red glow upon his head slashing through the dust and ruin.

Now indeed, he had to run. Clutching his injured hand, Dorilian lunged up the steps to the doorway. He dove at it even as the frame exploded outward. Debris slammed his body while objects sailed through the air along with him. Searing heat licked at his clothing, skin, and hair before he landed hard and rolled down a flight of steps. Something in his right shoulder cracked. Blood dripped along his scalp, sticky on his face and hands. He raised his head to see that he had fallen over the gallery level railing onto the atrium floor. On the landing above, soldiers running to the commotion screamed and burned as a swell of wind fire caught them. Fragments of the blasted doorway and wall rained down like hail.

Dorilian's ears rang as hands grasped his clothing and shoulders, hauling him to his feet, and a voice shouted at him to get out of there. Something, someone, propelled him down a corridor. He stumbled through noise and smoke, then belatedly realized that the upper levels of the High Citadel were afire. Dazed, he ran through the press of other bodies—soldiers, women, citizens—some moving toward the devastation, most running away. The groaning of the wounded Citadel, its Leur-imbued matrix straining to cope with the damage, added a sonorous horror to the screams of men. *Run!* Dorilian heard Marc Frederick's voice repeatedly and turned to look for him but saw only strangers, stares and terror, pale faces mouthing words. Fighting through the shooting pains in his shoulder and ribs, Dorilian pushed them aside and forced his way from the scene of horror until he found himself in the open. More people. More stares. None knew who he was, though a few offered help or asked questions he would not answer.

*Dead, all dead!* And those not dead were dying. Highborn bodies—even when paralyzed, even when bleeding out their lives crushed by stone or wrapped in fire—took a long time to die. Their last throes snagged at him like talons. Already the Mind shriveled, withering as its losses tugged at the fabric of the Creation. Every agony, every death, peeled away more skin. In a world where Dorilian had always heard the hum and buzz of others like him occupying a familiar firmament, the emptiness left him grasping at threads of distant, hollow grief. A few of his kind survived, so few... and the only fate he wished to know for certain, he could not feel.

*The offspring of gods... snuffed out like vermin.* And Marc Frederick, too, lost in the very trap he had unwittingly crafted. Dead... surely dead. Dorilian could find no trace of him at all. Nammuor had turned triumph to ruin, and for what? To feed a power never intended for man.

Iridescent arches upheld citron ceilings, and water ran down the walls. Dorilian didn't recognize where he was, and wondered, vaguely, if he might be underground. For a moment only, he stopped and rummaged at his waist to pull the blood-soaked pouch from his belt, then peeled it open. The Rill Stone burned vivid green, singing against his skin with power and causing his open wounds to throb. The finger on which the Hierarchs usually wore the ring was intact. He slipped the Rill Stone onto his left third finger and swallowed a cry as ice-cold pain engulfed his hand and traveled up his arm. He turned his head aside and retched, vomiting bile.

As before, the pain helped; it cleared away all but itself. He looped the Wall Stone over his head, outside his garments, and leaned back, absorbing the pulses of communing power. The Entities protected all his blood and would protect him. The rough wall he leaned against glinted with gold—a mosaic depicting the fall of Iddolea. White towers gleamed upon a high mountain above a distant blue sea, recalling another City... one he called his own.

*Sordan.*

Dorilian jolted. Nammuor's plans were far from complete.

He must get to the Rill. His nausea had receded; things felt... clearer. Dorilian started running again, following the Entity's pull on his skin. Pale columns soared overhead to ghostly heights. *Where is Marenthro?* The question mattered, though he could not say how. Everywhere he turned, his mind found only images of death, of fingers curling into black wraith claws, of gases whistling through paralyzed flesh writhing in flames. Even though the Malyrdeons had foreseen an attack, they had not believed it would strike them here—not at Permephedon, not in the High Citadel under the auspices of their race's immortal guardian...

For generations, they had trusted Marenthro to protect their kind.

Never again.

The way opened onto a plaza Dorilian recognized, a paved court separating the City's grand buildings from its attendant Rill structures. Handfuls of people stood in the open, staring at the smoky plumes rising from the High Citadel's destruction. He battled through them. As he ran up the steps that led to the colonnade and the platform beyond, Dorilian saw only a translucent sea-green wall. The Rill's shields were raised. He had never seen the Entity sheathed before, and he stopped, staring. A screaming throng milled in front of the shimmering barrier, crying out to the guards stationed before it and screaming at the Epoptes for access or explanation. Some called for Marenthro. A few beseeched the god.

A hand closed about his arm. Turning to fight, he withheld the blow only as he saw Tiflan's concerned face.

"Thank Leur!" The big man was breathing hard. "I came from the Archhalia. I thought I saw you running, but you outdistanced me!"

"I must get to Sordan!"

"Dor—"

"I cannot stay here!"

Taking him at his word, Tiflan forged a path through the crowd. Though it bruised his arm, Dorilian did not fight his cousin's hard hold on him and doggedly kept his face lowered, hating the mindless confusion. *I can't stay. Nammuor wants me dead or taken... my fingers, my blood... the worst kind of monster. They don't understand... they'll never understand...*

He had to get to Lev before Nammuor did.

If he could not reach the Rill, or if it would not help him, he would die here along with the rest of his kindred, captive in Essera, hunted by enemies and betrayed by unbelievers. Tiflan battled aside a soldier to thrust him toward the barrier. "Touch it!" Tiflan cried. "Derlon will shield you too!"

Dorilian placed the bloody mangle of his left hand on the Rill shield. The Rill Stone blazed green. Upon his bloody shirt, the Wall Stone burned white-hot. He feared the shield would hurt him, but green flickers appeared at his touch, and the energy veil parted. Tiflan's big hand pushed at his back to send him stumbling, into it and then through.

A violet-robed Arch-Epopte hurried across the platform, the ends of his white stole snaking like banners: Quirin, the Psilant, wearing the First Ring of Order on his finger.

"What have you done? Permephedon is disturbed, and the Rill is armed." Suspicion clipped Quirin's words into sharp edges. "Some great calamity has befallen us. You cannot travel now."

"I am Sordaneon."

"I know who you are. You are going nowhere."

Dorilian barely heard Quirin or any mortal voices. He listened to monsters instead. The Mind contorted as the Highborn lives to which Leur had tethered the Creation screamed to each other— fathers, sons, friends, and lovers still dying, still burning. Perme-phedon's living structures struggled to repair themselves, their haunting moans echoed in the Rill's icy sheathing and the Wall's distant, palpable grief. It seemed he saw through Levyathan's eyes again, his vision distorted by the sight of Rill energy streaming outward into the wounded City along root lines of plasm, flowing freely except at the point where he stood. Here the energy pulses converged in glowing miasmas... vortexes he might master and command. He raised his maimed left hand, showing Quirin his wounds and the Rill Stone bright upon his finger. The Psilant's eyes widened.

"My father is dead. I am Hierarch now." Dorilian sensed in the man's mind the thought that he had played some role in the catastrophe, the details of which none but he yet knew... might never know. He would be blamed for it somehow, of course, because he had survived—and because Marc Frederick was dead. People would only remember that they had been enemies.

"Thrice Royal, you cannot—"

"I will not stay here to be murdered!"

Drops of his blood fell to the snow-white floor and suddenly burned bright blue. Beneath his feet, subterranean relays activated, and he felt them in his bones. The Rill would not listen to Epoptes now. Dorilian stepped to the edge of the run and jumped down into the slip itself. No one would follow. Only fools and dead men stood within a Rill path.

"Thrice Royal!" Quirin's golden gaze flashed wide with alarm.

Dorilian blocked them all from his mind: the Order of Epoptes, Essera's nobles, and the vast sea of its commoners. None of them mattered to him. All he wanted in the World was to leave Permephedon, never to see it again, and to go to Sordan to undo the ruin of this day. He could not fight Nammuor from here.

"Father!" he cried. He lifted his arms high and released himself to the god.

# 60

*or.*

*D*Dorilian felt a presence, a pinprick on his mind's skin, amplified by a god. Lev sought him in the chaos, needed to know he was safe. But he wasn't safe.

No *charys* surrounded him. The Rill was pulling him apart.

Plasm streamed through his body, bathing every part of him with itself. Skin too thin, too vast... not his skin at all, and yet it was... skin like none he had ever worn. Towering pylons sprouted like hairs, monumental structures strung like organs astride arteries of power. The Rill pulsed, and Dorilian pulsed with it, flowed into it. Glowing coils of plasm peeled back skin and fascia, snatching the muscle away from his bones, unraveling his entrails. Blood vessels and nerves uncoiled in delicate skeins.

*No!* Here in the Rillstream, there was no death.

He pulled it all back, every living shred that was *his*. The Rill Stone, glowing like a star. The Wall Stone, like a moon filling his hand. His flesh strung out like a galaxy. As much as the Rill ripped from him, he pulled harder, snapping invisible tendrils and gathering his remains back to his corpse. He curled stripped limbs into his hollowed belly, his chin tight to his breastbone shielded by ridges of exposed spine. The healing was instantaneous. Flesh again wrapped his bones, fixed his viscera in place, and sheathed him in remembered skin.

The Rill was immortal, all-healing, and so, while in its body— while he retained memory of himself—was he.

Whole again, Dorilian slammed ego shields into place, battling a thousand incursions. What the Rill saw of him, it wanted. It laved his terrors. It promised him safety, eternity, power... all he had ever wanted, this god could give. To be safe, without pain, in the one place no enemy could reach, freed from his memories and promises. He would live forever. All he had to do was let go of his insistence on retaining his painful shell of flesh... all he had to do was forget.

And he would never forget.

*You... can't... have me...*

But he was too small. Naked to the Entity, he could not endure.

Sordan shone on the horizon of his senses, splendid and imperiled, shadows converging upon its highest places. Something dwelt there, unborn but aware. Something to fight for. Something to lose.

He seized the brightest spire-bone in the Rill's all-body and held it in his mind, brilliant and unalterable, and ordered his dwindling life will toward Sordan. *I am Dorilian.* He differentiated himself from the intelligent plasm that sought to persuade him otherwise. *Dorilian. And I go... here!*

Sordan.

Pain ripped through him again.

Dorilian inhaled sharply, gasping warm, fragrant air that flooded his greedy lungs and lifted his hair. Blue arcs and sharp angles filled his vision, and he used them to cut himself free from dreams of being limitless. When he sprang to his feet, he realized he was naked—his body restored and intact. Even the fingers. He extended and curled them, saw the Rill Stone glinting on his left hand, the Wall Stone clasped in his right. Blue tracery flowed in new patterns beneath his skin. All his skin. He had not hauled back his life from the Rill without bringing more of it with him. His body felt puny and false, a lie. Looking up, he saw the serene pillars and white surfaces of Sordan's Rill terminal. Faces peered into the run where he stood. A host of flesh-things yelled at him, extending their hands.

"Out! Out!" they shouted. "Out before the Rill comes!"

They did not know that he was already there.

Ignoring hands that sought to aid him, he leaped out of the pit. The platform surface felt porous under his feet. The warm air tasted like sweat and decay. Every sound, every touch on his skin vibrated to his core, and he screamed at them to stand back. They did. Someone recognized him, cried his name aloud, and soon it flew from every lip. Always before, when he traveled, the platform had been cleared. To be this near to him was momentous for the mortals; for him, it was like being surrounded by flies.

He looked toward the heights of the City, where he needed to be.

Because his nakedness attracted attention, he took the light cloak someone pulled from a travel bag and thrust at him. He knotted the fabric under one arm and at the shoulder of the other, so the crisp linen skimmed his skin and hung the Wall Stone about his neck. So clothed, he elbowed his way through the remaining crowd and ran toward the guarded portal leading to the Va Haira. A battalion of soldiers wearing Sordaneon colors barred his way.

As his name resounded at his back, shouted in warning, jubilation, and alarm, Dorilian raised his left hand high. The Rill Stone device of the Sordaneons burned with green light upon his hand.

"You know who I am!" he told the captain. "Your Hierarch Deben, my father, is dead—slain by Nammuor the Mormantaloran, who also tried to slay me. The Esseran King is also dead, as are the Wall Lords of Essera. Our enemies will now descend upon us. Keep Sordan free! Secure the City, every part of it. Believe no Epoptes! Believe no Esseran masters!"

He did not stay to hear their answer. He knew what it would be. Sordan's people, hundreds of thousands strong, would be his army now.

He ran, his legs carrying him not toward the Dekkora where the Rill passengers even now were spilling into the City with the news, but through the portal. The Va Haira would take him to the Serat. Another contingent of soldiers—this one wearing the bands of the Heir's Bodyguard—met him on the other side, with Legon Rebiran at their head. Dorilian had placed him to secure the route for his and his father's return.

"Dor! What evil strikes?"

At Dorilian's back, Epoptean guards already vied for control of the Rill platform.

Dorilian took note of Legon's small force. He had only a short time to seize his enemies unawares. "Take every man you can find to the Triemperal barracks," he ordered. "Disarm them or, if they will not lay down their arms, barricade them within. Stefan will seek to use them against me. Do the same with this station! Do not let Essera send reinforcements by Rill. Do it!" he snarled, and even Legon dared no hesitation. "Find Pandaros Vidyamemnon. Tell him to travel to Hestya by whatever means, take command of my troops there, and secure the Rill mount."

And then he left them as well, running with all the speed he could command.

Dorilian knew Daimonaeris was in the Serat, and he knew where to find her. The child she carried could not be hidden from him. Now the Mind had been all but emptied, that life glowed like a nova in the firmament, fixed as an island where all humanity was a sea. He raced along the Va Haira until his lungs burned and his limbs begged him to stop. His forefather Amynas had outraced the wind to capture Felarro. Now he outraced his own heartbeat to reach Daimonaeris before she knew that he lived.

*I'm alive, you unholy bitch! Your brother failed to kill me. You will not make Sordan the jewel in Nammuor's crown... or give him the blood of Derlon to feed his unholy dreams of power.*

High as the towers of the Serat were, his legs conquered them. Guards scattered from his path. He was Sordan's Heir, a Sordaneon, never to be stayed or touched. Gasping, he stumbled out onto the terrace overlooking the Dekkora, the same high terrace where he and Daimonaeris had coupled once and once only. Gossamer veiling floated on the breeze from the pillars of the Royal Barge, reflecting like clouds upon the mirror surface of the lily pool. Daimonaeris stood with her back to him. She looked slender, poised, and beautiful as she gazed at the Dekkora below. What did she see? Turmoil? Confusion? She would no doubt think it fitting, the desired consequence of all her handiwork.

Seeing a guard at hand, Dorilian grasped the stunned man's sword and pulled it free.

He had nearly reached her when she turned to attend the sounds of men running with shouts onto the terrace. He savored the look on her face when she saw him.

"Dorilian," she whispered.

*Alive!*

She had envisioned Dorilian dead, destroyed, out of her life at last. The man she saw before her, mad-eyed, wild-haired, a commoner's sweat-soaked mantle clinging to his skin, was not her husband but a creature of nightmare. He should not have survived to come after her... and now he stood between her and safety with sword in hand.

"Lies," he said, advancing upon her. "All lies."

*Nammuor!* Her mind shrieked, but there was no one to hear. Her brother had said he could not come to Sordan from Permephedon, that his power would be depleted, that his transport crystal, like hers, was linked to Mormantalorus. That she would not need him and could seize control of Sordan in the name of her unborn son. But Dorilian lived, and the City's soldiers would be loyal to him, not her... protect *him*, not her. He—not Nammuor—would claim her child now. Claim her son and claim the throne.

Barely thinking, blindly obeying a path practiced so many times, she sought the band of the gold-jeweled coronet on her brow with her right hand, and her fingers pressed the stones.

"I hate you!" she screamed at him. "I want you dead!"

The crystals released tendrils of power, spinning them into a cocoon about her body. For a moment, Dorilian stared, breathing hard, then his silver gaze locked on hers and hardened as he recognized what she was doing. He raised the sword, and she screamed... and screamed... until her voice suddenly stopped. Everything spun, and her vision grew tight and small, and the last thing she saw was Nammuor turning toward her, a look of horror on his face.

Every man on the terrace saw the flash at the moment the sword struck. Now the body at Dorilian Sordaneon's feet had no head. The men who reached him first found their prince covered in blood, a sword at his feet, looking down silent and unmoving at the woman he had slain. They turned aside, knowing she was his wife and carried a Highborn heir. Their alarm deepened when Dorilian knelt in the rapidly spreading red pool and grabbed the sword again. Turning to them, he scanned their faces.

"Elor," he demanded of the white-faced guard. "I am no midwife. Get Noemi! She will know how to do this!"

"Sire—where is... her *head*?" Elor choked on the word.

"With her brother, and they can both burn in Mormantaloran

hellfire. The bastard slew us all. Quickly, I tell you, we must act now. Fetch Noemi—"

"I cannot. I—Noemi—your Lady told us she is dead."

Dorilian stared at the man. In a day heavy with loss, this one seemed the least comprehensible. Then he wrenched aside from questions for which he had no time and attended again to his dead wife's swollen belly. "I will do it then."

Yanking up the blood-splashed gown, he laid sword to the distended, stained skin and made a shallow pass of the blade. The soft flesh parted and bled, though slight. Dorilian sliced again, deeper, parting fat and severing muscle. He no longer thought of her as human. "A knife!" he shouted, and one of the guards produced one. This time he cut into the womb, working the incision until it was wide enough for him to reach within. Dorilian eased the child forth with both hands, still encased in the dense, blood-filled chorion of Highborn gestation. The babe was fully formed. Just as he had done so long ago with his too-soon-born brother, he tore away the membrane and cleared it from the newborn's mouth, nose, and eyes. He gently rubbed the tiny chest.

*Breathe, little one!* he enjoined silently. *Don't leave me alone among them!*

The infant's chest lifted and filled, and the tiny eyes opened—blue-gray human irises with dark pupils that focused on his. Though it drew breath, it did not cry. It stared at him wide-eyed.

*Dor.* The thought was light, barely a flutter on his mind, but it was sure, and the origin of it was unmistakable.

*Dor! Dor!* The newborn crowed again, lest there be any doubt, and Dorilian pressed the tiny body close with a fierce joy and hope.

# 61

Soldiers met the *charys* bearing Essera's delegation when it arrived at the private Rill dock. Emyli stepped between armed men onto a smooth white terrace, and gazed past the pillared colonnade at the white buildings framed against a backdrop of lake and sky. Banners of green and blue, silver and gold still draped balconies and fluttered from gutters and window frames. The air smelled of oranges and flowers. Everything about Sordan was sharp and bright, from the City's vivid colors to the crisp voices and ready weapons of the soldiers assigned to escort her party. It had been a week since the City had celebrated the ascension of the twenty-third Hierarch.

Dorilian had consolidated his grip on Sordan and its provinces with astonishing speed. In the first hour following the slaughter at Permephedon, he had led five thousand soldiers and a mob of armed citizens against the Triemperal garrison, told them their King was dead, and demanded its surrender. When the commander had refused, Dorilian had ordered the garrison put to the sword. Not a single man had been spared. He had then led his army against the Epoptean guard at the Rill sanctuary in Sordan, where he breached the doors by using the Rill Stone. The Epoptes, at sword point, had allowed him to send reinforcements to Hestya and Randpory. Before nightfall, still wearing a garment blood-stained from his Heir's violent birth and bearing the infant in his arms, he presented himself in the Dekkora upon the Rill terrace and asked the populace of the City to endorse him as their Hierarch. They acclaimed him without hesitation. The next day, he had met with Quirin and secured unimpeded Rill transit within his domains from the Brotherhood of Epoptes in exchange for hostages and agreements. Additional troops were deployed under Pandaros Vidyamemnon to bolster garrisons in Teremar and Suddekar. When Nammuor had attacked Mokkasa a few days later, thinking to find the outpost weak and poorly defended, he had encountered fierce and well-commanded opposition.

Emyli marked how, even though its liberation was secure, Sordan remained on high alert. Sordani soldiers, as well as Epoptes, carefully scrutinized Rill manifests. Cargoes refused for warehousing occupied portions of the platform and Dekkora, and detained passengers formed long lines in the terminal. According to reports that had reached Essera, warships patrolled the inland sea, stopping and searching vessels before they could enter the harbor. Emyli could see for herself that access to the City was tightly controlled. She wondered how much of it was for Dorilian's protection and how much reflected the new Hierarch's iron-willed seizure of every mechanism of control. He saw enemies to every side of him now.

*It should not have been this way. Father would have spared us this division. If only he could have spared us all that Nammuor will yet unleash.*

She sensed hostility from the soldiers. Distrust in all camps had prevented Esseran guests from attending the formal coronation of the new Hierarch. Stefan had denied Rheger and Elhanan's requests to travel and had issued a direct forbiddance for all his subjects. The slights had been noted.

"Stefan must compromise." Sinon Kouranos settled beside her in a sleek horse-drawn carriage that rolled along the Va Haira as silently as a ghost. A score of soldiers rode pale horses ahead of them, with another score riding behind as they passed beneath gold ceilings hinting at glories past. "This Sordaneon need not be a Stauberg-Randolph enemy."

"I know that."

"Stefan does not seem to. His stubbornness but fuels an already unsustainable situation."

"Spare me your counsel, Sinon. Stefan sees only his destiny now." The forces that afflicted her son chilled Emyli to the bone.

Mysterious shapes unfolded in the shadows, curves and lines flowing into patterns for which men had forgotten all meaning. The Va Haira was crowded with such things, with passages secret and lost, and songs without words. Sinon did not say what he thought of Stefan's destiny.

"My son is Marc Frederick's Heir," Emyli reminded him, "and

in two weeks' time, he will be crowned King. If you loved my father, you will follow his wisdom in choosing Stefan as his successor."

"I'm not certain it was wisdom, although it was certainly his plan."

"Then honor his plan." Because Stefan already had too few men he could trust, she gentled her reprimand. "You stand high in my son's esteem, Sinon. He has entrusted you with me, and with this task, where he would trust no one else."

For the first time since she had known him, she saw Sinon's diplomatic face. The reservations in his voice unsettled her. "Your son only entrusted me, Princess, when Dorilian refused others permission to enter Sordan. A Kheld, not I, was initially enlisted as your companion. Indeed, you were your own son's second choice as an emissary after Dorilian rejected his first choice."

*Because Erenor Tholeros is not royal enough to bespeak a Sordaneon.* Emyli shivered to think of the arrogance she was about to confront. She regretted that Stefan so feared Highborn machinations that he would not entrust this business to Rheger or even the widowed and grieving, but willing, Palaistea. *They always side with each other, Mother,* he had said. *I will take at least one page from my grandfather's book and require that bastard to deal with me, not them.*

*Ah, Stefan, don't you see?* She gazed upon smooth subterranean passages and water-bright floors from which staircases vanished upward into shadows. *You misunderstand the lesson. It is you who should require yourself to deal with him.*

Dorilian met them at the Hierarch's private quarters, in a beautiful open throne room from which Sordan's rulers had conducted their personal business for over a thousand years. Emyli was thankful for the less public setting, as well as the shrewdness that Dorilian saw fit to keep their first exchange discreet. She had not known what to expect, coming from him. As she and Sinon walked the secluded corridors of the Sordaneon Serat, her black mourning skirt and veil floated like ink against the expanses of marble in pale, unearthly hues polished to sunlit warmth. Nothing about Sordan was cold, save for its rulers. It surprised Emyli to find Dorilian seated on the plain white marble throne with only two courtiers in attendance and a painter working his brushes at what looked to be a portrait or study. The painter focused on his subject's face, the stark planes of which seemed especially austere given the Hierarch's bare head and short hair. Emyli saw for herself that Dorilian had shaved his head in mourning. The new growth looked darker and distinctly not Staubaun, adding to the surreal impression.

For days she had pondered what damage so many violent Highborn deaths might have done to Dorilian's mind. In the aftermath of the Highborn slaughter, Essera was overrun with rumor: that Dorilian had slain his own kindred and for that reason had attended none of the funerals... that his wife had died not in childbirth but by his own hand... that he believed the child to be his half-minded brother reborn... that he had killed thousands, not slept for weeks, and had gone utterly and irredeemably mad. It relieved her to see no hint of such affliction upon the youthful, handsome face she remembered only too well.

Noting their entrance, Dorilian waved the painter away, and the man left with the ease and diffidence of one for whom such interruptions were both commonplace and understood. A momentary pause, like an indrawn breath, accompanied the man carefully laying down his brushes and conducting a short bow. As Emyli studied the room and its occupants, she noted that the wall behind the seated Hierarch was surprisingly bare, hinting at something removed and its replacement not yet hung in place. The two men who remained with the Hierarch, Tiflan Morevyen and a scowling Legon Rebiran, stood in attendance at their ruler's right hand. Reaching the steps ascending the dais, Sinon knelt upon the floor, upon which he placed his hands and lowered his head and body deeply in formal prostration. Emyli conceded only to bowing her head.

"Thrice Royal." She murmured the title politely and properly, still not sure how well he would receive her.

"Princess," he acknowledged. That he granted her title was more than he had done for her before, and she lifted her eyes to his at hearing it. What she saw in Dorilian's face then shocked her. All that had ever been warm in him was now invisible—or destroyed. His silver gaze had the impact of an assault. Something in that scrutiny devoured her unnaturally, as if he might somehow strip away her features and find something... or someone.

"Thank you for receiving us." By hand gesture, she included Sinon in her greeting.

Dorilian glanced cursorily at the kneeling man, then returned his attention to her. "On whose behalf are you here? Yours? Or your son's?"

Emyli drew a deeper breath before answering. What she was about to say was a risk. "My father's."

She marked the effect: the way Dorilian froze; the way what little color remained in his face drained from the taut, high cheekbones. When he drew breath again, she heard a jagged edge of pain. *It is true, then. You loved my father, whatever others may say, and whatever you may say from this day forth.*

"There is a limit to what I will consider"—Dorilian's voice was darker than it had been, at once more beautiful and more terrifying—"even for his sake."

"I would speak with you of other things... difficult things that pertain to both our realms. But my first request of you, though it may be my last, will be for him. My father's memory, like his life, is doomed to fall to the cruel erasures of time. Yet, I would have the meaning of his life honored. I wish to inter his remains with those of his grandfathers—and your forefathers as well—in Permephedon, among princes and kings."

Dorilian barked with laughter, the sound strangled and mocking. "You *dare* ask this of me after telling me I was unwelcome at the funeral—"

"That request—"

"Is held by all Essera as testimony that you and your stupid son consider me his murderer! You have branded me his enemy and his killer! Did you think me not hated enough already that you had to go and embellish the lie?"

Despite the outburst, he remained controlled, Emyli noticed. *Part of him understands why he could not be there, but part of him resents it to the core. The part that loved my father.*

"We regretted—"

"Regrets are hollow. The deed is done, so make no plea to me about appearances. You lost your chance at compassion."

"Would you have come?" She wanted to know.

He eyed her unhappily. "Yes. I had prepared a death gift."

Emyli closed her eyes. Her father would have celebrated such a demonstration. *Was I wrong?* But she knew she could not have made that decision—not then, not against Stefan's fervent opposition and that of an entire nation wallowing in accusations. And there had been the additional concern for Dorilian's sanity—and safety.

His survival mattered too much to risk for the sake of display. She would not apologize. She clung to words of hope.

"I know what my father meant to you, and that is why—"

"You know nothing of that."

Her anger flared. "Do you think he never spoke with me?"

"I think you never listened."

*And you did?*

But he had. He alone among the Sordaneons had ever truly listened to Marc Frederick Stauberg-Randolph. Emyli looked upon the hardened face of Marc Frederick's greatest convert—and pupil. A Highborn pupil, all that her father had hoped to achieve. Her heart broke to think those hopes had led only to failure and ruin. "Please, I beg you. Don't deny my father in death the honor he was denied in life. He was as great as any of you."

"Yes. He was."

To hear him say it finally unleashed the tears she had refused to let so many others see. She blinked them from her eyes but could not prevent them from spilling down her cheek.

"What say you Sinon Kouranos?" Dorilian said in the ensuing silence. "Does the shell of the late Stauberg-Randolph King deserve such an honor?"

Sinon calmly met the eagle gaze of the young Hierarch. "The shell itself does not. But the memory of the man... deserves that, and more."

"The Malyrdeons have no objection?"

"The remaining princes convey their consent, Thrice Royal." Sinon extended the cylinder he carried. Legon stepped forward to take it from him and examined it closely. He gave it to Tiflan, who extracted the document then handed it to Dorilian. But the Hierarch had recognized what it was.

Dorilian resumed his study of Emyli's tear-stained face. "Do it," he pronounced. "Inter your father with the Malyrdeons, and I will not object to it. But do not think to ask the same for Stefan when his time comes."

Emyli bowed in profound thanks. No mortal man, not even the loftiest of heroes or those closest to the Highborn in birth, had ever been interred in the Vault of Incorruption alongside the god-born. What Dorilian had done was to elevate her father above any man who had ever lived, aside from his own kind.

"Out of my regard for your father, I grant this honor," Dorilian said. "He, at least, is now removed from the sordid little conflict into which his death has cast us all." His voice, however, sounded burdened by grief and hurt. "Tell your son that my good will extends no further than his grandfather's final resting place. He has himself not earned my regard. Now is his chance to do so. I demand that he cease his attempts to regain Sordan as a chattel state—that will not happen while I live. Nor will I countenance his efforts to remove me from power. If he will concede that Sordan and its domains are no longer Essera's to command, formally recognize my borders, and declare my sovereignty over my traditional lands and domains, there is a chance we may exist without confrontation, and preserve the form of the Triempery."

"And what of the other terms of the Permephedon treaty?" Emyli demanded. Dorilian had just invoked one of the articles of that agreement. "Will you also demand that those be duly enforced?"

"To which terms do you refer?"

She damned him for being facile. He knew that the full text of the treaty had not survived. He alone—and possibly Marenthro—knew all of what that agreement had been, or even if it had been signed or its oaths voiced. "The ones that stipulate you will recognize the Stauberg-Randolphs as Essera's legitimate rulers, that you acknowledge Stefan as Essera's King and his descendants as Heirs after him. That Khelds be permitted to ride the Rill—"

"I would be a fool to initiate such a measure at this time." Opening the Rill would but alienate him further from the Staubaun aristocracy and elevate a new class of enemy.

"Then my father's treaty with you is dead?" she asked tightly.

"I did not say that."

*No, just that you will not now honor all of its known provisions.* Dorilian meant only to hold to those parts that benefitted his position.

"Don't perpetuate old mistakes," she warned. "You have what you wanted. Stefan cannot take Sordan from you the way my father did from Labran."

"Then have him recognize me publicly as Hierarch and declare this feud at an end."

"And will you also recognize Stefan as ruler over my late father's domains?"

It was the crucial question. Dorilian's own claim to Marc

Frederick's throne was ancient and legitimate. He now possessed the legal power, and the military might, to act upon that claim. It had been as a counter to that possibility, more than for any other reason, that the Seven Houses had moved quickly to proclaim their support for Stefan—and also why Essera's Halia had voted so strongly to denounce the Sordaneons and reaffirm their Stauberg-Randolph alignment. And it was the only reason the ever-cautious Epoptes, fearing the loss of their Order's already tenuous influence over Sordan and Hestya, had yet to announce their choice. Everyone waited to know what Dorilian meant to do. To Emyli's dismay, the young man shook his head.

"The man to whom I would have promised that is dead."

"My father—"

"Stefan is not your father. Even he could not teach that bramble to become an oak."

His disdain for her son stung in places she had not known were tender. "You think us upstarts, usurpers still, for all that we came by our power legitimately. But you will find that we are stubborn and tough—as stubborn and tough as you yourself can be—and we will not be uprooted."

"Prove it. For the moment, I have my hands full with Nammuor's incursions into Suddekar."

Was he letting her know that Stefan would have a time of reprieve, an opportunity to show what he could do with his inheritance? The only expression she could read was indifference. Emyli found herself once again biting her tongue.

"You are not alone in the World, Dorilian Sordaneon." She dared to use his name, and it pleased her immensely to see him snap out of his pomposity. His gaze upon her suddenly sharpened, if only in irritation. Her father had taught her the value of familiarity as a means of gaining a subject's attention. Dorilian had never fully considered her as an adversary. "You can have allies, or you can have enemies. Some will seek you out, but all are yours to create or choose. I am here to ask you to consider your position. Stefan is not your enemy."

"Then let him demonstrate it," Dorilian said at last. "Can you not be satisfied with that?"

"Have I a choice?"

"No." He reached behind his neck and drew over his bowed head a cord that had been hanging there. He handed it to Legon, indicating that he should pass it to Emyli. She took it from the man's gloved hand. Still warm from Dorilian's body, the cord rippled against her palm. In the room's rich light, the dark gold color glinted with bright strands. Emyli ran it through her fingers, knowing now what had become of Dorilian's shorn hair. At the end of the cord hung an amulet, a bone cylinder, sealed with gold. She dared not ask, or guess, what it held.

"Place this in your father's hand," he said. "It is my death gift. May it comfort him, if the dead can be so comforted."

"You made this."

"I did. Of my own bone and hair, and the promise within is written in my blood."

Marenthro had told her that he had returned to Dorilian a severed finger recovered from the ruin of the Jewel Tower. Whether the product of madness or overwhelming sorrow, the object in her hand was not merely personal—it was sacred.

"I will do as you ask. Thank you."

Dorilian shook his head. "You thank me now, but you forbade me to make this gift in person. It would have meant more then than it does now. You have no idea what we had promised each other, your father and I. You think we played the casual games of men who seek power: that I dangled lies and he dangled compromise; that he withdrew troops and I opened borders; that I promised peace and he promised autonomy; that he kept his bargain where I renege on mine."

Now, indeed, Emyli felt the chill of his disdain. Dorilian sat upon the Eagle Throne of the Sordaneons as though he had done so all of his life.

"The World will never know the things we meant to do. I will strive with all the strength that is in me to make them forget. But I would have his remains honored. Among your kind, he would be reduced to foul corruption and white bones, even beneath a mighty sepulcher. Let him lie instead among those he protected, and let their descendants be reminded of his deeds."

Dorilian rose and signaled that he would go. He was taller than Emyli remembered. In the way of his kind, he was still maturing even at twenty-one years. But the Hierarch who looked back at her was no longer a youth—he was adult and dangerous and stood upon the threshold of power unimaginable. The only men who had ever been able to govern him were dead, and he would attain his final shape in a World which to him would seem limitless. She dared hope he would know how to ask for help when he needed it.

"You cannot defeat Nammuor alone." She spoke before he could leave her standing bereft in the vault of this room of sunlit beauty. "Don't cast aside what my father worked so hard to give you."

He turned to face her, a man more royal than any of the legions who opposed him.

"I know very well what he gave me. He would understand what I will now do."

"No. You will destroy everything he lived for."

"But not what he died for. That, I will turn into his monument." He left the room with his companions trailing like ships pulled in an unbreakable current.

Emyli curled her fingers over Dorilian's death gift. A bone and promises. Her father had opened a door, and Dorilian had just handed her the key. But a door to what?

In her mind, she heard Marc Frederick telling her the answer. *The Rill.*

Always the Rill.

# END

## TO BE CONTINUED IN BOOK II,
## THE KHELD KING

Turn the Page
For a Preview of
The next chapter in

# The Triempery Revelations

Emyli sat at one end of a table so long it could have served for a game of balls and pins. Dorilian sat at the other end, still robed in state attire. The beautiful room, its elegance so understated as to be piercing, announced that this meal was itself a performance. Waterglobes suspended above the black marble table cast gentle light upon plates of roasted fennel and sweetmeats, pungent cheeses, creamy flans, and fruits so exotic most inhabitants of Essera had never eaten of them. All Highborn princes ate richly and in great quantity, and Dorilian was no exception. Indeed, his affiliation with the Rill broadened the menu. He had access to the foods of a hundred lands. Emyli stopped herself before asking why there was no meat. Her stomach turned when she realized the answer.

"Why should I grace Stefan's coronation?" Dorilian's question landed gracelessly between them. They had not spoken the whole while. "He didn't come to mine." His silver gaze narrowed. "Neither did you."

"I told you at our last meeting that I regretted Stefan's decision and why I honored it. Things happened too quickly, too violently, for all of us."

He averted his gaze.

She decided to proceed. "Perpetuating a slight resolves nothing. Heals nothing."

"Healing." He shook his head.

"The Triempery cannot survive another amputation."

"You imagine I care."

"If you did not care, we would not be here."

Dorilian had not broken formally with the Triempery. He had threatened. He had raged and postured and had done everything except say the words or pen them in official ink. On the same day of the Demise, he had answered Stefan's order for his arrest with the corpses of Sordan's entire Esseran garrison. He had dismissed ambassadors, refused emissaries, and stationed what troops he could spare from his war with Nammuor along his northern border. He had commissioned and successfully recruited new armies. He had frozen assets, withheld payments dictated by the Archhalia, and was forcing unallied domains to choose between him and Stefan. He had become the single greatest obstacle to the free flow of Rill traffic. But he had not, yet, declared Sordan's historical bond to Essera null and void.

He also had not yet ordered her to leave.

"What does any of this have to do with me attending your wretched son's coronation?"

"My father's dream for Essera and Sordan. It's in the letter. A united Triempery blessed by the Rill and the Wall. Strong, visionary, and true to his ideals."

"I never believed in a united Triempery. I believed in *him*."

"And now you can't believe in Stefan?"

He scoffed, a harsh sound. "The only thing I believe about Stefan is that he's an ass. For me to attend his coronation would be a sideshow, a distraction—we'd probably just have another fight."

"It would be a statement. You swore to my father two years ago that you would not oppose Stefan as his successor. Would you now take that gift away?" If looks could kill, she would be dead already. She leaned forward, willing to match him glare for glare. "Don't make worthless the deaths of my father and yours, and all those other men."

A hundred men, all dead in a single act of murder, sorcery and fire. The Highborn and human rulers of Sordan and Essera, and of several allied domains also, not least of them the new young Kheld nation there to be brought into the privileged circle of Rill users. The new Rill treaty would have opened frontiers and changed the political landscape of the World. Dorilian knew better than she what had been lost that day, and how much had been taken from them. He was the only soul to have survived the slaughter, the only one to know what promises had been made.

"They didn't die for *him*."

*No. They died to advance the plans of a monster.* "They died for a future. My father died for wanting something more than this."

His face hardened. "And now you want me to give Stefan legitimacy."

She had expected that insult. "Stefan's not asking for legitimacy. He has that already."

Dorilian shrugged. He knew better than anyone the shaky pillars upon which her son's kingship rested.

"Please, consider this opportunity." She was not yet ready to concede failure. "Stefan can be an ally. My father spent the last months of his life with him, imparting a greater vision and sharing all he knew. My son wants to cease these hostilities between our realms—"

"Hostilities *he* started—"

"Yes. He recognizes that he was unfair. That is why he is taking this extraordinary move. He's asking that you put your hard feelings against him behind you, and he will do the same with his."

"He accused me—in Archhalia—of *murdering* your father—"

Just as it had in Sordan two weeks ago, his pain at that accusation slammed against her nerves. "He'll withdraw the charge—"

"—and my kindred! He is seeking my arrest. Maybe my execution." He stabbed at his food.

Anger. So much anger. The World itself might not be vast enough to hold it. "He wants neither! If you will meet with him—"

"Only if we meet with swords in hand."

And that was that. Every encounter with Dorilian meant having to overcome his formidable hostility. Emyli steeled herself. Her father had showed that it was possible.

"You read the letter. Both letters. Stefan is willing. He wants peace and to keep his grandfather's vision. The accusation withdrawn and promises of cooperation given. Permephedon is the only city where such a meeting would be possible. He promises your safety and freedom. I will do the same."

His gaze bored into hers, asking if he could believe her. The gulf of distrust between their families was deep. Just because her father had bridged that gulf did not mean it had ceased to exist. Dorilian had reason to be wary. Betrayals had hardened him—but too many deaths had also left him in need of allies. Of peace. Emyli knew herself guilty of playing on those needs. She would have been ashamed had the stakes been less high.

*I'm contending for my son's survival.*

"You hate me less than he does." Dorilian had finished eating.

"Stefan doesn't hate you, he—"*Fears you.*

---

# THE KHELD KING
Coming in 2022 from FOREST PATH BOOKS

# AUTHOR'S
# ACKNOWLEDGEMENTS

So many people have helped bring this book, the first of a six-book series, to life, but I would be remiss not to start with my sister, Mary. She was there not only at the beginning where the writing began, but the conception. When we were just kids, before I put pen to paper, I used to tell her stories with these characters. She read the very first drafts, and she always encouraged me. If she hadn't dared me one day to send in a book for publication, I might never have actually done it or gotten published. I think of her often when writing in the Triempery universe, and always when I am asked how I became a writer.

My wonderful husband supported me and never suggested I do anything but write what I love. He's been my first reader, first editor, and best fan. Numerous characters and bits of dialogue owe him a debt of thanks.

My three sons suffered through the writing of this series while they were children and contributed more to the story than they will ever know.

Special thanks to Joe Dascanio and Victor Pane, who read this series in manuscript and offered insights and encouragement. Christina Wooden is the book's patron saint; she read the final manuscript and also made a wonderful map from my hand drawn sketches. Aliette de Bodard and Elizabeth Hull read and edited the very earliest draft of this book and encouraged me to finish it. A thousand thanks to Jeanine Hennig for believing in this book. I bow humbly to Larry Rostant for the amazing cover art. And my deepest gratitude to Peter Stampfel for suggesting I write Dorilian's backstory in the first place.

## CHARACTERS

*MALYRDEONS—PAST*

**Ergeiron** one of the Three, son of Leur and Amynas-Malyrdys. After his brother Derlon gave life to the Rill, Ergeiron founded the Wall, sealing dangerous Time Rifts opened during the Gweroyen War, protecting the Malyrdeon stronghold at Stauberg, and serving as a means by which his descendants could discern past and future events.

**Cienorr** son of Ergeiron and founder of the Mormantalorus Nuarchate.

**Emrysen** Wall Lord and great-grandson of Ergeiron, who bestowed a conditional pardon on the Hen Kyon.

**Erydon** Wall Lord and great-great grandson of Emrysen, who granted the Khelds the wilderness of Amallar for their homeland.

**Endurin** last true Wall Lord and last Malyrdeon King of Essera. Endurin's Heir died unexpectedly, leaving only a natural daughter, who fled to sea and was caught in the Rift. Endurin later brought her son Marc Frederick back to the World.

**Ariande** Granddaughter of Endurin. Mother of Marc Frederick.

*MALYRDEONS—PRESENT*

**Apollonia** Queen of Essera; daughter of Elegiros, Prince of Tahlwent. Wife of Marc Frederick and mother of Jonthan.

**Austell** Wall Lord, third cousin of Endurin and distaff cousin to Marc Frederick. Brother of Enreddon.

**Elegiros** Prince of Tahlwent (family name, Halasseon); third cousin to Endurin. Father of Apollonia.

**Elhanan** son of Rheger; Wall-gifted; one-time tutor of Stefan and Dorilian at Permephedon.

**Enreddon II** Prince of Stauberg; cousin to Endurin and distaff cousin to Marc Frederick. Scholarly, but not Wall-gifted, Enreddon supported Marc Frederick to be Endurin's Heir. This infuriated the Sordaneons, who felt their claim more valid. Both of Enreddon's wives died in childbirth, failing to produce living sons.

**Ionais** Princess of Merrydn; daughter of Regelon and betrothed of Jonthan Stauberg-Randolph.

**Ostemun** Prince of Dannuth (family name, Dannutheon); distant cousin to the Stauberg Malyrdeons.

**Palaistea** Princess of Lacenedon; daughter of Lakron. Becomes third wife of Enreddon.

**Regelon** Prince of Merrydn (family name, Merrydeon); matrilineal cousin to Sebbord Teremareon. Father of Ionais.

**Rheger** Bas of Hespera (family name Dannutheon); brother to Ostemun and Estevan. Father of Elhanan. Possesses strong spatial ability and is one of few Malyrdeons who can use an enhancer for translocation.

## SORDANEONS—PAST

**Derlon** One of The Three; known as the Rill Giver because he integrated his immortal body and lifeforce with the remnants of the Rill, facilitating its rebirth. Epoptes believe his integration still directs the Rill's actions, though he has lost the ability to interact with other beings.

**Deben I/II/III** grandson and great-grandsons of Derlon (collectively known as the Three Debens), ushered in a Golden Age of Rill expansion and Triemperal growth that secured the Sordaneon dynasty. Builder/creators of Leseos, Gignastha, and the Vermillion Aqueduct.

**Peleor** Son of Derlon; slain by the Aryati, who poisoned his blood and spilled it on the mount at Simelon to be absorbed by the Rill. His blood still stains the platform and Rill structures.

**Tarlon** Hierarch of Sordan during the Second War with Ardaen. The youngest of his three sons wed an Ardaenan princess to secure the truce. Tarlon was the last full Rill Lord able to communicate with and influence the Entity. Opened the Rill node at Randpory Crossing.

## SORDANEONS—PRESENT (and associated characters)

**Daimonaeris** Daughter of Camas, the late Highborn ruler of Mormantalorus; half-sister of the current ruler, Nammuor. Marries Dorilian.

**Deben IV** Sordan's Heir and regent. Son of the captive Hierarch, Labran, and Ermenthalia, daughter of Mezentius, Prince of Suddekar. Deeply paranoid, he has not set foot outside of Sordan's Serat in thirty-five years. Married Valyane, daughter of Sebbord Teremareon. Father of Dorilian and Levyathan.

**Deleus** son of the Heir to Suddekar, great-grandson of Mezentius and grandson of Sebbord. Although a first cousin to Dorilian, Deleus is not Highborn.

**Delos** Deben IV's twin brother. Son of Labran. Used the Lacenedon Crown to destroy the Vermilion Aqueduct and end the siege at Gignastha. Died after that deed from plasm shock.

**Dorilian** Son of Deben IV and Valyane. Brother of Levyathan. At the age of seven, witnessed his mother's murder. His precocious physical and empathic gifts allowed him to save his neonate brother. Determined to right wrongs done to his family.

**Ermenthalia** Daughter of Mezentius and a Mormantaloran princess. Wife of Labran, mother of Deben IV. Bears title of Gracious Hierarchessa. Favors alliance with Mormantalorus, from which her mother hailed.

**Labran** Grandson of Tarlon; his mother was a princess of Ardaen. He wed Ermenthalia, daughter of Mezentius, Bas of Suddekar, and is father of Deben IV and grandfather of Dorilian. He objected to Endurin Malyrdeon naming Marc Frederick as Heir to Essera and at Marc Frederick's coronation refused to acknowledge him as King. Labran fought his way into Permephedon's Rill node and commanded the Rill to stop running, creating widespread panic. Taken captive by Marc Frederick and considered too dangerous to release, Labran continues to be held in Stauberg, far from any active Rill nodes.

**Levyathan** Son of Deben IV and Valyane. Grandson to Labran and Sebbord. Brother to Dorilian. When enemies poisoned his mother, Levyathan was born months too soon to survive. Although saved by Dorilian, Levyathan's development was affected and he suffers neurological deficits.

**Mezentius** (family name Suddekeon); Bas of Suddekar. He wed a princess of Mormantalorus. His eldest daughter Ermenthalia wed Labran and gave birth to Deben IV.

**Nammuor** (family name Varehos) Ruler of Mormantalorus, half-brother to Daimonaeris. Reputed to have Aryati blood and to dabble in forbidden arts. Has recovered the lost Diadem of the Devaryati.

**Sebbord** (family name Teremareon) Prince of Teremar. Although not Rill-gifted, Sebbord trained as an Epopte and rose to the level of Archmage in service to the Rill. He wed twice and sired three daughters. Grandfather of Dorilian, Levyathan, Deleus and Tiflan.

**Tiflan** (family name Morevyen). Grandson of Sebbord, but not Highborn. Seven feet tall, he is Dorilian's first cousin and a loyal ally.

**Valyane** Princess of Teremar. Sebbord's daughter, wife to Deben IV. Mother of Dorilian and Levyathan.

**Endelarin** (family name Nemenor) King of Ardaen, brother to the throne queen. Romantic and rumored to have one hundred wives. Cousin to the Sordaneons and fond of reminding them of it.

**Legon** (family name Rebiran) Son of Terveryen, Bas of Anit-Rebir. Youngest of six sons. Sent to Sebbord as a boy to enter Sordaneon service. Dorilian's friend.

**Tutto** (family name Rhunnard) An Estol serving as Sebbord's sword master. Later serves Dorilian.

**Noemi** Wet nurse to the infant Levyathan, later his governess. Mother of Fahme.

**Heran** (family name Albos) Weds Noemi. Has secret ties to Daimonaeris and Nammuor.

**Fahme** Noemi's daughter by Heran.

**Quirin** (family name Chrysolemnos) Psilant, or leader, of the Brotherhood of Epoptes.

*STAUBERG-RANDOLPH (and associated characters)*

**Marc Frederick** King of Essera; great-grandson of Endurin Malyrdeon
through his son Estevan and Brenna Almarresda. Son of
Ariande Malyrdeon and William Randolph. Considered a
Malyrdeon in recognition of his relation to and support from
them, but he is not Highborn. Marc Frederick first
married Thora, a Kheld woman. After Thora's death, he
wed the Highborn princess Apollonia as a condition to
becoming Endurin's Heir. He has two children: Emyli, his
daughter by Thora, and Jonthan, his son by Apollonia.

**Emyli** Daughter of Marc Frederick and Thora; was betrothed to Deben
IV Sordaneon but ran away at age 14 with charismatic
Kheld rebel Erwan Cedrecson. The pair wed and Emyli
gave birth to Erwan's son, Stefan. To free Erwan from
prison, Emyli helped Kheld rebels gain access to the
stronghold of Gignastha, resulting in three Highborn
deaths and the bloody siege of that city. She later gave birth
to her second son, Handurin.

**Jonthan** Son of Marc Frederick and Apollonia. Betrothed to Ionais,
princess of Merrydn. Prince of Dazunor and Heir to Essera.

**Stefan** Son of Emyli and Erwan; grandson of Marc Frederick. Stefan has
no inheritance of lands or titles but is considered a royal.

**Handurin** (Hans) Son of Emyli, reputed son of Erwan. Grandson of
Marc Frederick. Brother to Stefan.

**Gareth** (family name Morgan) Marc Frederick's steward, in charge of his
household.

**Trevor** (family name Allen) Captain of King's Guard.

**Marenthro** Wizard of Permephedon; ageless and possibly immortal. No
one knows much about him save that he is apparently
benign and possesses both Wall and Rill affinity. Responsible for finding Marc Frederick for Endurin and bringing
him back to this World.

*SEVEN HOUSES (and associated characters)*

**Chyralane** (family name Rannuleon) Denizen of Phaer, most prominent
of the Seven Houses. Daughter of a Highborn prince of
Rannul. Opposed to any action that would lessen cartel
control over the Rill. Very tall.

**Philemon Leander** Wealthy Staubaun merchant, not noble but aspiring
to the nobility. His daughter married the Denizen of House
Haralambdos.

*ESSERAN STAUBAUNS (and associated characters)*

**Asphalladra** Youngest daughter of the Enlad of Chennor; in love with Cullen Brodheson.

**Eldonus** (family name Kastryon) Enlad of Velsitha; husband to Palimia. Very old friend of Marc Frederick.

**Erenor Tholeros** Cousin to the Halasseon rulers of Tahlwent; grandson of an illegitimate daughter of Elegiros. Captain of Marc Frederick's cadets at Stauberg; friend of Stefan.

**Kathanos** (family name Niarchos) Friend of the Stauberg-Randolphs.

**Machon Epirosi** Archon of Penrhu. Breeder of bloodhorses.

**Alban Eskeros** Gignasthan lord whose lodge Dorilian uses during his rebellion.

**Palimia** Daughter of a high-ranking Sordani noble killed to facilitate confiscation of his estates. Later married Eldonus Kastryon.

**Phellan Illarion** Bas of Serrain, married to one of Ostemun Dannutheon's daughters.

**Sinon Kouranos** Marc Frederick's administrator in Sordan, and then Neuberland.

*KHELDS (and associated characters)*

**Cullen Brodheson** Cousin and best friend to Stefan.

**Erwan Cedrecson** Son of Cedrec Aelfricson; ran off with young Emyli Stauberg-Randolph. She later bore his sons, Stefan and Hans. Died at Gignastha.

**Tobold Forbasson** Thegnard (leader) of the Thegnkeld, the foremost clan of Amallar.

**Cedrec Aelfricson** Kheld representative to the Triemperal Archhalia. Father to Erwan. Grandfather to Stefan and Hans.

**Robdan Aelfricson** Cedrec's youngest brother; a scribe.

**Trahoc Caddenson** Neuberland rebel whose son and brother died at Gignastha. He meets Stefan at the inn in Bellan Toregh.

**Krigan** One of Trahoc's companions

**Lorn** Another of Trahoc's companions

**Neddig Darronson** One of Stefan's friends.

**Mahon Gormladson** Another of Stefan's friends.

**Reard Argllson** Another of Stefan's friends.

*OTHER CHARACTERS*

**Baran Redharg** Hen Kyon leader, Lord of Gloanneach. Looks nearly fully human.

## ENTITY-BOUND DEVICES

**The Leur's Ring** Fashioned from the body of The Leur as last living act. Rejects non-Leur flesh and can only be worn by the Highborn. Used at coronations to identify the true king of Essera (Heir of

Ergeiron). Manipulates real world/Leur's Creation. Removes barriers. Opens doors. Reveals truth and restores Leur's reality.

**The Rill Stone** Device created by Derlon, who encapsulated his immortal blood in Rill matrix. The Rill Stone will identify a Sordaneon who wears it by glowing green. The Rill recognizes Sordaneon wearers and will not arm itself or lock locations against them. Taps into Rill energy. Can be used to burn a permanent Eagle mark onto any surface, including human skin.

**The Wall Stone** Shard of the Wall containing Ergeiron's immortal essence. The Wall Stone connects directly to the Wall, regardless of proximity, and must be used carefully by individuals open to its gifts. Allows wielder to peer into discreet temporal flows and walk the Wall when inside Aidion. The Wall Stone unlocks the Aidion and provides access to the Archive, which it assists in revealing.

## OTHER ENTITIES

**The Diadem** Undying Crown. Also known as Diadem of the Devaryati. Pre-Devastation device created in secret by the Aryati from the immortal core that remained of Vllyr after that god was destroyed by Amynas and the Leur. Generates and commands arcane forces. Vastly powerful when fully tapped into an immortal being. Retains vestige of Vllyr's godhood. Malevolently self-aware and fixated on destroying that which destroyed Vllyr. Succeeded in corrupting the Aryati, destroying Mulsor, then the First Creation.

### GREATER ENHANCERS

**Sordan Coronal** Also called Derlon's Crown. Most powerful of the Greater Diadems. Now in possession of the Sordaneons.

**Stauberg Coronal** Also called the Star Crown, Ergeiron's Crown. Now in possession of the Malyrdeons.

**Mormantalorus Coronal** Also called the Crown of Fire, Ciennor's Crown. In possession of Mormantalorus and its ruler.

**Lacenedon Crown** Also called Ulnossi's Bane. Used by Delos Sordaneon to break the Vermillion Aqueduct.

### OTHER DEVICES

**Derlon's Armor** The fabled Eagle Breastplate, helm, and gauntlets. When activated sheaths the wearer's torso and limbs. Kinetic negation. Any blow to the armor is absorbed. Invincible to nearly all weapons.

**The Sword of Amynas** Also known as Derlon's Sword or the Gweroyen Sword. Greatest of the *tullun* blades made from Vllyr's skeleton. Most effective when paired with more powerful enhancers.

## HIGHBORN ORIGINS

**Aryati** human strain engineered to replicate the powers and immortality of Leur. Creators of greater and lesser devices that generate quasi-magical powers. The Aryati rose to extraordinary advancement through technology but were arrogant and acquisitive; they ultimately destroyed their world. A remnant of the Aryati survived into the new Creation but most were slain following their defeat by the Highborn during the Gweroyen Wars. No pureblood Aryati survive but the strain persists in noble Staubaun lineages.

**Leur** immortal beings that created the World. Elusive and mostly hidden from humans until technological advances revealed them. Leur magic built the Five Cities, each in a day, and, combined with Aryati technology, engineered the living matrix of Rill. During the Devastation brought by the Aryati, the Leur race sacrificed itself to create the temporal disjunction that preserved the Creation. The lone Leur survivor merged his immortal bloodline with that of the Aryati clone-prince Amynas, with whom he conceived three immortal sons known as the Three.

**Malyrdeon** descendants of Ergeiron, one of the three sons of the gods Amynas and Leur; Ergeiron settled in what is now Stauberg, where he created the Wall as a barricade against the Rift. The Wall exists throughout all Time. Some descendants of Ergeiron are able to "walk the Wall" and by that means can divine future events or reveal the truth or import of past events.

**Sordaneon** descendants of Derlon, second of the three sons of the gods Amynas and Leur. Derlon settled Sordan, home to one of the surviving Five Cities of Leur, from which he restored life to the Rill by melding his immortal body with that of the vast machine. The descendants of Derlon carry the potential to connect with and communicate with the Rill, giving them the potential to alter the god-machine's operation and physical structure.

## HUMAN RACES

**Highborn** males descended from the three immortal sons of Leur and the human Amynas. Only male offspring of Highborn males possess the Leur bloodline, and they must mate with human females to reproduce. For this reason, the adage is that the Highborn take the race of their mothers. Almost exclusively, the Highborn have chosen to reproduce using Staubaun lineages

**Staubaun** a people originally created by (and from) the Aryati and still manifesting some of the gifts of the parent race. Tall, fair-skinned, brown or gold-eyed blondes, beardless (with little body hair), Staubauns are intelligent and long-lived. They also, after generations of success and prosperity, tend to be rich and privileged.

**Estol** an amalgamation of races, the general population. Disdained as mongrels by Staubauns, Estols nonetheless rise to positions of influence and become minor nobility. Most are servants, laborers, soldiers and craftsmen. Because they are of mixed blood, Estols can have any human color of eyes, hair, or skin.

**Kheld** a people (considered 'barbaric') that entered Essera through the Rift during a period of instability. Khelds generally have blue or green eyes. They also have dark hair, sturdy builds and are shorter. Adult males are usually bearded. Their language is completely separate, as are their ways of life. Kheld naming differs from the Staubaun, as does their system of inheritance.

**Nemenor** a sea-faring people that forms the ruling families of Ardaen, Callorn, Lahgael, and the Isles of Maskos. Traditional enemies of the Triempery in the past, a marriage by treaty to a younger son of a Hierarch of Sordan instilled Ardaenan Nemenor blood into the lineage of the Highborn Sordaneons.

## NON-HUMAN RACES

**Leur** magical race, as explained above, creators of the original World and the tripartite Creation they fashioned to salvage it from destruction. Originally the Leur people inhabited the area now known as the Bogs, a marshy delta where the Dazun River flows into the sea. The last Leur was slain by the Devaryati and the race is now only legend.

**Hen Kyon** the Dog Men, created by the Aryati as hunters and servants, specifically to track down and kill the offspring of Amynas and Leur. Intelligent and reclusive, the Hen Kyon are bipedal with fur covering parts or all of their bodies. The most true-to-breed have long, wolfish faces with well-developed olfactory organs. They have incredible stamina and strength. The Hen Kyon can interbreed with humans, from which race they were originally fashioned. The Hen Kyon nearly eradicated the young Highborn race. Even though they later repented their deeds, the Dog Men were abhorred and hunted nearly into extinction until the Malyrdeon King Emrysen cloaked them in obscurity and gave them the haunted wilds of the Kragh in which to live unmolested. They have since become feared and avoided.

## PLACES

**(Mena)trohjana** The Second Creation. The present World that moves forward in Time.

**(Mena)tantaureus** Archived world/Past world, living remnant of the First Creation. Birthplace of Marc Frederick.

**Gsch** The World of Fire. The moment of Devastation, forever happening, never completed. A single moment in Time that has both already occurred and will never occur.

**Five Cities** Eternal cities built in the First Creation by Leur and continuing in the Second Creation. Îs (vanished), Permephedon, Sordan, Mormantalorus, and Mulsor (destroyed).

**The Rift** Transient instabilities in the Daln Barrier that permit passage between the Past World and the Current World. The appearance of Mulsor is one such occurrence.

**Gweroyen** Domain in Essera, north of Stauberg. Former stronghold of the Aryati.

**Iddolea** Destroyed city in Gweroyen. Former capital of the Aryati.

**High Citadel** Principal tower of Permephedon's city core. Also called Marenthro's Tower. The Leur Arcana is here, as are the Archhalia Chambers.

**Rillhome** Sordaneon palace in Dazunor-Rannuli

**Customhouse** Seven Houses seat in Dazunor-Rannuli

**Illystri Palace** Malyrdeon palace in Dazunor-Rannuli, located on island in the Lago.

**Lago** Large lake in heart of Dazunor-Rannuli near the Rill mount.

**Emrysen Palace** Monarch's residence in Dazunor-Rannuli, on the Upper Canal

**Tahlwent** Principality in Essera. South of Stauberg and east of Dazunor. On the sea. Home to the Halasseon Princes.

**Aral** Capital of Tahlwent. Major sea port.

**Golden Palace** Highborn palace in Trulo.

**Kragh** Badlands of high hills and dangerous gorges near Trulo. Home of the Hen Kyon.

**Bellan Toregh** Town on eastern edge of Amallar. Site of a dormant Rill mount.

**Orqho** Mines in southern Amallar near Leseos.

**Gignastha** Former Principality in Essera that included Neuberland. Made a Crown Protectorate after its Highborn Princes were murdered by Kheld rebels.

**Vermilion Aqueduct** Raised by Deben II Sordaneon to provide water to Gignastha and also power the locks of the impregnable Waterglit Palace. Broken by Delos Sordaneon during the Gignastha War.

**Telarkan Mountains** High mountain range separating Esseran domains from Sordan.

**Maskos** Client island kingdom northwest of Gweroyen.

**Pitiless Isles** Archipelago near the edge of the Fallen Sea.

**Sordaneon Serat** Palace of the Sordaneon Hierarchs, in Sordan. Portions of the palace are part of the immortal Citadel forming the core of the city.

**Viridian River** Man-made river contained within the Serat. Site of numerous features, including a waterfall over the Serat Walls.

**Va Haira** First Creation underground passage connecting the Rill, Citadel, Serat and other pre-Return structures in Sordan's city core.

**Ilmar** Domain of Sordan. Located at mouth of Sorandruil.

**Kolpos** Gulf between Sansordan and Ardaen. Also known as the Gulf of Mulsor.

**Tiris** Estate on Sordan island given by Dorilian to Daimonaeris.

**Rhondda** Sordaneon estate on Sordan island. Personal estate of Dorilian.

**Dzalarad** Volcano upon which Mormantalorus is built.

# L. L. STEPHENS

has been writing science fiction and fantasy full-time for several years. Published works include a debut science fiction novel in the deep dark past and a medical journal, as well as lots of short stories, and local brochures, newsletters, and pamphlets for everything from local politicians to an international airport.

The Triempery series, which includes *Sordaneon*, is a six-part series and life's work.

*https://triempery.com*
Twitter: *@triempery*